ISBN: 979-8-9877706-0-3

Printed in the United States of America

Zerocruh

The Return of the Muted

By X.V.V.

Important message from the author:
It would greatly be appreciated if you, the treasured reader, would leave a handsome review on the selling page in which this story was sold...if you want that is. I am just a message not a code of conduct or legally binding contract.

This book is dedicated to Steven K. Satterfield, a man who always teases the idea of becoming an author but when asked about the journey replies with, "It's all up here..."

Table of Contents:

Chapter One. . . . . Page 1

Chapter Two. . . . . Page 17

Chapter Three. . . . . Page 28

Chapter Four. . . . . Page
41

Chapter Five. . . . . Page 56

Chapter Six. . . . . Page 75

Chapter Seven. . . . . Page
93

Chapter Eight. . . . . Page 116

Chapter Nine. . . . . Page 130

Chapter Ten. . . . . Page 138

Chapter Eleven. . . . . Page 160

Chapter Twelve. . . . . Page 173

Chapter Thirteen. . . . . Page
190

Chapter Fourteen. . . . . Page 215

Chapter Fifteen. . . . . Page 242

Chapter Sixteen . . . . Page 258

Chapter Seventeen. . . . . Page 301

Chapter Eighteen. . . . . Page 325

Chapter Nineteen. . . . . Page 334

Chapter Twenty. . . . . Page 354

Chapter Twenty-One. . . . . Page 376

Chapter Twenty-Two. . . . . Page 388

Chapter Twenty-Three. . . . . Page 406

Chapter Twenty-Four. . . . . Page 410

Chapter Twenty-Five. . . . . Page 439

Chapter Twenty-Six. . . . . Page 450

Chapter Twenty-Seven. . . . . Page 460

Chapter 1
Chaotic Chase
Sartan

Their need to hook a catch was desperately visible. Most merchants struggled to get anyone from the stream of bodies flowing through the market to buy from their individual shop, yet every vendor had lots of potential buyers loitering around the stands. It was obvious that very few were interested in purchasing anything this early in the morning, as most were simply gazing before heading to work. Some were already there. Within the crowded market square some buyers weren't interested in buying, rather taking. Many of the robed citizens were waiting for a chance to steal or less likely barter, and the merchants, although they had just finished setting up, were aware of the intentions of their riskier clients.

Since it was a young January, Sartan could still feel the chill of the previous night creeping away with the moon despite being so close to the equator. As the sun rose over the buildings it slowly beamed across his face, and the warmth it possessed made him want to fall asleep. The sun's glare had yet to reach the dusty market itself. He enjoyed the few moments of peace upon the roof of a clay building, for he knew from the previous few weeks of living in Dursnia that once the city starts to warm up so do the crimes. Below him inside a home residents stirred. They probably wouldn't endorse him sleeping on their roof, so his actions had to become silent and hasty. With an empty stomach and nothing but a small bag of coins to his name, Sartan watched the crowd attentively. It wasn't long before something grabbed his gaze. A woman, conspicuous to the rest of the crowd, seemingly came out of nowhere. All of the men and women around her wore dirty, black thawbs and tunics. However, this female wore black leggings and a blue hoodie. Instead of a hijab her long black hair ran down her back. Unlike the woman he wore the long, black robes that all the natives were accustomed to. This was a tactical decision that allowed him to easily disappear within the crowds. He quickly realized that she was entirely aware of how much she stood out. In fact it had to be all part of her plan. The locals around her, as hostile and aggressive as ever, were too focused on her odd attire or place of origin to notice her hands effortlessly slip in and out of their pockets. One by one she waded through the sea of sardines that was the middle path quite easily. Sartan wanted to steal food from a vendor because bartering with them was infeasible, but this short and agile woman seemed to be accumulating quite a sum of currency. As his stomach began to grumble, thoughts strafed through his mind, and he decided that he would follow her. She had done all of the work for him anyways. He just needed to collect the cash.

Sartan, determined not to lose view of her, quickly slid down a shaky, wooden ladder that was attached to the clay home. With splinters in his hands, his dirty sneakers hit the sand in the alleyway, and he scanned the crowd for the lady. It didn't take long to find her as, although short compared to the crowd, the ever shifting background contrasted well with her bright blue sweatshirt. Sartan entered the market following her path. With a slight height advantage, Sartan could see over most of the crowds. She was only a few stands away from him when she slipped up. The woman grabbed a wallet from a man's pocket. However, another pedestrian bumped into them causing her victim to spin around. Caught red handed with his wallet in her hand, the man was enraged. Without hesitation, the man viscously lunged a knife, that seemingly appeared out of nowhere, at the thief. Before the blade made landfall she ducked and dodged away, missing a fatal blow by the width of a hair. The inertia that built up from the lung sent the man stumbling forward in the densely populated crowd.

It was bound to happen. Sartan had closed a lot of distance between them before the knife dove into the arm of an onlooker. The citizen cried out many ghastly slurs before striking back at his attacker with multiple jabs. Unfortunately, that is all it would take to rouse the established tension in the market to an all out riot. Sartan had to catch her if he wanted to eat easy for a while, and if she valued her life she wouldn't be in the crowds for much longer. He followed her around punching pedestrians and out of the rioting market. Behind him he could hear merchants dropping bags of coins. It would be easy for him to steal enough to survive another day, but his tunnel vision had already started to form on his prey. He hadn't seen anyone that was from distant lands since he arrived here about a month ago, and if she kept walking around like this she wouldn't walk much longer.

Eventually he caught up enough to be in earshot of her. "Wait! Come back!" he shouted.

The woman glanced back to see who had called for her while slowing down slightly, but much to Sartan's dismay she didn't wait for him. Instead she sped up now knowing that she was being chased. She was surprisingly fast, but he was faster. Being a streetwalker, he was no stranger to a chase. In order to survive his type of lifestyle one must have great speed to evade threats or to become the threat. The woman noticed he was gaining on her quite quickly, so a different path was created. She decided to take the chase into the alleyways of the city. She consistently made tight turns around multiple corners. This prevented him from reaching his top speed. Sartan noticed this, but more importantly he noticed that she was now weaving through tight corners faster than he was.

This charade went on long enough for Sartan to feel a wincing pain in his side. Determined not to let her escape, he ignored it. He was actually quite close to losing her as each time he hugged a clay building's corner he could barely see her turn the next one. After a while the woman ran down an alleyway and ate a left. By the time Sartan rounded that turn all he could see was a black pant leg quickly disappearing around another corner. Afraid this might be the last time he saw her Sartan turned one last corner not expecting to know which way she went. To his surprise the woman was running towards him, but upon seeing him she stopped. Behind her was a tall, clay building. The alley had come to a dead end.

"I'm not going to hurt you," said Sartan. The woman didn't reply. He watched her analyze possible routes around him all to no avail. "All that I ask--"

Sartan stopped speaking when she turned away from him and started running deeper into the alley. She was completely ignoring what Sartan had to say. At first he just stood there and watched knowing that he blocked the fastest way out. The fastest way. He quickly sprinted after her, and a sharp pain struck his side once more. Sartan bottled the pain away and kept on with the chase in spite of what his body was telling him. She ran straight towards the building at the constrictive alley's end. She didn't even slow down, and for a moment Sartan thought she was going to jump through a window. Astonishingly, the short woman in the blue hoodie seemingly ran straight up the side of the building, jumping from clothesline to windowsill. He heaved a heavy sigh as he stopped at the base of the building before him. Sartan continued to follow the path that she had set for him opposed to accepting defeat. As he looked up for the first window sill to grab on to, the blue hoodie flashed over the peak out of view. Instead of gracefully running up the side of a building like a praying mantis, Sartan caused a few problems and took his time while doing so. On his way to the top he knocked over flower pots in the windows, he snapped the clotheslines, and nearly fell when a cat scratched at him with excessive hissing.

When he was just about to reach the roof a softly tanned face, hidden under a blue hood and behind strands of black hair, poked out over the side to look down at him. Her crystal-blue eyes widened under thick black eyebrows when seeing Sartan stapled to the side of the building, and like a frightened deer her lightly freckled face disappeared over the summit once more. Aware that she was fleeing across rooftops, Sartan doubled his efforts and refused to look down, as the fall would easily break his legs from this height. When he threw his arms over the top of the building to pull himself up the sun streaked across his face so brightly that he could barely see the blue hoodie in the distance. *Is this really worth it?*

It was almost as if the pain in his side reminded him about everything that was at risk here. If he made one little mistake it could be his last at this height. His victim, however, looked like she wasn't struggling at all. She obviously was still great on stamina, unlike Sartan, and she easily leaped between roofs. *She made one mistake though, it's all an open stretch.* His abdomen was begging for mercy, but Sartan had trained his body to obey. With the last bit of energy he had left, Sartan's long legs went into overdrive. As they were on the rooftops he could easily get going fast. There still was the occasional long jump or drop as they went from a tall building to a shorter one, but almost instantly Sartan was only seconds away from her. Sartan waited for the perfect moment. Now merely arms length from each other, Sartan could have easily caught her. He kept this game up for a while waiting for the perfect moment.

Unfortunately, that moment might never come for him. He had been within arm's length of her for over four rooftops, sprinting at her pace so as to not pass her. Afraid that when he lunged for the tackle they would fall off the side of the building to their doom, Sartan had been taking his time. A burning sensation had started in the soles of his feet. His mouth was too dry to speak, and the pain that originated from his side had now corrupted his back. A disease that was spreading throughout his body. She clearly wasn't going to stop for as long as there was another rooftop to jump to. He couldn't hear her panting at all which could only mean that she could keep this chase up for hours. Then again he couldn't really hear much over his own hefty exhales. Regardless, she wasn't slowing down. He was. Knowing he couldn't keep going on like this, it was now or never.

  With no other options left and so many resources invested into this chase, Sartan lunged forward in an attempt to collect some coins shortly after he began to slow down. He aimed for her waist to bring her down the fastest, but as his arms locked around it she kept moving, sending his grip down past her thighs. She almost ran right out of his tackle, but in the mere instant she went to take her feet over his arms he caught the end of a sneaker with his hands. The two of them were both moving with some speed before the fall. The inertia sent Sartan sliding forward on the dried clay, instantly losing his grip on her foot all the while leaving scratches on his arms and sides. She wasn't as lucky. Acting as an untied shoelace, he tripped her which forced her to flop ahead. She went flying face first into the rooftop. The woman managed to catch herself with her hands, scraping cuts into them. That protected her face, but she didn't stop moving entirely. The female in the blue hoodie continued and rolled over the side of the building down into the alleyway below.

  Sartan quickly gathered himself up off the rooftop to look over the edge. She landed in an open dumpster rear first and was still recovering from the fall, quite loudly. High pitched shrieks pierced through him. This of course was alarming as now others might attempt to steal from her. At initial glance one might think that the pile of trash softened her fall by the way she landed on her rear, and there might just have been enough cushion between those two factors for it to be a safe landing from that height. However, when Sartan's gaze drifted on he saw that her right leg was sitting on the metal edge of the dumpster. Even from three windows up Sartan noticed the black leggings around the injury quickly turning a darker shade as they became drenched in blood. The shrieks that came from that dumpster turned his stomach upside down, but he had to eat just like her. *An injury like that translates to death in Dursnia though.* He frantically looked for a ladder down or at least a safer alternative to how she got down. With no other options he broke through the door on the roof to get to the ground through the building itself. Residents screamed as he barged through kitchens, bedrooms, and bathrooms with a small trace of blood on his arms and clothes.

Unsure whether or not she would still be in the dumpster, Sartan busted out of the front door. He looked to his left and then to his right. He was on a road. There weren't any cars, but it wasn't the alleyway his victim fell into. The city only used the streets for service vehicles and banned citizens from using personal cars unless on specific streets. Because of this almost everybody in the town walked to and from points of interest. Sartan refused to waste energy thinking about the codes of the tyrannical mayor while he walked around the building looking for the injured woman. In the alley the overflowing dumpster sat against a building. There was almost as much trash outside of it as well. Cardboard, plastic containers, trash bags, and beer bottles all lined the walkway, and in his frantic rush Sartan accidentally shattered a few of the glass bottles on his way to the dumpster. A startled, old man murmured something to him, but it was ignored when Sartan noticed the woman was no longer in the dumpster.

There was a patch of blood or trash juice leaking over the side of the container, and when it stretched further into the alley its origin was without a doubt connected to him. Sartan ignored the grumbling of the homeless man behind him and followed the trail. As he went further the buildings on each side of him grew further apart, and the alley evolved into a road. The road was not in use of course, reserved for emergency vehicles that Sartan had yet to see once. The blood trail began to fade as it led across the street and down through a long underpass. Despite his thumping heart, he ran through the street and took his first step into the tunnel before he noticed that the homeless man was still following him.

When he realized his presence, Sartan gave him a few seconds of attention. The continuous mumbles changed into unnecessary complaints about a broken beer bottle. Sartan then disregarded the man's incoherent babble and continued tracking down the hoodied individual. The man didn't go away, but instead started getting angrier. Sartan could hear cursing and gurgling behind him. In front of him he could hear the faint echo of a whimper. Knowing that had to be who would pay for his lunch, Sartan jogged slowly under the request of his burning abdomen. The muffled cries got louder as he continued down the tunnel. Sartan got wrapped up in his thoughts and everything around him started to disappear. *There has to be a more peaceful existence. Far from anyone else. Unaffected by the decisions of others. This town clearly isn't that, but where is?* A valid question indeed, but at the time Sartan had yet to realize the true answer. Nevertheless, it wasn't long before his thoughts were shattered.

"You aren't even going to say sorry?!? Just keep running from everything, see where it gets you!"

Sartan came to a complete stop as the sound shattered his train of thought. He stood there in silence for a few seconds thinking about what just happened. "You're right. I won't say sorry because I didn't intentionally smash your bottle," said Sartan impatiently as he turned back to follow the person he truthfully owed an apology to.

The man didn't care too much for Sartan's reply. He just continued with his lecture, "That's what's wrong with the youngins these days. Their parents didn't teach them proper morals. Now we have people like you loose in the streets. Sickening!"

If your parents had done any better then why are you on the streets too? Sartan only listened to about half of his lecture before quickly walking further down the tunnel allowing the man to drone on in the background. That's when he saw the blue hoodie in the distance by the exit of the tunnel. Sartan willed his legs to go as fast as the sharpness in his side permitted and ignored the screaming of the hobo behind him. The woman was limping ahead of him, swallowing down all the tears, blood, and pain that she had just endured. He was catching up to her when he yelled, "Wait, I can help!"

The woman heard him and started limping a little faster. She screamed back to him, "Have you not helped enough? What more can you possibly do?"

Sartan stopped only feet behind her caught by the truthful sting of her words. The pain in his side, thirst in his throat, and hunger in his stomach froze him in place allowing his emotions to run freely. Sartan rarely had been in a situation where he severely injured someone…when he didn't intend to. He had to do questionable things to survive almost everywhere he has been, but he knew the pain he inflicted on this woman would lead her down a path that ends slowly and painfully. He rapidly came to a final conclusion. *She must be put out of her misery.* Sartan then proceeded to walk after her but this time with different intentions.

Behind him the possibly drunken hobo had enough of being ignored. "If you care so much about her, help her with this!" As the man screeched this from beside Sartan, a busted bottle flew through the air towards the injured woman. It exploded on the back of her calf. Shrapnel shattered on the walls and ground around her while she collapsed with a shriek. Thick glass shards stuck out of her leg, and Sartan noticed that it was the same leg that got hurt from the fall.

The hobo then ran past them slurring, "I'm a baseball p-p-player mom! I don't have a curfew any-ymore!"

A brief heat fluttered through Sartan as he chased the man out of the tunnel and into the street up ahead leaving the critically injured woman behind. The road was more populated than the tunnel, so there were lots of people meandering around. The gristly hobo quickly blended into a small crowd, and Sartan was fuming with determination to show the man that violence was a way to survive, not a way to entertain himself. When he slithered around the pedestrians he saw the hobo leaning up on a house. He would have ran up to the hobo and taught a hasty lesson, but two officers unknowingly walked in between the two of them, stopping Sartan in his tracks.

"Wait, this is the guy who stole food from the mayor a few weeks ago," whispered the first guard to the other. "I nearly got demoted because of him."

"Hey! Hands in the air now!" demanded the second Dursnian Guard.

During all of this confusion Sartan looked up and down their robes to see that neither of them had a gun, just batons and cuffs. *I refuse to run anymore.* Sartan quietly backed away from the two guards as they ranted about who would get the pay raise for catching him. Surprisingly, the two officers noticed his attempt at a sly escape and yelled, "One more step and you get a beating too!"

Sartan stopped, knowing that they would beat him regardless. He glanced down the tunnel where the woman watched the arrest begin. He stared as two men dressed in silky, black sweatpants and colorful hoodies ran to help her from the other side of the tunnel. They grabbed her and helped her limp back towards the dumpster. She glanced back once before pedestrians gathered around Sartan, blocking her from his sight. The guards had yet to put him in their cuffs, and Sartan noticed the crowd was particularly agitated. Many people circled around them intrigued by who the officials were abusing this time.

He only had a few options left, and he wasn't ready to try the one that left him in cuffs. Refusing to run anymore Sartan did what no man in Dursnia would do. He slowly pulled out a brown cloth bag from his pocket. Both officers pulled out their batons and slowly started to creep their way towards him. Sartan smiled as he opened the bag and turned it upside down. Gravity took effect and every last coin that resided inside the pouch clinged down on the ground by the guards' feet. A brief second of silence passed before every pedestrian around him lunged forward in a visceral attempt at free coin and started fighting each other for the right. Even the hobo who had thrown the bottle got caught in the pile, and there was barely enough money to buy one cheap dinner.

The officers weren't happy with the interference of the arrest and began batoning the crowd that formed between them and their fugitive. Naturally, that only forced the crowd into a mob, and because of this Sartan was able to wander away uncontested. Sartan knew that he made a few enemies today. Now that the woman had assistance, chasing after her would be futile when his aching gut groaned for mercy. The blood in his body was warm, but the cold, desert winds slowly cooled him off. With the officers distracted by greater matters he casually walked down the street. His body thanked him immediately for finally slowing down, but the cracks in his throat demanded softening. His hunger went unnoticed physically. However, he was well aware that upon cooling down a bit more, it would rear its ugly head once more.

With not a nickel to his name and so many simple survival problems to fix, Sartan strolled further down the street. Usually he was the one being chased for stealing something such as food, but he never had to run that much in order to lose his predators. The officers usually gave up after the first or second quick sprint, but now he knew what it was like to chase and not catch. It wasn't worth it at all. He had gotten nothing out of it other than cardio, and he was sure that he would get that later in the day regardless. It wasn't long before his stomach began to confront the parched peace with a grumble similar to that of a stressed cow. Sartan had wandered down the street long enough he realized he had no clue where he was. There was a bubbling conflict within his body. His legs demanded that he rested, but his stomach and dry mouth wanted to be soothed.

Knowing that he couldn't please both of them at once Sartan took a seat on the steps of a house. It was such a relief to relax for a few seconds. In Dursnia that didn't happen often. Sartan zoned out on the building across the street while his legs melted into the sidewalk. The dusty building had blue towels in the windows preventing him from seeing inside. *What even keeps these people from absolute anarchy anyway? The police are a joke, and everybody hates the mayor.* Sartan peered around his surroundings. The street itself was empty of vehicles like all the others. Instead the citizens walked aimlessly through the roads. Personally the no driving law didn't bother Sartan, but he learned the hard way that the citizens did not approve. The buildings were mostly made of clay bricks and wood which at first seemed fine to him since every direction eventually leads you into bleached sand dunes, but Sartan had been inside the mayor's complex with its marble buildings, giant clock tower, and personal library. The citizens weren't blind. They knew that their liege was living a life of luxury while they suffered from disease, famine, and overworked stress. *Unfortunately, the mayor has a monopoly over his city, and all of his subjects put the blame on eachother for it. Surely, this only gives him more power over them.*

Sartan was still staring at the building across the street contemplating politics of a city in which he wouldn't stay much longer when the door of the building flew open. Out stumbled a police officer who obviously hadn't been on the job long, as Sartan noticed three different batons on his waist. He was followed by the beefiest guard Sartan had ever seen in the city. They both stood on the sidewalk by the building for a minute talking to each other until a third officer came out. Sartan wasn't too worried about the presence of the officers until this one came out. It was the police chief of the city himself. Sartan knew that if he saw him sitting on the steps across the street he would recognize him. Earlier that week Sartan had broken into the mayor's complex looking for hoarded food. The complex was huge, but Sartan snuck into the main building through an open window in the library. He made his way into the mayor's kitchen before this very man caught him. He barely escaped persecution, and this time there was no way he could run away from anything without busting a hole in his side or dying of dehydration.

Across the street the police chief smacked the scrawny guard across the face before whispering something into his ear. The beefy guard lodged a piece of bread in his mouth as the whole thing happened. Sartan was trying his hardest to not be seen, but at the same time he tried to hear what they were talking about. Despite the small distance between them Sartan couldn't make out anything that they were saying. They were trying to be as quiet as possible, and random citizens flooded the street, making it harder to hear them. He knew that if the passing pedestrians weren't in the road, the officers would see him, so not being able to hear their chatter didn't bother him that much. However, it did inspire curiosity in him. The three officers walked down the sidewalk quickly, but the chief led the other two all the while gripping his head with both hands. The chief looked more distressed than any man that Sartan had ever seen in his life. It was not the type of stress that slowly sneaks in over time but the kind of stress that follows a discontent, death-row inmate. Impending doom.

Once the guards were completely out of sight Sartan stood up from the sandy steps and crossed the street. He was unnerved by the way that all of the citizens walking around watched him. They viewed him as simultaneously a potential threat and a potential exploit, and the veils nor robes hid the hatred that flowed freely from their eyes. Then again what wasn't there to hate in this overpopulated, desert death-trap. Sartan overheard one of the locals talk about how there was another riot in the district again he had just left, and he scoffed to himself knowing that there was a riot in the main market area shortly beforehand. There wasn't time let alone energy to waste on such thoughts. He already knew how bad this city was, and he wanted to begin his journey to the next town. Sartan got across the sparsely populated sea of bodies and twisted the doorknob that the officers had recently closed. It was unlocked. The chief must have been in such a hurry he forgot to lock it. The sandalwood door slowly crept open when he pushed it forward. He checked the room before entering to make sure that he was the only one in it. After finding out nobody else was there he quickly closed the door behind him and locked it hoping that nobody cared enough to follow him.

The building couldn't be a police station. First of all it was quite some distance from the center of the city. Not to mention that the inside looked nothing like a police station, and Sartan knew what that looked like from unfortunate experiences. There was a rotting sofa to the left that had a small lump moving under its tarnished green fabric. The flies failed to blend in on the walls as they were bare with the exception of a singular light switch that had all of its circuitry exposed. There was a kitchen towards the back wall. When Sartan noticed that, everything else in the house disappeared. Sartan ran into the kitchen and under the slowly rotating ceiling fan that failed to tick away at the stillness of the room. On the center table sat a lone bowl of grapes that barely seemed edible even to the beetles that scurried around them. Even though his stomach grumbled at the sight of the grapes his nose had an emetic tantrum.

He hesitantly grabbed the bowl and dropped the first peeling grape in his mouth. The grape was sour and furry as it slid down his throat. The whole process made him gag, but its juices soothed his dry mouth way more than his spindly spit could. Looking back at the bowl he realized that they were mostly brown with hair on them, and despite his conscious warning him against it, the grumbling in his gut made the decision for him. Sartan swallowed down every last questionably colored grape with a sting of uncertainty heavy in his mind. After cringing as the last one went down, Sartan's own face briefly turned into a raisin as he fought off the bitter taste. He glanced around the counters looking to find a chaser for the fruit. Instead he only found a piece of parchment in the other corner of the kitchen. Sartan slowly made his way across the room feeling the sharp pain tingle as it finally faded away from his side. When he got close he realized that it was actually a letter. He figured that if he ate their food he might as well read their letters. It was only fair. Sartan snatched the letter and slid down onto the cool kitchen floor. The letter, already ripped open, was addressed to the chief officer that he just saw. It read:

Omar,

I task you with the retrieval of one of the Tansiq Scrolls. My informants have come to the acknowledgement that the Sagittarius Palace Scroll is within your very city. I do not care if Strelec allowed your liege to keep it in your shabby, intolerable city. He is gone now, so you won't have to worry about his opinion. Regardless, his scroll is somewhere within Mayor Khalil's personal library. Retrieve it and bring it to me. Do this quietly as I am not in the mood to have my image tarnished by the historical values of your mindless lands. If you fail to accomplish this task you will be dealt with quickly and indefinitely. Upon receiving this letter Lev will be arriving within a few days to retrieve the scroll for me. You better have it when she arrives, or else you will be at her mercy. Don't whine about the snail mail, but we just couldn't squeeze your lands into our budget. In the future we will have more reliable forms of communication.

Your Liege,

Kozoroh

Sartan sat there knowing that he wouldn't remember all of those names. *I know who Lev and Kozoroh are, the Leo and Capricorn Zodiac respectively, but what do they want with the Sagittarius Tansiq Scroll? Shouldn't they already know where the other Zodiac's Palaces are?* He figured it could be useful, or at the very least a bit of leverage over the police chief if things took a turn for the worse, so he took the letter and slipped it under his robes. The strange thing was that he went through the mayor's library, and he didn't see any scrolls. Then again he rarely saw what he wasn't looking for.

It was at this very moment when the grapes started to cause problems. His stomach didn't sound like it was accepting the delivery, so he hastily stood up looking for something to help him. With the acids bubbling up from his stomach, Sartan swiftly opened every cabinet in the kitchen. He opened the first one, nothing. He opened a second one, plates. He opened the final cabinet to find two jars of curdled milk and a pile of hummus on a cracked plate.

His first instinct was to drink all of the milk, but his nose punished him severely for opening the glass jar so hastily. Sartan closed his eyes, held his nostrils shut and chugged the whole jar. Upon the last gulp he gagged and spewed the rest of the not so creamy, curdled milk all over the countertops. Desperate to hold down any liquids, Sartan forked the hummus into his mouth a handful at a time in hopes of neutralizing the urge to vomit. While reaching for the second jar of milk, which somehow looked worse than the first, Sartan heard some shuffling near the front door.

The doorknob twisted as he lunged down under the counter knocking the empty grape bowl down to the cracking tiled floor. A guard entered the doorway and gagged. Then a second guard shoved him while preaching with great vigor, "You are gonna want to turn your nose off recruit!" Sartan could recognize his voice. It was the police chief, Omar. Sartan needed to get out of here and fast. He looked past an island bar to see stairs leading up into the building.

The recruit asked, "Why is there milk all over the countertops?"

"What!" bellowed a third guard as he charged into the room knocking down Omar. The third guard was a bit too excited to get into the building, especially over some spilled milk.

At this point Sartan decided he was done visiting. He picked up the empty grape bowl lying by his feet and chucked it at the first guard he saw after rising up from under the countertop. It landed right on the forehead of the beefy officer, cracking into one hundred pieces and sending him stumbling backwards into the recruit. By now Omar had crawled over his companions and to his feet to chase Sartan, who was already up four of the steps on the stairs.

Sartan yelled out behind him, "Thanks for the food!"

Without looking back he heard angered grunting and one of the guards screaming, "Omar! Don't let him get away! The letter is gone!"

When Sartan made it to the second floor he nervously looked for a way out of the building. He was hoping that there would be windows by the stairs, but he couldn't see any. With the only other option being to run back down the stairs and into Omar's grabby hands, Sartan impulsively sprinted up the next set of stairs which had so many steps missing it was more similar to running up a slide. He could hear Omar trip over the steps behind him. Sartan knew he wasn't in the clear though. By the time he made it to the third floor his palms were sweaty and the pain in his side was starting to return. He didn't drink enough. Not to mention running after eating fruit with grizzly fur wouldn't help. Fortunately, he could see light entering from a window on the opposite side of the room. Without even thinking about it his legs involuntarily took him to the window. There was a brief moment of struggle as the window refused to budge. The footsteps grew louder behind him. The glass had yet to budge. Sartan's fingers started to tremble as he knew there wouldn't be a trial if he were caught. With no other options left he started to punch the glass. His first blow only made it wobble, but when his right fist landed on it the glass shattered across the alleyway onto the rooftop of another building. He glanced back to see Omar standing there in astonishment. There wasn't any time to spare, let alone explain how he had done that, so Sartan started crawling through the sharp and jagged mess of transparent spikes.

Sartan crawled right out the window and slid down the side of the building grabbing a clothesline just above the second floor. Hoping to lose them in the crowd which by the smell and sound of it was getting agitated in the heat, he let go and quickly fell to the ground. His feet hit the sandy, hot alleyway right as a baton flew past his head, clanging off the wall of the adjacent building. Looking back at the window he saw Omar slowly crawling out. *Glad that this Mayor Khalil didn't have tasers in his budget.* He turned towards the main street and jogged quickly to gain distance but slow enough to maintain pace.

His side immediately showed displeasure at his decision, but Sartan knew that Omar wouldn't chase after him much longer. Anybody could figure that out just by looking at him. Omar's rolling stomach didn't always obey the constraints of his uniform, leaving a bit of the pudginess slipping out over his trousers. Once Sartan was deep into the main street he stopped to see the other two officers coming out of the building's front door. They didn't see him luckily, but Omar wasn't ready to give up that early.

"Brick Brain! He's right there! In the middle of the street," yelled Omar in a hasty squeal as he started falling off of the side of the building. Omar wouldn't be that much of a problem anymore. At least that is what Sartan hoped and concluded.

'Brick Brain' located Sartan during the yelling. He assumed that Brick Brain was the dimwitted and muscular officer who made it possible for him to escape the building, so there really wasn't a challenge at all. This officer's veins bulged in his arms as he approached, but Sartan had dealt with many overconfident police officers before. Even better, he was accompanied by the recruit officer. The fear on the recruit's face was visible as this was probably the first time he ever had to actually do his job. From what Sartan has seen there is no academy for officers. Instead the mayor probably just smacked them in a uniform and told them to shake feathers until gold falls out. Sartan glanced back to Omar who was still writhing in the alleyway. He decided that he wouldn't need to run after all.

As Brick Brain and the recruit approached him with batons in hand, Sartan stood still and spoke just loud enough, so that they could hear him over the crowd, "If you let Omar die there will be no police chief to do your paperwork, and it will be your fault for letting him die."

Brick Brain didn't think about what he said at all, but the recruit did. It had to be the recruit's first day. He tugged on the big officer's sleeve whispering, "He's right we can't let Omar die."

The recruit then ran away from Sartan to help Omar. Meanwhile Brick Brain stood in front of Sartan disoriented for a few seconds before finally deciding to assist the recruit with their chief. Sartan could feel his stomach flutter with an absolute urge to stop and laugh. He held back the urge while walking away, but then he realized that Omar was the most respected officer in Dursnia and completely lost it. Between his chuckles he could hear Omar arguing with the other officers to keep chasing him instead. *The police force here is a joke.*

A wanted man, Sartan easily escaped the sights of any nearby officers. He kept going in the same direction until he knew that Omar wouldn't be able to find him within an hour. To his surprise he had made it all the way to the outskirts of the city. It was a given he chased that woman quite some distance away from the city market, but he didn't think about it until now. It wasn't necessarily a bad thing to be on the outskirts because he wouldn't have to deal with the police as much, but there wouldn't be as many opportunities for stealing food. The clay buildings were more spaced out from each other as he continued down a dusty path. The dunes began rolling all around him, and oil pumps could be spotted in the distance whirring away autonomously. Clay buildings grew shorter and thinner compared to the taller and wider ones in town. Most citizens must have been terrified of the desert that surrounds the city, as they all pile up towards the center of the town. Then again that could have just been where all of the action was.

Sartan neared a barn when he heard a strange grunt coming from inside. He slowly crept up to the window on the side and peered through it. What he saw was not what he expected at all. There was a small caravan of camels eating in the barn. A few camels weren't about to stop him from getting a nap though. Sartan crawled through the window and snuck past the camels trying not to startle them. He slipped into a separate room, and glanced around the deteriorating barn. A pile of hay bales layed on the ground in the corner. He wondered how the farmer even got straw in the desert for a few seconds before deciding it was an import and plopping down on the straw. The caravan was munching away unaware of his presence in the other room, but within moments Sartan was able to drift away into a quick and much needed nap.

Chapter 2
Treacherous Stone
Sartan

Splat! Splat! Sartan was startled to the waking world when a thick, mucousy liquid slugged its way down his face. The camels had found him, and they didn't seem too fond of his presence. Sartan could feel the soreness in his legs while wiping away the slime. He tried to inch backwards away from the onslaught of slobber. On the other side of the room he could see orange light shining through the doorway onto the ground before completely being swallowed by the dull and dusty cement floor. The camel who still hovered over him grumbled with wet lips. Sartan slowly looked back to the camel that rudely woke him from his sleep and saw more camels surrounding him. The closest one stared at him grunting a soft warning of incoming spit. He grabbed a handful of hay, and before the camel spat again its face was thrown to the side in a flurry of sun-burned strands of hay.

Unfortunately for Sartan, these camels weren't very fond of hay to the face shenanigans, so they responded with enough hostility to convince Sartan that he had stolen one of their children. The herd started moaning in anger and showering Sartan in saliva. Drenched and sticky, there was no hope in getting back to sleep. Instead he decided it was time to head out. The only problem was that they had encircled him in a corner, and Sartan struggled to squeeze past their brown bodies. Their gritty, sandy hides pressed up against each other so tightly it prevented him from escaping, and there was no way he was about to crawl under them to be placed at the mercy of their stomping. His pasty punishment for sleeping in their barn had endured quite long enough, as his shirt became soaked in camel slobber the patience within him melted away. Sartan curled up into the corner of the room holding his hands over his face to prevent a headshot.

Upon pressing his hands over his face he could feel the cold buzz of the large ring on his finger, and he refused to let it be tarnished by these mindless camels. The 10 carat gemstone drowned him in its milky-white, swirling clouds that were confined by the oval frame of the gem. The gem itself was locked into a black chassis that heaved down Sartan's finger by its size alone. Sartan went to cover it with his other hand, but right before he could, the camel directly in front of him dropped the juiciest and creamiest loogie known to mankind directly on the ring. Sartan's hand involuntarily formed a fist, and that fist shot right into the side of the nearest camel. Time seemingly froze while Sartan remembered what was about to happen. His fist had curled into a ball at the side of the camel, but nothing moved. Nothing happened. He never felt the impact of punching the hide, and the camel stood motionless before him. He was able to observe all of this without being able to move himself.

Suddenly, strong winds quickly charged up circling behind Sartan cooling the room down to a chilling shiver. In an instance the frigid winds channeled their way into a concentrated and singular gust. That thin gust then found its way into Sartan's back. It chilled him to his core, but fortunately, the gails weren't directed at him. The wind continued through his body, quickly making its way through his chest and down his arm to the ring on his finger. Once the energy reached the gemstone all the winds that had been violently building up suddenly erupted out of the gem directly into the side of the camel. All of the camels that surrounded the victim that he hit were immediately launched away from Sartan so quickly he missed it by blinking. They toppled over each other in the corners of the room, but a few of them actually crashed through the walls ending up further in the barn. Simultaneously, the camel that Sartan involuntarily punched out of annoyance got the brunt of the winds. He suffered a much less desirable fate than the others. While all of the others got chucked through the cold air within the barn this camel was launched straight through the ceiling.

It was all done within three seconds. Silence ensued as the camels that remained in the barn were all killed by the explosion. Sartan fell to his knees, trembling at the mercy of the sudden arctic temperatures. Frost had already coated the floor and walls when his limbs went numb. He had only used the ring to its full potential once before, but he quickly remembered why he tried every other option first. As his torso and head started to go numb, he wondered whether or not he would survive this and rose to his feet to reassess the situation. The room looked nothing like it did when the camels were attacking him. There was a thick pile of snow covering everything around him: the remaining walls, the floors, and even some of the camels. Their extremities had already gone black with frostbite, and Sartan knew that would be his fate too if he remained in the barn. No more snow accumulated out of seemingly nowhere, as Sartan suspected all of the moisture in the air had already frozen. However, the air had to be getting colder because his eyes began to gloss over with a thin film of ice between each blink.

It took every muscle in his body to push himself just one step forward. The whole room pressed down on him as he trudged ahead. His blood began to slow when he passed the camels. Dead without a doubt, a few of them twitched before giving in completely to the cold, but the only thing that Sartan could think about was his heart slowly going numb from frost. Within the silence he could easily hear a steady internal thump. The thump faltered and failed at fending off the closing walls of the coffin that the powerful ring had created, and with each failure the consistent thud of his heart slowed allowing the frost to eagerly creep into major arteries. The longer he was in the barn the less he could hear. Once Sartan made it to the entrance where the camels undoubtedly entered from his ears were ringing so loudly he started to feel dizzy. He made it through the door into the main room of the barn. There was still a thin layer of frost all over the floor, but Sartan could see convection currents flutter rapidly at the large, barn-doors that stood wide open.

As he hiked through the barn, his senses continued to fade almost as quickly as the gemstone froze the heat of the barn. Sartan couldn't feel anything other than his numb heart faintly beating through the blizzard. He was slowly approaching the giant barn doors that opened up to a sandy path when his vision began to wane. Sartan looked down at the white gem that had caused so much damage within such a little time frame. The white clouds continued to swirl around. They were so thick it was impossible to see through the stone. Then the black that steadily devoured his peripherals took total control over his eyes. Sartan could still feel his heart fighting, but the ice was slowly creeping up through his gut and down his throat towards it simultaneously. He remembered he was walking straight out of the barn, but with failed vision that path twisted and turned over itself in his mind. All he could hear was this continuous ringing that pierced right through his iced brain. Attempting to walk in the straightest line outside without any sense of direction or feeling, the blizzard only grew in strength. With every breath his lungs slowed as the icy air froze them shut.

Nothing burns like the cold, so when he miraculously managed to exit the barn he could tell instantly. The thing that gave him hope was that his feet began squishing the ground that was now made of sand. The air outside was perfect for a patient fighting tuberculosis, but that didn't mean there wasn't any water at all. At first he thought it was death splotching itself over him, but the droplets forming on his exposed skin felt like tiny needles of heat pricking him. His face, arms, and literally anything that was exposed to the air was drenched with condensation. The water warmed him drastically, but it wasn't enough to keep him on his feet. The edge of his skin had the slightest tint of heat fluttering about it, but on the inside his heart still resisted the blizzard. It finally thumped so slowly that his legs could no longer support him. Without warning Sartan collapsed into the sand barely outside of the barn. Sartan had flailed a bit going down, throwing one arm over his head. Then there was nothing. All he could feel was his heart. Thump. Thump…Thump……Thump………Thump. Almost as if it were a miracle the very tip of his longest finger burned. *This is it.* Sartan thought unsteadily. *Death is creeping in.* The burning sensation slowly crawled down his finger spreading to the rest of his hand. Sartan reached further to hasten his demise, and his wrist began to burn as well. With the last bit of brain power and energy he had left inside of him Sartan kept crawling and reaching out for the end. Suddenly he regained the ability to feel in the hand that was burning. Then it all dawned on him.

Now with every fiber in his body he crawled out of the barn's shadow and into the sunlight. Each lung into the sunlight engulfed him in heat that violently stripped the cold out of his body. He didn't stop crawling away from the barn until he could feel the sun shower every portion of his body. Eventually the ringing in his ears subsided completely. The whole time Sartan was waiting for his ears to stop ringing he kept thinking the same thing: *Never again I am going to this thing. I don't even remember how I got it, but unless I want to die I will never use this weapon again.*

The gem's origins didn't matter that much to him when his vision started to flicker back into existence. As the darkness faded away hesitantly, Sartan came back to his senses. He struggled to rise to his feet, but the fact that he was breathing air that didn't freeze and crack his lungs was enough fuel to keep him fighting. His insides felt wet almost as if ice had formed and melted within him, and his movement was still sluggish and choppy delayed by whatever powers the stone cursed him with. Before walking off from the scene he looked back at the barn, and anyone could tell something vicious had happened. There were multiple holes in the sides with deceased camels laying not too far from each hole, not to mention he could literally see blurs in the air as the desert heat fought its way in through the many entrances.

He had just nearly killed himself destroying some random farmer's barn. A camel spit on his hand and in response he accidentally slaughtered the entire caravan. *I don't trust myself with this ring, but there is no way I trust anyone else with it. They will just abuse it like me.* Sartan took the ring off his finger. He placed it on the sand at his feet, and within the blink of an eye the entire gem cleansed itself of the white fog that haunted its insides. There was no swirling mist in the white tinted stone. Instead it was so clear Sartan was almost blinded by the reflecting sunlight. He then grabbed the ring and placed it on the same finger that resided on his opposite hand. *Letting someone else get their hands on this is not an option.*

Sartan needed to get away from this barn. Now that all of his senses had returned he began the long walk that would take him to the center of the city. He hadn't even melted off the frost that slowed his movement yet when he walked by a camel. He didn't want to see another camel for at least a month after leaving the barn behind him, but when he approached the camel he saw that it had been severed in half. He took a deep breath. Frostbite riddled its front two legs as well as its face, but the rest of its body was nowhere to be seen.

Sartan exhaled slowly and crouched down next to the frozen camel, more accurately the upper portion of this frozen camel. On his side dangled a sheathed dagger used mostly illegally. Sartan unsheathed it and ran his finger across the inscriptions on the gold plated blade that already had dried blood on it from a previous encounter. He took one last deep breath before sinking the dagger into the camel's side. When he finished with the act he put the dagger back in its leather home and held a meaty chunk of camel that was still frozen, but as the desert heat continued to flood him with rays the meat wouldn't be preserved for long. His plan was to sell the meat to a vendor to get some quick cash even though the vendors in this city are intolerable when it comes to any interaction with them. He would have to act fast, as the sun was finally falling below the sky. Shops would close, and the end of day riots would ensue. He didn't want to think about how far the camel must have flown to end up here, but there was no question that this was the one he punched. Otherwise it would be an entire camel instead of a half.

Sartan ended up walking down a paved road further in the city still holding the frozen food. The clay homes were posted on the sides of the street, and the sidewalks fed into the alleys between the buildings once more. Sartan had been walking long enough for the sun to dip further towards the horizon when a crowd of women and children ran away past him. They startled him, but once he came to, he assumed that it could only be another riot. Sartan didn't find any shops on the way so far, but where there is chaos there is usually money involved. He must have been near a city market.

Sometimes things just are too predictable. Sartan followed the screams and cries until he found himself at an entrance to the peaceful market. When he showed up the riot had simmered to a few small pockets of squabbles where law enforcement continued to exert control over the citizens. The merchants and vendors had already started to re-establish their carts and venues. It didn't take long for Sartan to find one that would take his meat. It was a shop owned by an old man who knocked out an opening in a clay shed. This was where he showed off his product. The scraggly facial expressions of the vendor nearly deterred Sartan from even saying what the man obviously already knew he was about to ask.

"Do you want some meat?" said Sartan while he approached the vendor.

The vendor knew what he was doing. Before Sartan could even throw out a starting price the vendor was already speaking, "20 for the meat! Take it or leave it."

He glared at the vendor with a deathly stare of annoyance, and the vendor simply stared back ready to counter. Sartan hated bartering, especially with strangers, but then again everyone in Dursnia was a stranger. He stared at the vendor for a few more seconds before deciding to play his game, "75 or the next vendor will have it."

"35!"

"50, let's meet in the middle"

"35!" denied the vendor with quite vigor. "I have a family to feed. I don't care if it is the best meat ever no more."

"50, or I'm gone! It isn't my fault you have liabilities," spouted Sartan.

"Fine! Fine! I'll take it," cried the vendor. "You are really an evil individual. Your type makes me sick, do you know that?"

"Welcome to Dursnia. The money?"

The vendor handed him a wad of cash, and Sartan handed him the meat that was dripping blood. Without counting the money he started to make his way towards the pool of people in the center of the street, and once he was engulfed by the crowd the vendor he just sold meat to started bellowing.

"Grade-A camel meat! All of it for 100 or some of it for 25! It's a deal because nobody is stupid enough to kill their camel for food. Hah!"

There was one good thing about living on the streets, you barely have to talk to anyone. Given there is always the occasional talk with the stubborn merchant or law enforcer, but overall it is a lifestyle Sartan has been forced to be proficient at. He wanted to make it through the crowd and into the alleys before counting his money because this town was unwilling to allow funds to flutter safely in open sight for even brief periods of time. Before he disappeared into the shadows once more Sartan peeked at the giant clocktower that stood proudly over everything. The clock tower itself was at the center of the mayor's complex, and that was only a few blocks away which meant that the police were highly concentrated here. Looking back at the market there were still officers beating on people in tiny corners of the street. Their uniforms were like bright spots in the market. Some must have been new to the whole police thing because two officers refused to stop their beating on their citizens, and that started to attract onlookers.

Sartan, who remained in sight of the beatings, counted his money as more people gathered around the beatdown across the street. He kept his eyes on the market with his back to a wall. It grew harder for him to see anything as more locals gathered around the guards. Sartan didn't have to see anything to understand what was about to happen though. He counted the last bill realizing that the vendor had only given him 40 mostly in ones, but it wasn't worth it to go back into the market now. The guards weren't beating anything at this point. Instead they received their first few fists to the face. The squeals were muffled by the growing hunger of the crowds, and Sartan could tell that another riot would be ensuing. However, this one was directed at the officers. *Usually the riots are more spread out. That last one couldn't have been more than twenty minutes ago.* Sartan turned his head but made sure his ears remained alert while he let the alleys absorb him.

Traveling deeper into the alley Sartan shoved his money back into his pocket before trying to get the camel's dried blood off of his robes. *I need to leave this town.* He didn't want to dwell on that idea for too long as he was going to leave soon, but it was hard not to think about it when he heard pained screeches echoing off of the walls. Dursnia, no matter what anyone thought about it, taught Sartan an important lesson. Sartan had learned a few new things to watch for in the streets. The most important were the quiet strangers that nobody noticed and the officials. The officials had to be watched with three eyes. Regardless, when he heard the autocratic and mindless voice of an officer around the corner he didn't have time to stop and walked right into the open.

Down the path he walked into he saw a tight dead end with no other exit. In the alley stood four police officers all wearing their shiny uniforms, two of which were interrogating a man who looked barely of legal age. The man was very short from Sartan's perspective, and was wearing silky black sweats and a neon orange hoodie that probably was melting him. His sandy blonde hair was wet with sweat that trickled down his flat, freckled face. The man struggled to keep a bag filled to the top with food from falling into one of the officer's hands, and although the officer was taller he was making no progress. It looked as though the official was trying to pry a hive of honey out of a short bear without any facial hair.

Then an officer saw Sartan and instantly proclaimed, "Get him, he must be the other one!"

There was no time for talking, so Sartan decided to make the first move instead of running back into the riot behind him. A left wing into the first guard sent his aggressor back into a wall. The guard looked down and spat out a spindly string of blood before he stood up. Another guard approached, but this one wasn't as lucky. Like a plank the beefy man fell backwards all at once.

By now the first guard had pulled out a baton and was on his way over to Sartan. He swung the black rod around vigorously, but his prey kept dodging until Sartan slipped on the fallen guard. Sartan quickly scrambled to grab the fallen guard's baton, but he simply wasn't fast enough. A baton blasted him on his shoulder making the rest of the arm go limp. Losing control over himself, Sartan's reflex was to just swing his other arm towards the guard. The swing thwarted any attack from the guard but missed the landing. It didn't matter though because the guard stumbled long enough for Sartan to regain ground and crack a swing into his forehead. The officer slumped into the wall leaving just two more officers.

The two guards who were interrogating the boy finally granted Sartan their focus. One of them had red stripes on his black robe instead of white; it meant he was important in some arbitrary way. Sartan simply scoffed at the presence of the captain.

"Put your hands up and turn around!" screamed the captain as he took out his baton in one hand and some cuffs in the other. Sartan looked past the guards to see that the boy wasn't shackled or in any restraints.

"Okay," said Sartan as he slowly brought his hands up past his head.

In front of him on the ground rested a fallen guard's baton giving him an idea. Before they told him to turn around he kicked the baton hoping to have it slide right under the captain's legs to the feet of the foreigner. Since his aim was stretched as much as his imagination, that didn't happen at all. Instead the metal baton flew off to the left striking the other official in the stomach. Instantly, the man fell to his knees writhing in pain. His own baton followed him, clanking on the ground with an echo that shattered off the walls.

"Really? Run off now and I will forget all about this," said the captain while looking at Sartan.

Sartan stared at the man wondering why he would ever offer freedom to him, but before he could come to a cohesive conclusion the official let out a piercing squeal. The victim behind the officer had reared back and launched his foot between the guard's two legs. The last officer fell down onto his knees and then to his side weeping the whole while.

"Why did you do that? He was about to let you go," asked Sartan.

"That's unlikely scruffs. That was a typical type two guard. I don't think he would've. Plus this is faster," claimed the man as he gathered himself. "That was amazing though! You took down almost all four of them by yourself!"

"Right…but what did they want from you?" asked Sartan while looking down at the beefy officer that slowly was inhaling and exhaling. "Who are you?"

"Well my friend…my friend and I borrowed some food and medicine. It is for his sister who was really hurt," said the man as he pointed to the hefty bag that was still in his hands. "The officers didn't take too kindly when they caught us on our way out. My name is Caleb Tariq by the way."

"That makes sense. Food is more valuable than money in this town. Not to mention how corrupt the police are," said Sartan while he watched Caleb find a small capsule of pills in the pile of food he had recently acquired.

"This town is the worst place I've ever been to, and we just came from Hapopelma! We've only been here for about a week, and some freak already tried to kill our friend for apparently no reason!" exclaimed Caleb.

This city surely is filled with anguish and despair. "That happens a lot here. It is kind of an eat or be eaten mentality in Dursnia. Speaking of food, can I get some?" asked Sartan.

"Of course of course! You should come home with me too. Not like that, but you could really help us out. We will give you a place to sleep and eat for the time being," replied Caleb.

"I don't know. Are you sure that your friends would be okay with it? I don't want to be intrusive or anything."

"Of course they will let you! Once they find out you saved my cheeks, why wouldn't they? Ferran doesn't really have a say in it if you saved my life," said Caleb.

Caleb had gathered himself and began walking away from the chaotic battleground where officers laid on the ground crying in pain. "We have been sneaking into houses on the Northern side of the city and using their showers the whole time we have been here! We won't be here long. Once we get some things I will gas up our ride for us to leave."

"What?" said Sartan. He was more surprised by the fact that Dursnia even had running water let alone gas stations.

"How else would we stay clean? We will let you stay. It is the least I can do. Maybe you could even help us with some things."

"I will check it out, but I don't know about staying or helping you with your issues. I would say that we are more than even if you let me have a portion of the food you borrowed."

"Nonsense scruffs! You have to meet my friends. Ferran would love you!"

They continued down the alley as Sartan countered, "Dursnia is a scary place. It may not be the smartest idea to let anybody on the streets into your home."

"I trust you! Like I said you saved my butt just now. So what do you say?"

I don't care if you trust me. I don't trust you. What if your friends jump me? What if---

"I will take your silence as acceptance!"

"What?! Okay, fine I'll meet your friends, but I am not going to stay longer than I wish."

"Perfect! It isn't too far from here. My friend is probably waiting there for us already because we split up before the police caught me!" exclaimed Caleb as he walked out of the alley leading Sartan towards his fabled home.

Chapter 3
Familiar Face
Aqila

She was looking out the window of a camper upon the smoldering city that laid below a hastily descending sun. The distant sun still bleached the curtains as she closed them. On the inside of the camper she rested on a creaking leather couch, and opposite of her sizzled a small pile of dirty clothes intertwined with a few scarce DVD's and comics. Next to the pile an unfinished, model car waited for somebody to complete its final bit of assembly. Her gaze eventually drifted down to her leg. Upon slightly rolling up her black leggings to assess the injury, the throbbing pain in her calf started chewing at her consciousness again. The bleeding finally stopped a few hours ago, but there was a lingering pain of a wincing nip reverberating all throughout her leg. It only grew stronger with the more attention she fed it. In an attempt to distract herself she spoke out, "Ferran, do you think Caleb got caught?"

A man, wearing a neon green shirt, was standing on the other side of a small counter in the kitchen of the camper. His softly freckled face was similar to hers, but his large ears dwarfed those that she wore. She could hear him quietly panting through the still air, and that is all she needed to assume something went wrong on the mission. He quickly ran a sweaty hand through his brown hair before his green eyes frantically glanced over to reply, "I could've sworn he was right behind me."

Without replying she just looked around the aged camper that was shaking in the weak, desert winds. *A pebble could probably pierce through the thin walls.* She then tried to stand up. *This is not going to work!* She barely prevented herself from falling down by grabbing the curtain rod on the window.

Ferran failed to notice her flailing, as he was looking out the camper's door for their friend. However, when she was unable to hide the squeal of pain that came out of her gut, he turned around and instantly said, "Aqila! Sit! You aren't ready to get up." Before he could reach her the curtains she grabbed folded under her weight, and she flopped down onto the ripped couch with a thud followed by loud squeaking and creaking. He said possibly out of annoyance, "I'm not impressed. You are only prolonging your recovery."

"I am fine! You act as though you know me or something," replied Aqila in a stark manner as she fought for independence from the couch. "We know the bone is intact, so what does it matter to you anyways?"

Suddenly, the front door slammed open. Ferran instantly unsheathed a hidden knife, as Aqila watched Caleb excitedly wander into the camper with a big duffle bag of supplies. Caleb hesitated at the front door, but eventually entered and put the bag down on the counter. Behind him, however, entered a man in a hoodless, Dursnian robe.

"Who are you!" yelled Ferran who was about to stab the intruder. Aqila on the other hand did not say anything, but instead she just stared at him. The man's foggy brown eyes gazed about the room quickly assessing the situation until they reached hers. She allowed him to stare into her retinas where his brows quickly grew pensive. Something he saw scared him as he shrank back towards the door uncomfortably. Then again Ferran was holding a blade out on him, so that may have had a profound effect on his behavior as well.

"What are you doing here?" questioned Aqila. She stared at his face, eating all of his features. He must have been forced to remain in the sun, as his tanned face devolved into dark patches that successfully fought off any attempts of acne under his eyes. He had scratches on his arms and a black ring on his finger with a white, oval-shaped stone. Perhaps it was an opal.

"I'm on my way out," replied the man.

"Nonsense!" exclaimed Caleb. "He helped me fight off several officers. Saved my life!"

"And?" started Ferran. "He still needs to leave!"

Caleb shut the door with him inside and continued, "Sartan can help us if we give him food and housing. I don't see a problem with that."

"It is about time Sartan leaves," said Ferran, disregarding Caleb who was now unpacking all of the food and supplies.

"Nonsense, he can stay as long as he would like." replied Caleb who approached Aqila with a bottle of pills. "Here take two," he whispered to Aqila before jumping right back in the conversation with, "Scruffs saved my life. If it weren't for him I would be in a jail cell right now."

"They don't use their jail cells here; he would be executed." said Sartan who was standing strategically in the corner of the camper by the door.

"Do I know you?" asked Aqila as she gulped down four pills to ease the pain. By now she had gathered herself and slowly stood up off the busted sofa with a wobble. Sartan's voice echoed in her mind when she looked back at the scrapes all over his arms. Then it dawned on her. Before Sartan could answer her previous question she blurted, "You broke my leg!"

Sartan stood there flabbergasted. Both Ferran and Caleb stared at him. Then once again before Sartan could reply Ferran said, "Well how about we break both of his legs then!" Ferran jumped next to their culprit holding a knife to his neck.

"I didn't break your leg. The hobo broke your leg!" exclaimed Sartan in a last ditch effort.

The whole situation became a game she was determined to win, so she began hypothesizing his reasons, rather…excuses, when she stated, "Wait! Let him explain himself."

To Aqila's surprise Sartan replied, "I did knock you off the roof. I will admit that. It was unintentional, but it happened. However, I was trying to help you once you fell off the roof. The hobo was not, and that is where most of the damage came from."

Ferran, without loosening his sharp grip on Sartan, turned to Aqila and exclaimed, "See! He is obviously lying. He could've killed you. Grab the wrench from under the sink!"

She looked down to her leg which was covered in red bandages beneath her pants. *He tore it which is unforgettable, but then he saved Caleb…who had medicine.* She noticed that Caleb did not seem to be that concerned about the whole situation before asking, "Caleb, are you not concerned about this intruder?"

"He isn't an intruder. I invited him here. If you think he doesn't belong here then that would be your decision Aqila."

Aqila's eyes glared forward at the thought of his ability to just go with the flow so easily, but he did leave the decision up to her whether or not Sartan could stay.

"This is what is going to happen. You will answer my questions, and I will decide whether or not you have to leave," demanded Aqila. She watched Sartan nod slowly as he fought back her oppressive gaze with his own.

"Are you serious!?" exclaimed Ferran. "You can barely even walk because of this guy, and you're giving him a chance to stay! Not even a chance to leave safely but a chance to stay!"

"First question," started Aqila, disregarding Ferran completely. " Where did you come from before you got to the city of Dursnia?"

"I came from Hapopelma, a city to the North. It is way more developed there," replied Sartan.

Caleb quickly interrupted, "That is where we came from before here! What are the chances?"

"Quite slim," added Ferran who mentioned a red flag to Aqila with his face.

"Why did you come here?" asked Aqila who picked up on Ferran's cues.

"Because the police in Hapopelma were making survival impossible."

"Where are you going next?"

"It depends if he even survives here," laughed Ferran.

"Silence! 'Sartan' if that is even your real name, why do you want to stay with us? We have an agenda," said Aqlia, who was opening a cabinet under the sink. When Sartan saw her pull out a rusted, old wrench he kicked back Ferran and turned to the door. Ferran was quick to act, as he managed to rustle him to the floor and tighten his knife's position. A small drip of blood escaped Sartan as the knife just barely pierced through the skin on his throat. Aqila watched the whole ordeal come and go, as she limped towards them wrench in hand. "Why do you want to stay with us?"

"I DON'T!" exclaimed Sartan from the floor. "I'll stay to help you with this agenda since I unintentionally hurt your leg, but I really don't want to be here!"

"I see," said Aqila slowly. The wrench was cold and heavy in her palm. "Not everyone is able to chase me across rooftops, so you will be retrieving something for us before you can leave."

"Wait, now you want me to stay? You were asking questions to see if I get to stay, but now you are asking questions to see…"

"I am asking questions to see if Ferran kills you now or you leave with your life after doing some work for us," stated Aqila abruptly without letting Sartan finish. She watched as a faint frown gave birth on his face.

"I understand."

"We need to find the Palace of Strelec, or Sagittarius if you know little about the Zodiacs. It is somewhere within this desert, but other than that we know very little about its location." She knelt down over him while smacking the wrench in one of her hands.

"You obviously are having issues meeting your goals. Especially since you just exposed them to a random stranger. I however, might be able to assist you with that," replied Sartan whose frown quickly faded away.

Stupid! Why would I tell him that? Aqila, knowing full well that she wanted not to kill him, quickly replied in an attempt not to lose the little mind game she created, "I know you can help me find Strelec's Palace. Why else would I tell you about it? You nearly did catch me after all. You will help us with anything we need, understood?" said Aqila as she hinted back to the wrench that now rested peacefully across her knee.

"I will help you. I suppose it is the least I can do after hurting you like I did, but why do you want to do something with the Zodiacs? They are more dangerous than Dursnia itself," asked Sartan.

Aqila stared deep into his eyes for a few seconds before saying, "Good, good. We like to avoid accidents whenever we can." She smiled a cheeky grin. Then in an attempt to stand up on her own, violent purrs of electricity sliced through the neurons in her calf, locking her in the kneeling position she was in. She distracted herself from the pain by graciously answering his question all the while swallowing the internal fire that trembled from her injured calf and up to her fingertips, "Because they are all dead. All of them except for Kozoroh, Lev, and Blizenci, but I am sure you knew that as well as their identities. We will explain the rest later."

The confusion that creeped across his face reaffirmed her mental victory, but the victory was short lived as his gaze was now fixed on Ferran who must have noticed his confusion as well. Ferran had let out a question for him, "You don't know anything about Zodiacs do you? You're telling me that you never even realized that almost all of the night's stars are gone?"

"What? I haven't really had the time to notice. When you don't even know which Zodiac you are, retaining information about them becomes daunting and unimportant."

Aqila resumed her interrogation with, "When is your birthday?"

Sartan stared hesitantly before replying, "I honestly don't know the exact month, but it was around twenty years ago that is for sure."

"You don't even know what your own birthday is?" asked Caleb from the background.

"No. I can't remember much of my childhood either. A few random memories pop up occasionally, but most of it is blank until just a few years ago."

After a long moment of awkward silence Aqila finally said, "Alright, you can stay with us. You just need to figure out whatever that thing with your memory is because that is quite odd." Aqila watched the relief flood across his face for a few seconds before putting down the wrench and offering him her hand. Reluctantly, he took it. Once they stood up she victoriously kept herself from laughing as she watched him realize she used him as a crutch for her leg rather than offering to help him up. In an impudent tone she said, "Thanks, my leg is killing me."

"Of...course," answered Sartan slowly.

"Are you serious Aqila?" blurted Ferran who was still standing next to them holding a knife. "This guy broke your leg! How can you forgive him that easily?"

"I forgive him," said Caleb who was already in the bathroom with the door conveniently left open. "He saved my rump. As long as Aqila is cool with him I'm okay. I mean after all it's her leg not mine."

"Caleb has a point," claimed Aqila. "If Sartan can hurt me like that then he could be a great asset to the team, and he might teach us something. Nobody has ever stayed on my trail that long let alone catch up to me. How did you escape those officers anyway, Sartan?"

"I literally threw money at them. It was kinda fu-"

"Nobody cares if you dodged a case, 'Sartan', and there is no way you can teach me anything!" shouted Ferran as he busted through the camper door murmuring under his breath, "Unbelievable, just unbelievable"

"Don't worry about him. He tends to get a little...overprotective." said Aqila who plopped down on the sofa. She propped her injured leg up on the wall of the other side of the camper to ease the pain.

"Do you need anything? The bone didn't break, did it?" questioned Sartan while he stood there awkwardly, and after reading him Aqila assumed it was because he didn't want to sit down next to her.

Caleb groaned in the bathroom and screamed, "Oh, don't kiss her ass Sartan. Just tell us where Strelec's Palace is." Then everything went quiet as

Caleb groaned again before murmuring something incoherent under his breath. Within seconds the silence was disturbed once more. "HEY! Sartan, come bring me some toilet paper!"

"It's under the sink," said Aqila while fighting back a blush of embarrassment that was caused by her friend in the other room. "And yes that would be more important. We believe the bone is fine, but do you know anything about the Zodiac Palaces? Or anything about Zodiacs in general."

Sartan had the toilet paper and was trying to vault over her injured leg without touching it. That was a challenge in the first place because the camper was so small. Aqila noticed his discomfort, but chose not to do anything about it other than restate the question.

"I know practically nothing about them, but I actually have something right here." He reached for his pockets, but within seconds Aqila could tell that whatever he was looking for was gone. "I could've sworn I---It was a letter from Kozoroh to Police Chief Omar about some sort of Tansiq Scroll in the mayor's library. Not too sure what that is about but I do know that Police Chief Omar is supposed to retrieve the scroll by the time Lev arrives," said Sartan unsteadily as he finally got around Aqila without touching her. She watched him realize that the worst was yet to come, as now he had to go to Caleb. She failed to hold back her laughter when she saw the pinched face he made upon smelling the dread that was in the other room. Unfortunately, the outburst of laughter made the festering pain in her leg rear its ugly head again.

"Lev's involvement, let alone Kozoroh, means that they must be searching for the palace just like us. Regardless, this is Amazing! A Tansiq Scroll is basically a map to a specific Zodiac's Palace. We knew Strelec's scroll was somewhere in this city. We will need to steal the scroll before Omar can because if Lev gets it we are never going to see that scroll again. I also don't want to be here when Lev arrives," said Caleb, sounding like he was excited to see the arrival of Sartan to the bathroom.

"Why don't you want to let Lev get it?" asked Sartan. He walked back out of the bathroom scarred for life, and Sartan looked as though he had a bit less eyebrow when he returned to her eyesight. Aqila watched as he finally decided to sit down next to her. After a moment he said, "How do you know that Lev won't help us either? She might be able to help you."

"I can assure you her allegiance lies with Kozoroh," said Aqila.

Caleb continued from the other room, "Yeah, I would rather not meet the fabled Lev. She has a reputation for hunting down and killing those that willingly or unwillingly learned too much…"

"Well…we don't know too much do we?" asked Sartan with uncertainty in his tone. "At the very least I don't know too much."

"That reminds me," started Aqila as Caleb returned from the wash room. "What do you know about the Zodiacs? Give us your quickest summary of them."

Sartan hesitated and glanced at Caleb for assistance. When he found none he slowly answered, "The Zodiacs…well there are twelve of them."

"Great start scruffs!"

"There is…they each are a rightful ruler of one of the twelve empires of the planet. Each one belongs to an elemental family of Fire, Earth, Water, or Air, and…they are real people who live somewhere in the world."

Aqila nodded before continuing with, "Is that all that you know?"

"What else is there to it?" asked Sartan as he looked to the left and the right with a hesitant smile. "Every single one of us on the planet is part of a Zodiac, and I am quite certain that each Zodiac is immortal too," answered Sartan.

"Well, yes…and no," laughed Caleb.

Aqila replied, "Everyone is part of a Zodiac. That is how the Zodiac gets its power, from everyone who is a part of it. Zodiacs usually are immortal but not always."

"Okay, but how is this relevant if all you need me to do is help you steal a scroll?" asked Sartan.

"Don't be rude scruffs! She is trying to teach you something!" exclaimed Caleb who was in the kitchen searching through the large duffel bag that he had stolen.

"It is important because you broke my leg, and I want you to know this if you are going to help us at all," said Aqila hastily and unmercifully. "Where was I? Zodiacs are only immortal if they are an Active Zodiac. From our understanding, to be an Active Zodiac you have to fulfill three requirements. One is going through the ritual-like inauguration at a Zodiac's palace. Two is having the powerful gemstone of the same Zodiac as the palace. Three is, and by far the easiest, to be a part of the Zodiac that is both the palace and gemstone."

"That isn't confusing at all," laughed Caleb who now had pulled a few cans out of the bag and lined them up on the counter. "He said he knows nothing about them."

"Fine Caleb," responded Aqila. "To appease you I will give an example."

Sartan said, "An example probably won't be necessa-"

"Here is the example," stated Aqila as she continued without listening to Sartan. "Lev. Lev is an Active Zodiac that possesses great powers, one of which being immortality from human means. Lev was born a human quite a few decades ago as a part of the Leo Zodiac. In order to become the Active Zodiac she is today she had to remove the previous Active Leo by means of death. Then she had to be inaugurated at the Leo Palace and hold the Leo Gemstone. All of this can be done for each-"

"Like I said I think I got it," interrupted Sartan.

"What about the ones that aren't immortal?" asked Caleb with a tauntful laugh.

"What a wonderful question," replied Aqila who happily enjoyed Sartan's visible disamusement. "Let us take Kozoroh as this example. Kozoroh was, like Lev, born a normal human. He is part of the Capricorn Zodiac, so he would never be able to become the Active Leo like Lev. Kozoroh however is not immortal. This is because he is not the Active Capricorn rather an inactive one. The only difference here is that he was able to be inaugurated at the Capricorn Palace, but he has yet to touch the Capricorn Gemstone since that date. He is still more powerful than a normal human, and he still acts as the Zodiacal representation for all of the Capricorns throughout the world, preventing anyone else from becoming an Active or inactive Capricorn."

"I could only imagine if he had the powers of an Active Zodiac though," whispered Caleb who was stirring something on the small but clunky stovetop that jutted out of the side of the camper wall.

"So that is what you guys are really trying to do here?" asked Sartan. "You are basically trying to become gods by replacing all the Zodiacs that have died mysteriously."

"No. No. No. No, not in the slightest!" exclaimed Caleb. "We want to revive them all."

"I'm not too sure I believe that, but how do you know they want to be revived in the first place?"

"How do you know they wanted to die in the first place?" countered Aqila.

"That's fair," answered Sartan. "I still don't see why it is relevant for you to go out of your way to resuscitate the Zodiacs that have died. If you wait long enough somebody surely will just replace them and do as little work for their people as the predecessors did."

"Nonsense," replied Aqila. "If we are able to bring these ancient rulers back to their rightful thrones then I see no reason why they would view their subjects as peasants rather than choosing to serve them diligently."

"How did they die in the first place if they were all immortal?"

"Were they all Active?" asked Caleb from the adjacent kitchen.

"All of the ones that have died were, but even an Active Zodiac can still be killed by other Active Zodiacs. They can even be killed by inactive Zodiacs or the gemstone of another Zodiac in extreme cases," replied Aqila whose nostrils were besieged by an array of herbs and spices.

"I see," said Sartan. "Why did they die though?"

"I do believe you are unready for that lesson," said Aqila before she realized where the questionable scents originated from. "Are you seriously making turtle soup in this heat!?"

"What? I'm hungry…"

"Sartan, you said that you knew where Strelec's Tansiq scroll was, correct?"

He instantly gave her a reply. "The Chief Officer Omar received a letter from Kozoroh. I don't remember everything, but it said that the scroll was in the mayor's library at the center of the town. I've been in the complex before, so I could get you there easily."

"Perfect! Here is the plan. Tomorrow night you, Ferran and I will sneak into the library and grab the scroll. Ferran will be a lookout for any guards that try to stop us while you lead the way. Lastly, Caleb will wait for us at the entrance to the complex with the camper."

Sartan processed the plan before countering, "The entrance to the complex is right on the interstate in and out of town, and we shouldn't wait that long if an immortal beast is on her way to retrieve it from Omar. He probably doesn't have it yet, but I have no doubt that if we wait much longer it won't be there when we get to the library."

"Plan B! Same plan, but we do it tonight and Caleb parks on the other side of the interstate."

"Are you sure you can handle this with your leg Aqila?" asked Caleb with sincere concern plastered across his face. Perhaps Aqila misjudged the concern for hunger, but either way Caleb continued, "I usually don't try to tell you what to do…maybe you should sit this one out though?"

"I will be in the mayor's library when they get the Tansiq Scroll," responded Aqila. "A minor injury will never stop me from the main goal."

"Well that is reassuring to hear," slurped Caleb. "The stew is done if you guys want any."

"No thank you. I don't really have an appetite," said Aqila.

"I will. I haven't eaten well in days," said Sartan so quickly he nearly cut her off. He happily made his way across the room towards dinner.

Aqila was starting to feel numb as the painkillers took effect. She blurted to them from across the room, "Caleb, don't forget we are moving on Strelec's scroll tonight. You will need to fuel up the camper and wait for us at the entrance to the mayor's complex."

He replied with a mouth full of soup, "At what time?"

She didn't reply immediately. Aqila zoned out as a wave of weariness crept across her mind. Aqila knew that the painkillers had to be drowsy, but she did not read the bottle. "We should leave here at ten till 11:00 p.m. That way we have an hour to get the scroll before the midnight chimes go off on the clock tower. By the way, what medicine did you give me?"

Caleb laughed when she asked that question. "I gave you some 'supreme' painkillers. You probably won't be awake for much longer."

"Tell Ferran our plan if I fall asleep before he returns. He is going inside with Sartan and I to help." Caleb nodded with his mouth full, and she watched as Sartan stuffed his face full with rolls and nasty, turtle soup. It looked as if he had failed to eat in weeks. "Sartan, who are you?"

He glanced up and gulped down the oddly colored water before replying, "What do you mean?"

"What is your story? Everyone has a story. What do you want to do in life? Who-are-you?"

Sartan's eyes widened as he stared at her. Before Sartan could manage to muster up a response Caleb interrupted him saying, "You don't have to answer those. Her medicine must be kicking in." Sartan quickly grasped his statement and nodded before returning his full attention back to the soup. "Aqila, you should probably go get some rest," said Caleb.

She hesitated before sighing, "I could use some rest. Can one of you help me get to the bedroom?" Caleb subtly whispered a few sentences to Sartan. Then Sartan got up to help her. She could feel the inability to feel just about everything in her body, so she quickly made it to the back of the camper without feeling the slightest wince of pain. As soon as Sartan helped Aqila into the bed she turned to see that he had already started to make his way out of the bedroom. In an attempt to keep him in the room she said with a giddy inflection, "This is going to be an intense *steeeaaal* tonight." For some odd reason she said the word steal with great emphasis. Upon realizing this her face was lit ablaze with a burning red hue. *Why did I say it like that?*

"Yeah...that is kind of how it works," said Sartan speedily without even turning around.

While he thudded back to the soup she thought, *Why am I so stupid? What the hell is wrong with me!?* She then looked down at her injured leg. She felt no pain, but a throbbing sensation on her calf of the same frequency as her heart melted her pants to her skin. Aqila rolled her pant leg up to see that the bandage was mostly red. She screamed, "Hey, can someone get me another bandage and some scissors?!"

Within what felt like a delayed instant Caleb entered with a fresh bandage and scissors in one hand while a dripping spoon was tightly held in the other. He tossed the bandage and scissors onto the bed before he told her, "Try not to waste this one, it's the last."

He walked off closing the door behind him leaving her alone in the bedroom with her injury. In the other room she could briefly hear Sartan asking Caleb things about her. It dawned on her that she never even told him that first thing about her. *I will have to introduce myself to him when I wake up.*

Aqila sat there for a few seconds contemplating this issue before removing the dirty bandage. Her leg was mostly drenched in red and brown. The wound itself resided on the upper portion of her calf. She threw the bloody bandage onto the floor next to the bed then the clean one was quickly swathed around her injury. A few dribbles of blood made it to the bed itself, but Aqila was too tired to worry about it let alone notice. She then took the scissors and slid the rusted, bottom blade through her black leggings at the middle of her thigh. After sitting up a little the scissors snipped all the way around her thigh in a barely complete, disorganized circle. Aqila slid the bloody black pant leg down past her foot. Then the piece of clothing along with the scissors, her socks and her shoes ended up on the floor next to the bloody bandage that had already laid on the crusty brown carpet. All of this happened at an extremely slowed pace.

Aqila figured that the throbbing would stop when it was no longer being choked out by the fabric. *Now that over half of my leg is out I can cool down in the heat of this godforsaken desert. Tonight will be big for us!* She toyed with the endless possibilities that getting to the Sagittarius palace and reviving their first Zodiac could bring, but she was so buzzed by her meds that time slipped by before she could actually think about it. Before even thinking about what the inside of the palace might look like, sleep softly consumed her in its crackling, warm embrace.

Chapter 4
January Nights
Ferran

Ferran returned from the outside of the camper. He had already returned hours ago, but he wanted to take a glance at the hike they were about to make before leaving with a stranger helping them. That stranger of course had nearly maimed his sister within the past twenty four hours. Once inside Ferran was hit with a plethora of sounds, sights, and scents.

"It is time we go," said Caleb who had just finished lacing his shoes.

"Where is Sartan?" asked Ferran who scanned the room for any trace of the sturdily malnourished fool that had connived his way into their group. The room smelled like rotten, sweaty soup from their dinner earlier, but the camper wasn't nearly as warm. Ferran followed with another question, "And why is it getting colder?"

"I told Sartan to wake up Aqila, and it's cold because it's a January night in the desert." replied Caleb with a subtle chuckle.

Sartan then shuffled out of the backroom with Aqila stumbling behind him. Aqila used one hand to prop herself up against the wall and another to rub the sleep out of her eyes. Ferran instantly noticed that Aqila had cut off over half of her pant leg as she reached for her hoodie and shoes. *What is she thinking! Why would she show much skin in a city as dangerous as this one, especially at night?* Ferran then focused more on Sartan. *He probably told her to cut it.*

Ferran watched Sartan slip into three shirts, a hoodie and two pairs of pants while shivering the whole time. Just watching someone else shiver made him even colder. Ferran looked around the dark room for an extra shirt. It took him a few seconds to find it, but when he did there was no hesitation putting it on. He slipped into his sneakers and stood up to stretch before the hike.

"We should move soon. It will take us a minute to get to the mayor's home," said Ferran while he grabbed a knife and a wallet off of the counter. "Caleb, take this and gas up the camper. We might need a getaway vehicle."

"Who'll be the lookout?" questioned Caleb who was rummaging through the cabinets for food.

After a moment of silence Ferran replied, "Sartan can be the lookout when we get the scroll," *He needs to stay away from Aqila anyway.* He started to think about ways to get Sartan to leave after this but was promptly interrupted.

"No, that-at isn't going to-to happen. I know my way around th-the mayor's compound more than you," slurred Sartan with great disdain. Sartan had possibly been the most affected by the cold and clearly struggled to form a sentence without it breaking from his shivers or shakes.

"You really are that stupid aren't you! You have them fooled, but I know why you are really here," shouted Ferran while his voice cracked from excessive exercise of the vocal cords. "Plus, I don't care if you were living on the streets, you can go back to them after today."

"Why are you screaming and arguing?" demanded softly Aqila who had spent the past minute zoning out watching Caleb struggling to open a container of oats. The room went silent, and everybody watched as she stood up slowly with great wince in her wobble. Aqila then threw her hood up over her head and continued, "I just woke up, and my ears are already ringing because of you. We will deal with whatever problems you two have later. Right now we must not stagnate. Ferran will look out while Sartan helps me look for the scroll. Caleb go get some fuel. Then wait for us on the main road near Mayor Khalil's complex in about two hours. We will need a quick getaway if things get hairy."

Caleb stopped dumping raw oats into his mouth when he heard someone utter his name. "Agreed, I'm ready to leave Dursnia," he squabbled with a mouth full of food, if one could call it that. Then he opened the cabinets looking for something once more.

"Wait-t, we are leaving D-Dursnia after this?" asked Sartan quite selfishly while still being haunted by the frigid air.

"Would you rather stay here after stealing possibly one of the mayor's most prized possessions and escaping the entire town's pitiful police force," asked Ferran rhetorically, allowing a few seconds to pass. "That's what I figured. The fuel container should be outside Caleb."

Caleb stumbled off outside with one of his hands stuck in an oats container while laughing, "I mean…he has a point."

Aqila, even in her groggy state, was smart enough to suggest leaving for the complex before allowing Sartan to respond. Ferran walked out the door after Caleb saying, "At least we won't have to deal with any riots at night. Come on, it will take some time to get there, especially with Sartan slowing us down." Ferran didn't wait one bit. Without looking back at either Aqila or Sartan he continued out of the camper. *This is ridiculous anyway. I hope he gets caught tonight.*

***

The three of them made their way away from the camper and towards the center of the town. The dry winds pierced through his clothes in the cold, open streets of suburbs of the town that in reality consisted of multiple scattered clay huts rising just barely enough to shield them from the full force of the winter winds. Ferran looked to Aqila who was limping along while shivering with most of her leg out. Of course it was her injured one that she decided to cut away the cloth from. A bandage wrapped around her calf hiding almost all of the damage that had been done, but he could tell just by how tightly she gripped Sartan's arm that the icy gusts slashed straight through the bandage and possibly even the flesh, freezing her fibula that she claimed was intact and uncracked. *We should probably get her a cane.* In an attempt to passively soothe his younger sister Ferran told them both, "When we get closer to the city the larger buildings will stop the wind."

Neither of them showed interest in what they had heard. Sartan was shivering more than Aqila even though he had piled clothes onto himself like a rotten, little child. Sickened, Ferran spat on the ground cursing at the relentless wind. Seconds later a strong gust knocked all of them down like bowling pins just as they made it to the first few tall buildings of the city.

Before Ferran could get back up he heard Aqila cry out in pain, "Ouch! Ouch!"

He quickly rose to his feet to see that she was holding her exposed calf and watched as she held down tightly on the bandages with her hands.

"We need to keep going, Omar is probably already there," whispered Aqila, choking back tears as she struggled to rise against the wind.

The three of them scrambled to their feet, and shuffled forward to the safety of the buildings leaving the howling whispers of frosted air behind them. The roads were lit up by the occasional street lamp which reminded Ferran how strange he found Dursnia to be. There were so many alleyways, but only a few streets where cars could drive. Hapopelma, the city he was in before here, had so many cars revving through the city it was a miracle he didn't end up in a vehicular homicide. This city on the other hand has multiple riots everyday in the foot markets. Ferran was sure that everyone wanted to leave Dursnia sooner than later. *Even Sartan wants to leave this unforsaken town that spawned him, but he will only jeopardize our operation.*

As they continued the buildings clustered together both vertically and horizontally. Sartan then whispered to them, "At night there are usually a lot more guards lurking around. Something is wrong." Ferran looked around and realized that they hadn't seen a single officer the whole time. In fact they hadn't even passed a citizen yet. He and Aqila were usually asleep at night, but in this one circumstance he trusted Sartan's expertise who found this to be extremely strange for Dursnia.

"Where do you think they are?" asked Ferran when he looked behind him to see an empty street with flickering shadows cast on the pavement from street lights that weren't working properly.

Before Sartan could answer, Aqila whispered, "Regardless, we need to stick to the shadows and get off the main streets." She tugged Sartan softly with little energy and pulled him into the nearest alleyway shrouded in darkness. Ferran followed, but he watched how weak her strides had become.

Ferran stated, "If you keep pushing yourself like this Aqila you won't heal."

"What do you want me to do then? Go wait with Caleb? Try to make it all the way back to him by myself all the while leaving you unsupervised?"

"Unsupervised?!"

"It matters not," whispered Aqila. "We must keep going. I have already committed."

He shrugged the comment off and followed them in the shadows. After weaving through the alleys for a while Ferran noticed that the sky was getting brighter. Either the moon had tripled in size or they had arrived at the walls of the mayor's personal complex. After rounding another alleyway corner Ferran had his answer. They all stopped dead in their tracks when they saw the walls. The walls towered over the group as they stared upward. Down the alleyway to the right the wall ended at a huge street which he presumed the main entrance sat on, but the main entrance was way too obvious to be safe. In no way was Aqila capable of climbing over these walls with her current state, so instead, Ferran looked for an alternate entrance. One that could be accessed from the ground level that at the same time wouldn't alert anyone on the inside. "How do we get in?" asked Ferran as he searched for an opening somewhere.

"There is a backdoor around here somewhere," whispered Sartan.

The crew circled around the complex looking for anything that would defeat the purpose of the gigantic walls. Then he saw it. A tiny door on the rear side made for trash disposal, and the area around it definitely smelt like it was a space for waste. The door itself was dripping in a rancid green liquid while the ground around it was permanently stained both visually and olfactory. Black trash bags were scattered around the door, some of which had been ripped open and spilled their contents out all over the ground. Ferran ran up to the door to see if it was locked, but right before he could reach it, the knob started to twist. Being so close he had nowhere to run. Ferran turned to see Sartan struggle shuffling Aqila into an adjacent alleyway, but he knew there wasn't time to join them. Instead, he lunged behind the door as it swung open

A chunky, dirty man stumbled out holding two soggy trash bags. The chef's apron that constricted his billowing belly was all brown and saturated. Ferran watched from behind the hinges as the door swung out completely hiding him from the man's vision. The man didn't walk all the way out. His fingers gripped around the thick, metal door holding it open just enough. Then the chef decided to fling the bags at the building across the alleyway. Everything within them exploded upon impact, and bits and chunks of the leftovers from at least a week ago splattered back onto Ferran who crouched down trying to dodge the incoming artillery. The giblets steamed their way down his arms sizzling when they dripped onto the frosty asphalt. Ferran gagged when some of the matter landed on his face and started to drip down over his lip and off his chin. Luckily, while he was gagging the chef let out a belch that could silence an air horn. The chef rubbed his greasy chin and turned around facing whatever was on the inside of the wall. Then, following a mighty sigh, the metal door clanked shut once more.

Ferran couldn't stop gagging though, but he was able to hold it in while the man was standing there. When the door slammed right next to him the chef trudged back to his work, and things changed. Knowing that the insider no longer could hear him, Ferran choked down the following gags, spat up as much saliva out of his throat as possible, and wiped his lips off on his sleeve several times.

Finally, when Ferran came to control his bodily functions he tried to twist the knob, insisting to Aqila and Sartan that everything was fine. It didn't budge under the pressure of his sweaty hands. After wiping his hands off on his shirt he said, "We aren't getting inside."

"We can still get inside. We don't need to use this door," said Aqila who had left the stability of her third leg for a seat on the ground away from Ferran's spit and the piles of fresh and fermented trash.

"No, Aqila. It's over," replied Ferran.

"I could get us through the door if it weren't for my leg," said Aqila as she stared at the goosebumps that violently took up residence on her bare thigh. "We could scale the wall and unlock it from the other side."

"You aren't going to try it. Not with your injury," demanded Ferran. Aqila was struggling to keep eye contact with him, and he noticed quickly. "You're so naive."

A second passed before she continued the argument. "Then what was the point of sending Caleb for fuel?"

"He is getting fuel for the camper so that we can leave Dursnia," replied Ferran in an angered tone. "We shouldn't be messing with the Zodiacs anyway. Look what happened to dad!" Aqila froze for a second, and he knew that she would stop if they started talking about that.

"Are we dad? We told Caleb to come pick us up on the main road once we got the Tansiq Scroll. I will not put him in danger for no reason. The only cars on the main street travel through Dursnia. Nobody pauses there contentedly and safely. I am not putting Caleb to the test," argued Aqila while shivering. Ferran noticed that she wasn't getting any better.

"We can get back to the camper before Caleb leaves," said Ferran. Before he got a reply from his sister there was a pile of dust that landed on his shoulder. Aqila instantly tried to say something in order to distract him, but he had already turned around. At first he didn't see anything, but then he looked upward a bit to see Sartan clinging to about two-thirds of the way up the wall. "What the hell Sartan!?"

Sartan didn't look down, instead he slowly inched his way upward while holding on to the few cracks. Regardless, he looked like an ant climbing a flat wall. He appeared to be only two arm's lengths from the summit, but when

Sartan tried to put his hand on the next slouch in the bricks his fingers didn't hold. Behind him Ferran heard Aqila gasp as Sartan lost his grip. Now watching him hang on to the wall with one hand and two feet Ferran started to think. *Maybe we will get in. If he can get over the wall and down the other side safely. But do I really want that? That will just create more problems.*

After a few nerve racking seconds Sartan managed to lock his flailing hand onto the wall. Both siblings watched without taking their eyes away from him the whole while. Unsure of whether or not he would survive all they could do was watch. Well all that Ferran would do was watch. Aqila quietly and consistently instructed Sartan, "Do not look down. Do not move forward until you know your grip will hold. Do not put your feet somewhere they will slip."

Ferran knew Aqila was quite agile, but he had forgotten that she scaled buildings and such all the time. He looked back at her. She was now standing up against the side of a building staring up at Sartan. Ferran whispered, "I don't trust Sartan, and you shouldn't either." Aqila looked over to Ferran with an irritated glance before looking back up at Sartan.

Ferran turned just in time to see Sartan's right hand flop over the top of the wall. "Now crawl down and open the door!" shouted Ferran, completely unaware of his surroundings. He cupped his hands around his mouth and was about to shout something else up to Sartan when something stung the back of his head sending him stumbling forward.

When he turned around he saw Aqila struggling to stay standing up without support. Then he saw that her left hand was turning red. "Why did you smack me?"

"Why are you shouting right next to the walls? Do you want to get caught?" demanded Aqila. She looked at him with a furious glare that successfully melted some of the goosebumps off his arms. "It is literally freezing out here, you are intolerable, and Sartan is doing all of the work while you are about to get us caught. I might as well slap you again!"

"Doing all the work? We literally just got here!" argued Ferran, rubbing the back of his head. "All that he has done is make problems for us."

"You are wrong! Sartan has found the location of a Tansiq Scroll, something we failed to do for such an extended amount of time. He has helped me with my injured leg the whole time which is something I know you would never even contemplate," ranted Aqila who undoubtedly was tired of Ferran for some unknown reason.

"How do we even know there is a scroll here? Sartan could've just lied to get us arrested. I might not have helped you walk as much as him, but we could get you a cane or something instead of some random person who likes to break stuff. I'm done trying to help you. If you and Caleb want him to hurt you then I won't stop you, but if he tries anything with me then it's over!"

Ferran spun around before Aqila could reply to notice that Sartan was completely gone. The wall was bare and dusty just like it was before Sartan straddled it like a bull. Then Aqila must have noticed the same thing because she said, "Where did he go?"

"I hope he fell," said Ferran. "That's what he deserves."

Aqila didn't get enticed by what he said like he was hoping, instead she just limped back to the side of a building to lean up against. *What now? Do we just wait here for someone to find us?* Ferran walked a bit away from the rancid region which was the back door and plopped down on the ground against an adjacent building. Looking upward the building towered over him, but it was nothing compared to the skyscrapers that breached the atmosphere in Hapopelma. *Other than our hometown, Hapopelma is probably the best city we have been to so far. The police force there didn't mess around as much. They actually did something, and they nudged us in the right direction by telling us there might be a Tansiq Scroll here in Dursnia.*

He sat there reminiscing on the easier times before the doorknob quickly twisted. The door slowly creaked open interrupting the enjoyable reminiscing he was doing. Luckily, it was just Sartan behind the door. He got up and tried not to step on any sloshing trash that had started to freeze. Once he got to Sartan he didn't say anything but instead walked past him into the complex. In the background he could hear Aqila wincing in pain as she limped towards the door saying, "Thank you, Sartan." Ferran tried to ignore their childish behavior.

Ignoring them was not a problem. Once he took a hungry glance at the inside of the compound he realized that finding the Tansiq Scroll would be harder than anticipated. The world on the outside of the walls was in another dimension. People struggled to even get a meal a day or a place to stay at night, but inside the walls it was an entirely different story. Multiple buildings congested the complex all of which were made out of polished marble or at least something that looked like marble. Every single light on the inside of the walls was ten times brighter than any of the few flickering lights that were scattered through the rest of the city. Ferran noticed that each building had a specific purpose. One of the buildings was an industrial mill, and another was a greenhouse growing wheat. Down to the left of the wall about in the corner was a large generator powering the whole complex, but he knew that it wasn't powering the city. *This complex is almost entirely self-sufficient.*

"I see why you stole from here before Sartan. This place is amazing compared to the rest of Dursnia," said Ferran who stood there intoxicated by the sheer difference in environments. "How did you even get in last time?"

"This place is the best part of Dursnia. At the same time it's the worst," said Sartan while he shuffled into the complex with Aqila. "I snuck in through the front door during the day. That wouldn't work again though because there are three of us, and they buffed security since they caught me doing so."

"Then take us out of the open please," whispered Aqila.

As the group trudged behind the nearest building they could find, Sartan said, "The library should be towards the center."

Ferran opened the back door to an industrial greenhouse. The inside of the greenhouse was way warmer than the cold desert night. The warmth that nearly burnt his eyebrows off melted away the frozen fears that he had. Before they even closed the door behind them, his feet began to scream in the heat, and sweat dripped down his skin. Well it wasn't sweat rather the water in the air sticking to him, but either way it was a welcomed change in temperature. He watched Sartan's eyes nearly roll back in his head from the heat, but Ferran didn't dwell on it too long because Sartan was weird to begin with. *What kind of freak would chase someone and then help them?* Two long rows of pots lined the walls on either side of them. Each pot had one lamp hanging above them and thin hoses running through their soil. Tiny green sprouts stretched upwards out of the black dirt, a contrast of colors that Ferran hadn't seen in quite some time since arriving in the Great Desert.

Unfortunately, the three of them quickly made their way through the greenhouse. The whole group stood at the front door for a few seconds preparing for the cold that awaited them on the outside. It was an unspoken agreement that all of them surely were aware of, to take a few moments in the safety of the greenhouse before continuing onward. Ferran's hand hesitantly reached to slowly open the door. He peeked his head around a thin gap to see two guards come around the corner of a nearby building. He quickly closed the door and whispered, "Two guards."

"Are they approaching us?" whispered Aqila.

Ferran slowly opened the door again, but this time he didn't see anyone. He poked his head out and glanced to the right and left. "They're gone, but I don't like this."

Aqila replied as the group crept out of the safety of the greenhouse, "I agree. I want this to be as fast as possible. Preferably unnoticed as well."

The complex itself was a maze to Ferran. They ran through it like maze rats, and the cheese at the center was just a key to a bigger maze. He had no clue how close they were to the library, but upon a quick glance to his flank he realized it shouldn't take that long because there sat the greenhouse barely visible around the corner of a few buildings. He then asked, "Sartan, where is the library?"

"Shhhh! It is by the tall building at the center. With the clocktower," replied Sartan who was starting to appear tired from carrying a portion of Aqila's weight for so long.

Ferran saw the twisting structure barely creep up above the peak of the building in front of them. He sighed at the sight of the somewhat distant objective. Then he couldn't look away from it. The tall clock tower was a beacon of hope for him. As they silently snuck around tall marble buildings of various unknown purposes, the glow behind the clock began to fail at growing out above the marble structures. This was good as the tower itself was probably the tallest building in the small city. They rounded another corner allowing him to see just how far its sharp-pointed peak really was. *It's 11:50 at night. We left about an hour and a half ago. Caleb surely has fueled the camper by now, and it is only going to get colder until the sun rises tomorrow morning.*

"We have to hurry. Caleb probably has the camper on the mainstreet by now," whispered Ferran as they took a left into the shadow of another building once more. Sartan nor Aqila gave him a reply, and he was about to restate the question when he saw two guards a few yards ahead of them. The guards had their backs to the group, but if they made a single wrong move the whole complex would be on lock down. For a few seconds nobody moved at all, then Sartan slowly backed up with Aqila. Ferran followed his lead and quickly lunged back behind the side of the building they just came from.

"Luckily it was really dark in between those buildings behind the officers. Otherwise that might have been the end of Zodiacs as I know it," whispered Ferran.

"Okay?" stated Sartan rhetorically with flexed eyebrows. "We have to knock them out."

"Why would we have to do that yet?" asked Ferran.

"They aren't going to move. We need to get through the center of the complex unseen."

"We can go around them though."

"Yes, but the library is in the center. They will see us heading for it."

Ferran poked his head around the side of the building and looked past the guards. He hadn't realized how close they actually were to the clocktower. Past the guards was a large empty road that encompassed two large buildings. The first building had the clocktower on top of it. It was shrouded in parking spaces for cars. A few were occupied, but most of them looked like they were there purely for drop offs or something. He assumed that it was the office and or living quarters for the mayor. Then his attention shifted to the bigger building attached by a footbridge to the smaller building. This building was way larger than the other one, and its height dwarfed that of the other. It rose at least half way up the clock tower while the other building seemed to be only one or two stories, excluding the clock tower that dwarfed everything of course. What really got his attention though was the windows of the large building. They were spaced out quite a bit, but in every one of them resided rows and rows of bookshelves. He then looked back to the road. It was so wide that they would definitely be seen if they attempted to cross it, especially since towering fog lights illuminated every blotch of pavement.

When Ferran returned his attention to Sartan he said, "Okay, if we have to we will. Just don't make any mistakes."

Sartan gave him a glance of pure annoyance before helping Aqila sit down on the cold ground. Sartan then stood up and watched Aqila grimace upon lowering her leg to the cold ground. The two of them left her there as they rounded the corner quietly. While steadily creeping up on the guards, the conversation they were having became more audible.

"Yeah, Omar acted terrified."

"Can you really blame him though? If Lev was on her way expecting me to have something I would be too."

"You think. Though if he was this scared of her he would not be late to this thing."

"Right! He was supposed to be here 20 minutes ago."

Both Ferran and Sartan glimpsed at each other knowing that they had less time than expected. If they didn't hurry then there might not be a scroll to steal. *I am not going to let some corrupt cop stop me from-*. Ferran slipped his knife into his hand, holding the blade in his palm. By now they were a few feet behind the guards and in arms reach. Ferran stopped thinking and didn't even notice that Sartan was counting down with his fingers right next to him. He cracked down his hand right on the back of the guard's head. The guard toppled to his knees, and he dropped the clean knife back into his pocket.

In his peripheral vision Ferran saw the other officer take out his baton getting ready to swing it at him, but he didn't even have time to flinch. He was jolted when there was a heavy crack to his right. The other officer toppled down next to where Sartan stood.

"We need to get them out of sight, come on grab one," whispered Sartan as he tried to grab both arms of the officer that he just knocked out.

"Why bother? They won't be causing us issues anytime soon," said Ferran.

"Are you being serious?" asked Sartan as he began dragging an unconscious officer into the darkness of the alley. "There is no time to dwell on this. Just pull your cop into the alley," whispered Sartan in a deep voice.

Ferran dragged his guard back towards Sartan who by now was deep into the darker part of the alleyway. As he pulled his victim into the dark shadows Ferran avoided looking at the guards. The cold wind stung his face, and he closed his eyes to shield them. He didn't open his eyes again until his rear hit the wall of a building. When he opened them he saw Sartan approaching. Sartan grabbed the legs of the guard and pulled them towards the corner where two adjacent buildings merged.

Ferran glanced to his right to see where one guard already laid askew in the corner. His gaze drifted to his left to see Aqila watch in slight discomfort from the cold. Then he finally peaked forward to see the clocktower and library loom over them. It nearly invited him into the library just with its sudden ominous presence. When they got to the darkest part of the alley the two of them threw the officer into the corner where it flopped onto the other officer. Ferran slowly watched Sartan close his eyes for a few seconds before walking back to Aqila.

"Are they okay?" asked Aqila.

"They will be fine, but it's best if we keep moving," said Sartan calmly while helping her up. Aqila stared at Ferran for a few seconds. The three of them kept silent as they all staggered towards the open street. Ferran was anticipating more guards to be lurking around watching the street, so as Aqila and Sartan stumbled forward unsteadily he stayed back in the safety of the shadows. He watched briefly waiting for a surprise attack, but when nothing happened he hesitantly followed them into the open.

When he left the safety of the dark alley in between two buildings of unknown purpose it was almost as if he had walked out from the night right into a mid-day market. The fog lights beamed down onto the group like the sun baking a scorpion in the desert. Ferran was enamored by the pure heat that the fog lights were capable of producing. Had he been barefoot then his feet might have burned as he walked across the sandy pavement. *It isn't that hot, it's just because we have been in the cold so long.* Ferran's eyes started to get dry as bursts of cold, dusty winds, in spite of the heat produced by the fog lights, pierced him, ushering small tears to flood his face.

After what seemed like an eternity the three of them finally made it out of the street and into the yard of the library. It was so weird to see grass growing in these extreme conditions, but then he realized it was fake. More importantly Ferran was just glad to be out from under the overbearing fog lights even though the yard was still considerably illuminated. Sartan limped with Aqila up to the first window. Ferran watched as he tried to budge it open with no triumph. While Sartan continued to fumble with the lock Ferran peered through the glass. On the inside there were rows of bookshelves taller than himself. The only thing Ferran found odd was that the window was a basement window. *What kind of library is in the basement?* Not being happy with his presence in the open, Ferran went over to the next window to try it. Naturally, it didn't budge.

"Bust the glass Ferran," said Sartan as he slowly trudged over towards him with Aqila.

There was not any hesitation. The glass shattered after one hit. It was only when it fell in shards all over the floor of the library's basement did he wonder if this might have been a mistake. "Do you think that was too loud?" asked Ferran.

"It doesn't matter; we need to move. Get in," whispered Sartan.

The window itself wasn't that roomy. It took Ferran a few dreaded moments to squeeze through. The hardest part was getting his hips through. Ferran found that strange as his shoulders were definitely wider, but when Sartan started to push him he realized that the window had plenty of width but hardly any length. Once his hip bones made it through he slid into the building like a piece of budder sliding out of a wet hand. His feet landed on the ground, and he heard cracks and crunches. There were still shards of glass scattered everywhere. *Good thing Caleb is with the camper.*

Upon his rotation back to the window, Aqila's foot nearly hit him in the face. She was already sticking one leg through the window. Ferran wondered if she would even be able to squeeze through as it was a challenge for him. Once her feet were in his reach he grasped onto them and started to tug while Sartan pushed. It only took a few seconds before Aqila said to stop, but by then it was too late. The shards of the window that were still intact sliced into her hips as she barely slipped into the basement. Not expecting her to make it through the window, Ferran didn't catch her as gracefully as expected. She avoided landing on her right leg, but when she got cut by the glass it was obvious any plan of a graceful landing disappeared. Instead she flopped straight into Ferran.

The two of them toppled over on the basement floor. Ferran felt a few shards of glass pierce into his left arm. He tried to get up, but Aqila whimpered on top of him. Luckily, Sartan had already made his way through the window and with much more grace than either of the siblings combined. He pulled Aqila off Ferran and away from the shards of glass on the floor, but before tending to her newly established injury Sartan helped Ferran to his feet and told him, "We really need to hurry. She isn't going to get better if we are here."

Ferran glanced over to his sister. There were tiny shards of glass sticking out from all around her hips, arms and legs. Small traces of blood were slowly trickling out from cuts that lined half way down both of her thighs. All she could do was watch as Sartan pulled fragments of glass out of her arms. *She is going to die.* Ferran then felt the pain inside himself bubble up. He realized that his own arms were in jeopardy. As he slowly plucked glass out from his arms there was an acute pain that bounced through his whole body. "Sartan, we need to find bandages or she won't make it. Look how pale her face is," said Ferran after he threw the last piece of glass to the floor.

"Use your shirt and tie it around her," commanded Sartan.

"My shirt? You have at least two on! use yours!" argued Ferran.

It was obvious Sartan was not in the mood to argue because after staring at Ferran for a few seconds he took off his hoodie and tried to wrap it around most of Aqila's new injuries. Within a few seconds the shirt was bundled up around her waist tightly like a makeshift skirt. Ferran knew that it wouldn't be much help though, especially since they took the glass shards out. Sartan tried to help Aqila to her feet, but she didn't move.

Instead she just stared at him for a few seconds before whispering, "I can't walk."

Sartan glanced at Ferran and sighed, "We will need to carry her."

Without arguing Ferran helped Sartan pick her up. "Aqila, you know the most about Zodiacs. I need you to tell us what the scroll looks like," said Ferran.

"The map should be in a black scroll with the words 'Tansiq' and 'Sagittarius' written on it."

Ferran and Sartan carried Aqila down the aisle of the library towards the main walkway that should lead to an exit somewhere. When they got to the middle of the room he peered one way to see a spiral staircase that advanced into the upper floors of the building. "We are never going to find it," blurted out Ferran.

"But we already have," whispered Aqila in a faint and weak voice.

With what appeared to be the last of her energy she pointed in the opposite direction of the staircase towards a glass box. The box held a large black scroll with the words 'Sagittarius Tansiq' inscribed in gold across the side of it. The scroll itself was sitting on a golden pedestal that clipped to the ends of the scroll within the transparent enclosure. The group was then startled when they heard the midnight chimes ring out twelve times from what sounded to be right above them. Relieved that it was only the clock they made their way to the scroll. After everything Ferran had been through he was especially glad to see the prize that was worth coming to this intolerable town for in the first place.

That's when he heard the footsteps clanking down the stairwell behind them. They quickly sat Aqila down on the floor with her back to the scroll case. Ferran opened the casing which for some reason wasn't locked. He gave the scroll to Aqila who instantly put it behind her under her shirt. Once the scroll was hidden out of plain sight they all put their focus on the stairs. Knowing there was no way they could squeeze back through the window in time to escape whoever was approaching them, they watched patiently as the footsteps echoed louder and louder down the stairs.

Chapter 5
A Special Scripture
Sartan

The footsteps were getting heavier with every step. Sartan glanced at his companions. Aqila was sitting down in front of the glass box that no longer held the Tansiq Scroll while reaching for something on her neck. She had cuts all up and down her arms from the glass that ripped up her blue hoodie, and her natural caramel color evaporated from her face where a pale, moon colored tint now rightfully reigned. Ferran didn't look like he was doing much better. He was standing next to Sartan sweating a puddle on the floor while watching the spiral staircase that truly was the only logical way out. Ferran's face was almost as pale as Aqila's. They all were bleeding a bit, but there was no way either of them were as bad as Aqila. She looked like she wasn't going to last much longer, and black circles hung heavy under her eyes that unsteadily fluttered shut and open. *It's up to me if we want to escape alive tonight.* At that moment Sartan finally realized the weight in which he held on his shoulders.

Behind him Aqila whispered to Ferran, "It is gone Ferran!" The footsteps were only seconds away by now, and Sartan knew they had no time to talk.

"What do you mean? Isn't it on the necklace?" asked Ferran.

"The whole necklace is gone! I know not where it!" exclaimed Aqila, stopping mid sentence when she saw the men entering the basement from across the room. Officers piled into the room from the spiral staircase. All of which were in riot gear holding heavy, metal batons. By the time the tenth officer entered the room Sartan saw him. *Omar.* The fat police chief still walked with a limp after his incident that Sartan was fortunate enough to witness and was followed by the mayor himself. The mayor was armed with a revolver in one hand and a majestic, crystalled cane in the other, and it was obvious to Sartan that he was more familiar using the cane just by the angle at which he held the revolver.

"Glad to see that you came back, Sartan," said the mayor. "I was starting to think that I wouldn't be able to use my newest gun. After all, nobody deserves it more than you."

"Do you really need all of these officers then?" asked Sartan who wasted no time replying.

"Well of course I do. We both know how elusive you can be, but let's get to the point here. What are you doing in my library? There is nothing in here for an illiterate such as yourself."

"We know exactly what he is here for Mayor Khalil. He already took your Tansiq Scroll. Look it's gone," said Police Chief Omar without letting Sartan speak for himself. All of the officers and the mayor followed Omar's pointing finger to see that the scroll indeed was missing from its case. "When we deal with this minor inconvenience I suggest that you let me watch over it. A scroll of that value shouldn't be taken this easily, and we both know that."

"Mayor, if you give that scroll to him then he will just give it to Kozoroh," interjected Aqila with barely any energy left.

"And who might this fine young thing be?" questioned the mayor as his warts bubbled on his face. "Your graceful looks might have spared you into a life of concubinage had you not interrupted our conversation. Even in your current condition with all of that nasty peasant blood on you, apparently destiny had something else in mind for this one. I mean seriously, Kozoroh? Do you know how far away he is from our lands? You might have said that Omar was actually the Capricorn Zodiac. That would've been more believable," laughed Mayor Khalil as he looked to his guards to see if they were laughing too.

"No! You fail to understand Lev is on her way!" exclaimed Aqila while breathing heavily.

The mayor calmly said, "Detain her." Within seconds she was on her feet wincing in pain with an officer holding her tightly from each side. *How has the scroll not fallen out from her shirt yet?*

"No you can't do that to her! That's my sister!" screamed Ferran as he took his fists attempting to swing at Khalil.

"Detain the mouthy man as well," continued the mayor while he backed up pointing the gun at his skull. Sartan watched as the two siblings were straddled by police officers. When Ferran and Aqila were gagged and cuffed the officers found the Tansiq Scroll on her. They then walked towards Sartan presumably to do the same thing.

"Wait! Sartan still can stand freely. Until he explains what is really going on here," commanded the mayor. "It will be his last time doing it anyways; now be gone with most of you! It's too crowded here."

While the extra officers were leaving, one handed Khalil the scroll on the way out. During this exchange Sartan started to think of ways to get out of this with his life, with the scroll, and with his two new acquaintances. He noticed that he still had the ring on his finger, but using it would definitely kill everyone in the room including himself.

"Sartan, I'm waiting for one hell of an explanation," said Khalil with a click of the revolver.

Sartan looked at his fellow thiefs, gagged and cuffed under the tight grip of two officers to his left. He knew what he had to do, but he also knew that they wouldn't agree with it, at least Ferran wouldn't. "Fine. I will tell you, but only on one condition, you take them out of the library. They are too innocent to see what is about to transpire." He could see Aqila shaking her head in disapproval, but he had no other options left at this point. "That is all I ask."

The mayor seemed to contemplate this offer for a while before coming to a verdict, "You know what? I will grant you this one, and only one, wish. After all, I have never seen these peasants a day in my life. However, they are acquaintanced to you, so their morals must be just as muddled. Remove the irritants from my sight and leave us alone!"

As Aqila and Ferran were removed from the building, Sartan tried to buy some time. "Have you seen what is going on in your streets? The consistent riots everyday?"

"I am well aware of the status of my city. If my subjects want to be heathens then they will be met with my military force. They are in no position to question my rule, and neither are you. Let's not dive into such topics as I am sure the last conversation you want to have isn't politics."

"Very well. What will my last conversation be about then?"

"Don't play dumb with me boy. Explain to me why you remained in my city after your banishment? Explain to me what it is that you want with the Sagittarius Tansiq Scroll?"

"Banished?" asked Sartan hesitantly. "How could I be banished if I was never caught? I was never told of my banishment."

"Your fate has dwindled lower than disgraced banishment since then. Why the scroll?"

Sartan sighed knowing that he was running out of time. "Khalil, do you see this ring?" The remaining guards in the room immediately stepped back, not believing their eyes. "So you do know what it is capable of right?"

"Libra's Gemstone! How did you find that? All of the Zodiacs hid their gems," said Khalil.

Sartan struggled to maintain his facade, as he just now realized which Zodiac the stone belonged to. He blanked briefly in an attempt to fabricate a story in which he acquired the stone, as he truthfully had no recollection of obtaining it. Its origin predated his memory issue, but luckily he didn't have to explain himself down that direction.

Omar foolishly interrupted the conversation, "So you are going to try and become a Zodiac. If you are an heir to Libra then why would you even have any need for this scroll?"

"My motives are beyond your simple understanding Omar. Mayor Khalil, may I ask you kindly to hand me the scroll before you see what this stone is capable of, and trust me it is capable of more than that revolver in your hand."

The remaining two officers crept behind nearby bookshelves to brace for what might come. Mayor Khalil and Omar however remained unphased. "Useless guards! Leave us if you are going to be that frantic," demanded Omar. The guards were confused by the statement, but they weren't confused for long. Not once did they look back on their way out of the library.

The mayor then began to speak again, "Your ring does not incite fear in us, Sartan. Had you been the real Libra the constellation would light up the sky, but we both know that to be false. Instead of continuing your shenanigans, why don't you explain to us why the Sagittarius Tansiq Scroll is so important to you. Maybe then I will grant you a quicker, painless death."

Sartan stared around the room. The dust bookshelves were taller than he was, and they were filled with books that appeared to be older than time itself. The library was tightly cramped and Omar nearly had to stand behind Khalil just to fit in the center aisle. There were isles that split off from the main footpath that ran all the way to the exit. The library was almost like a maze of books. Sartan refused to use the ring indoors fearing that he wouldn't survive, so a new plan was quickly created.

"How about I continue my shenanigans and you give me your slowest, most painful death," said Sartan as he casually walked into the nearest aisle grabbing a book without them seeing.

"Do you know who you are talking to?" asked the mayor when seeing Sartan slowly creep out of the aisle and back into his vision. Sartan leaned up on a bookshelf hiding the book behind him. "Give me a reason not to shoot you right now!" The gun was now pointed directly at Sartan's chest. Khalil's plump face had turned red with anger and in the library's oversaturated lighting it looked as though he might burst before the gun did.

Sartan fully slowly pulled out the book from behind him. "Because you need answers from me," he whispered while pointing at the title of the book. The moment the mayor put the gun back down to focus on the title Sartan chucked it at him. The book flew through the air hitting the mayor in the stomach. As a reflex he flailed backwards into Omar's hands, pulling the trigger. The gun rang out firing not one but two rounds into the air. Sartan sprinted towards him and took the scroll that had fallen out of the mayor's grip during the commotion. Omar, who was struggling to manage the mayor's weight, attempted to take the gun from Khalil in order to do things himself. As they fought, a third round was fired into Omar's arm. Omar cried out in pain as a pool of blood formed on the ground in front of him. When Omar fell to the ground Khalil followed, and the gun let out a fourth round that shattered through a window high up on the wall.

Now with Omar squirming in pain in his own puddle of blood and Khalil regaining his surroundings, Sartan decided that it was time to leave. Before the mayor could stand back up he ran down a nearby aisle looking to dodge any shots. Sartan quickly ran to the edge of the library. Going through a window wasn't an option as that would give Khalil too much time to fire. Instead Sartan ran down the side of the library planning on making it to the front of the room by the stairs. Khalil must have heard him running because when Sartan passed the aisle that Khalil was at, another shot rang out, grazing Sartan's face.

"Give me that thing!" shouted Omar.

Sartan couldn't see what was happening while he was running to the other side of the room, but there was a rustle and a few exchanges of smacking skin before Sartan heard a body fall to the floor. By now he was right next to the stairs. The only problem was that going up them would put him in the view of Khalil and Omar again. The room went silent. A string of sweat dripped down Sartan's forehead. He stood there trying not to make too much noise and calm down his heartbeat at the same time. Sartan tried to silence his panting, but it didn't matter.

"Sartan. We need to have the real talk now." The deeper impact of those words shook Sartan to his core as he knew that Omar knew a lot more than Khalil. "You aren't very good at stealing, so why don't you just give up while you're ahead. You didn't even get away with that letter yesterday, so what makes you think that you will get away with something today? " Omar laughed the sentences out, and Sartan tried to be as quiet as possible. Omar's heavy boots clopped down the library slowly, but with each step they got louder and closer. He seemed to trail on, but Sartan did take interest at first. "We both know that Lev wants this scroll. Try not to forget that Lev always gets what she wants, and if you stall her then you will become her prey. Do you really want that Sartan? She has a nice track record when it comes to catching her prey. The lioness is better at hunting than even the most balanced Libra. I mean what do you think happened to the last Libra Zodiac? I will give you a hint. It wasn't a suicide."

Omar doesn't want to know anything from me. He just wants to close up loose ends before Lev arrives. I need to leave now. Omar began speaking again, but Sartan didn't listen as the proximity of those words melted the complex thought straight out of him. Sartan took a deep breath and lunged out into the main aisle. With a hasty glance Omar trudged on less than an arms length away from Sartan, and Khalil layed on the floor in the middle of the aisle. Without any time to focus Sartan threw his small knife at Omar. The blade failed to penetrate anything, but it distracted Omar long enough to get a few steps up the stairs. POW! The sixth shot rang out as Sartan was sprinting up the staircase. It ricocheted up the staircase, and pierced through a wooden step in front of him. With no time to think Sartan kept running. The staircase was tight which would explain why it took so long for the officers to get in and out of the library. He didn't look back down the staircase, but he could definitely tell Omar wasn't done by the hefty footsteps that followed him.

When he reached the first floor Sartan ran straight through the nearest door that he saw. On the other side he quickly realized it wasn't the best choice. Half a dozen confused kitchen staff wearing dirty stained aprons stared at Sartan in wonder, making him stop dead in his tracks. The bright white lights burned his retinas when it bounced off the silver utensils all over the room, and the exit sign at the end of the long room shone like a beacon of hope for him. The grunting behind him was enough to turn on his legs again, and the kitchen staff stared in disbelief once Sartan began to sprint. Omar wasn't that far behind him, and Sartan desperately hoped that the revolver was only a six shooter. The door busted open once more, but this time he didn't stop to stare around.

"What is he paying you for? Catch that heathen!" Omar yelled at the kitchen staff making Sartan's job ten times harder.

Half of the cooks didn't even do anything after seeing that Sartan had already passed them, but the ones in front of him tried to block his path. Sartan had to jump over slippery, silver tables in order to dodge the gloved hands of the cooks. At one point forks were thrown at him, but Sartan didn't slow down at all. After jumping over another silver table, Sartan only had one person in the way. A cook stood in front of the exit door with his hands formed into fists. Without thinking Sartan continued to run at him. Upon impact the man stumbled backwards swinging at Sartan. One of the hits landed, but the cook was pressed up on the door with enough inertia to open it. The two of them flopped onto the cold pavement outside of the building. Sartan quickly rose to his feet despite the grabby hands of the cook that remained aimlessly grabbing at the air from the ground. The grip was only strong and accurate enough to rip off the laces of his shoe. He sprinted out into the road that surrounded the clocktower, and as Sartan went further he heard Omar cussing at the kitchen staff that remained behind him in the building. He ran around the street until he arrived on the other side of the building where they had entered via illegitimate methods. In the front of the buildings, right next to the window that they had broken into, sat Aqila and Ferran gagged and cuffed with many officers surrounding them.

Sartan slowed when the riot shields were posed towards him. Stopping only feet in front of their formation, Sartan spoke to them while trying to catch his breath, "Let them go....or I will have no other choice but to use it."

Most of the guards didn't react at all, but two of them slowly stared at Sartan before turning to Aqila and Ferran. There was a great fear on these two officers' faces. One of them removed the cuffs and gag from Ferran's mouth and wrists while shaking and looking back at Sartan every few seconds. The second officer uncuffed and ungagged Aqila, but only after dropping the key to the ground twice. The rest of the officers stood in disbelief.

The officer that released Ferran said to them, "This scroll isn't worth my life"

"But there are more of us, what are you doing?" said another officer.

"THIS IS NOT WORTH OUR LIVES DEPUTY!" screamed the other officer who must've been of a higher status.

"Now leave before I change my mind!" shouted Sartan without letting the guard explain himself to the rest of the squadron. "Go to Khalil. He needs your help."

All of the officers ran straight through the front door with no questions asked. While Ferran gathered himself. "What did you do to those guards?" asked Ferran while frantically looking around.

"Herd mentality. It doesn't matter, we need to get away from Omar," replied Sartan.

Ferran helped Aqila to her feet, and she threw herself onto him to use as a cane. *At least it isn't me this time.* Her face was ghastly white, and she appeared to be struggling to keep herself conscious. There was blood still clotting on her blue hoodie and goosebumps on all of her exposed skin, well the exposed skin that wasn't occupied with dried blood, bandages, gushing slashes from the glass that is. *How does she have goosebumps on her under these fog lights?* The cold wind pierced through his thoughts, answering his question and reminding him of more important issues. Omar was probably still close on his tail, and if not he is looking for the officers.

"Let's go through the main entrance at the end of this street. Caleb is probably already there waiting for us," said Sartan.

He looked forward ahead of Ferran and Aqila to see the giant mechanical door that reminded him of a moat gate standing tall in defiance. The bright fog lights lined the street all the way to it. They began walking down the heated strip of street. About halfway to the gate Sartan looked to a chunkier building on his left. The sliding doors were open, and upon peeking through the opening, he saw at least twenty utility and squad cars for the officers of the city. *Why haven't I seen any of these patrolling the streets or in use at all? If Khalil was smart he might actually use these to fix the domestic unrest of his city.*

"Let me see the scroll," said Aqila, sounding like she was about to collapse under her own weight. "I wa-want to know what it---what way there--- what way it is and how far we are."

Sartan looked down at the crisp, golden lettering all over the black sheath that contained the scroll. He slowly handed over the scroll to her. As the soft leather slipped out of his hand he finally realized how valuable this ancient map might actually be. They kept walking steadily to the gate, and Aqila opened the container holding the scroll. She gracefully took an aged, brown parchment out of the leather black sheath. The thing that surprised Sartan the most was the fact that he could smell it the second Aqila took it out of its container. It was almost as if the air had fermented in there for centuries, and he was quite a stretch away from the actual scroll.

"Yes!" whispered Aqila.

"What?" questioned Ferran instantly.

Aqila put the scroll back into the black, leather container before replying, "Strelec's Palace is a lottt closer than we thoughttt! Itttt is in a village called Furictown. It is to the North-Easttt, but I-I have never even heard of that place, have y-you?"

Her excitement visibly dripped out of a runny nose at the realization of this revelation, but expressing it was obviously a challenge in her current shape. With every word her shivering tongue twisted the syllables to a point where they were barely comprehensible. Fortunately they were quite close to the gates by now. Sartan glanced up to the top once they reached the base of the gate. He used to be petrified of heights years ago, and even now the summit brought back those shivers. The walls weren't even half as tall as the gate, and he couldn't see a lever nearby.

"Sartan, go pull that lever," said Ferran.

"What lever? I don't see anything."

"I think there is something in that tiny building right there," said Ferran as he pointed to a small glass window with a bunch of levers and buttons on a panel within it.

"No, there wouldn't be a lever to open the massive gate in the shed with tons of buttons and levers," laughed Sartan sarcastically. "I bet that Khalil doesn't even have it locked."

Sartan walked around to the back door which was conveniently unlocked. Once inside, and after fighting back the laughing fit that attempted to consume him when thinking about Khalil's security, he could see Ferran and Aqila look back down the street in surprise. He needed to hurry, but the console had more buttons than he had cells freezing. In a panic he just pressed and pulled the largest buttons and levers. Nothing happened, and he could see Ferran screaming at the glass from the other side. It was too thick to hear him. That's when he saw a key sitting next to an abandoned, brown mug. Sartan grabbed the key and frantically searched the console for somewhere to jam it into. The fact that Ferran kept yelling and banging on the glass only chopped his focus more. He looked up for a second to see Aqila struggling to stand with all of the movement her human-cane was making. Upon looking back down at the panel he saw a small, golden key-insert. Without hesitation the key plunged into it and twisted. Instantly all of the buttons lit up flashing in hundreds of different colors. It was at this point that Sartan tried his previous strategy: pressing and pulling all of the largest buttons and levers.

After mashing about a fourth of the controls loud sirens went off alerting the whole complex, but maybe those were just warning beeps. The giant gate slowly split in half receding into the walls on each side. Red flashes blinded him on his way out of the operator's shed.

When he finally got to the other side Ferran didn't need to debrief him on what he missed. Omar and half of the officers were running towards them from down the street. Omar held the revolver in his hand. Spinning around Sartan could see Ferran already trying to squeeze Aqila through the little opening in the gate as it grew. They undoubtedly would be going faster had she not needed stabilization, but the beacon of hope wasn't that the gate was open. Past the two siblings Sartan could see their friend's RV across the interstate that the gate was opening up to. However, there was an unknown man loitering by its front door. He would have to be taken care of, but other than that it looked like they might just escape with their lives.

Sartan returned his attention back to Omar while Ferran squeezed through the opening door. Omar's proximity had been cut in half, but more importantly his officers were acquiring vehicular transportation from that warehouse Sartan passed on the way to the gate. Right before he turned back to the gate to escape, Sartan noticed that a few officers were climbing up a ladder to the top of the warehouse. His gaze raced them to the roof where he realized things were going to become a lot more intense. On the roof rested a fully functional helicopter. The sleek black sides reflected red beams of light from the warning sirens of the gate opening, and the tinted glass made it impossible to tell if there was weaponry inside. Its heavy thwupping grew louder.

Spinning around to see Ferran and Aqila already on the other side of the gates, Sartan yelled, "We need to leave now!" He ran through the gate which was wide enough to fit a car by now and continued to yell, "Start the camper." To his surprise the blindingly blonde man who was standing by the camper actually went into it. *That can't be Caleb...can it?* All that mattered was that the lights on the camper quickly turned on only after some nasty black smoke puffed out of the exhaust.

"Let's just get past the median strip," said Ferran shakily when Sartan caught up to him. "They can't drive through it."

Sartan took a deep breath and spoke, "Ferran, we will have to carry her then, this isn't fast enough." Ferran didn't say anything to that, and thankfully Sartan asked for forgiveness before permission. He already knew that Ferran would hate every second of carrying Aqila with a complete stranger just by his behavior towards him earlier, but it would be better than facing the herd of officers behind him. "Grab her legs, we need to carry her."

Aqila glanced at Sartan, and he could instantly tell she was growing delirious from blood loss. She was smiling at him while her eyelids slowly closed and opened with every other step. Naturally, Ferran didn't listen to anything he said. Ferran's eyes were wide and windowed on the median. His face was smothered in a contagious fatigue that nearly forced Sartan's legs to plop onto the ground right where he stood. *Once we escape I need to get away from these people. I've helped them enough. They will turn on me shortly.*

Luckily Ferran was assisting Aqila in walking with her injury. Sighing at their incompetence, Sartan grabbed Aqila by her ankles and lifted her up. Sartan made sure that he would touch her as little as possible, throwing most of her weight onto Ferran who still was her human crutch. As if taken out of a trance, Ferran frantically struggled to keep his sister from face-planting the ground, and she giggled while it all happened. Once he was sure Ferran had a decent grip on her, Sartan picked up the pace quickly approaching the concrete median strip. At their new pace they might just make it in time to escape Omar. The only question Sartan had in his mind was getting over the concrete divider.

When they got to the divider in the middle of the interstate, which if it hadn't been for Dursnia's motor restrictions might have been flooded with vehicles, the concrete rose up out of the ground all the way to Sartan's waist. There wasn't any time to argue with Ferran, so he propped Aqila's feet up on the divider. Without any restraints, Sartan easily vaulted over the divider and told Ferran to put her over it too. To his surprise Ferran somewhat listened while trying to balance her on the divider. *How is she so gone? She literally just got excited while reading the scroll.* As Sartan thought this he realized that the scroll was no longer under her grip. He was not about to let the one thing they came here for, escape them. Looking back at the officers who by now were driving their squad cars towards the gate, Sartan saw the black leather scroll resting in the street far from the divider. *She must have dropped it when we picked her up, great!* As Ferran climbed down from the concrete divider, Sartan went back to the other side.

"Take her to the camper and quick," commanded Sartan.

Without waiting for a reply, partially because there probably wouldn't be one, Sartan ran as fast as he could to get the scroll. He zoomed across the dusty freeway, and as soon as possible he bent over to pick it up. His fingers shook as they curled around the ancient, gold letters, and a bright searchlight beared down on him. Sartan stood back up looking up at the light. Apparently they took longer to get to the divider than he thought. The unquestionable sound of a helicopter accompanied the overbearing beam of light that nearly flattened him into the street. He stood frozen like a deer in headlights long enough for the first squad car to get through the gate, and they were driving to kill rather than capture.

Sartan had been in many life or death situations before, but he rarely had to race a car for his life. Regardless, standing still wasn't going to help him at all. Turning around he sprinted to the divider as fast as his genetics allowed, and the spotlight easily followed him every step of the way. The sound of the motor behind him grew louder as every second passed; the concrete divider that would mean life if he could pass got closer with every second as well. With the scroll in hand and a heart rate that could kill a mouse, Sartan jumped over the divider, but he didn't stop once on the other side. He could see Ferran and a somewhat conscious Aqila limping up the steps of the camper across the rest of the freeway. That same random guy that was wearing the same type of black robe Sartan ran in helped them into the camper. *It honestly doesn't matter right now as long as he helps.*

After Sartan made it about a dozen steps, the car that was chasing him didn't slow down and ended up crashing into the divider. Chunks of concrete flew towards him as the car busted through to the other side veering out of control. The car spun to the left, narrowly missing him. He got a glimpse of the driver being smothered by the airbag, but the passenger flew out of the front window landing next to the camper's exhaust. Sartan knew better to look at the body. He jumped over chunks of the divider that landed in front of his path while making sure he covered his head and neck in case of falling debris. As he approached the camper the guy he saw from a distance appeared to be less and less of a threat. He was short with blonde hair so white it almost looked like he dyed it with the sand from the desert. The important part was that he had already helped the two incompetent siblings into the camper. While climbing up the stairs Sartan glanced back behind him. The divider in the center of the interstate was entirely shredded from the crash the first squad car made, and there was now an opening wide enough for the rest of the squad cars to squeeze through. That is exactly what they were doing. Right before Sartan closed the camper door he saw Omar hanging out the window of the next squad car to get through to this side of the interstate. *Omar is trigger happy.* When he closed the door it bulged as a bullet ricocheted off it on the other side.

"Caleb! Aqila said we need to go to the North-East," shouted Sartan as looked at the couch where Ferran was attending to Aqila's wounds.

"Did you get the scroll?" shouted Caleb.

"Yes, let's go!"

The conversation ended there as Caleb put the camper into gear and pulled off. Sartan fell and almost everything in the room shifted backwards as the camper accelerated. When Sartan rose to his feet and stabilized his position within the vehicle he realized that the random was missing. It didn't take long to find him in the passenger seat, but now was not the time to get to know him.

Instead, now that he knew everyone was in the vehicle, Sartan made his way through the camper into the back bedroom. The bed where Aqila had slept still had traces of blood on it, and the sheets were scattered throughout the room. Realizing that he still had the scroll in his hand he opened a dresser and placed it in before closing it once more. Looking back to the bed, right above it there were blinds that covered a dirty glass window on the very back wall of the camper. He instantly jumped on the bed and shoved the brown blinds out of the way to see through the window. On the other side of the window the mayor's complex slowly started to shrink as they rode further away from it. Unfortunately, the officers chasing them didn't shrink at all. At least six squad cars and an armored truck clogged the Eastward side of the interstate, but that was just on the ground. Above the camper Sartan could see the helicopter through the skylight. The most frightening thing was the fact that the Dursnian officials could even afford a helicopter.

It was obvious that their pursuers weren't stopping anytime soon, so Sartan ran back to the front of the camper to inform Caleb. After passing through the bathroom and entering the living room section, Sartan saw that Aqila was in much better shape already. Her face was still whiter than the moon, but Ferran had managed to wrap ripped cloth and band-aids over most of her wounds preventing any more blood loss from occurring.

"Ferran, when she wakes up, tell her that the scroll is in the bedroom's dresser," said Sartan as he passed by the two of them entering the kitchen.

"Shut up! I'm trying to focus," said Ferran while tending to the largest wound on her leg.

Without replying Sartan continued into the cockpit of the vehicle. Caleb was already dripping with sweat and the random man in the passenger seat must have pretended not to realize the intensity of his current situation. Looking out of the front window the street grew darker as they approached the suburbs of Dursnia. Luckily, the camper had lights, but that was of little concern to Sartan.

"Caleb, they are still following us, and they aren't going to stop!" yelled Sartan so that Caleb could hear him over the deafening music that he had on for some reason.

"What do you want me to do about that? All I can do is drive!"

"Well if we don't do something about it we are all going to die!"

"I can't do anything other than continue to drive! I mean we are already going 85 miles per hour, and my camper is probably going to explode!"

"They have a helicopter!" shouted Sartan.

"Of course they fucking do, but I can't do anything about that! J-Juice go help him because all I can do is drive!"

Sartan looked at the guy sitting in the seat next to Caleb, and he realized that he had to be no older than himself. He looked like the stereotypical Dursnian just with less robes than usual, but one thing caught Sartan's attention. The strange tattoo on his forearm. A long, black arrow with a cross halfway to the bottom. Sartan didn't focus on the tattoo for too long, and when the character stared back at him he realized he would be of little to no help. Without wasting any more time in the cockpit, Sartan turned around to make his way back to the bedroom. "What the fuck is 'J-Juice' going to do to help us!?"

Once he got to the bathroom he heard footsteps behind him. *It's just Ferran complaining under his breath.* Upon turning around he saw the alleged J-Juice following him, and it looked like his confidence was back.

"Do you have any master plans to take down a helicopter J-Juice?" asked Sartan. The music wasn't as loud in the back, but Sartan decided to continue into the bedroom before the alleged J-Juice could respond.

Behind him he heard the man speaking, "Actually my name is Jaako."

"Okay? How are we going to stop the helicopter?" replied Sartan after jumping on the bed to look out the window.

Behind them the suburbs of Dursnia disappeared into the rear lights of their pursuers. They soon would be on the dusty, flat roads that take travelers through the desert over the sandy dunes. It wouldn't be long until they were no longer in Dursnian jurisdiction, but something told Sartan that wouldn't stop Omar from continuing the chase. He couldn't tell which squadcar Omar was in because of the blinding headlights blasting into the camper, but it didn't matter as the helicopter wouldn't ever lose them if it was operational. Meanwhile,

Jaako was standing behind Sartan analyzing him. Then as Sartan turned around with a slight defeat in his posture Jaako spoke.

"Why don't you just use the ring?"

Sartan stopped. He was naive to assume that people could only notice it when he brought it to their attention. While glancing down at the murky, white clouds swirling in the gemstone he replied, "I'd rather not. Plus, the helicopter is all the way up there, I have to make contact for it to work."

"Do you know nothing about Zodiacs? You don't need to make contact for it to work. Not to mention that looks to be the Gemstone of Libra, an Air Zodiac. Why wouldn't that work to stop a helicopter?" ranted Jaako over the swear filled screams Ferran let out after hitting a bump in the road.

"Then why don't you use it yourself then?!"

Jaako exclaimed quickly, "Certainly not! I would probably die because I'm a Sagittarius!"

"Why do you know so much about Zodiacs? Most of them are dead, so why would you waste time learning something like that?"

"That's exactly why you're here. You are here with me because you want to revive the Zodiacs."

"No! I'm here because I made a mistake. The Zodiacs have nothing to do with my everyday life, and I don't understand why people care so much about something that means so little. They seem to be corrupt anyway."

"They have little direct impact on the populus because they are almost all dead right now, and if you don't want to make another mistake I suggest using the ring to save us all. Who is to say you might not become the new Libra?"

Sartan looked down at the ring again. Just watching the milky clouds bubbling over each other gave him chills. *Us is a stretch. Using it would save everyone but me, and I know too well what would happen if I use the gem. Then again Jaako seemed to know some stuff about the Zodiacs.* After assessing the current situation Sartan finally looked back up at Jaako to reply.

"Who is to say it wouldn't kill me either?"

"Well, if you are a Libra you should be perfectly fine. Even if you aren't, the cops will surely kill you before the ring does!"

"Fine! I'll die on my terms, but I don't know how to hit it from here though."

"Oh that's easy. Just do what you always do with it."

Sartan looked at him with a face that contained so much frustration it could melt Mars. After a deep breath Sartan finally conceded, "This is the last time I'm ever using it."

"That's perfectly fine. I respect that. You don't abuse power."

After a quick 'whatever' facial response, Sartan glimpsed up to the skylight and heard the loud rotors of the helicopter bearing down on them. He jumped up grabbing the bar that hung right below it. With almost all of his upper body strength he pushed the top open, and once he heard the frame clank on the top of the camper at its full angle Sartan dropped back into the room.

"Omar has a gun. I'm not doing it from the roof," Sartan said.

"Okay," said Jaako as if he could care less how Sartan dealt with the helicopter.

Sartan took a few seconds to focus on the helicopter which he could barely see the front of through the opening in the camper. A long moment of silence passed or what Sartan tried to make silent over Caleb's music, the burning of the RV's motor, the shots that had begun digging into the back wall of the camper, the sirens of the police, and Aqila's screams as Ferran made a mistake in tending her wounds. Forming his hand into a fist, Sartan wondered if it would even help to take down the helicopter. Regardless, everyone was depending on him to save them, and he didn't get himself into this situation just to die from Omar. *This is it. Rather die to this ancient, Zodiac shit than Omar.* With his fist already clenched up Sartan took his stance and thrusted the ring into the air. Expecting the cold air to engulf him, Sartan was pleasantly surprised when nothing happened. He tried again, punching at the air multiple times, but no burst of air came to the rescue.

"What are you doing?" asked Jaako, who was watching Sartan flail about the whole time. "I think you might be a little too tense. Try to relax, and let the air flow through you."

"Try to relax? Do you not see our current situation? We are all about to die!"

"You have so much to learn if you want to become the new Libra. You are resisting the air as if you are afraid of the recoil," said Jaako.

"I am afraid of the recoil! You will be doing it if you keep talking!" shouted Sartan vigorously as he began punching into the air once more. Sweat began to drip down his face, and he could begin to hear himself panting. He jumped up and punched. He threw his arm out to its full extent and punched. He even took a deep breath before throwing his fist at the helicopter, but nothing seemed to work. In a final effort Sartan punched at the air angry and sweaty saying, "Screw it!"

That must have been a trigger word because Sartan regretted everything that very second. Time itself seemed to freeze around him, and like pulling the trigger on a heavy rifle, Sartan was aware of the recoil that was about to explode in his face. Frozen in time, he couldn't look behind him, but he could hear winds picking up within the camper. They would be strong enough, after time resumed, to pick up light objects that were all over the room and scattered them once more. He got a glimpse of Jaako who stood there amazed and in slow motion, yet completely unaware that he was about to die. As the winds continued to ravage around him without causing any physical harm to anything around him yet, Sartan could already feel his sweat freeze on his skin.

Like before, once the winds were charged enough they would want to pass through him. There was enough time for a single tear to sneak out of Sartan's socket just from realization of the end that was to come, but it didn't even get halfway down his face before it froze in the quickly cooling room. Then it happened. Time sped up three fold to even itself out, and the frozen winds pierced through his back. Going straight through his heart and up his arm which still was at its full extent from the jab at the air, the energy froze him to his core. When it reached the gemstone it exploded out of his body. Sartan had never made this happen without contact, so he was extremely surprised to see that the air itself turned white when leaving the gem.

It was as if the gemstone itself was emptied of the white, milky clouds that inhabited it. The large burst of air glowed in the cold night as it merely missed the side of the camper's hatch and continued up into the sky. Bubbling over itself and expanding, the white cloud quickly made its way up towards the helicopter. Upon impact Sartan struggled to see exactly what the frosty explosion did, but it was obvious the helicopter wouldn't be working anymore. The helicopter instantly consumed the clouds, and ice filled dents were left all over the outside. That alone would've been enough to destroy their pursuer, but the knockback from the clouds sent the helicopter spinning up further into the sky. It shattered into multiple pieces and the operators fell out.

Since the camper was moving quite quickly Sartan didn't see anything else from the skylight, but Jaako jumped up on the bed moving the blinds away from the window. Sartan couldn't see much around Jaako, yet he still witnessed the debris falling behind them on the ground. Most of it landed on the freeway, blocking the rest of the squad cars. One of the rotors went through a squad car, and the rest of the cars braked. While watching their pursuers shrink behind them Sartan realized that Dursnia itself had already disappeared completely. There weren't any streetlights anymore, and they had already driven past countless sand dunes meaning that they were already far into the desert.

The whole time watching this however, Sartan had been struggling to stay standing. The intensity of his situation kept his heart warm enough to watch their escape unfold, but his adrenaline quickly froze up mid pump through his veins. The gust of frozen, white clouds had left him shivering since the second they left his body. Jaako seemed unphased by the change in temperature, and maybe that was because the gust exploded on the helicopter. Regardless, Sartan didn't feel as warm as Jaako. The ringing in his ears had already begun, so when Jaako jumped up screaming something with joy Sartan couldn't understand anything. He tried to speak, but his tongue froze and was too slow to even form comprehensible words. Just like last time it felt as though ice was creeping towards his heart, but this time it was already at his heart. As his vision began to fade he could see Jaako's face go from excited and happy to confused and concerned. Losing feeling in his limbs, the last thing Sartan saw was Jaako shaking him. He didn't even feel it because by then everything was numb. The only thing Sartan could feel was the burning cold all throughout his body, and his heart slowing down as it struggled to keep beating. He wanted it to stop completely; that way it wouldn't continue to spread the frost throughout his body. Unfortunately, Sartan's heart pumped the frost into his mind, forcing it to go numb before his body gave out, actively taking him out of the conscious realm.

Chapter 6
The Traveler
Aqila

When Aqila opened her eyes the first thing that she saw was the burning sun coming through the camper window. She realized that she was laying on the couch in the camper, and the midday heat of the desert had left her sweating under the thin sheets. Throwing the sheets off to cool down, Aqila saw that there was a bit more than sweat on her. Band aids and cloth were tied all over her wounds, of which there were a lot more than she remembered. Dried blood was all over her, and she failed to remember how most of it got there. She tried to sit up feeling pain all over her body. There were scrapes on her hips, arms and sides. After she tried to sit up things finally started to come back to her.

It was the glass in the library! How did I end up here? Wait, where is the scroll? Despite the wincing pain that flowed throughout her whole body Aqila sat up and looked around the room. The timer on the microwave flickered and said that it was just after noon, but she did not see anyone in the room with her. The last thing that she could remember was the giant complex doors opening and going through it. She did not even remember getting in the camper. *Too bad my body remembers the pain.*

Aqila slowly rose up off of the couch to retrieve some painkillers. Her chopped calf hurt slightly less than it used to, but keeping her balance was still a bit of a struggle. The frequent stabs of pain that remained forced her mind's train of thought as she walked into the kitchen. *Where are my painkillers?* She opened cabinet after cabinet and for some reason everything was scattered around on the inside. Almost as if Caleb crashed the camper into a firestorm while she was asleep. After a brief search she found her medicine, and then she grabbed a flask off the table in the kitchen and popped two of them. When they went down she realized that whatever was in the flask was a little more potent than water. In fact, a lot more potent than water because she gagged the whole time it burned down her throat.

"Yeah, if I were you I wouldn't want to swig that this early in the day," said an unfamiliar voice as a blonde haired man walked out of the cockpit.

"Who are you?" questioned Aqila while she patted at her side for her knife. Realizing that it was missing she grabbed a fork off the table and held it at him. "Where is Ferran? Where is Sartan? Actually, where is everybody?"

"Relax, Ferran and Caleb left to get some gas for the camper."

Aqila glanced out of the window for the first time to see endless and sandy, white dunes getting smoldered by the bright sun. The dunes bounced along the horizon for as long as she could see. There were no buildings or streets, other than the one the camper was sitting on, and just the width of it told her it had to be an interstate. A poorly constructed interstate riddled with potholes that seemingly led to and from nowhere. Looking back at the man, who seemed strangely calm, Aqila realized that she was stranded in the middle of the desert and alone with him.

"WHERE ARE WE? WHO ARE YOU?" shouted Aqila as she slowly backed away from the sudden stranger.

"Shhh! You're going to wake him up. I'm Jaako, Caleb's friend. We were on the way to the Sagittarius Palace which is part of your guys' plan, but the camper ran out of gas. It's okay," The man in black, Dursnian robes stared at her with great concern on his face. She tried to remember if she had ever seen him before, but nobody came to her mind, nor did she remember Caleb having a friend in Dursnia.

"Wake who up?"

"Sartan. Don't you remember what happened?" asked Jaako.

Aqila put down the fork after deciding he was no threat and replied, "I don't even remember seeing you at all last night. Where is Sartan?"

"He is in the bedroom wrapped up in almost all of the blankets. If it weren't for him the helicopter and convoy would still be chasing us. Also, you've been asleep for about a day and a half."

"What? There was a helicopter? What even happened? Where is the Tansiq Scroll?"

"Calm down with the questions. You lost so much blood we honestly didn't think you were going to make it, and I'm pretty sure your brother had a mental breakdown at some point. Caleb and I had to do everything. He had to keep driving to get away from the officers, so I actually did everything."

"What is everything? Why are you so calm about all of this?! That still cleared nothing up at all. Why is Sartan in blankets?"

"It's just part of life. Speaking of which, I honestly think he might be dead or something but---"

"WHAT? Can you just explain what is going on here!?"

"How far back do you want me to go?"

"Featuring I have never even seen your face before, all the way!" emphasized Aqila sarcastically.

As if he were dealing with a child, Jaako heaved a heavy sigh before speaking again, "I helped Caleb get his camper back from thieves last night. Then he surprises me with what looked to be an entire prison break from the mayor's complex. You, Ferran and Sartan all come running out of this giant gate with a convoy of officers and a helicopter following you. Ferran didn't tell me much of what happened before you got out of the gates other than 'Sartan screwed things up for us in there.' I couldn't ask Sartan because he froze up right before we were in the clear. Anyway, all three of you got into the camper with the Tansiq Scroll, and we took off trying to escape the police."

"Sartan never screwed things up for us on the inside! If it were not for him we would never have even gotten inside the complex! What is wrong with Ferran and why are we in the middle of nowhere?" interjected Aqila.

"I was going to get there had you not interrupted me!" sighed Jaako as he grabbed the flask off the table, putting it in a hidden pocket. "While we were escaping the officers, Ferran was working on stitching up your wounds and all that good stuff. Trust me you should be glad you don't remember it because your piercing screeches still haunt our ear-canals. Anyway, the helicopter and officers weren't slowing down, so Sartan used Libra's Gemstone to destroy it, preventing the rest of the convoy from following us. I still don't know if it was luck or skill, but we are mostly still alive so who cares?"

"Wait! Libra's Gemstone? Since when did he have that?"

"I was going to ask him, but right after he used it he literally passed out. He stared at me for a few seconds before collapsing to the bedroom floor. His body was colder than a night in the arctic, so we wrapped him up in all the blankets we could. Caleb told Ferran to cuddle him back to warmth, but somehow that led to an argument about how I even ended up here instead. Caleb and I then took turns driving and sleeping so that we could put distance between us and the officers. Now we are about a day and a half East of Dursnia. A few hours ago we ran out of gas entirely, and Caleb and Ferran went ahead to get gas."

"Where is Sartan now? Do you understand what we can do now that we know he is a Libra? We need to keep him alive for so many reasons," interjected Aqila once more. She looked around the room trying to find Sartan, and ignored Jaako's humorously small ears as she stumbled towards the bedroom to find him. "When was the last time you checked on him? Has he even been drinking water?"

"I wasn't done talking," said Jaako while he followed her through the bathroom and into the cold bedroom.

The questions continued even once she got to the bedroom and saw quite literally every single blanket in the small camper wrapped around him. It was almost as if he was webbed up with only his head and neck showing. She walked to him and with every step she could feel the room getting colder. As she put her palm on his pale forehead the contact of their skin put goosebumps all over her arms and legs. There was no question that he should be dead, but upon checking the pulse in his neck she could feel his heart slowly fighting for life every few seconds.

"He is alive! Wait, how is he still alive?"

"I have no clue, but I fear he won't last much longer. There might not be anything we can do at this point, and you have no clue how cold it is in the middle of the desert at night despite how close we are to the equator."

Jaako kept talking, but it wasn't long before she tuned him out. *We can't let him die. Not after everything he has done for us. Not with all that he can do for us. There has to be a way to save him.* With a torn blue hoodie and ripped black leggings that were nearly missing an entire pant leg, of which she had no clue whatsoever as to where it went, Aqila could really feel how cold the room actually was. Letting the cold distract herself from Sartan she decided it was time for a change of clothes. While Jaako, in his Dursnian robes, was murmuring about how the Great Desert should not be this cold at night regardless of season, she rummaged through the room looking for anything to wear that would cover her up a bit more. The rest of the camper was warm enough to continue on in her attire, but she really felt quite uncomfortable with being that exposed and alone with Jaako. It was hard for her to believe she had been dressed like this for days now.

While in Dursnia she refused to buy, or steal, any of their women's robes. *They just are too restricting on movement. I wouldn't be able to move as fast as I can now.* Some of the shops had normal clothing that was more aerodynamic and suited for her agile lifestyle, but she just never had enough time to make any attempts on them. After Jaako finished his little rant about the nickname Caleb gave him she found something that might work. She managed to rescue a pair of black jeans from under a pile of Ferran's dirty shirts and socks. They wouldn't allow her to move as quickly as her favorite outfit, but with the wound on her calf still healing she had to ask herself if it really mattered.

"Jaako, could you leave for a moment? I need to change," said Aqila while pointing to the bedroom door.

"What about Sartan? Are you just going to change in front of him like some weirdo?"

She had completely forgotten about Sartan, and she could only attribute that to the cold room or her need to have any type of personal hygiene. "I will change in the bathroom then, but I still need you to get out."

"Fine, let me know what you think we should do about Sartan when you're done," said Jaako.

Aqila found an old top that would not melt her in the heat or freeze her at night. Looking over at Jaako she realized that he did not know that she had been wearing the same thing for a few days. "Look, I wish to be quick. We should focus on how we are going to save Sartan, but I have been wearing these blood stained clothes for like a week."

Agreeing with her desires Jaako disappeared into the other side of the camper while Aqila changed. The second she was able to lock the bathroom door on Jaako she scampered through the drawers in the bedroom looking for a knife, or any sharp tool that could fit in her pocket. She found a small dagger, and slid it into her pants pocket after changing. Still, a shower was way past due for her, especially with all of the dried blood and bandages. When she finished changing, Aqila unlocked the door and called for Jaako to come into the bedroom. Once he arrived she explained to him what she believed would save Sartan.

"If we take him out of this cold room and place him in the heat of the sun then he might get better faster," said Aqila while grabbing at what seemed to be Sartan's feet. She could not tell exactly where they were under all of the blankets, and Jaako was helping very little.

"I doubt it is going to do anything," said Jaako as he watched Aqila struggle to grab the living corpse wrapped in blankets. "He has been like this for over a day."

"Then help me change that!" shouted Aqila after failing to move Sartan with her injury.

It took no more than that to get Jaako to help, even if he believed that Sartan was unsavable at this point. Both of them carried Sartan out of the freezing bedroom. Before they even got out of the camper there was already condensation all over Sartan's face and even on the blankets around him. The second Aqila pushed the door open and slowly trudged out intense rays from the sun flooded down on her, melting away any concern that this would not heal him. Once in the sun the blankets dried up quite quickly as the dry desert air added little humidity to the cold package. The air was not that warm itself, but as long as he was in the sun he should get hot quickly. With every step on the pavement her bare feet burned a little bit, and she realized she forgot to put her shoes back on after changing. *The pavement is definitely warmer than the back bedroom of the camper, so this should work quickly.* Aqila and Jaako decided to place Sartan a bit in front of the camper so that they could keep an eye on him from the front window. He was placed on the pavement, and Aqila stood on top of some of the blankets to ease the slight burning sensation in her feet.

"I might get blisters because of this," said Aqila while staring at Sartan's pale, frozen face.

"It was your idea to put him out here, why didn't you put shoes or socks on?" asked Jaako sarcastically.

"I know not! I woke up five minutes ago," replied Aqila in a friendly tone. "Not that you would have been paying any attention."

"Okay, sure. Anyway, you can stand out here and watch him all you want. I'm going back to the camper where it is a little bit cooler," said Jaako before walking off.

Aqila could hear him complaining about how the temperature here is too intense as if he were still having a conversation with her while he walked away. *It's only like 70 degrees or so outside. The coldest month of the year was just last month. It is just hot in the sun, and our orbit is too far from the sun right now for the heat to stay throughout the night, even at the equator.* She glanced down at Sartan for a few seconds, and figured he would be fine without her supervision before going back into the camper. She quickly made her way into the camper after Jaako to prevent any blisters from forming on her feet. Once inside she found Jaako shuffling through the cabinets.

"Jaako, what are you looking for?" asked Aqila as she sat down at the tiny table in the kitchen.

"Something to eat. Aren't you hungry?"

She hadn't really thought about it that much as more pressing things had been thrown into her lap upon waking, but once it was brought up her stomach roared and refused to let her forget. "Yes, very. I do not know how to make anything though, so have fun finding something and making it."

"You really don't know how to cook? Neither do I to be honest, so this should be fun."

"Nobody really showed me how. Our parents always had servants who made our food for us. I did try once, but I almost caught the camper on fire. Now I leave that stuff for Caleb," said Aqila while she watched Jaako attempt to prepare some sort of canned vegetable.

"We didn't have servants, but when I got older my job was to get the food, not make it."

Aqila glanced out of the front window to see that Sartan was still wrapped up in blankets laying on the ground peacefully. "Why does Caleb keep adding random people to our group?"

"What do you mean?" asked Jaako. "He didn't add me to the group. I decided to join. There is a difference."

"Yeah, totally. If he never ran into you would you be here?"

"Well no, but if he didn't run into me you wouldn't be here either? No, he wouldn't even have his camper anymore."

"I guess not, but he brought Sartan here as well. I would be surprised if he does not bring another random person when he gets back with the gas."

"Probably. After talking to him for the past day I can totally see that. He really knows how to get people to speak."

"I believe that, but I do not think that he could get Sartan to actually talk about his history."

"Why? Is Sartan impossible to talk to or something?"

"No, but he told us that he hardly remembers anything from his childhood. He claims to not even know his own birthday, and I struggle to believe that one bit."

"That's really strange. Why wouldn't he tell you that? It doesn't even matter that much. Mine is November 10th. What are you going to do with that knowledge? Nothing!"

"Exactly! All I can do is figure out your Zodiac, and I think the month of November is Scorpio. Maybe he is embarrassed about it or something."

"No, November, from the first to the thirtieth, is all Sagittarius. Scorpio is all of October."

"What? I thought that Scorpio went into November."

"Eh, not anymore. Ever since the Arkurvian Shift each Zodiac has its own month. Caleb told me that you knew a lot about the Zodiacs, but that is some pretty basic stuff."

"I have been learning as I go. Apparently you know more than me. Would Caleb's change then?"

"It depends on timing. What is his birthday?"

"His birthday was the fourth of this month."

"January? He is an Aquarius, but I don't know why Sartan would want to hide something like that from us. Do you think he might actually be telling the truth?"

"Of course not! Who does not remember their own birthday? He has to be hiding something from me! Something from us!"

"I don't know. A lot of people don't remember their birthday. I don't think I told you, but my dad is an unlicensed hypnotist. It is really common to be brainwashed or hypnotized. That would make sense too because subjects don't die when they use their own Zodiac's Gemstone."

"First off, Sartan is not dead. Secondly, Sartan would not let himself get brainwashed," argued Aqila as she watched him put two bowls of green into the microwave.

"Okay he isn't dead, but if he was an actual subject of the Libra Throne would he really be laying in the street right now?"

"But there is no way he would let that happen to him," argued Aqila.

"Anyone can be brainwashed Aqila. It isn't that hard, especially if the subject is young. He easily could've been captured and hypnotized. I don't believe he is a Libra," said Jaako. They watched the microwave spin for a brief couple minutes before Jaako took the steaming broccoli bowls out of the microwave and placed them on the table.

"How can we be sure though?" asked Aqila. The vegetables were shriveled and small. By far not her favorite, she spooned it into her mouth quickly to sooth her feral stomach. "There has to be a way for us to figure that out right?" she asked after gulping down the warm tree like structures.

"There are a few ways to tell. Is he cautious of what he says or does? Can he think for himself?"

"I am unsure. I have barely even talked to him since he got here. Not to mention Caleb brought him to us about a day before you, so we do not really know him at all," replied Aqila whilst finishing off her nasty greens.

"Well if his hypnotist was here then it would be really easy to tell, but as long as he is unconscious we will never find out."

"Let us not bring it up with anyone else. I wish for Caleb or Ferran to remain oblivious to this."

Jaako nodded in hesitant agreement as he took the two bowls off the table and into the sink. Aqila watched him wash the dishes before her eyes wandered back to Sartan. To her surprise Sartan was no longer alone anymore. On the other side of the glass stood a scraggly lioness. That alone was enough to send Aqila into a heated panic, but this weakly looking lioness was an abnormal animal. As she sniffed around Sartan her black fur glistened in the sunlight. Almost everything on this lioness was space black. From her bony legs to the snotty black nose everything shimmered under the light. There was however white on the large cat. Streaking from the underside across the exposed ribs and all the way up to the mouth there were two thin, white streaks. The blinding fur stopped at the mouth quickly changing to the opposite shade. The white fur also continued down the front side of the animal's back legs only stopping right before its rear paws. Enamored by the mere rarity of the lioness and unpredictability of the situation Aqila struggled to voice her vision to Jaako.

"Jaako!" whispered Aqila. "There is a--! Quick look at Sartan!"

"What?" said Jaako before putting the last dish into a strainer. He then glanced out of the front window. "Wha-"

I don't understand. I thought that black lions were extinct. Not even! Why is there a random lioness in the middle of the Great Desert? Aqila had gathered herself a bit by now and had stood up and began walking towards the door.

"Wait!" whispered Jaako. "You can't go out there!"

"I will not let a random, malnourished lioness eat our friend," replied Aqila.

"You have a broken leg! You won't be able to fight her off."

Aqila felt at her chest realizing that something was missing. *Where is it? Oh no!* She quickly looked at her injury while thinking about just how long it took her to get up out of the chair. *He might be right. It is gone...It is gone!*

"What can we do then?" asked Aqila, successfully distracting herself from the missing necklace.

"If we can turn on the camper then we might be able to scare it away," replied Jaako as he began to look for the keys to the camper.

While he looked for the keys Aqila made her way to the cockpit of the camper. She sat down and watched in pure fear as the lioness sniffed around Sartan on the other side of the window. Many thoughts ran through her mind. *Do we not have a gun or anything we can use? Where are the keys?* The black, sickly animal sniffed Sartan's face a few times. *I WILL KILL THIS BEAST IF IT EVEN NIBBLES HIM!*

"Aqila, I think Caleb took the keys with him," shouted Jaako as he came out of the bathroom on the other side of the camper.

Aqila ignored him and kept watching the animal. Strangely enough, the lioness seemed to be playing with her food. Instead of eating Sartan, she yawned over him showing off her broken teeth. She must have sensed something was wrong with Sartan because she circled around him sniffing and patting at him with her bloodied paws a few times before limping off out of sight. Aqila, in disbelief, stared at her unconscious friend who is oblivious to how close he just came to death. Then she remembered that vehicles have rear view mirrors. To her surprise and confusion the scrawny animal had already disappeared. *Where did it go? She came out of nowhere and disappeared just as quickly.*

"Where did it go?" asked Aqila frantically.

"I don't know! I was looking at Sartan to see if there were any bite marks," replied Jaako who was now standing next to Aqila in the cockpit of the camper.

"It is not in the mirror!"

"It probably just isn't in angle. You will see it when it gets further away. Do you see anything wrong with Sartan?"

"There are lots of things wrong with Sartan, but I am unable to tell if she did anything to him. Go outside and check."

"Why me?!"

"Because you told me that I am unable! I doubt that weak thing could hurt you anyway," argued Aqila while pointing at her injured leg. "It probably is hiding under the camper or something, so just go check really fast."

Jaako chose not to reply to Aqila. Instead he rolled his eyes and exited the camper to check Sartan. While Jaako went outside to make sure that Sartan was still alive, Aqila frantically looked for the lioness again. She adjusted both of the mirrors multiple times to capture every angle. There were no prints in the sand off to the sides of the interstate, so Aqila knew that it was still on the road somewhere. She tried to get every angle behind the camper, and it had been long enough for the lioness to go into view at some point. A few minutes passed, and she realized that it had to be hiding under the camper because she would have seen something by now.

Randomly, the door began to shake. She turned around in her chair grabbing at her pockets. The door flew open, and Jaako ran into the camper. He wasted no time to shut the door behind him and began ranting.

"Aqila! Something isn't right!"

"What did it do to him?" asked Aqila before Jaako even finished his sentence.

"Aqila, he's fine, but the lioness is gone?"

"That is precisely what I have been trying to tell you!"

"No, you told me that it was under the camper, but it is gone!"

"I know not where it went! What do you want me to do about it?"

"No, you don't understand."

"I am just as concerned about it disappearing as you are, but if it left Sartan alone why does it really matter that much?" asked Aqila while she stood up from her seat slowly.

"Just follow me."

Aqila sighed in annoyance as she followed him outside. Strangely enough it felt warmer than it had been, and the sun seemed to be shining brighter than earlier. Her injury did not hurt as much, but she knew that was an entirely unrelated thing that probably stemmed from the medicine she took upon waking or at the very least her adrenaline. Aqila continued to follow Jaako around to the back of the camper. There was a strange bubbling sound, and when she finally came into sight of it Aqila was left speechless. On the ground about five feet behind the camper was a small, dark-red puddle of fire that twisted and turned over itself. She finally realized where the extra heat was coming from as sweat broke out all over her forehead.

"What is this?" asked Aqila as she backed away in order to prevent her skin from burning.

"Something very dangerous…even in its weakest state," whispered Jaako while he slowly looked to the endless road on which they had just come. "And it is heading straight for Dursnia."

"What?" asked Aqila who was still confused.

"Lev."

Aqila stared at Jaako with raised brows for a few seconds. Then it all dawned on her. *What does Lev have to do with this? She is probably on her way to Dursnia…to get the scroll…heading straight for Dursnia. A lioness heading straight for Dursnia. A weak lioness heading straight for Dursnia. January is the detriment month for Lev. Lev is a Fire Zodiac represented by a lion. A weak lioness just passed us heading towards Dursnia in the month of January, and left a random puddle of fire on the ground.* There was no way to rationalize any defense in Jaako's conclusion. No other reason as to why all of this just happened was plausible. *Lev was just here.*

"We need to go catch her, now!" exclaimed Aqila as she turned and ran down the interstate away from the rear of the camper. "If we can deal with her now Kozoroh will not be as difficult to kill later on!"

From behind her she could hear Jaako calling out to her, "Aqila! Stop! You can't catch her!"

She did not hear the following words let alone heed to them. There was only one thing that was coursing through her mind at the time. *Lev!* With the camper and the strange fire puddle to her back the heat quickly stopped pressing on her mind as much. Everything around her disappeared from reality while she focused on finding the mangy lioness that cursed her with her presence not even five minutes ago. *I will find her and strangle her with my bare hands if that is what it takes.*

Out of nowhere she was brought to the ground hastily by a quick tackle to the side. This external force brought her out of her dangerous mindset. Jaako had just tackled her. The only thing that she could think of doing was slapping him across the face. SLLLPPCK! The sound seemingly echoed throughout the endless desert, and it was enough to get Jaako to back up. SLLLPPCK! This time the sound echoed all the way to Dursnia for good measure. It worked because whatever Jaako was rambling about was squeezed out of his throat with a high pitched squeal.

"Why!"

"Do not touch me! Or better yet, never get in MY WAY!" shouted Aqila as she raised her hand lining up for a heavy slap. Jaako scrambled backwards while sitting up from the sandy street in order to avoid receiving another hit. "Good you are not stupid!"

"You're lucky I can't hit you back," replied Jaako as he slowly stood up.

"No, you are lucky that you are too afraid to hit back!" shouted Aqila while she rose to her legs, which began throbbing angrily at her for running on them.

"Whatever, you still can't chase her though"

"You do not make the decisions here Jaako!"

"Aqila, you physically can't catch her, and even if you could, what would you do after that?"

"After we catch her we will interrogate her for information. Then we will kill her."

"Zodiacs can't be slain by traditional methods, and why would you want to kill her anyway? Aren't you trying to revive all of the Zodiacs? Killing her would make that harder."

"There are things that you are violently unaware of. We must remove her if we are to achieve anything. When she gets to Dursnia she will find out that we took Strelec's Scroll, and then she will hunt us down until she gets it," replied Aqila as her rage started to dissipate. She no longer was tunnel visioned on Jaako. Her surroundings started to come back to her peripherals. She also no longer viewed him as a threat, and began listening to what he was actually saying. *How far away from the camper did we go?* Aqila glanced back to the camper to see the bubbling pool of fire slowly melting out of existence only a short stretch away.

"There are things YOU don't know about either! We can't kill her. Do you not understand that Lev is immortal?" argued Jaako.

"I know that, but why not help me by telling me how to kill her then?"

"The only person here who can even harm her would be Sartan," whispered Jaako as if trying to prevent someone from eavesdropping.

"Why is that? He is unable to even stand up right now. What makes you think he can kill an immortal Zodiac?" shouted Aqila as she lost confidence in Jaako's ability to assist her.

"Shhh! She might be able to hear you!" whispered Jaako aggressively while he looked around the empty interstate. "Just because you can't see her anymore doesn't mean she isn't here."

"What are you talking about?"

"That puddle of fire back there...that's where she went through. We can't see or hear her. We can't even touch her, but she can see and hear everything normally."

"Since when could a Zodiac go invisible and untouchable to the human realm?"

"Aqila."

"You still did not tell me why Sartan is the only one who can kill her," said Aqila, reminding Jaako of more pressing matters. *He can not stay on topic very well.*

"Sartan is the only one here that could even harm her because he has the Libra Gemstone. It would be possible to kill Lev with just that but extremely difficult because he nearly died by just using it on a helicopter."

"If we are not going to kill her right now then we need to leave like right now! As soon as she finds out that someone took the Tansiq Scroll she will realize it was us," said Aqila as she began to walk back towards the rear of the camper. Jaako followed her. "How much time do you think we have?"

"Well, it will take Lev about eighteen hours tops to get to Dursnia. Then the officers there will provide her with anything she needs to catch us, so I would say that she will get back here within a day and a half for sure. Probably more like one realistically."

"That is how long until she gets to this exact spot?"

"Yeah, but Lev has multiple advantages over us even in her weakest form. For her, sleeping is optional, and she is faster than us no question."

"So she is able to get to Dursnia from here and back in the same amount of time that it took for us to get here from Dursnia?" asked Aqila with widened eyes.

Jaako laughed, "Yep! Doesn't really sound fair to me, but I guess that is what happens when you are an Active Zodiac."

"But we do have one advantage over her, Jaako!"

"Yeah right! Lev is literally immortal."

"She does not know where the Sagittarius Palace is though."

Jaako thought about it for a few seconds before responding. "You're right! After the Distancing Act of 6700 N.Q. all of the Zodiacs were prohibited from even stepping foot in each other's lands. Lev became the Leo Zodiac after that, so there would be no way that she knows where the palace is!" exclaimed Jaako as he continued to rant about politics from sixty years ago. "The Leo before Lev probably knew, but she has no clue! That has to be why she wants the Tansiq Scroll. In fact none of the living Zodiacs should know where the other palaces are. They were all born after the passing of that act!"

"It is very cool that you know your politics, but what are we supposed to do right now? If we are not at the palace right now then we are still in danger," said Aqila while they stopped where the puddle of fire was raging only minutes before. Now it was entirely gone, and the heat that it produced was being blown away by the winds. They both turned to the road that led to Dursnia, where possibly the most dangerous thing on the planet was slowly getting closer to acquiring information on its new prey. "Not to mention Sartan is still on the street."

"Yeah, why is he on the street? And why are you two behind the camper?" asked a familiar voice from around the side of the camper. "Also, which one of you melted my camper?"

Aqila and Jaako quickly spun around to see Caleb sticking a large, red container into the side of the camper. He looked tired and weary from walking, but Aqila was just glad to see her old friend once again. She then glanced at the back of the camper. Strangely enough, it did look as though the metal on it had turned into icing, got smeared, and turned back into metal.

"We had to put him on the street because that backroom felt like it was literally freezing," said Aqila. She then began to walk away from Jaako and towards Caleb. "Do you know where the scroll is?"

"Yeah, of course. Ferran has it in the camper, but before you go get it I have something to give you," said Caleb as he finished pouring fuel into the hungry camper.

"Oh…okay? What is it?"

Caleb put the canister down on the ground and stuck his hand under his shirt. He slowly pulled out a black-gold chain. A pendant followed the chain out from under his shirt. On this pendant was a knuckle sized red scarlet gem that had bubbly red clouds swirling around within it. Aqila instinctively reached to her chest to realize that there still was nothing there.

"My necklace?" gasped Aqila as she stared deep into the mystical, swirling clouds that she didn't remember occupying her gemstone. Caleb nodded before handing the necklace out to her. She did not hesitate at all and quickly grabbed it to get a closer view. "Why is it so clou---" Aqila stopped mid sentence as she watched the bright, scarlet clouds disappear from the gemstone almost instantaneously. Confused, she handed the gemstone back to Caleb.

"It isn't mine Aqila," said Caleb as he backed away from the stone.

"I know, but I just want you to hold it for a few seconds."

"Why?" asked Caleb in a confused tone. "You must've dropped it before leaving for the mayor's complex because I found it in the camper before picking you guys up. You almost lost it in Dursnia, but I don't want that kind of responsibility any longer."

"Just do it Caleb."

Caleb obliged and stuck his palms out to Aqila. She gracefully placed the necklace back into his hands, and all three of them watched as red clouds swiftly appeared inside the gem seemingly out of nowhere. Making it impossible to see through, the clouds filled it up as if the inside was hollow. She then took the necklace back from Caleb, and as she predicted the gemstone instantly turned clearer than scarlet tinted glass. It shimmered in the sunlight, and the many small cuts on it were now visible once more.

"Now, I was completely unaware that you had this, but it is obvious that you are a subject Aqila," said Jaako as he stared in astonishment. "It's red so it has to be a fire one. Can't be Lev, so that leaves Sagittarius or Aries. Here let me hold it for a few seconds."

Aqila stared at him for a few seconds before handing the necklace over to him. The second her fingers left the metal chassis and the gem fell into Jaako's hands, red clouds swirled back into the stone. Jaako stared up to Aqila with a cheeky grin on his face.

"What?" asked Aqila.

"I'm an heir to Sagittarius. That means that you are an heir to Aries, and we have the late Beran's Gemstone right here!"

"Yeah, okay?" asked Aqila while she took back her necklace. *I need to keep a better eye on this.*

"Who the hell is Beran again?" asked Caleb as he bent over to pick up the canister off the warm interstate pavement.

"Are you serious right now Caleb?" asked Aqila.

"It is just the name of the previous Aries Zodiac," said Jaako while he began walking towards the front of the camper. Aqila followed him along with Caleb. "Where do you guys keep getting these things? Like there are only twelve of them in the world, and we have two of them right here!"

Jaako began to rant about how rare this occurrence is when you factor in Lev being here not too long ago, and Aqila could still hear Caleb's surprise at that news as they went inside the camper to probably talk about it some more with Ferran. Aqila however decided to go check on Sartan, his fabled ring specifically. He was still unconsciously laying on the interstate in front of the camper. She was almost sent into shock when she felt his skin. It felt warmer than the last time she checked on him, but he was still frosty to the touch. Aqila began removing all of the blankets in order to get to the ring. *Please don't be cloudy! Please don't be cloudy!* She checked his hand searching nervously for the ring. His frosty hand was numbingly cold, but it was also void of any ring. She quickly went to his other hand holding her breath. She saw the black chassis, but there wasn't any gemstone on it. She slowly turned the ring around on his finger, and the longer she held his hand the colder she got. The white gem began to shimmer under the sunlight as it was finally exposed. *Jaako was right. Sartan is either lying, or he was brainwashed.* The gemstone bubbled with white swirling clouds just like her necklace did when Caleb or Jaako held it.

She wondered if removing the ring from his finger might take the clouds away. His icy fingers made it really easy to slip right off. The clouds persisted while the ring laid in the palm of her hand next to her necklace. One odd thing that she noticed was that the gemstones were identical in size. The only differences were color, clouds, and what they were held in. She placed his ring down on the ground next to him, and the clouds slowly dissipated as nobody was holding it anymore. Aqila then quickly put her necklace on, so she wouldn't lose it again. Cusping his hand with both of hers, she could feel her own hands going numb from the cold. *Where did you come from? Why did you sacrifice yourself like this? Are you brainwashed....or are you lying to us? One of these days I will figure you all out.* Aqila laughed to herself after thinking that, but she could swear that his hand felt warmer. *Maybe my hands just have gotten colder.*

"Hey, we are getting ready to leave! We need to get off of the interstate if Lev is on the loose!" shouted Ferran as he hung out the side of the camper's door. "Do you need me to help you get him off the street?"

"Yeah, just give me a minute," shouted Aqila as she turned back to face Sartan.

What is wrong with Ferran? Why would he offer to help Sartan? Then again I would not want to stand around while Lev is about to make us her new prey. Aqila looked at Sartan's hand that lay lifeless in between hers. Looking up to his face she was about to stand up, but something froze her in place instead. His eyes were wide and glaring right at her. Aqila blinked a few times to make sure that he was really staring at her, but his eyes blinked too. She was unsure if he was conscious because his lifeless eyes were white with frost. She watched as his gaze went down to where she was holding his hand. Out of nowhere he flailed and kicked her in the side through the thick blankets. She instantly fell to her side in pain letting go of his hand, and Sartan quickly scrambled backwards away from her.

In a deep, groggy voice he tried to shout, "Don't touch me!" It looked very hard for him to produce just those three words, and they were barely audible.

She writhed in pain on the ground holding her side as he tried to get to his feet. She could hear the others running out from the camper to try and calm down the situation, but Sartan had already begun to limp down the interstate away from them. Caleb was the first one to get to Aqila and he said something while he pulled her up to her feet, but she was unable to hear a single word. They watched Ferran and Jaako chase after Sartan, but before they even got to him he collapsed onto the street shivering.

Swallowing the pain in her side, Aqila bent over and picked up his ring quickly slipping it into her pant pocket. She motioned to Caleb to grab all of the blankets insisting that he took them inside and that everything was fine.

Jaako shouted at her from where Sartan collapsed on the ground saying, "He's out again!"

"Good! Take him back into the camper," shouted Aqila as she slowly walked towards the camper's door. "We still need to get away from here!"

Chapter 7
Involuntary Submission
Ferran

The sun was setting over the distant sand dunes, and Jaako had been driving ever since Sartan attacked Aqila. That was many hours ago. Now the cold January night was fast approaching while Ferran mindlessly stared out of a cracked window from the ripped sofa. He knew they were getting closer to the palace because Aqila and Jaako were trying to use the scroll for direction, but the aged parchment didn't seem to help that much because it was written before roads were even invented. Luckily, Caleb had an old atlas, and they used to decipher their location in the world.

"How far until we get there?" asked Ferran.

"Once we get to a village called Furictown," said Aqila from the passenger seat. "There is an exit about a mile ahead, and I bet that is probably it."

Ferran then stood up from the sofa and began walking towards the back of the camper saying, "I'm going to go check on Sartan."

"Wait, was that the turn!" shouted Aqila without taking her eyes off the scroll.

Ferran walked to Sartan who was still unconscious in the bedroom. Instantly, Ferran noticed his heavy breathing. *He wasn't breathing like this earlier. I swear if he dies like this I'll have to kill him again.* There was a glass shaking around on the desk next to the mattress. The water in it rocked back and forth aggressively making him think that it might spill. *Caleb doesn't know how to drive at all.* Ferran then decided to pick up the water in an attempt to prevent a spill. With one hand he poured a little bit of it into Sartan's mouth. After about half of the cup was emptied into Sartan's mouth, Ferran placed it back on the shaky table and backed away. Sartan's breathing slowly returned to normal, but he didn't wake up. Impatient, Ferran gave up on reviving him then and returned to the front of the camper.

"There's another exit right there!" shouted Aqila as she pointed to an offramp.

"I see it," replied Caleb instantly.

The camper awkwardly pulled to the right lane and speedily swerved back and forth. As they progressed away from the interstate and onto a sandy gravel road a small village appeared in the distance over a few sand dunes. The village itself looked old and weathered by the years, but then again the sunset factored with the distance might have twisted Ferran's initial observations. Unsurprisingly, as the crew crossed over a few more dunes the city looked more ancient. It appeared as though there was only one actual road that passed through the tiny town. In fact, the road could barely even be considered a road at this point. There was a thin trail of discolored sand that sat lower than the rest of the endless desert, and the camper followed this path between many small stick tents. In the distance he could see tiny clay huts blotched together forming the bulk of the village. The clay huts were very similar to those in Dursnia but much smaller, even from a distance.

"Are you sure this is the place Aqila? I don't see a palace anywhere," asked Ferran who was now standing behind Caleb's seat.

"Yeah, I know that the Zodiacs have been dead for a few years, but I can't believe that things got this bad so fast," said Jaako who was standing behind Aqila overlooking the scroll.

"It has to be. The interstate would make a sharp turn South had we kept going on it," said Aqila without looking up from the world atlas that usually Caleb kept in the glove box. "Maybe we should ask the locals to be sure."

Ferran's stomach turned after he watched a slight curl in Jaako's lips form and dissolve within seconds. As they passed the first few clay huts they realized that the town was in dire need of help. The wooden doors and windows were all rotten and hanging off the hinges, but that was just the few homes that had doors or windows. Most of the clay huts didn't have anything other than a few holes in the walls. A few scraggly muts trotted behind the huts as the camper came further into the village. Strange old men in red robes were walking around staring at the camper. The whole town had begun clustering around them by the time the vehicle came to a halt in the center, and their unaccepting faces pierced through the glass as they stared curiously into the camper. In the center of the village was the source of the town's survival, a rusted old well sat at the end of the road in the middle of an oasis. Palm trees and shrubs grew around the well, and Ferran could see all the way to the edge of the village, in any direction. As the rumbles from within the battered and beaten camper subsided, the townsfolk waited patiently outside.

"This is strange. Something is going to go wrong," said Ferran while looking at all of the frowning faces through the windows.

"Relax Ferran. They are just wondering who we are," said Caleb as he turned around heading towards the door.

"There is only one way to find out," said Aqila as she got up to follow him with the scroll.

Ferran and Jaako stared at each other with a brief hint of shared annoyance before Ferran decided to follow the others outside. He caught up with Caleb and Aqila who were already trying to talk to the robed individuals when a tall, wrinkled man with a large, red headpiece walked through the crowd.

Aqila was already talking to the others and didn't notice him, "Is this the town of Furictown?"

"What are you doing here?" said the tall, frail man with a red-robed cone shape on the top of his head. The headpiece had pink strands of lace wrapped around it in a disorganized, webby mess.

"We are looking for the Sagittarius Palace," replied Caleb while pointing at the Tansiq Scroll in Aqila's hands. "This says that it is in the town of Furictown. Can you help us---"

"Where did you find that scroll?" asked the elder as he snatched the scroll right out of Aqila's hands. "And what business do you have here?"

"Why would you show him the scroll Caleb?" questioned Ferran. "Why do you have to be so open with strangers?"

"He has to be open with us. This is our village not yours. Now answer my questions," boomed the leader of the desert town.

The three of them glanced at each other silently for a few seconds before Aqila finally pushed back in front of Caleb and replied, "We are going to revive Strelec. That is why we need your help finding his palace. Please forgive my friends. They have had a long week."

"And we have had a long three decades! Where did you find this scroll?" pressed the robed elder.

"We found it in Dursnia," replied Aqila.

"It has been in Dursnia this whole time! Where in Dursnia?"

"We stole it from the mayor's library," interrupted Caleb as he walked back next to Aqila.

The elder's face crinkled like a can upon hearing that fact, and the rest of his companions seemed just as disgusted. Regardless, Caleb was about to throw the conversation when the omission of a single fact could've saved them.

"We had to steal it because Lev was on her way to take it. Why does it matter how we got it? After all we brought it to you didn't we?" interrupted Ferran as he tried to gain the trust of the elder.

"Lev was trying to get it? None of you had permission to have it, but we all know that it's better you got it instead of her," said the elder.

"You know why we are here now, can you help us revive Strelec?" asked Aqila as she looked around the tiny village. "I have yet to see the palace anywhere. Is this even Furictown?"

The red robed elder sighed and looked at the other townspeople before replying, "This is Furictown, but we can't revive Strelec. Master is gone for good."

Ferran thought about what he meant by 'master' before asking, "Can we not revive him?"

The elder began talking in a broken voice, "My master may have been immortal, but we can't take him back from the grave. Ironic is it not?"

Ferran realized that Jaako had finally grown the balls to come out and talk to the locals. He noticed this when Jaako replied to the elder from behind him, "So there will never be another Sagittarius Zodiac again? What was the point of all the drama we just went through then?"

"There can be a new one, but none of you will live long enough to see that happen. We would need his stone to inaugurate a new Sagittarius, alas we still have no clue where that went. Filthy thieves might as well have put it on the black market by now."

"Could we use a different one instead?" asked Aqila.

The elder sighed as if her optimism was poisonous to him. "Yes, we could use any Fire Gemstone to create an inactive Zodiac, but they would be hundreds of times weaker than the active one. If you are going to look for a Fire Gemstone you may as well look for Strelec's."

Ferran watched as Aqila glanced around at her companions, smiling that cheeky smile she smiles when she has the advantage in literally anything. He tried to stop her from speaking, "Aqila wait---"

Aqila, while clearly holding back her excitement, pulled her necklace out from under her shirt exposing the shimmering red gemstone under the cold, setting sun. All of the elders gasped in surprise as they instantly recognized the significance of her jewelry.

"Where did you get that?" questioned the main elder instantly.

"Aqila you are going to get robbed or worse if you keep showing off your things," said Ferran.

"It is not Strelec's so I am not obliged to answer that now am I?" taunted Aqila as she put the necklace back under her shirt. "Now will you bring us to the palace so that we can create an inactive Zodiac before Lev finds out we took the scroll?"

The elder nearly jumped with joy as he looked around at the rest of the villagers. "Masculine signs can't be inaugurated during night. It is too late for us to do it now, so we must wait until tomorrow."

"Okay so we do it tomorrow?" asked Ferran.

"Hold on now. We need to figure out who will be the new Sagittarius Zodiac," said the man as he looked around at everyone. "Only valid subjects have the possibility to become the new one."

Everybody went silent as selfish thoughts rampaged throughout the group. All of the elders looked around at each other whispering so softly that Ferran nor his friends could make out anything that they were saying. Ferran looked around at Aqila and Caleb knowing that they aren't subjects. He himself wasn't one, so that just left Sartan, Jaako or the townspeople. *Jaako? Jaako is a subject, but we didn't come here to create a new Zodiac...we wanted to revive the old one!*

Breaking the silence the eldest elder spoke to the whole group, "There is only one thing that I fear more than death...the inability to succumb to it. I was dealt that curse on the orders of young Strelec and do not wish to hold the responsibility that he did. Are any of you a subject of the Sagittarius Zodiac?"

"I am," said Jaako as he stood next to Ferran.

"We will let you replace Strelec as an inactive Zodiac on two conditions," said the village's leader.

Of course here is where selfishness returns. "Why can't we just revive Strelec?" asked Ferran with audible skepticism in his voice.

"Believe me if we could revive Strelec we would, but once he passed the event horizon of Zodiacal mortality there was no saving him," said the elderly leader.

"I'm quite confident that I am the oldest one here," said Ferran as he tried every option available to him. "Jaako surely is no older than I! How is he supposed to control an entire empire?"

"Did age matter with Kozoroh? He became an inactive Capricorn at only five years, and we all know…" The man stopped to prevent himself from saying something that he wanted to keep private. "Governments have changed because of Kozoroh. Lands have been conquered, and Zodiacs have died since then. He has yet to become an Active Zodiac, so what makes you think your friend here isn't fit for the job?" questioned the leader as he pointed at Jaako. "Not to mention Strelec has no land now. His empire has fallen into the hands of Lev and Kozoroh, so that won't be an immediate issue."

Ferran didn't reply instantly. Instead he took his time to think of something that might stop what was about to happen. Something that would prevent Jaako from becoming a Zodiac, or something that would prove Strelec was still savable. With little hope left Ferran pushed harder, "Why can't Strelec be revived? There is something you aren't telling us."

"I already told you boy. Strelec is gone for good. If there was a way to revive him do you think he would be gone right now? Of my six hundred years as his right hand not once was a Zodiac revived from the dead. Your cause is just, but impossible."

"Forgive him old and wise one. He just really wanted to make things the way they used to be," said Caleb as he tried to calm down the ancient elder. "You said something about two conditions?"

"Ah yes! If you want to prove to us that you are worthy of replacing Strelec, you must defend our village tonight!" exclaimed the elder. "For the past few nights we've had increasingly large packs of wild, desert foxes sniff around and pillage the village's livestock. If you deal with them then why wouldn't your Jaako be worthy?"

"Desert foxes? That shouldn't be much of a problem," said Caleb.

"It usually isn't, but recently a few lives have already been lost to their sheer numbers," said the elder as he wiped his shaky brow.

"Well, do you have any weapons?" asked Ferran.

"All we have is a few swords, bows, and lots of arrows, but that alone isn't enough to stop the onslaught that awaits us. I suggest you take some time to get ready for their assault. The sun has nearly set, and if you can survive the night then we will discuss the second condition."

After the statement most of the shorter, robed men dispersed from the group. They quickly disappeared back into their clay huts and chicken coops. Where they got all of the supplies to sustain the village was beyond Ferran. The gray, rusted well in the center of the village can support some life, but there was no way it could support enough life for chicken coops, palm trees, mutts and a bunch of ancient monks.

"I have things to take care of prior to tomorrow's inauguration, but I will be back before the foxes attack," said the elder right as he turned to walk away.

This is great. Now we have to kill desert foxes. Ferran didn't wait for the rest of the crew to finish talking. As soon as he entered the camper he realized that they would be entirely lost if they actually managed to create a new Zodiac. He took a seat on the tattered and torn couch and began thinking. *What do we do after this? This is the only lead we have. We won't be able to find another palace or gemstone after this. I still have to deal with Sartan whenever he wakes up, and now I also have to deal with this Jaako guy. Why do I always have to do all the work?*

He closed his eyes and began rubbing his temples. The pain within his cranium echoed off the walls of his skull with every heartbeat. He could hear the rest of his allies entering the camper, but their noisy presence only made things more painful.

"How much time do you think we have until they arrive?" asked Aqila.

" I don't know he never said," answered Caleb.

"Is Sartan up yet?" asked Jaako. "We could really use his help about now."

"Probably not, but somebody should go check on him," said Aqila.

There was then a loud thud a few feet away from Ferran. When Ferran opened his eyes the first thing he saw was Caleb quickly scrambling back to his feet. Gravity must have won another match against him, of which there have been many.

"Can't you guys see what they are doing to us!?" exclaimed Ferran as he rose off of the couch. All of his supposed allies stared at him cluelessly. "That elder just wants us to do his dirty work for him. Do you really think that he will give that title to Jaako?"

"We have no other options Ferran," replied Caleb as he strode off to check on Sartan. Gathering himself after his unexpected fall.

"Exactly, we have finally made it to a palace. This is what we have to do in order to revive them," said Aqila who was looking inside the cabinets.

"So I am the only one who actually sees something wrong with this place?" continued Ferran.

"Well there is definitely something strange about most of this, but what else would we do?" asked Jaako before taking a sip out of his silver flask.

"What do you actually find strange about this place?" asked Aqila while she found an orange bottle.

"They are skeptical of us. Why aren't they showing us the palace first, and why do they want us to do work for them?" asked Ferran.

"Oh, so it is okay for you to be skeptical, but when somebody else is skeptical of you they are up to no good?" asked Aqila who was now entirely focused on Ferran.

"No it isn't that. Why aren't they proving that they can help us? Do you not remember that they literally took the Tansiq Scroll from us? We don't even have it anymore!" exclaimed Ferran.

Jaako interjected before Aqila could reply, "Maybe they did that because it is literally THEIR scroll, THEIR palace and THEIR land. We know the palace is here. Do we still need it?"

"And since when were you part of our family? Didn't Caleb just find you on the street or something?" shouted Ferran. "I am tired of him just randomly bringing people into our lives!"

"Leave him alone! We need him to revive Strelec, and it is not good to be this torn before the foxes attack or whatever that elder said!" shouted Aqila as she literally stepped in front of Jaako to separate him from Ferran.

Ferran walked up to them and yelled, "No! We aren't reviving Strelec! He is trying to be the new Sagittarius! I thought the plan was to revive the Zodiacs, not become them!"

"Things change Ferran! Since when does that mean we have to?!"

"Our goal was to revive them! How can you just accept this change so easily? It isn't even change! You've sacrificed our goal entirely!"

"We are still making sure that their subjects have a leader! Why does this matter anyway?"

"Because I don't trust him at all to become a Zodiac let alone the leader of about one-twelfth of the entire world!"

"Well, who would you trust to replace Strelec?" asked Aqila.

Ferran stared blankly at them as he actually considered the question. Unfortunately, he didn't have time to provide an answer as Aqila continued to talk.

"If you were in Jaako's position you would not be complaining at all now would you?"

"I actually---"

Caleb's unexpected voice stopped him from defending himself, "Hey guys guess what! Sartan finally woke up from his little nap!"

Ferran spun around to see Sartan groggily standing in front of him scratching his head. Sartan yawned then rubbed his ears as if he couldn't handle a bit of volume this early in his late-night morning, and Ferran could feel his heart rate instantly triple. Behind Sartan stood Caleb who was smiling excessively for such an unimportant event. Ferran felt his face snarling at Sartan, so he turned back around to Aqila who grinned sincerely. Even Jaako seemed relieved to see a guy who had only exchanged a few sentences with him standing again. It didn't matter that he saved their lives.

"Good thing you woke up. We were all worried about you, Sartan," said Aqila with a large smile on her face.

Without thinking, without hesitating, Ferran spun around and swung his right hand directly at Sartan's face. As it landed on his chin and the head swiveled back, everybody in the camper started to scream and attempt to end the fight that had swiftly passed the prevention phase. Caleb was able to prevent Sartan from falling, so after recovering hastily from Ferran's blow, Sartan instinctively threw two hits at Ferran's stomach, both of which landed. He swallowed his pain and involuntarily held his breath as his stomach ringed. Ferran lined up another shot, but Aqila and Jaako grabbed his arms, preventing him from defending himself. Unfortunately, Caleb was a little slow to do the same, so the unrestricted Sartan sent a fist missile straight into Ferran's nose. Realizing that Ferran had been detained, Sartan stopped his left hook from putting a second bruise on his face.

"Why is this tiny camper more dangerous than the whole city of Dursnia!" shouted Sartan.

"I'm sorry Sartan, he looked like he was about to do the same to me," said Jaako while tying up Ferran's hands with a thin piece of rope that Aqila hastily handed him.

"Why would you do that, Ferran!?" shouted Aqila.

Ferran could feel the blood trickling out of his nose as he murmured, "I don't have to tell you my motives!" Ferran took a few breaths before continuing. "He is no longer welcome here, and that is all you need to know!"

"I'm perfectly fine with that," said Sartan as he began walking towards the camper's door.

Aqila quickly ran to get in front of him insisting, "We still need your help reviving the Zodiacs though!"

Sartan walked to the door, and with the only thing in his way being Aqila, he calmly spoke in a monotone voice, "It is obvious that your leg has healed. I don't need to stay here any longer." He then grabbed Aqila and moved her out of the way before opening the door.

"See Aqila, he doesn't even want to stay," taunted Ferran. Without even looking at her face he knew she was distraught at Sartan's departure. Ferran basked in the joy for a few seconds until he heard Sartan's muffled voice from outside the camper.

"Wait…where in the hell are we?" asked Sartan. He closed the camper door and turned back to the group.

"I can explain everything. Everybody needs to just calm down and relax," insisted Aqila as she put her hands on Sartan's shoulder.

"CALM DOWN?" shouted Sartan while he backed away after throwing Aqila's hands to the side. "I'm not the guy who randomly punches people that just woke up! I'm not the one who thinks it's a good idea to revive Zodiacs! I'm not even the guy who randomly picked up whoever this blonde guy is back in Dursnia!"

"Sartan, you are just dazed and confused. I can explain everything if you just let me," said Aqila in an attempt to pacify him.

"You have no clue what I am! I don't even know. I should've left when I had the chance."

"Who hurt you?" asked Aqila.

"Who hurt me? What does that mean? Was I supposed to be keeping track?" asked Sartan. "Ferran literally just punched me if you want to add that one to the tally!"

"I'm sorry, I do not mean it like that. I just want to help you," said Aqila as she went in to hug Sartan. "None of us are enemies. We are all here to help."

Sartan instinctively rejected Aqila's embrace and continued to speak, "None of us are enemies? I just got clocked for waking up, so we definitely aren't allies."

Caleb interrupted, "He didn't mean to Sartan. There are still some things that we have to fix, but we are going to get closer to our purpose tomorrow."

"Yeah, and what purpose is that?"

"Jaako will become the new Sagittarius!" exclaimed Aqila. "That is why Ferran has been so moody recently. He is just jealous."

"Jealous? I don't think Jaako is fit to be a Zodiac. I'm not jealous at all," said Ferran as he tried to stand up with his hands tied.

"Jaako to be a Zodiac? Didn't you just grab him off the street like me? I don't want to say anything about his abilities, but you guys must really be out of options if you are hiring random people to become Zodiacs. Then again it doesn't even matter, so who cares anyway," said Sartan.

"Well what is your purpose, Sartan? What were you working towards before now?" questioned Aqila vigorously.

"My purpose? All I could focus on was surviving," said Sartan.

"Then who are you to criticize our goals?" asked Aqila.

"Well when your goals conflict with my focus I believe that I have every right to criticize you!" screamed Sartan while he wiggled his fingers in one of his hands. Aqila started to speak again, but was interrupted by Sartan. "And where is my ring!"

Ferran had finally managed to rise to his feet while his hands were restrained behind him, and Caleb and Jaako had managed to slither to the other side of the room. They watched Aqila and Sartan argue from a distance. Ferran didn't quite feel comfortable in this camper either, especially when detained.

"I took it from you so that you could not hurt yourself anymore!" screamed Aqila.

After waiting a few seconds for Aqila to stop screaming, Sartan calmly asked, "Where is it?"

The whole camper went silent. With a raised finger Aqila opened her mouth and almost shouted once more at him, but something persuaded her to stop. She looked at Ferran and the others before glancing back at Sartan who was waiting for her reply patiently. Goosebumps quickly formed on Ferran's skin as the silence continued. Then Ferran felt a strange shiver go through his spine as Sartan spoke again.

Even calmer than last time Sartan asked, "Where?"

"I will give it to you if you help us," said Aqila in a calm voice.

Without raising his tone Sartan continued, "Give me one reason I shouldn't take it from you by force. None of you hid your weaknesses very well."

"What do you mean?" asked Ferran.

"You are restrained. Jaako has no reason to stop me. Aqila just needs one hit on the calf before she crumbles, and that just leaves Caleb who won't be a problem at all," said Sartan.

Ferran finally grasped the situation that he was really in. He had no control. At the complete mercy of those around him, he hastily spoke out, "Aqila! Stop him by any means!"

Sartan stood in front of the camper's door waiting for Aqila's attack. She however wasn't moving into a fighting stance. Instead, she slowly pulled out her necklace while keeping distance from Sartan. Unamused, Sartan said, "Go ahead and kill me with that. You'll die too."

Aqila smiled at him as she tilted her head to the side a little. "Nope. Just you. I am a subject."

As Sartan stared at her Ferran could only imagine what was going through his mind, but there was only one thing that mattered: if he would submit. Sartan didn't say anything, instead he just stared at the necklace. Perhaps there was a question of its authenticity, but Aqila didn't waste any time solving that mystery. Without using her hands, she willed a small, neon-red flame to come sparking out of the glowing red gemstone. It flickered on the stone as it slowly grew larger. Sartan briskly stepped back, but he instantly bumped into the door of the camper. Ferran could feel the camper quickly heat up. Within seconds the flame had stabilized and grown like a plant to the sun, directly towards Sartan. Sweat broke out on Ferran's face, and he wasn't nearly as close as Sartan.

Aqila grinned as the little space between Sartan and her flame steadily decreased. She then commanded Sartan, "Stay and help us if you want your ring!"

Sartan looked around the room at the witnesses. Ferran felt a smile take a seat under his nose as he watched Sartan press himself further into the wall. He watched as the sweat on Sartan's face began to drip down his chin, and then the fabric on Sartan's shirt began to curl.

"STOP!" choked Sartan.

The flame stopped growing, but it did not fall back towards its master. Aqila then commanded, "The choice is yours!"

"FINE!" shouted Sartan without hesitating.

Within less than a second the entire rod of fire retreated back into the gemstone, which proceeded to glow for a few seconds before returning to its normal clear appearance. Only now there was steam surrounding it as it cooled down. Sartan stared at Aqila with a frown. They all watched as Aqila stared back, only breaking eye contact briefly to slip the necklace back under her shirt.

"I wish not to harm you, Sartan," started Aqila.

"Yet you treat me as though I have no basic human rights I see."

"What do you mean?"

"I can't leave as I wish and you possess my belongings. Oddly similar to imprisonment is it not?"

Aqila spoke once more, "You can leave if you want, but we need the stone for our purpose. It nearly killed you, so it helps you with your current focus of surviving very little.

"You are no better than anyone else."

"Jaako, can you get him some water?" asked Aqila as she rolled her eyes.

Ferran glanced behind him at Jaako who nearly tripped over his own feet as he scrambled to get water for Sartan. *I don't think I will have to deal with Jaako or Sartan anymore.* Even Caleb's eyes were wide with surprise. Aqila had promised them only to use the necklace if she really needed to, and Caleb must have forgotten its raw power.

"Caleb, untie Ferran," said Aqila as she turned back to Sartan. "There are desert foxes that are going to attack this tiny village in high quantities very soon. What we are doing right now is helping the villagers protect their home. Then tomorrow we make Jaako an inactive Zodiac."

Sartan still glared at her, but Ferran's cheeks started to hurt from maintaining a smile for this long. *Glad to see people get what they deserve. I wouldn't have let him live however.* Jaako had finally obtained some water and handed it to Sartan. After some gurgling resistance the entirety of the bottle was emptied into Sartan. By now Caleb had untied Ferran. Any remaining tension in the room was shattered at the sound of somebody knocking on the door. Aqila being the nearest, other than Sartan of course, answered the door. On the other side stood one of the red, robed elders.

"Marcus, our leader that you spoke with earlier, told me to warn you when we first spotted the foxes," said the short man nervously.

"Thank you. Ferran and Caleb, would you go and follow him to the foxes," said Aqila. "The rest of us will catch up in a minute."

"Okay, if you say so," replied Caleb as he walked in front of Ferran who slowly followed him out of the camper. Aqila didn't hesitate to close the door on them, but the aged man who guided them through the town was just as polite, refusing to initiate conversations.

"Ferran, you do know she feels really bad about being that cruel to him?" questioned Caleb as they passed between two clay huts.

"What was cruel? What do you mean Caleb?" asked Ferran while looking over the dunes. Strangely enough, in the far distance he could've sworn that there were multiple mountain tops. They covered every spec of the North, and fell back far into the East. Their frosty white tips had merged with the industrial gray of the rest of the mountain under the setting sun. He knew little about geography and even less about maps, but surely another nation sat on the other side of that barrier.

"Do you not know who your sister is? She never wanted to hurt him, and now all he is going to do is resent us," said Caleb as they walked between a few more huts.

"So? He will leave if he doesn't want to stay," replied Ferran.

"But what if he wants revenge?" continued Caleb.

"Then he can try all he wants? She basically controls him now for all I care."

"She doesn't control him, she just made him mad!"

"I am certain that she will try to make him adore her rather than resent her," replied Ferran.

"Adore her?" asked Caleb.

"Adore her," restated Ferran slowly as he thought. "He has to go. We need to force him to leave or get rid of him!"

Caleb asked, "Wait, if Aqila wants him to adore her and also help us with our mission why does he have to leave?"

"You don't understand Caleb. He can't help us with our mission. He has to leave because now he will only cause bigger problems for us."

"Are you sure?"

"Certain. We need to deal with him for the last time"

Caleb didn't reply as quickly as Ferran had hoped, and instead the elder leading them spoke, "If you must do that, wait until you depart our peaceful town."

"Of course. Of course," assured Caleb. "But Ferran, I don't want to hurt him."

"What if he hurts you though? You found this guy in Dursnia, and he has no interest in reviving the Zodiacs like us. Sooner than later he will cause massive problems, and that will happen faster if he adores Aqila."

"Do we have to hurt him?" asked Caleb.

"It is either him or me," started Ferran. "His life or my life. A very easy question if you ask me. An easier question if you ask him, and I am sure of that one fact."

"Well, when you put it like that…"

Ferran nodded barely hearing what Caleb had just whispered to him. They had finally followed the elder through the town to the outskirts where the rest of the elders stood. The tall, old man with the red headpiece wasn't there but weaponry was, sort of. They had put up a few tables and covered them with bows, arrows, and a few swords. The elder broke the crowd up before turning around to face Ferran and Caleb.

"We don't have any guns. What we do have is better though, so just grab whatever you think you can use," said the elder. "We have only seen a few foxes in the North so far, but the rest of them can't be that far behind."

"What exactly is to the North? Why would they come from there?" asked Caleb as he grabbed a quiver full of arrows off of the table.

"If you go straight to the North there isn't anything but desert until you reach those mountains," replied the elder.

"And what is past the mountains?" questioned Ferran while examining what appeared to be an ancient bow crafted centuries ago.

"If you pass the mountains then you will enter the Gemellian Empire, and if you continue North I believe those mountains curve back around. Pass them again back into our lands, well what was once our lands," said the elder while slowly looking down at his feet.

"Then let's take it back!" exclaimed Jaako as he shoved his way through the crowd to Ferran and Caleb. Sartan trailed behind, and refused to even glance at them. He slipped a dagger into his palm from under his sleeve as he walked closer to Ferran. Concerned, Ferran backed away while Sartan continued through the crowd straight towards the dunes. Jaako however ignored this as he grabbed a bow off the table.

"What is he doing?" asked Caleb.

"Who knows? He is pissed, but I couldn't imagine why," said Jaako with a quiver in his hand. Seamlessly he slid it over his shoulder and pulled an arrow into the bow.

Ferran glanced up to watch Sartan storm off towards the North. A few dunes away more foxes had gathered, but it was hard for him to tell with the fading sunlight. The elders were starting to shuffle around hastily, and Ferran had yet to grab a weapon. In the distance the moon had already begun overpowering the weakened sunset forcing the few remaining dull oranges into the already thrashing sea of deep purples and blues. A few of the elders lost patience and grabbed some of the bows. In fact, not a single sword was touched. He reached for the last quiver on the table as a short, plump elder grabbed it frantically, and the elder didn't spare the bow that went with it either.

"Hey!" exclaimed Ferran as he picked up one of the rejected swords.

The fat elder ignored Ferran, and right as Ferran was about to make sure he heard it the second time, a loud scream echoed into his left ear. A different elder was on the ground squirming with something. With a pile of light, brown fur stapled to the man's leg, a mix of dark red and dark white quickly assaulted Ferran's eyes. Then out of nowhere a thwish from behind them was followed by a quick crack as an arrow landed in the pile of fur. Within an instance the pile of fur released the injured elder from its grip and slumped to the ground. Ferran glanced between the random elder who shot the malnourished animal and the light arrow that had pierced the eye socket effortlessly. Everything then hit him at once.

"They're flanking!" exclaimed an elder from somewhere in the crowd.

With a quick glance past the injured elder, Ferran witnessed endless amounts of foxes trotting around the dunes. Each and everyone had patches of fur missing as well as grizzly, rotted teeth, and Ferran could easily see their rib cages writhing under their skin as they ran closer to him. They seemingly overflowed the land. There was more fur than there was sand on the ground, and they toppled over one another as space quickly became an issue.

Caleb then drew an arrow and unloaded a shot into the flaming tornado of desert foxes. To Ferran's surprise the shot landed directly in the head of one unlucky fox. At this point the whole pow-wow of villagers had already reacted accordingly by shooting as many arrows at them as possible. The foxes' advance was slowed but it definitely wasn't stopped. Every single arrow fired from the bows pierced a skull. Ferran decided that there had to be something peculiar about these bows. *Caleb has never even picked up a bow or arrow in his life, there is no way he can land multiple headshots on a moving target.* The overanalysis of the situation quickly devolved into primal, mechanical motions as the wave of lion like creatures advanced close enough to harm him. The foxes jumped on the nearest elders as soon as they got a chance. Initially, they would be executed by that elder, but after six or seven managed to hold their position on the victim, resistance was futile. Ferran realized this and backed away as the few villagers between him and an endless storm of fiery teeth got their throats ripped out.

"We have to get on top of the buildings!" shouted somebody from behind Ferran.

There wasn't any arguing with that command because one of the elders standing between Ferran and the foxes just had his arm tossed to Ferran's feet. Knowing that he would soon end up like the townspeople if he tried to fend off the onslaught with a sword, Ferran turned and ran towards the voice when he felt a sharp pain sink into his left arm. He struggled to keep his arm off the ground as the weight of the fox tugged on him. He swung the measly sword that remained in his right hand, but it barely even scratched the fox. Jaako must have seen this happening during the chaotic battleground, and luckily, he also must have seen an opportunity to shoot. Like all of the previous shots from the bows, the head of this fox was just as elusive as the rest of its fallen comrades.

The fox loosened its grip on Ferran while he continued to try and put distance between himself and the attackers. As it died he finally managed to pull it off of his arm, which now had a gash the depth of a grave in it. He then squeezed between a few elders that were unloading more shots than Caleb when he turned 17, except all of them were sticking firmly in the place they landed. He regrouped with Caleb and Jaako. A few of the elders at the rear of the formation had dropped their weapons and ran away from the rest of the fighters.

"Guys! We need to follow them!" shouted Ferran over the numbing sound of one hundred foxes growling. "NOW!"

"Just one more shot we can win this!" shouted back Jaako who had figured out how to fire his bow more rapidly than most automatic rifles.

"If you try to get one more shot it will become your last!" screamed Ferran.

Deciding that Jaako was not necessary to save, Ferran grabbed Caleb by the arm and pulled him after the fleeing villagers. Out of the corner of his eye he could see Jaako follow suit, and Caleb said something but there was no way that he could hear it over the screams of the elders that were behind them. After rounding a corner of a few clay huts, Ferran saw a ladder sitting on the ground by the side of a hut. The elders were nowhere to be seen, but that didn't matter now because he had access to everything they needed to survive the night.

"We need to get on to the roof!" shouted Ferran while he pulled the weak ladder closer to a taller building.

There was a brief moment of silence, and Ferran quickly recognized it as the final elder dying near the weaponry tables. The foxes would now come for them, so with sweat on his forehead and a painful panting within his lungs, he propped the ladder up on the side of the building. Without hesitation he started climbing the frail wooden structure. It wobbled the whole time that he went up it, but luckily Caleb stood at the base acting as a support for it.

Once at the top, he looked around the village realizing that there were many more foxes than he had initially thought. Like a forest fire they blazed around all the nearby huts. Caleb had begun climbing up to him when the ladder started slipping to the right. Ferran grabbed for it unsure whether or not he could save it in time. It took all of the force remaining inside his damaged arm to save it from falling to the ground and shattering upon impact.

"Hurry up!" shouted Jaako who was still on the ground shooting at the first few foxes that ran around the corner of the homes.

Caleb had gotten halfway up the ladder when his footing slipped. One of the steps in the ladder snapped in half while Caleb desperately tried to save himself from the force of gravity once more. Ferran was just glad to not be in Caleb's position, let alone Jaako's. After he got in reach Ferran pulled him up so that Jaako might be able to use the ladder and live, and upon finding his footing on the roof, Caleb pulled his bow back into his hand to assist his so-called friend.

Jaako didn't climb the ladder at first. Instead, he continued to shoot the foxes while hesitating to turn his back to them, but little did he know, the foxes were closing in on him from every angle. Ferran had to remind him once more to focus on the high ground rather than one more shot. After a few more shots Jaako must've realized that the foxes were really getting too close. In an indecisive manner Jaako turned to run towards the ladder while still slinging a few arrows at the foxes. He made it to the second step, but the foxes were only steps away from him. Ferran watched, and as Jaako climbed up the ladder the foxes jumped up snapping at his feet. Ferran witnessed Jaako's hanging robes get ripped and torn by the jumping sets of jaws. Like before when Caleb was trying to get up, another step snapped, and Jaako nearly fell into the hungry mouths of the desert predators. Jaako's hands gripped the wooden brace of the ladder. He climbed further up, safe from the reach of the hungry predators but not quite on sturdy ground. As Ferran watched the relief flood Jaako's face he knew that the foxes weren't done yet.

Even though they all were out of reach from the foxes, Jaako was still on the ladder, and they seemed smarter than the usual animal. The foxes must have known how weak the ladder really was because within seconds they started to compromise its position. They congregated around it while one or two of them ran into the sides. It didn't take more than one attempt to knock the ladder over. As the ladder exploded into a thousand splinters on the ground, Jaako was hanging over the side of the building just by one hand. Ferran dropped his sword in order to grab the reaching hand of Jaako. It clanked on the roof, but as he pulled Jaako up to safety it was knocked over the edge. Piercing right through the side of one of the foxes. The three of them gasped in relief on the roof. After catching his breath, and heart, Ferran glanced over the ledge to reassess the situation. His sword glistened in a fox's side under the moonlight. However this fox was not a normal one. This fox was visibly mangy and sickly like the rest, and it appeared weak by nature. However, unlike the others, it was larger than the rest, and instead of the reddish fur the others had, it was covered in deep, maroon hairs that were barely visible under the moonlight. The animal did something that none of its dying comrades had time to do. Unlike its brethren it had time to feel the pain, and as a result it let out a burst of heated roars.

The three of them watched as the rest of the foxes whimpered around with it, giving the giant plenty of room. A waft of heat flew up to them when the injured fox stood up on its hind legs. Unsure of whether or not he was actually seeing this happen, Ferran glanced over at Caleb and Jaako. Both of which had eyes wider than the wound in the fox. When he looked back at the fox however, the fox was gone. In its place stood a muscly, yet sickly man with short maroon hair on the top of his head. The only thing that was constant was the sword piercing right through the man's stomach. Ferran watched in disbelief as he grabbed the hilt of the sword and pulled it out of his side with nearly no resistance. There were showers of blood on the blade when he threw it to the ground, and all of the foxes around him sat down. He breathed heavily while the gash in his side slowly began closing, and the man then looked up to the roof.

"Is Marcus here?" he coughed loudly almost as if he was attempting to scream.

"Hold on," started Ferran. "What the f-"

The beastly man coughed blood onto the wall of the hut interrupting Ferran. He then continued, "Have you seen Marcus here. Yes or no?"

"Why?" countered Ferran from the top of the building.

"Do you value life or not?" replied the ailing man as an endless skulk of weathered foxes sat patiently around him.

Whispering on the roof Caleb quickly said to Ferran, "He just pulled a sword out of his side. I think we should just tell him."

"Not to mention he was just a fox!" exclaimed Jaako.

After staring at Caleb and Jaako for a few seconds Ferran finally replied to the man, "Is that the really tall and old man with a strange headpiece?"

"Yes, where is he right now?"

"We don't know. He disappeared right before the foxes were spotted."

The man didn't reply to Ferran, but instead he walked up to the side of the building that they were on. He then pulled out a piece of paper and dipped his fingers into the wound of one of the fallen foxes as the wound in his side had already clotted shut. Ferran tried to make out what he was writing without falling off the roof, but the lighting and distance made it difficult. The awkward silence was broken after the man rolled up the paper and put it in a satchel.

While looking at one of the foxes the man spoke, "Take this to master." The fox grabbed the bag in its mouth before turning around and running away into the night. The man turned back to the roof and began speaking once more, "Poor service out here right? I apologize for the bloodshed, but the rest of the villagers refused to speak to admit it. All we needed to know is that Marcus really was here. Now that I know this place isn't a hoax, you can tell him that we will grant his final wish soon." The mysterious man then turned away. All of the foxes rose up to their feet and began walking away from the building with him.

"Where are you going?" asked Jaako from the top of the building.

"Yeah, and who are you?" questioned Caleb.

The man stopped to stare at them again. "My orders were only to find the palace, not to capture it. I'll let Marcus enjoy what little remains, until my master arrives."

"But who are you?" asked Ferran.

The man said, "My name is Jiry, but that is all that you need to know my friend."

Jiry then walked into the desert that he came from, and all of the foxes went with him. All that was left behind were the multiple bodies of slain elders and foxes. Having the high ground never really was a problem until now. They needed to get down, but with the ladder shattered on the ground that was a difficult problem to solve. As his heart rate steadied at the mirage of post battle safety, Ferran remembered that Sartan walked towards the first pack of foxes right before they flanked. *Well we got rid of him quicker than I thought we would have.* Right as he thought this there was movement near one of the shadowed buildings. Behind one of the buildings appeared a short figure disguised by the shadows. It walked past the buildings unaware that they were on the roof. Once it walked into the moonlight Ferran instantly recognized it to be Aqila.

Relieved that it was her, Ferran shouted down from the roof, "Hey!"

She looked around confused for a few seconds before finally spotting them on the building. After she spotted them she replied, "Where is everyone?"

"Dead or missing," replied Caleb. "Can you find a ladder for us? We are kind of stuck."

Aqila looked around the ground, but all that was on the ground were piles of dead animals and shattered splinters scattered around the base of the building.

"There is nothing here. Can you just climb down?" she asked.

"I'm sorry, we aren't as 'cool' as you," said Ferran seconds before Jaako climbed over the side of the roof. "Have you seen Sartan at all?"

"No. I was just about to ask that," replied Aqila as she looked around the battlefield.

"He probably didn't make it. After all he just walked out into the open by himself," said Jaako as he managed to find a hole in the building that supported his foot.

"That's a shame, but at least he helped us get this far," said Ferran.

"No! Ferran you never just give up like that. He is part of our team, so we have to find him!" shouted Aqila as she turned towards the open desert.

"He *was* a part of our team, but we can't let this loss slow us down Aqila," continued Ferran as Caleb began climbing down the building after Jaako.

"It was probably for the best anyway," whispered Caleb while looking up at Ferran.

Aqila walked off towards the weaponry tables that were the most chaotic place just moments ago. Once she was out of sight and Jaako had made it off the house, Caleb lost his footing and fell at least halfway off the side of the building. Ferran laughed until he realized that he was still on the roof and Caleb wasn't. While Jaako was helping Caleb to his feet Ferran finally climbed over the side of the building. It was at least a third taller than it was when he climbed the ladder. Ferran made it about half way down the side of the building before Aqila returned with Sartan. He turned to make sure that it was actually him, and then he instantly fell off the side of the house. Unlike Caleb, he fell from a much higher position, and the second he landed on the bodies of the foxes the air inside his lungs retreated into his stomach. He gasped aggressively for air whilst coughing uncontrollably.

"How did you survive Sartan?" questioned Jaako while Ferran choked on his own breath. "There were so many of them, and you were all by yourself."

Sartan glared at Jaako for a brief moment before replying, "There were only five foxes on that dune. The rest went for you."

Ferran rolled over with the persistent wheezing in his side preventing him from forming a single word. The rest of the group just ignored him as they marveled at the fact Sartan survived. Tears streaked Ferran's ghostly face as everything around him seemingly disappeared. He could no longer hear his companions over his own gasps, and the smell of blood sent him into a nervous shock. An eternity passed before breathing became easier, and the whole time everyone was just talking, not even worried.

Once he finally caught his breath Ferran shouted from the ground in a broken voice, "Screw you guys! You'd really just stand around watching me die?"

They all stopped speaking about whatever was more important and stared at him. Sartan nodded in affirmation while the rest stood clueless to what he meant.

"I nearly just died falling off the house. All I can smell is blood, and I have no clue where it is coming from!" shouted Ferran as he rose to his wobbly feet. Blood streaked across Ferran's face and body, and everyone noticed the instant he stood up.

"Ferran, you are fine. You literally just fell into a pile of bloody animals. Of course you will have blood on you," said Aqila before returning to her conversation and completely ignoring Ferran once more. "We have to find Marcus and revive Strelec before the foxes come back."

"But it is night time. We can only do that during the day," replied Jaako, who was not worried about Ferran either.

Then as Ferran's adrenaline dissipated, he could feel the stinging sensation in his arm again. Without paying anyone attention he trekked out of sight to the nearest elder that suffered a less fortunate fate. He ripped a part of its red robe off before swathing it around his wound. The indifference to pain Aqila felt towards him was distasteful to say the least. Upon returning they were still talking about the same, less pressing, matter.

"Well like I said, we have to find Marcus either way. If we do it now then we might survive when the foxes come back," countered Aqila hastily.

"If they wanted us dead they would've killed us by now. I say we just sleep until the morning," interrupted Caleb. "Not to mention all of the fighting MOST of us did has been very tiring."

"I told you I was unable to even push the door open!" insisted Aqila.

"Whatever. You can look for Marcus now, but I am going to sleep my wounds away," said Caleb.

Aqila exclaimed, possibly in surprise, "You did not even get bit!"

Jaako didn't leave enough time for Caleb to answer and began speaking over the two of them, "Well if Caleb isn't doing anything then I'll be asleep too."

Aqila lost control over the situation, and Ferran noticed this as Caleb and Jaako turned away. *I can't sleep, but I'm definitely not going to help her.* The three of them walked to the camper leaving Sartan and Aqila alone. Ferran could hear Sartan talking behind them as they walked away, "I haven't been awake for too long. I really need to find something to eat."

Good, you can starve.

Chapter 8
Swimming in the Sand
Sartan

The sky had already begun warming up to the light in the East, and the unnecessarily low temps would follow suit soon. Aqila and Sartan sat against one of the buildings on the Eastern side of the village staring off into the distance. A few scattered foxes layed less than three buildings away, and Marcus has yet to emerge from his hiding spot. Aqila had been sleeping on and off, but after finding out how long he had been out, Sartan understood why it was so hard to fall asleep. Everytime she fell asleep Sartan considered searching the camper for his ring. *I can't try anything while stranded at this village.* There were no visible burns on his body, but Sartan felt pain on his skin just from the touching of the fabric of his shirt. The cold wind soothed the pain for less than a second before burning a different type of burn.

"Where do you think the palace really is?" asked Aqila in a groggy tone.

Surprised that she was still awake, Sartan turned to face her as she sat a short reach to his left. Then after staring at her with a twitch in his eye he spoke, "Does it matter? Marcus will show us when he is ready."

"Why do you have to be so difficult all the time?"

Sartan didn't want to answer that question, let alone be in the vicinity of Aqila, but in order to appease his captor he replied, "I think we both know the answer to that Aqila."

Everything went silent as she failed to respond, and he turned to look back at the endless white sand dunes. They curved up from the ground like tiny hills leading to nowhere. Only a day ago he was practically dead. The gemstone might as well have killed him because the indifference in the drifting dunes sparked a question inside of him. One that he didn't know the answer to. *What now?*

"When will you give me my ring?" he asked, knowing that she would distract him from his own thoughts if provoked.

The cold wind pierced through him as the silence continued. Without the stone it would be harder to defend himself on the streets, but she was right. *Using it would only kill me...but maybe I could use it without using it. Threaten people if they attack me as long as they don't call my bluff. That still doesn't help me though. What now? I can't go to Dursnia. I don't want to go there, but there is nothing but sand in every direction. Maybe I could escape these Zodiac vigilantes and become a nomad.* His train of thought derailed at the rustling Aqila made not too far beside him.

"I told you," said Aqila after a moment of silence that was so long Sartan forgot what he actually asked. "I need it for our mission. You can have it after we no longer have a use for it."

"Your mission will get us killed before that happens."

Another moment of silence passed as Aqila didn't deny his statement. Then she said, "You do know that I did not wish to use my gemstone against you yesterday, right?"

"Well my skin doesn't care what you meant to do. It cares about what you actually did to it."

"I did not get mad at you when you hurt my calf, so why do you have to be this way?" asked Aqila as she scooted closer to Sartan reaching for his shoulder in an attempt to comfort him.

Sartan intercepted Aqila's hand before laying it down on her leg and returning to his initial position. He then replied to her questioning, "You remember what happened when I broke your leg. It was not intentional, and I felt guilty enough to break back into the mayor's complex. Living on the street usually trades the ability to feel guilt for the ability to survive."

"I feel guilty too! But you choose not to be receptive to my help," argued Aqila.

"What help?" asked Sartan as he scooted away from her. "Maybe that is because you intentionally harmed me. And not for survival."

"It could not have really hurt that much, and I already told you that it was unintentional!"

"The pain is primal, but the act instilled distrust. The difference is vital," said Sartan as he stood up to catch some silence.

"I am sorry Sartan! I had to calm things down!"

"Just stop talking," said Sartan stoically as he turned away from her.

Silence finally returned after Aqila sighed. Sartan decided all that he had to do was wait for them to go back into a larger city before escaping with his ring. After that the only things that would be problems are the menial, usual tasks that revolve around living to see another day. *Only then could I put this behind me and attempt to find peace. Whether that be eternal or mortal.*

"I want to be your friend not your enemy," said Aqila interrupting the silence. Sartan stared at her wondering what kind of trap this could be. "We could really use your help with the Zodiacs."

"No you don't. Jaako is going to become the new Sagittarius today. You have accomplished your goals, so why do you have to keep me around," argued Sartan as he watched Aqila stand up with no problem. "Not to mention your leg was not as severely wounded as we thought, so what do you really want to keep me here for?"

She sighed before replying, "Sartan there are still eleven other Zodiacs. Not to mention that we will probably need to kill the three that are alive right now. We have a lot of work to do before our goals are accomplished."

"Kill the three that are alive? And you want me to believe that what you are doing is right?"

"Need I remind you that they are the reason that we must revive the other nine in the first place?"

"There is no way that only three of them could kill all twelve of the Zodiacs. Why can't you just revive the ones that are gone and be on your way?" asked Sartan as Aqila stepped closer to him.

"Even if the three living Zodiacs do not actively try to stop us we still have to think about how they treat their subjects."

"What if their "subjects" were born days away in foreign land?"

"They are still part of their Zodiac and can be affected by their Zodiac's decisions."

"Okay, but even if all of this is true then why do you need ME to help you with it? I don't know anything about them, and I care even less!" exclaimed Sartan as he persistently tried to keep physical distance from Aqila.

Aqila didn't reply instantly. Instead she stopped walking towards him and stared deep into his eyes. The cold breeze melted under her glare, and she finally replied, "I also want you to stay because there is-"

"There you are! Where is the subject?" boomed a loud voice completely cutting her off mid sentence. The man was dressed in red robes with a gargantuan red headpiece. The headpiece towered over the high and wrinkly face it sat on. It was a wasp nest of pinks and reds that surely meant something to the elder before them. Sartan had no recollection of speaking with this man prior. Apparently Aqila did.

"He is in the camper. Where have you been all night?" asked Aqila.

"I have been in the palace preparing for the inauguration. Let us retrieve him," replied the elder. "I am surprised that you survived the night. You must've seen all of the dead foxes scattered throughout the Northern homes."

Aqila began leading the man to the camper where their companions were sleeping, completely ignoring his question of why he must stay to help. Marcus followed her, and Sartan did as well. The sun hadn't even peeked over the horizon, and Jaako said that they could only begin the inauguration during the day. *Just another thing to make the Zodiacs more complex than necessary. Another thing to slow me down and keep me in this forsaken desert.*

"How long does this usually take to complete?" asked Sartan as they weaved in between the buildings on their way to the camper.

"It shouldn't take that long, but then again I haven't seen this happen in over many centuries," answered the elder.

They approached the camper that was still sitting in the middle of the village right by the well. By now the sun was high enough to hit the huts at just the right angle to make them shimmer a creamy white color. Beams reflected off the camper, yet shadows still ran long and wide. The many vast differences in lighting were almost enough to give Sartan a headache as they walked in and out of the sun's rays.

When they entered the camper all three of the boys were fast asleep, and unaware of what they were about to do. Upon seeing this Marcus slammed his hand on the opened door of the camper as loudly and quickly as he could. It only took about eight slams before all three of them were startled awake, and it took another eight for them to get up and try to stop whatever was creating that awful banging.

"Stop it! Stop it! I'm awake, what do you want?" exclaimed Jaako as he rolled off the couch landing face first into the carpet.

"It is time for your inauguration!" boomed Marcus as he turned to exit the camper that reeked of sweat, blood, and salty feet.

Jaako jumped up off the ground, and Caleb made a quick bounce out of the bedroom in the back. Ferran however was the slowest and last to stand up from the floor cot. When Sartan turned to face the elder once more he was no longer in the camper, and Aqila wasn't that far behind him. Everybody followed Marcus out of the camper and towards the well in the center of the village.

After everybody finally gathered around it, Marcus spoke, "Have any of you ever been in a Zodiac's palace? Do you know what they look like?"

A moment of silence passed before Aqila replied, "I do not think any of us have been inside one, but I know that they all stretch for a super far and can be huge."

"That can be true! You must have done some research," said Marcus with a crescent smile on his wrinkled face.

"If it stretches super far from then how far do we have to walk to even get close to it?" asked Ferran with visible disappointment on his face.

"Not very far. Featuring that we are already at the center," said Marcus as he slowly crawled over the edge of the well. Looking back at the group he pushed himself into it. His voice trailed off as he fell down into it, and everyone quickly ran to the well to see where he went.

When Sartan looked over the edge of the well he saw Marcus standing on what he assumed to be water down half the length of the camper into the well, but after staring at it for some time, Marcus's reflection revealed it to be a mirror or thick glass at the very least. The well was way too tight for anybody else to jump into it with him, but just as he thought this Marcus opened a door into the side of the well. Sartan didn't notice the door until Marcus opened it just like he didn't notice the water wasn't water until Marcus stood on it.

"Jaako you go first," said Aqila once Marcus went through the door.

Wide-eyed Jaako didn't argue with her as he crawled over the side of the well, falling quickly towards the glassy water at the bottom of the well. Sartan watched Jaako's feet splash into the mirror moving all of the standing water out of the way. Jaako stared around the well in surprise before walking through the doorway towards Marcus.

As soon as Jaako moved out of sight Aqila flung herself over the edge splashing down on the mirror just like Jaako had seconds before. She squealed quietly while grabbing at her leg. She then glanced around the dirty, rusted well before following Jaako through the doorway. After Aqila got out of the way, Caleb and Ferran stared at each other possibly wondering who would go next. Sartan's curiosity, however, told him not to wait any longer, so he vaulted over the edge and quickly fell towards the mystical water-mirror. The second his feet pounded into the glass a watery substance retreated away from his feet. Sartan then bent over to pick it up. The wet substance was clear on the ground, but the second it touched his hand and was separated from the floor it turned into sand. The sand fell out of his hand back towards the mirror where it turned back into clear water. Sartan then glanced at the door that Aqila just walked through. He couldn't see anybody, but he could see pink-red torches lighting the way down a spiral staircase. *But how do we get back to the surface?*

With no other way out Sartan made his way through the doorway, out of sight of Caleb and Ferran. The stairway went on for what felt like hours, but he could hear the echoes of Jaako and Marcus coming from ahead of him. He then heard a thud echoing from behind him as somebody else dropped down into the well. When he started to hear Aqila's voice echoing up the stairway to him he knew that she must've caught up with Marcus and that he would catch up soon. The moldy, rock stairs slowly turned into pinkish-red marble blocks, and the further he went the brighter the torches became. The walls also changed the further he went down. Initially they were streaked with sand and cracks, but the lower he went they eventually changed into those same pinkish-red marble blocks that the steps were made of.

After what felt like thousands of steps, Sartan finally came to a door at the end of the staircase. Upon entering the door he found himself inside a dimly-lit, clean, pink-marble room with multiple marble doors on almost every wall. The floor was made out of obsidian, and the ceiling was made out of white quartz. On the ceiling there were black slits that let out the smallest trace of pink light. The room was warmer than the surface that Sartan found himself on only a few heavy moments ago. In the corner of the room he saw a single door that was cracked slightly, and it had to be the one that Jaako, Marcus and Aqila went through. Sure of it, Sartan breached through the door slowly.

On the other side he witnessed the ceiling rise endlessly towards the surface. The walls followed suit leaning into the center of the ceiling where a circular, blue window supplied the entire chamber with its only source of light which was fainter than the previous room. Hundreds of feet directly below the window was an enormous throne with a tall wall slithering around it providing a barrier for attacks from behind. The shiny throne stared directly at the entrance to the chamber, and a long, pink-velvet carpet stretched all the way from it to

Sartan. Halfway to the throne stood Jaako, Aqila, and Marcus on the middle of the carpet.

Something told him to catch up with them as they approached the throne, but instead he stared around the chamber a bit longer. The pink-velvet carpet had many tributaries connected into it. They extended away from the center of the room towards many tables and chairs. One of the tables had a map of the entire palace in it. The map however, was three dimensional, as Sartan walked down the carpeted lane away from the main stretch to the throne, he saw the model of the current floor stretch out. He could see every room on the floor, and he could see an extremely small model of Ferran entering the tiny room that he just exited. Sartan could also see Caleb walking down the spiral staircase as a micro model. He then looked for himself. Within seconds he found the micro model of himself standing next to a table labeled mapping on the table he was standing right in front of. With wide eyes he then noticed a lever on the table next to the modeled map, and without thinking he pulled it up. All of the modeled rooms and architecture that filled the tiny center of the table disappeared for a mere second before a new set of pinkened holographic models appeared above them.

Sartan looked at the newly appeared holographic models and realized that it was the village above the palace. He saw everything that he saw on the surface prior to jumping in the well. All of the dead foxes were scattered around the Northern side standing as a memoir to the previous night. The clay huts that were sitting next to the camper shimmered in and out of reality as the hologram flickered unsteadily. He then trailed his way into the palace through the map. The well on top of the surface flickered slightly, but he could still see a small stairwell exiting the side of it. Strangely, the stairwell didn't spiral at all. Instead it went straight around the walls of the chamber he was currently in until it reached the room that Caleb had just entered. The same small room with all the doors and pink walls, but now Sartan knew where each door led, nowhere. Confused, Sartan pulled the lever down twice, and as he expected the holographs for each floor rose upwards from the table as the level below him appeared slowly. Some of the doors in that first room led to this floor via a spiral staircase, but most of them had spiral staircases that kept going deeper in the palace.

He pulled the lever multiple times until the entire palace was shown on the table. The surface village, that was still being projected, hovered about five feet above the table. The very bottom floor filled the entirety of the table, which stretched at least five feet on each side. He stared at the hologram looking back at each floor once more. As he went up each floor got small and smaller until he reached the chamber he was currently standing in. The pyramid shape completely peaked upon the ceiling of this chamber however, and that is when Sartan realized the top of the entire palace is actually the well in the middle of the village. He was standing on the smallest floor of the entire palace, the throne room.

Suddenly, a hand landed on Sartan's shoulder forcing him to jump forward. Instantly, he spun around ready to disarm the attacker. Behind him stood the red-robed elder whose hand was slowly falling back to his side and behind the elder stood Ferran, Jaako, and Aqila. Sartan could see Caleb entering through the entrance merely twenty feet away.

"The map is very interesting indeed. Not a single palace is built the same as another," said the elder.

"When are we starting the inauguration?" asked Aqila.

"Patience, bold one. I want all of you to be able to witness it. Your companion is still on his way," replied Marcus as he gestured towards Caleb who was walking towards them on the carpet.

"What about the foxes? Will they come back tonight?" asked Aqila.

"I don't think so. You killed almost all of them didn't you?" questioned Marcus as Caleb finally regrouped with them.

"No, they said that they accidentally injured one that turned into a man," replied Aqila.

"What?" boomed Marcus.

"I did not see it happen, that is just what they said," claimed Aqila as she pointed to the three boys behind her. "I failed to even get out of the camper."

"What really happened last night?" demanded Marcus as sweat started to form on his brow.

Jaako hesitated before replying, "A big red fox turned into an ill yet beefy, red-haired man."

"And what did this man do?!?" bellowed the elder.

"He just asked us if you were here. After we told him he wrote something down and left with all of the foxes," whispered Jaako so quietly Sartan could barely hear the vowels in his speech.

"Jiry! Why would you tell him I was here!?" exclaimed Marcus. "What did he do with the letter?"

With wide eyes Jaako slowly replied, "He gave it to one of the foxes and told the fox to take it to master. He said he only killed the other villagers because they didn't tell him you were here."

"This is worse than I thought!" exclaimed Marcus as he trudged away.

Jaako tried to add context by saying, "He survived a sword in his side, maybe that is---"

"Follow me!" shouted Marcus as he interrupted Jaako.

Everybody followed Marcus down the carpet towards the throne, and another few elders appeared out of nowhere. Once they got to the throne Marcus stopped, and turned back to the group.

"I don't know exactly how long it will take that fox to get to Lev, but I know it won't be long! I knew the attacks were abnormal!"

"Wait, that fox is going to Lev?" asked Aqila.

"Yes, Jiry is one of her subjects. She values him so much she has granted him some of her own powers, and once she finds out that I am here she will come. If I am here then the palace is here, and she will want to secure it for herself!" exclaimed Marcus.

"Lev is in Dursnia to pick up the scroll," replied Aqila.

A moment of silence passed before Marcus spoke again, "I suppose it is always best to assume the worst. I only hope that she is not there yet."

"No, she really is. We saw her," replied Jaako.

Marcus stared at him as if he were speaking in tongues before saying, "You SAW her?! How could you omit such a detail?! Then...she already knows! She already knows! We need to start immediately. Jaako, sit down on the throne!"

When Jaako sat down, Sartan finally paid more attention to the centerpiece of the palace. The throne shimmered under the scarce light coming from the window hundreds of feet directly above it. Its red-pink, crystalline structure towered over him as a command point for the entirety of the palace, and he could've sworn that it began to glow when Jaako sat down. The throne was elevated off the ground by a slab of black stone, but the seat in which Jaako rested was made of a thick, silver metal with crystal-like lines on the back and sides of it. These crystal structures were windows into the throne, but on the inside a dark void crept outwards, consuming any excess light that got caught in its path.

Meanwhile, Marcus was frantically chanting another language at the few elders who were running around the throne. He then turned to Aqila demanding, "Give me the stone!" She hesitated, and the elder sensed this. "You wanted this to happen, it's now or never!"

Aqila unhooked her necklace from her neck and pulled the stone out from under her shirt holding it out to Marcus. The wrinkled, old man grabbed the fiery, neon-red stone. He began chanting something drenched in guttural and throat sounds, but before Sartan could even try to decipher it, Marcus thrusted towards Jaako with the stone. A large red burst of flames exploded out of the stone in an instant, spiraling straight towards Jaako sitting on the throne. The heatwave knocked nearly everyone back, but Jaako didn't even have time to recoil before the shot landed directly in his chest. Sartan witnessed the heated energy flow throughout Jaako's body. The neon-red color of the shot quickly turned pinker as the throne began glowing the same light red hue through all of the crystal slits that were previously engulfed in darkness. Jaako started to twitch as the energy radiated out of his skin. Suddenly, Jaako sat back into the throne stiffer than a plank whilst looking straight up towards the ceiling. His eyes shut, and his whole body trembled. A loud ringing was now screeching out of Jaako forcing Sartan to cover his ears, and the whole time the throne kept glowing brighter. Sartan watched as Jaako's eyes exploded open along with his mouth. However, bright pink light escaped from both his eyes and mouth. In fact, the energy even came out of his nostrils and ears.

After the throne finally reached a blinding level of light, Jaako was swallowed by a beacon of pink energy that beamed straight up towards the sky. The deep, eerie boom of sound knocked everybody off their feet, including Marcus. Sartan was sure that the beacon of energy would completely destroy the well at the summit of the palace, but after the light slowed bringing Jaako back into sight, Sartan was surprised to see the well still intact. In fact, it wasn't even tinted blue anymore, but instead it was glowing pink. Actually, everything was glowing reddish-pink around him. All of the black slits in the wall, previously invisible to him, now supplied the chamber with a pink glow bright enough to expose the corners of the throne room. However, Jaako remained slumped on the throne, unexcited by the lavish environment recently created.

As Marcus stood up, he handed the scarlet stone back to Aqila before speaking, "Thank you for bringing us hope." Aqila nodded while returning her gemstone to its hiding place. Marcus then placed his attention on the recently inaugurated Jaako saying, "Jaako, I do not think I will have to ask you for that second favor anymore, regardless your journey has just begun. Lev will not be able to create a Sagittarius under her control as long as you live, and I am sure that is what she wanted to do. She is surely on her way here now, so you really should get ready to embark on your journey."

Jaako, dazed, slowly stood up from his throne, which still was glowing incredibly bright, before replying, "What now?"

"Your family and friends, if you have any, must be kept a secret from the world for now, and the best way to do that is to avoid them until a safer time. Excluding our palace, all of your lands are controlled by foreign nations and-or Zodiacs," answered Marcus as he knelt down in front of Jaako. "Master."

"I didn't agree to this!" shouted Jaako as he looked around his companions.

"There is no turning back now master. You hold enormous responsibility to the world," said Marcus while still on one knee.

"Why couldn't you do it then if you know so much?" asked Jaako.

"I have held this responsibility since Strelec died, and I held a similar responsibility for six-hundred years prior to that. Now it is your turn to hold that responsibility," said Marcus.

"What about the other elders? Why can't they?"

"I already told you. They do not wish to hold such a responsibility indefinitely."

"So you are saying that I am immortal?!?"

"Not quite. You are only the inactive Sagittarius Zodiac, but the moment you touch your Gemstone, wherever it is, you will transform into the Active Zodiac, unlocking all of your powers and detriments for both you and your subjects."

Jaako stood in silence, perhaps intaking everything. After Aqila attempted to keep him calm, Jaako turned back to Marcus, who had yet to rise off his knee, and asked, "Then what are my options?"

"My master, the only option you have right now is to help your friends revive the rest of the Zodiacs. You must stay alive, for Lev will capture this very palace tonight if not earlier. If she catches you Jaako...you will be destroyed."

"We will prepare an ambush for her then!" interrupted Aqila.

"No, you must escape before she arrives. Jaako is still too weak to defeat her alone. He has no mastery of his newly acquired abilities, and Lev will arrive with more than enough troops to destroy us twelve times."

"Where do we go then?" asked Caleb.

"Retreat to the East. Over the mountains into the lands of Blizenci. It is safer to assume that most Gemini's will be hostile towards foreigners, especially if Blizenci finds out about everything that has transpired. It is still safer than remaining here in the desert with Lev on the loose. Once you cross over the mountains you will be in their empire. Go South from there following the mountain chain until it ends. After the mountain chain ends you will be in the lands of the late Panna. Before everything fell apart Panna and Strelec had a decent relationship. Replace her next. May I rise master?"

"You may rise," commanded Jaako. Marcus nodded as he finally stood up again. "How do we replace Panna though?"

Marcus had an answer for everything, "The same way we did Strelec. Find a subject that can be an heir. Find an Earth Gemstone. Find her palace. Put the heir on the throne and unload the gemstone into them. It would be preferred if you found Virgo's exact Gemstone, but if you can't then that is okay. As long as Kozoroh or Lev don't replace her with a puppet first we are making progress."

"And how are we supposed to find all of that?" asked Ferran. "It took ages to get here, and we had a Fire Gemstone. Now we have to find another Tansiq Scroll, another heir, and another gemstone?"

"Find the heir on your way to the palace. I believe that the Taurus Gemstone is somewhere in Garigo, a city in the Empire of Gemini. Some guy by the name of Dominick Kreet has the stone. I doubt he can be trusted, but since he is in Gemini lands you can get it from him on the way to Virgo's Palace. He was a part of the Shamal War, and the allies hid the gemstone on him for safe keeping," replied Marcus. "I know that you won't remember most of that, so I will write it down before you leave. All you need to worry about right now is getting over the Gemini border which is the mountain chain to the East."

"I didn't see any roads to it though," mentioned Caleb as his eyes doubled in width.

"There isn't. Leave the camper behind. You need to get to the mountains now if Lev is on her way," replied Marcus.

"Will the mountains really stop her though?" questioned Aqila while Caleb stared, trembling.

Once again Marcus had an answer, "At the moment you probably aren't her target, but after she captures the palace she will want Jaako. If you are still in the lands of a Fire Zodiac then escaping her will be nearly impossible because of Siphon Travelling. Trust me, just get to the other side of the mountains. The peaks are the border."

"Yeah, and how do you know all of this?" asked Ferran with crossed arms and an unrelenting gaze. "How do you know where the Taurus stone is if your master was Strelec?"

Marcus rolled his eyes and replied, "The late Taurus was an ally during the war. Dominick was assigned to keep the gemstone safe far away from the battles in a neutral empire. To this day I am positive he is still doing that very job. It just so happens he ended up in a not so neutral empire, so stop questioning my knowledge when there is such little time to spare."

"Wait! Did you say that I have powers?" asked Jaako with wondrous anticipation.

"Yes, but I really suggest that you focus on making it past that border first," said Marcus.

"Okay, but how do we get out of the palace then?" asked Jaako.

A smirk stroked Marcus's face before he replied with, "I suppose we have time for one lesson!"

Marcus did a quick movement with his hands. Nothing happened. Sartan looked around twice before realizing that Caleb no longer was standing next to him. Concerned, he glanced at Marcus and Jaako. Jaako was doing something with his hands when suddenly everything went black. Within a blink of an eye Sartan could see again and was no longer standing next to an enormous, pink throne, but instead he stood in a cramped clay hut with everyone. He stood still for a few seconds just to make sure that it wasn't a mirage. Afterwards, he walked through the doorless doorway to see the camper plopped down next to the well they previously entered.

"What the hell just happened!" shouted Aqila as she followed Sartan out of the home.

"Where are Jaako and Marcus?" asked Ferran as he came out into the early morning light.

Caleb was already standing by the camper door saying, "I don't know, but we should probably get some stuff from the camper before we leave."

Both Ferran and Aqila agreed with him and left Sartan to go get their possessions. Sartan leaned up against the clay home thinking about the palace he was just inside of. *All of the pink glowing. The relics. Maybe all of these things are a bit more serious than I thought. Strangely unusual. Unusually strange? They still are irrelevant to me though.* Suddenly Sartan heard a voice coming from inside the home.

"That was so cool!"

Sartan glanced through the doorway to see Jaako stumbling forward. There were pink flames quickly receding into his hands, and he could no longer deny all of the evidence. *The ring. Aqila's necklace. Now Jaako? This shit is real. Lev actually poses more of a threat than starving does.*

"Jaako, where is Marcus?"

"He said he had some stuff to take care of in the palace. Where is everybody else?"

"They are in the camper. Listen, we really need to get across that border. The sun is way higher than it was when we went into the palace!" exclaimed Sartan.

"Relax, we have plenty of time. It is still morning."

"But do you know how far away the border is from here?"

Both Jaako and Sartan glanced around the clay hut to see the endless white dunes drifting far into the Eastern horizon. The mountains were barely even visible from this distance, and Sartan knew that was just what Jaako needed to see in order to focus.

"And we are walking?" asked Jaako rhetorically. Without wasting another moment, Jaako ran to the camper screaming, "Hurry up guys! We have a time limit here!"

Finally alone for an undetermined amount of time, Sartan could relax without the extra stress that the group brings. Being up for so many hours at this point, he contemplated getting a headstart on the hike, but instead decided to take this time to relax for once. Relaxing would be the last thing he did. Goosebumps briefly fluttered over his skin as he was lost in thought. Even though Lev wasn't chasing him specifically, just the mentioning of her name made him wonder. As he thought about who this fable woman could possibly be, something deep inside of him began to twitch. His stomach felt as though he had been flung off a skyscraper, left to freefall. Something about it was tethered to his core by more than just simple Zodiac stories and stereotypes. Something his brain couldn't quite remember, but something his gut couldn't quite forget.

Chapter 9
A Meticulous Meeting
Lev

Ten minutes ago in Dursnia, she flung the heavy metal doors to the mayor's office open to reveal Mayor Khalil and Police Chief Omar speaking hastily and nervously about something. She looked into the mirror that stood next to them. Their conversation was cut short as she towered over them. Her dark-skinned glistened in the mirror, and she quickly analyzed her own figure before addressing either the mayor or police chief. The two separate white streaks that began under her bottom lip contrasted her space black skin as they ran down her face, across her neck, under her shirt, and across her stomach before finally disappearing under her black pants. As beautiful as her markings were, she was disgusted to not be in her best shape. Heavy eyelids hovered above a runny nose. When she smiled with teeth her grin showed broken and rotten ones. One of her ears was partially missing, and her hands were beyond arthritic repair even though she was immortalized young. Even the magnificent white streaks crossing her stomach couldn't hide her exposed ribs and malnourishment. Regardless, both of the men in the room stopped the second they saw her, and neither of them spoke to her. Instead they patiently waited addressment.

Slowly and formally her gaze drifted away from herself and she spoke, "After less than a day of inspection and personal analysis it is safe to say that your tourism sector needs significant work. Alas that is not my job, so if you would kindly sit down I must get back to work after this pitiful evaluation of your experimental feudal rule."

"But Lev, you have yet to explore the South side of town. There are many industrial tourist attractions there that you might be interested in," squeaked Mayor Khalil.

"My master is counting on me to secure the Sagittarius Palace as quickly as possible, so I feel no regret when I inform you that it was not a question. Sit down," said Lev as she stared deep into Khalil's weak eyes.

Both men took a seat before Omar hesitantly stated, "So, what is it that you want to talk about?"

"You received Kozoroh's message did you not?"

Omar nodded slowly while struggling to keep eye contact and saying, "Now I know that I didn't follow the orders to the point, but I did manage to get Mayor Khalil on board."

"Does obedience mean nothing to you? Kozoroh didn't want any low-life politicians or nobles to be aware of our actions and intentions unrelated to his experiment. Now you have forced us to place trust in this old man."

The mayor interjected, "Funny of you to call me old Ms. Immortal."

Lev turned her attention over to Khalil instantly replying, "Being immortalized at twenty-six does not make me old, it makes me strong and powerful. Whereas getting involved in something that you should have rightfully have no knowledge of does not make you younger, rather it hastens your withering." The mayor sat speechless long enough for Lev to return back to the focus of the meeting. "Omar, you were assigned to steal the Sagittarius Tansiq Scroll from Mayor Khalil here, but for some reason you have failed to. Now you claim that he is involved and willing to hand it over to me, am I right? Otherwise it would appear to me you have failed your assignment. Does he have the scroll?"

"Well, I am sure that he would be willing to give it to you if our situation was different," responded Omar as he trembled in the leather seat.

"I care not about a situation that could be different. I care about the situation we are currently living through, and if you value your title I suggest that you explain the current situation without any omission of facts," said Lev without moving her head even once.

Before Omar could explain, Mayor Khalil interrupted, "Lev, I am going to have to ask you to leave. I have a button under my desk that could have twenty guards in this room within seconds."

She stared blankly at Omar who held his hands up trying to distance himself from Khalil's actions. Her gaze then quickly shot over to Khalil who already had one hand under the desk. Without speaking she turned towards the door. She took two steps before grabbing the heavy door and slamming it shut in front of her. The sound of the button clicking was unmistakable, but it didn't alarm her at all. She turned around to see Khalil standing with a pistol aimed at her forehead.

"One more step and it's all over Lev!" exclaimed Khalil while he pulled the hammer on his revolver back.

"Call me Master," said Lev as she walked towards the table in the center of the room. The gun rang out, and the bullet flew across the room landing right on her forehead. Like a squashed ant the bullet crumpled upon impact before falling, dejected on the floor. Another shot rang out this time hitting Lev's eye. For her it felt like a grain of sand getting stuck in her eye, and within seconds the bullet hit the floor crumpled up like the first one. By now Khalil must have realized that he was in immediate danger because his tone shifted.

"Ha ha! I was just making sure that you were actually as powerful as they say you are, Lev. Glad to see that it is true, but we don't need to see how powerful your offense is," squealed Khalil as he backed away from the approaching Lev.

"I said to call me Master, did I not?" asked Lev as she walked closer to Khalil who had fallen backwards into the leather seat behind the desk. The desk of course was the only thing separating the two of them.

"Yes, yes you did! Master Le---"

"Silence! You will tell your guards that it was a false alarm when they arrive, and I will decide your fate at the end of the meeting," commanded Lev.

Khalil nodded and grabbed a microphone from off the desk, "False alarm disregard the emergency call guards."

Lev immediately returned her attention back to Omar, "Explain to me exactly why he is a part of this now."

Without any hesitation this time Omar squealed, "A few nights ago I went to steal the scroll from his library for you, my master, when I found a group of young adults native to the city that already had it. We ma---"

"Are you telling me that a group of peasant workers, SLAVES, took the scroll from a police chief?"

"No master, they were armed and skilled fighters!" exclaimed Omar.

"My disappointment is escalating. Finish your explanation."

"The three young adults had the scroll, but we managed to take it from them, detaining two of them. One thing led to another, some people got shot and the taller male stole the scroll again before releasing his friends. We chased them to the interstate where they got in a camper and headed North East."

"You just let them drive away in a camper? Really? Do you not have any squad cars?" asked Lev with disappointment that must have been so visible Mayor Khalil squirmed uneasily in his seat as a result.

"No, we chased them in the squad cars and helicopter, but suddenly a blast of white clouds came out of the camper. It crashed directly into the helicopter which then crashed into the squad cars preventing us from chasing them any further," answered Omar while all fidgety.

"White clouds? What do you mean?" asked Lev.

"Master. They have Vahee's ring and Gemstone."

"Vahee is deceased. Who are these young adults? Why do they have the Libra Gemstone?"

"We only recognized one of them, the tall one with Vahee's Gemstone. His name is Sartan."

"Sartan?"

Omar nodded a shaky nod while Lev took time to think. The name was familiar to her, but she couldn't quite remember why. She had never met a Sartan personally, but she had heard his name many times years ago. *It doesn't matter. I will have to catch him now anyway.*

Lev spoke once more, "So you have no clue where the scroll is do you?"

"None. We suspect that they have already made it across the border by now," said Omar.

"Why would they go across the border if they just found the Sagittarius Tansiq Scroll? They are still within my lands somewhere. Between you and Jiry we should have been able to find the late Strelec's Palace by the end of January. IT IS THE 19TH! Without the scroll the timeline is going to be pushed back, and when Master Kozoroh gets angry it isn't going to be my fault but yours!"

"If you don't mind me asking. Why do you want the palace anyways?" said Omar from his seat.

"There are only three living Zodiacs, Omar. If I can get to his palace I can convert every Sagittarius to become a subject of mine," replied Lev as she pounded her chest. "With all that extra power my master's goals will be achieved much faster."

"And your master's goals are?" questioned Khalil quietly from his seat of unsuccess.

"Neither of you have business with that knowledge, understood?" replied Lev slowly and formally. After they both nodded she spoke again, "Since you failed to retrieve the scroll for me Omar, I am going to take things into my own hands."

Suddenly a knock on the door interrupted Lev's meeting. She quietly turned around to open the door unaware of what may be on the opposite side. When the heavy door slid out of the way it revealed a shorter man with a scruffy brown beard panting and holding a letter. The man looked ill as she could easily see dark circles under his eyes and dried blood in one of his nostrils.

"What do you need, my weary subject?" asked Lev.

"My master," said the man as he kneeled down on one foot handing out a rolled up piece of paper to Lev. "Jiry has a message for you."

Lev grabbed the letter and opened it to see that it only had two words written across it in blood: *Found Marcus*. She stared at the letter for a moment before smiling. "What is your name?" she asked the messenger.

"Master, my name is Luke Hugo, and my age is thirty-four," said the messenger.

"Your age is irrelevant to me. Regardless, there are a few recently opened positions here if you would like a promotion," said Lev. "Just tell where exactly this letter was written."

"Of course my master," said Luke as he still kneeled down in front of his master. "Jiry wrote the letter in blood immediately after talking to three men on a roof in a village called Furictown."

"Furictown? As in…you found it!" said Lev methodically but aggressively at the same time. "These men. How old were they exactly, and what did they say to Jiry?"

"They had to be at least in their early twenties. Jiry talked to them about Marcus. They said that Marcus was somewhere around the village hiding. After hearing that he called off the assault and retreated back into the desert," said Luke. "Your boots are quite stylish."

"Thank you, but I am more interested in your opinions on the assault," replied Lev.

"Well, Jiry said that he didn't want to capture the palace since you never told him to. He let the four young men live even after slight losses," said Luke.

Lev took a second to think before finally replying, "Good! I want to be there when we capture the palace, but did you not say that there were only three young men?"

"There were only three on the building, but the fourth was on the ground alone after he defeated the distractions. There was also a female, but she refused to fight and hid in a camper."

Lev smiled wide. She soaked in the information before saying, "So boys, did you hear that? Jiry and Luke have found where your little mishaps have ended up. Now which one of you has a map to Furictown for me?"

"It isn't on any of the maps master!" exclaimed Khalil in fear.

"OF COURSE NOT!" shouted Lev. "IT IS A FUCKING ANCIENT PALACE WHY WOULD YOU KEEP TRACK OF SOMETHING SO IMPORTANT HERE?! Luke you may rise, and when you stand up you may consider yourself the new Baron of Dursnia!"

Khalil let out a high pitched squeal before screaming, "Wait! Don't kill me! I have a family!"

"QUIET!" roared Lev. The word echoed down the hall and Khalil's face went whiter than the white streaks on her body. "As much as the world needs it I won't kill you right now Khalil. Not as long as I have use for you."

The ex-baron glistened with joy momentarily before that very relief was consumed by more fear. "What are you going to do with me then? I thought I was the mayor of Dursnia?" asked Khalil with sweat dripping off his face.

"For now just write your letter of resignation stating that you are transferring the Barony of Dursnia to Lord Hugo here. I will deliver the letter to Countess Noel personally so that we don't have any mistakes or misunderstandings," commanded Lev regally.

Khalil's face turned red from the previously pale white perhaps from anger or disbelief, but either way Lev was more focused on the window behind him. The Northeastern facing window showed almost half of Dursnia, and the expanding desert squeezed the interstate as it advanced away. Far in the distance Lev could see an explosion of light. The pink beacon shot straight up into the sky. It was barely visible from this distance, but there was no way it was a natural occurrence. By the time everyone else in the room noticed the phenomenon the sound wave hit. A deep blair shook the building, vibrating the glass. The deep ringing was so forceful it knocked the flying birds out of rhythm, nearly killing them from a fall.

Once the sound wave popped and passed Lev roared, "Idiots! Why didn't you think that they would try something like this! KHALIL! Finish your letter now!" Khalil frantically looked for paper and a pen while Lev turned to Omar. "OMAR! Gather lots of supplies and a few guards! After that go straight to Furictown!"

"What just happened?" asked Luke from the door.

"We have a Zodiac to kill because of their incompetence," said Lev referring to Khalil and Omar. "You are going to take Omar to Furictown, and then you will come back here and manage the city. From then on you this city is your realm and main objective."

Luke smiled while replying, "Understood."

"OMAR! Move!" shouted Lev upon realizing he still stood in the room with her. He didn't need to be told twice. After he was out of the room Lev asked, "Are you done with the resignation yet?"

"Yes, yes it is written and signed," replied Khalil.

Lev snatched the paper off of his desk before he could put it in an envelope, and she quickly scanned over it to make sure it was accurate in text.

"STAMP IT!" she exclaimed while handing it back to him. "Then get some guards in here Khalil," said Lev as her temper began to cool.

"Why?" asked Khalil.

Without speaking Lev stared at Khalil raising an eyebrow. Instantly, he began to tremble and called for a few guards. His shirt was drenched in sweat, and now that the pillar of pinkish light had disappeared Lev grew more and more annoyed by his pitiful presence. She took the resignation after he stamped it and turned to face the door at the approaching footsteps.

The moment the guards arrived Lev commanded, "Take your ex-baron to his prison cell, for he has been caught conducting treason towards his liege. He has already admitted it and written a letter of resignation."

"Who are you to say that?" questioned one of the guards.

"I was sent here on the orders to inspect possible treason, and that very suspicion has been found almost instantly. Would you like to read his written admission and transfer of the Barony of Dursnia to Luke here, or must we waste more time on this fanatic?" replied Lev as she held up the paper. The potentially illiterate guards nodded in understanding as they took the unwilling and hostile Khalil to his cell. Lev and Luke still stood in his office alone now. "Luke, Uzaley might be the King, but I am your master, and I am becoming the empress of all the lands controlled by the late Strelec with every second that passes. Uzaley will soon be my vassal, so you will pledge your loyalty to me before even thinking about him. Do you understand?"

"Yes my empress," said Luke.

"It is a shame that we must keep my position as an ever growing empress a secret, but until Kozoroh says otherwise that is how it will be. Keep your mouth shut. Either way the feudal contract is still in place, and you have a lot of lieges. If I ask something of you that conflicts with your liege, you obey. Your new direct liege is Countess Noel. Do as she says until I give further instructions," whispered Lev as she put her hand on Luke's shoulder.

"My empress, what is the plan now?" asked Luke.

"I'm going to visit Countess Noel in Jerilo to deliver Khalil's resignation and transfer of power to you. After that I will go to Furictown and clean up this mess that Omar made. Don't worry about me, I'll just sniff down Jiry. That is all that you need to know right now. I want you to just focus on getting Omar to Furictown for now, okay?"

"Yes, my empress," said Luke as he knelt down in front of Lev.

Lev turned towards the door and gracefully walked out leaving the office fifteen degrees warmer than it was when she walked in.

Chapter 10
Bridging Borders
Aqila

Five hours after leaving Furictown for the border, Aqila glanced back at the distance she had traveled. Many miles behind her in the afternoon haze was the Sagittarius Palace, too far to be seen from her current position. She stood next to her allies at the base of the Arqet Mountains. The extreme heat from the desert had left excessive sweat on her clothes and aching joints begging for a break. She concluded the feelings were mutual among the group, as Caleb had already plopped down for a breather upon reaching the edge of the desert. They still had to follow through with the plan.

"Come on guys, we must get up and continue. Lev could be only minutes away from us by now," said Aqila with a dry and raspy voice as she turned towards her friends who had been resting in the sand for quite a few sweaty moments now. "I am being serious, we need to get past the peaks."

"We know, but what is the point if Lev could get here in only minutes?" asked Ferran while he slowly rose to his feet off the sandy white ground.

"The point is that if we do not try at all our chances of survival is simply that, zero," replied Aqila.

Caleb interjected, "We would have to get some distance from the border not just pass it. Lev can reach the border just as quickly as she can reach us."

"Exactly! Does that not concern you?" asked Aqila as she began walking towards the steep mountains in front of the group. "Lev is not the nice person you think her to be, and I prefer not to wait to be proven right."

"Who has the water?" asked Sartan as he stood up next to Jaako.

Without any exchange of words Aqila handed a small bottle of water to Sartan. She then walked off away from the group towards the steep terrain saying, "Drink it on the go, come on!"

The group may not have noticed her inner quaking, but she noticed that her hands instinctively had started to fidget around anxiously. Of course whenever she caught this happening she gracefully distracted herself with the group's conversation. Then her legs started to shake with every step she took, but when questioned she skillfully disregarded it as her minor injury reacting to the long hike. Almost as though she were the origin of a graph, Aqila's thoughts continuously crept back to Lev as they hiked. She had only seen Lev once before in her human form and it was the epitome of fear, but now she had seen her twice counting the chance encounter on the interstate. The coy smile that she remembered Lev sneering around incited nausea in Aqila. *Now that I am an adult though, there will be no hesitation to rip that smug smile right off her face. When the time comes at least.*

"Aqila," shouted Jaako from behind her as the rest of the group began to follow.

"What Jaako?"

"What do you think Lev will do when she finds Marcus?" asked Jaako who was now trailing behind the rest of the group.

"I am sure he will be fine, Jaako. After all he has survived the previous six hundred years or so has he not? Best not to think about that right now," replied Aqila as she walked past the first gray rock that sat on the white sand.

"What should we think about then? I'm stuck thinking about how the devil personified is currently hunting after us," said Jaako. The path began to grow steeper, and Aqila laughed to herself upon hearing he shared the same struggle.

"I am clueless, Jaako. My mouth is too dry to talk right now. Talk to the others about your hobbies or something," said Aqila as the thought of Lev aggressively forced its way into her mind once more.

Desperate to ease her worries, Aqila focused on the landscape. The terrain she was traveling over did not feel like it was changing, but it was slowly turning into a different environment. The warm winds from the world's largest desert pushed her further up the first hill. As they continued up the steep hill the pearly, white sand from the Great Desert quickly disappeared behind them as more gray rocks piled up on the way to the top. Upon glancing up to the peaks of the nearest mountains Aqila saw what appeared to be the same sand. Then it dawned on her, the peaks were covered in snow.

It must have dawned on Sartan as well because he spoke out from behind her, "How about we don't reach the summit of these mountains."

"Agreed, let's find a path in between the mountains," said Caleb as he nearly tripped over a rock. "That way we get through faster and before nightfall."

Aqila chose not to reply to them, instead she was distracted by the pure scale of the mountains. The way they seemed so dead to the eye was strange. Their frosty tips and melancholic gray bases were impossible to miss when placed next to the white sand from the vast Great Desert. The jagged rock faces that jutted out of the sides of the growing mountains towered over her, and the cloudless, blue sky sank down over everything like a heavy blanket. She knew that there had to be luxurious life and water on the other side. It was just the action of getting there safely and in time that was dangerous.

"Jaako, what were you doing before coming here?" asked Ferran.

"What do you mean?"

"What did you do?"

"I just survived in Dursnia. You know the grind," replied Jaako.

"Yeah, but how?" continued Ferran.

"I had to steal sometimes, but my dad had a market shop which helped out a lot."

"Okay, so you're just as bad as Sartan I see," said Ferran.

"Ferran, please just focus on something else," shouted back Aqila from the front of the group.

A few moments of silence passed before Ferran murmured something under his breath. Too exhausted to deal with it, Aqila just kept trudging forward up the side of the mountain. She was currently walking between two substantially more enormous mountains, but even without reaching the peaks of the adjacent rock clusters her elevation would be lifted drastically. With every step she took she could feel the heat of the sun melt into her back. Her legs were already sore from the previous five hour hike, but if she wanted to live she knew that she would have to continue until possibly nightfall. *I might be able to do that, but I can not convince Ferran or Caleb to.*

They were much further up the side of the mountain than when they began, but they still had quite some distance to go. Aqila could have sworn that only a few hundred feet away was a smoother looking path that could be traversed easily. By now every step she took was on a stray gray rock that had been shaken out of the mountainside, and with every few steps she could hear one of the boys behind her complaining about something. Usually it was Caleb and Ferran, and that fact alone heated her blood because she knew that they had survived much more dangerous feats than mountain hiking.

"I am certain there is a path up ahead if you guys can just make it there," she shouted back at the rest of the group without turning around.

"Yeah, but that doesn't mean we can stop walking," yelled back Caleb.

Aqila stopped walking and struggled to keep balance on the loose rocks as she turned to face the crew. Immediately behind her was Sartan and a few feet behind him stood Jaako. Caleb and Ferran however, stood at least five yards behind them with their eyes stapled to the ground below them. When they caught up to Jaako they failed to even realize that he stopped as they bumped into him.

"When we pass the border we can take a breather," she said. She then wondered if her lifelong friend and brother even understood the life threatening terror they all found themselves trapped in.

Before she could return her attention to elevating up the mountain Caleb spoke, "Why are you so worried Aqila? If Lev wanted to be here right now don't you think that she would've caught up by now? Not to mention that even if we do make it to the border she can catch up just as quickly."

"I do not know why she has yet to catch up. Perhaps Marcus is making things hard for her at the palace, or maybe this is all part of her plan. Do I need to remind you what she can do?" replied Aqila before turning away to continue the hike. "The pathway is not even that far from here. Mom and Dad would not have wanted us to die like this."

"Hold on what happened to your parents?" asked Jaako as he shoved his way past Sartan and next to Aqila. "Ferran can ask me about my past, but now that I think about it I don't know anything about any of yours' other than Sartan's!"

"Wait…what?" said Sartan quietly.

"That isn't a story for today Jaako," interrupted Ferran from the back of the group.

"He can know Ferran. It is not like he is going to tell anyone, or that he has not heard worse before," said Aqila calmly.

"You three are siblings right?" asked Jaako while they walked deeper between the mountains.

"No, Ferran and I are, but Caleb is just a childhood friend," said Aqila.

"Well what happened to your parents Aqila? Why would they 'not have wanted us to die like this'? As if they are a past tense themselves!" asked Jaako loudly with wide eyes and a wider grin.

Aqila did not reply at first. She was wondering how much she could tell without saying too much. She could feel Ferran's displeasement at what she was about to say without even looking at him. Finally after a bit of silence she answered, "Our parents were murdered just for knowing something."

Jaako gasped, "No way! Did they ever find the killer?"

"No, but I am always afraid that the killer might find us. We were just kids at the time. Luckily, I managed to overhear some of the stuff that they were talking about before it happened," whispered Aqila.

"Wait, you guys were there when it happened?"

"Ferran was gone at Caleb's, but I was in my bedroom at the time. The killer was unaware that I was home, but I could hear little parts of the conversation even from my bedroom."

"What were they talking about?"

Ferran interrupted, "That's all you need to know right now Jaako. She probably doesn't want to talk about that right now."

"Well you can ask me anything about my parents. I don't really care," blurted Caleb from the back of the group before Aqila could reply. "They housed Ferran and Aqila after the incident."

"What happened to your parents Caleb?" asked Jaako as prompted.

"Nothing. They are still alive and well why?"

"Well, I just figured…you said that I could ask you anything about them, so I assumed there was some event or something that happened."

Caleb replied, "Oh! Well they managed to get us all scholarships at any college in the world. Then they gave me the camper for my seventeenth birthday last year. Shortly afterwards we left which began our mission to save the Zodiacs. The rest is history. Also they might think we are just studying prestigious courses abroad but…the less they know the better"

"Where have you guys been so far over the past year?" asked Sartan.

Before Caleb could answer, Aqila replied, "We left our hometown of Mirisburg, a small city in the heartland of the Aries Empire far far to the West. Then we traveled North to some cities in the Libra Empire before traveling East for ages ending up in Hapopelma where we spent a few months before going to Dursnia. Now, the rest is history."

"That is like almost half of the world. That must've taken forever," replied Jaako.

"I am more concerned with how they managed to fund that for a year," said Sartan.

Caleb answered, "We have had a lot of people help us with donations, and we also borrow with the intent to return if donations are scarce."

"So you stole?" asked Jaako.

Caleb replied, "Not quite, we always would've given back the things if the owners asked us."

"Be real Caleb, we have had to steal some things more than you would like to admit. Just like those who live in Dursnia, it was for survival," interjected Aqila. She bit her tongue immediately when she saw Jaako's eyes glow in triumph.

He hastily proclaimed, "Then why are you so worried about Sartan and I stealing to survive in Dursnia then Ferran?"

"We had to steal. You could've found another way to survive," answered Ferran.

Sartan shouted, "That is too fucking hypocritical Ferran! Do you see how skinny Jaako and I are? If we didn't steal we would not be here today."

"Still, we stole with purpose while you stole just to survive," countered Ferran.

"Well now look at us! I'm an inactive Sagittarius, so how dare you belittle me!" shouted Jaako as he rolled up his sleeves. "Do we need to settle this right now?"

"Maybe, but you know that even if you do win Aqila has her gemstone and will kill you afterwards!" shouted back Ferran as he cracked his knuckles. "Not to mention if it weren't for us you wouldn't be a Zodiac anyway!"

"And if it weren't for me, you wouldn't be alive right now!" argued Sartan with crackling volume.

"Nobody is going to get killed," said Aqila as the whole group failed to listen to her.

Before she could speak again, Jaako had swung a fist into Ferran's side forcing him to wince in pain. Then Jaako threw a jab that was quickly caught by Ferran's hand. It was at this point Aqila realized something was off about the fight. Even though only two punches were thrown, Jaako's hands had a slight pinkish-red glow to them, similar to that which emanated out of the entire Sagittarius Palace. She could barely see the tiny flames resonating off of his hands, and when Ferran noticed it as well, he jumped back away from Jaako quicker than she could scale a building. Sartan grabbed Jaako, detaining him by bringing Jaako's awareness to the flames, but Aqila wasn't focused on that. Instead she stared at the damage the pink flames had done to Ferran. The side of his body where Jaako landed the first hit was virtually untouched, but Ferran's right hand obviously carried the peculiarity of the flame.

Ferran fell to his knees screaming at his hand before rolling onto his side. Aqila quickly ran over to help him put out the flames that raged on his palm, but when she reached for them she realized that they were abnormal not just in color. The flames burned, but they did not burn hot. Instead, they burned so cold that her own hand retreated before even touching skin. Ferran waited not to put the pinkish-red fire out, but after the flames were gone and he stopped screaming, Aqila could finally address the situation.

"Sartan, take Jaako forward up the path and wait for us. Caleb, hand me some water," commanded Aqila who successfully took reigns over another fight. Jaako and Sartan gladly left Ferran behind, and once Caleb gave her the water, Aqila took Ferran's cold hand and put the warm canteen in it. "Drink it!"

Ferran gulped it down, and after a small swig of uneasy silence he spoke, "We really have to get rid of Sartan."

"What?! How is this Sartan's fault? You are the one that keeps causing problems with our newly acquainted friends. You have fought Sartan and now Jaako both for no reason. Just accept that they are going to help us and open up for once."

"So what is your plan? Get a whole bunch of people off the streets to replace the Zodiacs?" coughed Ferran as he slowly tried to stand up.

"No, but we have done that which is necessary to advance us. What do you want me to do now? Jaako has to stay now that he is an inactive Zodiac, and I want Sartan to stay because he easily seems to be more and more rational than you."

"I am way more rational than he could ever be! What benefit does Sartan bring to us from this point on? He was only supposed to stay until your leg healed," said Ferran who was now standing up, towering over Aqila. "But it turned out it wasn't even that injured in the first place, so why is he still here with the group?"

As she glanced up at him she said, "There are eleven more Zodiacs to deal with, and I am sure he could help us replace at least one of them. Do you realize what we have done? Like Caleb said, we are 'college students' that have single handedly recreated one of the Zodiacs that has been deceased for decades. Find a way to deal with Sartan because he is going to stay in the group!"

"Fine! Fine, I will think of something then," replied Ferran as he handed her back the canteen.

Aqila sighed and turned around to catch up with Sartan and Jaako assuming Ferran and Caleb would follow, eventually. She took a few steps before she heard Caleb murmur, "It's okay Ferran, I know you will find a way to deal with him."

When she caught up with Sartan and Jaako they were already talking about something.

"Yeah, but I feel so tired now," said Jaako as Aqila came into earshot. When they noticed that she had arrived Jaako jumped a few feet back pleading, "I didn't really mean-"

"Relax. He thinks that you guys do not belong in the group any longer, but that just can't happen," replied Aqila. "Now that you are an inactive Zodiac you have to follow us on our journey."

"What about me?" asked Sartan. "When can I leave with my ring? I'm not a Zodiac."

"Not yet. I still need you," answered Aqila.

"For what?"

"Your rational thinking and your emotional support," replied Aqila as she began to walk up the smooth path.

"No. I am not your or the team's emotional support pillow," said Sartan. "From what I have seen that is what Caleb is for."

"Why not? And Caleb!?"

"I don't do emotions. It's for your own safety."

"What do you mean?" asked Aqila.

Sartan replied, "Listen, how about I just be rational for a day or two before you give me back my ring and let me go."

"Where would you go? We are nowhere near Dursnia, and even if you do go back they will probably kill you," added Jaako who was trailing behind them.

"He has a point, Sartan. You are better off just staying here with us," said Aqila.

"Stay with the girl who got us to the top of Lev's hitlist, that makes plentiful sense."

"I never intended to do that! I also could have let you freeze in the back room of the camper. In fact, if it were not for me you would have frozen to death there. You used the ring to save us from the police, which certainly would have burned through you with bullets. I barely even burned you with the gemstone. Is it not better to be burned than to be frozen?" questioned Aqila.

"Usually it is, but I'd rather freeze than be burned by you," answered Sartan as the path became so steep that Jaako was using his hands to help him trudge up it.

"If I really wanted to burn you I could melt you down to a puddle on the floor, and you would absolutely love every second of it," taunted Aqila jokingly who placed her hand on his shoulder to balance herself atop a jagged rock.

Sartan was far less receptive to the joke than she thought he would be. He threw her arm off his shoulder and glared back at her wordlessly while frowning. Shaking his head he looked back to the path.

Aqila shrugged off the rejection as Jaako broke the silence, "Well that was beyond weird, but honestly Sartan, it is probably smarter to just stay with us. We are going into a new country with a crazy lioness chasing us all. None of us have been here before, so we might as well stick together if we want to survive."

Aqila said, "Exactly, we can help each other survive in the Gemini Empire. Not to mention we probably are going to survive like you did in Dursnia since we no longer have a camper."

"Fine, I will stay with you guys for a little bit longer but on two conditions," said Sartan while the path began to level out. Jaako stretched briefly as he no longer used his hands to help him climb.

"What conditions?"

"First, promise me that I won't have to deal with Ferran's bullshit," replied Sartan with a smile.

"That's a good one! He has my vote!" laughed Jaako before Aqila could answer.

"Hey now. Ferran is his own type of person. Even I have to deal with that sometimes too!" exclaimed Aqila with an unsteady laugh.

"Second, you give me back the ring."

"I would not be able to do that," said Aqila.

Sartan raised an eyebrow and stared at her silently. Then in a deep tone he slowly yet methodically whispered, "Why not Aqila…do you not trust me?"

"Not at all after you said it like that," laughed Aqila as she infected Sartan and Jaako with her laugh. They all laughed together. Whether or not the laughter was genuine or not Aqila could not tell yet, but the fact that they were enjoying themselves was an important start in the right direction.

They walked further up the path before Sartan compromised, "Okay, but I want that ring back eventually. You taking it away from me is like that murderer taking your mom from you."

Jaako gasped, "Woah. That was a cold card to play."

"It is fine this ring must be as important to you as your own mother is."

"Yeah, but I didn't really know her," stated Sartan.

"Why?" asked Aqila.

"I don't know. I told you that I can't remember much of anything prior to life on the streets," replied Sartan.

"Do you even remember your mom?" asked Jaako.

Sartan answered as they reached the top of a rocky hill, "Of course I do...vaguely. She was tall...I think. She had black hair and always had the most soothing voice when she read bedtime stories to me. Which was rare by the way. She was always busy doing work or something like that."

Sartan continued to speak, but Aqila was enamored by the landscape. They had reached the peak of the path that crossed over part of a ridgeline, but they were nowhere near the summit. Instead she looked onward down the path to see the beginning of a long bridge resting only a short gallop away. This bridge was old and made of wood and rope, but it stretched up towards the highest ridgeline which had to be the border in the distance. Obviously, it would be the fastest way across. However, Aqila wondered if they would survive it as she could already feel the bridge swaying in the wind. The bridge started only feet above the ground, but the end of it was pinned on the edge of a steep cliff far above the rocky, gray ground below.

Jaako's voice trailed off next to Aqila, "We have to cross that? I think we can take a breather. We made it to the top of a mountain I think. We deserve a second."

Without replying Aqila glanced back towards the Great Desert. Ferran and Caleb were walking towards her, but behind them was a blissful, white desert quite far down the rocky, gray hill. Then she turned around and looked down the path. When Sartan began walking down the path towards the base of the bridge she followed him.

"Do you think that the bridge can support us?" asked Aqila as Jaako started following them reluctantly. "It has to be the fastest way right?"

Sartan replied, "I will happily find out."

"It doesn't look like it can, guys," said Jaako from behind them.

As she stopped next to Sartan right in front of the bridge, Aqila spoke, "We either die like this, or we die because of Lev."

"We might have better chances with Lev," argued Jaako as he twitched once so slightly that Aqila would not have noticed if she were already looking at him.

Aqila noticed something peeking out over the top of the gray hill behind Jaako. *Lev! I thought we had more time!* As her thoughts ran wild she could feel sweat forming on her palms. She patted at her side with one hand to make sure she at least had a knife and scratched at her chest to make sure she still had the necklace. She glanced at her two companions to confirm they were seeing the same threat approach before focusing her entire attention on Lev. As the figure walked further into view she realized that it was just Caleb with his mouth wide open pointed to the sky. He was either panting or complaining. Relieved, Aqila's face blushed as she tried not to be noticed. It was easy because they all could start to hear Ferran shouting profane language from directly behind Caleb.

As Ferran and Caleb slowly caught up with the group, Aqila said, "Come on guys. I do not want to try and convince them." She trudged her way past Sartan and slowly onto the first few planks of the bridge. The first few planks strung into place by the ropes seemed fine, but as she took a few more steps Aqila noticed that the planks were not all as healthy. Looking back at Sartan, who was directly behind her, she said, "Watch your step, not all of these planks are sturdy."

He nodded, and she glanced back at her feet. The ground beneath the bridge had already started to grow distant. Her hands gripped the rope railing so tightly that when she let go the ropes uncompressed with a quiet wheeze. She shimmied her way up each plank, and she could start to feel the bridge sway in the wind. She could also feel it vibrate frantically whenever Sartan or Jaako took a step forward. The whole thing started shaking suddenly, and she glanced back to see Ferran finally getting on the bridge. However, when Caleb walked on it, Aqila thought it might collapse so badly that she stopped long enough for Sartan to bump into her backside.

"Why did you stop?" asked Sartan as he took a step backwards.

She slowly replied, "Do you feel that?"

"I feel the vibration of the bridge, but that is what it does."

Aqila closed her eyes and focused on the vibrations within the rope she gripped so dearly. They had yet to even make it a fourth of the way across, but she could already feel the wind ripping at the bridge up ahead. It swayed back and forth so much that it almost made her sick. In fact she did feel sick. Sudden chills overcame her as she refused to look down, and her stomach slowly turned into a clothes dryer as soft pings of pain began emerging from her injured calf. *I will need a painkiller soon.*

"I really don't want to be on this thing longer than I have to Aqila," said Sartan from behind her. "And I think I speak for everyone when I say that."

She gulped down salty saliva and nodded. Every step seemed heavier than the previous, and the planks began to squeak under her weight. Closing her eyes, Aqila slid across the planks further up the inclined bridge. Before she knew it the squeaking planks no longer made any noise. Well, that was unlikely, but she was unable to hear it over the wailing winds that now pierced her ears and threatened her balance. Aqila decided to open her eyes once more to not only have more control over her balance but also to reassess the situation and the distance to the bottom.

The moment she opened her eyes a strong gust of wind running across the mountain chain slammed into the bridge. The ropes and planks trembled at the touch of the dry, merciless winds, and Aqila could feel the whole bridge sway three times its width to the left before quickly hurdling back to correct itself. Of course, her eyes were now glued open, and she was staring straight down in disbelief. Nearly one hundred feet down layed millions of shattered, sharp rocks waiting to pierce right through her soft skin, and she was barely even half the way to the end of the bridge that rested gently on the steep ridgeline. Suddenly, a loud snap cracked from behind her. She instinctively held the ropes as tightly as possible before looking back to see two arms tightly gripped around Sartan's stomach. Jaako's foot had busted through one of the planks, and he was now holding on to Sartan for dear life.

"It's slipping!" shouted Jaako from his compromised position. Aqila's heart melted as all she could do was watch "Don't let me fall!"

Sartan held the bridge firmly while Jaako used him to re-secure himself on the bridge. During all the commotion a shiny object flew out of a pocket. Aqila didn't notice it at first, but it only took a second before she saw the silver flask shimmer as it fell down towards the baseline. She watched as it slowly made its way to the hungry rocks, and by the time it reached the bottom Aqila could only see the shimmer being reflected back to her from many different points. As expected, upon impact, it was ripped into multiple shiny pieces that bounced back up towards the sky before disappearing into the gray graveyard of lifelessness. When she looked back at her companions, Jaako was already standing up with white knuckles gripping the ropes. Despite a heavy wave of sudden chills, Aqila could feel sweat dripping down her face. She turned around to continue up the bridge unsure of how slow to go, and by now all she could think about was getting to the peak so that she could stop the ever growing aching of her muscles and immediate threat to her life.

"Come on whoever is in the front! Please go faster!" shouted Caleb from the very back.

Aqila put each foot on the roping where the planks were sewn into the bridge, so that if the planks snapped she would still be standing on the ropes. She picked up her pace as the added sturdiness gave her all the comfort she needed to convince herself she was safer than she really was, but the sweat dripping off her freezing nose failed to cease and instead grew. Hot and salty saliva quickly formed in her mouth as she persistently tried to keep her stomach from cartwheeling out of her body, but seconds after succeeding she heard the unmistakable sound of somebody failing to hold on to their stomach behind her. Jaako was spewing chunks over the side of the bridge, and desperate to not follow suit Aqila quickly swiveled her head around and tried her hardest to ignore the aches and pains as she continued up the heavily compromised bridge. The winds only intensified as she went further. At the worst part she was almost certain that the whole bridge would flip over on itself, and if it did she knew that she would not be able to hear herself scream over the winds.

Before she knew it she was only a few planks away from actual ground, and by far at the highest point of the bridge. *If I fell now at least I would hit the side of the mountain before the sharp rocks at the bottom.* That thought did little to ease any pain, but at least it brought some sick sort of comfort. Aqila refused to look back at her allies until she was settled on hard ground, and as the wind died down near the ridgeline she could hear planks squeaking behind her.

The very instant her right foot landed on the ridge she bolted forward in attempts to put the slightest distance between herself and the bridge. There were many mountains with higher peaks to her left and right, but luckily straight ahead was an easy downhill journey from now on. Down the easy sloping hill, well easy compared to what Aqila had just climbed, she could see the mountain slump down back towards the Earth, and in fact, she could also see green closer to the bottom, a color that the Great Desert had deprived her of seeing in its purest form for nearly a year. Rivers flowed downhill from the peaks of the higher mountains, and she immediately felt relieved now that she had crossed the border.

Then it hit her. The cold chills and aching legs returned along with the sweating and the nausea. Without glancing back she dropped her backpack on the ground to grab it from inside. After unzipping a side pocket and pulling out the small orange container, Aqila nearly fell over when something poked her shoulder twice. She jolted back and was even more surprised to see Sartan standing behind her as he returned his hand to his side.

"I thought your leg finished healing," said Sartan while pointing at her calf.

As a droplet of sweat fell off her nose and onto her shoe Aqila replied, "I think it has for the most part, but after our hike I could definitely use some painkillers in case I overworked it. Do you have the water on you?"

As he pulled the bottle out from his pocket Sartan sighed, "Just leave some for me."

While nodding, Aqila took the bottle in his hand and quickly threw two of the pills in the orange container into her mouth. The last ounce fell next to the pills on her tongue, and with one quick swig it all went down. She then hustled to hide the orange tinted bottle back into her backpack before handing the empty water bottle over to Sartan.

Wiping the water off her lips Aqila exclaimed, "We made it to the border Sartan!"

"Yeah take a photo because I'm not doing that again," replied Sartan once the bottle of water was back in his pocket. "I'm just glad I wasn't behind Jaako."

Aqila turned back to the bridge when she asked why, but the question then became rhetorical. Jaako was just walking onto the gray Earth when Aqila watched his partially wind-dried shirt drip with vomit. The wind obviously was blowing strongly when he threw up because when Ferran walked off the bridge there was not any lack of liquids or chunks on him either. Caleb managed to dodge most of it, or more likely, used Ferran as a human shield.

"Please tell me that you guys took clothes from the camper," said Aqila.

"I thought Jaako was going to bring our clothes," said Caleb with a strange bit of relief in his tone. Perhaps it was because Ferran took most of the blast, but more likely Aqila concluded his relief to be derived from surviving that cursed bridge.

Jaako replied, "I only own what is on me. Why would I take the clothes?"

"I actually brought some extras," said Ferran while he took his shirt off letting it drop to the gray ground beside his feet. "Not enough for everybody though."

"At least we made it to the border in time," said Aqila. "You guys can figure that out, but I want more distance between us and Lev. I am going to start the hike down the mountain now."

Before Aqila turned to begin the long trek into the Gemini Empire she glanced back at the Great Desert one more time as it hid between the peaks of smaller mountains. It was almost like looking at an entirely new desert from her height. What felt like days away was the base of the mountains, and what felt like light years away was a small vibrating speck in the white sand that had to be Furictown. After spinning to face Sartan, Aqila took in the beautiful sight behind him. The mountains slowly receded back into the ground, and the gray rocks that she currently stood on, quickly crumbled into nautical blue rivers and green shrubs that led all the way down into a lush forest. There was no waiting. Aqila picked up her backpack slinging it over her shoulder and meandered down the gentle slope glad to be off the bridge.

Sartan was walking right next to her, and for the first time she noticed how ill he actually looked. The black crescents under his drooping eyes contrasted his unusually pale skin that still had a tint of red to it perhaps from sunburn or maybe even when she barely burned him with the gemstone, by the way that he carries on about it. He stumbled every few feet, and she really wondered if under the black robes his ribs pierced through his skin. *I have been up for at least one day. The weariness has slowed me down, but he looks like a zombie. When was the last time he ate?*

"Sartan, when was the last time you ate?" she asked while they slowly approached the first few green and brown shrubs hanging on the hill.

"The food from last night. It hasn't been that long," replied Sartan slowly and without any interest in the conversation.

"Sartan there is a small bag of chips from Dursnia in my backpack if you want it," whispered Aqila so that the others couldn't hear. Upon glancing back at them however, they were already quite a bit away. Not to mention that they looked as though they were arguing about something irrelevant, so Aqila continued at normal volume, "It is in the second pocket on the side if you want it. I know it is not much, but it is better than nothing."

They continued walking for a few seconds. Silence ensued briefly before Sartan gripped the zipper, opening the tiny pocket. She kept walking as he took it out and zipped the bag up once more. Aqila watched in amazement as Sartan, almost like a feral animal, ripped the bag open and began feasting on the chips as if it were his last meal. *The sad thing is, he probably thinks it might be his last meal.*

Aqila tried to speak over the sound of Sartan's possibly expired, chip bag rustling and crinkling, "Sartan, if you ever need anything just let me know, okay? It is the same with Jaako and the others. I do not want any of you guys to suffer."

Sartan swallowed his mouthful of chips before replying, "History would argue with that statement and so would I."

"Come on Sartan. I never meant you any harm. In fact, I forgave you after you broke my leg, and let us not forget you did not really represent a good reason for doing that in the first place," said Aqila in astonishment while Sartan crumbled the empty bag into a ball.

"You forgave me after I helped you get that Tansiq scroll, but I was basically an indentured servant prior to that. When you woke up and your leg healed, if it was even broken in the first place, I tried to leave debt free, but now I am forced by multiple events to stay with strangers that trust me as little as I trust them. Not to mention they stole my ring."

"What do you want me to do about it now? All I can do is apologize. I'm sorry."

Sartan dropped the empty bag onto the ground while saying, "I don't want your apology. I want actions, and I just can't understand why you would want me to stay if you can't trust me. If you really trusted me then I'd have the ring back."

"I do trust you though. I just think that it is best for you not to have the ring after the accident."

"Who are you to make that decision?"

"I am the one who saved you after you froze."

"Yeah! But now I am on death row, execution method LEV!" exclaimed Sartan as a stream peacefully flowed next to them. Happy frogs hopped around from lilly pad to grass splotch completely unaware of what they were talking about. "Look, it took more than just an apology from me, so it surely will be that way for you. I literally had to break you into the mayor's complex, steal a scroll, break you out of the mayor's complex, and destroy an entire helicopter to be even. Now I can't leave the safety of the group, but staying is equally as dangerous."

Aqila looked at his face that had crumbs all over, "Fine, what do you want from me then? Other than the ring of course?"

"Really?"

Aqila smiled while nodding her head, "You do know that there were two bags in my backpack right? If that is not enough I could also help you with your memory problem…"

Sartan did not reply to her. Instead he casually opened the backpack while looking back at the others. Aqila glanced back as he zipped the pocket closed and to her surprise they had finally begun to catch up. Not too far away stood Ferran in a brand new shirt that was clean and vomit free. Caleb and Jaako however were in the same outfits as before, and Jaako still was drenched in his own charf. *I bet he is just glad he is off the bridge by now. I doubt it would slow Lev down though. LEV! I forgot about that.*

Upon remembering the whole reason they are here right now, Aqila yelled up the mountainside to them, "GUYS! Come on! We crossed the border, but Lev is never that far away!"

Behind her she heard Sartan murmur, "How far do you want us to go? I didn't get any sleep last night, and we have been at it all day."

Aqila spun around and looked past Sartan. At the base of the mountain a very lush forest started. It looked thick enough to keep some of the day-time heat in, but she knew that would be a problem. Without the camper and its heat, things can get colder than the arctic. Maybe the heat would hold a bit better than the desert, but that was a problem for when night fell. *Right now I just need to get us all away from Lev and the border.* Aqila finally answered Sartan while pointing down the side of the mountain, "Do not worry Sartan. Once we get off the mountain we can set up camp in that forest down there. The faster we get there the more time we will have to relax."

Without speaking she watched Sartan roll his droopy eyes momentarily before turning and trudging down the slope, which by now had green, leafy chokeberries all over it. She followed suit, noticing that the sun had already begun its slow descent one or two hours ago. It boggled her mind that Lev had yet to show up, but realistically she knew that it was only a matter of time. *She had to have made it to the palace by now. Marcus must have sent her on a false lead, or she thinks that we are hiding somewhere in the palace. Truthfully, it was a gargantuan construction, and it probably would take her forever to search through all of those pinkish-red rooms and chambers. Then what? How would she know which way we went? Unless Marcus tells her. UGH! Who am I kidding? Lev is coming after us right now, and there is no doubt about it. They don't call her the hunter Zodiac for nothing.*

Out of nowhere Aqila heard footsteps run up to her from behind. Suddenly Jaako appeared next to her with his vomit ridden shirt still reeking of his insides.

"Aqila!" exclaimed Jaako.

"What? What is it?" asked Aqila in nervous surprise. *He spotted Lev!* "What is wrong?"

Jaako rubbed his eyes before replying, "Everything is starting to get a little blurry!"

"What do you mean?"

"My eyes, I can't really see that much now!"

"When did it start?"

"I don't know! It happened so slowly that I couldn't really notice, but now I can barely see the ground!" exclaimed Jaako as he stumbled down the slope.

"I do not know Jaako. Do you have anything in your eyes?"

"Just my contacts," said Jaako while nearly tripping over a small rock. "Do you think that they dissolved or something?"

"My vision was always fine but try taking them out. They may be dirty or dry," answered Aqila as they stopped to assess Jaako's problem. "Can you see without them?"

"Of course not! If I lost them I wouldn't be able to even walk upright let alone go down the side of a mountain regardless of how gentle this slope is," said Jaako with his finger in his eye.

Aqila watched Sartan walk ahead of the group as Jaako fingered his eyeballs out. Jaako was frantic about the sudden failure of his vision, but Aqila never could blame him for something like that. *I have never really had to deal with poor health. Everything was always fine with the exception of the occasional injury. I can only imagine what it would be like to be deaf or let alone blind, and there is no way I could stab my own eye with my finger like that. DID HE ACTUALLY JUST TOUCH HIS!?* After a few gut wrenching seconds of watching Jaako poke at his own eye, a small clear contact sat on his fingertip.

In an astonished voice Jaako exclaimed, "I still have them!" His excitement distracted Aqila from the rancid smell wafting off his shirt for a few seconds only to be crushed by confusion. Jaako covered his eye that still had the contact in it before asking, "Why can I see without it though?"

Aqila shrugged, "Maybe they went bad or something. Take them out if they are making you blind." Aqila cringed as Jaako took the other contact out, and before she knew it Ferran and Caleb caught up to them.

"What are you guys doing?" asked Ferran as he slowed down his pace.

"Apparently his eyes are broken or something. He was blind with his contacts in but perfectly okay once he took them out," replied Aqila.

"Well then. We're going to catch up with Sartan," said Ferran while he walked right past Aqila.

Aqila instantly spun around to say, "Do not cause more problems Ferran. You have already been in a fight today."

She watched as Ferran shrugged her off, and Caleb followed him down the slope. Upon returning her attention back to Jaako she realized that something was off about him. Now that his contacts were out his pupils were dilated too much for the amount of sunlight present. He was staring around intensely at the most random things like the grass on the ground or the peaks of the mountains behind them. She never said anything to him until he started to stare directly at the sun.

"Jaako! What are you doing?" exclaimed Aqila as she grabbed his arm and tugged his attention to her. "Do you want to go completely blind?"

Jaako stared at her for a brief moment before exclaiming, "WOAH! WOAH!"

"What?" asked Aqila as curved brows burned across her face.

"Aqila your face! I never knew it looked like that!" exclaimed Jaako as his hand slowly reached for her cheek. "It looks so soft!"

Aqila quickly smacked at his hand and backed away while asking, "What is wrong with you?"

"Hey! You knocked the contacts out of my hand!" exclaimed Jaako as he backed away from her assault. "But if this is how the world looks without them I can get used to it for sure!"

Aqila stared at him in curious confusion as he slowly brought his hand to and from his face. It was as if he was a child viewing the world for the first time. A new set of eyes gobbling up every trace of light there is to see. *Is he okay?*

Slightly concerned Aqila said, "So you can see now?"

"Oh my yes! I can see everything! Every blade of grass, every particle of snow on the mountaintops, and even the sun. I don't remember the sun shining so much ever in my life!" exclaimed Jaako as his gaze ran uncontrolled all over the scenic mountainside.

"At least nothing is blurry anymore. I am going to try to catch up with the others. You good?" asked Aqila as she took a few steps backwards down the mountainside.

"Never better!"

Aqila gave him a smile before spinning around and making her way after the rest of the boys. Sartan had made quite some distance already, and the others were not that far behind them. Next to her was a very small stream that trickled all the way down into the forest, but by the time it reached the forest it was a completely full river of fresh water. The lush forest awaited them, and despite the fact she was operating on practically no sleep, Aqila continued down the mountain.

However, after only a few steps she heard Jaako holler from behind her, "WHAAAT!"

Alerted, Aqila spun once more to see Jaako's jaw at his ankles. He was staring at the river just ahead of her. Unamused and unphased, she turned around down the slope again lost in her thoughts. *What is wrong with him? His contacts just randomly stop working, and he can see perfectly without them. And perfectly would be quite an understatement. I mean he stared at the sun just because it was bright. He is strangely unique.*

It wasn't that long until they all reached the entrance to the forest, and from the base of the slope, the roped bridge looked so far away. Not to mention that she could only see the very end of it, but that was now behind them. In a small patch of neon yellow forsythias, they all stood arm's length from the first few low hanging hawthornes that lined the entrance to the deep, dense forest. The forest seemed so much livelier than anticipated as Aqila could already hear cicadas and various, chirpy, forest dwellers from within.

"How far in do we have to go?" asked Caleb while stroking his hairless chin.

"Not that far. We just need to get out of sight of the border," replied Aqila as she took the first step towards the forest. "It is still going to be very cold tonight though."

Nobody replied. Instead the whole group watched her walk into the forest alone. After she passed three trees she finally realized that nobody was moving. Aqila glanced back and could barely see her companions through the foliage. They slowly followed suit behind her, but the forest had an eerie glow to it. Maybe she had grown accustomed to the colorless Great Desert, but the amount of green in her vicinity made her uncomfortable. With every other step she would check over her shoulder to make sure someone was right behind her, and she could barely see, through the green, Jaako behind her.

There were too many thorn bushes attacking her sides, and there were way too many birds chirping in her ears. Even the sharp breeze that was almost hotter than the winds on the other side of the mountains kept slicing through her with heated malice even within the safety of the forest. Every time that the winds picked up Aqila could hear all the leaves dodge out of its way giving it as much space as it needed to barrel into her. It was almost as if the forest breathed in and out every few seconds because once the winds passed through her, they returned to pass once more only seconds later. Although they nearly knocked Aqila on her butt every time they passed by, the warmth that the currents of air brought to her made her realize just how tired she really was.

"This should be good enough," announced Aqila after walking far enough into the forest to not remember which way she entered. "We can set up camp here tonight, but just no fires."

"What is a camp without fire?" asked Jaako.

"Yeah, how are we going to keep warm at nightfall?" questioned Sartan after stopping next to Aqila. "Do you want us to freeze?"

"Lev will definitely find us if she sees smoke," replied Aqila as she leaned against a tree.

"She won't see the smoke at night though," argued Sartan.

Jaako said, "Unlikely, Lev is an Active Zodiac, remember?"

"So?" asked Ferran as he appeared through the foliage.

"The Fire Zodiacs have really impeccable vision. I know for a fact that one has night vision and another has thermal vision. I think Lev has thermal, but I can't remember which one had night vision, whether that be Beran or Strele---well...me," said Jaako slowly as his eyes widened. "I forgot! I'm a Zodiac now! This makes so much sense!"

"Relax, you're only an inactive one. Marcus said your powers would be really, really weak," interjected Ferran who crunched down some violently green tall grass to sit on.

Aqila overheard Sartan whisper, "But he did say that you'd have powers..."

"How do you know all of this Jaako? Where did you learn it all?" asked Aqila curiously as she attempted to change the conversation.

"My parents enrolled me in a Fire/Air Zodiac club before we had to move to Dursnia."

"Isn't that illegal though?" questioned Caleb who already sat down on the ground. Aqila watched Jaako smile and nod without replying.

After a short moment of wondrous silence Aqila spoke, "Well let us not take any risks. No fires."

"If we aren't having a fire I'm going to bed now," said Sartan as he walked away from the group.

"The sun isn't even down yet," said Caleb.

Sartan quickly replied, "You can try to sleep once the cold comes, but I'm not."

"That's a fact!" exclaimed Jaako as he followed Sartan's train of thought.

Aqila sat down on the dirty, grassy ground. *Damn.* She watched Caleb rip into his bag to recover a sandwich as if he thought it might have been stolen. Meanwhile, Ferran sat down to sip some water. *At least the shivers are gone. The aches and pains soon to follow. I'm just glad Lev has yet to catch us. It still is quite displeasing to know that she can use thermal vision though. I have to stop. I will only make myself sick if I keep worrying about these things. Everything is great right now.*

Aqila randomly broke the silence to say, "Caleb, do you remember that one girl from Mirisburg? The one with the red hair?"

Ferran immediately shouted for him, "YES! I remember that! Poor Caleb!"

Chapter 11
Stranger Strangers
Ferran

Ferran rested under an enormous pine tree that loomed over everyone else. The warm breeze kept him stuck in a comfortable position where he could see the entire group. With itchy skin from the army of plant life that had yet to give way to a road, he took note of the direction Sartan had gone, in search of a river. Everybody else was still sound asleep in the bedding that was created the previous night by smashing down all the waist high grass. The early morning light struggled to shine through the treetops, but with sprinkled success, it landed on Ferran's face. Disgruntled by the excessive heat, Ferran moved out of the way of the beams. The sun no longer ruined his morning, rather a pinkish butterfly that fluttered energetically in front of his yawn ridden face. He swatted at the pest hopelessly missing every swing of his open palm. As if rejected, the pink butterfly flapped its large wings over to Jaako, who still slept peacefully. The nuisance landed softly on Jaako's face and stretched its wings in the sun. Ferran watched the bug flutter incessantly about on Jaako's nose and was content with it no longer assaulting him. Delayed rustling of shrub and grass ensued as Jaako was startled awake by the bug. He sat up and rubbed his eyes with heavy yawns. The bug drifted away, back and forth with the warm breeze before eventually disappearing into the deep forest once again.

Seconds later Ferran watched Jaako rise to his feet and fight his way through the shrubs to the rest of the group. Jaako scratched his armpits clearly unaware that Ferran was watching him, and when he did realize that he attempted to speak. Jaako opened his mouth and closed it slightly. He then breathed in heavily, licking away at crusted lips.

Unsure if Jaako was going to talk at all, Ferran decided to ask, "What? Are you hungover again?"

Jaako stared glossily while yawning before saying, "No, but very thirsty for some reason. What time and day is it?"

"It is early in the morning on the 20th of January," said Ferran as he stared at Jaako. The two of them lived in silence after that, with the exception of the never ending screams of birds from every direction. Ferran listened to the forest breathe while he watched Jaako take two sips of water before emptying his canteen. The scraping of the leaves in the wind was interrupted by heavy, clopping footsteps coming from nearby.

"Someone is coming!" whispered Jaako as he knelt down in order to hide his puffy eyes below the tall grasses around them.

"Relax, it is Sartan returning with water," replied Ferran without searching for the first sight of the approacher.

Suddenly, a tall figure appeared out of the foliage showing itself off to the two of them. Ferran stared enamored by shock, as he realized the figure hovering over them was not Sartan at all. Instead it was a thin, elderly man who looked as though he should not be this far into a forest at all, let alone unattended. His narrow, wrinkled face was dull with disappointment, and there was a sense of impatience under his short white facial hairs as he began to speak under a twitchy smile.

"Ah! What may bring you to…these parts my children?"

Ferran watched dumbfoundedly, unable to reply to the man's question. Luckily, Jaako managed to squeeze out an excuse, "We were going on a hike and got lost in the forest. Is there any way you can help us get back to the nearest city?"

"Wh-which city did you come from? You know there ain't really any towns this close to you?" asked the man as his unnaturally slim body inched closer towards them. "As people of the Genil…Gemini Empire you must know that…the borders…borders have closed for the better part of this century."

Jaako and Ferran exchanged glances before Jaako finally got the guts to answer his question, "You see we were assigned to survey the borders. We

Started all the way back in Garigo, but to be completely honest we don't know how much further we got a bit lost on our way back."

The strange man's eyes widened as he heard the story. Staring directly at Jaako the man took a few heavy steps towards him. Ferran saw something glimmer inside his pocket momentarily, but with the flash of an eye the glimmer disappeared back into the man's black wool coat. Regardless, Ferran held his hand on his knife just in case.

Right as the man's arthritic hand reached out to Jaako's shoulder Ferran interrupted, "Who are you, and why are you so far from any towns either?"

Startled, the man backed away from Jaako and tried to muster up an answer, gasping for breath multiple times, "Heard some noises…from over…was wondering if…you need help? Now that I know… you are friends…I help you."

"Great! Can you help us get back to Garigo?" asked Jaako with a smile.

"You didn't answer either of my questions," pressed Ferran as he stood up preparing to defend himself from the strange man. "Tell us who you are? Where did you come from?"

The man's cracked smile had waned away with the request, and he slowly stepped away from the two of them. Ferran heard the sound of more footsteps not too far away through the foliage. The man sensed them too and quickly looked around as if he felt the reaper breathing down his neck.

"Hunt! Go down…fast! Hunt! They hunt you!" exclaimed the man with a soft yet stern whisper. He dropped down to a shaky squat to hide himself from the view of anyone outside the bedding. "Attack them! They want kill us!"

Ferran's mind could only think of one thing. *LEV!* Both Ferran and Jaako hesitantly abided by the man's demands and dropped below the grassy foliage that might hide them from their attacker's view. The footsteps quickly grew louder, and the bony, old man began counting down in one hand. The moment that last arthritic finger fell into his fist, a tall figure wandered into their bedded campsite. All three of them sprang up to attack, sending the wanderer into reflexive defense. Jaako got instinctively punched in the nose resulting in him stumbling backwards onto Caleb who still layed sleeping on the ground peacefully. Ferran was too far to attack, but close enough to watch the man reach out for the hunter. That hunter's face, however, was the face of Sartan. Ferran screamed for the man to stop, knowing that Sartan might kill him if he kept attacking. Sartan jumped away from the attacks of the strange, old geezer. The elderly man, however, jumped forward still trying to attack Sartan.

Jaako stumbled and shouted at him, "Relax he is with us!"

The man did not heed the call, and continued to swing after Sartan, who was actively trying to simply distance himself from the ailing fighter. Jaako continued to yell the same sentence at him until he finally stopped, and by the time he finally stopped both Aqila and Caleb were standing with groggy eyes and yawning mouths.

"My sorry…I thought---"

The oddity stopped mid sentence when he realized that Aqila and Caleb were now awake. Ferran watched as the stranger's lips flared into tight curls. This man's wrinkled face scrunched up as he stared around at the concerned, curious faces that watched him groggily and inquisitively. Without warning he started shaking and vibrating aggressively.

The whole group took a few steps back as Caleb asked, "Are you okay?"

The peculiar man never replied but instead continued to shake vigorously until the skin on his bones turned to bloody gelatin from the excessive vibrations. As his skin slowly melted away, a skeleton mostly similar to the human's quickly appeared beneath the steaming mush that was his skin. However, a long, sharp bone slowly erected itself upwards and out of what seemed to be the bottom of his face. Everything above that sharp pike of white transformed as it moved upwards on his skinless face. A large opening widened in the middle of his skull leaving room for tiny sharp teeth to excrete themselves from two head sized jawlines. Lastly, one of the only two things that didn't melt into the steamy puddle of skin, organs, and clothes that now pooled at his bony feet, were two small eyes that now were positioned in the very summit of his cracked, alien skull. His eyes were light gray in tint. There was no pupil. There was no iris, and there definitely weren't any eye whites. The whole eye ball was a light tint of silvery, shiny gray, and it was impossible to tell just who they were focusing on.

Unfortunately, that was just the ex-human's head. His skeletal form slithered all the way down to sheer bone feet. A strange sack of flesh and blood hung within his exposed and cracked rib cage, and the arthritic hands of the man were now nothing but long, crooked bones, without any trace of flesh other than the steam resonating off them. Now an additional two limblike-excretion of bones jutted out from beside the lone sack of flesh hanging from its torso. Apparently the creature's gaze was fixed upon that of Jaako because the very first thing the creature did was lunge forward towards the blonde man.

Ferran jumped away from the threatening creature as it hunched over after Jaako. *There is no way this sick fuck doesn't have lethal motives!* At this point the entire campsite was consumed by chaos. Aqila and Caleb had been rudely awoken by this thing, Sartan returned just to get attacked, and Jaako was currently being chased away from the campsite. Luckily, Sartan and Ferran's instincts kicked in as they followed the hungry creature into the woods. Ferran struggled to keep up as the creature slithered around husky trees with ease. *How can Jaako stay ahead of it at this pace?* Ferran lost the beast as it slipped between several thick, thorn bushes while hunting Jaako, but the explosion that followed led him right back to the monster. He ran around a seared trunk to see two birch trees falling to their sides and a glob of gray gelatin jiggling on the ground with pink flames fluttering around the base. Sartan was just as shocked. The creature no longer had any legs, well leg bones whatsoever. It was using its four arm bones, if it was even right to call them that, to inch itself closer to Jaako as it dragged its fleshy-ribcage across the wet ground. Jaako was slowly backing away from the dangerous creature. The thing snarled and crackled despite being so heavily damaged.

Aqila quickly shouted from behind, "What is this thing?! Have you guys killed it yet!?!?"

"Jaako ripped its legs off somehow!" exclaimed Ferran as they all watched the creature chase Jaako. "Jaako! Kill it!"

"I don't know how I did that! HELP ME KILL IT! PLEASE!" shouted Jaako from a few trees away, but Ferran could barely even hear the scream over the sound of his own heart racing.

For some reason the creature was fixated with Jaako. Even when Jaako circled around the creature still crawled after him despite only being a few feet away from everyone else. *It is as if it knows he is powerful. Does it know he is an inactive Zodiac?* Ferran watched Jaako randomly punch at the thing while he walked backwards in a circle. The punches were way too far to make contact with it. Regardless, Jaako kept trying as if something would change. Eventually Jaako began punching towards his persistent predator so aggressively that he accidentally bumped into a tree. Within an instant Jaako fell over onto the ground, and the thing capitalized on this opportunity. Before Jaako could get back up and away from the thing, it lunged forward with an unexpected burst of energy. Like an ant on a wall the creature latched on to Jaako's legs with both of its bone hands, and Ferran could do nothing but watch.

"AAAAAHH!!! IT'S GOT ME!!!!" screamed Jaako loud enough to make Ferran's ears bleed.

Sartan grabbed it by a conglomerate of bone that held the flesh sack in place. The fiend failed to notice this as it attempted to crawl closer over its prey, but it still tried to force the large, piercing face-bone into the soft skin just beneath Jaako's chin. Ferran, however, was stuck in trance by the sheer strangeness of the entire situation, and he wasn't the only one. Half of them didn't even react to Jaako's screaming. Both Caleb and Ferran just stared in frightful wonder as the scene unfolded, but Aqila ran towards their fallen ally the instant she realized what the thing was about to do to him with its face sword. Alas, she was too slow.

Jaako's fist shot straight towards the thing's alien skull in a final thrust for survival, and a gust of pink-red fire flew straight down the open throat of the creature before dissipating back into the air just how it appeared. Its tight talon-like fingers slumped off Jaako's calves leaving behind bloody scratches. The raging fire completely froze the thing's skull along with most of its organs that resided in its exposed ribcage. Sartan jumped away from the blast which let the monster fall, twitching on the ground next to its prospective prey.

Strange to Ferran, was the fact that Jaako's fire froze the creature instead of burning it. The fact that Jaako shot out a small flame straight out of his hand was no surprise to him. After all he had Aqila who could create similar flames with the gemstone that hung around her neck, and he was aware that actual Zodiacs possessed some power, even the inactive ones. The thing that confused Ferran was that Jaako's fire was different in the fact that it wasn't really hot at all for fire. In fact it was the opposite. The flames froze him in their scuff the previous day, and once again they have failed to produce heat. He could already feel the cold air pierce through the forest, and he was a safe distance from the burst of flames that froze this creature in its place.

He could see ice forming on the bones, but that didn't last long. Seconds after Jaako jumped up to put some distance from himself and the attacker, the entire skeletal system that had transformed, mobilized, and attacked them, now was crumbling to pieces. He stared in wonder as each fragment of its skull slowly turned into gray mush. When all the bones deformed into a silver blob, the dark pulp began to jiggle around suspiciously. All of the material wiggled over itself repeatedly until it was all connected in one slop, and once the matter was all one it stopped moving and slowly began evaporating into gray steam.

He stared at the cold, steamy blob wondering if he might vomit before Aqila screamed, "What the hell was that?!?!"

Jaako was now standing with a face almost as pale as the one he wore on the rickety, rope bridge less than a day ago. Ferran watched Jaako squeeze his nose with his fingers, and he quickly backed away from the blob and covered his own nose that was still a virgin to the scent.

"NO WAY!" exclaimed Jaako as he walked around the steamy pile of goo to get closer to the rest of them. "I completely forgot that these creatures existed! That was an Eveharris! We must have got an elderly one, but I can only imagine what would've happened had it been in its prime!"

"We would be dead no doubt!" exclaimed Aqila.

"I'm definitely awake now," said Jaako as Ferran felt his heart rate slowly return to normal. "I thought I was done for!"

"What is an Eveharris?" asked Sartan with a raised eyebrow as he ran a hand through his short, black hair. *He is obviously trying to pretend like he is used to things like this. Almost as sickening as the creature. Too bad it didn't go for him first.*

Regardless, Jaako replied, "An Eveharris is one of the naturally occurring phenomena in the lands of the Gemini Zodiac. They spawn in rural areas, and shapeshift in order to hunt. They only exist within the lands of the Gemini Zodiac, but they can be a real threat to country folk, livestock, and hikers. Some of the other students took a Gemini course, so they knew a lot about this kind of stuff and told me about it. I know there is more to it, but I can't remember."

Sartan replied with haste in his voice, "So they are like those naked women who always swim around in the ocean?"

"What?" asked both Aqila and Jaako simultaneously.

"What do you mean? The naked women that always swim next to the big freighters at sea. They are so beautiful that most grown men can't even look at them or else..."

"Or else what?" asked Jaako with a smile as he taunted Sartan jokingly. "Do they kill them with their beauty?"

Sartan nodded while replying, "Just about. One man couldn't control himself and jumped over the edge of the freighter for a closer look. Once he splashed into the water one of the women swam up to him and locked her arms and legs around him. I assume for a few seconds the man was breathing pure euphoria, but once she had him locked down they both sank straight to the bottom."

Ferran watched as Jaako's face went pale once more, and the smile that previously resided there turned back to the extremely nervous face that he wore when being attacked by the Eveharris. Ferran could even swear he saw a sweat droplet fall off his chin, but then he got distracted by the fact such a creature exists. *Why does there have to be so many dangerous creatures in the world? I didn't even know the Eveharris was a thing and now this? Wait if Sartan has seen one before then---*

"Wait, you have seen one?" asked Aqila, cutting Ferran's train of thought off instantly.

Sartan replied with a grin, "I saw an entire pod of twelve. Only one guy jumped off, and when he did a large portion of the pod surrounded the one that caught him. Every one was beautiful beyond belief."

"Why didn't you jump in?" asked Jaako with wonder on his face.

"I was a child. Children are immune to the weapon of lust, and believe it or not most women can stare at them all day without being tempted to even lean over the railing," replied Sartan as he started walking back towards the campsite.

Everyone followed as Ferran asked him a question, "You were a child on a boat? I thought you said you couldn't remember anything from your childhood, so what is up with this?"

Without turning around Sartan replied, "I haven't lost memory of everything. I couldn't tell you why I was on the ship, where I was going, or even my age, but I can remember the creatures. Especially since they were so…different. They don't really look like women, but they look a lot like women. It is hard to explain, but even as a youngling I could tell they were abnormally attractive…I suppose. That kind of event stuck with me."

"Why are you just now telling us these stories?" asked Caleb from a few trees back. "You haven't mentioned hardly anything about your backstory at all."

Sartan replied from up ahead, "That is not true. I have said a little bit, but Ferran was quite skeptical of me when I first got here. It wasn't really an environment where I could just tell you stories that you wouldn't believe anyway."

"I'll never change Sartan!" exclaimed Ferran.

"Guys let Sartan finish his story!" exclaimed Aqila who was obviously trying to calm things down. *Maybe she really just wants to know about these naked women who kill people with their beauty. I don't blame her, but what if this is all another lie? How do we trust--*

Sartan continued, "Anyway, these naked women are naturally occuring phenomena just like the Eveharrisses. My mom said that we can't kill them because they are a natural part of the food chain in the ocean, but she also told me repeatedly to never become part of that food chain. Apparently they feed on weak-minded men, and when they die they fertilize the ocean floor or something. I can't remember everything she said, but they seem similar to the thing Jaako just killed. In the way that they feast on weak minded men…it must've sensed Ferran."

Jaako's stomach must've exploded because he chuckled and coughed for the following seven seconds. So loudly in fact that Ferran decided it wasn't even worth it to prove Sartan wrong. Aqila then exclaimed with a quick laugh, "I am just glad that the thing Jaako killed was not mind-controllingly beautiful or roaming the forest in pods of twelve!"

"Do you think we will encounter any more?" asked Caleb as they made it back to the campsite that was void of any campfire. "After all, we are in the middle of nowhere."

Jaako replied, "It is very possible, but hopefully we won't have to make that encounter."

"I don't plan on it," added Ferran as he reached for his backpack.

"So what are we going to do now?" asked Jaako. "We obviously can't stay here for long with Lev on the loose, but where do we go now that we crossed the border?"

Aqila stared into the deep forest before saying, "Well, we need to make our way to Garigo. I know Marcus said to follow the mountains South until we got closer, but I wish not to be asleep again when another Eveharris shows up." Everybody nodded in agreement as they grabbed their belongings.

"Then what is your plan Aqila? Go through the forest until we reach a town?" questioned Sartan with a smirk. "My chicken legs are going to melt by the time we make it to Garigo if we walk."

"I can agree with that," said Jaako.

Caleb added, "I third that."

"Let's find a city so we don't have to walk as much," said Ferran from behind the tree he had begun urinating on.

"That is what I was thinking," replied Aqila. "We trek through the forest until we find a city. Then we obtain a vehicle and drive all the way to Garigo. It should be a lot safer for us, and it also should make things way more difficult for Lev, assuming she has already crossed the border."

"That seems cool and all, but how do we exactly know where we are and how to get there? I don't know which way is North or South from here," said Ferran as he zipped up his pants behind the tree, refusing to be left out of the conversation.

"We only need one direction. Somebody climb a tree and find where the mountains are. The mountains are in the West now, so we just need to go the opposite direction," commanded Aqila as she took some of the medicine for her calf.

"Why can't you?" asked Jaako as he walked off to find somewhere safe to pee.

"Why she can't. Her calf is 'obviously' still healing, can't you see her taking her medicine?" insisted Ferran.

Aqila put away the meds and said, "I can try to, but just give me some time."

"No. Have Sartan do it. He obviously knows how to climb, so just have him do it instead," argued Ferran as Aqila tied back her hair.

"Stop worrying Ferran," said Aqila after her black hair was securely tied behind her head. "I will be fine, so just make sure no Eveharrisses show up."

Ferran thought about arguing with her, but chose not to when he saw that look in her eyes. The look. The one where her eyes go flat, her face goes blank. He has learned that whenever she makes this face nothing can be said to sway her. She won't listen let alone think about changing her mind. He looked away from Aqila as she disappeared into the tree's leafy branches. Ferran's gaze drifted to Caleb who was grabbing the front of his sandy, blonde mop and tugging it over his face. The longest strand stretched down over his eyes, and right before he let the hair go back to its curly formation on the top of his head he noticed Ferran's gaze.

"What the hell are you doing Caleb?" asked Ferran.

Caleb quickly tried to reply with something logical, "My hair is long!"

"Yeah?" continued Ferran as now both Jaako and Sartan were watching in confusion as well.

"Hair is overdue. With the shave. UGH! We need haircuts!" exclaimed Caleb as his social skills malfunctioned momentarily. "We haven't had a haircut in over a year, Ferran!"

"We can get one soon," replied Ferran as the tree Aqila climbed began to sway.

Suddenly Ferran could see two dirty, white sneakers descend from the tall tree, and of course the rest of Aqila followed them down to the ground as quickly as she could. He could see a few scratches and scrapes on her exposed arms, but they seemed miniscule compared to the scabs that were already there from when she broke into the mayor's complex.

"Alright guys!" exclaimed Aqila only seconds after her legs stabilized on the hard ground. She then pointed to her left while exclaiming quite loudly, "We need to go this way!"

Instantly, Aqila searched for her backpack, and once it was strapped around her arms she began walking in the direction she pointed at. Everyone else already had grabbed all of their things, so they slowly followed her, aware of how long this hike may be. Ferran pulled Caleb to the back of the group and waited for the rest of them to walk ahead a little bit.

Once everyone was out of earshot, Ferran whispered, "Okay, what should we do?"

"I don't know, but you should probably make the move before it's too late," whispered Caleb as he watched to make sure the others couldn't hear him.

"I say we do it when he is asleep."

"Hey, remember that I am not a part of this. You can do it when he is asleep, but I'm not going to help you. I don't want that blood on my hands, but trust me I won't say anything to anyone," whispered Caleb as Aqila and the boys walked out of sight into the forest. "I just think that there are better ways of getting rid of him. Ways that don't compromise our innocence."

"Caleb, this is the real world. It is for real now! Lev is chasing us. We nearly died just by waking up this morning. You might be the only one I can trust right now. Aqila letting these two random guys come with us is not usual for her. I'm thinking she did it just because she thinks they are cute," whispered Ferran while they both glanced in the direction the rest of the group walked away towards.

"That definitely is a reason, but Jaako has a purpose in the group now."

"I know! I know! But we still could have found someone more reliable."

"Could have! We can't anymore, so let's focus on Sartan because Jaako needs to stay until we can find a replacement and until Lev doesn't have control over the Sagittarius Palace."

"Fine! How do we deal with Sartan though?" asked Ferran quietly. "If I straight up kill him the others will attempt to prevent it."

"Don't kill him!" exclaimed Caleb.

"SHHHH!!!"

"Sorry!" exclaimed Caleb with a whisper. "We can get rid of him without getting rid of him you know? Right…right?"

Ferran sighed, "If we don't kill him he will follow us for the ring, remember?"

"Then have somebody else kill him."

"Like who? We are in the middle of a forest nobody is here except for the Eveharrisses. The Eveharrisses!" exclaimed Ferran quietly.

"Exactly! But how?"

"I'm not sure. I guess we can try to leave him behind. Have the whole group walk off without him, and make sure he can't catch up. Act like we were going in separate groups. Have Aqila and Jaako walk in the front and tell them we will be a few minutes behind them."

"Yes! We can knock him out and then leave him behind for the Eveharrisses, but give him a fighting chance. Get him twisted and confused, so that he can't follow us. We have to knock him out though. That is the hard part to do discreetly."

"Possibly, but what if he is already asleep?" asked Ferran with a grinching grin. "If Aqila and Jaako walk off while he is still asleep we can tie him up while he is unconscious. We could catch up with Aqila and Jaako later that day, and when we don't have Sartan with us, say he wanted to rest a few more minutes. In reality, he is tied up ready for the next Eveharris to walk by him a day's hike away!"

"It's perfect! Tonight he will be exhausted from all the walking, and will sleep like a baby."

Ferran continued, "We will have Aqila and Jaako start the hike early, and we can tie up Sartan!"

"We probably won't even need to do that. If we get far enough away he won't be able to find us, and at that point we wouldn't need him to be tied up. Right?"

"Yes! I agree, but I want to see him suffer first. I want him to be punished for what he has done!" whispered Ferran as they began walking again after the rest of the group.

"Punished for what?"

"For hurting Aqila! For destroying our dynamic! For trying to get with Aqila!"

"Oh…"

"It won't be long now until he no longer poses a threat to our group!"

"Threat to our group?"

"Don't act stupid Caleb," whispered Ferran as they climbed over a mossy trunk that sat on its side defeated. "Sartan is here to fuck us. Both figuratively and physically. He will take Aqila and steal from us when the opportunity arises!"

"Does he have to die though?" asked Caleb while trying not to fall face first into the foliage.

"Not necessarily, but we are better safe than sorry…are we not?"

Caleb hesitantly replied, "We can untie him after you punish hi---"

Ferran interrupted, "Better safe than sorry…ARE…we…NOT?"

"I suppose…"

The sun sprinkled through the canopy above them onto Caleb's curly hair as his long time friend stapled his gaze to the ground. Ferran, feeling pleased at their heroic plan, could hear the chirps of the birds much louder now as well as heavy pecking of the woodpeckers on a distant tree. It had become bearable for him, but he laughed to himself knowing that the liveliness of the forest would soon induce great pain in Sartan. Not because Sartan had weak ears, although that very well may be true, but because the headache that he planned on forcefully fisting into Sartan's skull would make the softest of whispers tear at his ringing ear drums. The softest chirps. The sneakiest Eveharris.

Chapter 12
Lies with Legs
Sartan

It was the next morning after the long hike that followed the killing of the nasty Eveharris. Sartan could feel something shaking his face by the chin, and he was startled awake from the sweet world that was utterly void of consciousness. Upon opening his heavy eyelids, Sartan saw Ferran's light, caramel hand fall to his side as he stood up next to Caleb. He was screaming about something, but it was hard for Sartan to focus immediately after waking up. Not to mention there was great strain on his limbs, which was of more concern to him. With a groggy gaze, Sartan looked over his shoulder to see that his arms were stretched and tied around the trunk of a thick tree.

Now he was very confused. *What is going on? Where is everybody?* Sartan hastily looked for Jaako or even Aqila at this point. Neither of them were in sight, and neither were any of the bags. Caleb and Ferran had their bags thrown over their backs, and the fact that he was tied up and basically alone with Ferran was even less comforting. He could feel his brows burrow down towards his nose as his gaze finally drifted to Ferran, who was still yelling about who knows what. Sartan's ears rang at the sheer volume of every sound that came out of the man's mouth, especially after rising.

"LIKE WHO DID YOU THINK YOU WERE KIDDING?!?!" shouted Ferran as Sartan began listening mid sentence. "AS I'VE SAID JAAKO IS A PROBLEM, BUT YOU NEED TO BE DEALT WITH FIRST!!!! AND DON'T WORRY THEY CAN'T HEAR US FROM HERE!!!!"

Where are they!? Did Jaako and Aqila already leave for Garigo? What the hell is happening? Why am I tied up, and WHAT IS FERRAN SCREAMING FOR THIS TIME?!?!? Sartan could barely even think over Ferrans persistent yelling. "SHUT THE FUCK UP FERRAN!!!!" shouted back Sartan as his ears rang from all the noise so early in the morning.

"SO YOU WERE PAYING ATTENTION AFTER ALL!!!!" screamed Ferran while he quickly slapped Sartan's mouth shut. It was painless, but the real pain, Ferran's incessant screaming, persisted. "DON'T WORRY!!! AQILA AND JAAKO WILL NEVER KNOW EXACTLY HOW YOU DIED!!!! BUT REST ASSURED YOU WILL DESERVE IT!!!!"

"YOU WOULD BE SCARRED FOR LIFE IF YOU TAKE MINE!!!!" shouted back Sartan while stringy saliva flew out of his mouth and onto the dewy ground. "GO AHEAD AND DO IT!!!! YOU'D BE DOING ME A FAV---"

A stinging sensation was left on his face as Ferran cut him short with a much heavier slap. Once Sartan's face readjusted to its previous position, he could feel blood trickling over his lip. His tongue licked it up and spat it out onto Ferran's shoes. Almost as expected, Ferran returned the favor with a heavy crack to the face. Sartan's vibrating head hung down over his chest as he felt his right eye begin to fill with drip with water.Surely there would be a bump on his head, but the bump that was to grow easily would be dwarfed by the crack that was left in the bark of the tree.

Ferran wasted no time to continue speaking, "Now that you won't be defiant you should know some things."

"They're irrelevant," whispered Sartan as tears mingled with blood on his lips.

"I don't care. You're going to listen," said Ferran with sudden calmness.

Sartan then said, "There is nothing of value that could possibly reside within your empty skull, and even if there was I would never be able to access it by your failure to understand it yourself along with your failure to translate it to me."

Ferran closed his eyes and took a hefty breath in. Without opening his eyes he held it before exhaling just as loudly as he inhaled. Afterwards he opened his eyes and tilted his head to the side with a smile. Ferran then continued as though Sartan had said nothing, "I know that the only reason Aqila let you stay is because you were 'cute', but I know your intentions with her are simply sinful. Secondly---"

Sartan interrupted with, "You think that my intentions with your sister are sinful?!?! What makes you think I'd even waste my time doing something like that with someone like her?"

"Don't lie to me, Sartan! I know what people who live on the streets like to do, and you know that you would love to do something like that to her!"

"Are you joking?! Is that what you think of doing to every woman you pass on the road because you have strategically failed to mention that you live on the streets too, so how dare you act like I am beneath you and my intentions are deplorable because of that!"

Sartan refused to glance up at Ferran, but there was an obvious sound of shuffling in front of him. When he looked up he saw Caleb preventing Ferran from sending a heavy punch into his dome. Ferran's anger pumped through his veins like oil, and the fear on Caleb's pale face dripped away with his sweat.

"Ferran, just leave him for the Eveharrisses like you said," whispered Caleb with a broken voice. "I don't want to be a murderer. Let's just leave him here, and whatever happens, happens."

Ferran stared at Sartan with a sneaky snarl resting above his chin. His frown scared the bugs that were crawling on the tree away, and the birds stopped flying through the forest. They all sat and watched the two of them. They locked eyes for what felt like eons, and Sartan knew that his bloody, tear-filled face was probably just as unforgiving.

Finally Ferran spoke, "Sure! But I just want him to know one thing." He crept towards Sartan putting his mouth right next to his left ear. A few hot breaths came and went before Sartan finally heard Ferran whisper, "You're right Sartan...we aren't really that different after all. We both are homeless now. I may not be able to see my parents ever again, but you won't be able to see anyone you care about ever again. We both have gone through great pain and loss. It just so happens that I've already dealt with pain and loss, but for you, you're just about to go through it all. I'm sure the pike-like bone on the Eveharrisses has some great importance for hunting..."

Ferran then stood up to stare at Sartan one last time. As they stared at each other Ferran must have felt the need to slap Sartan one more time because that is what he did, repeatedly. After all of the violence faded, Sartan watched him walk directly away from the tree he was tied to. Caleb followed suit, and

Sartan assumed that was the direction Aqila and Jaako went. They disappeared into the dense foliage of the forest quickly, but they didn't get very far before Sartan overheard them.

"I'll catch up with you, Ferran. I left my canteen," said Caleb. Within seconds Caleb trotted back to Sartan, and quickly knelt down in front of him whispering, "I don't want you to die out here Sartan, so if I let you go will you not follow us?"

"If you let me go the first thing I'm going to do is BEAT FERRAN'S ASS!" exclaimed Sartan quite loudly in contrast to Caleb's hushed voice.

"No, let's not have that then. I really don't want you to die though," whispered Caleb as he frantically looked around to make sure Ferran wasn't coming back. "I'm going to put this knife down here by your feet, and I'm going to leave some of those berries we found yesterday next to it."

"Can you take my shoes off then? How am I supposed to get loose with shoes on? Just untie me now and I won't have to hurt you," said Sartan as a drip of the salty, iron-flavored mixture streaked into his mouth.

Caleb nodded, but by the way he kept looking to the woods for Ferran, Sartan wondered how much it would take for Caleb to get scared and run off to Ferran. He chose not to say anything when Caleb comically took forever to untie his shoes with his frantic fingers, but before he could get the right one off Ferran screamed for Caleb through the dense forest grass and foliage. He didn't risk getting caught helping Sartan, and Caleb instantly stood up to run towards his friend. *Typical.* The blood trickling off his chin and onto his shirt didn't slow up at all, and before the sounds of Caleb and Ferran disappeared into the forest, Sartan already attempted to use his one foot that Caleb had emancipated to grab the knife. Of course this didn't go too well for him, and he nearly stabbed himself thrice.

Angered, Sartan kicked at the knife for not cooperating with him. The unsheathed blade flopped a short distance from him, entirely out of range. "FUCK!" shouted Sartan as escaping would be much harder now. With the knife now out of reach Sartan focused on loosening whatever was tying his hand behind the trunk of the tree. Wiggling his wrists, he could feel fabric rub on him, but with each quarter rotation of his forearm the bark of the tree chewed into his skin. The scratching of the moss on his wrists made them beg feverishly for just one itch, but with the way that they tied the shirt rope around him that soon proved more difficult than initially concluded.

Sartan took a few seconds to catch his blood scented breath before he attempted anything. Then when he felt his heart rate starting to slow, he flailed and wiggled as aggressively as humanly possible. The cloth that stapled him to the tree stretched slightly, but not once did he hear it snap or rip under the pressure. Regardless, he pulled further away from the tree feeling the bark begin to scratch at his wrists through the thick moss that sat vicariously on it. Sartan screamed the whole time refusing to let the fabric keep him locked down to the tree. He kept wiggling and flailing away from the trunk until he realized that he no longer could feel his hands.

He slumped back to the tree, which he hadn't made that much distance from in the first place. Sartan stared at the bit of berries next to his feet. The fruits mocked him as he knew that even if he wanted to eat them it would be practically impossible. *What the hell Caleb. You don't want me to die, but you don't do anything to help me at all. Where the hell is Aqila when I need her? The moment I let my guard down she let this shit happen. She was just distracting me. Now I am going to die. And for what?*

The very second that thought crossed his mind a warm breeze blew through the forest. It was the first time he actually listened to the chirping of the birds. Until now nothing in the forest actually resonated with him. Nothing in the forest caught his attention for more than a second, but now that he was forced to just sit, it was much harder to be distracted. The deep thwups from a distant woodpecker echoed from far away, and the buzz of cicadas sizzled off to his left. A soft breeze whispered its way past him carrying the occasional butterfly and bird with it. Even down to the barely audible crinkles of the leaves and pine needles of all the nearby trees constructed an orchestra with him at its very center. He enjoyed the surreal environment for what it was, but his thoughts slowly crept back in after the brief distraction.

But wait! What about the ring? Was this just all part of Aqila's plan to take Vahee's gem? It can't be. She was the only one who really wanted me to stay, so it has to be the rest of them. Although Jaako seemed to have lots of problems with Ferran, and Ferran said---screamed that he would be dealt with later. They have to be clueless! That leaves Caleb and Ferran, and there is no way that Caleb would have actually wanted to kill me, but nonetheless he didn't help me escape. He was persuaded by Ferran. Ferran! This is all Ferrans doing, and Aqila still has my gemstone!

He stared at the berries feeling his skin start to heat up. Sweat droplets formed under his arms and on his face. The bitter-salty taste of blood and sweat only made him hungrier, and Sartan breathed louder as he felt the heated wind breathe the warm air with him. The birds chirped so much louder, yet their specific locations still remained impossible to locate within the windy, dense forest unless they flew right in front of his face. It was at this moment Sartan lost his ability to hear anything around him, not from supernatural reasons but because of the amount of screaming that splattered out of him. Droplets of saliva flew all over his legs and feet, and all of the nearby birds flew out of their trees.

"I'LL KILL YOU FERRAN! OR SHOULD I KILL YOUR BELOVED SISTER! OR BETTER YET, I'LL BEAT THE SHIT OUT OF YOU BEFORE DOING ANYTHING AQILA WANTS ME TO DO WITH HER, AND WE KNOW IT CAN TAKE A LOOONG TIME TO REVIVE EVERY ZODIAC! I WILL HAVE ALL THE TIME IN THE WORLD TO DO EVERYTHING IN THE WORLD WITH HER! ALL THE WHILE RUINING YOUR INNOCENT IMAGE OF HER!" screamed Sartan while scaring all of the nearby wildlife away.

However, Sartan quickly ran out of stamina. He choked on his own exclamations before coughing up an entire lung. The blood pulsating through his head dizzied him to a steady breath. After recovering from his fit, Sartan's logic finally returned to him, and he was forced to be alone with his thoughts.

Shit! Caaalm dooown. You'll get through this. I just need to figure out what to do from here. Step by step, what do I do? Sartan rolled his eyes as he felt the tight restriction of the only thing that prevented him from chasing after Ferran in the first place. *Escape. Step one, escape. Step two, regroup with them and beat the shit out of Ferran physically. Then for step three I'll beat the shit out of Ferran mentally and emotionally. Lastly, leave them all when they need me most.*

He had so much to do, but he knew all too well that these plans would take more than one week, more than one month, possibly even more than a year. Strangely enough, Sartan had an urgent sense of tranquility flow over him as his gaze slowly drifted off to the thick branches of a tree. The veins in his body were no longer bulging at full capacity, and all of the sweat that still left a questionable scent, had now dried on his skin or been absorbed by the cloth. Unfortunately, his bloody face still taunted him, growing itchy and sticky as the blood dried. It reminded him of what he so desperately needed to do. The beating of Ferram would be impossible to execute while restrained, and with every second he remained in tethers, his prey got further from its rightful punishment. From an onlooker though, Sartan would surely be the prey not the predator. A prey of a merciful predator at that.

Speaking of onlookers, as Sartan stared at the branches of a tree that towered in front of him a mountain bluebird fluttered onto the branch Sartan was gazing at. It squawked insistently at him without letting up. He stared at it, and the nearly neon, blue bird sang away telling him an entire story's worth of chirps. The strange twists of the bird's head as it watched Sartan in his prison cell were disgruntling to say the least. It was similar to watching an owl twist its head around. The bird squawked some more as it flew between branches, each of which were closer to Sartan. Enamored by the pure colors of the creature, Sartan simply stared in awe. After the bird told him its entire life story, it fluttered away happily back into the vast forest. Now that his bird buddy was long gone, Sartan looked back at the bunch of berries. The berries that the bird probably wanted to steal from him and would have had he not been there. The berries that Caleb left for him made him start thinking again.

Jaako is the only one who could have been trusted. Caleb is clearly still too young to make his own decisions and follows Ferran, blindly. Aqila is-- Aqila is most likely loyal to her goals. She said I could basically have a favor though! She offered to help me with my memory. She will have to let me help them revive every Zodiac, and she WILL let me beat Ferran when the time comes!

***

Several hours later Sartan was still sitting down. He was still seated in front of the same tree, and despite what he had anticipated doing, he had not made it an inch closer to Ferran or any of his goals at that. The sun was definitely on its descent once more, and the thirst in his throat was beyond quenching. Despite furious hours of wrestling the cloth that kept him tied to the tree, all that he had accomplished was the burning of a thousand calories. The growling of his stomach surely would alert any Eveharrisses that were hungrier to his presence. Other than the never ending rumbling from within and the occasional bird chirping in the distance, Sartan had nothing to do, nothing to do but think, and he had grown exhausted with himself for doing just that for the first time in quite a while. He had given up on thought at this point and aimlessly stared at the berries on the ground. He hoped for a bear to find and maul him over an Eveharris, but that hope evaporated instantly.

"And who may this unlucky individual be?"

Sartan's stomach fell like a rollercoaster after reaching its summit. The sudden voice completely froze him in his already restricted position, and he could only wait to see who the stranger could be as moving to view them was impossible. Chances of it being an Eveharris were incredibly high, and Sartan could do nothing but wait for his own demise now. He kept his mouth shut hoping that the stranger would simply pass by, but the lack of any footsteps, grass crunching, or even breathing disposed of such hope.

"How have you ended up in this peculiar position? Not by chance I assume." asked the same feminine voice as it grew closer. "Or are you not with me anymore my fellow lone wanderer?"

"Who are you?" asked Sartan as he figured he may as well let the stranger know he was alive.

"I just so happen to be the person who can save you from your peril, but I assumed you were polite enough to answer my questions first. I was mistaken," said the woman. Her calm tone resonated with the peaceful chirps and hums of the forest, but it also tickled a nerve that reminded him of the absolute mercy he was at to her. He was at the mercy of a naturally occurring phenomenon. The mercy of an Eveharris.

"I was betrayed for an unjust reason," replied Sartan as the figure finally stepped into view.

The woman stared at him for a few seconds before speaking, "How did that happen? My boy, what is your name?"

He glanced up to see the woman standing in front of him. The dark-black hair that coiled down her back in one thick strand was tattered and messy. Her skin was the same tint as her hair, darker than the most moonless nights, and she had a toothy white smile to offset her skin tone. However her teeth were chipped, broken, shattered, and even missing at certain points showing how inflamed her gums were. Regardless, that did not stop her from smiling her wide smile as she looked Sartan up and down with bloodshot eyes. Whoever this woman was, she did not look well. She had arthritic fingers, yet strangely enough her face was that of only a woman in her late twenties, free of wrinkles or worry marks but heavy with sleep deprivation and acne. Her exposed stomach showed just how malnourished she really was. Her skin wrapped around her ribs so tightly that it actually turned light gray from stretching so much. Other than that one instance, Sartan realized that her skin wasn't entirely uniform with one color everywhere else either.

Sartan noticed that this woman had white streaks going down her body, possibly all the way to her feet. There were only two white streaks on her, both of which started on her colorless lips on each corner of the mouth, but by the time they reached her ribs the streaks ran on opposite sides of her stomach. The woman was wearing black pants that covered all of her legs, but he was sure that these same streaks did not stop at her waist. Either way, he couldn't tell if the streaks were painted. Sartan began to wonder if the bright white coloring was her actual skin color.

"My name---my name is Sartan," said Sartan as he struggled to create a coherent sentence. "You don't look…you look ill."

"What fortunate circumstances! I thought that I had lost the scent. As for my health…I could say the same for you, Sartan. Not in health though, rather in circumstances, but rest assured, like your's, my current state is only temporary," replied the woman with a voice that nearly put Sartan to sleep. "Now Sartan, could you tell me just how you ended up like this?"

"If you're an Eveharris just kill me now."

"An Eveharris? Preposterous! Trust me Sartan. I am not a pitiful creature of the sorts," replied the woman slowly and regally. "Now would you politely inform me how your fate left you tied to a tree in the middle of nowhere? Certainly, this would not have happened if you were traveling alone."

Sartan nodded slowly as he acknowledged being truthful might be the only way to make it out of this forest. "My friends turned on me. They stole my ring and left me for the Eveharrisses that roam this forest. One beat me and left me here to die."

"These so-called friends of yours, why would they do something like that?" asked the woman.

"It was mostly the brother. He thought I wanted something to do with his sister and freaked out on me. He tied me up while I was asleep, and I am positive that if my eye turns black it is from his fist."

"So it was only this brother that caused problems for you?"

"It was only him. He is going to get a beating the moment I catch back up to them."

"I see, so what brought you guys to the middle of a forest in the Genillian Empire? Surely there could have been better ways to travel," said the unique woman as she knelt down next to Sartan. "Could you have been running from something?"

Sartan happily replied, "Actually, we were. Aqila kept insisting that this Zodiac would kill us if she ever caught up with us, but I never really was that into their goals. The Zodiacs never helped me in my times of need anyway, so why should I go out of my way to revive them all."

"The Zodiacs you say? You intended on reviving them?"

"I didn't intend on reviving anything. I simply wanted to survive another day. Helping them with their goals enabled easy living or so I thought."

"Do you know exactly who the woman is that you were running from?"

"Personally I do not know her, but everytime I hear her name it sounds familiar."

The woman tilted her head to the side as she spoke regally, "And what might this hunter woman's name be exactly?"

"Apparently she is the Leo Zodiac. Like the actual Zodiac. I think they called her Lev though," replied Sartan as he watched an unwarranted, large grin quickly appear on the woman's sickly face.

"Do you know which way they went?"

"Of course!" exclaimed Sartan as she infected him with her smile. "I've been staring at the direction they left in for the past several hours, and the moment I get free I'm going to hunt down Ferran to beat his ass."

"Excellent! Now you claimed that their goals were to revive all of the Zodiacs. Have they already created a new Sagittarius Zodiac? How many traitors are there in total?"

"Yeah, we turned Jaako into the new Sagittarius Zodiac," said Sartan while the woman's grin turned into a more attentive smile. "Counting me, there was: Caleb, Jaako, Ferran, Aqila and me."

"So there are four of them left, and this Jaako is the new Sagittarius? Which Zodiac will they go for next? If they have a Fire Gemstone then they would probably go for Aries next, but then why go East?" asked the woman rhetorically. She stared past Sartan for a few moments as she presumably thought about everything he had just told her. Eventually she asked, "Sartan, why were you with this group in the first place. You said that you don't really care about the Zodiacs, so how did you end up creating a new one? There is no way you did it to survive alone as reviving Zodiacs is inherently dangerous. Did they pay you? Or are you in debt to them some other way?"

He stared at her momentarily before sighing out his answer, "I accidentally injured Aqila, so I gave her my word I'd help her with this Zodiac crap. I got knocked out after stealing the Tansiq Scroll, and woke up in Furictown. I tried to leave then, but she still had my ring."

"This ring that you keep bringing up, is there anything special about this ring?"

Sartan did not want to answer that question. He hesitated before saying, "I suppose…they said it had Libra's Gemstone in it."

"Peculiar. I do have to admit you are quite an interesting individual to speak with Sartan, but I suppose anybody who has been tethered to a tree in the middle of a forest and left to die all alone would have some exciting things to share. All of my vassals have been so close minded and selfish recently, but you do things you don't necessarily care about for those you have pained," said the woman as she stood up next to him. "Sartan, can you tell me your mother's name?"

"My mother's name? I---I can't remember her name," said Sartan sadly as he failed to keep his head up. He closed his eyes figuring that the woman won't believe him. "I'm telling the truth! I can't remember her name! I'm sorry!"

In her most calming tone yet, the woman said, "Relax Sartan, for I already was aware that you would be unable to remember her name. That is perfectly okay, and I'm sure she thought it would be for the best. Your identity eludes me no longer, young one."

"You knew my mother?" exclaimed Sartan as he wiggled in his restraints. "What are the chances of that? Do you know where she is?"

"Yes, I knew your mother well. Very tenacious, she would be very disappointed in you."

"I'm so confused. Wait, who are you? How do you know my mom?"

"Your mother had a…business…work that was done in my lands back in the day," replied the woman as she stared off into the dense forest. Sartan could only imagine what those encounters were like, but he was quickly consumed by his own thoughts.

"My mother had a business!?!?"

"Roughly," said the woman without returning her gaze to Sartan.

Sartan exclaimed in pure wonder, "Wait! If she had a business why have I been homeless on the streets for most of my life? What is going on? And did you just say that you have lands?"

"Sartan. I can bring you to your mother, and I can help you remember everything about your past. I just need you to help me right now. I'll untie you, and we will deal with these once friends who hurt you. They possess something I yearn for."

"I never said anything about not remembering my past. I only said I can't remember my mom's name. Who are you?" questioned Sartan as he felt more and more uncomfortable in her presence.

"Sartan please. We both know your brainwashing took away a portion of your history. The intensity of such a procedure I have yet to determine, but with time these issues will…well transpire. Luckily, time becomes an ally once you learn the virtue of patience."

"Not once has time been my ally," replied Sartan.

"Perhaps, but you being forced to endure it has led me to you. A mutually beneficial coincidence dare I say. If I let you go," the woman continued. "You will become my subject until I relieve you of your duties. If you refuse to those terms...then I am sure the next Eveharris to pass by would be much more merciful."

"So I am a slave now?," replied Sartan sarcastically.

The woman's face crinkled up as she asked, "Certainly not! You will help me with my current objective, and I will help you live easy and possibly remember all that was so wrongly taken from you. I am so sorry I could not make it here before now, for I was occupied with other campaigns at the time. You need not fear any type of tyrannical treatment from me."

"As long as I am obedient, right?"

"If your obedience becomes too…defiant…for my liking then I won't ever prolong your pain! Sartan if you fail to follow my orders then I'll simply imprison you or kill you. Extended suffering is something you've endured long enough. I am sure of it," said the woman as she put her thumb on his forehead. "Sartan, you do realize that your so-called companions left you in the middle of a highway for hours all alone."

"Huh?"

"A few days ago I was traveling to Dursnia, one of my campaigns was requiring attention, when I saw someone unquestionably similar to you laying in the road next to this shabby looking camper," said the woman as she walked behind the tree and out of view. "I stopped to see if you were alive, but when I tried to wake you up, your friends chased me away. It was almost as if they were trying to sacrifice you to the sun. They all attacked me with their weapons insisting that I not take their bait. I didn't recognize it to be you until long after the incident."

"Aqila mentioned that multiple times. I think she was trying to warm me up." asked Sartan.

"Do you hear how foolish you sound?" laughed the woman as she walked behind the tree. "Why would they not just give you a blanket? From what I saw they were attempting to do some sort of sick Zodiac sacrifice. They wanted to take the raw power that flows through you for themselves! I can sense it in you, it is boiling! With nowhere to go!"

"Are you sure that was it? I was literally froz--"

The forest suddenly got hotter. Then it began to fizzle with heat as the winds swayed around them. It was hot and for no reason. REALLY HOT. Suddenly the woman began yelling from behind the tree, "THE BROTHER WAS ABOUT TO SLIP THE KNIFE INTO YOU SARTAN! HE WAS SACRIFICING YOU TO THE ZODIACS, AND I'M POSITIVE HE WOULD HAVE KILLED YOU HAD I NOT STOPPED HIM!!! WHEN I LET YOU GO, WHAT ARE YOU GOING TO DO TO HIM!?!"

"Why are you yelling?" asked Sartan as the woman continued to scream at him. He doubted that was what really happened, but how could this woman remember such a specific event if it had never happened, especially after Aqila previously mentioned she put him on the highway to 'unthaw' him. Sartan couldn't hear anything over her screams, but he could feel himself getting agitated at the thought of catching up to Ferran. Then his hand felt it too. His hand felt it a little too much.

"OUCH!"

His reflex was to move his hands away from whatever was causing the burning sensation. To his surprise, he flew forward as the cloth restricting him no longer held him down. Sartan fell face first into the berries that Caleb had left him. The moment he realized he was free, Sartan brought his hands into view to assess whatever happened to them. Two burn marks were on the tops of each hand, but it was a light price to pay in order to escape the restraints.

The woman stepped out from behind the thick tree and said, "My apologies Sartan. My lighter lit the shirts a little faster than I thought it would." This woman who may have just saved his life then walked up to him with her hand out. "Come on my friend, let's go get this brother."

Sartan reluctantly took her hand, and once he was standing on his feet he finally realized how tall she really was. His eyes were just barely at her chin, and if she were wearing heels there would be no doubt that Sartan would have to tilt his head back just to look up at her. The female smiled a proud grin into Sartan's face, and he realized that he had to help her with whatever she wanted since she freed him.

"What do you need me to do?" asked Sartan as he thanked the woman for freeing him. "And you never told me who you actually are."

"My most sincere apologies, my friend. You may call me Lev," said the woman with that same regal and calm tone she had spoken for the majority of their conversation.

"Lev? Like, the Active Leo Zodiac?" asked Sartan as his heart dropped. *This is the woman we have been running from this whole time? Aqila and them all said that she would slaughter us just for knowing a little too much, let alone creating an entirely new Sagittarius! Then why did she just free me from my shackles, and why hasn't she slain me yet? In fact she said she would help me find my mother if I helped her! Unless...*

"Yes, Sartan. I am who you think I am, and I have seen you many times before on our paths to greatness. Your mother and I have a reputable history, and even though our last deal didn't end in a positive light I always promised her that I would help you if you needed it," claimed Lev with a smile. "This is what is going to happen: We are going to go back and regroup with the others to stop them from securing the perimeter. Then we will make a b-line for your ex-allies."

"As long as I get my revenge on Ferran, and I get treated for my 'alleged brainwashing' in the end I'm okay with that," said Sartan as the woman began walking ahead of him. "You do know where my mother is right? Can she help me with my memory problem? You won't kill me with malnourishment or sleep deprivation will you?"

"Certainly not! I am aware that humans have needs unlike myself, and I am sure it wouldn't be that difficult to find your lovely mother. Alas those aren't immediate concerns. Currently we are focusing on catching your so-called friends. Only then will I help you with your problems. After all, I did just save your life right now, did I not?"

Sartan nodded at the woman who claimed to have met her before. Whether or not she is telling the truth, who else could he trust? In Lev's defense she was an Active Zodiac and had no need to lie. Her word is worthy by nature, and she does whatever necessary to protect her subjects…or so they say. He was now walking behind her when he realized it. *Nothing has changed. I am still following someone else. I still am not free to do as I wish. I might as well still be strapped to the tree! What the hell! Lev doesn't owe me anything, in fact I owe her now! At least she will be willing to help me later on, but that is also what Aqila said she would do. What if Lev doesn't even know how to find my mother? That's unlikely, but what if she isn't willing to? Does she really know my mom?*

"Lev...can you tell me my mother's name?"

Instantly Lev stopped in her tracks. A brief second passed before Sartan heard her reply. "I think it is best that you wait to receive that information my friend, for it would only make our current goals much more difficult to achieve." Lev took a moment to think of what she would say next. "You must find Leucemie first. Only then should you allieve your brainwashing, and after that, only then can you even think about your mother."

"Who is Leucemie?"

"Oh…Oh I fear your condition may be more intense than I had expected."

"What?"

"To protect you from yourself I am sure…she thought this through more attentively than I had anticipated. I will gladly take it."

"I don't understand," said Sartan as they traveled through branches and bushes.

"Leucemie was a close friend of yours. Not in reality, but nearly blood by how much you both endured together."

"Wait, who is that? How do we find Leucemie? And how will this help us remember my past?"

"Such a selfish young man you have become Sartan! I suppose your position required that of you for survival however," said Lev as she began walking once more, now beside Sartan. "I'll gladly tell you everything I know about Leucemie. You shouldn't need to ask about her anymore once I tell you everything I know, and then you will keep your mouth shut about your brainwashing and your mother until we deal with these traitors. Do you understand?"

"Completely," said Sartan hesitantly as he agreed to Lev's terms.

"Leucemie, from what I was able to witness from afar, was your closest ally. She and you trained together, learned together, and even fought together. Inseparable, I rarely saw you without her. The fact that such a relevant part of your life goes completely unremembered in your brain tells me how frightened your mother truly was. If we find Leucemie then perhaps that will spark a mental recovery, but we should not rely on that alone. If I remember correctly, she was not brainwashed like yourself. However right after the time of your brainwashing, she was captured by the then Active Cancer Zodiac. She was enslaved and forced to the dungeons of one of the Water Zodiac's Palaces. Which one I can't recall, but I am positive that Leucemie is still at a palace carrying out her futile sentence. Futile of course because all the Water Zodiacs are now deceased," laughed Lev as she continued steadily but not without sighing. "I would assume that Leucemie is at the Cancer Palace. If not then she is definitely at the Scorpio Palace. From what I've heard both of those places are like vaults. Even if you manage to get in, you would only be able to get out with the consent of the respective Zodiac, and of course they are no longer with us."

"Why did the Cancer Zodiac imprison Leucemie?" asked Sartan.

Lev was hasty to reply, "Who knows. Cancer might have seen some value in Leucemie and imprisoned her as a result, but more than likely Cancer slipped down an irreversible path of lunacy. After all if it weren't for Cancer every one of the Water Zodiacs would still be well and with us. She killed both Stir and Ryby in an outburst of rage. Ryby had been alive for tens of thousands of years, so that day was a great loss for the entire world as we know it today. Unfortunately she couldn't even be punished. Just like Maeiz, Kozoroh's predecessor, Cancer committed suicide," said Lev hesitantly. She bit her lip while slowing her pace nearly to a halt.

"What happened to the other Zodiacs then? That explains why three of them aren't with us anymore, but what about the other six that have died?" asked Sartan as he figured she would have the most insight to such a question.

"I've told you everything I knew about Leucemie and then some. Now keep up your end of our deal and squelch your curious mouth. I wish to focus on less depressing concepts, shall we? Let us regroup with the others before they get too far."

Sartan agreed with Lev, but couldn't think about anything to speak of with an immortalized Zodiac other than Zodiac related things. Ironically, those concepts were the ones she didn't want to speak of. Silence ensued as Sartan got lost in his thoughts once more.

If Lev was a violent and evil being why would she assist me so much? She claims she promised my mother she would protect me but at the same time refuses to tell me her name. Could this weak and ill woman really have killed Aqila and Ferran's parents just for 'knowing a little too much'? Is there something that I don't know? Is there something that is---

Lev blurted out as a large man approached them from out of the woodwork, "Jiry! We have found our lead. Cancel the perimeter. I plan on dealing with the rest of them personally…with the assistance of Sartan of course!"

Chapter 13
Fleeting Feelings
Aqila

With one more heavy step Aqila's left foot landed on the pavement. Finally, she had escaped the end of the dense forest, well maybe not the end but the edge. The forest edge sat patiently behind them about a minute or two away. These nine hour hikes had been really taking a toll on her. The only thing that ached more than her legs were the bottoms of her feet, and as she glanced quickly over the long stretch of treeless grass between the road and the forest, she felt more and more soothed to have distance from Lev. The sun always seemed to be on the descent, and Jaako's eyes had only been growing wearier with everytime Aqila looked back at her companion. *I can only imagine what I look like after this past week, and if we keep this up I will be too fearful to want to look in a mirror by next week.*

"Finally!" exclaimed Jaako as he flopped himself onto the pavement. Aqila sighed and sat down next to him on the cracked, grayed road, hauling her backpack over to the side for the first time in what felt like years. With all of his limbs spread out over the pavement, Jaako continued, "Laying down has never felt so good before."

"I know. Hopefully we can get a car or something because I doubt we are even a sixth of the way to Garigo," replied Aqila as she began searching through her backpack.

"At least there weren't any fights today. You seem to be a lot more chill than your brother, but then again I bet you're too tired to get loud," said Jaako.

Aqila kept looking through her backpack until she managed to find a small bottle of pills. She quickly threw two white pills into her mouth to relieve the persistent aching such a hike had brought, leaving only three in the bottle. After chasing them down with a gulp of water Aqila replied to Jaako, "Yeah...we all are tired...but Ferran can be really cool..." It was hard for her to speak with her friend because of the consistent onslaught of yawns attacking her consciousness. "...once you get to know him of course."

"I don't know. So far I have found him to be a...well he does things that he doesn't want us to do ourselves," said Jaako lazily as Aqila's yawning fit infected him. "Not fair in the slightest."

Aqila laid back onto the lonely road as she stared towards the spiraling sunset which was hidden behind a soft, drifting cloud. The darkness of the nearly night slowly crept in as the light faded. She had no clue how far away the rest of the group was, but she figured it could not take but an hour for them to regroup. Both Caleb and Ferran insisted on waiting after she left with Jaako. She wanted to wake Sartan to have him walk with her and Jaako, but Ferran argued a good point that he desperately needed rest after his incident with the ring. *Regardless, the three boys should not be that far behind us. I do not want to move any further away from the forest without them, but which way do we go?*

Aqila glanced back towards the sunset that was quickly receding over the enormous forest that she just came from. The light struggled to escape the dense leaves, and she assumed that way was West. *That means the street we are sitting on runs South and North. Coming from the forest, I would be going East-ish, so I need to go right. Right? Good enough. The road will surely lead to some sort of town, and that is all we would need. I just do not want to walk there, but how are we going to get a---*

"You guys are rich aren't you?" questioned Jaako as he derailed Aqila's train of thought. "Well not you but your parents...well Caleb's parents I'm sorry."

"I suppose...I mean they could handle raising two extra children with ease," said Aqila without taking her eyes away from the sunset.

Jaako continued after a few seconds of silence, "Caleb got a whole camper for his birthday? Do you realize that simply being able to afford that makes him rich?"

"No it doesn't. Almost everybody had vehicular transport where we lived. Caleb got it for his birthday, but his parents definitely are not rich just because they could afford that. I know we would not be able to afford one now though, and now that I actually think about it, Caleb probably has yet to realize the significant loss we took when we left that camper in Furictown," lectured Aqila over the sound of birds fluttering away in the distance.

"Aqila. If you had a car in Dursnia then you would be considered a high value target, and if you could afford three then you wouldn't waste your money on them. Instead you would find a way to ditch towns and live somewhere else."

"Is Dursnia really that poor?" asked Aqila.

"Dursnia isn't poor, but the citizens are. It is like that for most of the cities and towns in the Great Desert. The entirety of the Sagittarius Empire is in shambles. We can't blame that on the passing of Strelec, but my whole life things always seemed easier in bordering nations."

"You know what they say, the grass is greener," laughed Aqila as she thought about what it might have been like to live in the Great Desert for years on end. It could not be that much harder than living in the far West. Of course the lands of Aries were never eroded into unfarmable desert, and there was always a steady source of income at any of the understaffed businesses in town.

"I don't know about that Aqila," stated Jaako quite quickly. "Sometimes you just really have to look at it from all angles. I know I'm going to be able to drink legally soon, so my opinion is still completely unimportant to everyone else but hey! The whole liege after liege after liege thing might not be beneficial to everybody."

"Oh nonsense! Your opinion matters Jaako! Do you not realize that you are the new Sagittarius Zodiac? The entire empire is yours to reclaim. Yours to rebuild and yours to maintain. Yes you may be inactive right now, but when we defeat Kozoroh and Lev, the first thing you can do is fix everything that has gone wrong in your homeland!" exclaimed Aqila with inspirational intent.

"I know. I know, but how long will that take? Who said I even know how to do all of those things? Even if I did know how to reclaim the empire, how would I physically reclaim the empire?" asked Jaako as he slowly sat up.

"What? If you knew how then you would know how," replied Aqila as she watched him stare at her with weary eyeballs. "You would just…know how."

"But how?"

"What?"

"I don't know Aqila," replied Jaako as he layed back down in the street. "You're really just confusing me right now. I've been exhausted ever since Furictown, and I think I'm too tired to even worry about things like that right now."

"Well then what do you want to think about Jaako?" asked Aqila as she felt her meds slowly start to relieve her pain. Without the constant shivers she could easily hold a conversation now. "Do you want to talk about…your adventures?"

"I don't have any exciting 'adventures' Aqila. Why would I want to talk about that?"

"I do not know. I am just trying to make you feel better here Jaako. Would you like to talk about your parents? Ooh what about your aunt? I bet you have got some pretty cool aunty stories?"

Aqila swore she saw Jaako roll his eyes under his closed eyelids before he blindly replied, "My aunty only ever saw me once, and I am pretty sure it was the day I was born."

"Well when was that Jaako? I need to know so I can get you a present on time," laughed Aqila as she laid back onto the pavement next to him. "Would you like a birthday hat for your birthday?"

"My birthday is November tenth, seventy-six forty-one, and no I would not like a hat for my birthday. For my birthday I'd prefer something a little more exciting."

"Are fashionable hats not exciting to you? That's what I'm feeling!" exclaimed Aqila jokingly. Then her mind slowly drifted back to Lev and her missing allies. "Jaako! Why is it taking the others so long to get here with us, and where could they possibly be?!"

Jaako's eyes turned into two large eggs in their sockets as he stared at Aqila. Finally he replied to her, "Aqila. They are on their way. Relax. They probably let Sartan sleep in an extra hour or two, so they will show up by the time the sun sets. Or at least an hour afterwards."

"What if they got lost? What if they got captured by Lev?!?!" exclaimed Aqila.

"Nobody got captured by Lev, and nobody got---well they will eventually show up. That seems to be what Ferran and Caleb do. They disappeared and reappeared frequently on our previous hikes. This is just them being them. I have a raging headache that is seeping into my eyes. Quite frankly I think you took a little too much of the meds, and I think that you should have shared one or two with me instead," said Jaako as his two hands rubbed his temples over and over again. He remained sprawled out on the pavement as Aqila began rummaging through her backpack once more. This time however she stopped mid search as soon as she opened the zipper with the pill bottle in it.

Without even opening the bottle Aqila claimed, "I think I just took my last two pills though."

"Ouch. Whatever, just calm down and wait for them to arrive. I am going to take a nap."

"Had I known beforehand I would have…"

She stopped mid sentence knowing Jaako did not care and chose to leave him in peace for his sudden, cranky nap. Aqila thought vaguely about a circumstance where a car could drive by and run them over, but at this time of day it seemed that shouldn't be a problem. Also, their location was surely still quite some distance from any towns, so traffic shouldn't be that much of a problem. Regardless, Aqila was still too nervous to sleep on the road like Jaako was attempting to do.

***

Hours later Aqila was startled when a random voice spoke out nearby. At first she did not realize that it was Caleb, under the now sunless sky. In fact, she never even saw him leave the forest or walk across the treeless ground. She was unable to even see the forest from the road, so when Ferran spoke it scared her briefly.

"I don't know Caleb," said Ferran after Aqila rose to her wobbly legs to try and find him. "She said they would stop upon nightfall, but I think we went too far."

"Ferran?" shouted Aqila from the side of the road. "Where are you guys?"

Everything went quiet. Nobody was moving, and Aqila could no longer hear Caleb and Ferran having a conversation. *Am I hallucinating, or are they just hiding from me?* She took one quiet step into the grass that had already started to get dewy, and she closed her eyes in attempts to hear them better. It was not like her eyes were being of any support under the lightless sky. As she stood still in the grass just a few feet from the road she tried her hardest to listen, but unexpectedly there were no sounds for her to listen to. Not even the birds were chirping anymore.

"Ferran! Caleb!" shouted Aqila. "Sartan?!"

Her heartbeat began to pump faster as she could have sworn that Ferran and Caleb were just speaking right next to her. She nervously backed away from the grassy ground back towards the road where Jaako still laid asleep. She refused to turn her back to the vacant field as now she could hear whispers echo throughout the treeless landscape between her and the forest. *An Eveharris!*

With no other explanation for what had just happened, Aqila quickly turned to find Jaako. He had yet to move an inch since falling asleep, and would be quite angry if she woke him up for no reason. *But if I wait we both might die!* With that on her conscience she did not hesitate to shake his face in her tiny hands. She aggressively whispered to him, "Wake up Jaako! Wake up! I think there is an Eveharris! Please wake up! Please!"

With the combination of that and her constant face shaking, Jaako was quickly startled awake. It was obvious he had been living the life in his dream world, or he was just very unhappy to see Aqila in the waking world because the first thing that happened after he awoke was a quick barrage of profanity, slurs, and references to his headache. She tried to convince him that there may be an Eveharris in their precinct, but Jaako refused to get up. He kept rolling over on his sides until Aqila finally said something that grabbed his attention.

"Come on Jaako! We are going to die if you stay asleep! I will replace your flask when we get into the next town! I know you dropped it when we crossed the border, so if you get up right now--"

"Alright fine!" shouted Jaako loudly. If the loud response from Jaako did not alert the Eveharrisses to her location then what he did next definitely would.

Jaako slowly struggled to grab his footing while rubbing his closed eyes. A brief moment passed where he just stood up stretching with his eyes closed while Aqila nervously tugged at his arms to take this seriously. When he finally opened his pupils to the nightly world Aqila was assaulted with another onslaught of verbal tyranny.

"What the actual FUCK!?!?" screamed Jaako as he looked around. He was barely visible to Aqila as she stood a few feet away from him, but the expressions on his face were of pure fear. "What the hell did you give me Aqila?"

"I did not give you anything Jaako! Please focus! I heard whispering over there," insisted Aqila as she backed away from the possibly enraged Jaako.

"Oh you mean those two nitwits over there?" asked Jaako as he pointed into the darkness.

Aqila stared at the end of his finger, but could only see a few more yards out past it. She wondered what kind of headache he could possibly have had to make him this confused, so with great concern she asked, "Jaako, you do realize you are pointing straight into the dark, right?" He continued to stare off into the black night as she wondered if he was still having his migraine.

"No. I can see Ferran putting his hands on both of Caleb's shoulders. It looks like he is giving him a prep talk or something. Can Eveharrises even take the form of our friends?"

"Why would they not be able to, but I also do not see Ferran, Caleb, or Sartan at all," replied Aqila while squinting into the deep, black darkness that engulfed her. "Are you feeling okay?"

"Sort of. The headache is gone, but the body aches are still here. Not to mention I am desperately hungry now," said Jaako calmly. "Also, everything is a little green right now."

"Nothing is green Jaako. Everything is either black or barely visible. Are you sure you are okay?"

"Yeah, I'm fine, but I definitely see lots of green. I definitely see your brother and his friend having an anxious little conversation over there too," said Jaako. "HEY FERRAN AND CALEB!!! I CAN SEE YOU GUYS!!! COME OVER TO THE---"

Aqila smacked Jaako across the face to stop him from screaming at the Eveharrisses. "What the hell are you doing Jaako?!?!" she exclaimed in a whisper. "How do you know they are not Eveharrisses? They are acting quite strangely, are they not?"

Jaako turned around with a stinging, red handprint on his cheek, "I didn't know! I just thought that they were talking about something."

"Ugh! We need to get away from them!" exclaimed Aqila in a whisper as she frantically looked into the darkness unable to figure out where she was.

"That might be a problem," said Jaako who was still staring into the black abyss as if he had tunnel vision that melted it away. "They are on their way towards us right now."

"You are kidding!" whispered Aqila. "How do they know where we are?"

"Probably from all of the noise you were causing," said Jaako.

"Me?! You were the one yelling at them!"

"Yeah, well you slapped me."

"It was a necessary action."

"Right, well if they are Eveharrisses I'm sure I can just kill them like the last one. I'd rather find out soon instead of waiting around to get surprised. Especially with how anxious you look right now."

I'm not anxious. I'm not nervous, but I definitely am not happy! Aqila frowned at Jaako for a brief moment before looking back into the darkness that gulfed around the two of them. "Jaako," said Aqila. "Where are they now?"

"They are walking to us," said Jaako as he peered through the dark night with ease. "I don't think that they can see us though. They seem a little bit lost."

"How close are they?" asked Aqila when a stiff breeze blew past the two of them.

"HEY! FERRAN! CALEB! OVER HERE!!" shouted Jaako at the top of his lungs completely ignoring Aqila's question. "COME TO THE ROAD!!!"

Aqila did not stop him this time. Instead she just stared at Jaako. She felt goosebumps arise on her arms and legs as her heart rate increased. Then again it might have just been the temperature decreasing as the night went on. After all it was January, and the Earth will not be this far from the sun again until November. *I miss spring.* Aqila shook that thought off and her chills away simultaneously, but once she heard heavy footsteps in the grass the goosebumps returned.

"Where the hell have you guys been?" asked the voice who resembled Ferran.

"We've been in this same spot since before the sunset," replied Jaako. "Where the hell have you guys been?"

"We got lost," said Caleb with a pure voice.

"That would explain a little bit," replied Aqila suspiciously. "But what is my last name?"

"What?" asked Ferran as he finally came into view, well a silhouetted view.

Aqila continued her analysis of her allies with, "Come on, say it. My last name."

"You mean our last name?" asked Ferran with obvious confusion resonating out of his throat.

"Our last name, what is it again?" continued Aqila

"Aqila, our last name is Rih," said Ferran suspiciously as he turned to Jaako. "What has she been doing while we were gone?"

"She thinks you guys are Eveharrisses," answered Jaako as he sat back down on the road. Caleb and Ferran did not hesitate to join him either. Completely disregarding Aqila's suspicions, Jaako asked them, "So when did you guys get lost?"

Apparently these two are authentic. Ferran began with profanity, and Caleb was blatantly honest about their mistake. Not to mention he knew our last name, but then again can Eveharrisses acquire such knowledge without talking to us? Or do they get that knowledge once they consume us? I'm tripping. These are the two boobs I've had to deal with for decades.

"It was right about an hour after sunfall," said Caleb dryly. "We came to the edge of the forest and figured you guys were still in it."

Ferran interjected, "So then we went back into the forest thinking that you guys had set up camp inside it. We didn't know you went this far."

"How long did you guys stay at our last camp spot?" asked Aqila while still standing. She looked around the group realizing that Sartan was not with them. In fact she never even recalled Jaako saying he saw Sartan when he spotted these two goons just a minute ago.

"I'd say we stayed about another hour before we left," answered Caleb who hung his head down. "It's probably almost midnight now, so that had to be, what, about thirteen hours ago?"

"We really hiked for that long?" exclaimed Jaako in wonder.

Caleb refused to look up from the pavement as he replied, "I know right. I feel like I'm about to fall apart and crumble into a puddle."

"Sooo," interrupted Aqila. "How far behind is Sartan?"

Neither Ferran nor Caleb replied to her statement. An awkward moment of silence came and went as she watched the two of them stare nervously at each other. *He could be in danger if he is all alone. Sartan is a little scrawny, and if he got caught alone with an Eveharris. I do not want to think about that outcome. He surely will be fine, and I bet he is not too far behind them.*

"Yeah, I haven't seen Sartan since early this morning. Where is he?" asked Jaako curiously.

Ferran slowly sighed, "You see..."

"I do not see. Literally, It is pitch black out here just tell me," said Aqila aggressively.

"Sartan didn't think that our cause was that relevant to the world anymore," replied Ferran with transparent shakiness in his words.

"So you killed him for it did you not?!?!" exclaimed Aqila as she felt her blood begin to boil.

"No!" exclaimed Ferran. "I would never do such a thing!"

"Then where is he? Where did you paralyze Sartan at? Can he even walk right now?" asked Aqila with more and more pressure. She could feel anger building a bridge across her mind. A bridge that would soon enable her to cause lots of physical harm to her immediate surroundings, and soon it would be the only bridge she can cross as the others were quickly being burned by Ferran's hesitation in answering these very important questions.

"Relax Aqila!" insisted Ferran as he leaned back to dodge any spit that might fly out when she responded. "He can walk perfectly fine."

"WHERE IS HE?!?!"

"HE LEFT!!" screamed Caleb as he unexpectedly interrupted the conversation. "He didn't want to help us anymore. He and Ferran got into an argument before he left."

"That is bullshit Caleb! Why would he leave, especially right after I convinced him that it would be way smarter to stay?" questioned Aqila feverishly. "And what about his ring? You act as if he would just leave something that valuable to him behind?"

"Nothing is valuable to Sartan," said Ferran slowly. "Not even you Aqila."

Aqila was startled by the accusation and struggled to speak. "What? What. You are lying. I saved his life! He cares about the group! He cares for me. Even if it is the slightest bit of affection he does! I saved his life! He has to!"

Ferran continued, "Not everybody thinks like that Aqila. Some people are just cold, heartless individuals. I think it is best off that he is gone now. He caused too many problems."

"I don't want to listen to this right now. Jaako do you want----"

"I DID NOT ASK!!! Not once did I ask if it is better that he is no longer here, and even if I did that would never be true one bit! He solved more problems than he caused! You are just too dense to see that when he solved one problem it created others! Problems that we would have to deal with regardless of whether or not he was here!" exclaimed Aqila as she completely ignored her surroundings. "He found the Tansiq Scroll we were looking for almost instantly and nearly killed himself to get it and saved us in the process! Problem solved! It led to Furictown. We got to Furictown and had to deal with the foxes' attack. New problem, but it was solved was it not?"

"He barely even helped with the foxes! He killed their decoys while the entire onslaught nearly killed the rest of us!" argued Ferran with sweat and hasty anger. "If he wasn't there then we still would've surviv---"

"JUST STOP!!!" pierced Aqila as she cut him off. "You still are not getting it are you? We might have survived all of this without him, but even if he is gone we will still have the same problems! Look at us right now Ferran! The four of us are alone in the middle of who knows where with no transport. We still have to go all the way to Garigo just to find someone who might not even help us with creating the new Virgo Zodiac. Lev is probably in that forest right now sniffing after us like a bloodhound, and the amount of food we have left should frighten you way more than it is!"

"So what does that mean?"

"Ferran, it means that Sartan is not causing more problems than he has solved. Are you seriously trying to say that the biggest three problems we are dealing with right now have been caused by him?" asked Aqila. "No! In fact if he were here he would end up helping us solve those problems. Or at the least he would make things less stressful for me. You know, it is hard being the only responsible one here?"

"Being the only responsible one here?!?!" exclaimed Ferran. "He CHOSE to leave! You can sit around and let anybody you want come and go from our little 'party' while I have to make sure they can be trusted enough to even stay a night with us! You hardly do anything but order and command us around like you are some sort of queen, and don't even get me started on why you let Sartan stay in the first place!"

"I let him stay because I knew he could help us find the Sagittarius Tansiq Scroll!" argued Aqila.

"LIES! FALSEHOODS! CAP! Whatever you want to call it you know damn well you didn't let him stay because of that! You didn't even know he knew anything about the scroll until after you let him stay."

"HOW IS THIS RELEVANT?!?!" screamed Aqila as loudly as humanly possible.

A moment passed before Ferran slowly answered, "It is the most relevant thing ever. You and I both know that first impressions create the entire relationship."

"Okay, and?! Your first impression of him was finding out he hurt my calf. That explains a lot now does it not?"

"Maybe it does. Maybe it doesn't, but tell me what your first impression was of him and we will learn a lot more," said Ferran confidently.

"The first time I saw Sartan was when he chased me across the rooftops of Dursnia. I had never seen someone actually be able to keep up with me, so of course it made sense to let him join us on our journey. Why would it not?"

"I'm talking about the camper."

"Ferran, I have no clue what you are getting at!"

"SARTAN IS YOUR LOVER!!!!!" screamed Ferran.

"What the hell Ferran," said Aqila loudly. "What are we fourth-graders? Even if he were my lover, what makes you think that would be any of your business?"

"Oh really? First off, you're my little sister, so that makes it all my business. Secondly, and more importantly, that would be too much of a distraction for our purpose. We can't have you getting emotional and lovesick when he leaves you while we recreate all twelve Zodiacs!"

Aqila sighed as she began walking towards the forest, "I understand what you are trying to say, but it is blatantly wrong. Even if I had any interest that decision would be mine, and if I want to make that decision you are nobody to stop me. I am going to go look for him"

"I think it's a little too late for that Aqila."

She stopped with one foot in the grass. "What?" She turned to see Ferran smiling back at her under the little light there was. Instead of answering her, he smirked and slowly turned around. As he began walking away Aqila screamed after him, "What do you mean it's too late for that!!!! What did you do to him?!?!"

"I did what I had to."

"WHAT DID YOU DO!?!?"

"I didn't hurt him, but by now there is now way he can be saved..."

"YOU LIED TO ME!!!"

"I wouldn't say that. I was just protecting you from the truth."

"I WANT THE TRUTH!!!"

Ferran stopped, but still refused to turn around and face her. *He probably knows I'm WAY TOO TEMPTED TO PUNCH HIS SMUG ASS FACE RIGHT NOW! Who is he to kill our ALLIES!? He better think long and hard about how he replies to me.* Suddenly, breaking the brief silence Ferran said, "He is strapped down to a tree near our last campsite...well he was strapped down to a tree near our last campsite about twelve hours ago. I have no clue where he is now."

Aqila could hear a chuckle sneak out of his mouth when he finished his last sentence. Even the shortest, most transparent hairs on her arms felt like they were burning. The quickly cooling, night air was heavily pressing down on her, but the only thing she could think of was how much she had been betrayed. *Sartan could be in great danger right now, and it would take us hours just to get there. He is strong though! He could have broken out of the restraints and followed after us! Then again he was awfully thin. HE BETTER BE ON HIS WAY HERE!*

Ferran forced Aqila back to the conversation by saying, "It's all going to work out in the end just perfectly, trust me."

Instantly Aqila bursted, "What's going to work out just perfectly?! The fact that you literally killed one of the very few people we trusted!? Or the fact that we still have so many more problems to fix now that he is gone?! It just so happens we have less resources to fix them now!"

"What problems have been created by getting rid of him?" asked Ferran as he visibly tried his hardest not to scream at her. "From my point of view we have fixed most of our issues by getting rid of that freeloader. Now we can focus on more important things."

"Nobody cares about your point of view, Ferran!" exclaimed Aqila as she began to walk away from him. She trudged down the road as she tried to get her thoughts together. "Shut up Ferran! Every word you say is just another lie!"

"And every lie you hear you believe. I can't help it, you're gullible."

Don't reply. Don't reply. Don't get angry. Okay, get angry but don't reply. Aqila refused to glance back at her brother. Even if she couldn't see him under the dark night sky, his silhouette would still be just enough to piss her off even more. *What should I do? How do we save Sartan? I still have his ring. I don't even care at this point! Where the hell is Sartan, and what the hell is wrong with Ferran. I don't go around trying to kill his friends, so why can he just do that to me?*

"Aqila...where are you going?"

"Shut it!" shouted Aqila almost instantly upon hearing Ferran's tauntful voice. "You're evil!"

"I am what the group needs me to be, Aqila," said Ferran from a few feet behind her. Apparently he had been walking down the road too. "I am simply making sure we are safe. I am making sure that we are capable of making the world a better place in the future. Capable of morality and understanding."

"THE GROUP?! SAFETY?! CAPABLE OF MORALITY!?!?" screamed Aqila as she spun around to confront her older brother. "You just killed a completely innocent man just because he was your sister's, and I know you can not be dense enough to believe this but---I quote your words, LOVER! I don't want to hear anything about morals from you. You're an immoral, jealous, dick!"

Ferran was not slow to reply, "Aqila this isn't necessary. We are beyond petty issues like this. We both know that Sartan was a good for nothing thief. He was a possible murderer and a definite liar, but for some reason you wanted him. For some reason you thought he was wronged like us. No, he was probably the kid who ran away from home because he didn't get a green street-racer but a blue one instead."

"Thief?! Liar!? So you are telling me that you have never committed any of those 'moral' crimes yourself Mr. Perfect?!" yelled Aqila while she turned away from him to continue down the road. The road was filled with tiny potholes just waiting to pop a tire. Each pothole tried to swallow her feet with every step she took, and with every step she took she could feel her foot coming down harder and harder on the cracked pavement. "You know what Ferran? I do not think I have EVER seen someone more hypocritical than yourself! And that is really saying something featuring I live with...oh wait I can not compare you to the most hypocritical person I live with because that is YOU! I understand perfectly now! You have nothing! You are nothing, and you will be nothing. When somebody else that comes into the group is also nothing you feel threatened. You feel like you will lose the pity of the squad anymore since you did not have it as 'rough' as him," explained Aqila without turning to face him. She continued to walk only assuming that he was still following. "To FERRAN, and FERRAN alone, Sartan was nothing! This is why you felt as though he was causing problems. Your little pity party would no longer be focused around YOU!" She took a quick breather to catch her breath before she continued derailing Ferran's entire argument. "You are a jealous, hypocritical brother! You are a lonely loser, and you want me to fix all of your problems! Well, you might not want that, but you certainly have been taking it out on me! There have been countless instances where you completely screwed a relationship I was forming with someone, some of which were never even romantic. SO many of them could have been! I could have actually fallen in love several times by now if it were not for you, but NOOO you have to go out of your way to make my life miserable because you are lonely! Or even at the very least we could have a trustworthy companion that can help us, but NOOO he is tied up to a tree half a day away! Grow up Ferran! What now? Am I gonna shack up with Jaako?! Have I not treated him with the same human decency and respect that I showed Sartan? Oh wait, you would never know what that means let alone what it looks like! If you are implying that I am overly promiscuous then you have to accept the fact that you are: for one wrong and for two overly celibate! At least that is what it looks like from my perspective, and we both know that your perspective is visibly twisted and untruthful, otherwise you would have understood the real reason for letting Sartan help us. Therefore your opinion is completely disregarded in the argument as logically flawed and rationally irrelevant!"

When she finally spat out that last word Aqila felt as though she had cracked the case wide open. She panted from the excessive yelling and arguing, but she still managed to hold her hearty smile as she knew he could never reply to that. Well, Ferran would always deny things true or not, so his reply was as irrelevant to her as he is a sore loser.

After waiting a quick few seconds, Aqila victoriously stated, "Now let's go get Sartan back before your own pride pins you to your pity again."

When he refused to respond to that Aqila felt her stomach drop off a rollercoaster. Ferran was not one to take shit from people, and she was the sole valedictorian of her class in pissing him off. What she said must have heavily resonated with him, but that was very unlikely. He probably just was not listening at all, but it was more likely that he was thinking of a smarmy remark to deconstruct her statements. Then a dreaded thought scraped the side of her mind. The thought tore through her brain leaving a trail of blood down her neck. *What if he is not even behind me at all anymore?* She slowly turned around, expecting the worst but hoping for the best. The foggy moon still illuminated her surroundings in the slightest bit, but even with that faded light it was nearly impossible to see more than five feet ahead of her. There was no light pollution for potentially miles upon miles, and luckily she had never been afraid of the dark. However, being alone like this never would have been a problem for her in the past, but she was in the lands of Gemini. Apparently Eveharrisses could only exist within Gemini lands, and apparently they roam these parts in high numbers. That thought was the least bit comforting to her. Especially after seeing one for the first time only a day ago. *Surely, other Zodiacs have creatures like Eveharrisses lurking in their lands. Gemini can not be the only one. Sartan even talked about the gorgeous sirens in the oceans. SHIT! How is this relevant right now? I am in the lands of Gemini, and I know for a fact an Eveharris could be lurking nearby.*

"Ferran?..." asked Aqila as slowly and quietly as possible because when she turned around...no one was behind her. "Are you there?"

There was no reply. All of the heat created by her fit of rage instantly retreated back outside of her body, and like a transaction, it was all replaced with shivers and chills. Jaako and Caleb were nowhere in sight, and she knew that Sartan was hours away from her in the best case scenario. *When did Ferran disappear? He was arguing with me one moment, and then he just teleported to the North Pole. That is what it feels like. He is going to try and leave me for an Eveharris just like he played Sartan!* Suddenly, Aqila heard footsteps approaching her. There was no time for her to react because the approacher quickly whispered out to her.

"Aqila!"

Every square inch of her body trembled in goosebumps for a mere instant, even after she realized that it was Ferran's voice who was whispering to her.

"Aqila!" whispered Ferran aggressively but quietly as he came into a silhouetted view.

"What?! Where did you go!?" whispered back Aqila as her sense of insafety began to burn away in the stiff breeze. "What is going o---"

"Shhh! I was listening for the most part, but when you began blabbing about thieves and some Mr. Perfect I stopped listening and realized how far we had walked," whispered Ferran as he stepped close enough for Aqila to see the details on his face. "I ran back to get Caleb and Jaako to follow us, but when I got to your bag they were gone!"

"What!?" exclaimed Aqila in the quietest whisper ever heard.

"Your unnecessary screaming scared them away Aqila."

"Mine!?" whispered Aqila loudly. "You are the one who wants to kill Sartan, and I only say want because we are going back to rescue him as soon as we find Jaako and Caleb."

"That would be quite possibly the dumbest thing for us to do. We would literally be walking towards Lev putting our hands out and giving up."

"So just how you gave up on Sartan? 'Ope, he isn't worth the time! I'm putting my hands out and forcing him to stay behind!' I do not believe a word you say Ferran!"

"Well Jaako and Caleb are missing and that's a fact."

"THEN GO FIND THEM!!!" yelled Aqila as she no longer worried about volume. "If anything happens to them I am blaming you and you alone! As if blaming you for leaving Sartan behind was not enough today. You need to find them!"

"I will go grab your bag then," replied Ferran calmly. It was almost as if he were playing with her at this point. She could sense it.

"FERRAN I SWEAR TO---"

"We can't just leave it on the road. I'll go get it then I'll help you find Jaako and Caleb."

"Help me find Sartan and I might not let him beat the crap out of you when we find him!"

Naturally, Ferran never replied. Instead he just disappeared back into the dark night as she listened to his hasty footsteps quickly fading away. He must have ran towards her bag because within seconds all that Aqila could hear was the quickly cooling breeze that consistently sliced her. All of the chaos had left her exhausted, but she still stood short. She still thought about how to save Sartan, and she refused to think about what might happen to him if nobody untied him by the next day.

We have to regroup. We have to regroup. Lev. Caleb. Eveharrisses. Jaako. Garigo. Sartan. Ferran. Fucking Ferran! He is slowing us all down drastically! Who even thinks about doing something like that? WHY!?!? I have so much work to do now. I had so much work to do, but this just ten X'd it. I will have to delegate. Delegate most of it to Ferran and take a sick day. Wait, that will never work! If I want things to work out smoothly I will have to do it myself. Or at least oversee him. He would just end up killing Jaako or some stupid shit like that. Okay, we have to get Sartan. We have to find Dominick Kreet in Garigo. WHYYYY! That is going to be impossible! We also have to find the stupid Virgo Tansiq Scroll because I have no clue where this palace is. Oh! Lest I forget that I also need to find some random person who I can trust, and apparently Ferran too, who is a Virgo to make the inactive Virgo Zodiac...then we move on to Pisces...and after that we are just barely one-third of the way done. I am going to lay down and cry.

That is what she felt like doing, but when her back was sprawled out all over the cold pavement Aqila could not manage to pull a single tear out. She could feel another headache en route to her previously beaten and battered brain. The only thing that she could do is wait. She would not go look for Caleb or Jaako because even though they were still her responsibility, Ferran needed punishment. He was the reason they disappeared. It was Ferran who started the argument, and there was no way in hell she was about to go help him find them after finding out about Sartan. Of course she would like to just warp over to Sartan and untie him at this very moment, and then warp back to Caleb and Jaako leaving Ferran lost on his own for a short moment. However, she would never even dare go into the forest alone, especially at night. She would wait until they were all together before going back to get Sartan, and even going back might jeopardize their entire plan.

What if we run into Lev? Will she notice us? Of course she will, it is Lev! She would slaughter us all on the spot. She would take the Aries and Libra Gemstones off me and do who knows what with them. She would probably destroy them so that those Zodiacs could never exist again. If we are fast enough we might be able to sneak back into the forest, get him, and get out before Lev arrives. UGH!! But every second I waste laying here on the road makes that less and less likely. What if only two of us go back for him? Jaako and I because Ferran would---no. That would not work though because Lev is specifically after Jaako. If she finds him then we would have to recreate another Sagittarius Zodiac, and if she finds me she will get the gemstones. That just leaves Caleb, and I highly doubt he has what it takes.

Her thoughts played tennis inside her skull, and with every crack of the ball her headache worsened. She lost track of time as she focused only on ways to get Sartan back without compromising their mission. No good ideas came to mind, and the few that did were just too irrational to put into plan. The midnight sky beamed down on her as for the first time in what felt like ages she could finally see the stars. They did not provide enough lighting to see anything properly on Earth, but with no light pollution anywhere nearby she could see them perfectly fine. There were tiny stars scattered throughout the sky, but for the most part no major constellations could be seen. Almost all of the constellations that should be in the night sky during late January were no longer present. All of the Zodiacs who ruled them had been slain. There was no Pisces in the night sky. There was no Taurus. There was no Aries. She could see a cluster of stars peeking over the treeline that she assumed was Gemini, but the next constellation that would exist in the night sky would be Leo. That was it.

Blizenci. Lev. Kozoroh. The reasons all of the other Zodiacs are dead. They are all fake. Too much politics. Who even cares about politics. I know I could care less if it ends in slaughter, but for some reason that seems to be the way to enslave an entire nation. Well, the easiest way to enslave a nation. What would be the hardest? UGH! It does not matter! Lev is a manipulative, deceitful animal. Blizenci is...I am clueless as to what he has really done, but Kozoroh is the puppet master. How did any of this even happen in the first place? Oh, I know! Because people are stupid. The masses are stupid. Most of the world still has failed to even learn how to read, so no wonder these three Zodiacs exploit us so much. If there is the only thing I learned today, it is that people are stupid! Which is blatantly obvious after dealing with Ferran!

Aqila thought for what felt like hours about how screwed the world is. Regardless of which Zodiac ruled over them, from what she has seen on her travels, none of the citizens of any empire seemed to even try to change it, and it only made her headache more aggressive when she thought about how easy it must have been for Kozoroh to steal the world and Lev to steal so much from her. Her heavy head filled with heavier thoughts burned a hole into the cracked pavement as she lazily gazed around at the stars. Aqila's eyelids drooped, and before she knew it she caught herself counting how many stars there were in the night sky. She chose not to stop herself. Instead, she persistently counted away knowing that her mission was futile. No matter how much time she elapsed or how much energy she wasted, she would never count all of the stars. Not to mention there were ten constellations completely missing from the night sky. All of which could only be seen during certain times of the year which meant that, even excluding those constellations, most of the stars in the sky were not even visible at the moment. Even against all of the odds, she kept counting. From 27, to 45, to 68, all the way up until she lost track of her count...and had to start all over again.

When she felt herself nodding off she turned on to her side. It was an attempt to keep herself awake, but she was entirely aware that this position was more comfortable. Without fighting nature, Aqila slowly dropped her eyelids, and no more than two minutes later she opened them. The road beneath her shook. Her first instinct was to open up her tired eyes in case an Eveharris had found her. She quickly remembered that her vision was of no use to her in this lighting, so she angrily closed her eyes and rolled over to her other side to fall back asleep. However, upon rolling over her she saw a faint light pierce through her eyelids. With slight confusion and extreme weariness she pulled open her gazers one more time. In the far distance she saw two small yellow lights. They beamed brightly, but it was obvious quite some distance separated her from it. *Good, they found some flashlights and are going to look for me, then Sartan.* The lights quickly grew brighter and closer as Aqila attempted to keep herself awake until her friends got to her.

These beams became blinding, and Aqila soon was startled awake by the consistent rays. Once her consciousness was entirely online again, she realized what was happening. *Shit! No! No! No!* Aqila hastily scrambled to her feet, and by the time her legs shot her up towards the stars, the lights had already grown exponentially closer. Whoever was driving the vehicle must have been in a rush because within seconds they were only seconds away from Aqila. With no other options or time to think of one, she thrusted herself into the dewy grass off the side of the road. By now the light was so bright it blinded her completely, and she could see as much as she could without any light. A quick screeching sound followed a face full of grass as she landed in the ditch. The truck squealed out into the other ditch nearly flipping over itself. It finally came to a stop several spins away from the road, and Aqila desperately hoped that the driver did not see her. Of course, if that were the case then the truck would probably be on its merry little way, clueless to her presence. Aqila quickly stood up patting away the dirty dampness off her. The passenger door of the truck was the first to open, and her eyes were still adjusting to the lighting which made it difficult to profile the individual.

"Are you okay!" shouted a man as he stumbled out of the truck.

Instantly Aqila shouted back while walking to the road again, "What the hell Ferran!"

"Hey, I wasn't the one driving!" shouted Ferran as he jogged through the grass to meet her back on the road. "Why were you just laying in the middle of the road?"

"I got tired, and you just disappeared for no good reason!"

"I told you where I went! I was looking for Jaako and Caleb!"

"You should be looking for Sartan!" screamed out Aqila. "Ugh! Did you find them?"

"Well who do you think was driving?" asked Jaako as he stepped around the other side of the truck. "I wouldn't trust Ferran with my life like that."

"I could never agree more with you Jaako, but where did you guys find a truck? And why did you just leave us in the middle of nowhere?" asked Aqila as everybody slowly regrouped on the road.

"We stole it!" exclaimed Jaako.

"From who?"

"Oh, Caleb and I went on a walk North until we reached this old looking house. We found a truck, hotwired it, and took it," replied Jaako as they all began walking to the prized truck.

It was a tiny, white truck that had obviously seen better days. The tires kissed the ground and must have been leaking air. The back headlights were completely broken. The muffler was missing. The passenger window was also missing, and there was only one windshield wiper. The rear view mirror on the driver's side was shattered, and like the passenger's window, the passenger side rear view mirror was completely missing. Somehow the front lights worked perfectly fine, but the driver's door had six bullet holes in it. The paint had mostly peeled around the edges leaving a nasty, brown rust behind. The bed was black and dirty like a usual truck bed, but in the very middle there was a large phallus spray painted in white. Aqila could only guess who might have wasted their time spraying that piece of art. She coiled in disgust because the more she looked at it, the more she realized the artist might have had some actual artistic talent with all of the detail they put into the piece. All of the capillaries seemed to pulsate when she looked at it which only grossed her out more. She realized that whoever created this horrendously, decent piece of 'artwork' or 'graffiti' had signed it with their initials. *DS. Who the hell would sign their initials on something like this?*

While they showed the entire truck off to her, some things they had failed to notice until showing her such as the piece of artwork in the bed, Caleb spoke out, "We did just steal this however, so let's not just stare at it while the owner possibly finds out it is missing."

Ferran quickly jumped in on the conversation, "I agree! We need to get far away from here as quickly as possible."

"What about Sartan!" exclaimed Aqila as she refused to let Ferran get away that easily. "The further we get from him the longer it will take to save him!"

"Sartan is too far gone!" exclaimed Ferran.

"Stop lying!"

For the first time in what seemed like ages, Ferran finally abided. He did not argue with her, possibly out of fear that Caleb might wander off again. Instead, he stood there without purpose, just letting Aqila rail into him. Again.

"This is all your fault! Could you imagine how much closer we would be to Garigo right now had you not thrown us off?!? I know you are tired of hearing my constant complaints, but I SWEAR FERRAN YOU ARE CONSTANTLY CAUSING PROBLEMS!!! Unnecessary problems. WHAT THE HELL DID HE DO TO YOU?!?! Awww, did he not like you? Well nobody else does either!" screamed Aqila as anger quickly flooded her pours.

"Aqila---"

"NO! I'm tired of your bullshit Ferran! We are all supposed to be on the same team here!"

"And what are you supposed to be our leader or something? Screw that!"

"Yeah well if you were the leader we would still be in Mirisburg!"

"Oh so you're saying you ARE the leader? How selfish of you! But what else could be expected from someone as disappointing as yourself? Mom and dad knew that you would burnout, and recreating all of the Zodiacs has made it obvious that they were right!" exclaimed Ferran, making the argument much less avoidable.

"What do you mean burnout?!?!" screamed Aqila as she completely ignored the terror she burned into Caleb and Jaako's face. "The only one here that is going to be a burnout is you! Scratch that! You are going to be a blowout! Shot dead by the ripe age of twenty-one if you fail to get your shit together!"

"I may die from a bullet this week, but you'll have two-hundred STD's by then," whispered Ferran with a smug grin on his face.

The heat that resonated out of her head emasculated magma, but she knew the heat that stung her hand must have been shallow in comparison to the flame that burned red on Ferran's face. The smug grin was instantly smacked clean off him as his entire head swiveled to the left. Aqila raised her voice along with her hand again, but before she could land the second smack Ferran surprised her. She went stumbling to the side before tripping over her own feet and falling in the wet grass. Her hands quickly cusped her face as she felt tears rolling down her chin and blood trickling out of her nose. Ferran's knuckles might not be the boniest out there, but they certainly would be leaving more than a bruise on her face. While she buried her face in the grass she could hear Jaako arguing with Ferran. Stuff about hitting a woman. If he should or should not be allowed to do that. To her it was irrelevant as he did it anyways, and it hurt way more than she hurt him.

Even as the voices behind her began to amplify, Aqila still refused to take her head out of the grass. It was almost impossible, and even if she did manage to stand up she would surely collapse from the dizziness. *I will never defeat Lev. I will never defeat Kozoroh. I will never be able to if I can't even handle this.* Amidst all the chaos that ensued the fight that was surely about to break out between Ferran and Jaako, Aqila could hear someone whisper to her.

"Aqila, are you okay?" asked a soft voice.

She hesitated to respond. Aqila did not want to let him know she was in tears, and speaking would only make that ten times more difficult. Regardless she attempted to hold a conversation even after the impact, "Yes Caleb, I am---I am fine. Just make sure--" her voice cracked and she had to stop in order to prevent the shaky tone that one gets when crying. "Just make sure they do not kill each other."

"Okay let's get you in the truck," whispered Caleb over the increasingly loud exclamations from Ferran and Jaako. "Come on, stand up."

"I can't," whispered Aqila.

"What? I couldn't hear you."

"Okay!" whispered Aqila shakily.

Caleb slowly helped her to her feet, and when all of her black hair, drenched with a mixture of dew and tears, flung forward in front of her face she did not attempt to put it behind her. The two of them slowly made their way towards the passenger side of the truck where Caleb placed her. She sat down on the crusty leather seats that had more burnholes than the moon had craters. Her nose was stuffy, and her vision was mostly compromised with all of her black hair in her face. The headache that had quickly moved into her head had doubled in size after receiving Ferran's generous stimulus. The headache had enough time to invite its entire family over into its one bedroom apartment where they would have a party all at the detriment of poor Aqila. The dashboard was spinning, and when Caleb shut the truck door on her she nearly fell over onto the steering wheel. Since the passenger window was absent from the door, she could still hear everything that was going on outside of the truck. She could hear it, but she definitely could not listen to most of it. The constant ringing that plagued her head made it hard to think, let alone eavesdrop on their arguments.

"Just get in the goddamn bed Ferran!"

"I'm not riding on tha---"

"---id you even care about being clean?"

"Caleb, I've always worried about hygiene. Unlike Ja---"

"Wow! Well---definitely not riding in the---so figure something out Mr. Clea---"

"---isn't enough room---always just leave Jaako---"

"Caleb, I think Aqila is---he makes the group---toxic than it has---"

"I agree with you Jaa---"

"---it! You two can go kiss her fat------or all you want! I'm going to-----in the back------can actually leave!"

Suddenly Caleb hopped into the truck from the driver's side. He slid all the way to the middle seat where he sat next to Aqila who refused to look up from the dashboard to acknowledge his presence. She felt the truck shake, and before she knew it the truck was on. She glanced over to see Jaako behind the wheel. She had no clue where Ferran was, but that did not matter to her anymore. Not after today.

"Jaako," whispered Aqila as she slowly began to regain her vocal abilities. "Are you taking us to save Sartan?"

"Not yet Aqila," replied Jaako as he attempted to reverse back onto the road. "Caleb, what way did we come from?"

"I think that it was…that way?"

A brief second of silence passed before Aqila exclaimed quietly, "Sartan is gone now. Please tell me that he is not."

Another awkward moment of silence passed before Caleb exhaustedly whispered, "It doesn't look good. There is a pretty low chance at this point to be honest."

"Low?" asked Aqila in a defeated whisper. "But his chances are not zero."

Caleb hugged her as he exhaled, "Not zero, but sadly his chances are very low."

She closed her eyes and pushed away her friend. *Not zero but very low. Very low but not zero.* When she opened her eyes again one final tear tore away from her duct and trickled down her face leaving a flameless trail of ash and despair. *My brother is a murderer. He never even cared. Ferran killed a whole twenty percent of our team. A whole fifth of the cause is gone because Ferran was---not right now. Not yet.*

She looked out of the windowless door next to her and witnessed the dark winds pierce through to her face. In the far distance she could barely, just barely, see the forest from which they all came. The trees swayed back and forth under the mere glimmer of moonlight, and it was difficult to imagine how long they might have been there for. With every one of her breaths she shared with the forest her ability to see the trees breathing in the wind decreased. As Jaako drove South both Lev and Sartan would be further away. Possibly even Ferran too as Aqila still did not know if he was in the bed of the truck or not. She could have cared less after tonight. The sun would be up before she knew it. She would deal with everything when that happened. As for right now, right now Aqila was enjoying a peaceful ride. For once neither Jaako nor Caleb had enough energy to talk, and Aqila could not have been more pleased.

It was not long before Caleb began snoring next to her, and she desperately wanted to join him on his peaceful journey. She couldn't. Her mind raced with questions. It raced with worries and doubts. Missed opportunities and regrets. Anger filled-hatred towards those who have done her wrong in the past made it too difficult to sleep. She knew that her companions would not leave her behind if she fell asleep the next morning, but after Sartan anything seemed as if it were possible. Those closest had turned. Aqila rested her head on the dashboard trying to ease the headache, but she quickly remembered Jaako was driving. All of the bumps in the road made it futile, so eventually she just leaned back in her seat. She sat there wishing. Aqila wished for many things, but the most recurring wish was to forget. To forget everything and finally sleep away her problems like she had seen so many others do in the past.

Chapter 14
What a Windy World
Sartan

Over three days later the bright lights beamed down on Sartan. In an unnamed city, as she insisted on keeping things anonymous, he was alone with Lev. It certainly wouldn't be difficult to figure it out, but the question was if he cared enough to. Around him were many pedestrians walking through the night streets. The tall concrete buildings had shiny glass windows that reflected the red glow of the stoplights. Cars honked and beeped all around him, and the bags under his eyes along with the souls of his feet so desperately wanted to rest. That wouldn't be an option however. Lev stood right next to him as they walked closer to the center of the metropolis. They had walked a fair portion of the way there. Not too long ago Lev practically stole a vehicle from a local farmer, but he seemed more than pleased to lend it to her when she told him who she was. They had left it on the side of the road when they got into thicker traffic closer to the city, much to his dismay. It had been about four days since she rescued him, and she hadn't been nearly patient enough for his mortal needs as he thought she would be. The amount of sleep Sartan had managed to steal from Lev was criminal, and he wondered how shaky his mind would have grown if she hadn't taken up driving a bit of the journey. Lev still appeared as rugged as she did when he first saw her. Nothing had changed within her sickly physique, but with only six days of January left he was expecting some sort of miraculous change. He was expecting to see if she was lying or not.

Sartan was most certainly surprised to find Omar lurking around the forest for her. Omar was now re-searching that forest for Aqila and the others, but the fact that he was working for Lev now made him concerned. Then again he was the one who received a direct letter from Kozoroh. *None of it matters anymore. Lev will help me find this Leucemie character and I will help her find Ferran and the others in return. I will finally restore everything, and Lev will do whatever she needs to…whatever that may be.*

The two of them steadily approached the center of the bustling city, and when they finally did Lev must have decided it was time to let Sartan understand a little bit of what was actually going on. "Sartan," spoke Lev softly as they stopped at a crosswalk. "When we arrive in his chamber you must give him your utmost respect."

"Who's chambers?" asked Sartan.

"His majesty of course," replied Lev before they began walking across the street.

"Do you mean Blizenci? Gemini?"

"Well I would certainly hope not! This city would be the worst place to make your capital, and if this were Blizenci's capital then his empire surely would not last much longer," Lev laughed out those last few words as she glanced around the metropolis. "His capital lies on the coast between here and Garigo."

They stood in the middle of downtown. There were multiple skyscrapers erected all around them. Most of them were hundreds if not thousands of feet high with lots of aerodynamic designs. One skyscraper in particular had a hollow section right in the middle. Four very thin metal frames connected the top half of the building with the bottom from the corners, and within that fifty foot space where the skyscraper seemingly disappeared was only four elevators squeezed into the very center. The space around them was wide enough for an entire fleet of helicopters to come through the building and not cause a single cent of structural damage. It was only then that Sartan realized what the skyscraper really did. Several large turbines were spun by the gusts, and while doing so they directed the wind that passed through the building down through tubes. These same tubes shot out air at several spots throughout the downtown section of the city. It was almost a free form of air conditioning, but during late January nights, even near the equator, that might have cooled the city down just a little too much. *Surely they take advantage of that wind and turn it into power somehow.*

Sartan finally stopped awing at the city when he remembered the vague conversation he was having with Lev. "If it isn't Blizenci then who is it?" asked Sartan who attempted to chase after Lev. She had cut off traffic when she decided to cross the street during a green light.

"We are having a meeting with Herton, the King," replied Lev with carelessness burning in her eyes. "He rules as king over the Northern half of the Genillian Empire. He will assist in faster transport to Garigo as well as acquiring Blizenci for the cause."

"What do we need Blizenci's help for?" asked Sartan.

Lev sighed in annoyance before replying, "Blizenci will help us locate the Virgo Palace if our campaign fails in Garigo. Its location eludes my memory."

"Wait, I thought you knew where every palace was. Is that not true?"

"I have no time to dilute my intelligence with such bleak questions, Sartan. I am obviously a Leo, so I was forbidden from leaving my homelands until the fall of the Zodiacs because of some ill-advised act my predecessors agreed to. How could I figure out where the Virgo Palace was if I grew up during an age of secrecy between the Zodiacs? I also have not had the need to until now either."

Sartan did not reply. He glanced up at the skyscraper in front of him. It towered over the two of them as it sliced through clouds on its way to the stars. Small pinholes of light could be seen growing ever so slowly behind the opening in the thin clouds that blanketed the sky. The skyscraper seemingly breathed in the clouds because whenever one would get near the windows, it would get sucked into the building by some unseen machinery or mechanic, but it would never make it to the other side.

He followed Lev through the spinning doors of the building, and was instantly hit in the face with the smell of laundry detergent and the sound of hundreds speaking over one another. The lobby of the building had so many people inside it, but not one of them smelled of fresh laundry. Wherever the scent was coming from was hidden, but Sartan smiled at the staff's choice to keep the lobby clean. However, upon seeing the gargantuan line ahead of them his frown was less than flattered. Lev made her way through the pool of people skipping the line to the front desk, and Sartan followed her trying not to look at all of the people who began getting angry at them. Before they made it to the front desk, a sickly, old woman grabbed Sartan by the shoulders.

"Excuse you! The line starts back at the door buddy!" exclaimed the woman as she dug her bony fingers into Sartan's shoulders.

Sartan stared at the woman in shock. A bloody tissue hung out of her left nostril, and her yellowed teeth stunk of mildew. Conditioned by the streets of Dursnia, he instinctively thought that his life was being threatened, so when his fists flew up to her face in reflex he had to calm down and quickly. Luckily, Sartan did not punch an old woman for little reason. Instead, he managed to throw his balled hands on to her shoulders. He stared at the veins bulging in his arms as his hands rested on her shoulders. This strange stance where the two of them grabbed each other tightly by the shoulders went on for a few steady seconds as the elderly woman looked up and down Sartan's face in confusion. Sartan was just as lost, and he struggled to control his reflexes. His thoughts quickly escaped reality as he got distracted by how his initial instinct was to beat her senseless. She must have been uncomfortable with the situation because the woman quickly pushed him back.

"Are you deaf?!" shouted the woman as she choked blood on his face. "Back of the line grabby!"

Sartan looked around at the other people in line. Their faces were cowled and angrily focused on him. One of them praised the old woman, and two of them pointed to the door aggressively. Their dirty suits and dress pants certainly could get dirtier. A few of them looked just as ill as the elderly woman. A rare few of them looked just as ill as Lev. They had bloody noses, rotten teeth, hunched shoulders, scabby skin, black circles melting the underside of their eyes, and a few of them had even gone bald as if they had cancer treatment. Though most of the people in line did not look unwell let alone deathly ill, most of them looked fatigued, and all of them looked angrily at Sartan.

The old woman grabbed her purse and began swinging it at him. He tried to dodge her attacks, and he did for the first few swings. Eventually the woman landed a few hits on him, and for some reason Sartan didn't fight back. All of the angry onlookers would make sure that wouldn't end well for him if he did choose to defend himself. Suddenly, Lev must've noticed Sartan was trailing as she grabbed the purse of the woman, preventing her from hitting Sartan for the eighth time.

"Get your hands off me you slits!" shouted the elderly woman.

Sartan by now had scrambled to his feet to see Lev leering the woman deep in her eyes. Lev's irises were no longer brown. Instead she gazed deep into the old woman's eyes with fiery, shiny, maroon irises. Sartan stared in awe as

Lev began muttering something inaudible to the woman. He noticed that the irises of the old woman were now maroon in color. The old woman stared at Lev as her mouth slowly gaped open, and her focus was undivided. Sartan looked around the room and noticed that a few other sickly looking individuals that previously cursed him to the back of the line were also maroon eyed and focused on Lev. He felt the room warming up quite quickly, and by now the victims of Lev had begun muttering silently in response to whatever spell Lev was commanding into them. Sartan wasn't the only one to notice it either. Most of the people in line looked around at the situation with great confusion. They looked at Sartan. They looked at Lev and back at the people who were seemingly in trance with her. The whole time Lev muttered under her breath. It was so quiet that Sartan could barely hear it even though he stood right next to her. Not to mention that the room had gone silent. Whatever Lev was doing had distinguished the conversations of the entire lobby, and the few whispers Sartan could hear were definitely not of the human language.

"Isen whyiuc gretuiz cherquinva looyiiq..." Out of nowhere all of the maroon eyed people knelt down on one knee. They bowed their heads, and Lev's eyes slowly returned to brown. She glanced at Sartan while smiling, "Let us continue Sartan. We have a time frame to fulfill, and I desperately wish not to get behind schedule."

Everyone in the room who wasn't affected by Lev's strange ritual stared nervously at Sartan as they awaited his reaction. Sartan slowly nodded, and Lev turned around to face the front desk. The two of them skipped the line, and this time they didn't have anyone try to stop them. Once they got to the front of the line, the person who was previously being helped stepped out of the way to let Lev and Sartan go ahead of him. The women behind the giant counter all shook as they shuffled their papers around while trying to look organized.

One of them quickly spoke out to Lev with a tremble in her voice, "How may I assist you?"

"We have an appointment with the king," stated Lev punctually.

"What time are you scheduled to meet with him, and what are your names?"

"It is an unannounced appointment."

The woman behind the counter swallowed a ball of spit before replying, "I'm sorry ma'am, but the king is a very busy man. If you want to have a meeting with him you will have to schedule one, and he will have to accept it."

"We will do no such thing."

Another woman dropped her papers all over the floor behind the counter. The secretary talking to them then said with a broken voice, "Then-then I'm afraid I can't let you see him."

Lev glanced at Sartan and rolled her eyes before she replied, "Where is your boss? I need to speak with him."

The secretary gladly ran off through a door in the back to find her manager. Meanwhile the other secretaries began helping those people in the line behind them. Sartan still was stuck on the strange ritual Lev randomly executed on those sickly looking people. Everyone else seemed to just move on from it as if they had already forgotten, or if they had already repressed it deep into their subconscious.

"Blizenci's citizen response sector is quite a disappointing department. Is it not?" asked Lev with her arms crossed and her foot tapping the floor repeatedly. "What even is this lobby? A place where a whole bunch of random people stand in line to find out they wasted their time entirely. At least in my empire they don't have the option to try and speak with nobility."

"Then how do you know what your subjects want?" asked Sartan.

"The subject's desires are unimportant to me. However, it is necessary to keep the labor force happy and distracted, so we have set up anonymous voting sanctions where they can anonymously ask for certain amenities. Whether or not they get them is up to me," said Lev quickly.

"Won't that just make them resent you?"

"Certainly not!" exclaimed Lev. "I make sure that my subjects are all well fed, employed, and generally happy. If they are unwise enough to respect my wishes or if they fail to meet those three requirements, I will deport them to a less fortunate nation such as this one."

Sartan replied, "Well at least there hasn't been a riot here today."

"Yes, that is quite a valid statement. Dursnia, and the rest of the late Sagittarius Empire for that matter, needs lots of administrative change for it to become even close to as unstable as the Genillian Empire. At least Blizenci is ruling over his empire. The absence of an almighty ruler has caused many internal problems for the shattered Sagittarius Empire."

Suddenly the two of them were interrupted by a sniffling voice, "Now what seems to be the problem here ma'am?"

Sartan watched as Lev hastily replied, "Of course. As a divine ruler I was on my way to speak with the king, but your secretary is making such appointments difficult to complete."

"My sincerest apologies my lady. Of which vassal may you be to the noble King Herton?" asked the man. Just like the elderly woman who had assaulted Sartan in line, this younger looking man was sickly beyond belief. Sartan deduced that the face mask straddling his mouth and nose was to prevent himself from getting sicker rather than others from getting sick, and Sartan had no clue as to what the strange piece of tissue that stuck out of his ear was for.

"I am not a vassal to the king but rather a foreign noble," said Lev as the man began writing things down on a piece of paper.

While the man checked his computer for names he slowly spoke out, "I'm not seeing anything scheduled for a foreign noble."

"It just so happens to be a surprise meeting of great importance. We did not have the time to set up an official meeting."

"Right. Well what is your title then?" asked the man with rising skepticism in his breath.

Lev waited a second before sighing and replying regally, "I am Lev, Empress of the Leo Empire."

The man stared at her. A smirk ran up his chin before he said, "You're kidding right? Lev the Active Leo Zodiac? As in ruler of the Leo Empire to the North? And with your appearance? My lady, I was born quite a while ago."

The man laughed as Lev rolled her eyes and shook her head to Sartan. She then decided to stare the man down until finally asking, no stating, "You do not believe me. I can prove it. After all, you are one of my subjects."

"Exactly! If you were the real Lev I would definitely be able to tell as a Leo myself!"

Lev raised her left hand while muttering more words from a non-human language. The man quickly reacted as both of his hands shot straight up to his nose. He plugged his nostrils with his mask, but when that didn't stop his discomfort he took it off entirely. Beneath the mask was now a nose gushing with blood. He scoffed as it poured out claiming that it burned. It sprayed over his papers and nearly short circuited the computer's wireless keyboard.

"You see, during our month of detriment everybody has to deal with the weakness that showers over us so kindly, the Active Zodiac, everyday Leo's like yourself, and even six month old babies. However, as the Zodiac I can always choose who has to bear the worst of it. I can even make the pain cease to exist for you. I could shift your load onto every other Leo in existence. Of course they would never notice such a small change," stated Lev. She then whispered so that only the three of them could hear her in the once again silenced room, "If you are smart you will lead me to the king."

The man stared at her as bloody tears began to trickle out of his eyes. He murmured something under his breath not realizing that blood was also leaking out of his mouth as well.

"I can also do the opposite. I could shift the load, the detriment of every other living Leo to you," said Lev as she raised her hand once more. "Although carrying that much pain…that much detriment…you would only last a few seconds before you succumb. Rather, I believe it would be instantaneous. I could even obliterate your levels of sobriety right now if I wished. Making everyday functioning absolutely impossible."

"Fine! Fine! I'll lead you to the king!" exclaimed the man as blood began running out of his ears.

Lev lowered her hand, and within a second all of the blood stopped gushing out of this poor man. He instantly grabbed tissues to wipe himself off with, and the crowd watched with open jaws as he cleaned himself up a bit. The other secretaries were distracted briefly before attempting to get the citizens to do whatever it was that they came here to do. A few of them complied while others stepped out of the line to watch what Lev did next.

"Follow me," cracked the man as his bloody mask was tossed to the side. He grabbed some keys from under the desk before allowing them to walk around the counter. After they were on the same side as him, Lev and Sartan both followed him through the back. They made their way to an array of elevators that formed a half circle in the wall. Pristine elevators at that. The quartz finish left an airy feel for the whole room as the minimalist walls widened out leaving the three of them standing in a wide carpeted lobby. Except, the only thing different about this lobby was that nobody else was present. The quietness was eerie especially after having to deal with the aggravated civilians of this city.

The man that led Lev and Sartan to the elevators walked up to the center elevator. He fumbled around with the keys for what felt like an eternity. Sartan witnessed him drop the keys once, and the man attempted to use the same key for the lock twice. Eventually he must have found the correct key because the elevator door suddenly whooshed open pouring a leathery smell out into the vacant lobby, and a monotone buzzing preceded a silver light which illuminated softly from within.

"This is the one," stuttered the man as he let Lev go first.

While Lev walked past him she gracefully reminded the pained man, "There are merely five more days of detriment. We thankfully have almost four days left until the first."

Sartan trailed into the roomy elevator, and the door nearly nipped him as it quickly shut behind him. The inside of the elevator was just as deluxe as the door. Shiny metal lining ran up and down every side of the elevator while a glimmering, gray light emitting from the top of the box buzzed softly above him. When Sartan's eyes eventually drifted towards the buttons with numbers on it he realized that he had never been inside a building that went so high into the sky. Well…not with righteous intentions at least.

The man now had dried blood all over himself, and he pressed button number fifty-five. Which just so happened to be the second highest room. The ticker instantly began counting upwards from zero to fifty-five. Lev didn't say anything, and Sartan's ears began to pop. Sartan had noticed that she would interact with a good portion of people they passed on the way here, but for some reason she wasn't speaking with this man that much. Sartan then focused on the man himself. The man had streaks of sweat running down the back of his neck. His body would twitch randomly, and he stood in front of them refusing to look back. He quietly mumbled to himself counting each tick as they ascended higher and higher into the building. Lev noticed this as well. Sartan watched as her face scrunched up in confusion before relaxing again.

"My loyal subject, why do you fear me so?" asked Lev while she put her hand on the man's shoulder. "I am not your enemy, rather your guide. Your leader. Your Zodiac. So what reason would you have to fear me so much?"

"I-" the man stuttered before dropping his keys. After hastily bending down and picking them back up off the beige marble floor of the elevator he quickly replied with, "I don't know. I'd just feel safer far away from you. I really enjoy our month of benefit in July, but the Zodiacs are a thing of the past now. I think it would be better if---"

"I did not ask for your thoughts on what the Zodiacs should be doing," interrupted Lev while she walked closer to him, placing both of her hands on his arms.

Sartan watched as the breath that came out of her nose, with extreme heat, curled the hairs on the back of his neck. She kept speaking to him moving from ear to ear, and Sartan was certain that had she whispered into one ear the whole time, this man's skin would've caught on fire.

Lev continued to breathe down on the poor man, "I merely asked why you feared me, not why you believed the Zodiacs should no longer exist. It is obvious we are not a thing of the past as the most powerful Zodiac to ever live has cornered you in an elevator...all by your lonesome." Lev tightened her grip on the man's arms as he began to writhe. "You call yourself a Leo? Then you should be able to handle a tad bit of heat…my whiny subject!"

Sartan could instantly feel the airy elevator heat up. He could see the flames in Lev's eyes as she gripped the man even tighter, possibly burning him with her hands. Sartan stepped back from the two of them, but when his back hit the wall behind him he realized that there was nowhere to go. Sweat began to break out on his forehead, and he could already see small traces of steam beginning to accumulate at his feet. However, it quickly rose towards the ceiling of the elevator. Looking at the ticker he hoped Lev could keep herself from killing him before the door swung open. They were already at floor forty-six and rising, but the elevator was no longer an elevator. Instead, it had turned into a sauna, for the steam had quickly expanded stretching from both the floor to the ceiling. Shortly after the time they reached the fiftieth floor Sartan could no longer see the ticker, and when he felt the elevator come to an abrupt stop he could barely even see Lev through the mist.

The doors swung open. All of the steam paraded out of the elevator into the room before them, and as it billowed out Sartan still couldn't figure out what Lev had done to the man. She let go of him, and he ran out of the elevator away from Lev and Sartan whilst flailing his arms. Once the steam cleared Lev stepped forward into the vacant hallway. Glistening, golden lights lined the short hallway, and large, glass windows rested between the lighting. As Sartan followed Lev onto the marble flooring he glanced out of each window. The night sky shadowed over most of the city, but the street lights far below maintained illumination quite well. He could see thousands of car lights moving in hundreds of different directions. The adjacent skyscrapers looked up towards his position as he watched the antennas and wind meters shake violently in the strong winds.

Unfortunately, there wasn't much time for Sartan to gaze at the modern city or watch the wind turbines spin vigorously on that one skyscraper. His mind was focused on what the man was going to do now. He walked past six or seven windows before entering through an opened glass door after Lev. On the other side stood a sharp marble desk with a young secretary sitting behind it. She was talking to the man that led them to the elevator, but there was quite a bit of confusion on her face. As Lev and Sartan walked up next to him, he became more aggressive in his gestures, but he was stuttering and struggling to make sense. He stumbled around as he tried to stand upright. He pointed at Lev while desperately trying to keep his distance from her. He slammed his fists on the secretary's desk multiple times, and he barely mumbled a few curse words while doing it all.

Eventually the secretary spoke out, "Do you two understand what is going on with him?"

"I am afraid we do," replied Lev as she pushed the frantic man out of her way. "He told us that he would bring us to the king for our unscheduled meeting, while slurring and swearing the whole time may I add. However, once in your unbearably slow elevators the scent of alcohol assaulted us with every breath he took. It was quite upsetting for us to witness, as when the doors swung open our host stumbled forward completely forgetting about us."

"My most sincerest of apologies madam. I will deal with it immediately," said the woman as she picked up a thin, oval-shaped sheet of glass. The glass lit up, and she tapped it a few times before speaking again. "Can you send security, Reginold needs detained."

As the woman put the paper thin sheet of glowing glass back down on her black-glass desk Sartan couldn't help his intrigue and asked, "Wait, was that a phone?"

"Indeed it was. The mark three's from series two. My boss wants us to have the most efficient and updated services. After all that is what Blizenci wanted the Northern Kingdom to focus on, technology."

"Blizenci split up his empire into separate districts to focus on certain tasks?" asked Lev as an obvious abundance of intrigue paraded over her face as well. "Do you happen to know what the South's focus is?"

The woman stared off for a second before getting distracted by Reginold's consistent flailing and inebriated presence. She then continued with, "I am not too positive, but I do believe that if the Northern Kingdom's focus is on technology and the sciences, the Southern Kingdom's focus must be on agriculture, processing, factories, and all of the necessities to keep the empire functional."

"How does Blizenci depend on defending his nation then if there is no military sector?" asked Sartan as he tried to get back into the conversation.

"Blizenci should not require a military, for the only two Zodiacs left are both allies to him. Every other nation is desperately leaderless and thus poses no threat to his empire," replied Lev.

The woman behind the desk opened her mouth, but then shut it while suddenly pointing over towards Reginold. Sartan spun around to see two beefy guards walk up and carry Reginold off back to the elevator. The secretary then continued with what she was about to say, "That may be true, but after everything that has happened over the past forty years it is better to be safe. Blizenci does have a small Eastern sector of the empire where he reigns over the cities with less vassalization. There are no kings over there, but only a few dozen barons. Even less counts and dukes. It is this sector that focuses heavily on militarization and government as it is Blizenci's noble wish."

"I suppose you do learn something new everyday," said Lev as she glanced over at Sartan. "Our talk has been quite intriguing, but I do fear we are on a time limit here. Could you so happen to lead us to King Herton, so that we can solve our trade agreements and diplomacy issues?"

"But of course," said the woman. She picked back up her paper thin phone, pressed a single button, and said into it, "My liege, you have visitors.....I don't know?.....Are you sure?.....As you wish." The secretary put the phone down as it ceased to illuminate itself on her desk and said, "You may go on back. He is waiting for you in his office."

Lev nodded to the woman and walked past the desk. Sartan followed her down what seemed to be another hallway, but this one was shorter than the last being only a few feet long. They quickly ended up in a vast, white-carpeted living-room that had enormous windows that you could view the entire city with. Deluxe sofas and loveseats sat scattered around the room. Some of them faced a large sheet of paper thin glass that hung on the wall while others faced the windows. Sartan realized that it was a TV made of the same material the secretary's phone was made of. Not to mention the fact that there were practically no wires whatsoever. In fact, there were no wires whatsoever.

He looked down towards the right to see the living room stretch to the end of the floor where it finally turned into an array of cubicles where workers sat. What those workers were doing was beyond him, but their monitors were of the exact same material as the TV and as the secretary's phone. There were several workers sitting at their own personalized desks completely unaware of both Lev and his presence. Sartan then glanced to the left as he realized Lev had already begun walking that way. A few black, glass tables were scattered as the living room quickly turned into a tiny little bar with lots of drinking equipment sitting around neglected. Looking past the evidence of a nearby liquor enthusiast, Sartan saw the room end at a large glass door that was too dark to peer through. It was chipped and chiseled with two equally large mirrors on the walls next to it. The mirrors reflected the light that came through the windows as well as the light that came out of the interior walls. Sartan then noticed the plate at the summit of the door. On the shiny yellow metal stood the words, *King Herton,* chiseled in bold golden letters. As Lev reached for the golden door knob that jutted out from the black frame, he realized that the door wasn't even glass. It was chiseled obsidian.

On the other side of the door was an airy room with lots of photographs resting on the many silver shelves throughout the office. The wall directly to the left after entering was covered in royal paintings of the king with what appeared to be his family. The wall directly to the right after entering was completely absent, being replaced by the same large windows that stretched the whole side of that wall. The back wall however, had hundreds of small valuables and photos on the many silver shelves. Most of the valuables were awards, knives, jewelry and coins, but there was still a large amount of pictures and random things that could only have sentimental value to one person. On the very center of the wall was a large, canvas painting of what Sartan could only assume was Blizenci. The man wore royal robes, and stood with his arms crossed. No crown rested on his short, slightly ginger hair, and no necklace hung below his goatee. Instead there was a ring on one of his fingers. The ring was strangely familiar even in painting. The black chassis held in a gray gemstone. Even within the painting the gemstone itself looked clearer than the air he was breathing. It was so clear in fact that at first he figured the ring had no gemstone in it at all.

Sartan's eyes finally wandered to the black, obsidian desk that sat in the center of the room. Three chairs rested in front of it, and behind it sat a big, hairy man. The grayish white hairs that jutted out of his arms ran all the way up to his sleeves. A combed bush of white hair sat on the top of his head, and the mustache that surely should've been white, was stained brown in the middle for some reason. The man didn't look up from his desk as he asked both Lev and Sartan to take a seat. Instead he was focused on the larger version of the paper thin monitors that all of his workers had as well.

"Now what unscheduled business do you require of me?" groaned the man as he took a sip of his black coffee. Once he placed down his coffee, the king pressed a button on the screen and it lowered into a slit within the obsidian desk. He first glanced at Sartan before quickly moving his gaze over to Lev. When the king looked at Lev, Sartan instantly saw the surprise on his face as he nearly spat out his coffee.

"Is it not acceptable for me to visit my acquaintances without notice?" asked Lev with a smile on her face. She stared him up and down for a brief second before continuing, "It appears time has not treated you well my friend. Blizenci has still yet to grant you immortality?"

The king glanced over at Sartan before replying to Lev, "Unfortunately, he does not think that I am ready for such responsibility yet. I keep reminding him that if he had given it to me thirty years ago I would've been thirty-seven forever. Now if he gives it to me I'll be sixty-seven forever."

"Well isn't that just ironic? He should know that since he became the Active Gemini at a mere twenty-two years of age. I sincerely do apologize, Herton, but it appears our friend Blizenci does not plan on granting you immortality," said Lev as she kept looking at the aged man's body. "When was the last time we spoke? Fifteen years ago?"

"Just about. At the end of the war with Beek and Vodnar," said the king as Sartan watched him zone out looking at the obsidian desk. "It has been a looong…minute."

An awkward bit of silence passed where both the king and Lev sheepishly glanced at Sartan. Then Lev said, "Well, I suppose we should get down to business then."

"Of course, of course, and what is it exactly that brought you here on this fine night?" replied the king without moving his gaze away from Lev.

Lev hesitated before admitting, "Herton, we have a group of fugitives that have escaped into the Genillian Empire."

"Well that doesn't seem to be a problem at all. Why do you need my help finding them?"

"We both know that I don't need your help finding them, but since they have escaped into the Genillian Empire I legally can't chase them anymore," replied Lev.

"Oh well you have my permission to arrest them. They haven't made it into the Southern Kingdom yet have they?" asked the king as he pointed behind Sartan.

On the wall above the door that they entered through sat a large map of the Gemini Empire. The city that they were currently in was the capital of the Northern Kingdom, Palilverton. All of the names of the nearby cities were too small for Sartan to recognize from his seat. The important thing was that they were practically at the Northernmost tip of the map. Sartan knew that Aqila was planning on going to Garigo, the capital of the Southern Kingdom. Garigo was on the map, but it was nearly all the way on the Southern border of the entire empire. There was a border line in the middle of the empire which split it in half, but that appeared to be nearly as far away as Dursnia…if Dursnia would have been on the map. It took Sartan more than eight days to get to this city from Dursnia, and about half of that journey was in a camper. *Half of that journey I got to sleep through thankfully. There is no way Aqila has made it across that border yet. It has to be at least fourteen walking days away, but then again that's from here. I doubt she went North like Lev and I, and if she finds a vehicle she probably could get there in five or six days. That's only if she is constantly moving though, and I know Ferran will slow them down somehow.*

Sartan said without taking his eyes off the antique map, "Even if they found a car there is no way they have made it to the Southern border yet."

"Yes Sartan, we both assumed this, but a problem still persists," said Lev quickly and sharply.

The king said, "Well then what may the problem be? They are in my lands, so you have full legal permission to chase them."

"Herton, it is still my month of detriment, and I am unable to siphon travel within your lands as they are lands of an Air Zodiac. The very few personnel I brought with me across the border are too limited to do anything other than secure a perimeter."

"Your personnel are limited?" asked the king sarcastically with a smile on his face.

"They are practically peasants of the late Sagittarius Empire, so I am not surprised by their inability to assist me. A third of them didn't even survive the Eveharrisses within your Western forests. The few that remain are too exhausted and incompetent to stay on the trail of my fugitives," replied Lev as she rolled her eyes.

"I see...so how may I assist you then?" asked the king. "And what makes these particular fugitives so important to someone like you?"

Lev quickly said, "Their crimes are of no concern to you. All that matters is that I require your assistance in hunting them down efficiently and effectively."

"Of course. What do you want me to do, dispatch a warrant for their arrests and have my best detectives work the case?"

"No, wait yes. Actually no," said Lev indecisively. "Send out a warrant for their arrests, but don't have your detectives work the case. I don't wish for them to make any unnecessary mistakes."

"Our detectives don't make mistakes Lev," interrupted the king. "They have the most advanced technology in the world to assist them, so mistakes are simply not a part of their calculations."

"I am uncertain. I need to keep this out of the public's eye."

"Well my detectives are sworn to secrecy, and even if they weren't you still wanted me to publicize their presence with the warrants. After all, if the public knows of them we could have people turn them in, especially if it is incentivised."

"Fine, Herton, you may attempt to impress me with one or two of your best detectives, but after the case they must be brainwashed," said Lev hesitantly before going on. "The warrants for their arrests must be for something horrendous, and the cash prizes for them must be exponential, that way your citizens might be more inclined to turn them in."

"I'm perfectly fine with that, but I do have an entire kingdom to budget. Not to mention the taxes Blizenci requires of me," replied the king. "I can offer one-hundred for each of them, but if you want it higher you must finance their capture."

"Only one-hundred? You are the king of one of the strongest kingdoms in the world, and you can only offer one-hundred dollars for your old acquaintance Lev?"

"Fine Lev, I'll warrant one thousand for each of their arrests, but you'll finance anything more. After all, you are the Empress of the Leo Empire and the Leo Zodiac."

"We can start at that then. Issue four warrants for mass genocide," replied Lev hastily.

"Mass genocide!?!" exclaimed the king in confusion. He quickly took the monitor screen back out of his obsidian desk, and began tapping on it as it floated before him. Sartan couldn't see what was happening on the other side of the glass, but on the side he and Lev could see, there was a light blue glow coming out of the thin glass. That wasn't nearly as important to him as the fact that Lev claimed Aqila committed mass genocide. Before Sartan had any real time to think about it the king continued, "Lev, had you started with that I surely would have been moving a bit faster! What are their names and ages?"

"Sartan, would you be kind enough to describe our fugitives to the king here?" asked Lev as if she were talking to a young child.

Sartan stared at her wondering what was really going on inside her head before hesitantly replying with, "Yes, of course. The oldest, Ferran, is twenty one."

The king must've typed it in as he tapped on the screen. He then asked Lev, "Wait! The oldest of these fugitives is only twenty one, and they all committed mass genocide?"

Lev quickly replied, "Yes those are the unfortunate circumstances we are currently dealing with."

"You really have let the Fire Empires fall apart haven't you Lev?"

"Silence Herton! You have but one kingdom to focus on. I have ten kingdoms and three separate empires to rule over. Lest we forget that eight of those kingdoms are not even kingdoms within the Leo Empire, and six of those have yet to realize I am their new secular liege!" exclaimed Lev as she nearly stood up out of her seat. "My domestic issues squelch the microscopic troubles you have within your kingdom, Herton, and the fact that I am even here and not fixing things within one of my three empires is a bigger issue than both of those combined."

"No need to get so fiery Lev. I understand. We all have problems to deal with. Can I get the info on the rest of them then?" asked the king as his gaze rolled over itself once before making it back to Sartan. "First names, last names, ages, appearances."

"Caleb. He is the youngest at eighteen…I believe. He is short, chubby with the curliest, blonde hair you'll ever see. He has pale skin and a flat face with no facial hair whatsoever," said Sartan slowly. The more he spoke the slower his words came out. He realized what he was doing, and after Lev claimed they committed mass genocide he knew that things wouldn't end well when she catches them. It was almost as if he had become the narc that he hated dealing with while on the streets, but if he was going to be there with Lev and possibly assist with Ferran's demise is it really considered snitching? After all, Sartan didn't run off to the police. A stronger individual appeared and decided to help him if he helped her. It just so happened that they both shared a common goal...or a common enemy.

"Alrighty Sartan, what about the other two?" asked the king as he finished the warrant for Caleb. "And I still need more info on Ferran."

"I don't know Ferran's last name, but I remember him having brown hair. He was average height with green eyes, and he was wearing black sweatpants the last time I saw him. He never frowned, but there was rarely ever a smile on his face either. He isn't chubby like Caleb, but he isn't really that thin either. I suppose there was a bit of stubble on his face too, and he was slightly tanned."

"Okay what about the other two then?" asked the king without moving his eyes away from his screen. "Do you know their last names?"

"I do not, but I do know that Ferran is the brother of Aqila," replied Sartan.

"Perfect. Tell me more about this Aqila."

Sartan hesitated, long enough for the king to actually look up from his screen. Sartan then felt the guilt run through his stomach as he said, "Aqila is twenty. She...is black haired…black and thick eyebrows. Long black hair, but then again she is quite short. She isn't chubby like Caleb, but she seemed very fit. Just like Ferran she was kind of tan, if not more than him."

"I see. Now do you remember what any of these people were wearing?"

"I do not. I'm sorry," said Sartan as he wondered if he had just made a mistake.

"No need to be sorry Sartan," said Herton as he tapped away on his screen. "Can you tell me about that fourth fugitive?"

"Yeah...the last one is Jaako. He is nineteen, and has white, blonde hair. Kind of like Caleb's except it isn't curly and it's way whiter. I do remember that he was wearing white robes, but that might've just been the fashion of towns in the Great Desert. I doubt he is still in the same clothing right now."

A brief second of frantic tapping passed as King Herton wrote away on his screen. He then asked, "Sartan, is there anything else that might help us find them?"

"Not that I can think of," replied Sartan slowly. "Actually...Jaako has a tattoo on his forearm."

"Which arm?" asked the king instantly.

"I'm not too sure. I just remember it being on one of his arms. It was a long, black arrow with a tiny black line going through the middle of it," replied Sartan slowly as he tried to remember the tattoo.

"The Sagittarius symbol?" asked Lev who was now staring deep into Sartan's soul.

"I don't know," answered Sartan. "It is just an arrow with a short, perpendicular line going through the middle."

Sartan watched as Lev glanced back over to the king to say, "A tattoo of the Sagittarius symbol."

"Alright, is that everything?" asked the king.

"I think so," answered Lev without letting Sartan speak.

"Okay, so I have the descriptions for your fugitives written up. I'll have a detective gather more information from Sartan on their faces soon, and then an associate will work on creating a digital image for them based on what Sartan said they looked like. Now is there anything else you need from me Lev?" asked the king as his monitor fell back into the black obsidian desk.

"Actually there is," replied Lev. "I'm going to require transportation, your two detectives and a bit of capital to make sure we can keep on the chase. I'll pay you back of course."

The king pulled out a small, thin piece of glass that instantly lit up. He tapped it twice before taking it up to his head. Within an instant he spoke into it,

"Hey, can you get me two detectives--scratch that. Summon my best two detectives to my quarters right now?...Yes I'm sure...Well I don't care if they are asleep, they are paid on salary not hourly!...Fine just make sure they get here ASAP." The king then put the phone back into the hidden compartment in the desk from which it came and said, "We have two detectives on their way to us right now. Here is five-hundred. Spend it wisely Lev. I know you've had your struggles when it comes to budgeting."

Lev took the cash out of his hand while rolling her eyes, "Nonsense. What about our transportation?"

"I have two squad cars in the garage that are full of gas right now waiting for you."

"That won't be fast enough. Do you have anything that is not ground dependent?" asked Lev.

"Of course I do! I'm the King of the North Genillian Kingdom. Who do you think I am? A baron of some Earth city?" laughed King Herton as he leaned back in his chair. "On the roof is a helicopter. Just like the squad cars she is filled up to the brim with fuel, but the only difference is you will need a pilot."

"That would be preferred," said Lev as a smirk snuck across her face.

The king pressed a few buttons on his phone once more before it magically disappeared back into a drawer in his desk. He then yawned out, "Your pilots will be on the roof by the time you get there. The detectives might beat you to the roof as well, and I will have your wanted posters ready for distribution by tomorrow morning, assuming of course the detectives get with Sartan for further detailing."

"Excellent!" exclaimed Lev.

"It is going on eleven-thirty though, so I do wish to call it a day if you feel the same," said King Herton as he slowly stood up while making lots of groaning and bone crackling sounds. "Don't worry about the money. You need it way more than I do right now. All---"

"What do you mean I need it way more than you do?" exclaimed Lev in confusion.

"Just take the money, and don't worry about it," said the King while rolling his eyes.He had placed a wad of cash on the desk, but Lev refused to grab it until he explained himself. "All I ask of you is to please not get my citizens roughed up too much, and that even goes for the detectives and pilots. I know that you don't need to eat or sleep since you're an Active Zodiac, but they will require such basic needs. Try not to forget this again on your journeys Lev."

"Of course not Herton," replied Lev hastily as she decided to grab the cash. "I have a time frame I must squeeze through, so try to rest well my old friend."

Lev stood up and made her way out of the office without any other words and without waiting for the king's reply. She left Sartan sitting in his seat, and by now he was just looking around confused.

King Herton said, "If I were you I'd catch up with her. She usually doesn't wait around too long, especially when she has loose ends on the run."

"What do you mean by loose ends?" asked Sartan as he slowly stood up from the leather seat.

"These fugitives surely have something she wants, or they have done something that she wants nobody to know about. Even if they did commit mass genocide, which I presume is her cover up, Lev wouldn't chase them into Blizenci's land without permission," whispered the king as he looked through the open door. "Lev is a very busy woman, so these young fugitives the two of you are chasing must be causing extremely disruptive problems for her and in large quantities at that."

"What is she going to do when we catch them?" asked Sartan as the two of them slowly made their way out of the office.

"That's a question for her my friend, but let's just say that their families will not be happy. That is if their families even find out," replied the king with a whisper as he began closing the door to the office behind him. "Now run off before she leaves you here! I wouldn't put it past her."

Sartan didn't reply, but instead walked very quickly through the building. When he passed the receptionist she was on the phone yelling at somebody, and when he made it into the hallway he could see Lev standing in the elevator about to press a button. He ran down the beige, marble-floored hallway reaching out for the elevator doors as they began to close. Just in time he grabbed them before they closed. As they slid open again Lev stared at him scornfully.

"We are on a schedule here, Sartan. Try not to slow me down."

"Well the king was talking to me as if the conversation was still goi--"

"I don't want to hear your excuses. I didn't ask you any questions," stated Lev boldly as she pressed the button that would bring them to the roof. "We will be required to cover quite a bit of land over a very immediate window. I am hoping these detectives are already on the helicopter. If not, we will be leaving them behind."

"Your patience is very low isn't it Lev?" asked Sartan once the doors to the elevator closed completely this time. "You didn't even sleep at all on the way to this city did you?"

"Is this a rhetorical question?" asked Lev without looking away from the door. "You do realize that if I had slept as much as you did we would be nowhere near this very elevator yet? You should be thanking me for dragging you along in your sleep."

"What about that farmer's blue truck?"

"What about it?"

"He said that he wouldn't be able to sell his harvests without it."

"And? He was a loyal Leo who supported his Zodiac without question. Even if I wanted to I wouldn't be able to return the vehicle. That would set us back another few days," said Lev as the elevator came to an abrupt stop. "He sacrificed himself for the greater good of this world, and his loyalty to me most likely will not be forgotten any time soon."

"I...I suppose it is only January. It's not like he is going to be harvesting any time soon," replied Sartan as he watched the doors open slowly.

"Exactly, when the time is right he will be rewarded for his loyalty to me. If he is still alive after I capture these fugitives then we will go get him a brand new truck," said Lev while she began walking out of the elevator onto the windy roof. "All I ask of my subjects is their absolute loyalty."

Sartan followed her out of the elevator, but had to scream in order to keep the conversation going over the howling winds, "Isn't that what all the Zodiacs ask for though?"

"That's all that the Zodiacs truly need from their subjects," yelled Lev as the two of them made their way up a staircase leading to the helipad. The helicopter's rotors were already spinning uncontrollably, and there was already one of the detectives seated with his feet dangling next to the landing skids. "This is simply the way of the world Sartan. If you aren't loyal to your own Zodiac then you aren't loyal enough to be trusted by anyone."

Sartan didn't reply to Lev. It was partly because he didn't know how to but also because she had already begun speaking with the detective onboard the helicopter. As they got closer to the helicopter the spinning blades were so loud Sartan couldn't hear anything. The two of them quickly got on board the helicopter, and Lev did not hesitate to close the passenger doors. Once the doors were closed it was a little bit easier to hear things.

"Let's go!" shouted Lev to the pilots in the cockpit.

"What about my partner?" asked the detective who was still rubbing his eyes.

"He isn't onboard, so we are leaving without him!" said Lev as Sartan's ears adjusted to the decreased violence of the blades.

"Right! Where are we going exactly?" shouted a pilot from the cockpit.

"Take us to Garigo," replied Lev with less scream in her voice.

"The Southern capital is quite far away. We may have to refuel at some point," shouted the pilot.

Lev quickly regained urgency in her tone, "Then I suggest we leave now! Full throttle!"

The pilots understood what to do even if Sartan was completely confused as to what was happening. The helicopter abruptly took off and began to float upwards off the already high skyscraper. Sartan looked out the window to see straight down to the cold city below. Hundreds of lights moved and glistened on the streets below, but the vast distance between Sartan and the ground made sightseeing quite difficult after the dizziness started to hit. Instead of letting himself get so dizzy he threw up, Sartan glanced around the black, leather passenger seats, most of which were abandoned, to see the young detective white knuckling the seat belt that held him down to the chair. On the other side of the roomy helicopter sat Lev who stared out of her window.

Sartan could only imagine what she was thinking at the moment. *What does an Active Zodiac even think about anyways? World domination? Taking over all of the late Fire Zodiac's Empires? Catching Ferran? It's probably all three to be honest, but she said all she wants from her subjects is loyalty. All she wants from anybody is loyalty, and I know for a fact I'm not her subject. She surely would've said something about it by now, or I would've felt the pains of her month of detriment. Why am I still here then? If she was the cold hearted killer Aqila claimed she was, why hasn't she cut me off now that I've helped her as much as I can? Unless there is still something that she wants from me...still something that I can be used for. Does she really hold up on promises? I just want to see Ferran suffer.*

"Lev, do you think that this Leucemie you told me about really could've survived all these years?" asked Sartan over the loud blades of the helicopter. She didn't reply. Lev continued to stare out her window as if she didn't hear him, and the detective looked around with obvious confusion crawling about him. "Lev--"

"I'm positive she will be fine, Sartan!" exclaimed Lev as she scowled upon turning to face him. "She is a water sign so as long as her mind isn't broken there is no way she'd die. You have to keep your side of the deal though. I told you everything I knew about her, so you have to stop asking me certain questions relating to my history."

"I'm not asking you questions about your history," argued Sartan. "In fact I don't think I ever did. I just was wondering how all of the Zodiacs ended up dying."

"That had nothing to do with me," replied Lev.

"I never said it did. I was just wondering--"

"Well stop wondering. I held up my side of the deal, so you must hold up yours. When we catch these fugitives I'll consider pointing you in the direction of Leucemie, and once you find her she can help you with your brainwashing. After that you'll come back to me, and we'll work things out from there! If you fail to catch these fugitives though..."

"You didn't hold up your side of the deal though because I just learned something about this Leucemie person that I never knew, so that means you didn't tell me everything you knew about her," argued Sartan as he realized how dangerous the game he was playing truly was.

"How was I supposed to know you were unaware of her watery, June birthday? Did Ryby himself brainwash you?" replied Lev rhetorically.

"What?" asked Sartan who now was confused.

"Nevermind that, but I'm sure that you didn't tell Herton everything you knew about our fugitives! The more you tell me about our fugitives the more I'll tell you about your Leucemie. Do you understand Sartan?"

"Yes, but why haven't you killed me yet? Why do you still want to keep me around?" asked Sartan as he tried his hardest to keep his voice steady and to keep the nerves from expressing themselves.

Lev instantly replied with, "Why does this group have both the Sagittarius Gemstone and the Libra Gemstone? Why did our fugitives create a new Active Sagittarius Zodiac?!"

"They didn't!" exclaimed Sartan.

Lev stopped. After a brief hesitation she replied with, "Wait what?"

"Jaako isn't an Active Zodiac. We didn't have the Sagittarius Gemstone, so we had to use the Aries Gemstone instead. He is only an inactive Sagittarius Zodiac."

"Well that is quite good news Sartan," replied Lev without screaming for once. "So our fugitives merely have the Aries Gemstone, but not the Sagittarius Gemstone?"

"Correct."

"Well if that is the case then why didn't they create a new Aries Zodiac? Or even Libra?"

Sartan took no time to think about the reply for Lev's question. He quickly stated, "I don't know why Aqila didn't try to become an Active Aries Zodiac because she herself is an Aries, but I do know why they didn't start with Libra."

"And why is that?"

"Because the Libra Gemstone was mine. They didn't even meet me until they got to Dursnia, and I think they started all the way in some small town in the Aries Empire."

"So they started in what used to be the Aries Empire, and went all the way to Dursnia instead, why would they do that?" asked Lev who was now more focused on Sartan than the city below them.

"I don't know why they didn't start with Aries, but they went to Dursnia because there was a Tansiq Scroll there," said Sartan as he noticed the detective sitting next to him. The detective had been typing things down on his phone for who knows how long.

"Yes, the Tansiq Scroll to the Sagittarius Palace. They still have it right?"

"They still have it. Don't worry though, I doubt Kozoroh will get too mad if you can't get it to him in time," said Sartan with a smirk on his face.

"WHAT!?!?" exclaimed Lev as a drop of blood escaped her nose. Perhaps it happened when she got angry, or maybe it was just because of her detriment month.

"Is that not why you went to Dursnia in the first place?"

"No, that is not the reason at all! What would make you think such a thing?!"

Sartan smiled before replying with, "Just an assumption. Omar didn't really seem too happy after realizing I read the letter though."

"Your kind is always sneaky!" exclaimed Lev with a snarl on her face.

"I doubt Omar would want to tell you he slipped up."

"I'm pleased that his loose end is tied now, but why didn't you tell me you knew all of this?"

"I just did?"

"You could've told me a long time ago, Sartan!"

"And I'm sure there are things that you could've told me as well," argued Sartan. "It would be hypocritical for you to play the omission of facts card on me."

"My knowledge is not for your simple mind! You know exactly what you need to, whereas I must know everything you know!"

"Well then how are we to help each other Lev?" asked Sartan. He knew that arguing with Lev may end in his death, but after going on for this long he may as well try to win the argument.

"You are so much like your mother, and you don't even realize it," replied Lev with a longing face. "She was definitely one of my favorites."

"One of your favorite what? Business partners? Key-word partners, as in working together. She probably demanded shared information like I am," argued Sartan as Lev's reminiscing smile slowly faded.

"Well...unlike you she had earned that!"

"And how did she do that? I'm willing to tell you everything, but you aren't."

Lev took a moment to reply with, "Do you not value your life?"

"I don't."

"What?" asked Lev who obviously wasn't expecting that.

"Lev, I live on the streets, can't trust anyone, and am currently arguing with the Leo Zodiac who refuses to help me remember my brainwashed past," replied Sartan as he desperately tried not to falter on his front. He knew that if she sensed he was lying his body would go spiraling out of the helicopter's door, and perhaps there was a slight bit of truth sprinkled in his statement as Lev didn't press in the direction he feared she would.

"I've told you numerous times that you'll get to find Leucemie and fix your brainwashing," said Lev with less fury in her voice. "We need you alive. I have grand plans for you, Sartan. All I ask of you is to be willing to work with me here."

"What are those plans then? That's what I was asking to begin with."

"Fine Sartan, I'll tell you the very minute details of what we need you to do," said Lev as she rolled her eyes. "The fact that there is not a single Water Zodiac alive right now is a huge problem. I have decided to turn Leucemie into one, but in order for that to work we need you alive."

"Why Leucemie?"

"Because when we save her from the late Cancer's Palace she will be willing to work with us more than any random water subject that lives on the streets," said Lev, completely unaware that the detective was getting all of this down.

"Won't you have to find a Water Gemstone to do that?" asked Sartan while trying not to look at the detective.

"Yes, but do you not remember the late Cancer killed both Ryby and Stir? She had all of the Water Gemstones on her when she died," said Lev as she zoned out temporarily. "I have all three of the Water Gemstones, so all we would need is a loyal heir."

"You would also need a palace for her," said Sartan.

"Exactly. Leucemie is an heir to Cancer, so we'd have to find her and then the Cancer Palace. Luckily, I am quite positive that she is locked away in the Cancer Palace, so quite literally all we need to do is find the Cancer Palace. After dealing with these fugitives of course."

"Why don't you want to let them create new Zodiacs if that is your plan as well?" asked Sartan as his gaze drifted off to the detective once again. The detective still was writing away on his phone, recording every last word down to the letter.

"We can not let everyday citizens become Zodiacs. That will surely end in a corrupt world governed by serfs. I have decided to become the Firgustus of the Fire Empires. Absolute ruler over the three combined fire lands. This way we can advance as a society in this world much faster."

"Then what about Leucemie?"

"She is to become the Wagustus of all the Water Empires, but only after she has proven herself to be trustworthy to the cause. If there are only four Zodiacs worldwide then we will not have to worry about backstabbing and betrayal as much. I would be able to focus on what is important," said Lev with a smile on her face.

"We have to execute revenge on Ferran first though."

"Speaking of Ferran," smiled Lev as she stared deeper into Sartan's eyes. "How about you tell me everything that happened between you and this group during your last few days with them. I haven't had much time to talk with you about them without worrying about getting to our destination or without you demanding information on my side."

Sartan sighed a heavy, deep breath before gasping, "And I suppose you've told me a few things now. Well where do you want me to start? Furictown? Or when I met Aqila?"

"Start from the very beginning."

He glanced over at the detective, now with much less enthusiasm for him to get every last letter down. Regardless, Sartan held up his side of the bargain by starting with, "Ten days ago, well more like eleven now, I was sitting on a rooftop in Dursnia…waiting for the morning riots…"

Chapter 15
Vigor in a Bottle
Ferran

Many miles away and many days later, Ferran was seated while waiting for the return of his sister and Jaako. They had stopped for gas on their way to Garigo, and the little, beat-down truck that they had stolen from an unaware farmer still managed to run. Merely hours away from their destination at this point, Ferran's legs had grown a mind of their own, shaking uncontrollably. Assuming that they would take a while in the gas station he got out of the truck to stretch them. He quickly glanced over at Caleb who was completely oblivious to his exit, as whatever day dream he was currently enduring engulfed his entire awareness.

Ferran slammed the door shut as he stepped out next to the pump. It was the last day of January, and the four of them have been on the road for nearly weeks. At least that is what it felt like for Ferran. He pulled his knees up to his chest one at a time while balancing himself against the side of the truck. All around the gas station were fields and farm houses scattered between thin roads. A large highway that they had been riding along slithered through the landscape of green and blue just down the street they came off, and by now Aqila and Jaako had come trotting out of the nearby building.

"What took you guys so long?" asked Ferran as he directed the question towards Aqila. As expected, he got no reply from her. For the past few days she refused to say a single syllable to him. Jaako, however, did not hold his grudge for nearly as long.

"We got behind an old lady who paid with nothing but spare change."

Ferran nodded at Jaako as he slowly approached him, and he watched Aqila out of the corner of his eye. She completely avoided his presence all together, heading straight into the truck to sit down next to Caleb. Meanwhile, Jaako had started to pump the gas into the tiny, white truck.

"The people in there thought I was of age!" exclaimed Jaako with a smirk on his face.

Ferran stared at him briefly before replying, "Okay? What does that have to do with anything?"

Jaako then took out a bottle from the bag he was holding in his off hand. The words, *100-Proof* were plastered on the front of the glass.

"How much did this cost?" questioned Ferran. "I literally could have bought that legally!"

"I forgot about that!" laughed Jaako. "Well, it was only forty something wh--"

"Forty for one bottle?!?!" exclaimed Ferran while the gas pump began to slow down.

"Not exactly. It was forty for two bottles," said Jaako as he put the bottle back into the paper bag with a few clanks.

"We only have so much money! We can't be spending it on useless things like alcohol!"

"It isn't useless. We need this. After all, why can't we celebrate for making it this far?"

Ferran sighed before glancing at Aqila who was quietly sitting in the truck. He then whispered to Jaako, "How long has she been out of her medicine?"

"It's been a about a few days now. She was begging me to get her a bottle to numb the pain in her leg, but I don't trust her with a whole bottle," whispered Jaako as he put the pump's nozzle away inside the machine.

"Wait, if you don't trust her with one bottle why did you get two?" asked Ferran while Jaako closed the gas cap.

"Look! It's been over ten days since I've relaxed a bit. I need this okay?" whispered Jaako aggressively. "And Aqila needs a little bit for the injury on her leg."

"What injury? The only injury on her leg was from Sartan, and that was over two weeks ago," whispered Ferran as they walked behind the back of the truck. "Aqila has healed since then, trust me. The first few days she couldn't walk without a human crutch, but now she can sprint perfectly fine. She doesn't need anything, but somehow she still ran out of her medicine." Jaako stared off into the flat farmland distance without replying, so Ferran continued, "When was the first time she started talking to you about it because we got that medicine all the way back in Dursnia."

"I don't know. She just mentioned she had leg pains in the store, so I snuck us some drinks."

"Come on Jaako we are almost to Garigo!" shouted Aqila from inside the truck.

Both Ferran and Jaako looked at each other briefly. Jaako then galloped away to the driver seat, and Ferran rolled his eyes before trudging into the truck. Jaako got in the driver seat, and Ferran squeezed in between Caleb and the passenger door. The midday sun beamed down on them heating up the inside of the truck momentarily, but as soon as Jaako would peel off onto a highway the wind would freeze them through the missing window. Not to mention the pure distance South they have traveled will make things much colder now that the equator is literally about a week's worth of driving away. January hasn't been helping them either. They had already traveled through heavy rainfall and, according to Caleb who drove them through a night or two, 'a dicey storm where a tornado nearly ripped through them.'

The fact that Ferran was back inside of the truck made him angry. He no longer could glance out the window to watch the landscape scutter on by as that got boring after the first day or two. There were no car games to pass the time as Aqila ruined those by not responding to anything that he and he alone said, but it didn't matter because after a while the games started to feel childish to him. His legs wouldn't stop jumping around, and the worst part about it was that there was no room in the tiny vehicle for his legs to jump around. The whole traveling thing was getting old for him, especially since they lost the camper back in Furictown. *Lev probably burnt it to the ground when she got there. I don't even remember signing up for this now that I think about it. I kind of just ended up here.* Ferran then looked around at his allies who sat in the truck with him. Caleb had drifted off into a slumber before they had even stopped, and Jaako was hyper focused on the road now that they were trucking along. Aqila was zoning out and shivering like usual, but he knew that soon she'd have to help Jaako navigate as they came into Garigo.

"Who is it that we are supposed to look for again?" asked Ferran as he tried to break the awkward silence. "Some beet guy? Cheat? Donald? Or was he a dominatr-"

"We are looking for a guy named Dominick Kreet. He has nothing to do with cheating or beets, and he has nothing to do with whatever you were about to say," replied Jaako as quickly as possible.

"And he has the Taurus Gemstone right?"

"Yep, we have to steal that from him somehow, but first we have to find him. Before that we have to get to Garigo," answered Jaako without looking away from the road that was speedily merging into an interstate. "We also have to find an heir and the Virgo Tansiq Scroll, but we can leave that up to Aqila and Caleb since they are better with people."

"We certainly can," laughed Ferran as he looked out his windowless window again.

The bushes and trees beside the road blipped by as Jaako accelerated on the highway. Ferran began dozing off into a sleep-like state as he watched and observed the objects quickly pass by. *A leafy tree. A red house. Another batch of leafy trees. An off ramp. A really tall tree. A cop car. Another leafy tree. A wheat field. WAIT!!* Ferran stuck his head out the window and looked behind them. As expected the car had already peeled out onto the highway. Just as he mouthed the first word to tell Jaako the sirens flicked on. They were so loud that they jolted Caleb awake. Ferran really didn't want to deal with this right now, and he quickly realized what Jaako was probably still clueless of.

"We aren't stopping, are we Jaako!?" screamed Ferran over the loud sirens that were steadily growing closer.

"Should I?!" asked Jaako over the ear piercing sirens.

Ferran took no time to reply, "We have alcohol in the car with us, and you are all underage! But more importantly this truck is stolen!" Jaako must not have understood what Ferran said because he slowly began pumping the brakes letting the cop get closer to the back of the truck.

"THAT AS A NO JAAKO!!! GO FASTER!!!" screamed Aqila as she tried to grab the wheel out of his hands. "LOSE THEM!!!"

At this point Jaako obviously understood what to do because the engine nearly exploded with volume. The cop car behind them temporarily began to recede away before an all out chase began. Caleb was frantically looking around, still quite unaware of his situation, and Ferran had no time to explain. Well, he didn't have the mental capacity or the lung strength to scream over the sound of the truck breaking down or the sirens speeding up, but he definitely could explain it in one sentence had he wished.

Ferran attempted to look at the speedometer every once and awhile because from what he saw the police car behind them was not getting farther away at all. The occasional glance he did manage to get when everyone moved out of the way showed the truck slowly accelerating. *80mph. 85mph. 91mph. 98mph.* Eventually, Ferran stopped worrying about the speed at which they were going. *There is no way we lose them. They are in a squad car built to keep up, and we are in a broken down truck that surely can't keep this up for more than another minute.*

That's when it hit him. The scent of something foul assaulted his nostrils, and he wasn't the first to notice it as both Aqila and Caleb already covered their nostrils with their fingers. The burning scent of metal and oil made Ferran certain they were about to die, and it was blatantly obvious Jaako felt the same because the amount of sweat dripping off the newly created inactive Sagittarius Zodiac seemed inhuman.

"JAAKO! SLOW DOWN THE TRUCK IS BURNING!" screamed Ferran over the roars of the engine and exhaust brawling together.

"NO I'VE GOT THIS!!!" exclaimed Jaako as he whipped the car into an offramp.

Ferran desperately held on to the truck's door as they semi-safely took the exit at one hundred miles per hour. Ferran frantically witnessed Jaako make sure the cop behind them was still following. *How can he watch the cop behind us when I can barely even focus on the road in front of us?!?!* Without hesitating Jaako faked out the cop by pulling back onto the highway, missing the cement divider by a mere inch or two. Ferran couldn't even think about looking back to see if the cop was still chasing because he was too focused on making sure he didn't fall out of his passenger window while Jaako tried to get the truck back on all four wheels.

As they barreled over the grassy bumps next to the street Ferran thought it was the end of their journey. He vigorously gripped the outside of his door to keep himself in the truck since there was no seatbelt to do that job for him; Caleb took the only one that still worked and gripped on to it for dear life. Usually this would be fine, but when Ferran glanced out his window to find something better to grip the quickly passing grass was closer to his hand than a mother bird is to her nest. Caleb had begun squishing him, as the two wheels on his side of the truck were the only ones touching solid ground. His instinct for survival threw him around Caleb, and Caleb quickly realized what was about to happen as well.

"JAAKO!!!!!" screamed Caleb as he tried to throw his own body towards the driver's seat.

Jaako's instincts must've kicked in and done something to fix the two wheel issue because Ferran quickly felt himself becoming weightless for an instant. When gravity regained its almighty power, which was almost instantly, Ferran quickly slammed down on Caleb and Aqila. Now with his grip on nothing, he was at the mercy of Jaako's driving. Luckily or rather unluckily, Jaako couldn't do much at the moment, for when Ferran looked out the front window all he could see was the world quickly spinning around in circles…repeatedly. Holding down the vomit as if he was at an amusement park Ferran scrambled to get in his seat again, and as he expected, Jaako didn't wait to take the truck out of neutral when the world stabilized around them.

The moment they stopped spinning on the road, the truck was aggressively thrown into drive, and it squeaked out on the pavement leaving trails of tire marks behind them. Ferran knew it was coming. He could no longer focus on the cop chasing them. He could no longer try to stay inside the vehicle. He could no longer even mouth a word. In fact he couldn't witness the rest of the ride. Before he could do anything like that he threw his head out of the window and threw the rest of his poor man's breakfast up on the pavement that had already begun to zoom by. Not once either. If he didn't close his eyes he might have even been able to see the few chunks of last night's come back up as well.

Eventually, Ferran pulled himself together and was able to focus on his companions' conversations once more. He wiped his mouth dry with the gray sleeve that quickly turned brown, and he glanced back expecting to see the cop still behind them. To his surprise he couldn't see it at all, but that never meant they were in the clear. The sirens still wailed off in the near distance. Wherever the cop was, he was too far to be seen, but not too far to be unnoticed.

"There, take that exit, quick!!!"exclaimed Aqila as she pointed at the next exit on the right.

"I've hardly even passed any cars though!" replied Jaako. "They surely will see us exiting."

"How much longer do you plan on staying on the highway?" asked Aqila aggressively. "If we stay on this path for too long we will surely run into a blockade or a tire strip."

"I know, I know! But this is the fastest way to Garigo!"

"Jaako, that does not matter if we get there in the back of a cop car!"

"Or dead!" exclaimed Caleb as he laughed a laugh Ferran knew was only half jokingly.

Ferran watched as Jaako checked his mirrors quickly before he said,"Okay you've got the atlas right? I think it is in the bag."

"The bag?!?" exclaimed Aqila in response. She frantically looked around the floorboards of the truck. "There is no bag! There is Caleb's backpack and my backpack, but the bag from the store is missing! A bottle is still in here, but the bag is gone!"

Ferran looked back to see if the cop had gained on them any bit, but upon glancing back he regretted everything. In the bed of the truck was a brown paper bag shaking endlessly in the wind. It was rolled up at the very end of the bed stuck to the bed door, and it appeared to have a bottle inside holding it down. A few feet away from it sat the atlas they must have bought at the gas station. The wind threw that around just as mercilessly, and the tiny window in the back of the truck was the only explanation Ferran could think of for this reindeer game the atlas had played.

"How badly do you guys need the atlas?" asked Ferran as Jaako swerved into the oncoming exit lane. "Can we get to Garigo without it?"

"I don't know where I am!" exclaimed Jaako as sweat dripped down onto the ripped up, rubber steering wheel. "We need it in order to get to Garigo!"

"Calm down Jaako. Calm down," insisted Ferran.

"I'm trying Ferran!" yelled Jaako while he swerved a hard right off the highway.

"We still have the atlas!" screamed back Ferran while he tried to keep his entire body from slamming into Caleb again. "It's just a matter of how we are going to get it."

Jaako did not look up from the road. Instead he wiped sweat off his brow while quickly saying, "I thought you said we have it!"

"We do," said Ferran as Caleb pushed him back a little. Ferran looked at Caleb angrily before respecting his need for personal space. "I don't know how but it is in the bed of the truck."

"What?!" asked Jaako as he accelerated down a country road.

"Look in the bed of the truck!" replied Ferran.

"I'm driving! Let me focus!" exclaimed Jaako as he ironically glanced into the rear view mirror.

The tuck hastily sped up and passed a whole forest of trees before getting back to what felt like lots more farmland. Ferran decided not to bother Jaako while he was driving and glanced out the passenger window. For hundreds of thousands of miles farmlands stretched onward without ceasing. Tired of the same sight for the past chunk of days, Ferran looked out the front window to see the same exact sight but all the way to the opposite horizon. Angered, Ferran looked to his left to complain about the agrarian centered economy of the South Genillian Kingdom to his friends, but before he could finish his first sentence he saw it. In the far, far distance, past Jaako's rolled up window, hundreds of light gray skyscrapers contrasted with the light blue sky. A few pitch black skyscrapers became outliers from the rest, one of which towered over all others.

"I don't think we will need an atlas anymore," said Caleb calmly as he smiled over at Ferran.

Jaako kept his eyes on the road when he exclaimed, "I don't know where I am!"

"And on your left you will see the ancient city of Garigo," taunted Caleb as he pretended to be a pilot on a first class flight over rarely seen geographical amazements. "Merely miles away from us, hundreds if not thousands of skyscrapers will tower over tens if not hundreds of millions of people. Most of which are subjects to Gemini."

"Who are you kidding Caleb, there can't be that many people in Garigo," laughed Aqila as she glanced over at the city too.

"No, but there will be way more people there than the pocketed gas stations we have seen on the way from Dursnia," said Jaako as he took a brief second to look at the city too.

Ferran tried his hardest to ignore his allies for a quick second. He tried his hardest to listen to the silence between their happy words. After a few attempts he made his conclusion. "I've got even better news!" he exclaimed as he finally came to his conclusion.

"I don't know Ferran, we've been on our way here ever since Furictown," joked Caleb without looking away from the distant city and its modern towers. "Nothing can really beat the sight of Garigo right about now."

"I don't hear any sirens any more do you?" asked Ferran with a slight smile on his face. The whole car went silent as everyone tried to listen to their pursuers.

"Finally!" exclaimed Jaako. "We are in the clear!"

"I would not say that just yet Jaako," began Aqila with a bit of disappointment on her face. "We still have Lev who is probably not even minutes away."

"Stop it Aqila!" exclaimed Caleb. "You are always so worried about Lev catching up to us. You haven't even seen her since before Furictown. How are we going to know if she is still chasing us?"

"This is Lev we are talking about Caleb!" argued Aqila while sitting up in her seat. "She was in Dursnia when Jaako became Sagittarius, so she surely would have heard and or seen the shockwave."

"Wait, there was a shockwave?" asked Jaako who had a gleamy smile plastered above his chin.

"Yes Jaako, how do you not remember this? You were literally at the very center of it all," replied Aqila with a slight laugh.

"I didn't know that happened," said Jaako as he finally started to decelerate the truck. "All I remember is everything quickly going white for what felt like an eternity."

"I am here to tell you that things were a lot more intense than that," said Aqila with a smile.

Ferran broke the lighthearted conversation, "So, when are you going to take a left and start heading towards Garigo? It isn't like we've been anticipating getting there forever or anything."

"You actually anticipated getting to Garigo?" asked Jaako while slowing the truck down even more. "I didn't think you anticipated anything good."

"I anticipate the end of Aqila's silent treatment," said Ferran with a blank face.

Everyone glanced at Aqila who looked away from Ferran while pretending to still be in awe at the large city across the fields. There was nothing but winter wheat for as far as the eye could see, with the exception of the city and a few random tree patches. The cloudless, blue sky bounced off the light, green plains, and the dusty gray roads formed a gridlike pattern in every direction. A few random farm houses were scattered on the roads, but the majority of the land was vacant. Through their whole journey they had been doing this. They never went to the major cities, but instead they brought this tattered down truck all over country roads and highways to get this far. *In fact, the largest city that I had ever been to would probably be Hapopelma back in the Great Desert. That city seemed so small compared to the behemoth that awaits us. If this is the capital of the Southern Genillian Kingdom, I could only imagine how large the capital of the entire Genillian Empire is. I wonder what is going on back in Mirisburg. That town is so small, so who actually cares anyway. I hated it there. Glad I'm gone. Not to mention that--*

Suddenly, Jaako threw the truck into a hard left which nearly put them on two wheels, again. The tires screeched as everyone held on for dear life. Unlike last time however, Jaako overcorrected the truck. This time the whole truck went spiraling out of control into the wheat fields. Ferran gripped Caleb's seatbelt after learning the hard way his door was not a safe handlebar, and this time, instead of watching chaos ensue in front of him, Ferran closed his eyes and hoped that Jaako wouldn't kill them. *He has twenty twenty vision if not bette--HE HAS NIGHT VISION! And he still doesn't know how to drive!*

When Ferran felt the car come to an abrupt, slam-filled stop after spinning, rotating and what he could easily argue was flipping over itself, Ferran slowly opened his eyes to see that wheat and grass had been mopped all over the front window. The truck had managed to end up in the ditch. The very front part of the hood was not visible as it was beneath so much wheat and grass, and the headlights surely were a foot or two under the dirt. Jaako's head rested on the steering wheel that had failed to shoot out an airbag, and Ferran had a sinking feeling that not even Caleb could get them out of this situation. It was at that very moment that Ferran could smell it. The same scent that he smelled when the truck was testing itself at one hundred miles per hour assaulted his nostrils once again. However, this time the scent was much stronger and more metallic. Before he could cover his nose or comprehend what Aqila had screamed, Ferran saw a small flicker of light within the air vents.

"GET OUT!" screeched Aqila the very moment Ferran saw the first spark hold on long enough to become a weak flame.

Jaako was the first out because Ferran could hear him swing his door open as he struggled with his own. He kept jerking the handle hoping it would open without any luck. He felt Caleb thrashing in his seat next to him, and from what Ferran heard the seatbelt was winning the fight against Caleb. He couldn't say anything though because the door was winning the fight against him. He felt a droplet of sweat land on his forearm after struggling with the handle long enough for Aqila to jump out after Jaako. The weak fire that had sparked to life inside the engine quickly grew to a steady flame, and this flame was steadily heating up. At this point he was about to go through the window to get out of the explosive death trap he found himself in when Caleb tapped on his shoulder aggressively.

"Ferran!" shouted Caleb with a red, sweaty face. "I'M STUCK!"

Ferran looked down at Caleb's seatbelt to see Caleb's chubby fingers persistently pushing down on the red button that should be setting him free. The harder he pushed the further it went in, but when Caleb removed his fingers the button didn't fall back. Ferran didn't understand how that wasn't freeing him though. Regardless, Caleb's worried face had begun to drip sweat-mingled tears. With no other options Ferran quickly tapped down his pockets looking for the pocket knife he always kept on him. The left one was empty. The right one had his wallet. *THE KNIFE ISN'T IN MY LEFT POCKET?!?!*

"HEY!" shouted Ferran to whoever was listening. "I NEED A KNIFE!"

Ferran stuck his arm out his window waiting for someone to get him a knife as he watched the flames in the air vents steadily grow. *Why didn't Jaako turn the truck off! It is still running! And what is taking so long for a knife?!* Ferran tried to glance out the back window without breaking his neck. He saw Jaako running around the back side of the truck, but he couldn't see Aqila anywhere. *I know Aqila has a knife! Where the hell is she?! I swear if I die because she is still holding a grudge over Sartan-*

"Here!" exclaimed Jaako as he placed a knife in Ferran's hand.

Without thinking or thanking, Ferran instantly took the blade to Caleb's seatbelt. All of the squirming Caleb had begun doing didn't make things easy either, and by now there were large flames shooting out of every air vent in the truck. He glanced away from cutting for a mere second to see flames coming out of the hood now. *The truck is going to blow! It is going to explode!* There was nobody who would argue with that statement, and the second Caleb's seatbelt snipped Ferran began throwing himself out the window. There was an air vent right next to the window that was not hesitant in roasting Ferran's side while he tried to crawl out, and by the time he was half way out of the window he heard it. A high pitched squeal had begun ringing somewhere under the hood. What it was or how it started was beyond him. All he needed to know was that he needed to get away from it. Fast. That's exactly what he did after barely catching himself from landing face first into the wheat.

He stood up and didn't look back until he ran the first five feet. Upon looking back the entire hood was engulfed in flames, and Caleb was just now crawling out of the driver's side. Certain he was about to watch Caleb get blown to shreds, Ferran refused to gaze any longer and looked forward while running as quickly as his body would allow. With every step the world felt cooler, and he would not stop running until he felt his side hurting. Well, that is what he planned on. After about twenty yards he tripped on the crops and landed face first into some wheat. Quickly scrambling to gain his feet again, Ferran glanced back to see quite some distance from the truck and quite some distance from his friends as well.

Ferran blinked. When his eyes opened the truck was no longer intact, and his eardrums took a slight hit from the explosion. Shrapnel and parts of the vehicle flew all over the barren field. Glass and chunks of metal then began raining down all around the ditch Jaako drove into. While falling from the sky the debris glistened as the sun bounced off it. Ferran's mouth slowly dropped while he took in the sight, but when the first few chunks of shrapnel and glass began landing in the dirt next to him, the sight quickly became less entrancing. He stepped backwards from the explosion without removing his allies from his field of vision. Ferran watched the rest of his friends regroup on the other side of the street far from the incident. The debris stopped falling from the sky, and Ferran trudged through the dewy field to his friends, grabbing one of the pricey bottles that survived the blast on the way.

Upon finally meeting them in the road next to the explosion, Ferran was equally surprised and relieved. Neither Aqila nor Caleb had any major damage done to their bodies. There were a few cuts and bruises on Caleb, but they both would survive. Jaako was fine. All that was left of the truck was a thin strip of the bed, a singular, half melted tire and many chunks of debris all in the ditch. They had to find another way to the city, but luckily Garigo was in sight at this point.

The entire group stared at the ditch where a few small flames nibbled the field before Aqila spoke out, "Why? Why Jaako? Why?"

"I didn't mean to!" exclaimed Jaako as he patted out the few flames that had yet to go out.

"Well, now we have to walk," moaned Ferran while turning to face the city. The city itself could be seen, but Ferran knew that if they wanted to reach it by nightfall they would have to begin the dreaded hike towards it now…and while walking faster than usual.

"At least it isn't that far," said Jaako optimistically.

Aqila spun around and exclaimed, "That far!? We could still have a vehicle if you knew how to drive, but no you crashed into a ditch for literally no reason!"

"Hey now," argued Jaako.

"Let's start walking so we can reach it before sundown," said Ferran as he glanced at the city on the horizon again.

"It won't take us that long to get there," said Jaako while walking past Ferran. "The city can only be, what a few miles away?"

"Did you guys have anything important in the truck though?" asked Caleb without glancing away from the debris. "I know that at least two of you left your bags in there. Then there were the groceries."

Ferran held up the bottle pointing to it with wide eyes. He stared at Caleb momentarily before responding with, "This is Jaako's fault. All we have to our name now is the cash in our pants and a tall bottle of...JORGLES! What the hell even is JORGLES!?"

"How is it my fault you left your stuff in a burning truck?" argued Jaako.

"And how is it my fault that you put me in a burning truck?" snapped back Ferran.

"JUST STOP!" shouted Aqila. "It is obvious we have nothing to our names now. Not like we did to begin with."

"So you're done with my silent treatment now?" taunted Ferran.

Aqila glared past Ferran ignoring his question and avoiding his eye contact. She replied, "I have the stones. We have the strength to make it to Garigo. Once we make it there we can find ways to survive the long term."

"You're just going to ignore me I see!" exclaimed Ferran in a fit of rage. "You know what Aqila, I will just do the same then!"

And with that Ferran began trotting down the road towards the not so distant city of Garigo. The looming sun was definitely past its peak in the sky as Ferran's shadow was long enough to nip at Aqila's feet even after many long, vigorous steps. He knew that they would follow. It was part of their plan to get to Garigo and whatever the hell they needed to do after that, so they would follow him, eventually. It didn't matter to him if he got there before them. More time to be alone. More time to think. More time to breathe, for Ferran was drowning from carrying their responsibilities.

Murdering Sartan might have been a mistake. It might have been rash and emotional. Had Aqila learned how to puppet him then I wouldn't have needed to do it, but then again would things be more stable with him still here? They surely aren't now. There is no way he would've stayed with us this long though. Especially if I refused to treat him as an equal.

He is of the past now. There is no need to worry about him. Aqila is still here, and it is obvious that she is in more need than he ever has been. Why didn't she just tell me though. There was no need to hide it. It wasn't as if I'd never find out eventually.

Ferran walked across the first lonely four-way stop without even looking up from his feet. As the sun beamed orange droplets over him he continued to think. The large power pylons that seemingly crept up from nowhere were now walking next to him, and they ran across the hundreds of acres of fields all the way into the distance. A rabbit hopped around in the ditch across the street, but Ferran was still unbothered by it all. His mind swamped with concerns of Aqila and if she was strong enough to continue with their goals. Whether or not she cared about him. How much she truly cared about Sartan. Whether or not she still respected him as an older brother. And most importantly, whether or not he should even worry about these issues in the first place.

The thinking was getting him nowhere though. As his mind tackled the problems he was faced with, those same problems stood around open armed inviting the tackle. They would change the rules of the game entirely until he wasn't even playing football anymore. Now the problems had been tackled by his mind, but they rolled on top and began pinning his thought process for a win in an unfairly rigged wrestling match.

Ferran quickly realized that his troubles would only stress him more as he tried to solve them. The only way to be at peace was to simply not think about that. To internalize the issues for a moment, hopefully until they disappear. They weren't as easy to kill as his Sartan problem, unfortunately. He glanced up from his toes for the first time since his mind went off on a tangent. The first thing to attack his eyes was that he was closer to the city than he was closer to his friends. In fact, upon checking his six, Aqila and the rest of them were nowhere to be seen. They surely had started walking to the city by now, and there was no way a wild Eveharris caught them this close to a city.

Oh well. Their loss. I will just revive the rest of the Zodiacs without them. Ferran quickly came to the realization that Aqila had the gems required to do that, but the joy he felt when understanding that she had yet to acquire an Earth or Water Gem was childish at the least. An immature notion to think that even though she had made progress she hadn't made exponential results. He made it to a street where the first few cars began to pass by him whether they were coming or leaving the city. *The answer is ahead. I'll just have to recreate Virgo without their help, and if they die then that is Aqila's fault for not respecting me enough. Caleb didn't deserve to die just because of her misguidance though. Actually, he had a choice. He could have followed me like a man with a brian would've done, but no, Caleb stayed with Jaako and Aqila. Why did they stay though? Probably some stupid reason to be honest. I'll just have to carry them and find Domidork or whatever without the...like usual.*

Ferran trekked on with a smile on his face and determination in his pocket, remembering he had vigor in a bottle too. There was no longer a fear of being hunted down by the ravenous, murderous pig that Lev was. She would go after Aqila and Jaako. Ferran looked up to the tall buildings, of which were only a heft jog away. By now the sun was barely strong enough to curve around the Earth and bounce off his glossy eyes. The cars multiplied beside him, and the traffic grew louder as he approached the metropolis.

In his mind, he was struggling with the death of his sister and Caleb, for he knew if he took one more step into the mind-bogglingly enormous city they would never find him. He tried to hold back his feelings, but unfortunately that was never his strong suit. Water welled up inside his eyes. Ferran stared forward coming to a complete stop on the side of the first road that splintered off between buildings.

The fields beside him were no more. Now stood long arrays of grass organized in aesthetically pleasing formations. The rows went on for miles possibly even circling all the way around the city, with openings for roads of course. Each row was a different shade of green. The grass rows furthest away from the city were almost yellow. They were so bright to his eye he couldn't tell if they were naturally lime or just tinted by the setting sun, but the rows of grass further down the road were dark green, possibly even blue. The few pitch black skyscrapers had begun lighting up with golden entrails. Half of the remaining skyscrapers shot out purple lights from their windows. The other half, to Ferran's confused surprise, glowed cherry red. There was not a single skyscraper that had different lighting. The short buildings between the thin titans were all beaming an array of random colors mostly orange and white, but Ferran did notice that the taller buildings all followed three colors: red, purple or gold. The only few buildings with gold lighting were the black ones though.

After regaining his eyes after a quick scenery admiration, Ferran continued down the road. Cars zoomed past him going both ways, and a large sign stood over the entire road. It was mostly for directions telling drivers technicals and such, but Ferran was more focused on the sign above the green, direction-oriented one. An erect, yellow sign hung above the green one. Instead of telling drivers where to go, it told drivers where they were. *WELCOME TO GARIGO* read the top line in black bold letters. Beneath it stood five words in smaller, black text, *THE WORLD'S CAPITAL OF AGRICULTURE.* As the first tear quietly dripped off his chin, his heart panicked to convince him to wait, but once the second tear, and the last, was softly stroked away by a calloused hand, he took the first step into the grand city.

Ferran, young and alone, decided to do what his sister had been doing secretly over the past few weeks or so, numb his pain beyond the ability to differentiate between reality and fiction. Tonight that would be easy. He wanted it more than Lev wanted to catch him and his friends. He wanted to forget for just one night, JUST ONE, everything that has happened to him recently. In the world's capital of agriculture there surely would be some mind altering foods to try. Scratch that, Ferran would take mind altering anything, and by the sheer size of the city, finding that would be easier than finding an actual job. With a crack the bottle popped as the cap fell on the ground. Fizzy vapors floated over the lip of the glass, and Ferran threw back the bottle, beginning his first night in the new city.

Chapter 16
United in Isolation
Sartan

Fluffy white clouds rolled past him. Sartan leaned back in his chair and gazed out of the tinted window to see the endless waves of the Acian Ocean to the East kiss the endless sky above it. The bright midday sun was a sign of spring growing nearer, a welcome change. The end of January reminded him that the Earth was spiraling closer towards the sun everyday. Then there was Lev. Lev was transformed into an entirely new person overnight. Yesterday, when Sartan helped her parade the streets looking for Ferran and the others, everything was normal. Today however, for the brief moment he saw her, she was entirely different.

Apparently, Lev's skin was a bit pale previously due to her month of detriment, but now that it was February all of her ailments vanished. Her skin gained even more color and a bit of shine making it comparable to obsidian, but color didn't explode just in her skin. Lev's hair, lips, eyes, recently gaunt face, practically everything Sartan could imagine had blossomed with flavor, and he saw her briefly only ten minutes ago when he was called to the office. Her malnourished form massed away to create a slightly more feminine stature that must have been taken from her at the start of January. The arthritic hands, rotten teeth, and even her mangled legs had respectively straightened, whitened, and thickened with muscle. Lev's ribcage was no longer visible, and there was no trace of blood under her nose anymore. Regardless, the Active Leo Zodiac no longer appeared to be on the verge of death at every given moment. Sartan knew from first hand experiences that she was capable of causing lots of damage in her previous condition, so he could only imagine what kind of powers she regained over this past night, let alone what powers she will possess after the last day of June.

"THEN WHAT WOULD YOU DO?!?!" screamed Lev from the other room.

Sartan failed to hold back a cheeky grin as the secretary on her phone call went silent. The secretary looked at Sartan with wide eyes as if she wanted him to react accordingly. However, all he could do is smile and take his gaze back out to the distant ocean hundreds of stories below and an hour of walking away from him. He no longer was wearing the black robes that he wore in Dursnia. Lev had sourced a more fitting uniform for him to wear on their journeys, and of course he didn't care as long as functionality wasn't compromised. The urban-camo, military pants he wore easily had the most pockets he had ever seen in his entire life, and the warm, black jacket that Lev claimed she had more of was great at fighting the wind. With his back to the office Lev was arguing brutally in, Sartan peacefully, taking a sip of his water while watching the many skyscrapers hover below him, realized that Lev was going to catch Ferran for him. There was no way that a handful of young adults with no military history or connections could escape an Active Zodiac known for hunting down its prey.

"YOU HAVE THEM ALL ON YOU?!?!" screeched a woman from the other side of the wall that Sartan's head currently rested on. "YOUR LIEGE WOULD KILL YOU IF HE KNEW THAT!!!"

"WELL DO YOU WISH TO INFORM HIM NOW?!?!?" snapped back Lev without hesitation.

Lev rarely spoke of her liege to Sartan, so naturally he was now suddenly as intrigued as the secretary was. *Kozoroh must be in loose communication with her because she hasn't spoken with him the entire time I've been helping her. I don't understand how he is both her and Blizenci's liege though. He isn't even an Active Zodiac right now while both of them are.*

"Does he know you have any of them?" asked the woman on the other side of the wall with much less aggression in her tone this time.

"He is aware that I scavenged Ryby's gem when Canc---killed him, but I told Kozoroh------Stir nor Cancer had their Gemstones on----when---," whispered Lev so quietly Sartan was only able to pick up a few phrases. "Shall I grant----oy his own-----iac's----tone or not?"

There was a brief moment of silence in the other room before the Queen of the South offered her opinion very quietly, "If I were you----give the boy his----iac's Gemstone nor one----isn't."

"I have to get rid of one! Now that it is the month of Pisces the energy is already overwhelming. It's making the other ones quite energetic as well!" exclaimed Lev loud enough for him to hear perfectly.

"Well can you really trust him to hold onto it? What if he loses it or uses it against you? If he tries you'd be the one that armed him," replied the Queen. "Do you want to give him the virus, the theoretical parasite, or the antibody to both?" Sartan opened his ears as wide as he possibly could while listening to Lev's response.

"Well what good is a cure if the two most potent ailments are nonexistent?"

"So there is your answer Lev, but how would you explain that to Kozoroh if he finds you with two gemstones that were missing and without the one he thought you had?"

"He won't, and if he does then I'll just lie" whispered Lev from the office room. "If it isn't the boy's Zodiac's Gemstone would it kill him if he uses it?"

"The Active Leo Zodiac coming to me for questions on Zodiacs!"

"I've had no such need to hand out gemstones until now! Just answer my question!"

"He will survive Lev. As long as he is a water sign Ryby's stone won't kill him."

Lev then said to the queen, "I suppose I shall bear the news to our friend before Blizenci arrives."

"Just don't forget that my loyalties lay with Blizenci, not you," replied the Southern Queen.

"I am aware, Adreia. Luckily, I doubt that he will ask you about this specific conversation. Omission of details can come in very handy," said Lev as Sartan heard the doorknob to his right twist.

He quickly jumped forward to regain his relaxed and oblivious posture as he hastily thought of something to say that was unrelated to their conversation. The gray skyscrapers outside of the gold tinted window all had either ultraviolet or neon red lights coming from the windows, and that was all that he needed to distract himself.

When Lev walked towards him, he began the conversation with, "We've been here for nearly five days, and I still don't understand why the gray skyscrapers have red or purple lights inside."

The Southern Queen who trailed behind her was eager to answer his inquiry, "Well sweetie, my skyscraper plantations are the most innovative architectural accomplishments on the planet! They are growing crops. The combination of ultraviolet lights and infrared lights ensure that our crops grow faster and have larger flowering seasons. Our city always has crops in the flowering and growing phase thanks to our skyscraper plantations. I didn't create the world's largest agricultural city by accident."

Sartan gazed over to the Queen. Unlike with the King of the North, the Southern half of the Genillian Empire was ruled by a queen. Her silky black hair fell down her spine, and the matte orange paste on her thin lips contrasted the yellow robes of royalty that glistened in the light. Lots of rings, bracelets and necklaces covered her body, most of which were purely made of sparkling gems. The queen's shiny, bright colors were reminiscent of the bright, yellowing sun. Her small face stared deeply back at Sartan, and her mouth hung half open as she waited for Sartan's response with an anticipating smile. There were faint wrinkle marks popping up on her face, and Sartan was nearly blinded by the large golden crown that rested on her head.

Before Sartan could reply, the secretary across the bright, airy room interrupted, "Master, your Blizenci is currently in the elevator on the way up to our office."

Both Lev and the queen stared at each other intensely. Lev quickly pulled out a small purse from under her shirt. The purse itself was so small Sartan didn't think there would be anything in it but a few pencils at the maximum. When she zipped it open with shaky hands a fluorescent, cyan light beamed out onto her skin. Far on the other side of the room, through the hallway leading to the secretary's desk, rang a high pitched ding followed by the sound of large doors squealing open. Lev must've heard it as well because she dropped the small, red purse on the beige-carpeted floor. Right before Sartan's eyes sat three similarly colored, large gemstones. Each one was about the size of a toddler's fist curled up in a ball, and each stone was cut perfectly in a trilliant shape. None of them were in a chassis. They were all lone gemstones. However they were not all the same. The first one that rolled closest to Sartan's foot was a shiny and fluorescent, dark-purple stone with sharp edges just like the other two. The second stone sat merely inches away from the indigo one. It was more of a neon, cobalt blue colored stone that was slightly transparent just like the previous stone. The last gemstone, however, sat next to Lev's feet and was not transparent like the others. It glowed so brightly compared to the others that there was no way one could see through its baby-blue, cyan surface.

Lev quickly grabbed the two that were not glowing as intensely, and when her skin brushed against the stones they instantly fogged up with frothy waves of blue and purple, no longer transparent at all, no longer glowing. As she put the cloudy gems away in her secret pouch footsteps pounded towards them. Lev hid the pouch under her clothing once more after hastily zipping it up, and then she grabbed the remaining stone off the floor. There was a slight, cyan discoloration on the beige carpet after the stone was in her hands, and just like the other two stones, this one frothed up after meeting Lev's palm. The spot where the stone had been sitting was slightly soaked, and the region where the other two stones sat was unaffected. Lev wasted no time in hiding the last stone, but her method of making it disappear was not the best in Sartan's opinion.

"Quick! Hide this in your pocket!" whispered Lev as she held the stone out to Sartan.

Sartan grabbed the stone only noticing that Lev's hands were drenched too late. He saw the red hair on a pale face creep around the corner, and without hesitation he shoved the soaking wet gemstone into his left pocket. He palmed his entire hand around the stone in order to prevent the extreme light from escaping his pocket.

"Welcome Master Blizenci," spoke the secretary gratuitously.

The man waved to her as he passed by her desk staring directly at Lev. His long gray robes covered most of his body, and all of the gold pieces, yellow and orange accents, and gemstone-encrusted buttons on the royal robes did not match his red goatee one bit. The man walked closer as the Southern Queen of the Gemini Empire bowed to him, but now the emperor's two separately colored eyes were focused on Sartan, both the blue and the orange. The gold cane that he held in his left hand matched the large crown that rested upon the top of his head. There were many red rubies plastered on the crown's tips, and a large symbol was erected above all the other parts of the golden headpiece. The symbol was simple. An upward curved line sat at the very top, and it was propped up by two parallel lines. Those two parallel lines were held up by a downward curved line that was connected to the crown by a gold rod in the middle. On the front of the crown, just below the symbol of what Sartan could only assume to be the symbol of Gemini, was a large gemstone, and just like the three Sartan just saw scattered over the floor it was at least ten carats. However, this stone was not cut in the shape of a trilliant. Instead it was cut in a perfect oval and sat in the very center of the young emperor's crown. It was not cloudy, milky or white. This man's stone was transparent as ever, and it shimmered gray in the light. *It is the same shape as the stone I had before Aqila took it.*

"What exactly brings you to my wonderful nation?" asked the ruler who came to a stop in the center of the room.

"We have loose ends to tie…" started Lev who quickly became hesitant to continue. "And we require your assistance in finding them."

"I knew you would come to me for help sooner than later!" laughed the emperor.

"Nonsense Blizenci. I don't need your help, rather prefer it, as it will hasten the process."

"I see…but who is this man? Do you usually not travel lonely?"

Lev sighed, "He is my trustworthy agent, and he plays a vital role in locating a few fugitives that have escaped my paws."

"Trustworthy you say? Vital? Tis a shame you can't kill him is it not?"

Lev quickly replied, "I have no interest in killing Sartan if it is not necessary. He will soon enough play a very---"

"So you have changed," interrupted Blizenci with a sneaky smirk. "Sartan…doesn't really roll off the tongue now does it? Tell me Sartan, do you know why you were named that? What is the history of your name?"

Sartan was caught off guard. He assumed that, like most other conversations Lev has with someone of importance, he would only observe not partake in the conversation, let alone be questioned. He faked a shaky smile as he quickly thought of a story that was reasonably believable, for in reality he had no clue. "My name is…it is just a nor---"

Lev impatiently interrupted, "My agent remembers not of unimportant subjects such as that. I must ask you to leave my agent alone. Any quest---"

"Well then…he remembers not?"

"Precisely…he remembers not of UNIMPOR---"

"Clearly it is deeper than that. Which merely confirms my suspicions."

"Blizenci stop playing these mind games with me!" exclaimed Lev.

"What would Kozoroh do if he knew you had found Sartan?" asked Blizenci. "Would he want you to keep him around, or would he demand you kill him immediately?"

"Kozoroh Smozjoroh! He probably doesn't even know who Sartan is, so why would he want him dead? Not to mention he doesn't know I have found him, so what he doesn't know can't bother him."

"Stop lying to yourself. He knows who he is, and not telling our master of our statuses and advancements within his plan is defiant in nature. We certainly don't want that now do we?"

Lev began to grumble, "He is my liege; you are not. What happens between him and I remains between him and I. If I choose to do something that you wouldn't, you unfortunately have no power to demand a change in my trajectory. You wonder why I rarely visit your empire."

"I don't wonder at all Lev. I already know why you don't, but luckily for you I don't care if you don't like my way of governing. We are allies regardless," replied Blizenci. The Emperor of the Genillian Empire then turned to face Sartan once more. Before Sartan could think of what he would say if asked a question, Blizenci emphasized his current, distracted thought for him, "Are you really in safe hands with Lev here? Is she really here to help you?"

"Seriously Blizenci? Stop messing with my agent!" exclaimed Lev. "I need your help finding a few fugitives, so we can both go back to the current assignments Kozoroh gave me."

"To quote you, 'Kozoroh Smozjoroh'! I'm in my empire, and one of the things he told me to do was make sure that my empire stood strong and stable. The fact that you are here must mean there is some sort of problem somewhere, so I am just determining whether or not it is you…that is the problem. Perhaps my border patrol needs more budgeting?"

"Sartan and I are not here to stay, Blizenci. There is no need to worry about us interfering with your perfect 'population' at all. In fact we are hunting after some aliens that snuck across the border, dangerous ones at that my friend," said Lev as she walked into the office that she recently came out of.

"Perfect! Anything to help get my numbers up!" exclaimed Blizenci in excitement. "You say that the fugitives will end up in my city of Garigo, correct? Why is it that they want to come here?"

Sartan was unsure whether or not Lev would want him to explain. Then he wondered if Lev could answer accurately without insulting the emperor somehow. He quickly decided to say, "There is another fugitive in this city that they are looking for."

"Why would they cross the border just to look for someone? How important is this person?" asked Blizenci as he took a seat in the queen's chair behind a large, white-marble desk.

"He is quite important. They are looking for him because he has a Zodiac's Gemstone, and they know he is in this city," responded Sartan, who was not taking the last seat in the room.

"That would do it," laughed the queen who sat down in a swivel chair next to Lev after trailing behind Sartan.

"Which Zodiac's stone does he possess? Remind me again," said Lev without spinning around in her chair to face him.

"I am sure it is one of the Earth signs, maybe Capricorn or Taurus," said Sartan with uncertainty.

All three of the rulers glanced at each other with wide eyes briefly before Blizenci mustered up some words, "I don't think Maeiz would've gone this far to hide her stone, so I am sure it is the Taurus Gemstone that this man has."

"I agree," spoke Lev. "Kozoroh took Panna's Gemstone to become inactive, so this man must have the Taurus Gemstone."

"Hopefully." whispered the Southern Queen.

"Agreed…" muttered Blizenci to himself. "Welp regardless…we must find this man before our fugitives do. Sartan what are the fugitives going to do once they acquire the stone?"

Sartan wondered momentarily before remembering Aqila's initial purpose back in Dursnia, "Once they find the man and steal the stone, they would go search for the palace."

"The palace?" asked Blizenci. "The Taurus Palace? What are they trying to do? Create a new Zodiac? Regardless, they would have to go all the way to the North, through all of my empire and the wastelands of Aquarius. Then they would have to travel West through Lev's Empire. There is no way they would make it."

"What if they go South though?" asked Lev. "Garigo is almost closer to the Virgo/Gemini border than it is to the coast. If they acquire transport they could probably get to the palace in under a week."

Blizenci exclaimed, "Right! They are going to head South for Panna's Palace. We find the man before them, and then we arrive at the Virgo Palace before them."

"You know its location?" questioned Lev.

"Yes, but do the fugitives know where her palace is? Or will they look for the Tansiq Scroll?" replied Blizenci.

"Well what good is that if they don't know where the stone is either?" asked Lev.

Blizenci replied, "You want to let them get to the palace?"

"I want to be at the palace waiting for them when they get there."

"Wouldn't that just put you behind schedule if we waited for them?" asked Sartan.

"Right, we know that they are somewhere in this very city, if we wanted to ambush them we would need to find them in the first place to show them how to get to the palace," said Blizenci.

"That would put both of us behind schedule quite a bit, and I do not desire explaining this to Kozoroh," said Lev softly. "Where exactly is the Tansiq Scroll, Blizenci?"

"For the Virgo Palace?" asked Blizenci rhetorically. "I took it from her palace back in thirty-one right after---"

"Good we know where it is!" exclaimed Lev as she cut off Blizenci.

"Yeah there is no way that the fugitives can acquire the scroll from my palace," replied Blizenci as both his blue and orange eyes zoned out through the high rise window.

"Then what is your plan, Blizenci?" asked Lev impatiently.

A brief second passed before Blizenci mustered up his reply, "We split."

"What do you mean?" asked Lev.

"We can cover more streets if we split up," said Blizenci. "I can get the police to go into overtime and search for the fugitives, after all Garigo's crime rate has been very low recently. Adreia can work the inner-ring, Lev can take the middle-ring and I will search the outer-ring."

"Why do you get to search the outer-ring?" questioned Lev immediately. "I have to take Sartan with me shouldn't I get the outer-ring? Not to mention you would know your own city better than I do!"

"Fine! Take the outer ring!" exclaimed Blizenci in frustration. "If you find anything, bring it to this office and alert the others."

"Now how would I do that?" asked Lev.

Blizenci sighed, "Where is your portable?"

"I broke it," replied Lev.

Blizenci sighed even harder, "Adreia, go get her and Sartan a new portable."

The Southern Queen stood up and hastily walked out of the room. Sartan could hear some commands in the other room, and before he knew it the queen returned with two paper-thin sheets of black metal. She handed one to Lev before handing Sartan one. When he picked it up all of the black metal lit up the entire oval, and instantly the device took a photo of his face. Startled, he glanced up to see if Lev's device had done the same, but she had yet to activate it. Instead they all watched as Sartan put his first name into the device as prompted. It then asked for his last name. He stared at the shimmering screen. There was no way around the question, and a brief moment passed before Blizenci interrupted.

"Put in your last name."

"I don't have one," said Sartan.

Lev countered his statement, "Your last name is Vipen. Just put in Vipen."

The device then asked for his middle name, and Blizenci lost his patience, "Why aren't you in the database already Sartan?"

"I don't know," said Sartan as his palms began sweating.

Sartan watched as Lev picked up her portable. The oval screen lit up just like his did, and the device took a photo of Lev's face instantly as well. However, her device did not ask for any information. Instead, it instantly pulled her information from the database. The first thing that appeared was a blank white screen. Then four boxes phased into existence, each titled: *Liege, Vassals, Messages,* and *Assignments.* Lev tapped the box that said *Liege,* and the only thing to come up was a black silhouette of a man with the word Kozoroh under it. Above his blacked out photo was an arrow. She quickly tapped it. It took her back to the initial page where she tapped messages. Her fingers moved so quickly that Sartan didn't even have the time to understand what she was doing. He briefly saw an image of Blizenci with his orange and blue eyes. Then her screen went black as she turned it off.

"Give me the portable Sartan," commanded Blizenci as he leaned forward in the seat. Sartan did as he was asked, and Blizenci put the portable in one of his pockets. "You won't need one as long as you stay with Lev. Now we have a job to do. Lev, the fastest way for you guys to get to the outer ring of the city is to take the train. One will go out every fifteen minutes, and it will only stop twice before exiting the city for Greectomo. Make sure you get off on the second stop." Blizenci proceeded to hand Lev two tickets. "Use these. The train station should be right across the street from the entrance to this skyscraper. I have a few calls to make before I can help, so don't wait for us."

"I never planned on it," said Lev as she rose from her seat.

Sartan knew that he wasn't an exception to people she wouldn't wait for, so he quickly turned around to follow her out of the office. The secretary waved as they walked by, and Sartan did not hesitate one second after the silver elevator doors swung shut. With his fist still clenched on the stone he pulled it out of his pocket and opened his hand. His hand was glowing turquoise, and his fingers were dripping with luminescent water. The whole elevator lit up as the energetic stone could breathe once more.

"What are you doing?!" exclaimed Lev with a whisper.

"What is this!?" countered Sartan.

"What does it look like!?"

"It looks like a Zodiac's Gemstone!"

"Well maybe that's because IT IS!" exclaimed Lev, still without screaming. "Don't let ANYONE see it on you!"

Sartan still didn't understand, "Why do I have it though? Why not just keep it with the other two? Why do you have three in the first place?"

"I need you to have one of them," whispered Lev. Sartan glanced down at the stone once more, and it still was foggier than an April morning. "Even if you aren't a Pisces you need to have one of the Water Gems."

"Why is that?" asked Sartan.

"I said so. Eventually, I'll give you the other two, and you will help me. As for now I only trust you with the Pisces Gemstone," whispered Lev as the ticker above the door dropped below fifty.

"What do you mean, trust me?"

"You won't be able to use the Pisces stone to its maximum ability since you aren't a Pisces. You will be able to practice with it, but even though it is February you'd still be too weak and untrained to kill me with it."

"Aren't we looking for Aqila and Ferran?" asked Sartan without looking away from the stone.

"We are, but we have more than one assignment at the moment. We can let Blizenci and Adreia look for them for the moment. Chances are they aren't even in the outer-rings anyway," mumbled Lev.

"Then what is it that we are doing?" asked Sartan as the stone vibrated and twitched in his hand.

The ticker fell below twenty-five before Lev replied with, "I'm going to teach you how to use a Zodiac's Gemstone."

"No!" exclaimed Sartan. "The last time I used one I nearly froze to death. Never again."

"You only froze because it wasn't within your elemental family. Had it been a Water Gem you would've been perfectly fine," countered Lev. "As long as you use one in your own sign's family it won't kill you."

"Then what is my sign?" asked Sartan, remembering that the gemstone in his hand would be crystal clear had it been his. "Am I Scorpio or am I

Cancer?" The elevator beeped and the door slowly opened up on a large crowd of people in the lobby.

"Hide it!" whispered Lev as hastily as her mouth would move.

Within seconds the stone was back in his pocket, but there was still plentiful evidence that something was happening. Sartan's hand was drenched and stained turquoise. Lev pushed her way through the crowd in front of the elevator, and Sartan was not about to let the conversation end like that. He followed after her. They both bobbed and weaved through the lobby that was full of people. Curious faces glanced over shoulders and around backs as a violent, baby-blue light emitted from his pocket. Then right before he made it out of the building somebody must have noticed the effect the stone had on his new pants.

A man from somewhere within the crowd laughed, "D'you piss yourself?"

Without waiting for more comments, Sartan bursted through the front doors to see Lev waiting for him. Upon seeing that he made it out of the building she continued across the busy street, and Sartan was left with no other choice but to dodge the incoming traffic in order to keep up with her.

Once on the other side of the road, and finally after catching up with Lev, Sartan saw the chunky yet short building with the words 'Transportation Hub' smothered on the side of it. The sign glowed orange with energy as gusts of bodies blew in and out of the doorless opening in the side of the building. He watched Lev stare at the sign in what was either intrigue or disappointment for a few seconds before she trudged forward. Again, he followed her into the train station knowing that she had his ticket. They went down a set of stairs before ending up beneath the rumbling streets. She gave the tickets to the man behind the counter, and he opened the gate for them. They quickly walked towards the tracks where the absence of a train was a disappointing reminder of how high the population really was. At least eighty other people stood and sat around waiting for the next train. Sartan didn't forget about the stone though, nor did he forget about the question he had asked.

"So which one is it? Cancer or Scorpio?" asked Sartan. Lev stared back at him, without replying. "Am I a Scorpio or am I a Cancer?"

"Shhh!" shushed Lev as she began to whisper. "What you really are shouldn't be an immediate concern for you. We shall find out soon enough though."

"What do you mean!?"

Lev began countering his question, but Sartan couldn't hear most of what she had to say because strong winds knocked out his hearing. A low vibrating hum began to pick up in volume as the winds grew stronger. Some of the people standing around them lost their hats and purses because the gust was so strong. Then he heard the screeches and saw a bright gray light coming from the tunnel. The train screeched to a halt right in front of them, and by the way that the current passengers were thrown around on the other side of the large, rectangular windows, Sartan could tell that it would be a quick ride. The doors flew open, and the dazed passenger slowly stumbled out of the train. After that last passenger got off Lev and Sartan squeezed, with the crowd, into the electric train. It was a surprise that they managed to get on in the first place let alone get a seat. There were not any seatbelts, but Sartan did hear a countdown.

"Ten. Nine. Eight," counted down an automated female voice out of the train's speakers. "Six. Five. Four. Three. Two. One."

Upon that last syllable the doors of the cabs shut and clasped with an air tight lock. Sartan looked over to Lev and said, "Well this should be---"

The train shot backwards like a rocket taking off, completely taking Sartan's breath away. There was a little sign on the ceiling of the cab that told the passengers how fast the train was moving. It quickly exploded from 10 mph to 90 mph to 200mph before finally slowing down around 678 mph. The stone walls on the outside of the window zoomed past so quickly that Sartan struggled to notice when the lighting on the tracks changed. The vessel undoubtedly could move faster, but since they were inside the city max speed was, fortunately, not necessary.

Suddenly, their speed dropped acutely. The inertia nearly threw Sartan into Lev's lap, and a singular passenger who was standing fell over. By the time that middle aged man stood back up with his briefcase, the airlocked doors opened up. Almost all of the people on the train blew out of the doors almost as aggressively as the wind of the train blew in Sartan's face earlier before getting on. Then those on the outside rushed in, and just like last time the countdown began at ten.

"Three. Two. One..."

This time Sartan was prepared. Or so he thought. The train took off so fast that Lev was thrown out of her seat onto the ground, and in a last ditch attempt to save herself she grabbed Sartan's leg pulling him to the ground with her. They stayed there until they felt the train stop accelerating. After regaining their seating, with slightly red faces, they both looked at how fast the train was moving. 603mph and decreasing. All of the other passengers stared at them while others refused to look out of embarrassment. The train didn't even zoom for a minute this time before it started to slow down once more, and it slowed even more abruptly than the last time.

From 584mph to 253mph in a few seconds, Sartan struggled not to be thrown on the ground, again. This time when the doors opened Sartan was happy to join the crowd of citizens who were trying to go on with their lives in the city. Lev followed him out of the train, almost pushing him to go faster. The air tunnels for the trains radiated heat onto him, and as he glanced between the ocean of bodies in his way he could see the tacks glowing red for a brief few seconds. Like before, Lev used her legs, which were slightly longer than his, to pass him and walk hastily through the transportation hub. This forced him to walk-jog after her all the way to the surface.

"After what could be argued as the traumatic transportation system that Blizenci has created we made it back to the loving sun," laughed Lev as they walked out onto the surface.

Sartan didn't reply. Instead he looked around him to see mostly small factories, warehouses and cheap housing complexes. Lev began walking towards the least populated street as if she knew where she was going, so Sartan followed, leaving the city center behind him. Much less cars bristled through the roads, and if the few vehicles that remained were semi trucks and rigs slowly barreling around. There was actually graffiti on the buildings they walked by, unlike the part of town they had just come from. Smoke stacks puffed a bit of black smoke from every fourth building, and pedestrians practically disappeared after trudging across a few blocks. Some of the factories and warehouses had boarded windows. Their cement walls were covered in white and black spray paint, yet the doors and windows remained mostly intact despite the obvious lack of care. Even plants stemmed their way through a few bricks and up the sides of the buildings. Eventually they came up on just another warehouse that seemed abandoned, but this time Lev didn't keep walking past it. Instead she wandered away from the road for a closer inspection, and Sartan was surprised when she checked to make sure nobody was around. She inspected the building with a quick glance. Then Sartan followed her as she walked up to the front door. He watched her try to open the locked door to no avail.

"It's locked Lev," said Sartan. "Guess that means you don't have to train me."

"Nonsense!" laughed Lev as she formed a fist. She softly thrusted her fist into the gray door, and it buckled under the intense, dark flames that shot out of thin air. A loud bang followed when it fell backwards completely unhinged. "Come on in Sartan. You need training," said Lev as she stepped over the now ashy and scarred door.

Sartan sighed as he felt the heat radiating around him. He then gracefully stepped around the charred door into the warehouse. Once he was inside, Lev lifted the door and propped it up in the entryway lazily to give off the impression that it was still hinged and closed. The large warehouse was largely empty. Cement floors absorbed the sunlight that beamed through the windowed ceiling. A few spare crates lined the walls of the warehouse along with pallets and metal racks, but the center was entirely empty.

"Take out the stone Sartan," commanded Lev as she took off her top shirt revealing more of the two white streaks previously hidden beneath. "It's time to start training."

"And do what with it? Just hold it in my hand?" asked Sartan as he watched Lev take a martial arts stance. "Woah! Woah! Woah! Slow down!"

"No. You will need to break through first," replied Lev.

"How do I do that?"

"With ease, just form a fist around it and punch in my direction." Sartan obeyed and balled his hand in a fist around the Pisces Gemstone. He thrusted the stone forward, punching at the air. Naturally, the first time he tried this nothing happened. Sartan glanced up at Lev who just laughed in amusement, "Try it again. You need to connect with the stone before you can use its powers free handed."

A second try resulted in a small mist of light-blue water shooting out from his fist. Lev didn't even need to block his attack; it was still so weak that the mist dissipated into the air within seconds. Sartan repositioned himself to match Lev's more serious, martial stance, but before he could try again he noticed Lev was suddenly wearing a black suit with shiny, golden buttons. He could no longer see a majority of the white tattoos that ran down her whole body. In fact all he could see of that now was the section that started at her lips and ran down her neck. The suit however was very fitting. There were red strands of silk interwoven into the suit that glistened faintly in the sunlight. Golden buttons on her chest contrasted with the accented, dark-red trousers, and the entire suit made Lev look just a bit more regal. *As if she needed to feel any more royal.*

"Lev?!?"

"What?"

"Why are you wearing a suit?"

"What?"

"Why are you wearing a suit?"

"The vanity of a suit does not match my current needs. I have my sports bra on and my...well I might consider slipping out of my pants for this training session if the need arises, but you need not be distracted more than you already---"

"No, Lev you are literally wearing a black suit with gold and red accents," argued Sartan.

"Sartan, we have no time for your shenanigans," said Lev as she grabbed at her pants pulling them up before awkwardly retaking her stance. "Just strike again, Sartan. Focus!"

While trying to ignore the fact that Lev suddenly was wearing a suit, Sartan attempted once more. This time he left a small puddle half the size of his foot scattered about in front of him.

"Sartan, take this seriously."

"I am!"

He thrust the stone forward once more, but this time he had a successful strike. So successful in fact, Lev had to block. Her quick dark red flame shut down the weak, frosty burst of baby-blue water that came out of Sartan's clenched fist within an instant. Her block was so powerful it went through the frigid, ice water, and Sartan now had to strike at the scorching flame that barreled across the room towards him. Just in time, Sartan managed to shoot a blade of ice to defend himself. The ice vaguely matched the shape of the incoming flames, and both forces neutralized each other in the middle of the warehouse.

Lev began clapping from the other side of the ice rink. Suddenly the warehouse, as if it had been spray painted in an instant, froze over. The entire warehouse had a thick layer of sparkling ice glazed over every surface, whether that be the floors, walls, ceiling, or scattered crates and such. Sartan struggled to keep his balance on the new terrain. The boom of each clap echoed in the frozen warehouse, and Sartan began to feel himself get cold.

Sartan glanced up to Lev once getting his footing and said, "Tell me you see thi---WHAT IS ON YOUR HEAD!?!?!"

"Wait...you are serious...are you not?" asked Lev who now no longer had a head. Instead of the human head that used to reside on her body, now there was the head of a lioness. The fur was pitch black, and Sartan noticed that her white tattoos started at the lioness's mouth before going down into the suit. The suit of course was on a human body. This of course only confused Sartan even more.

"The entire warehouse is coated in ice, and you have a LIONESS HEAD!!!" exclaimed Sartan in utter confusion. "What is going on?!?!?"

The figure that stood before him hummed to itself before replying, without moving its mouth, "I am simply baffled. I figured you would've lasted much longer."

"WHAT!? What does that mean?"

"You see Sartan, the stone has already got you. It made it to your mind and you are being forced to succumb to its power on a mental level. You are breaking through to the stone."

"WELL WHAT DOES THAT MEAN?!"

"The first time using a stone, if it is in your elemental family, you will break through."

"I don't quite understand. So you are still Lev?" asked Sartan.

"Precisely, I am Lev. You must be looking at my lioness form, but I am Lev regardless. In reality I am what I looked like back in the subway," answered Lev as the lioness head atop her suited body softly growled. "You don't need to worry. The Pisces Gemstone is just playing with your mind right now. After you break through the stone won't distort your perception when using it."

"Are you sure?"

"Positive. Well actually there are ways to break through to a stone even after you have done it before. They are difficult to do and require certain circumstances, but there are perks of doing so. If you were an Active Zodiac and this was your stone you would be able to break through like you are about to as frequently as you wished. I am sure you can do the same with other stones of your elemental family, but I have never had the need. Look at it as more of a necessary experience you have to go through in order to grow. I myself have only done it once and NEVER wish to again, but let us focus! Use the stone again so you can break through!"

"You NEVER wish to again though? This is a lot. Let me think for a second," replied Sartan as he began tuning out Lev.

Lev's lioness mouth opened slightly to let out a low pitched growl, and Sartan blinked heavily. He rubbed his eyes and kept them closed for quite a while, but upon opening them nothing changed. He heard Lev speaking to him, but didn't see her mouth move. She kept telling him to use the stone one more time, but at this point that was the last thing he intended to do. His attention gathered around the stone itself. His hand was so cold that it felt as though it had fallen off. *What if it kills me before I can catch Ferran. I'm already confused enough. I'm going to wait a second to use it again.* Lev, however, had different plans. She sent a large fireball that seemingly came out of thin air, bustling towards Sartan. In preference to death, Sartan's reflexes decided to use the stone for him. Sartan had practically no clue what he was doing, so he just thrusted out his fist with the stone in it and held it out while he tried to hide behind his extended arm, all while stumbling backwards.

Small bubbles of icy water quickly appeared on his arms. He could feel the water instantly turn into ice, and this was when he felt the energy for the first time. Similar to when he used the Libra Gemstone to shoot down a helicopter back in Dursnia, he could feel freezing water pulsating in waves behind him. This was different. This was intimate. This was...colder.

As Lev's flaming ball of red hot fire flew closer, Sartan understood that he was already going to die, and there was no point in preventing it. *Either the stone freezes me, or her flame melts me...but my feet have already gone numb.* Giving in to the stone completely he let the frozen water slice through his back, straight through his heart, and out of his extended arm.

Sartan struggled to keep consciousness as blades of ice speared through the recently flaming ball of fire. The sharp blades stuck into the walls, floors and anything sturdy that got hit by them. Lev held out one hand and disintegrated three of the spikes that flew towards her with ease. she suddenly began running towards him. Startled, Sartan didn't understand why a black lioness with white streaks on its fur in a red suit was sprinting towards him in an abandoned warehouse that resided in a city he had never been to before, but nothing was making sense anymore.

It was at this point Sartan watched the floor climb him as he fell to his knees. His body told his brain that his knees made contact with the floor...several times. Perhaps his nerves overfired telling him he fell to his knees multiple times because it took seven seconds before he even felt it to begin with. Regardless, his brain had an obvious disconnect from reality as all of his senses took several seconds to register before firing off repeatedly. His back began to arch forward, and the floor turned black. Then everything turned black, and all he could feel was endless neurons firing in his hand that gripped the freezing stone and his heart beating multiple times per beat. The air he breathed in froze him further with every breath he took. He reached a point where he didn't even feel himself fall over, but he managed to open his eyes for a brief second to see himself fall face first into Lev's arms. Right before she saved him from face planting the frozen cement with his frozen face, he closed his eyes and was consumed by the blackness once more.

SPLASH!!! He was sinking quite quickly through dreadfully dark water. Holding his breath became a problem way too fast, for as soon as Sartan realized that he was no longer in an abandoned warehouse with Lev but instead in a lightless, arctic ocean, the water gushed into his ears and nose. He clenched his eyelids shut to protect himself from the ice water, and as expected he could see as little as he could with them open. With every second that passed in the polar pond his squirming grew violently, but in consistency with the warehouse, everything he felt...he felt multiple times and in slow motion before his brain was able to process the next physical stimuli that attacked him.

Simultaneously as the deep sea waves raided his ears and nostrils, Sartan blew out of his nose and gasped for air. Of course this would bring about his drowning much faster. His gasping for air only invited the invasive water into his lungs. He felt the water trickle through his nasal cavity to meet the water that molested itself down into his throat. He choked on small chunks of ice as the lethal liquid plunged down his throat into his chest. There was nothing he could do. He had already exhaled all of his air, and now his chest was full of water. Sartan began gagging on the little bit of liquid that swam around his uvula. The water around his face warmed up just barely enough to notice, but that was the least of his concerns featuring it was his own salty tears that were taunting him before peacefully swimming off leaving their sinking ship in the black void all alone.

That was when he saw it. The faintest of lights kissed the bottom of his eyelids. He opened his eyes to see a glow coming from his hand before quickly closing his eyes again to prevent the water from getting in. The blue glow grew brighter, and Sartan could feel his face turning purple when suddenly something touched his foot. Without warning all of the liquid around him vanished out of thick water. Sartan fell a few feet before landing on a hard surface.

No hesitation was present in him as he began choking up water out of his lungs. He opened his eyes to watch the water splat out all over a gray, carpeted floor. As confused as ever Sartan looked around as he tried to exhale the water that so violently raped him. He blinked once and there wasn't a drip of water anywhere inside his chest anymore. Somehow he had ended up in a strange white room. Large, white lighting-panels laced the ceiling, and comfortable, gray chairs lined the walls. The gray carpet was dry when Sartan looked back at it, and to his surprise he realized that there was not a molecule of water on him at all either. The whole room was oddly scentless and undecorated. Only a singular brown door stood in one of the walls, and in the background somewhere Sartan could hear classical jazz playing from a speaker.

Still on his knees from choking on water, he stood up and walked over to a counter. The other side of the counter where a secretary or someone similar was supposed to be was completely blocked off by a metal sheet. Sartan still had access to some of the counter. Unfortunately, there were only two things on it: a timer and a sign. Above the timer was a sign that said, "Place gemstone on the counter." Sartan glanced down to his fist that once held the stone, and somehow it wasn't lost in any of the commotion. The stone sat patiently in his opened palm. As he stared, wondering how he didn't lose it in the water, the stone began to vibrate. It kept vibrating and glowing brighter until he finally put it down on the counter. Time seemingly froze before the stone disintegrated into nothing. The electrical timer then beeped very loudly, and started counting down from five minutes. The sign then changed to say, "Your current wait:"

"Wait…what?" whispered Sartan to himself.

Before he could figure out what in the world was happening the door behind him flew open. Sartan swung himself around to watch two individuals walk in from a violently rainy, black void. One was a man. One was a woman. They both wore black suits with blue ties identical to a red one that Lev had on in the warehouse, and they both laid their drenched umbrellas against the wall next to the door. The individuals mumbled to each other without facing Sartan.

"You can't save him!" whispered the man frantically.

"I know I can't, but we can speak with him before Ryby realizes!" whispered the woman who sounded just as concerned.

"How hasn't Ryby found him yet?!" asked the man quietly.

"He is not in the same realm as us right now!" replied the woman with graceful worry. "He is speaking with the Pisces before him, but that doesn't mean we have a lot of time!"

The two individuals finally turned around to face Sartan, and he stared in disbelief as the man turned to face him. With great similarity to Lev, the man: had on a suit and sighed upon seeing the timer. He then murmured something about not having enough time. Unlike Lev however, the man had the head of a scorpion plastered on the top of his suited body. The suited woman behind him shut the door behind her before turning to face Sartan. Just like the man there was no human head on her body and instead sat the head of a crab with long rectangular eyes shooting vertically. As if Sartan was previously invisible, the two suited creatures suddenly ran over to him after staring in his direction for a few seconds.

"Sartan!" exclaimed the woman as she grabbed and held his hands. "I'm so proud of you!"

"What?" asked Sartan as he backed away from the two of them.

The man quickly spoke, "Yes. You have to listen to us, Sartan!"

"Yes! Ryby is on his way, and he will not be happy with you!" exclaimed the woman.

"Why? What have I done?!" asked Sartan as he backed into the corner of the counter.

"My boy you haven't done anything wrong, but he has been watching Lev. We all have. He knows what she plans on making you do!" exclaimed the woman. "He is extremely angry at me, and because of our close ties he won't be kind to you!"

"What is going on?" asked Sartan.

"Boy, you have broken through!" said the man. "You have broken through the Pisces Gemstone, and now you are learning the truth. Child, this is an unforgettable experience."

"Why do you keep calling me child and boy?"

The woman hastily replied, "Because even a fraction of our age dwarfs yours."

"LEV!" exclaimed Sartan. "LEV WHERE ARE YOU!?"

"Lev is at fault for a lot of things, Sartan!" exclaimed the man. "But she pushed you to break through! Her inexperience with breaking through will become a fatal mistake for her! Now that you are here we can help you."

"I don't want your help. I just want to---"

"I can help you find Leucemie! I can help you find your mother!" interrupted the woman. "Right now I NEED you to listen to us."

"Why do I keep getting told that!? I don't know any Leucemie's, and Lev is going to help me find my mother! Maybe once I get my memory back that would work on me!"

"He is so naive," murmured the woman in a tear cracking tone.

"It isn't his fault. Sartan, do you know who we are?" asked the man.

"No. I don't know what is going on at all!" exclaimed Sartan.

The whole room shook for five seconds. Paintings that previously went unnoticed fell off the walls, and the lights flickered. Sartan watched as both of them glanced at the timer. Then he himself took a peek to see that it had already counted down two minutes. There was only three more minutes until his wait was over.

"We don't have much time," said the man as he stared at the woman.

The crab headed woman looked back at Sartan and spoke, "He is Stir, the last Active Scorpio Zodiac to live, and I am the last Cancer Zodiac to live---"

"It was you who killed all the Water Zodiacs then!" exclaimed Sartan in understanding. "Stir, why are you helping her if she killed you?!"

"She didn't kill me," said Stir.

"What?"

"Lev and Ryby did."

"What the fuck is happening?" cried out Sartan as he once again thought about how he was cornered in a room with an ugly arachnid and a similarly ugly crustacean.

"He's right," said the woman. "And after I found out I killed Ryby. I didn't kill myself like you've been told either. Lev killed me."

"She told me that you went crazy and killed all of the Water Zodiacs including yourself," said Sartan in confusion. "Does that mean I'm dead right now if I'm speaking with you?"

"You aren't dead…but we are. She killed us just like she killed almost all of my children."

"What do you mean by children?" asked Sartan.

"All of my Zodiacs!" exclaimed the woman. "Lev slaughtered the Active: Sagittarius, Scorpio, Taurus, Virgo, Aries, Aquarius, Libra and me! With the help of Blizenci, Ryby, and Kozoroh of course."

The room shook again and more aggressively this time. Sartan spoke, "I knew she was lying to me. It was either that or Aqila lied to me, but she can die for all I care."

"NO! You must find Aqila again!" exclaimed the woman. "Her and her group are the best option that we have to stop Kozoroh."

"She literally left me to die whereas Lev saved me from that forest!" argued Sartan.

"Lev only saved you because you would help her hunt them down, and she knew it," said Stir. "We have been watching everything. Aqila didn't know about what Ferran did to you until it was too late."

"Why don't I just kill Lev?" asked Sartan. "I don't want to ever see Ferran again unless I am beating him senseless."

"You are too weak to kill Lev right now," answered the woman. "If you let Lev or Blizenci catch them then your chances of freedom are over."

"Why is that?"

"Let's say you find Aqila. Lev will kill them all instantly," replied the woman. "Well from the evidence we have witnessed, she will brainwash you to make you forget about as much as possible before forcing you to become the Wagustus of the Water Zodiacs. That would make reviving two of the three Water Zodiacs impossible, and if you refuse then she will simply kill you."

The room began shaking, Sartan nearly fell over when he asked, "How is that bad?"

"Stop it boy! You know both of those are bad outcomes! Do not forget who you are dealing with!" exclaimed the scorpion headed Stir.

"Exactly! Lev, Kozoroh and Blizenci will all team up against you to make sure you submit to them," responded the woman. "By becoming Wugustus of the Water Empires you would destroy the lives of all the Scorpios and Pisces!"

Holes began appearing in the walls as the room shook consistently. The timer began to beep as the wait time dropped below forty-five seconds. "What do I do other than die then!?" asked Sartan frantically.

"You must not trust Lev!" exclaimed Stir. "She is using you for her benefit at your detriment. We don't know what her exact plans are, but we are almost certain that is it. Either way she is not making them to help you. You have to---"

The carpeting beneath Stir fell into the void bringing him with it mid sentence. At this point there were more holes in the wall than there were walls. The woman picked up where Stir left off, "Sartan! Ryby is coming for you! He thinks that you are going to destroy Pisces once and for all since you are helping Lev."

Sartan could only stare at the crab headed woman as he held onto the counter while everything around him fell into an endless black void. Its beady, black eyes glistened under the flickering lights, and the thin stalks of red flesh or shell twitched to the left and right. Thin and tiny hairs rose and fell on the sides of the head, as a labyrinth of mouth parts jiggled and moved around while the woman spoke.

"Do not trust Lev!" continued the woman. "Survive Ryby! Stay away from Blizenci he is very good at implanting ideas in your head, and try to find Aqila. She will help you! Trust me! Most importantly, do NOT let Lev---"

The flooring beneath the woman was sucked into the void along with the late Cancer Zodiac. Sartan held onto the counter while taking the deepest breaths he's taken in his life, for it was unknown when he himself would fall into the watery void. He glanced over at the timer to see a seven turn into a six.

By now there weren't any walls in the room. The ceiling was gone, and all that was left was the patch of carpet he stood on and the part of the counter holding the timer.

Strong rumbling started shaking him, and with the last beep of the timer Sartan felt his floor give out on him. The fall was strange. No wind assaulted his face, and he didn't feel like he was falling. Sartan simply was there, and there was not anywhere specific. The everlasting black canvas he was stuck in was eternal because time stopped...or started. Sartan didn't exactly know which one it was let alone if it even existed. The conversations with the two suited individuals from the waiting room warned him of what he was about to endure, but the void blissfulness certainly was a comforting new concept.

Moving his left hand to scratch his face, Sartan suddenly couldn't move as freely anymore. He tried moving his legs and arms only to realize that he was stuck in a thick liquid. Molasses, syrup, honey whatever it was he couldn't move at all. Then the entire substance began vibrating. He figured keeping his eyes closed would be pointless, so when he saw a massive, shining fin swim by him the ignorant bliss he had been enjoying instantly drowned on him. The fish passed his vision once more, and Sartan knew that it was circling him. Just in front of Sartan's feet appeared dark gray jellyfish. They didn't really move too much, but they lined a path of light just bright enough for Sartan to see his own hands. The jelly-like substance melted away to normal water. Unlike the last time, the water did not attack his lungs mercilessly, but instead he was able to breathe normally. He then slowly floated down through the icy water, and his feet landed softly on the jellyfish.

"Go ahead," demanded an aged and deep voice as it laughed, simultaneously in the far distance and right next to Sartan's ear. The voice sounded as if a cigar had been roasting in the man's throat since the ripe age of twelve as it cracked and echoed off what could only be described as an oily, iron rebar lodged in his voice box which itself was drowned whisky. "Take a walk with me...my boy."

The man's voice was punctual and non-negotiable. Sartan couldn't tell where it was coming from, but he knew that the creature was directly speaking with him. While looking down at the trail of jellyfish leading into the abyss Sartan witnessed an endless, silver fin rip up in between some of the floating jellyfish as the enormous fish circled around him. Sartan was unable to see the entirety of the fish's fins that spiked up from its back, but that only was cause for more concern because he knew that the fin had to be six times larger than himself.

"NOW!" vociferated the fish as its impatience seeped into the water.

Sartan moved his limbs to abide by the fish's demands, but while he stepped on the bells of the floaters he struggled to move fast in the thickening liquid. Thankfully he was able to breathe while slowly moving across the sea of jellyfish in the deep, thick water that seemed to change consistencies over and over again.

"SARTAN!" boomed the fish as its fin towered next to his right side. "Tell me exactly what you are doing with Lev right now!"

Sartan struggled to communicate his response, "I-I-don't know."

"Did you speak with the crab or scorpion?" asked the creature with a deep voice. "You don't have to lie to this fish, my boy."

"I think...I think I did," answered Sartan reluctantly.

"You can not trust them!" yelled the fish while Sartan got a glimpse of its bright blue eye as it passed him on the left. The pupil itself was slightly larger than himself, and that was when Sartan finally understood his physical inferiority to the behemoth. "They are vile creatures who poison the minds of all they touch! Whatever they told you before I saved you...it was all lies!"

"I see," said Sartan. "Then who may you be?"

"ME?" asked the fish angrily. "You do not know already?! I am Ryby! The longest living Pisces Zodiac! My reign lasted for over ten thousand years."

"Lasted?" stated Sartan. Upon mentioning that, he could feel the molasses like water push him back and forth more relentlessly.

"Tens of thousands of years of service to the Earth! Tens of thousands years of knowledge became inaccessible within minutes because of that FUCKING SHELLFISH!" fulminated the fish with exasperation. "Oh, she cared about her little scorpion and all the other Zodiacs we exterminated! Well who cares about that sleazy parasite anyways! He was a toxic cancer to this world, and that is probably the only reason why Cancer cared about him. They both are parasitic pests to this planet!"

"Were..."

"Thankfully!" exclaimed Ryby. "Lev is overly incompetent, but at least she fixed that problem with her shaky fucking hands. Now Kozoroh has to depend on her and Blizenci for the rest of the plan! Despicable!"

"Lev saved my life though," replied Sartan after stepping on to the next bell in slow motion.

"Sartan, are you really that dense?!?!" boomed Ryby as he sent a current that nearly knocked Sartan off the jellyfish. "She only saved you because she recognized you, and you had knowledge she could use. How she knew you is beyond me, let alone remember who you really are. You do know what Lev wants you to do for her right?"

"She wants me to catch Aqila."

"She wants you to do a lot more than just that," said Ryby softly. "She wants to make you the Wagustus of the Water Zodiacs just like she is trying to become the Firgustus of the Fire Zodiacs."

"Why would she want me to do that?" asked Sartan.

"You are easily manipulatable in her eyes," laughed Ryby. "You are young and unknowing. Your memory has been removed which makes you the perfect mule for filling that position. Do NOT let her do this to you!"

"How do I do that? She is way more powerful than I."

"She is more powerful than you, but she is weak compared to me, especially during February."

Sartan kept walking on the jellyfish's bells. The jellyfish behind him swam up towards the surface while the ones in front of him floated up from the depths below him and waited until he passed. Sartan then replied, "You are dead though. How would that work?"

"Kill her!" exclaimed Ryby with a laugh. "If you kill her a certain way, and with my stone I can prevent her from coming to the afterlife."

"Why would I kill her?" asked Sartan.

"BECAUSE IF YOU DON'T SHE WILL MAKE A WATER AUGUSTUS!!!!" screamed the fish as the coldest burst of water Sartan ever felt hit his side. "She has become too focused on her own goals! She no longer is playing for the team!"

"I physically can't kill her," whispered Sartan. "I am not strong enough."

"YOU MUST TRY!" demanded Ryby. "SHE IS NOT TO BE TRUSTED!"

"What about Kozoroh and reviving all of the other Zodiacs?" asked Sartan.

"You mean that Awila girl and her posse?" asked the fish unseriously. "Well she is becoming more of a threat, but I would not help her with her plans. I don't want you directly acting against Kozoroh and my plans. Do NOT revive any more Zodiacs. Kill Lev instead. For fuck's sake at the very least steal all of the Water Gemstones from her, so she is unable to kill off two thirds of us! Does that not make sense to you? She wants to kill two Zodiacs and all of their subjects…PERMANENTLY"

"Hmmmm," sighed Sartan. The water around him began feeling warmer. He wasn't the only one to notice it either as Ryby began speaking with more haste.

"SARTAN!" exclaimed the deceased Pisces Zodiac. "HELP LEV KILL AQILA AND HER GROUP! THEN KILL HER, BUT DO NOT TRUST THE OTHER WATER ZODIACS!"

The water around him quickly warmed up, and the jellyfish began stretching horizontally. The sun began peeking through to him. Sartan stopped walking on the jellyfish. He glanced upwards towards the surface and saw a slight ray of sunshine coming directly from the sun. The jellyfish he stood on suddenly shot up as they swam into overdrive towards the surface, and he started rising up through the water, Ryby was not happy about it at all.

"NO!" fulminated the angry fish. "HE IS MINE LEV!"

As the jellyfish flew upwards through the molasses like water, Sartan stopped shivering as the cold depths were left behind him. Upon hearing Ryby scream for him, he finally pinpointed his location. While the jellyfish brought him closer to the sun the sound of an angry fish swimming after him haunted Sartan. He looked down into the depths of the arctic ocean to see Ryby's mouth gaped wide open. Sharp white teeth the length of two school buses lined his entire mouth. The fish's mouth itself could easily devour an entire mansion, and the tongue...the red tongue slimed its way through the whole mouth before extending itself out for Sartan. It could be the length of two or three power pylons once fully extended, and Sartan couldn't watch it grow closer to him.

"STAY OUT OF MY WATER LEV!" screeched the fish. "DON'T LET HER TAKE YOU SARTAN! COME BACK TO ME WHERE IT'S SAFE!"

A cold gust of water absorbed Sartan as Ryby's mouth breathed out on him, but the jellyfish got the last laugh. Sartan, while staring directly at the sun through the sea, was thrown out of the water into the fresh air, and the first thing he saw upon escaping the waves was Lev. Everything slowly came back to him as Lev stood up from her seated position on the cold warehouse floor. He no longer felt stimuli being received several times by his neurons which made breathing feel much less intense. Lev had a sports bra strapped on tightly around her chest instead of a suit, and her head was the human featured one that he recognized once more, thankfully.

"You have awoken!" exclaimed Lev.

Sartan did not reply to her. He was still looking around the warehouse to make sure nothing looked out of the normal. The boxes in the corners were not glazed in ice, and the floor was made of gray cement now. Nobody was wearing a suit, and there were no strange animal heads on anyone. There was no timer ticking in the background, and there was not any sense of urgency anymore. The only thing that was different was a few black burn marks on the floor of the warehouse, but Lev had to be the reason for that. She stared at him with anticipation.

"How long has it been?" asked Sartan.

"Not even twenty minutes have passed us," replied Lev with a smile on her face. "How was Ryby? Did he help you understand water powers more?"

"What? He didn't do that at all," answered Sartan.

Lev stared at him sternly before asking, "What did the two of you speak of then?"

"He told me---" Sartan stopped mid sentence. "He was very angry."

"What is he angry about?"

"He was extremely angry with Cancer and Scorpio."

"That would make sense," said Lev as she stared off into the distance. "Is that all the two of you spoke of, or did you speak of more in depth concepts?"

Sartan took a moment to think about how he would word this now knowing that Ryby himself was probably watching. He hesitated before replying with, "Ryby was not too happy with you either. He told me something about a Wagustus, and that he doesn't want you to install one for the Water Zodiacs."

"Wagustus?"

"Yes, he said you wanted to make me a Wagustus, but he despised that idea," said Sartan as he rose to his feet. "Something about how two of the Water Zodiacs would be lost."

"Who is he to make a decision on something like that!" exclaimed Lev. "He isn't even present in the living world, why would it matter to him? Keeping secrets from those Water Zodiacs was always impossible! I need to know everything he told you."

"He wants me to kill you," said Sartan unreluctantly. After leaking the previous information that he was told, Sartan figured it didn't matter to tell Lev everything. "He said that you are no longer helping Kozoroh, but instead you are focused on your own selfish goals."

Lev instantly let loose and screamed, "WHAT?! I've been helping Kozoroh more than he ever has. In fact he actually slowed Kozoroh down because he didn't have respect for us. He was going to be the Wagustus for the

Water Zodiacs, but now that he won't he is all pissy." Sartan stared at her unable to think of a response let alone squeeze it in between her screams. "My own selfish goals! All of my goals are tied to Kozoroh's plan! How is it my fault that I have to replace an entire Water Zodiac because he was killed by Cancer?!"

"Lev," whispered Sartan.

"You know what?! I am going to replace him, and not with a new Pisces! He will be the last Pisces ever to rule on this planet! EVER!"

"Lev."

"WHAT!?!"

"He told me something else too," whispered Sartan.

Lev suddenly became worried and less violent as she asked, "My friend, what did he tell you?"

"He told me that he was killed by Cancer, but that Scorpio and Cancer were both killed by you."

"WHY!?" exclaimed Lev. "He is lying to you! I had to kill Cancer, but we both dealt with Scorpio before he became a problem!"

"Wait! You said that they all died because of Cancer!"

"I told you all that you needed to know!" exclaimed Lev as she opened the small bag that hid away the other two gemstones once more. This time she took out the deep, purple gemstone that instantly muddled itself upon touching her skin. She stared at it while Sartan watched intently. The indigo colored gem must have stared back as Lev completely ignored their current conversation.

"Lev?"

"Huh?"

"Lev?"

"Oh yes, your training," replied Lev without looking away from the stone.

"Do you want me to break through this one as well?" asked Sartan half hoping she would say no and completely aware she had avoided the conversation.

She continuously stared at the stone before finally looking up at Sartan to say, "I am not sure yet. Possibly. The only problem is Stir. You need to break through all of them, but Stir will try and poison you. Quite similar to what Ryby would've done had you not came back to me."

"He told me the truth of what happened to the Water Zodiacs though," argued Sartan while he watched Lev frown. "There has to be some sort of insight from contacting Stir."

"I don't know. He might not have access to the living world like Ryby does, so everything he knows is from his malleable life," replied Lev. "Stir would not be able to assist you at all with knowledge on current world issues, so when you speak to him focus purely on learning techniques. I can't train you how to manipulate Water Zodiac powers as well as him, but if you have any questions about the history of Zodiacs he will be clueless and heavily misinformed."

"Ask him for nothing but techniques?" asked Sartan as he put his hand out to receive the stone.

"Exactly! If it is not technique oriented it is a lie!" exclaimed Lev while hesitantly putting the stone into Sartan's palm. "Stir can be very manipulative and depressive, so I advise you to not grant him access to your problems. Focus purely on techniques, as he may take you down other topics that are untrue. Otherwise you may not come back alive, and certainly do NOT let him know you just broke through to Ryby."

When Lev pulled her hand away to reveal the milky purple stone in his hand Sartan could almost see black specs within the gem. As the purple fog curdled over itself inside the stone he felt a sense of uncertainty arise in him. Sartan then exclaimed, "He could KILL me!?"

Lev was walking away from Sartan to retake her fighting stance far enough to give him any chance, but without turning around she nodded and said, "Ryby could have as well. Just never make them angry at you, and certainly do not let them feel your emotions. They are very skilled with that."

"How do I not let them feel my emotions? I don't even---"

"Enough questions! I am already desperately behind schedule!" yelled Lev from the other side of the warehouse. The command came with a hurdling gust of flames as Lev punched a beam of fire straight towards Sartan. Almost like a ray of sunshine the beam of fire did not stop. Sartan, of course, did not want to be melted to a pulp in the warehouse, so he instinctively punched out at the flames before they hit him. A cylinder of ice water large enough just to cover himself from the flames extended up from the ground. The dark, purple water defended Sartan from Lev's flames for about five seconds. Then he felt the water running out. Gallons upon gallons of water gushed out of the floor, and he felt his body temperature drop what felt like ten fold. Lev on the other hand kept up and with ease.

It wasn't even twenty seconds later and maintaining the flow of water pained him more than the few flames that managed to swirl around and snip at his feet did. Then it all started to fall apart. The dark purple water that had been preventing his death quickly faltered, and with each passing breath it grew weaker. Luckily for Sartan, Lev instantly recognized this and adjusted the strength of her flames accordingly, but even after the ray was less heated and oppressive Sartan still lost control of the water. It pained his joints too much to keep it up. The pure coldness of the water he was producing out of thin air took a toll on him. His tongue dried out while his fingers chubbed up from swollen skin. Before he knew it Sartan's increased heart rate contrasted the slow trickle of water that now matched a calculated-weakening trickle of flames coming towards him as Lev readjusted once more.

After what felt like an eternity, Sartan could no longer keep this up, and when he finally gave in, breathing was too difficult to even think about. He slowly watched the tiny flame fly straight into his shoulder. It burned of course, but he was already too numb to even feel it. Sartan patted out the fire on his shirt, and was instantly plagued with a gift of warmth. He was so weary that he didn't even notice Lev speaking to him from across the room. She murmured some sort of warning, but the increasingly warm feeling that melted away any concern was his primary focus.

Kozoroh. Ferran. Lev. Aqila. Stir. None of them mattered anymore. Not even the terrifying fish named Ryby was a concern to him. Sartan knelt down on the warm and comfortable cement and felt the pain from Lev's fire fester. It wasn't painful for him. Instead, it felt like someone was massaging his shoulder. The flames had burnt through his shirt, and the open air hitting his bare burn relaxed him even more. He glanced over to his shoulder to see Lev running towards him. The fire still crackled away on him, but it didn't warrant any immediate danger. With a smile, Sartan glanced away as he felt Lev putting the fire out. *This is nice.*

"Are you breaking through already?!?!" exclaimed Lev upon patting out the fire that had set up residence on his shoulder.

"Huh?"

Sartan didn't listen to Lev's next response as his own thoughts began running rampant. *What do you mean 'already'? I am perfectly fine where I am. Wait, oh! She must mean I'm breaking through! I may be. I'd rather just sit where I am right now. It's much safer here. Nobody is lying to me. No one is trying to control me. It's all good. Life is good!*

"SARTAN!" screamed Lev loud enough to startle Sartan. "Are you still with me?!"

The loud screams of Lev sounded like music to Sartan's ears even once she started shaking him. However, he did want to be left alone, so he responded with, "Yes! I'm here!"

"You aren't all the way through! You need to go further!"

"I feel fine though," replied Sartan while failing to keep his head up. "I just…know where the fuzzy is or feel…you know what I mean."

"What?"

Sartan closed his eyes and was suddenly in the water on a beach. It was warm and bright, and the waves crashing against the shore kept a rhythmic beat going. He felt the warm water lapping on his waist, and his feet didn't touch anything. Instantly he began flailing in the crystal clear water. "I CAN'T SWIM!" he exclaimed while quickly feeling the waves ride up to his chest.

To his left a man with a deep voice whispered, "Then why'd you get in the water?"

Without even thinking Sartan flung his head to the left to see no man next to him. On his shoulder sat a fully grown scorpion with its face directed at his head. He only had a mere second to question it as he sank below the waves. The water gushed into his openings, and he closed his eyes as quickly as possible. Failing to learn from any of his past experiences, the water managed to slip into him. It was faced with no resistance upon breaching his nostrils and ears, but Sartan did manage to keep his mouth shut for a brief second. It went down the pipes as he gagged for air. In the back of his mind he kept hearing, "You need to go further! You need to go further! Come on!" There was no way he could go further. The light from the surface of the water had already shrank to a little sliver, and Sartan's mind had already panicked itself into demise again.

SLAP!!! Spit flew out of Sartan's mouth as a flaming hand flew away. Sartan opened his eyes to see Lev, again. There was no water on his face. He was completely dry, and the air he gasped for was no longer watered down. The warm fuzzy feeling in his body was dissipating with every breath, and he choked on his own breath saying, "What is happening!?!?"

"You didn't break through," answered Lev while kneeling over him.

"How do you know?"

"I had a sinking suspicion!" exclaimed Lev. "I also found it necessary to reiterate that you only listen to what Stir has to say about techniques! Use the stone now and you will go all the way. Only speak with him about techniques, and do not tell him anything that I have told you!"

"I'm not using any stone ever again!" exclaimed Sartan as he shot his fist into Lev's side.

Time seemingly froze as Sartan watched Lev smile. She had caught his fist, and even worse, he was holding the stone in it. The strongest burst of cold water Sartan had ever felt in his life exploded into existence. Lev gripped his fist with both hands and prevented him from moving at all. Her hands were literally made of fire, and that fire was hot enough to evaporate the frosty explosion of water he produced. She didn't take a step back. She didn't falter her smile. She took the entire blow. Once the gust had finished Lev dropped Sartan's hands releasing him to collapse on the floor after exerting so much energy in such little time.

"Much to learn," taunted Lev.

Sartan didn't reply as the stone clanked onto the floor next to him. The only energy he had left was spent thinking. He managed to think one thought before he smacked into the cement. *Once I close my eyes, I'm going to drown.* With that thought on the tip of his mind, Sartan flopped onto the warm and cozy cement where he nodded off into a world of understanding...and...misunderstanding.

***

An endlessly unknown amount of time passed. Sartan drifted back and forth in the shallow water. This time around he knew he wasn't in the real world. It was too cold. It was too sudden. It was too dark. Too dark for him to see. He must've been in some sort of creek, for wet mud sloshed beneath him as a current trickled by. His head rested on something. What it was he didn't quite know. All that mattered was the fact that it kept his ears, mouth and nose above any water. The rest of his body sat in a cold, muddy current. Droplets fell into the water all around him. Some fell on his face. Some fell on rocks. Critters crawled all around him. Sartan could hear their tiny, exoskeleton legs clatter on the rocks, but it was so dark he couldn't see any of them.

Time went on, how much he didn't know, but time went on nonetheless. Sartan began growing more anxious with every drop of water that splattered on a rock or dripped into the water. There was no light. He was hoping things would go like they did after using the Pisces Gemstone: being in a perilous situation before suddenly falling into the safety of a waiting room. *At least I can breathe this time, and since when were waiting rooms the safest place for me to be?* The sounds of bugs crawling on wet rocks was as inviting as it was when he got here, not. When he arrived here was another question he couldn't answer. He remembered feeling quite euphoric before slipping face first into the concrete. Everything went black, and he woke up a few times in the exact creek he found himself currently in. Eventually he woke up after slipping in and out of consciousness, and now he waited. He found that the only non-stop constant was the water trickling past him. It didn't stop for him. It didn't wait for him. The cold water slushed by with ease almost as if he wasn't there at all.

Sartan's lips would glow blue had there been light on them, and his shivering would make any onlooker internally uncomfortable. He whispered to himself, "How did I get here? I was just in Dursnia living an easy life. It wasn't the easiest, but I knew how to live it. Why? I want to go back in time. I just want to go back."

"Then go back," said a deep-voiced man from straight ahead.

"Wha-wha-what?!" exclaimed Sartan who was unable to move or speak properly in the cold, unforgiving water.

A dark blue flame lit up on the top of a tall candlestick. The man holding it was tall and thin. His short and unkept black beard contrasted the pearlescent-purple dragon and pearlescent-purple buttons on his black military uniform.Thick black boots hugged his ankles, and he wore tight, white gloves made of leather. The violet lighting opened up the world to Sartan, who now could see his surroundings perfectly. Dark purple water flowed through a large crevice in the rocks, and a rock ceiling with stalactites dripping even more water throughout the rest of the cramped cave opened up to him. Hundreds of centipedes crawled up and down the walls of the cave, but even they refused to crawl too close to the man.

"Come on Sartan," said the man with an extended hand. "Get out of the water."

Sartan reluctantly grabbed the man's hand while asking, "Are you-"

"Yes," heaved the man as he pulled Sartan up out of the water. "I am Stir."

"You don't have the head of a scorpion though," said Sartan.

"That is because you are in my realm," said Stir monotonously. "I don't want to make you fear me like Ryby did. I certainly could, but I am not feeling like it right now."

"Oh," replied Sartan.

"Anyways, how was your encounter with Ryby? Exciting?"

"It was definitely interesting."

"Ryby has always been an interesting character, but he has been through a lot in his long, long life. There may have been some pent up emotion in him to unload on you," said Stir calmly while walking off into the darkness.

Sartan jogged after him to keep up and ask, "Is it really true that he had been alive for ten thousand years?"

"Of course, it was probably more like fifteen thousand, but all that knowledge is very difficult to access and even harder to coax out of the stubborn fish. Thankfully, it would probably be used for corruption again if it wasn't," answered Stir who was casually manipulating the water in the stream next to him with his free hand. "Now he can only interact with those who touch his stone, Cancer, and I."

"I haven't seen him or Cancer since arriving here. Why is that?" asked Sartan with wide eyes.

"That is because I won't allow Ryby in my realm, not after what he did to me," said Stir with more passion in his voice this time. "Now as for Cancer I don't know where she is. I allow her into my realm freely, but she does have a tendency to disappear for no reason. Usually at the worst times, for example, now."

Sartan shivered his mouth to ask, "Why are you so calm now? In the waiting room you were frantic to tell me everything as quickly as possible."

"Precisely," said Stir. "That is because we were trying to protect you from Ryby. He knows a lot but his intentions are not necessarily…beneficial to the masses anymore, you included. However, you are not in any immediate danger while you are with me, and I have lots more time to speak with you than previously."

"If I've learned anything, it's that I'm always in immediate danger."

"You haven't even seen the smallest bit of danger in your life," laughed Stir as all the water in the stream bubbled up towards the ceiling at the raising of his hand. "I've been watching you since Aqila recruited you into her group, and the few instances of danger you've dealt with are dwarfed when placed next to just one year of my childhood."

"At least you can remember yours," said Sartan with a smirk.

"Well then," replied Stir, dropping all the water back into the stream. "Cancer did mention that briefly to me, but I believe it has helped you out more than you realize. Do you not agree?"

"I don't know. We think it is brainwashing because Lev mentioned something about brainwashing, and to me that makes sense because I can still remember a few vague things."

"Lev would be correct in this rare circumstance. I figured Lev would have forgotten who you were or at the very least slain you upon finding you," stated Stir who was weaving the water after random centipedes that got too close.

"Unfortunately she didn't. Apparently Lev and my mother had connections. Trade routes or something. Business partners. I can't remember, but she mentioned that if I could find Leucemie my memory might get sparked into existence."

"Leucemie?" asked Stir. "The guard or whatever?"

"No, I don't think she was a guard. Lev claimed that her and I were close friends and that she had been locked away in the dungeons of one of the Water Zodiac Palaces. If I can find her she might be able to help me remember," explained Sartan.

"No. Lev lied. Cancer sent a girl named Leucemie to my palace for extra defense right before I died. I was never there to accept her to guard the palace, so my assistant forbade her from entering," said Stir who was practically talking to himself at this point. "I didn't find out until after Cancer and I died when Cancer told me, but I can assure you she is still there protecting the entrance to my palace. It will be four years since I died this July. Cancer gave her powers…but Cancer is dead so Leucemie must have had to…well my assistant must have had to…"

Stir trailed off into his thoughts as Sartan watched him think, and the water in the stream grew faster and choppier with each moment.

"No!" exclaimed Stir as the current of purple water splashed at Sartan's feet with the increased speed. "My assistant…my right hand…"

Sartan watched as the flame on Stir's candle flickered halfway down the stick. The water thrashed about beside him before it finally calmed down to a steady trickle. A cold breeze shot throughout the endless cave, and the centipedes tried to hide in any crevice they could find.

"This is quite an unfortunate turn of events. I try not to think about the feeding needs of those left unrepresented, but I must admit it gnaws at me if I let it. Let me focus on the task at hand. Lev, even though she is training you, is going to hurt you."

"How do you know that?" asked Sartan.

"Look, there are some things you just don't understand right now," replied Stir as he sat down to put his feet in the icy water. "I don't know if Cancer wants you to know everything or not, so I can't explain it to you without both of us in agreement. All that you need to know is that Lev is using you."

"She wants to make me powerful," argued Sartan.

"No, she wants to make herself look good for Kozoroh!" snapped back Stir. "She knows who you really are, and if she can manipulate and control you she will look really good in Kozoroh's eyes. It will make him even more accomplished if you fight for their side."

"I'm not fighting for any side," explained Sartan as he sat down next to Stir. "I'm just helping them while they help me. There isn't even a side going against Lev or Kozoroh. I mean, I know they aren't in it for the people, but neither am I to be brutally honest."

"You're naive. They truly don't have any resistance for their plans which is why they can gracefully do it in the background without anyone noticing. The closest thing we have to a resisting force would be Aqila and a few scattered rebellions, and the brutally honest truth with that is you know how dysfunctional each of those groups are. I know you just want to fix your memory and live a life happily ever after, but this isn't fiction, Sartan. That won't be possible if Kozoroh is around. Billions of lives are in peril, and the scariest part is that none of them even realize it. You are becoming a force that has a greater and greater influence on that outcome. You think you know what you are doing, but you are painfully lost, running in circles chasing a futile dream that wasn't meant for you in the first place."

"You don't know me."

Stir sighed, "Okay, this is what we are doing then. You are right to an extent. I don't know what you are thinking or feeling. I don't know what you may have been through in the past four years on the streets, but I do know who you are. I do know your history, and quite frankly I know more about your life than you do yourself. We've met before, and we will meet again. You act as though you don't want my insight, but it was you that came to MY realm for MY guidance. Even if you didn't mean to, Lev forced you to come here for MY training. If I wanted to I could make the rest of our encounter absolute hell for you, so how about you respect my insight for what it is, gold. If you don't trust me I'd understand, but you aren't even opening up enough to see if what I have to say may be trustworthy or not. Hiding in your shell won't save you from Cancer, Kozoroh, Lev, or even I. You've seen it all now haven't you? You know way more about what to do with your life than I. Well, I'd consider yourself lucky to be listening to someone who has been dead for the past three and a half years! Not everybody gets that privilege!"

"Wow, what a privilege!" exclaimed Sartan sarcastically. "I bet it is so hard being dead!"

"You have the slightest clue! I have been dead and unable to protect those I cared about from Kozoroh. Unlike your pitiful death, when an Active Zodiac dies they are sent to a realm where they replace the previous deceased Zodiac. I am forced to stay in this purgatory state until another Active Scorpio dies. I have to watch from the sidelines as Lev attempts to derail everything I set up via an irresponsible, young man who doesn't know his hip from his nip. Then this same man comes into my realm and disrespects my insight! I can show you what death is really like! It's one of my specialties…"

"I don't need this," said Sartan as he stood up to walk away.

Stir yelled from his seated position, "You are an inconsiderate---"

"You wish!"

Stir stood up while commanding all the water in the cave into a sharp strand. Then he yelled back, "Like I would waste a wish on that!"

"Fine!" screamed Sartan from a few feet away. "What MAGICAL insight does the scorpion have to offer me today?"

"Aqila is already in Garigo."

Sartan stopped. He took a deep breath, and watched Stir slowly return the indigo water back to the stream. Stir smiled a victorious grin while Sartan took a few steps towards him. The flame on the candlestick had melted through most of the candle by now, and he remembered that if he returned to Lev without learning a single technique she would crucify him.

"Do you know where she is specifically?" asked Sartan as politely as possible.

"Now you want to be docile?" asked Stir while Sartan stared at him resentfully. "It is so easy to understand people once you realize their primary motive. Your primary motive is as transparent as glass, and it is as pointless as a tinted window on a stormy night."

"Then what is your primary motive? World domination through me?" asked Sartan sarcastically.

"My primary motive is simple," said Stir without a stutter in his voice. "Kill Kozoroh, kill Lev and kill Blizenci. Then replace all the Zodiacs with new ones, so that the world actually has decent leaders unlike the ones it has now."

"That's it?"

"Yes," answered Stir almost silently. "I don't want my people to go through the pain that I have. If you could just fix the problems I never had a chance to then I'd love you forever. Give them Zodiacal representation that isn't controlled by the backstabbing, murderous fiends that killed me in the first place. If you protect my people, I will try to make sure that they return the favor. It's a simple request. Lev and Ryby killed me. Backstabbed me. They wanted my power. My throne. My people. Thankfully, Ryby lost his chance at that. Just make sure that Kozoroh and the rest of them lose their chance too. You'll understand where I'm coming from after you speak with Cancer, but just don't let Kozoroh take my people away. They've already been through enough."

Sartan stared at Stir in the dim light. A singular tear dripped down the once Active Zodiac's pale face before it got stuck in his short beard. There were many things he didn't understand about the Zodiacs. Never had he seen a Zodiac so invested in their subjects. Everytime Lev encountered a Leo on their travels she just used them as a pawn to advance her play, but it was obvious Stir had a deeper connection with his Scorpios. It was almost as if they were family. United in isolation.

"United in isolation," whispered Sartan as he thought to himself.

"What?" asked Stir as he pulled his cracky voice back under control.

"I'll help you," answered Sartan. "I just want to speak with Cancer before I make my final decision. Every single person I have spoken to…rather been forced to speak to, has told me something that contradicts with another. I want the final piece of the puzzle before I decide to frame it. Not to mention, if she really did kill Ryby then I want to know how to do it. How to take down someone who has so much more experience than I do."

"That sounds like a good idea to me. Cancer will certainly guide you in the right direction," said Stir as he tried not to grin. "Right now Aqila is in the streets with Caleb and Jaako, but they have decided they are going to Murphy's Stewlot after they stop searching for Dominick. It is some sort of soup kitchen or soup shop in the middle ring of Garigo. Aqila is looking for the Taurus Gemstone, but her group is completely falling apart."

"How so?" asked Sartan.

"They all arrived in Garigo last night, but Ferran quickly ran off on his own. He has been drinking and what not while Aqila has been frantically searching for him, running from police, looking for the Taurus Gemstone, and trying to maintain the posse," said Stir while he began playing with the water again. He barely even had to move his fingers to manipulate the water into doing fascinating tricks. "I really do fear that if Aqila doesn't pull herself and her group together then our only shot at saving the world will die."

"What do you want me to do about it then?"

"In all honesty it might be best to stay with Lev for the short term. Use her as much as possible without letting her use you. You are in desperate need of training, and she can do that for you. She has all of the Water Gemstones, and you will need all three of them to replace us. If you can steal them without Lev knowing then you would be giving your group's mission some assistance because we all know they need it. The whole world needs it."

"How long do you want me to stay with Lev?"

"Stay with her until she splits away from Blizenci. There is no way you'd be able to escape them both in Gemini lands, especially with all the extra officers he has looking for Aqila. Your best bet would be to keep them away from Aqila's group. They need to get the Taurus Gemstone as quickly as possible. All of the players are way too close for my comfort, so do not let Lev or Blizenci find the stone either. Then this group you found will continue looking here until she is captured."

Sartan asked, "So you want me to just sit here and wait for Aqila to escape Garigo?"

"Precisely, you can't get too close to them or else Lev will find them. You can't get the stone for them because they will continue searching for it, and you can't help them find Ferran because that would involve interacting with them. If you see them, distance yourself quickly. All you can do right now is train for when the time is right and slow Lev down as much as possible."

"Speaking of training, if I return to Lev without knowing anything then she will know I've been talking about betraying her," stated Sartan while he watched Stir manipulate the water.

"Crap!" exclaimed Stir as he looked at his candle burning away. "We don't have much time! Let's get up and do this then!" Stir took a defensive stance positioned towards the stream. He placed the remaining inch or two of the candle on the cold cave floor. "Now imagine Lev is ten feet in front of you about to blast you with fire."

"Okay," said Sartan as he tried to mimic Stir's stance.

"Good, now open your palm and have it face your target. Extend your opened hand outwards as far as your arm can stretch."

"Okay."

"After that, quickly clench your fist and pull it all the way back to your side."

Sartan attempted the maneuver without success. "Nothing happened," said Sartan sadly.

"That is because you are in my realm. Had my Gemstone been in your pocket, and had you tried that move in reality a gush of cold water would've hit Lev from behind her."

"So I don't need any water to begin with to do this?" asked Sartan.

"Not if you have the stone or are an inactive or Active Zodiac," replied Stir as he took a new more aggressive stance. "The water around you will only make your attacks stronger, but you do not need it to cause problems at all."

"Got you," said Sartan as he copied Stir's stance again.

"This time take both fists to your stomach and kneel down a little bit," commanded Stir while doing exactly as he said. "Hold it there for a few seconds before shooting both of your fists out at the target, and a large beam of cold water should fly straight at your target so quickly it could pierce through metal. Of course using that one on a person could wrap things up quickly if you're in trouble."

Sartan was about to try it when the light from the candle suddenly went out. Everything went pitch black within an instant, and Sartan kept whispering for Stir, without a response. The cold of the cave quickly became a problem for him once more, and in the distance he could hear whimpered screams of women and men. They screamed for help. They screamed for revenge. They screamed at each other. One thing was consistent with them all; their screams would echo in and out of reality as Sartan stood still like a stone. They begged for help, but as Sartan listened he could only start to hear their begs after their first few words. Before they could finish the sentence their pleas echoed out of reality leaving Sartan listening to an endless loop of half formed pleas.

Luckily, as the howls went on Sartan saw a bright orange light glow at the end of the cave. It grew closer, and it grew brighter. It gained on him until the entire cave had lit up enough for him to see the centipedes in their true glory. Human heads were plastered all over the centipede's bodies, which had grown significantly in size. The centipedes screamed out for his help, and he realized it was them who were howling over each other the whole time. Once in the light they all scrambled to him as quickly as their tiny little legs would take them, and by now Stir was nowhere to be found. The only ray of hope was the ever growing bright light at the end of the cave. Sartan sprinted into it over being at the mercy of the centipedes, and as it grew to a blinding level of brightness he closed his eyes only to open his eyes.

"You have awoken!" exclaimed Lev as her face was the only thing he could see. "It has been nearly three hours, so Stir better have taught you something!"

Sartan leaned up off his back to see the same abandoned warehouse, but now it had more damage to it than before. Before standing up all the way, Sartan reassured Lev, "Trust me...Stir taught me some techniques."

"Good. Good. Hopefully you had enough fun because you will not be breaking through the Cancer stone today. We need to focus on training now," said Lev as she backed away, taking an aggressive stance. A fireball quickly grew in her left hand, and Sartan scrambled to produce a counterattack.

Chapter 17
The Butcher
Aqila

The lighting could most definitely have used some work. Other than that Aqila enjoyed the atmosphere of Murphy's Stewlot. Constant chattering of happy, hungry people and continuous clattering dishes in the back of house made it difficult for anyone to overhear a conversation, but more importantly, with all of the people inside the store, officers would have a harder time finding her in here than if she stayed out in the open. Nonetheless, twelve crisp ones for a bowl of stew seemed a bit expensive, but since it managed to take away some of her chills and hunger Aqila gladly paid that price. When the price tripled, however, it would put her back a bit financially as she needed to find a way to feed Caleb and Jaako for the day, and she knew a little too well that Caleb could eat her coffers away. Across the dimly lit table sat Caleb who had finished his mushroom soup minutes ago. Jaako, next to him, kept getting distracted by all of the waitresses that were running food. Aqila finally gulped down the last bit of her own soup. The heated contents of her meal broke sweat on her brow, but she was fully certain there was another reason for her sweat as she still shivered in the hot diner. She simply did not want to waste twelve dollars on soup that she might throw up in half an hour.

Across the room next to the entrance was an electronic, billiton board. On the board were various notices: employee of the month, special of the week, hiring information. It all was unimportant, but as Aqila stared at it longer, attempting to ignore the conversation Jaako and Caleb were currently having about certain waitresses, she identified more important notices. Some were rewards for missing dogs while some were rewards for missing people. One was a reward for a botched sketch of…her? It was a poorly drawn image, but it vaguely matched her facial structure. *The eyebrows are a little thick, but at least they got th----WAIT! One thousand for the sorry soul who catches me? You have got to be kidding me! As if I need any extra stress. As if I did anything wrong to begin with. Now I have a warrant for my arrest, and these two simps next to me probably do too.*

"No you won't!" exclaimed Caleb with a full hearted chuckle.

"Don't believe me? Then watch!" replied Jaako slyly while raising his hand to get the waitress's attention. "Watch and learn Caleb!"

"What is he doing?!" asked Aqila frantically. Her face started beating red, and she was clueless to exactly what Jaako was doing yet.

"He's gonna get rejected!" laughed Caleb. "That's what he's doing!"

Aqila swiftly twisted her head around looking for their waitress that had served them. As expected, the young waitress strutted over towards their table. Her long brown hair kissed her round curves, and the paint on her face covered any acne that may have troubled her this morning. She smiled with perfect white teeth while gracefully walking closer like a swan, and wore the tightest possible clothes on the planet to further display her natural beauty. It was sickening. Aqila knew that most, if not all, of her beauty was fake all the while shaming that of her own, but she also knew that Jaako cared not. Despite having the keen eyesight of an inactive Sagittarius Zodiac, he still had managed to get himself hypnotized by the ancient art of attraction. It was obvious Caleb was under the same trance, possibly not as much, but he had quieted down an unnatural amount for himself as the woman approached.

"What can I get for you?" asked the waitress in an unnecessarily high pitched voice.

"Just a couple things," attempted Jaako as his face promptly went pink. An awkward moment of silence passed where Aqila watched her companions' faces go from peachy pink to tomato red. Jaako finally continued, "Well we can start with your number. Then I'll need your schedule, so we can find some time to waste together. After that I'll probably need your address."

Aqila watched the waitress look Jaako up and down like she was analyzing her prey: deciding whether or not it would make her sick to catch him, deciding whether or not he was really being serious, and possibly deciding whether or not she should call the police. It did not take long at all for her to make her decision. Her smile instantly faded, but she managed to fake it temporarily while replying, "I'm sorry, but I have a boyfriend." She then returned to her job probably as readily as she ever would. Aqila stared off into space not believing what just happened whereas Caleb had a more explosive response.

"HARGHHGARGH!!" squealed Caleb excessively. He seemingly choked on his own breath for a moment, or he turned into a broken record player that was stuck on the same 'WHAHAHAHAHA'. Aqila was unsure, but she did know that the red on Jaako's face definitely was there to stay.

"Ouch," whispered Jaako to himself. "Since when did people actually have long term relationships? Garigo is so strange."

"Jaako, long term relationships are common outside of Dursnia," answered Aqila with mellow. "You are just a creep who asked her for her address, number and schedule."

"No they aren't!" exclaimed Caleb who was desperately trying not to break down into another laughing fit. "That was just her way of telling you that you're uglier than a farm goat! WHAHAWHA!!!"

"Whatever you say guys. We all know that she just doesn't have any taste in men," murmured Jaako. He then studied the crowd for a new target.

Aqila stood up from the table and said, "I will be back." She did not want to witness Jaako make a fool of himself again, and she also needed to make it to the restroom suddenly. She breezed through the crowds of people who stood around adjacent tables while making her way to the bathroom. Aqila kept her head down the entire time, especially when she passed the electronic, wanted poster of herself. There was a narrow hallway with a few people walking out of it, and the door with a feminine silhouette on it swayed shut as she approached it. When Aqila pulled on the door warm, salty saliva flooded her mouth.

The inside of the bathroom was cleaner than the diner for some reason. All of the stalls were empty, and she was alone in the bathroom. Aqila sprinted into the first stall, barely managing to lock the door before she started gagging. She dropped to her knees and opened her mouth over the toilet letting all of the hot, salty saliva drip out into the bowl. The heated liquid dripped out of her along with a few tears for what felt like an eternity as a fiery pain slowly churned in her stomach. "Just do it already!" she exclaimed as her knees began getting weaker. "Just get ou--" The splashing echoed through the entire bathroom. Every last drop of soup came back up, and it never tasted nearly as well as it did the first time. It burned. It hurt, and most of all Aqila knew what would make it stop. She just did not know how to get any. Aqila threw up a few more times, and then flushed the toilet. She sat up on the toilet, and while holding back her tears, buried her face in her hands.

Now she had a headache and was hungrier than she was before eating. Suddenly, the door to the bathroom creaked open. The entering woman made haste to one of the stalls next to her, and as the black silhouette passed it was apparent she was in just as hurry as Aqila was. *Maybe she had the same soup that I did.* Naturally that was too good to be true. The woman simply sat down and sighed. *I need to go now before Caleb or Jaako get suspicious or, more likely, before they get kicked out for flirting with the waitresses.*

"Hello," said the woman who was a few stalls down. Aqila was just about to get up and return to her companions when the woman continued with, "Not...quite."

Aqila could hear a deep voice on the phone mutter intensively back at the woman, but she could not quite tell what he was saying.

"Someone beat me to it, but you can rest assured I will not sleep until they are dealt with," said the woman in a nervous tone. "They were a bunch of nobodies...Yes...I understand...A few weeks at the most...I know..."

The conversation was difficult to eavesdrop on when hearing the half of it was nearly impossible, but once Aqila leaned over to the side the man on the other line could be heard faintly.

"And where are you now?" asked the man stoically from the phone.

"I currently have been forced into Garigo. I am diligently looking for them. As a matter of fact I have already caught one, but the rest are right under my nose I promise," replied the woman whose voice teased Aqila to continue eavesdropping on this random woman's conversation.

"You were doing so well, but now after this I am unsure if you are capable of..." The man cut out, and Aqila could only hear the first half of his sentence.

"I am capable, I promise!" exclaimed the woman. "I have already found one for the Water--"

"Your job was to focus on your element and prevent a water sign from returning! What part of that did you misunderstand? What..."

Wait...

"I didn't misunderstand or disobey you at all! I was just attempting to help!"

"Do not raise your voice with me! If it were never for me you would still be nothing, and you and I both know I can take it all away," said the man violently yet methodically.

"Yes."

"I want information on this individual!"

"Certainly, he is a young man I found in a forest bordering the Ge…."

"That shall not cut it Lev!" exclaimed the man. "I need a name, a visual description and everything you know about this young man."

Lev! How did she get this close? I need to get the others and leave right now! Aqila stood up from the toilet while wiping her mouth dry. She unlocked her stall's door as quietly as possible and slowly pushed it open. Thankfully, the faint creak it made was masked by Lev's response.

"He is a subject of the Cancer Zodiac. I do not know his exact age. I assume he is either twenty or twenty-three. Within that frame."

"Stop wasting time telling me unimportant information," replied the man who was sounding more irritated with each second. "A Cancer subject who is twenty, what is his name?"

Aqila tip-toed towards the door of the bathroom stall trying her hardest not to get caught. She still had to gather up Jaako and Caleb before even attempting to escape through the backdoor. Merely a few feet from the door, Aqila stopped right next to the air dryers upon hearing Lev's response.

"His name is Sartan."

What!? Is she joking? There is no way. He died. Unless…unless she found him in the forest.

"What!?" said the man intensely. "Sartan as in?…"

"I believe so…" answered Lev hesitantly. "I have been training him to take on his position as Wagustus of the Water Zodiacs."

"How much does he know?" asked the man hastily. "Has he broken through the Cancer Gemstone yet? What does he remember?"

Aqila stood as still as a steadily burning fire and listened closely to Lev's reply, "Thankfully, he does not remember much, but he has already broken through the Pisces and Scorpio Gemstones. After he came back from his experience in the Scorpio Gemstone he had knowledge of where my fugitives were, so I believe that Stir may be trying to help him, help us."

"You fool! Why would Stir try to help us?!" screamed the man. "Ryby maybe, but Stir!? Do you know what Stir might have told him during his experience!? At the very least, Stir is helping him become more aware of our intentions! Has he broken through to Cancer yet?"

"No, I did not think that would have been a good idea this early on."

"It won't be. Ever! Does he know how all of the other Zodiacs died yet?" asked the man.

"Not all of them, but he knows the truth behind the downfall of the Water Zodiacs."

"If that is the case I want you to constrict his access to knowledge until we can get someone to brainwash him again. Your main priority, however, remains all the way back at the Sagittarius Palace, yet you are out there in Garigo, chasing an inactive Sagittarius? You have begun disappointing me at an exponential rate the longer I am on the phone with you. An interesting find indeed, but I demand you deal with these fugitives Blizenci told me about whilst simultaneously keeping Sartan out of the know. If you fail to do even one of these-"

While Aqila scratched her elbow she failed to realize how close she was to the air dryer. It suddenly went off and cut out the man on the phone. She knew not to risk staying in the bathroom with Lev any longer, so the door was instantly flung open. As she ran out of the women's room she could hear Lev murmur something as the dryer turned off.

"My liege, I must call you back…"

The bathroom door shut behind her as she hastily made her way through the hallway. The many bodies that stood in her way were way more antagonizing now that she knew Lev was in the house with her! Simply knowing that Sartan was still alive gave her enough hope to forgive Ferran. *Ferran could be forgiven, to an extent, and Sartan could be rescued from Lev in the future. We can get the whole group together, and this confirms he was never lying to us about his memory! But why is Sartan so important to Lev and this liege? Who even is Lev's liege? Wait…No!* An epiphany fueled Aqila grew closer to her table.

At the table was another waitress kneeling over writing something down on a piece of paper. She was very short, but certainly not as attractive as the previous waitress Aqila had seen. Her presence annoyed Aqila, but she was aware that she had no time for such trivial distractions.

She walked up next to the waitress and boldly stated, "Jaako, Caleb, we need to go! Now!"

"Hold on Aqila he's getting a number," laughed Caleb who was watching the waitress slowly write down each digit.

"You fail to understand! We need to leave!" exclaimed Aqila while tugging on Jaako's arm.

"Hold on Aqila. Let her finish writing down her number," replied Jaako who was not looking at her penmanship skills but rather the buttons on her chest that held together the shirt.

"Come on guys, I am being serious!" exclaimed Aqila.

"Please ignore her, she's just got jet lag," said Jaako, whose hand grabbed the piece of unused napkin the waitress had written on. "I'll call you soon!"

After Jaako got to watch the waitress walk off with his keen Sagittarius sight, he stood up slowly almost as if he were in a daze. Caleb followed, but neither of them were moving fast enough for Aqila's content. She glanced around the diner as they slowly made their way around the table. It was nearly impossible to see through to the opposite wall consistently with all of the happy people moving around next to each other, but on the far side of the room Aqila watched a tall woman gracefully step out of the hallway that extends to the restrooms, and ironically, the backdoor. It was undeniably Lev with her long and thick black hair, but more importantly it was the fact that she did not blend in with the crowd at all. It had to be Lev, and she had to be scanning the diner for her fugitives.

"HURRY!" screamed Aqila as quietly as possible. "Follow me!"

There was no looking back to make sure they were following. *If they get caught because they are distracted by women...that is their fault.* Aqila bobbed and weaved her way to the front door as speedily as physically possible, and upon reaching the fresh, open air, she took an immediate right turn to get out of sight. Even though she was now walking on the sidewalk of a busy road with lots of people next to her, there were still giant, clear windows that exposed her to all of the guests inside Murphy's Stewlot. Instantly upon clearing the side of the building, Aqila flung herself around the edge into an alleyway. She then poked her head around the corner of Murphy's Stewlot to see her two, entranced companions following her. The closer they got, the angrier Jaako looked.

"What was that for?" screamed Jaako as he followed her into the alleyway.

"What was what for?" responded Aqila. "I just saved our lives!"

"You know exactly what I'm talking about! You cut my interaction with that fine lady short!"

"I saved your life in the process too!" exclaimed Aqila while she kept walking further into the alley. "Lev is inside that building looking for us as we speak Jaako!"

"I'm sure she is! Just because Ferran killed Sartan doesn't mean you have to take it all out on us!" exclaimed Jaako who was pulling the napkin out of his pocket vigorously. "If it wasn't for that nice lady we wouldn't have a location to check for Kreet!"

"What?" said Aqila who stopped dead in her tracks.

"That fine girl didn't just give me her number," said Jaako slyly. "We asked her where to find someone like Dominick Kreet, an ex-war veteran, and she gave us a location. Even drew me a map too!"

A rough sketch on a piece of napkin was handed to her, and Aqila grabbed it to see that they were only a few blocks away from this girl's idea of where Dominick could be. Her government issued phone number was conveniently written on the opposite side.

"We can not use this. She might just be messing with you Jaako," argued Aqila who was taking the alleys that would slowly bring her away from Murphy's Stewlot and closer to the point on the napkin map. "How did you even get her to do this?"

"He just asked her if she'd know where an ex-war veteran may be," answered Caleb who trailed behind her. "What other options do we have?"

"At least she is giving us some sort of direction. We have been here about a day without any luck. What if he really is there?" argued Jaako.

"Fine! We can go there!" exclaimed Aqila in annoyance. "But when we fail to find him and have nowhere to sleep again tonight what do we do? What do we do when we still need a gemstone, a Tansiq scroll, a person to fill the Virgo role, and Ferran?"

"I have no clue," answered Jaako with a laugh. "It always works out though."

"Surely we will think of something," replied Caleb with slightly more optimism. "We didn't make it this far to fail here."

"Oh, and we can never forget about Lev being only a minute away, possibly chasing us right now. We can never forget about the warrants for all of our arrests I was oblivious to until just now," mumbled Aqila. "If they catch me there is a one-thousand reward. I did not see your posters, but I am sure that they have been posted somewhere."

"Being a wanted man is nothing new," said Jaako as he took back the napkin map straight from Aqila's hands.

Then Caleb walked up to Aqila's side and said, "Let's just focus on getting to the nursing home that the waitress told us about."

Aqila nodded without speaking, and she quickly let Caleb and Jaako lead the way there. She trailed behind them with sweat on her brow and a pain in her cranium. *How is he alive? What is an Wagustus, and why did I let this all happen?* Aqila rolled these thoughts around her head for a majority of the walk, not realizing how many streets they passed or officers they merely missed. With each step she wished it were her last, but Jaako and Caleb trudged on. She did not want to be alone, especially in Garigo with Lev simply missing her by seconds. *They seem to be getting along. Better than Ferran and Sartan at least. Ferran could learn something from this had he been here.*

Before she knew it they had arrived at the nursing home's entrance. A giant, gray skyscraper towered over them, and enormous, white windows striped the sides of the building. Not a lot of people came in and out of the building, and those who did were workers or family members of a patient. It did not matter what their story was because Aqila unfortunately did not plan on doing any talking, so when she followed Jaako into the building not much happened.

Once inside the air controlled room, the three of them stood near the door like lost dogs with no owners. A counter was centered in the lobby with a few secretaries working. There were lots of chairs and tables all around them, even vending machines, but there were also a lot of people sitting around doing nothing. It was not long before people began noticing them standing there, so despite her lack of energy, Aqila was forced to do something.

"Stop looking around and go talk to the secretary to see if we can see Dominick," whispered Aqila. Neither of her companions replied, but they did abide by her wishes, so she continued to look around the airy room. Two school buses could probably fit between the floor and the ceiling, vertically. The tall windows matched the height of the room letting too much sunlight gas the lobby, and the gray carpet that they walked on appeared insanely soft yet simultaneously worn down. After an awkward walk through the room they had finally made it to the secretaries in all white.

A man sat behind the desk on the phone. He took the phone away from his mouth for a brief second while holding up a finger. He then promised, "I will be with you in one minute."

Immediately after hearing that, another secretary in the square of desks said, "I can help you over here whenever you are ready."

"Yes, we would like to see one of your patients," replied Jaako as he walked around to her side of the box.

"Certainly, can I get a name?" proceeded the woman as she clicked away on her computer.

"Dominick," said Jaako who was blindly unsure. "Dominick Keef."

"Dominick Keef?" asked the secretary. "It appears we don't have anyone by that name here."

"I apologize his name is Dominick Kreet," interrupted Aqila who couldn't sit and watch this happen any longer.

"Perfect, now we have two Dominick Kreet's, but I'm assuming you are here for the recently admitted Dominick Kreet of the upper ring. His lungs still aren't doing that well, so here are a few masks for you," said the woman as she wheeled away to a drawer on her left.

"Is he a war veteran?" asked Caleb.

"Oh," replied the secretary who was in the middle of grabbing three face masks. She sat in the chair stationary before answering. "You must be talking about the Dominick Kreet from the lower ring. The one who claims he fought for Taurus as some sort of high ranking general in the Shamal War?"

Jaako started, "Yes that is exactly who we are looki-"

Aqila kicked Jaako's foot, stopping him mid sentence while replying, "Yes that is who we are visiting. Have not seen him in ages."

"Poor man. We have had to up his meds three times, but he still believes he fought in the war," replied the woman with a grim face. "There isn't one record showing that he ever did, but if you are here to visit him I am sure you are already aware of his condition. I do fear his condition is worsening by the day, so be patient with him. He is in room sixteen on floor thirty-six. Don't go higher than thirty-six as…well I'm sure you know the floors above that are designated for the crops. The elevators are right down that hallway next to the bathrooms."

"Come on, I wanna go see him," said Aqila towards Jaako and Caleb, loud enough for the secretary to hear. As soon as they walked far enough to be out of earshot she whispered, "I guess he is here after all."

She refused to glance at Jaako's smug smirk that surely was waiting for her had she turned around. Instead she led the way progressing into the hallway where the elevators were located. As they waited for the elevator to make it to the ground floor, Aqila zoned out while watching the secretaries working tirelessly. *What is taking so long?* The elevator then beeped quite loudly, stealing her from her impatient thoughts. The shiny, silver doors opened, and a woman in all black rushed out hastily. The clothes she wore did not match the citizens of Garigo. Her silky lab coat glistened with red accents in peculiar spots as the woman nearly ran past them, and her black pants were damp from an unknown liquid. She had deep brown hair that was completely slicked back from her forehead to her neck. It was visibly wet with gel.

As the woman disappeared out into the lobby, Caleb spoke from within the elevator, "Hey guys."

"What?" asked Aqila nervously as she lunged into the elevator with Jaako.

"Look at the ground button," said Caleb softly.

Aqila glanced at all of the buttons and saw nothing out of the ordinary, but when her gaze made it to the lobby button that changed. The button was completely stained red. Aqila hastily pressed button thirty-six, so that no one else got in the elevator with them. Then she looked around the rest of the elevator for any other signs of blood. Of course, the only trace was on the button.

"Did you guys notice the blood on her jacket?" asked Jaako during the ascent to floor thirty-six.

"It was on her pants too," answered Caleb quietly. "What was she doing here?"

"I am unsure," replied Aqila as they approached their floor.

BEEP! The elevator doors slowly wheeled open, and on the other side were two visitors looking to return home. Aqila smiled at the elderly women and exited the elevator with her companions. They walked down the hallway refusing to say a word until the elevator shut behind them, but when it did Caleb was not hesitant to say it.

"They'll think we got the button all bloody."

"I was thinking that," said Jaako as they passed room four.

"We have to hurry then!" exclaimed Aqila. "They will certainly tell someone."

"What if this is all in vain?" asked Caleb with growing uncertainty. "What if this isn't even the right Dominick Kreet? What if he isn't even in this building?"

"Then we are really putting ourselves at risk," laughed Jaako nonchalantly. "It wouldn't be the first time something like that has happened to me. Back in Dursnia my friends and I had planned to hit a house that had some decent stuff in it. We knew that the owners were on vacation, so we broke in."

"What are you talking about?" asked Aqila who was wondering why Jaako left Dursnia so freely.

Jaako continued without answering her question, "No listen. Apparently the owners were not on vacation, so when we broke in it was a mad dash to break back out. The father had a gun, and now one of my old friends has a bullet hole in his arm. Fun times."

"Jaako, why did you join us so freely?" asked Aqila as they passed room eleven. "With your home and life in Dursnia, you just joined us without notifying anyone."

"Well, I was tired of Dursnia," said Jaako simply. "I wanted something new."

"What about all of your family and friends?" asked Caleb.

"Eh, my parents never really focused on me that much. If I asked them for food they'd just tell me to look through their empty pantry, so the past few years I've been living on my own with my friends. My mother is never sober, and my father is always working, so I'm sure they haven't noticed my disappearance at all. If they did then good! Fuck them!"

"What about your friends? Surely you cared about someone," said Aqila who was becoming more concerned with Jaako's past.

"Not really. They were more of a necessary evil," replied Jaako with a cover up laugh. "They'd lie to me and sleep with my girl when I had one. I only kept them because surviving in Dursnia alone is impossible. The only friend I trusted was literally my clone. He was just like me, but he got killed by two of my other friends. One got a life sentence, and the other got a death sentence. Even though the cops only caught people when it was your friends doing the crimes, they definitely deserved it. From then on I just hung out with mutual friends when I needed food or money."

"That is fucked!" exclaimed Aqila. "I hope they all get what they deserve!"

"Look, it's room sixteen," said Caleb who was pointing to the slightly open door. "Are you guys ready for the truth? For the whole reason we came to Garigo?"

"May as well be!" exclaimed Jaako sarcastically.

Aqila knocked on the half open door softly, and when there was no response she slowly creaked it open. The inside was warm and stuffy, almost like nobody had been in there for days. There was a kitchen sink, a fridge and some cupboards to put stuff in. The cabinets were all ripped open and dug through. The shiny knives and silverware were scattered together in the drawer, but a few of them were stained red. A microwave sat on the counter, and a closet was opened on the left wall. All sorts of shirts and clothes were scattered on its floor as if a firestorm had just ripped through. The bathroom door on the right side of the room was ripped off the hinges and laying up against the wall. Aqila was about to venture through the empty doorway to see what had happened in there when she gazed further down the room to the large, glass window at the end.

There was a dark oak dresser that sat on one side of the giant window with a television posted on top of it. The television was cracked and the drawers were all torn out of the dresser. A twin sized bed was crunched up into the other corner of the room with the sheets trampled across the floor. An old man laid in the bed motionless. He watched Aqila come closer to him without saying a word. He was severely wounded. His face was tattered gray with scruffy facial hair, most of which was tainted red with his own blood. He looked aimlessly at Aqila as she stared at his zombified eyes. His malnourished neck had deep gouges in it, letting blood pour out as his throat wobbled when he began speaking. He was in pain, but he still managed to talk softly.

"Get out of my room."

"Are you okay?!" exclaimed Aqila in wonder as she rushed to his side. "What happened!?!?"

"The Butcher."

"What?" asked Caleb who was standing next to the window that took up the entirety of the fourth wall. "Do you know who did this?"

"Yes, the Butcher," choked the man as blood trickled out of his mouth. "And she will be back when she doesn't find the stone."

"The Taurus Gemstone?" asked Caleb out loud. "You are the right Dominick Kreet!"

"She will kill you if she finds you in here," coughed Dominick as his voice grew fainter. "Go now before it is too late."

"We came all the way from Mirisburg to find you," said Aqila who was now kneeling next to the man. "I am not giving up on you now!"

"It's too late to save me. Save yourselves."

"Don't give up, who is the Butcher?" asked Caleb.

"I'll never tell," said the man as he closed his eyes.

"Wait! Wait! Listen to me!" exclaimed Aqila. "We are trying to revive the Zodiacs and are looking for the Taurus Gemstone. Marcus told us to find you! We have already recreated Sagittarius!"

Dominick Kreet opened his eyes once more and replied, "Impossible."

"We really have!" exclaimed Caleb. "Jaako show him! Jaako?"

Aqila turned around not seeing Jaako anywhere in sight. The door to the hallway was shut behind them, but Jaako was no longer in the room. *Where did he go? Is he getting a nurse?*

Aqila started, "I think he is getting a nu-"

"What?" asked Jaako as his head poked around the bathroom doorway. "I was looking through the bathroom for clues."

"Clues!? Jaako! Quick, show Dominick that you are an inactive Zodiac!" exclaimed Aqila.

"How?" asked Jaako nervously.

"I don't know, use your flames or something!"

"I don't know how to do that on command!" exclaimed Jaako as he shook his hands vigorously. "I can't force it."

"If it were true he'd be able to create a flame on command," whispered Dominick Kreet on his deathbed. "Now let me go in peace."

FRRHHHSHHH! Aqila swung her head back to Jaako who was trying not to let the pinkish flame go out in his hands. The room slowly began cooling down, and Dominick would have no other excuse.

"See!" exclaimed Aqila whose attention was back on Dominick. "See!?"

"Aye, he is a freshly created one isn't he?" asked Dominick softly.

"At most a few weeks," answered Aqila. "Can you help us find the Taurus stone so we can stop Kozoroh? Can you tell us who the Butcher is?"

The man stared at her emotionlessly. Aqila stared back unsure what he was thinking. Then he finally answered with, "I'm going to die today."

"I can get you a nurse just hang in there!" exclaimed Aqila while pointing at Caleb to get a nurse.

"Don't waste your time boy," said the man in his loudest tone yet. "The stone will be safe once I am gone. Nobody will be able to find it."

"We need it to recreate the Zodiacs!" exclaimed Aqila desperately.

"I don't care," whispered Dominick as his eyelids slowly fluttered shut. "I have my orders, and a true soldier never falters."

"If you don't tell us where it is, then there might never be another Taurus again!" exclaimed Aqila in a last pitch effort to persuade him.

A long moment of silence passed before, while coughing up a bit of blood, Dominick let out, "How do I know you aren't with the Butcher or Kozoroh?"

"Who the hell is this Butcher!?" exclaimed Jaako from the doorway to the bathroom.

"They call her that because she butchers her victims! LOOK AT ME!"

Aqila obeyed the elderly man and took a step back to inspect his current state a bit more closely. The slices in his neck were plentiful but shallow, leaking blood slowly but steadily. Somewhere within his throat a blood clot was failing to form as the man continuously coughed blood down his chin and into his white beard. He had a gray shirt which housed several shallow slices in the sides. Blood stained the edges of these precise tears in the fabric a dark, moist color as the wrinkly skin beneath glistened red. All of the cuts that she saw down his legs and arms were tiny slits of red no deeper than the width of a hair, but the amount of cuts Kreet had on him were easily enough to cause concern, especially for a man of his age.

"I understand," sighed Aqila. "We can still get a nurse to save you though! Once we save you we can explain everything to you and hunt down the Butcher…"

"That is only if Lev doesn't catch us first," whispered Caleb just loud enough for the man to hear.

The dying man proclaimed, "You want the stone, right? Don't bother saving me then!"

"What are you talking about?" asked Caleb.

"I am dying!. I've been bleeding for too long, and I don't want to resist the pain anymore," replied Dominick softly. Brown stains were all over his sheets, and blood continuously trickled from his multiple wounds. His eyes widened as he began speaking more frantically. "The active Taurus Zodiac had me protect his stone with my life at the end of the war, but he is gone. We lost. It is all over. Take the stone. Bring back the Taurus Zodiac, and stop Kozoroh. Don't let my death be in vain!"

"Of course Dominick!" exclaimed Aqila. "We will stop Kozoroh for you, just tell us where the stone is…we will get a nurse in here."

Dominick coughed up a lot of blood all over himself before muttering, "In…side." His hands fell to his side, and he pointed towards his chest. With an angry scowl the old man then exclaimed, "It is…IN-SIDE!"

Kreet's eyes closed shortly after he finished his sentence. Aqila and Caleb glanced at each other briefly before looking back at him. His chest no longer rose or fell, and he laid completely motionless. Jaako stood behind them still with the flame in his hands, and Caleb choked in disgust at the sight of such an unfortunate death.

"The stone is inside of him…isn't it?" asked Caleb with a grotesque look on his face.

Aqila took a second to answer, "I...I think it is."

Jaako walked next to the bedposts while his cold flames retreated back into his palms. The body reminded them all of how much danger they were in. They would all share the same, bloody, fate as Kreet if Lev caught up to them. *Maybe Lev won't kill us. She never killed Sartan, but is that going to last?* She accidentally got distracted with her own thoughts or perhaps intentionally, and was brought back to the problem at hand when Jaako spoke out.

"We have to tear him open?!" exclaimed Jaako unsteadily.

"I'm afraid so," replied Caleb from a safe distance to the body.

Jaako continued, "Well we should do it before a nurse walks by or, better yet, that Butcher lady gets back. I doubt a woman called the Butcher would have any issue tearing him open."

"Agreed," said Aqila hesitantly. "Can you grab the knife from the drawer over there?"

"A butter knife...yeah," answered Jaako who trudged to the cabinets.

"And I'll go watch the door, so that we don't get surprised by anyone," exclaimed Caleb who muscled his way to the door. "Just tell me when you are all done."

Convenient. Aqila then stepped aside as Jaako attempted to hand her the knife. "Go ahead Jaako...he is all yours."

"Here is the knife you asked for Aqila," stated Jaako as he tried to hand her the tool once more.

"I do not want to do it!"

"And I physically can't do it. This is low...even for me," replied Jaako.

Aqila took one of the deepest breaths she has taken in a while and rolled Kreet's shirt up over his chest. His hairy body was frail and small. The skin on his bones had cuts and bruises all over as if he had been in a hundred fights. Right above his stomach was a deep scar that streaked his side. The scar had to be decades old, but it certainly had been a brutal experience. Jaako handed her a standard butter knife, and she gripped it in her hands.

"This is all we have...no way is this going to be fun," stated Jaako who was now watching over her shoulder.

Aqila turned her head to glare at Jaako before she faced Kreet. Kreet's fingers pointed just above his stomach before he passed, so Aqila inserted the blade at the most centered part of his torso. Surprisingly the knife plunged straight into his body, burning through any neglected muscles in the way. Unsure what she was even doing, Aqila closed her eyes and shoved the blade further down expecting to hit the stone. At this point the warm blood was all over her hands, and the sticky liquid endlessly curdled from the man's body.

"I think it might be further up," whispered Jaako, whose hand sat softly on Aqila's shoulder.

"Do you want to try it?!" snapped Aqila.

Jaako made no response, yet Aqila still ripped the knife up towards Kreet's chest. It took more of her energy to tear the muscle like paper than the initial stab did. She kept severing his skin until the knife bumped into the bottom of his ribcage. She pulled the knife back out, and upon exiting she saw a sliver of dark green light escape the man. The knife was dropped on the floor, and Aqila closed her eyes as she stuck her hand in the slit she cut. At first only a few fingers would fit, but the warm blood acted as a lubricant for the rest of her hand. The steamy blood and mushy objects smothered her small fingers. Without opening her eyes she felt around his chest looking for anything sturdy. The second her fingers bumped into something that didn't give way she clutched it and pulled as hard as her arms would allow.

CRRRCH! In Aqila's left hand sat a broken length of Kreet's bottom rib. Jaako looked at her with huge, unbelieving eyes, and Caleb refused to glance away from the peephole in the door. Aqila stared at the fragmented bone for a second before she finally realized what she had done and threw it to the floor in repugnance.

"At least you found the stone," said Jaako with curled lips pointing at the body.

She swung her head back to Kreet, hesitantly, and saw a glimmer of pine tree green in an inferno of bright red blood. This time she kept her eyes open as her hand squeezed into the tight incision she had made. The smelting guts of Kreet haunted her fingers again, but she gripped the stone strongly enough to rip it straight from the slit. Now she had a very bloody gemstone cupped in her palm.

"That has to be at least like ten carats!" exclaimed Jaako who must have been seeing straight through the blood that dripped off it. "It's a perfect emerald cut too!"

"I suppose," said Aqila who made her way towards the sink.

"I'm just trying to distract myself," laughed Jaako as he began walking towards Caleb.

"And I am just washing my hands. A very normal thing to do," said Aqila in a monotone voice. "Then we are leaving."

"Yes, I agree!" exclaimed Caleb who was no longer gluing himself to the door.

Aqila smacked the sink on, and desperately scrubbed the blood off herself. Naturally, the hot water was broken, and there was no soap in the room. She tried harder to get the blood off the stone. After some good scrubbing, the stone in her hand was clear of any blood. Clear itself was another story. The large gemstone was nearly black. She failed to see one hair into it past the faded, green edges.

"Can we go now?" asked Caleb impatiently.

"Yes," replied Aqila as she put the stone in her pocket.

They made their way to the door, but upon opening it they all stood breathless. On the other side of the door was the secretary who told them the room number. Her face lacked any trace of a smile, and the clipboard in her hand made her appear more important than she truly was.

"Dominick doesn't have any close relatives. I'm going to have to...ask you...to...leave..."

The woman stared past them into the room while repeatedly glancing down at Aqila's hands, which still had a few small traces of blood on them. She murmured something that was incomprehensible to Aqila before sprinting down the hallway.

"WAIT!" screamed Aqila as she began chasing after her. "LET ME TALK!"

Aqila kept running, but the woman did too as they all chased her to the elevator. "DUCK!" exclaimed Jaako from a few feet behind her. Aqila was confused by his suggestion, but complied. She ducked down mid sprint, and without warning Jaako jumped over her. In his left hand was another flame that trickled pink droplets on the floor. He chucked the flame at the woman, but instantly after leaving his hand, the flame disappeared into thin air. In his off hand was another flame that he hurled at the woman. This flame kept strong as it surged towards the secretary. However, before the second flame could hit the secretary, she was smacked with unseen energy forcing her face first onto the floor. A dark-pink flame shot right over her drifting off down the hallway.

Before Jaako could catch her she got up and ran around the corner into another hallway. When they caught up Aqila saw her, facing them, mouthing words as the elevator doors closed between them. Jaako barely missed the doors, and Aqila heard the elevator slowly squeaking downwards to the lobby.

"SHIT!" exclaimed Jaako as he palmed his forehead.

"There's another elevator!" screamed Aqila who reached for the call button. Shortly after pressing it, the doors slowly creaked open. "Inside! Hurry!"

She ran inside the adjacent elevator with Jaako next to her, and rested her finger on the lobby button as she waited for Caleb to trail behind yet again. He cleared the corner and struggled to make it to the elevator, but as soon as he had one foot in the doors began closing.

"She's going to tell them all!" exclaimed Jaako frantically. "We are screwed."

"Once the doors open we will have to make a run for the exit," said Aqila nervously.

Caleb panted and sighed, "She surely won't have told them that quickly."

Aqila replied, "She will when we get down there though."

The rest of the elevator ride was spent in gasping silence. None of them looked at eachother, and none of them talked about what had just happened. Until, of course, they reached floor two.

Aqila glanced at the lobby's button and stated, "We just killed someone."

"We didn't kill him!" exclaimed Jaako.

"The Butcher killed him, we just caught him in his final moments," argued Caleb who had caught his breath by this point.

"No, but we massacred his body, and that's all that the secretary saw," said Aqila right as the doors began opening. When the elevator opened up Aqila saw the secretary jogging away from them. "Quickly do not let her see us! We are sneaking out the front!"

They all began speed walking behind the woman who surprisingly chose not to scream. Aqila cut through the lobby where chairs and people sat peacefully. Jaako and Caleb followed while the secretary made it to the other workers behind the desk. Aqila could not help but glance over at her, and upon doing so she saw that the woman, strangely enough, was not telling anyone what happened. The lobby was quiet enough to hear her had she been talking, but instead she stood in front of the counter motioning her arms aggressively.

"What is wrong Rebecca?" asked another one of the secretaries.

Rebecca did not answer. She flailed miserably and slammed her hands down on the counter while pointing at the elevators, but no squeak came from her mouth. Aqila was merely a few feet from the front door at this point when the secretary spotted her. She pointed intently at them as Aqila opened the door.

She tried to just not think about the nurse while she walked out into the sun. For some reason she did not feel compelled to sprint away yet, but then Caleb mentioned something.

Caleb quickly whispered, "She's getting a pencil and paper!"

"RUN!" exclaimed Jaako as he followed Aqila through the doorway.

That is exactly what she did. With speed and urgency the three of them pushed their bodies to the limits while getting away. They dodged headlights, and they jumped over hoods. Most of the pedestrians they passed had no clue why she was running, let alone to where, and she was just as clueless as to where she was headed. Jaako and Caleb trailed behind her loyally, but truthfully, she had not been paying attention to the streets and alleys she led them down. Before she knew it graffiti lined the buildings next to her and trash floated through the streets uncollected. She was in a part of the city far from the nursing home they broke out of. Now the street lights hung from thin wires instead of being bolted straight on to the poles, and the cars that waited at them were missing windows, mirrors and even doors. By then the organs in Aqila's stomach demanded rest, so she stopped on the corner of the street and leaned up against a rickety pole. Her lungs went into overtime to make up for lost air, and behind her she heard what one could only assume to be Caleb laying down on the sidewalk.

Gasps for air and coughs prevented silence from ever creeping in on them. Jaako quickly caught enough breath to exhale heavily, "I don't think...huh...anyone chased us."

A long period of gasping followed before Aqila replied with, "Good."

"We didn't need to run though," gasped Caleb who was indeed laying down on the ground.

"Yes we did," said Aqila as her side refused to stop paining her.

Jaako insisted, "Not this far at least."

"We got what we needed," said Aqila roughly. "I am just disappointed that Kreet died before telling us more about The Butcher. I want to forget that even happened."

"Agreed," said Jaako and Caleb in unison.

The light signaled them to use the crosswalk. Aqila began walking across the street that only had a few cars waiting, and the boys hustled to catch up, still taking heavy breaths. The industrial grade graffiti made every boring warehouse and apartment complex look like they belonged in a garden rather than above the sewage treatment plant. Unfortunately, the illegal artwork failed to change the scent of the scene. Aqila knew not where she was going other than away from where she was. With every step on the cracked pavement she could feel herself getting angrier, but she could not tell why. *Sartan is alive. We have the Taurus stone. Now all we have to do is find...FERRAN!*

"Where the hell is Ferran!" exclaimed Aqila without looking back at her friends.

"I want to rest. Plus, I don't know what to do now that we have the stone?" asked Caleb from behind her.

Aqila walked faster and aggressively while answering, "We find Ferran!"

"How do we do that?" asked Jaako.

Aqila began jogging down the sidewalk as she replied, "I am unsure, but I will figure it out!"

She heard shoes smack the pavement behind her, and it was not but ten steps before Caleb spoke out, "I don't think we will find him like this."

"Yeah, I agree with Caleb," said Jaako as Aqila kept jogging down the street.

She kept running for a few more seconds. Then she stopped dead in her tracks, and after looking back at her friends who were staring in confusion, she knew they were not going to follow. *Fuck!* Aqila trudged to her allies in defeat. They did not follow her this time. *They did not follow.* She made it back to earshot and heard them mid conversation.

"I don't know, but I don't want to stay out in the open like this," said Caleb as he spat on the ground. "They surely will still be looking for us, right?"

"We still don't have a place to sleep yet either," murmured Jaako.

While crossing the street Caleb reminded Jaako, "Well we can crash at your new girlfriend's home. Assuming she's still not at work of course."

"That is a terrible idea," protested Aqila.

"Still better than running around with no sense of direction," argued Caleb.

Jaako jumped back into the conversation. "He has a point, but I don't know if she would or not."

"There is only one way to find out now isn't there Jaako?" asked Caleb with a cheeky grin.

"How will harassing a waitress help us find Ferran?" squealed Aqila. "She only gave you her number so you would leave her alone."

"Don't listen to her, Jaako. I have some change, and I saw a phone booth around a corner. Give me the number."

Unbelievable. Within moments a phone call concluded, and the entire group was on their merry little way to an apartment deeper into the Southside. This 'Emilia' was on her break but was too far to come home, so she insisted on the whole group going to her home to wait until she gets off work. When they arrived at the address hard knocks on the scraped door were not met peacefully or hesitantly. A short woman ripped the door open from the inside with so much force Aqila wondered if the hinges were still intact. Her brown hair complemented her freckle splotched skin, and Aqila's stomach instantly fell to her feet. The woman was dressed entirely in a Garigo police uniform. The muscles bulged out of the silk sleeves all while her walkie talkie squeaked at her side.

The freckled face demanded, "Are you Emilia's friends?"

"Yes, she told us to wait for her here," stuttered Caleb.

"Wait in the living room," commanded the officer as she muscled her way through the door. "I have to go. Someone tried to burn down a damn nursing home, and they need more units on the scene."

The awkward interaction came to a brief end, and the group struggled to trudge past the cluttered floor. Eventually they managed to sit down on the ripped couch in the living room. The apartment was definitely not upper class. Clothes and papers were thrown about all over the place. Aqila had to move an empty shoe box, a mousepad, and three rags just to secure a seat on the couch. By then Caleb had already figured out how to turn on the television without a remote. The television did not look as though it belonged in the room with them though. The screen itself was transparent and curved. At the base of the stand the entire device was illuminated by blue lighting, and the first thing that popped up on the screen was the view of a helicopter camera.

The news channel was either the default channel, or the officer they just met was way too into her profession. The volume was off, and Caleb was struggling to figure that out. A lack of captions on the screen made understanding the incident difficult, and just as Aqila was losing interest she realized what was going on. The helicopter actually was not anywhere near the nursing home that they undoubtedly caught on fire by accident, but instead it was monitoring a high speed chase Southbound. A black jeep bobbed and weaved through the streets while an entire fleet of police units followed it relentlessly. It was hard to see who was driving with the current pace and distance from the camera. Jaako stood up from the couch and pulled the remote out from the corner of his seat. He shot the signal straight into the receiver, and instantly a man screamed at them.

"Once again, these are some thugs that you do not want to escape!" exclaimed the newscaster in his radio perfect tone. "Officers found a group of six miscreants loitering on South forty-seventh, and when approached this smart bunch hopped in their car to bolt. Responding officers claim that this could be the group of felons that massacred an entire village within our Eastern neighbor's borders, the Sagittarius Empire. Or it could be those responsible for the inferno that is the Grounded Living Senior Facility. Their only chance of escaping judgment day at this point would be making it across the border merely miles away, but our police force will make it impossible to even escape the city," boasted the newscaster. The black jeep ran through stop lights and stop signs. As the fugitives sliced through the streets of Garigo, the helicopter stayed right on their tails. Aqila watched in surprise when the jeep blasted over a tire strip unaffected. Officers did not let simple miscalculations like that ruin their plans, however with each street sign the fugitives grew closer to the edge of town and, more importantly, the border.

"They might actually get away!" exclaimed Aqila with shortness of breath.

Caleb countered, "But are these people that you want to be free?"

"Yes, if they escape then the police will continue looking after them thinking it was us-"

"True!" exclaimed Jaako while Aqila was still finishing her sentence. "But how did the nursing home catch on fire?"

"That couldn't have been us…right?" asked Aqila as her stomach fell down a flight of stairs.

After their brief interaction with each other, they all looked back at the television which now showed the black jeep mid air, ramping over a river. Not a single patrol unit risked their lives to ramp over the river after the jeep, but the helicopter still kept its eyes on the prize.

One would think that they would drive more carefully after escaping the patrols, but that was the exact opposite of what happened. On the other side of the river, this little, black jeep zipped its way around buildings, between cars, and barely missed at least three pedestrians. Suddenly, a loud beeping noise went off on the helicopter.

"It looks like our helicopter is low on battery, but these criminals' parading days are over," laughed the newscaster who was slowly starting to sound more like a comedian than a serious representation of information. "We have the plates, so when they reach the border, their Genillian provided vehicle will self-destruct, killing all passengers." As the helicopter began turning around the jeep made a sharp right turn, and the camera finally focused enough to take a picture of the front seat passenger.

"This!" exclaimed the newscaster. "This man right here is one of the murderous fiends that plague our lands. Illegal aliens such as him will no longer..."

The voice of the newsman drowned off while Aqila stared at the photo that refused to move away from her eyes. There was no mistake, no misunderstanding, and no way. All her companions stared in shared disbelief beside her, for in that jeep, Ferran, with those constant green eyes and brown hair, stared with violently dilated pupils out the window at the helicopter which took his photo. He was completely unaware that the world just watched his death be announced for him.

Chapter 18
Convincing Characters
Aqila

It was hours later, and the sun had set. As the last bit of funds Aqila held filtered through her hands into those of a hooded stranger, she slipped the baggie of gray powder under her shirt. Immediately she spun around and sprinted back towards the apartment. A quick run through the dark and vacant streets of Garigo brought her back to her companions. Walking up to the door she checked behind her to reaffirm the fact that she had not been followed, and with three soft knocks she could hear loud screams on the inside of the rickety apartment muffle and quiet down. The door slowly creaked open, and Caleb stood on the other side letting her back into the messy abode. This time however, she was greeted with a warm scent of ham and leafy greens which steamed past her to the outside world. She entered the home to see Jaako firmly sprawled on the tattered couch, which still had so much domestic debris the act of sitting down next to him would certainly break ancient antiques of unknown origin or sentimental value. The television was on, but she could not hear anything that was on it due to the sounds of crackling steam and boiling water that conquered the kitchen.

The woman Aqila had met earlier was still in her police uniform as she stirred over a pot in the kitchen, "You do know that police hours started precisely five minutes ago."

"I apologize I am not completely familiar with the streets yet," replied Aqila who still stood awkwardly at the door.

"Then knowing that you should not have ventured out for some fresh air so close to lockdown. Certainly it couldn't have been that necessary for you. Imagine if you had been caught," continued the officer grimly as she wiped her brow.

"Don't mind Octavia," stated the waitress Jaako had spoken with at Murphy's Stewlot. She was the one that had invited them over in the first place. "My sister is just a little bit of a worrier when it comes to things like that." The waitress sat down on the sofa next to Jaako, somehow pushing all of the nicknacks and relics into a neat pile in one corner.

"So Emilia," began Octavia from the kitchen. "How exactly did you meet these interesting characters after all? These friends of yours?"

"Well…it's complicated," started Emilia hesitantly.

"Agreed," interjected Jaako. "Why not focus on how we are going to go forward?"

"I'd rather not," stated Octavia.

"What do you think about traveling the world?" asked Jaako with a smirk.

"What do you mean?" asked Emilia, who had more acne and freckles fighting for dominance over her face than a middle schooler who doesn't know how to bathe. "I would like to see the Forfnian Craters, but I could never afford that."

"Price is just a suggestion," mentioned Jaako from his seat. "Right now we are currently traveling the world looking for-"

Aqila quickly coughed loud enough to stop Jaako before continuing for him, "My apologies. As Jaako was saying, we travel the world without having to worry about money."

"Oh, that must be amazing! I bet you guys have the best of times," replied Emilia as she turned off the television.

Octavia dropped a large wooden spoon on the ground before saying, "That doesn't seem logical. Certainly it isn't all fun and games if you have no money. Do you steal for your food and shelter? Do you beg others for it? In what way is your lifestyle sustainable like that?"

"Octavia please. They are guests at our humble home. Do not treat them like this."

"I'm just saying. If they don't have money how are they surviving? I don't wish to house fugitives under my roof do you?"

Emilia opened her mouth but stopped before any voice was raised. Then Jaako interjected once more, "Would you like to come along with us on our journey?"

Octavia immediately stopped cooking the food and Emilia stared at him nervously before Caleb intercepted his question, "We can't just invite her to come along with us without asking Ferran or Aqila."

"True, but we don't know where Ferran is," argued Jaako who was ultimately not listening.

"I wouldn't be opposed to traveling the world with you guys, but the decision lies with Octavia," stated Emilia. Aqila easily noticed Emilia was just trying to keep everyone happy.

"I am absolutely not going to give up my position and possibly run the risk of losing the apartment just to travel the world with some broke nobodies!" exclaimed Octavia from the steamy kitchen. "Traveling the world for what purpose? And I doubt you have written documentation proving your legal presence in Garigo!"

"Don't do this to them Octavia," cried Emilia from the couch with widened eyes and a forward hanging face.

"The borders of the Genillian Empire are closed to non-Gemini's indefinitely," protested Octavia. Without wasting a second she proceeded with, "You should be aware of the punishment for smuggling yourselves into our nation. If you have no current warrants for your arrest, which I doubt is the case, you are subject to deportation to a location of our choice or execution depending on how much you've been exposed to."

"Are you arresting us?" asked Aqila as adrenaline began to pump. Jaako, however, did not ask. He had already stood up from the couch and was waiting for Octavia's next move.

"Don't arrest them. I invited them here," insisted Emilia.

"But you did not invite them into the nation, nor would you have power to do so!" snapped back Octavia as she stepped closer to the couch. Jaako stepped back as Caleb rose to his feet from his seat on the mildewy and cluttered floor.

"Just stop," pleaded Emilia with an exasperated gasp. "You aren't even a Gemini you might as well deport yourself for intrusion as well. You don't even know why they are in Garigo. We've been home not two hours, and you're already trying to arrest our guests!"

"I don't need your mouth right now!" screamed back Octavia. "Knowing work might not…work...I've been doing everything, and you just disrespect me like this! I need to just get away!"

"Then run away like you claim I always do!" yelled Emilia as Octavia ran off down the hall.

"Make your own goddamn dinner for once!"

The bedroom door down the hallway slammed loud enough to make the dog in the room above them start barking. The whole building shook as the boiling water in the kitchen steamed away unphased by the situation.

"Does this happen often?" asked Aqila.

"Only when her job is the topic," replied Emilia. "She has been a bit sensitive recently. Her police chief found out she wasn't a Gemini, and now she is getting laid off because officers must be Geminis. I'm just glad that she isn't getting deported, or worse. We won't be able to afford it here much longer, and she has struggled finding new work now that people know she isn't a Gemini. I really hate the city. It seemed nice at first, but you have to work so hard to stay here. Sometimes I just want leisure or a break."

"Have you been anywhere else?" asked Jaako. "When I lived in Dursnia I had to steal and rob to survive. There was a riot at least twice a day, and the police were almost as corrupted as the oil cartel's who refused to hire me."

Emilia stared in disbelief before replying with, "I used to live in the country, but it wasn't much easier. We had to make enough crops to survive the winters, and most of the money we made selling our excess crops was immediately taken in taxes for the development of the cities. I've never been out of the empire, but it is starting to sound better each time I think about it."

"We have never lived here, so I think it is fair to say none of us can make a decision of whether or not this is a bad place to be," said Caleb as he offered a neutral response.

"Nonsense, I could never stand it here," clapped back Aqila with a chuckle.

"Yeah, I would never stay here," said Jaako. "It's way too strict. Even in the bad parts of town there are still scattered cameras and officers lurking way more than I initially anticipated."

Aqila's heart dropped. She never noticed the cameras. She noticed the patrols, but not any cameras. Running through the streets even at the start of police hours is suspicious. If she was caught on camera then the police force would certainly have probable cause. *Scratch that if I am caught on camera Lev will be one step closer than she already is! Wait, how does Octavia not know? She is an officer after all! There is no way she is oblivious.*

"Nobody likes constant surveillance, but I can't deny the results it achieves," continued Emilia as she began finishing up the dinner that Octavia had abandoned. "The crime rates have never been lower, and drug overdoses have nearly been eradicated due to multiple legal sources. There are still illegal deals done all the time, and those drugs tend to be much more lethal. But crime is down as a whole either way."

"I still wouldn't stay here. I bet the drugs are administered to control the populus anyways. I don't know about your sister, but the police force is most likely just as corrupt as your government head," explained Jaako in his attempt to persuade her to come along on their journey.

"Maybe. It is literally a feudal monarchy," laughed Emilia with wide eyes. "It could always be worse though. At least we aren't in the middle ages this time. We have Emperor Blizenci. Then we have the King Herton and Queen Adreia of the North and South Kingdoms. Wait there is also the petty king who rules the small kingdom on the coast between the North and South kingdoms."

"This got complex pretty quickly," laughed Aqila lightheartedly.

"Yeah, it can get pretty confusing, especially when you get to the dukes, counts, and barons. The important thing is that Blizenci requires the barons to give us amenities and three days off a week. We are allowed to own land, but we still have to pay taxes to our liege. We can even form our own armies if we wanted to, but I've never seen that happen before."

"So the counts and up just take money and tell barons what to do?" asked Caleb with genuine curiosity. "What does Blizenci do?"

Emilia struggled to answer his question, "Well...I don't really know what Blizenci does, but he is our master and liege as a whole. We trust him, but as the power trickles down it isn't always distributed evenly you know? Some dukes and counts misuse the power to make themselves richer, but luckily most of the dukes put it back into their duchy. The counts use it to try to become dukes, but each duke is in charge of creating a police force for their entire territory. I don't remember much of anything else from my government class last year, but it usually just ends up in wasted time."

"Huh, well what we've seen so far was a very focused and organized empire. How many crops do you produce each year in the empire?" asked Caleb who was still interested in the logistics of the Genillian Empire.

"We produce more than enough to feed the world population eight times over, but a good twenty percent of that number goes right into scientific research on new technology."

"Would you want to come with us?" asked Jaako once more even though the conversation had nothing to do with that at this point.

Emilia stared at him with a tilted head for a good chunk of time before saying, "At this point? What have I got to lose? Why not?"

"What about your sister?" pressed Aqila. "You would just leave her behind?"

"She will come with me too," replied Emilia who was now bringing the steaming and glistening ham to a small counter in the kitchen. "She won't be able to stay in the city much longer anyway. I'll convince her before we leave. When do you guys plan on leaving the city?"

Jaako hesitated with uncertainty. Eventually Caleb stuttered out, "Well...we still have to find somebody before we can leave the city."

"Wait, who do we have to find?" asked Jaako with blatant confusion plastered in his eyes. "Ferran left the city. We don't have to look for anyone in Garigo anymore."

"I am more concerned about our time frame and Ferran. The cops gave up their chase after him when he escaped the city, but how can we get to him before he passes the border," insisted Aqila. She tried not to think about saving her benevolent brother from his fiery fate more than she had to, yet much to her dismay his absence made dealing with Jaako and the strangers a bit more difficult. *Adding someone to the group will only hurt us if we already have members leaving and turning on eachother.*

"Ferran is ornery. He will surely survive. After all he made it through Furictown alive, didn't he?" asked Jaako.

"Yeah? So did Sartan," replied Caleb.

There was a very brief moment of silence in the room before Jaako burst out in laughter, "Ha! At least Sartan helped us get away from the cops in Dursnia. Ferran didn't really do that much for us other than...Heh...get rid of Sartan. Ha! Ha..."

"Why are you laughing about that?" asked Aqila who was beginning to feel her blood boil.

"I don't know!" laughed Jaako in exasperation. Jaako's face turned red, and his body began to sweat. "It really isn't funny, but I don't know what else to do."

"Okay, we need to focus," started Aqila once she realized that Jaako was coping. "Are you sure you want to do this Emilia? Once you leave the Genillian Empire you will not be allowed back in from what I understand."

"That is fine by me. I really don't need to be convinced. As long as we can get along and live long I am happy," laughed Emilia as she began divvying up the main course to everybody.

"What about Ferran?" asked Aqila.

Jaako quickly spoke out, "Ferran's opinion on this needs to be completely disregarded after what he did to Sartan. Especially since we need to save him now."

"Exactly!" exclaimed Aqila who only half agreed with his statement. "We do not have enough time for them to get all of their belongings if Ferran is headed to the border. Once he gets there he is going to explode, so we must leave without them!"

"We still have to find a Virgo though, right?" asked Jaako.

"I mean we can just find one on the way there," replied Caleb.

Emilia jumped into the conversation as she choked down her food, "What do you need to find a Virgo for?"

"We are going to the Virgo Palace to revive the Virgo Zodiac," said Jaako and Caleb in unison.

"What? You mean? The-"

"Yes, they are being serious," said Aqila with a growing frown on her face. Since she was not fast enough to prevent the leaking of that information she continued, "And this needs to stay on the low if you know what I mean..."

"I'm in!" exclaimed Emilia who had already finished the tiniest portion ever. She put her cleaned plate in the sink and rolled her eyes while she stated, "I could even find a Virgo for you. It's just a matter of compliance with this one."

"Octavia is a Virgo?" exclaimed Caleb in wonder before he started scarfing down his meal. "What will it take for her to come along?"

"I don't even know, but if she doesn't then I will be kind of disappointed."

"Obviously, we have to get her on board!" exclaimed Jaako as the bedroom door opened abruptly.

"And how do you plan on doing that?" asked Aqila.

"They don't," said a raspy voice from the hallway. As Octavia walked out she had to of seen how happy Emilia appeared to be, but without waiting for a response Octavia walked into the kitchen to get herself some food. "Where exactly are you guys going from here? How can you afford feeding and transporting five people? Are you even considered adults in all nations? You are crashing at our home. What makes me think you are capable of maintaining all of us on your journey when you are struggling with the three you have right now?"

Octavia was relentless in her questioning. A part of Aqila could only hope that her intense questioning of their capabilities was not an attempt to stop them from recruiting her but rather derived from curiosity and interest. Another part hoped she would fail to recruit Octavia on their journey simply because Aqila was unready and had lost control of the group. Regardless, they went through all the possible questions, and Jaako managed to answer most of them. The few questions he failed to answer, he argued that Octavia's presence in the group would solve.

"What if all of this goes wrong?" asked Octavia slowly once she heard Jaako's last botched point. "What is our punishment if we fail or get caught? Surely Blizenci, Lev, and Kozoroh wouldn't want us reviving Zodiacs without letting them know."

"If they cared they would have done it themselves by now," replied Aqila swiftly.

"What if they have a reason to not revive any other Zodiacs?" asked Octavia.

Aqila swallowed her breath and thought heavily as even she struggled to answer the question. *What if there was an actual reason Kozoroh wanted to keep the Zodiacs dead. Something that they did not know of! Reviving the Zodiacs would cause no problems for the masses. It would bring balance to the world and prevent tyranny. Kozoroh would have no competition though, and-* It dawned on her. *He would be the only Earth sign. He wants that power.*

Aqila gracefully answered, "If they have a reason it must be selfish. Reviving them would only bring back some sort of balance to the world."

"Let my sister and I talk about it in private," demanded Octavia as she pulled her sister by the arm into a bedroom. After shutting the door behind them Aqila could only hear murmurs from the other side. They would not be leaving much behind if they chose to go with them. The apartment was the main possession, and Aqila knew it was cheap. The occasional hole in the wall hid as much evidence of poverty as it hid the heat from the outside world. Twice since they arrived, chunks of the ceiling had fallen on their heads as the upstairs neighbors walked around, and at one point they all witnessed a giant rat fight Caleb, who was sitting on the ground, for being too close to its nest. When the door finally opened again Octavia walked out with an immense frown splattered on her face. Emilia on the other hand simply could not hold back her joy as she trotted out of that bedroom with the largest smile the world has ever seen.

"We're going to leave the empire! We're going to leave the empire!" exclaimed Emilia while running around the room. She grabbed random items and threw them into her bag.

"Emilia, we agreed to only take things we needed for survival," said Octavia in a motherly tone. "Your old poster of Jazzy-J is not necessary."

Everyone smiled in amusement as they watched their new companions, one of which much more excitedly, get ready for the trip ahead of them. Octavia quickly gathered all of her things and stood next to them while her sister continued her parade through the home.

"We leave tonight," said Octavia dryly. "And I'll only go on three conditions."

Aqila quickly focused on Octavia as Caleb responded for her with, "Of course, go ahead."

"One, not one of you lay a single finger on Emilia. Two, we can leave the group whenever we want." Octavia looked around hesitantly before finishing, "And three, we don't have to commit any crimes along the journey."

"That shouldn't be a problem," agreed Caleb instantly.

Aqila caught herself mid facepalm as everything seemed to be moving way faster than it should be. Perhaps these two sisters were really in a financial pickle and needed a fresh start, but the speed and ease at which Caleb and even Jaako were able to recruit them seemed off to Aqila. She began to respect Ferran's thinking about new add-ons to the group slightly more, but now his fear was obvious to her...their mission had grown out of even her control.

"We are taking my squadcar because I have already turned off the tracker in it. Police won't bother us in it, and it can get past the border without self-destructing. We have ten minutes to get ready," said Octavia as she opened the front door and walked outside into the night.

Chapter 19
The Wild Child
Ferran

It was the next morning, and the sun had just begun lurching over the horizon. Ferran, however, was busy attempting to help his comrades out of the burning heap of metal and glass. He didn't know why the car spontaneously combusted, but it happened fast enough to take out their driver. He had yet to learn the name of that man, but the only reason the driver brought them this far was because the police caught him underage drinking. Now Ferran was fighting the flames that marooned him in the middle of nowhere. An outstretched hand from the back of the vehicle begged for mercy as its owner was being melted alive in the metal casket. Ferran grabbed it and tried to pull quickly, but seconds after the blood curdling screaming stopped he fell backwards onto his butt with the entire arm of the victim still in his grip.

"Ferran! Help!" screamed a voice from the other side of the vehicle. Ferran obeyed the cry and ran to the other side. A man stood there attempting to pull out another victim of the fire. The victim was halfway out of a busted window when the man said, "Help me pull her out before she burns!"

The two of them struggled to get the last person, who was still alive, out of the inferno, and with much luck, she flopped onto the pavement next to them, scraping her skin all the way down. The woman that crawled to her feet had burns all over her body. From her face to her melted shoes, not one inch of skin went untouched. *She won't last another day.*

"Is this everyone?" asked the man who called for Ferran. "Are these our survivors?"

"The driver died instantly, and I couldn't save the person in the back," said Ferran slowly, his headache still pounding.

"It must be then...we must have just passed the border. We better get a move on. We've got a long way to go," said the man.

The crash was sobering. Still parched and dehydrated from the alcohol that left traces of its presence in his bloodstream, Ferran blurred his vision around the two who accompanied him in the accident. *I don't know who this man is. I don't know who this woman is.* Ferran remembered speaking with someone in a pub who knew where the palace was, but if he were telling the truth he didn't remember getting in the vehicle with these two at all. He remembered being in the jeep when it got pulled over, but then the driver sped off starting a life threatening chase. Maybe the driver had warrants. Ferran didn't know. All that he knew was one of them was taking him to the Virgo Palace. One of them knew how to get there, hopefully not one that got melted, but one of them knew. The man was wiping the tears off the woman's face while Ferran began trudging down the dusky and flame riddled road, with a pounding headache, the product of endlessly dizzy vision.

***

Hours later it was still early in the morning. The grass was glazed with frost, and many cars had passed by. Not one of them was convinced to stop. Some of the drivers didn't even notice the three of them lurking in the ditches. Ferran had already inquired about directions and figured he could make it to the palace without these strangers anymore. The walk was more than sobering. He had time to think about everything from a new perspective along with time to flush out the rest of the alcohol. *Sartan wasn't necessary. Aqila and Caleb don't understand that the three of us could get by just fine. I've found the way to the Virgo Palace with nobody but me. Maybe I should leave them in Garigo until I revive all of the Zodiacs. Jaako will probably run away from them by the time I return with the old Zodiacs, and by then Kozoroh, Blizenci, and Lev will be long gone. I'll do it all myself this time.*

The ditches got deeper and the grass got whiter. With every minute the distant sun rose further into the air. Closer to the Southern Tropic than to the Equator, one might have thought that they were at the Antarctic circle with how cold the morning was. Breath was visible in the air, and the snot froze in Ferran's nostrils. A massive blizzard had just swept the region, and now Ferran trudged through the aftermath. He liked the cold, regardless of how annoying a runny nose is. It limited aggression as people tended to prefer conserving their energy when affected by it. The cold was a trusted friend of his. Very few of those existed.

With sore legs, sorer feet, and frozen throats, neither of the strangers spoke a word to Ferran, and affected by the same ailments, he chose not to break the silence either, until he needed to. From the front he could see two figures far ahead on the road. By now Ferran, the man, and the burnt woman had all gotten back on the road, for the frozen grasslands that were the ditches had quickly turned into snow ridden jungles of wetness. The figures appeared out of nothing, or perhaps Ferran simply looked away from the horizon too long. It didn't matter where they came from, Ferran knew as the figures grew closer they were heading towards him.

He remembered studying a bit with Aqila before they left Mirisburg around a year ago. They studied everything they could about three Zodiacs: Aries, Sagittarius, and Virgo. The plan was to go in a circle and get those three Zodiacs revived first. That didn't happen. However, from his brief time looking over shoulders, Ferran learned a thing or two about the Zodiacs. This was one of those few things.

The Craven Walker. Deadly. Swift. Hive minded. And usually in a group of two or four. These nude, half-human bastards are approaching quickly. Just when I was getting tired too. Ferran unsheathed a small knife and held it forwards. The man and woman bumped into him from behind not knowing he stopped let alone why.

"Craven Walkers!" shouted Ferran who watched the faceless, mouth-headed creatures' details appear more vividly. There was dried blood all over their splotched skin, of which looked unhealthy. They ran with a limp, and the green foam at their mouths was trickling down their nude bodies. Craven Walkers never looked starved. Every single one of them is fed and fit compared to the average living citizen. These two were no exception to that, their bodies still managed to look grotesque with all the dried blood and green foam, and Ferran knew by the rate at which they advanced, the creatures were very powerful.

He stood in front of his injured strangers when the Craven Walkers were ten feet away from him. No hesitation was present on their end as the moldy scented creatures sprinted up to Ferran. He didn't even have time to attack before his body was tossed into the ditch.

"Aaahhh-"

Ferran scrambled to his feet as the woman's screeches stopped faster than they started. Her body fell flat in the snow. At the same time the man managed to fire a shot off into one of the Craven Walker's foreheads. It fell almost faster than its prey did, and by now Ferran had his fist raised to the back of the second Craven Walker's head. POP! A bullet sliced through the mouth-face and out of the backside of the head. It zoomed right past Ferran's ear. Everything began ringing, and both of his hands quickly flew up to cover his ears. He fell on his butt next to his blade and let the ringing pass.

The first thing Ferran heard when everything calmed down thirty seconds later was, "Thank me later. Preferably with new rounds."

Ferran smiled at the man while he helped him up to his feet. Then it dawned on him...if it weren't for this man he would be dead. He tussled the thought around in his head before denying its accuracy. To distract himself from the thought, Ferran tried to talk to the man.

"Let's get away from them."

"Hold on. I'm going through her pockets."

Ferran sighed as he watched the stranger rob the other stranger's burnt yet frozen corpse. The man checked every pocket, twice. As he was doing this, Ferran noticed a slight movement to his left. The first Craven Walker had twitched. Thinking nothing of it, Ferran glanced over at the other one. Looking at it he could see the muscle fibers ooze green liquids. However, its bullet hole was nowhere to be found, and after looking for quite some he realized that the hole had completely healed. The carcass twitched before him just like the other one did, and suddenly, with another loud ring, a bullet sliced through its head for the second time. The twitching menace slumped further into the street with a freshly pierced hole in its head. Then with a soft plop the revolver landed on a thin layer of snow right next to Ferran.

Gazing over to the man, the other walker had gotten up and attacked him. The man's head was entirely in the walker's gaping mouth. Green saliva slugged down the man's chest and arms, both of which were constrained by the walker's off colored, muscly arms. Stunned, Ferran didn't know what to do. In a brief moment of reduced consciousness, he grabbed the revolver and let off two shots. The first ripped through the walker's leg, and the second melted a small bit of snow on the ground. Keeping the man completely in its mouth, the walker fell into the snow still making loud squelches with its prey. He heard a gurgle behind him and saw the other walker twitching again. His heart stopped. *I can't do it alone...I can't do it alone!*

He fired the final shot in the revolver into the head of the rising walker. Then he threw the revolver on the ground and ran as quickly as he could down the road. Knowing that they would finish eating those carcasses faster than he would run out of breath, Ferran decided he would throw up, explode a hole in his side, or burn his feet into the ground before he would stop for a breather. This is exactly what he did. Ten minutes later his vision began to fade as his heart skipped beat after beat. Everything turned black under the bright gray clouds, and Ferran tripped and face-planted into a ditch shortly after the moment his heart demanded rest. The threat was far behind him, but even if they were a breath away Ferran's mind was still consumed by one thought as he drifted into unconsciousness. *I can't do it alone.*

***

Hours later, Ferran woke up to a strong shiver that ran through his body. Snowflakes softly landed on his face. The cold breeze sliced through him. Then suddenly, four hands grabbed his body, lifting him out of the ditch. Once his consciousness returned, Ferran noticed who one of the men who lifted him was. *Caleb?* Ferran struggled to escape their grasps and found that it was impossible. Luckily, the oddly buff woman in the police uniform didn't cuff him when he finally made it to his feet. Confused, Ferran spoke to Caleb.

"How did you find me? You need to go back to the others. It isn't safe here."

"The others are all here," said Caleb while pointing to his companions next to the squad car.

In disbelief, Ferran replied sharply, "How did you guys find me? Did you kill the Craven Walkers? Do you have water?"

He got some water right as Jaako shouted, "Well, you were on the news, remember? From there we just went where the police didn't."

"The news!" exclaimed Ferran while spitting out the water in his mouth. He then finished the entire bottle of water before continuing, "What happened? Was it the chase? I know how it started and a few random things, but other than that it is a bit of a blur."

"So you don't remember what you have been doing in Garigo for the past few days at all?" questioned the officer with more seriousness than Caleb had displayed in his entire life.

"And who are these two?" asked Ferran who had lips dryer than Dursnia. "I don't have any warrants. Not to mention I'm out of your jurisdiction."

The officer didn't hold back her thoughts, "Oh yeah? And who is going to enforce my jurisdiction out here in the middle of nowhere? My name is Octavia by the way. Thank you for asking Ferran."

"How do you know my name?" asked Ferran almost immediately.

"Your friends just couldn't stop talking about you," said Octavia slyly.

"What are you doing all the way out here anyways?" asked Aqila who had been lurking in the back of the group. "Why did you just disappear?"

Ferran stared at her. He wondered if it was time to finally…well…accept her apology. Whether or not she was ready to apologize was the question. He got lost in thought and didn't realize that Aqila was actually mad at him this time.

"No response like usual!" exclaimed Aqila. "So typical! I will be waiting in the car!"

"Wasn't she the one that said we weren't leaving without this guy?" asked Octavia sincerely after Aqila slammed the door to the car shut. "I regret this, Emilia."

"What are you doing Ferran?" asked Caleb who with squinty eyebrows.

Ferran couldn't bring himself to reply, so instead all of them stared around awkwardly until Jaako broke the silence, "I'm kinda cold let's go."

They all decided to slowly make their way to the squad car as the soft fluttering snow slowed down. Ferran didn't understand what was wrong with Aqila. *I'll have to figure this out, but for now who are these two girls I don't remember seeing?* Then he finally realized how crowded things truly were. The two strangers took the front seats, which meant that Ferran had to squeeze into the back of a police car with three others. *Wouldn't be the last time.*

From the driver's seat Octavia asked, "Where are we going now?"

"Just keep going down the road I suppose," said Aqila with a frown. "We can't go back to Garigo now, so let's just hope we are getting closer to the palace."

"We are," said Ferran calmly. "It shouldn't be too far from here anyways."

"What?!" exclaimed Jaako and Caleb simultaneously.

"That is where I was heading until I passed out," said Ferran. "The old burnt woman seemed to know exactly where it was, but she didn't survive the walkers."

"Shit!" exclaimed Jaako in disappointment.

"I think I picked up the directions from her," whispered Ferran confidently.

"I literally love you!" exclaimed Jaako with a smile.

"Since when were you so touchy?" asked Ferran blankly. "Also, it doesn't matter if I know where it is or not. We still need to find an Earth Gemstone."

"About that...we have one," said Caleb as if he had just said the winning answer to a rigged game show. "We found Dominick Kreet, and he wasn't in the best of shapes to begin with."

"What do you mean?" asked Ferran with a stern look. "You have the stone on you? What happened to Kreet?"

"Yes, we have the stone on us," replied Caleb as he slipped the stone out of his pants pocket to show Ferran.

"And as for Kreet?"

"Kreet was on the verge of death when we found him. Someone had slashed him to bits before we found him, and we only had enough time to talk for less than two minutes with him. Apparently there is this woman who walks around slaughtering people like animals. He kept calling her The Butcher."

"The Butcher?!" exclaimed Octavia from the driver's seat. "As in the freak who wears black lab clothes? The same woman with slicked-back, black hair who has made countless of Garigo's homeless veteran population victims of cruel crimes?"

"I suppose. Kreet was terrified. He desperately wanted her not to interrogate him again," answered Caleb nonchalantly.

"Well this figure has created countless cases. All of which are unsolved," continued Octavia as she took the right Ferran told her to take. "She targets the homeless, aged adults, and war veterans. She has a target group, and she keeps killing without any reason."

"The Butcher is a problem for Garigo, we are headed to the palace now," pointed out Aqila.

"What about Lev?" asked Ferran.

Aqila was silenced. After glancing at Octavia very quickly Aqila replied, "I do not believe Lev is worried about us anymore."

"Why wouldn't she be? We are her main targets after Furictown are we not?" questioned Ferran.

"What?!" exclaimed Octavia. "Lev is chasing you, why?! I thought you said that the Zodiacs didn't care if we were replacing the other one!"

"That is true!" exclaimed Aqila. "The Zodiacs want us to replace them…just the ones that are already dead. The ones that are alive care a lot."

"You lied to me!" exclaimed Octavia who stopped the car abruptly. "I am going to turn this car around and turn you in then. I should've expected this from non-Gemini's like you."

"NO WAIT! If you turn us in then Lev will kill you too!" exclaimed Jaako.

"He's right," said Ferran. "Why do you think she is so dead set on finding us? You know too much to be kept alive already, and I've only been with you for a solid four minutes."

"We can't go back!" exclaimed Emilia in terror. "I no call, no showed for my shift today, and there is no way they would let me come back to work after that! They already are going to cancel my pay for the week because of it! Everything would just get worse from there!"

The car's windows muffled the screams of the wind, and the tires sat motionless on the snowy road. Octavia planted her head on the steering wheel, so Emilia rested her hand on her shoulder.

Then she told her, "Sis, if you want to go back I understand…I just didn't think-"

"No!" yelled Octavia. "We have decided to leave Garigo! We will leave Garigo! Blizenci doesn't know that we are harboring his fugitives, and he will never know we did. We are taking them to the palace, and then we are moving on with our lives."

"But these are my new friends," argued Emilia.

"Your new friends have very serious warrants if they are who I think they are!"

Emilia swallowed deep before she said, "If you think that it is for the best…"

"Then it's settled. How do I get to the Virgo Palace?" asked Octavia.

Ferran was the only one to answer, "Keep on this road. It should be in a dense forest of enormous, green pine-trees…"

After a very long road trip through the heartland of the Virgo Lands, Ferran found himself deep within that pine forest. There was no longer snow fluttering around, in fact there wasn't even a single flake on the ground or in the trees. The setting sun no longer had to fight to make it through the clouds as they all had been blown North. With purple skies above and white, shrinking, rock roads leading further into the forest, the destination was way easier to find than Furictown was. Strangely enough, there were even parking spots. *This all seems too good to be true.*

Railroad tracks ran right through the center of the forest town, yet most of the pines were preserved in the strangest fashion. Only room for small roads meant for bikes and the buildings themselves destroyed the plant life. Every other square inch had an enormous pine tree that stretched on for centuries above the ground or at the very least shrubs and vines. As they walked through the town, Ferran wondered where the Palace was, and the sky above them faded out of existence under the more closely clustered, towering pines. Tall poles with fires steadily roasting at the tops stood scattered around the dirt, walking paths. Lots of townspeople wandered the thin streets on foot closing up their businesses for the night.

A post office, a town hall, farmers markets, communes, and strange bike shops making futuristic looking motorbikes were all present within the town. The people of the town did not worry about the presence of Ferran and his group even after Jaako pointed out the palace like a tourist would. Naturally it was at the very end of the forest village up a long path. It dwarfed the town twenty times over...twice. Heavy, green stained-glass lined the walls, and from the hill it sat upon one could probably see all the way to the ocean.

A chrome material that made up the walls of the palace glistened in the setting sun, and Ferran briefly wondered if he had ever seen a more pure building brick in his life. The walls curved outwards slightly before merging into a roof, similar to a kettle upside down. When they passed the last few buildings before entering the path that would bring them straight to the palace, the pines nearly disappeared entirely. Because of this, Ferran could finally see the peak of the palace. Possibly thousands of feet above was the large flagpole with a strange array of colors and shapes he could only assume to be the emblem of the Virgo Zodiac.

The single path they walked down exploded into a labyrinth of paths going in and out of the forest around the enormous palace. One of which led to a somewhat open field with a large pile of wood in the center. Ferran looked around at his companions and noticed that he wasn't the only one in awe. Even the stone cold officer that claimed to be Octavia was flabbergasted by the pure size of the palace. *Standing next to such a creation makes you really see how small you are in comparison to the world. There are ten other palaces similar to this that I've never even seen. This is bigger than any of us.*

"I just hope they have a bathroom inside," murmured Aqila who weaved her way to the front of the group. "I have been stuck in that car for way too long."

"That's something I think we all can agree on," said Emilia with an unfamiliarly polite smile. "We'll go with you."

Aqila snarled after hearing that, and Ferran almost didn't believe he saw it because nobody else noticed. When they all stood at the front door to the palace he asked, "How long have you guys been helping us? When did they find you guys, Octavia?"

"Yesterday," said Octavia immediately. Her focus was obviously not on Ferran as she rang the doorbell with a gaping mouth and wider eyes.

When the doors opened, a tall man stood on the other side. He had perfectly cut brown hair, and it contrasted his soft, pale skin that resided on his ever so inviting face. Not a single freckle was plastered on his body let alone his face, and Ferran was too focused on how buff the man was to even hear what he said. Luckily, Ferran wasn't the only one to mishear his greetings.

"What did you say?" Caleb asked as he pulled himself together trying not to focus on the man's bulging muscles. "I couldn't quite hear you."

"And why might you be here?" asked the mysterious man.

"We are travelers looking for somewhere to stay the night," replied Aqila who was unphased by the man's underlying gym routine. "Is there any way we can stay here for the night or at least use your facilities?"

"Of course we never have visitors here!" exclaimed the man. He welcomed them into the palace and closed the door behind them. "Ever since Panna left for her mission she has never returned. As she would've wanted, we just kept on working like usual."

"Right, do you know...what happened to Panna?" asked Aqila who kept looking around the halls of the vast palace.

"Yes, I am aware of what happened. However, that doesn't mean we will stop our operations," replied the man without answering her question.

They made their way through delicately decorated corridors and through various different warehouses. The man claimed there was a barracks just down the hall from the throne room. Ferran found this all too strange. *The throne room is on the ground floor, and the entire palace is in plain sight.* Their host led them all the way to the barracks, but as they passed the throne room the closed doors made even the tallest of men feel inferior. Golden accents ran all the way down to the floor where they met the glossy, polished walkway. Bright lights lined the halls glowing almost a neon green, and the clacks of the host's shoes kept Ferran's mind from wandering too far.

Once in the barracks, Ferran found they were the only visitors in the room. Not another soul rested in the barracks as the host, whose name he presumed was Wal-Cede just by the amount of greetings he got from workers passing by on their way to various jobs, quickly moved along the process.

"I'll leave you guys to settle in for a few minutes. Our chefs have almost finished up dinner, so as soon as that is ready I will come retrieve you," said Wal-Cede so quickly Ferran had to think it through twice. "It won't be long now. I can already smell the venison!"

He shut the door on them as he exited the barracks. *Why did he shut the door?* Everyone else began taking off their backpacks and placing them on the silky, white bunk beds. Everyone except for Ferran and Octavia that is. Ferran glanced around the room looking for anything suspicious. There were no windows in the barracks, and the only source of lighting came from ceiling lights. The room was way too vast for him to analyze quickly. At least fifty bunk beds stretched out in three directions, and not one of the directions led to another door. *For a room this large that is supposed to hold so many people, why is there only one entrance?*

"Where are the bathrooms?" asked Aqila while she was rummaging through her backpack. "Is there not a restroom in this barracks?"

"Apparently not," said Octavia as she walked towards the door.

"I don't know, this seems pretty cool!" exclaimed Caleb as he hopped back on the bottom bunk. "I couldn't tell you the last time I got to sleep on a bunk bed!"

Jaako stared at his bed in confusion before murmuring, "Have I ever slept in an actual bed?"

"We're locked in!" exclaimed Octavia before she even took her hand off the doorknob.

"What?!" exclaimed Ferran. He jumped over to the doorknob and attempted to open it. It turned just as much as it did for Octavia, not at all.

"There has to be another way out! Does anyone have a bobby pin? I'll pick the lock!"

"You can't, there is no key slot on this side of the door!" exclaimed Octavia. "It's blank!"

"Relax guys," said Caleb comfortably from his bed. "He just doesn't want us going anywhere and getting lost right before dinner. There's no reason to be concerned."

"Caleb has a point," spoke Jaako who was crawling into his bed atop of Caleb's. "There is no way that he knows who we are, and even if he did, why would he try to lock us up in the barracks? Wouldn't they just arrest us on the spot?"

"No!" exclaimed Ferran immediately. "I don't trust this."

"Neither do I," said Octavia. "Emilia and I are leaving first as soon as he lets us out."

"Why so early?" asked Emilia with blatant disappointment. "Can we stay at least a few days? It doesn't seem right to leave our friends this early."

"We are leaving the moment we recreate Virgo!" exclaimed Ferran. "Which one of you is going to be the new Virgo?"

"What?" asked Octavia and Emilia in unison.

"I haven't told them about that yet," said Aqila who still wasn't concerned with what they were talking about. She sat on her bed zoning out watching Jaako act like a young child as he struggled to get under the covers of his bed. "They don't know that we need a Virgo in order to create a new Virgo. They were just helping us get off the streets in Garigo for a night."

"Maybe that's what we should've done then!" exclaimed Octavia. "Nobody is making me a Zodiac, and nobody is going to lock us in here!"

"I'm going to have to go with Jaako and Caleb on this one. You guys are overreacting. There is no way that whoever that guy was knows that we are wanted by Lev and Kozoroh. If he did then why would he want to help Lev or Kozoroh? He probably is just trying to be a good host," said Aqila uncaringly. "A good host without any bathrooms."

"How do you know he isn't working with them?" asked Ferran once more. "Lev had the police chief of arguably the least important town on the face of the planet working with her, no offense Jaako."

Jaako laughed, "It is just a dried up oil well after all."

"Please just stop Ferran," begged Aqila with a look of absolute exhaustion. As she began shivering in the unheated room she got angrier. "You go missing, and as soon as you come back you start acting the same all over again! When will you ever learn to be a man!"

Ferran stared at her in disbelief. He was unable to process what she had just said, and before he knew it he had begun sweating in the room. Ferran then turned back to the door while saying, "Fine."

Octavia looked him dead in the eyes and said, "Are you two…or…?"

"They are close siblings, don't let the way they act fool you!" laughed Caleb lightheartedly from his bunk bed.

"I see," said Octavia slowly. "Well either way we are leaving first thing tomorrow mor-"

The door swung open, and Wal-Cede stepped into the room with an assistant. The assistant was a kitchen worker, and she had a large, silver plate that held six glasses of water on them. Wall-Cede spoke, "Leaving so soon? You haven't even had dinner yet."

"We are staying for dinner but we leave in the morning," replied Octavia.

"Surely you will want to stay for breakfast then?" asked Wal-Cede as he offered them all the water. "You will also miss our festival if you leave so soon." Both Ferran and Octavia refused the water. Everybody else was making their way to the door and taking theirs. When only two waters remained, Wal-Cede took one and said, "I'm quite thirsty myself. Come along now. Dinner is ready."

The assistant disappeared down a hallway, and everyone followed Wal-Cede. They passed the throne room doors again, but this time the doors were wide open. The room was twice as large as the barracks they had just been in, but for some reason it seemed larger than the throne room of Sagittarius.

"Why does your throne room seem larger than the throne room of Sagittarius?" asked Ferran as he glanced in at the human sized bonsai trees and the hanging, crystal chandeliers.

Wal-Cede stopped in his tracks. "So you have been to more than one palace?" He quickly began walking again as he continued, "Most of the time the throne rooms are the same size among the Zodiacs, but a few of the throne rooms differ in size. However, the size of the palace is always the same. They may be in different shapes, made of different materials, having different interior designs, or in different places, but no matter what each palace is the same total size."

"Interesting," said Jaako. "Do the Active Zodiacs follow those same rules?"

"What do you mean?" asked Wal-Cede. "That is a much more complicated topic involving several completely different points of focus, but I applaud you for your curiosity. As we grow closer to the cafeteria, may you feed a bit of my curiosity, young ones?"

"Of course," replied Emilia who answered for Jaako.

"Did you come here to recreate the Virgo Zodiac?"

Ferran gulped silently as Jaako gladly answered, "I'm pretty sure we did."

They had just finished walking up a flight of stairs to the second story when Wal-Cede continued, "Now did you just come here hoping to convince us to recreate one, or did you plan on doing it yourselves?"

Now in another hallway the group walked towards a large set of metal doors. Caleb replied with, "Either way works for us, but if you guys don't I think we will do it ourselves."

Wal-Cede stopped in front of the doors, and without opening them he asked very softly, "Well in order to do that you need an Earth Gemstone and a Virgo to take the place. Do you have those?"

Octavia interrupted before anyone could respond, "They have a gemstone, but they do not have a Virgo that is willing because my sister and I are leaving first thing in the morning still. I am not about to be their guinea pig test Virgo."

"Relax my friend, it is very unlikely that we will be allowed to let a Virgo like you become a Zodiac. Anyways, you have the gemstone, am I correct?"

"Yes," said Ferran, who knew secrecy was now pointless.

Wal-Cede's eyes were wider than watermelons ripe for harvest, and after hearing what he wanted, he led them into the cafeteria. "There are two lines where you get your food and countless tables as the cafeteria stretches around this entire story of the palace. Right now you are in cafeteria B-2. There are four other cafeterias feeding all sorts of residents, but all I ask of you is to stay in this one."

Ferran had no problem staying within this cafeteria. By the sheer size of the room, and the fact that there were four other cafeterias all probably just as populated as this one made him think that the food would be rubbish. Several rows of uncountable amounts of tables curved in both directions, and just about every table had six or seven people happily munching away. The lines of people attempting to get their food was only a short ten steps from them, and all the chatter of everyone else in the gargantuan room made his own thoughts ricochet around his head a little more violently. *The food has to be bad.* However, as they passed tables on their way to the line, Ferran realized just how delicious the food smelled, and by the way the seated groups were feasting made him think that it tasted just as good as it looked. *And there are actually windows and multiple doors in here. This is a lot safer than the barracks; if we wanted we could leave right now.*

They got into the lines, and Aqila murmured something that missed his ears before walking off. Concerned he looked back to see her making her way to Wal-Cede who was tapping away on a phone.

"Relax Ferran, she is asking him where the bathrooms are," said Caleb whose eyes would not leave the plates of venison around him.

Ferran stood in line wondering if they were making a mistake, but every time that scent of perfectly cooked meat hit his nose those thoughts were abolished. *How do they supply all of this meat? Venison at that!? Surely this would have an impact on the environment if they hunted this vigorously every night. I just don't understand the logistics of it all, but then again maybe Panna did some Zodiac stuff that would make this possible. Maybe all of this isn't suspicious. Maybe I was wrong. No. There is no way. He pulled out his phone almost as soon as we walked away. Is it business messaging or worse?*

"I think that it's a three course meal," said Caleb, breaking Ferran's train of thought. "Ferran, if you don't want your berries will you give them to me?"

"Sure," replied Ferran who just wanted Caleb to stop talking to him so he could think again. *Maybe I owe her an apology. An apology for killing Sartan. An apology for disappearing in Garigo. An apology for not trusting her like I should've. Maybe I should ask her a few questions.* "I'll be back. I have to go to the restroom too."

I'll have to wait until she gets out of the bathroom in order to catch her alone, but that is if I'm fast enough to figure out where they went before she comes back. Ferran quickly forced his legs to propel him to the doors slow enough that he didn't look odd or draw attention to himself but fast enough to catch up to his sister. When he got through the doors there were three hallways up ahead: the one he was walking down that led to the stairs, one that went right towards who knew what, and one that went left. He had not yet reached the two hallways that went right and left, but he stopped just before them. He peeked his head around the corner of one to see a sign that said, 'Restrooms'. Before he lunged around the corner after Aqila, he heard Wal-Cede down the other hallway. Ferran immediately took his head back to be safe and listened intently to the conversation that Wal-Cede was having on his phone.

"Yes, I am aware of the threat they possess. This little affliction that Lev has been trying to deal with for about a month now has made its way to you," said the man on the other side of the phone with an inordinately deep voice.

"So what do you want me to do? Steal their gemstone? Kill them? Use their stone to make myself an inactive Virgo until we can find the Virgo Gemstone? What if they have the Virgo Gemstone!?" asked Wal-Cede nervously.

"No," replied the strange man. "You will do as I command. Take the Virgo that they intended to use and make her the inactive Virgo Zodiac."

"That is exactly what they came here to do though, master. Why would you want me to do that?"

"You do not have the right to ask for that knowledge. You will do as I wish. Take their Virgo and replace Panna. Immediately."

"Yes, my lord."

"Then make sure they stay at the palace for as long as possible. This will all be over within a few days. I must make Lev aware of my plans now. Can you handle the task at hand until she gets there?"

"I think-k I ca-can," said Wal-Cede who struggled not to stutter.

"Then you will be replaced if you can't. Go replace Panna. Now."

The mysterious man hung up on Wal-Cede, and Ferran could hear footsteps behind him coming from the cafeteria. He quickly walked towards whatever the sound may be and was surprised to see that Emilia walked towards him.

"Do you know where the restrooms are?" said Emilia as loud as day.

Nervous and forced to improvise, Ferran was unsure that what he spat out would be believable for both pairs of ears. "I don't know. I think they went this way." Ferran's face was beat red, and he could feel sweat pooling under his arms. They walked around the corner to see Wal-Cede holding his face in his hands. He quickly pulled himself together and began questioning them.

"What are you two doing?"

"I was showing her where you guys went because she had to go to the bathroom," replied Ferran who was lying to both of them.

Emilia started, "Wait a second you were already-"

"It's down that hallway. I have to take care of something really quickly," said Wal-Cede as he walked past them giving no concern to their presence.

Emilia began talking to Ferran about why he said that, but Ferran gave even less concern to her than Wal-Cede did. He immediately walked after his host leaving Emilia in the hallway. *She'll figure it out*. They barged through the cafeteria doors, and Ferran instantly saw his companions at a table.

Wal-Cede pulled up his phone and quickly murmured, "Ready throne room for a recreation of Virgo, and station extra guards there in case we have resistance."

"What are you doing?" asked Ferran who was right behind him.

"We are giving you what you want. To recreate a Zodiac," said the man as he gasped for air on the way to Octavia. "We must collect your friends and bring them to the throne room before we run out of time. It is of utmost importance that we finish the process immediately."

"What process?" asked Jaako who was chewing his food and heard the last bit of Wal-Cede's statement. The host had walked so fast that they were already at the table.

"You must go now!" exclaimed their host. "Hurry, follow me!"

The entire table stared in confusion. Whether it was the visible epiphany Ferran had on his face that got them to stand up or the urgency on Wal-Cede's, Ferran would never know. Once they all stood up guards muscled Octavia ahead of Wal-Cede, much to her thrashing dismay. One thing Ferran did know however, was that the man Wal-Cede just spoke with was Kozoroh or at the very least one of his goons, and that no matter what they did they would still need to recreate Virgo.

Ferran thought about it as they all ran to the throne room together. *We have to play into Kozoroh's hands. If we leave now we will have to come back later, and that would only cause more problems for us. Why would Kozoroh want us to get ahead though? He certainly doesn't want us to recreate Virgo, yet that is exactly what he told his minions to do!* He jumped off the last step onto the ground floor. *Lev was last seen all the way back in the lands of Sagittarius, but it is extremely unlikely she is still there.* He swung himself around the great doors of the throne room. *If she was actually in Garigo only a day ago she could get here within hours if she siphon travels! Wait! She can't siphon travel; she isn't in a Fire Zodiac's territory! That means she is at least one day away! She would have no clue how to get here though...right? Let alone where the palace is to begin with.* He stopped right in front of the palace's throne room and began panting along with all of his companions, most of which hadn't slept in over a day.

"Begin the process!" yelled Wal-Cede as he gasped for breath. "The officer is their Virgo! Which one of you has the stone?!"

Caleb looked at Ferran nervously as if he didn't know what to do. Without saying a word Ferran nodded to Caleb, and Caleb slowly pulled the Taurus Gemstone out of his pockets. Instantly Wal-Cede snatched the stone out of his hand and gave it to an assistant. Suddenly Ferran's hands were grabbed and cuffed from behind. He screamed out, but it was in vain because after looking around he saw Jaako and Caleb all getting handcuffed at the same time.

"This is for your safety during the procedure!" exclaimed Wal-Cede. "Put her on the throne!"

"NO!" screamed Octavia as she began bucking much more violently at her captors. It took three of them to get her on the throne, and two of the guards ended up with bite marks on their arms.

"Do it now!" screamed Wal-Cede. He could barely be heard over all of the chaos within the throne room, but the assistant who held the stone thrusted the tightly gripped Taurus Gemstone towards Octavia without letting it go.

"What!?" exclaimed Wal-Cede. "Why did nothing happen?" An assistant ran up to his side and whispered something into his ear. "Well how long until the sun is down!?" A moment of silence passed as the assistant whispered into his ear again. "Forty-seven seconds!? Are you kidding me?!"

"Let us go!" demanded Ferran.

"You will have your freedom after the procedure! None of you will die on my watch! I promise!" screamed back Wal-Cede without looking away from the throne. "Try it again!"

Nothing happened. Wal-Cede had his assistant attempt two more times until a voice was heard from behind them. "Something really bad is happening! Help!" screamed Emilia at the entrance to the throne room.

"Ignore the girl! She's with them!" screamed Wal-Cede. "Try it again!"

This time something happened. A deafening ring silenced the entire room. Every single leaf on the enormous bonsai trees, of which Ferran failed to truly notice amidst all the chaos, were blown off and began flying around the room. The three guards that were holding down Octavia disappeared into the blinding light that followed, but it didn't matter because shortly after everyone else had been thrown on their backs by the shockwave. A glistening, green beacon of light blasted through the ceiling extending miles into the sky above. Temporarily blinded by the light, deafened by the sound, and beaten by the shockwave, Ferran finally understood. Once the shockwave had passed no guards were holding him down. As everybody began getting up the beacon of light still glimmered powerfully from the throne, and Ferran's ears still rang too loudly to hear anything. All he could hear were his own thoughts.

The beacon. The beacon of light. It is so bright that it could be seen from the ocean. Lev doesn't need to know where the palace is or how to get there...she just has to follow the light. It all makes sense now...Lev didn't know how to get here to begin with, and Kozoroh wanted us to think we were safe here by letting us continue our plans, unknowingly...helping his. He just killed two birds with one stone...unfortunately for Kozoroh, Wal-Cede fucked up enough to make the others distrust him as much as I RIGHTFULLY do!

To his surprise, the guards uncuffed him, and he looked around at his companions. Octavia, barely breathing, sat lifelessly on the throne zapped of energy within the tower of light which hid most of her from view. Guards were watching her from all around to make sure that she didn't try anything, but oddly enough she wasn't the main focus anymore. Caleb and Jaako were already uncuffed and running out of the throne room next to Wal-Cede. They weren't running from him or after him but with him. There were also assistants who looked similar to doctors. They carried first aid kits of all different types and were running ahead of Wal-Cede and Ferran's companions. As Ferran's ears slowly stopped ringing he was startled when Emilia began shaking him by his shoulders. The fear in her eyes dripped onto his face in the form of tears.

"My sister is dying on that throne!" she screamed at the top of her raspy lungs while struggling to not let the tears cut off her voice. "My sister is dying on that throne, and this is all my fault!"

"Your sister will be fine," insisted Ferran who desperately tried to get her off him so he could stand up. "She will be weak for a short while, but she will not die because of this. Where is everyone running to?"

"Everybody is dying, this is terrible!"

"What happened?!" screamed Ferran as assertively as he could.

Emilia, who finally ran off to her sister on the throne, cried out, "I found Aqila..."

Ferran stopped standing up. "You found Aqila doing what!?!"

"She is overdosing!"

Chapter 20
Accepting an Apology
Aqila

Approximately twenty-four hours later, Aqila opened her eyes very slowly. The first thing that she noticed was a full glass of water on the counter next to the head of the bed. Sitting peacefully next to the glass was an empty syringe with a label on it. The letters read, 'Naloxone'. She knew not what happened, but her mouth was drier than Ferran's bubbling sense of humor. She sat up in the bed and gulped down the entire glass of water as if she were a parched camel. Still very weary, she zoned out staring at the blank walls around her. There were no windows in the room nor doors. There was a hallway that curved out of sight, and it had to be the way out. Multiple other infirmary beds lined the room, and on one of them sat a pile of neatly stacked clothes. At the top was a white piece of paper.

She struggled to command her legs to lift her out of the bed, but once she won the battle, the letter that was left for her became more readable through her dizzy eyes. When she picked up the folded piece her legs nearly gave out, and she stumbled forward attempting not to fall. Once she gathered her strength, she unfolded the paper and slowly read it to herself.

Aqila, we had no clue it had gotten this bad. I knew that something was happening when we went into Garigo, but I didn't think about how long it could have been going on for. I just figured you were still mad at me for...well you know. We understand that you didn't see how important it was to leave him behind in that forest, but I forgive you. Sometimes you just have to be the bigger man...I wasn't ready to point that out to you, and I apologize.

You didn't have to do this though. When did you even have time to find that? There is no way that you still were using the pills from Dursnia. Now all of the new people you insisted on bringing into the group: Emilia, Octavia, and Jaako are all very concerned for your health, and I haven't seen you since before Garigo. That's how you treat me when I return, when I return with directions to the Virgo Palace at that. High out of your mind the entire time. Had Emilia not gone to the bathroom you wouldn't be reading this right now. On top of all this, I think Kozoroh cornered us last night. Wal-Cede forced Octavia to be inaugurated as an inactive Virgo Zodiac. I'm quite confident that Wal-Cede is not here to help us, and I want to leave as soon as you wake up. I'll tell you more about it when you get up in case they read the letter. Hopefully this is all just a wake up call for you, and we can move on after this. Much love...your brother Ferran.

Aqila ripped the paper to shreds and chucked it into the corner of the room. *Just when I was beginning to understand his point of view! Bigger man!? He is so full of shit! The only one here that I do not trust is you! It was not important to leave Sartan behind at all! You are just an envious sack of shit!* Aqila itched at the thought of the intervention talks she might have to be a part of when they all found out she was awake. It made her want to rip her hair out, especially if Ferran is the one who decided she needs it. She could already feel the shivers kicking in as she stripped down out of the stained clothes she had been wearing since Furictown. Riddled with anger, Aqila threw her dirty clothes into the corner next to the rejected letter. Once nude, a faint sound of a door down the hallway clicking shut very quietly trickled into her ear, but it was loud enough for her to hear it. Hastily she slipped into new undergarments that clearly were provided by her host and not of her desired fashion. Instead of telling whoever approached that she was changing, Aqila tried to hop into the pants before they rounded the corner. Failing miserably, she fell backwards onto the bed behind her. With the pants on the floor away from her she tried to call out but was too late.

As she stood back up from the bed, a hooded figure stopped in the middle of the room. It was a man, and she quickly reached for the pants on the ground to use as something to cover up her bare skin. She gripped the infirmary sweats with her left hand and stopped half bent over when she heard the man speak.

"Aqila?" asked the man with uncertainty.

Aqila let go of the pants and looked up at the hooded figure. He threw the hood back off his head, and Aqila's heart stopped just as it might have the night before. Without saying a single word she dropped the pants and ran to the man grabbing him tightly in her arms.

"I thought you were dead! How did you get here!? How did you find me?! What happened!?" Aqila bombarded Sartan with questions before burying her face in his chest. She felt her shivers disappear the second he reluctantly wrapped his arms around her in surprise. "I am so sorry he did that to you! I never told him to do that, and I still have yet to forgive him for it!"

"I wasn't expecting that," laughed Sartan stoically before escaping her embrace. "But you should put your clothes on. It is already night."

Aqila blushed fire-red before walking away while refusing to make eye contact. She got dressed into basic sweatpants, a t-shirt, and a hoodie before continuing her conversation with Sartan. She instantly noticed the burn mark on his hand and asked, "What happened to your hand?"

"I had a training accident a couple days ago," replied Sartan who tried to hide the fresh burn. "Wal-Cede told me you had an incident last night."

"Who is Wal-Cede?" asked Aqila as she walked back to Sartan.

"He is the one in charge of this palace. He told me where to find you and the rest of your friends. I'm genuinely surprised that there are so many of you now."

"Yeah, but you are the one that kick-started everything," said Aqila as she went in for another hug. "You saved all of our lives in Dursn-"

Sartan hastily stepped away from her as he cut her off, "That is not what you want. Not to mention we should get going. I'm running out of time."

"All I want is a hug...we have enough time for just one hug..."

Sartan took a deep breath and sighed heavily before replying with, "There is too much to do right now. I must take care of a few things first." Aqila understood the truthfulness of his statement as she stared at the ground. She must have failed to hold back the visible disappointment on her face because he noticed. He embraced her in his arms while inside the privacy of the room before whispering into her ear, softly and slowly, "This is the last time I will be affectionate with an acquaintance."

Aqila nodded her head into his chest, understanding the sad truth that she had passed the boundaries of their relationship in his eyes. Unwilling to let go so quickly, the hug lasted until Sartan pulled hard enough to break free from Aqila's grip. His face remained mostly unchanged by the entire experience, yet a small frown sat on his lips right under the droopy eyes that rested on black pillows. She immediately knew what he wanted.

"You want to find Ferran now…do you not?" asked Aqila whose eyes were suddenly much more sensitive to the cold air around her.

"I know exactly where he is, but yes, I want to have a talk with him," answered Sartan with a slight smirk. "Wal-Cede has all of your friends gathered around the campfire for the end of his festival."

Sartan then turned towards the hall, and Aqila instantly grabbed his burnt hand, stopping him from leaving her in the room. She started, "Sartan…I know you want to hurt him…and I told him that I would not protect him from you…he deserves this, but please do not kill him or maim him…he still is my brother after all." As she let go of his burned hand, she begged, "Promise?"

"I won't kill or maim him personally…but I can't promise he won't die soon," answered Sartan as he began walking away again. "I don't make promises I can't keep. Let's go, they are impatient."

Aqila, silently analyzing his statement, kept her mouth shut as Sartan led her out of the room. She implicitly followed him through the vast palace. Long shiny corridors stretched through the building as they walked through them looking for their exit. Luckily, Sartan must have known where he was going because within a minute they walked out of the palace onto a rocky, gravel path. A large fire rumbled down the path in the distance. She walked behind Sartan scrambling on the path. None of the rocks were the same size, but it was not the path that really was bothering her. *How did he just show up? He was left to die in a forest nearly half a continent away.*

She heard a twig snap off into the deathly, dark woods next to the trail, but the moment she glanced towards the sound a short and plump worker bumped into her, returning her attention to the trail before the worker walked away on his mission. Aqila began sweating uncontrollably way before they reached the roaring fire. The enormous fire crackled in the center of an even larger opening deep within the woods. Several paths went off in each direction at the edges of the forest, and each of them was wide enough for a car. Small, wooden huts with workers coming in and out of them lined the edge of the woods between the paths, and there was also an awkwardly placed building not too far from the blaze. It obviously did not belong where it sat as tree branches went through various sections of its core. She saw various oddly constructed motorcycles sitting within the building on the other side of the giant garage door. Workers were inside constructing new bikes and fixing old ones. Several of the vehicles sat outside of the building waiting for a worker to fix them or take them back to where they needed to be. All of the bikes had transparent fuel tanks with green liquids inside them, and worst of all the headlights glowed an emerald green instead of the typical yellow or blue. The bikes were huge in comparison to most of the standard motorcycles Aqila had seen. They were large enough for two people to ride on one, comfortably.

Closer to the grand fire were several benches where lots of the residents sat around staring at the fireworks, which consistently yet chaotically exploded far above in the sky. Food service workers held trays and went around the separate benches offering locals snacks and delights during the festival. Off to her right one man was even surrounded by a crowd as he juggled flaming bowling pins. Surprisingly, it was not that hard to find the rest of her group among the masses, but then again Sartan must have known exactly where they were as he skipped looking around the dozens of benches on the front side of the fire. Aqila followed Sartan to the other side of the fire where she saw faces she recognized sitting down and staring at the endless flames and fireworks. Sartan had his strange, military-like jacket's hood up over his face, and he was not recognizable. She now noticed that he also wore urban-camo pants. Regardless, their friends were unaware of their approach until Aqila had gotten really close. *How did he get these clothes…how did he survive the forests…Lev saved him! Wait, how did he escape Lev to find us!?*

Upon that thought Ferran noticed her and ran towards Aqila with outstretched hands exclaiming, "You're awake! I was just telling everyone something very important!"

He went in for a hug completely disregarding Sartan who stood right next to Aqila, as a result Aqila ended up witnessing exactly what she feared would transpire. Once Ferran was only a foot away from her, Sartan sent his fist flying straight into Ferran's stomach. Ferran's body instantly dropped to the ground, and he exclaimed through blotched coughing, "I told you they can't be trusted! Get away Aqila!"

Aqila was frozen, but all of her allies jumped straight into an aggressive, fighting stance. Sartan was silent while he slowly pulled down his hood. The light from the fire, bright red and scorching, showed every little detail on his face to the group. Octavia rushed forward to neutralize the threat, but Caleb and Jaako stopped her before they could even stop their mouths from gaping. Emilia stood confused, unsure of what exactly was happening.

Ferran rolled over to glance at his attacker, and upon seeing a ghost hovering over him he asked in astonishment, "Sartan?"

Sartan whispered back so quietly that only Aqila and Ferran could hear him, "So you were paying attention after all..." Ferran stared in confusion unsure what Sartan meant, and Aqila was too in trance with the moment to process it herself. Sartan then smacked Ferran hard enough Aqila could hear the echo crack off a thick pine from deep within the forest.

"Stop that!" exclaimed Octavia as she struggled to break free from Caleb and Jaako. "Why are you letting him attack Ferran?!"

They watched Sartan punch and kick Ferran time after time while Aqila slowly answered, "It is only retaliation Octavia. Ferran...Ferran deserves this." Aqila looked away from the beating and tried to ignore her brother's screams for help. *He deserves this. I never knew it would be just as hard for me though. Sartan will stop before he truly hurts him...right?*

Upon looking back at the two of them that fact became apparently false. A red trickle dripped out of her defenseless brother's nose in the burning light. "That is enough," she said in a broken tone. Tears dripped down her brother's face as Sartan continued to beat him. Now fearing that he was not going to stop until after Ferran's drowned in his own blood, Aqila pulled Sartan away from her brother while exclaiming, "Stop! You've got your point across! Do not kill him!"

Jaako and Caleb released Octavia and the three of them began approaching Sartan to help Aqila when he finally stopped attacking Ferran. Everyone grouped up into a circle around Ferran who still laid in his own puddle of pain. Sartan then spat on him.

"Oh, I'm sorry, but...who the hell are you!?" asked Octavia, completely unaware of what was happening.

"Sartan was part of our group before we got to Garigo," answered Jaako.

"And?" continued Octavia who had knelt down to help Ferran. "That doesn't warrant-"

"Ferran killed Sartan," said Caleb in disbelief. "Or so we thought! How did you manage to live?!"

Sartan did not reply. Instead he looked at Caleb with a scowl on his face, so Ferran asked again from his compromised position on the ground, "I strapped you to that tree! There is no way you could've escaped on your own! Why are you here anyways?! I GAVE YOU WHAT YOU WANTED!"

"YOU GAVE ME NOTHING BUT PROBLEMS!" yelled Sartan.

"Have you ever thought that maybe you...ARE THE PROBLEM!?" snapped back Ferran after spitting out blood on Sartan's feet. "WHY DID YOU COME FIND US?"

"Why did you try to kill me just for your sister's attention?" asked Sartan as everyone went quiet. "You are the problem! I didn't even want to help you guys in the first place, and you still tried to get rid of me! As soon as I thought about staying with you guys to help with your bullshit agenda you left me for the Eveharrisses! All you do is lie!"

"We wouldn't have made it this far had it not been for me leaving you behind! Now that's the truth!" argued Ferran while Octavia helped him up to his feet. "You just wanted to bend over my sister!"

"And who are you to say that?!" yelled back Sartan. He began walking away from the group. "It doesn't even matter anyways!"

"Sartan wait!" exclaimed Aqlia. "Don't leave us again!"

"Again!? I did NOT choose to last time!" exclaimed Sartan.

"Please stay...even Jaako and Caleb want you to stay," continued Aqila.

"I bet they do," said Sartan sarcastically. "You know what though? I will stay and help you until the very end...the brutal, bloody end"

"Thank you!" exclaimed Aqila while Caleb walked closer to Sartan.

Caleb told Sartan, "I'm sorry I didn't untie you. I don't know what came over me, but I knew what Ferran was doing was wrong. I'm glad you're going to stay with us until the end."

"Bullshit!" shouted Ferran from behind them.

Sartan smiled and whispered, "Although that may be sooner than you think..."

"What?" asked Aqila and Caleb in unison as they were the only ones close enough to hear.

"I'm sorry Caleb and Jaako. I'm sorry Aqila," whispered Sartan while stretching his arms.

"Sorry for what?" asked Aqila as she walked up to his side.

"I brought her here with me...it was the least I could do after she saved me..."

"What are you talking about?" asked Aqila with the joy of Sartan's oddly-violent reunion quickly being replaced by concern on her face. "Who saved you?"

Sartan stared past her into the forest and winked slowly. Before he even responded she realized the answer to her own question, and her gut slipped at the thought of it. He then turned to her and whispered, "Lev."

Aqila's knees gave out and she fell to the ground. *WHAT? There is no way!* She looked around doubtfully unsure whether or not Sartan was lying. Then it all made sense. *He would never have made it out of that forest had nobody helped him escape. He would never have made it this far and known where we went without Lev. How could he even escape Lev!? She is here!*

Ferran screamed at Sartan and possibly even Aqila too, "YOU WHORES!"

Dozens of soldiers with guns and red-dot lasers emerged from the woods around them. They all had barrels being pointed at them except for Sartan. *How could he do this to me? Why?* Down one of the paths that stretched out into the dark woods walked a pale man bulging at the brim with muscles, yet somehow his height made him look thin in some respect. Right beside the man's dark hair stood the tall, relentless Lev. The two of them walked slowly towards the group, and the heat from the bonfire behind Aqila melted away her critical thinking. Even in the black of the night, the two white streaks on Lev's body radiated like a beacon. As she grew closer, Aqila could see the skin on Lev was clear of any blemishes or scars, and her hair was in one quite thick strand that hung down her back perfectly swaying in the breeze. Aqila never realized Lev was so tall, and the way Lev's eyes focused on Aqila finally made her realize how dangerous their situation truly was. Lev had a perfect form...perfect posture, and when she opened her mouth, the words that came out were more distinct and regal than the first king's.

"Aqila, Caleb, Ferran, Jaako, and two that I was not informed of," stated Lev as she stopped right before the group. The entire group was opened up into a half circle to view the threat with Sartan and Aqila at the center. "I presume that one of you recently was inaugurated as an inactive Virgo Zodiac, am I correct to assume it is the woman who is holding her head heavily?" asked Lev while pointing at Octavia with her eyes. Octavia nodded in defeat, but was not given enough time to reply.

"Silence, weary one," commanded Lev as Octavia attempted to speak. "I do not require your name this late in the game. All I care about is who had the bright idea to create two Zodiacs. Who is in charge of this rebellion?"

"I am!" exclaimed Ferran who was still using Octavia to stand sturdily.

Lev nodded with a smile before asking everyone else, "Is he your leader?"

Everyone mumbled around with unsureness before Aqila answered for the group, "No. No, he is not. I am their leader, and it was my initial idea to recreate the Zodiacs!"

Everyone continued to mumble around within the group. Lev then began laughing hysterically, "That answers your question Wal-Cede...they clearly have no leader. They have no central authority and were doomed to fail from the beginning."

"That does not mean anything!" exclaimed Aqila in anger. "I know who you really are, and if us doing this slows you down then that is all that matters!"

"Who I really am?" asked Lev with a grin. "I am eternal, and I am righteous. How dare you question my nobility!"

"July 18, 6750!" exclaimed Aqila. "Tell me Lev, tell me where you were that very day!"

Lev stared at Aqila with her eyebrows questioning the relevance of the question. "I shall humor you...how would I know where I was that day?" asked Lev.

"It should not be that hard. It was not even a week before Beran was assassinated under suspicious circumstances," answered Aqila. "Of course you would fail to remember that too."

"Nonsense, how could we forget the death of Aries?" asked Lev. "Strange thing is, I toured his lands that week before his death. Not once did I suspect civil unrest in his empire. What a tragedy that day was, but we can not change the past. Where are you going with this my child?"

"Where am I going with this?" laughed Aqila. "I know exactly where you were that day."

"Then why don't you inform us all, smart one?"

"You were at Mayor Rih's home. In the city of Mirisuburg? Were you not?"

Lev stared at Aqila with burning eyes. "Why do you ask?"

"Is this true or not?" pressed Aqila.

"Lying never gets anybody anywhere does it?" asked Lev rhetorically. "I was there, yes. I had a few loose ends to tie up, and a few things went wrong."

Aqila instantly was consumed with curiosity over what could have gone wrong that night, but she desperately tried to get a certain answer from Lev instead. "Was Mayor Rih that loose end?"

Lev stared at her before replying insensitively, "Perhaps. The wife however, was an unnecessary casualty. The mistake, have you."

"And for the kids?" asked Aqila who was getting the answers she feared. "What is your policy for the children of the incident?"

"I view it as a profession. If I get attached to every life I ruin then I would not be fit to run an empire now would I? I neutralize all witnesses regardless of gender, age, or importance, and in the end more lives are helped than harmed."

"Then that answers my question...you knew not that the child was a witness."

A strangely brief moment of epiphany passed before Lev laughed, "You were awake? Aw…you poor thing. I bet you have had a very difficult time grieving."

Aqila screamed out instantly, "You feel no guilt for what you have done to me, and I will NOT feel any for you when you are defeated!" She thrusted her fist forward knowing very well that the Aries Gemstone was tightly tucked in her palm. A burning spear of flames shot out into the air. It hurdled towards Lev who attempted to block the thin streak of fire, but due to the short distance between her and Aqila she was unable to. The scolding flames struck Lev right in the leg, knocking her onto the ground.

"Follow me!" screamed Aqila as she began running away around the fire.

Lev simultaneously screamed out to her goons, "DO NOT FIRE! I NEED TO CONTINUE QUESTIONING THEM!"

Aqila was already halfway around the enormous bonfire before she looked back at her allies, and thankfully, all of her friends were running after her with the exception of Sartan. In her brief glance back at her allies, she saw Sartan helping Lev up from the ground. *I do not even want to think about it.* "Come on guys, all we have to do is make it to the bikes and drive off! Lev is not that fast!"

By the time she made it to the motorbike building she saw on the way to the festival, the large warehouse doors were already halfway closed. She slid right under the door into the garage full of bikes all by herself, but the doors had already closed by the time that the rest of the group caught up. With no other options, and quite a lack of time, Aqila used her gemstone to melt a large hole in the door, but the hole was only large enough to wheel a bike out.

On the other side of the hole stood all of her companions waiting for a bike, and as she steadily wheeled all of them out one by one Lev jumped straight through the bonfire to cut corners. Aqila was wheeling the fifth bike out when Lev caught up to them.

"Your insurgence ends here after a brief interrogation!" commanded Lev as Aqila slowly came out of the garage to stand next to the bikes. "Who is Jaako?"

They all stood there unsure of whether or not they should fight back, flee, or comply with Lev's demands. *I am done running.* Aqila thrusted her gemstone in Lev's direction once more, but this time Lev was not caught off guard. With fire still burning peacefully on Lev's body from running through the bonfire, she opened up the palm of one hand and caught the entirety of Aqila's strike, nullifying any damage it could have posed to anyone.

"Give me your stone, NOW!" demanded Lev as she grabbed Aqila's wrist tightly. Aqila felt the blood draining from her hand, but she still kept grip on her stone. "CEASE!"

Suddenly a chilling blast released the tension on her wrist. From a few feet to the right, Jaako had struck Lev with an uncontrolled ball of fire. Freezing pink flames smacked Lev off her balance, and she stumbled away several feet in attempts not to fall on the ground again. The flames that riddled her body grew larger, yet they did not seem to affect her. There were only five bikes, and that would be enough for everyone to get away. As Lev was stumbling around, Octavia and Emilia were the first to hop on to one of the bikes. Caleb and Ferran shared one as well because Ferran was still struggling to walk let alone drive. It all happened so quickly. By the time Jaako got on his all of the other bikes had already revved up and were ready to go.

"Follow the river South until you reach the coast!" screamed Ferran from the back of a bike. Caleb instantly began looking at the stars for direction, and Aqila hopped on her own bike. *This will leave one bike for Sartan...if he chooses to help us.* By now Lev, who displayed even more flames running up and down her body, had already recovered and was stomping back towards them with quite a lot of frustration in her snarled lips. "There is a small city at the end of the river by the coast! It is our only bet! We just have to make it to the other side of the mountains first!"

"Not one of you will be getting to the coast!" exclaimed Lev right as Caleb began peeling off. She raised both of her arms quickly, and a ring of flames large enough to encompass all of them rose up straight out of the ground. Caleb and Ferran were the closest to the growing ring of fire, and Caleb swerved back around to avoid melting the metals in the bike. "Now cooperate!"

Lev stood in the middle of the ring of fire. The surrounding five feet around her had tiny flames begging her for more power, but the flames that made up the outer ring grew consistently. When they stopped growing, Aqila guessed that they were at least fifteen feet tall, and the flames all curled inwards at their peaks. Aqila could hear the garage behind them melting under the heat. Without getting off his bike, Jaako sent another ball of icy-fire towards Lev. Lev did not even attempt to block the attack, and everyone watched the tiny flames in the inner ring around her jump up from the ground to neutralize the fireball. *This is it…We are done for…*

"How many Zodiac Gemstones do you currently possess as a group?" asked Lev from her position of safety. Before any of them replied Aqila caught a glimpse of Sartan walking up behind Lev. *He can still save us!* Her hopes were destroyed when he stopped right next to her side. Lev had a few inches on Sartan, and Aqila finally came to the most undesirable conclusion when she watched Lev fade away some of the flames so Sartan could stand next to her unharmed. *He is not going to help us. Not after everything Ferran has done to him.*

"We have three!" exclaimed Aqila as she turned off her bike. "Taurus, Aries, and Libra…"

Lev whispered something to Sartan with a smirk before addressing the rest, "And Ms. Officer here is an inactive Virgo while Mr. Jaako is an inactive Sagittarius? How sad. You didn't make any progress."

"Maybe, but once we get rid of Lev things will be easier!" screamed Ferran on his running bike with Caleb. "You and Sartan are doomed to die!"

"Quite amusing, but I fear he has already become more powerful than any of you," taunted Lev. "I don't lie, now do I Sartan?"

Sartan stared at Aqila, and she read his lips mumble, "Precisely."

"Perfect, then it is the purest of truth that I am ready to put these cretans behind us. Do not fear young ones. The stones will survive…their legacies however…"

Lev raised her hands, and the ring of fire rose up to a point in the sky above them. They now stood in a giant hut of fire with no exit. The heat tripled around them, and Aqila could feel her skin turning red within an instant.

"HELP!" screamed Octavia as her hair caught on fire.

Jaako was quick to think and shot a beam of flames out of his hand onto Octavia's head. The fire was not put out at all. Instead the melting flames were replaced with freezing ones, and Octavia's screeching became deafening. Aqila glanced over at Lev who was grinning with her hands up.

"Dismiss the units, Wal-Cede! Our threats have been neutralized!"

Lev slowly lowered her hands, and the ceiling of fire fell down to match them. The extra bike that Aqila had left by the melted garage burst into flames and melted into a puddle of silver. A burning tear trickled down her face as images of her friends and family burning alive next to her refused to disappear from reality. Jaako was the only one not affected by the heat, but it had grown strong enough that he could no longer help others. Everyone, like ants on a crumb, had clustered into the center of the burning casket. Aqila stared at Sartan one last time before the end. His face was emotionless and analytical. As the flames neared Aqila's head Sartan slipped his hand out of his pocket and held a fist, facing Lev, parallel to his stomach. Her last hope was that he launched it into Lev's side. That alone would give her enough time to save everyone, but unfortunately, that is not what Sartan did.

As a red aura closed in around Aqila's sight, she watched Sartan quickly pull his fist away from Lev pointlessly. She closed her eyes. Then all of the heat vanished. *Am I dead?* Aqila opened her eyes, and to her surprise the flames were all gone. Little flames crackled on the ground where the giant ring had been. Both Lev and Sartan laid on the ground next to each other in a puddle of icy water. Aqila's companions either saw what happened, or were too focused on survival to care because they all revved up their scorching hot motorcycles and drove off down the nearest path. Aqila's bike was not on yet. She left it where it stood and ran to Sartan who had already stood up and stepped away from Lev.

"YOU TRAITOR!" screamed Lev who was rising to her feet. "I WILL TERMINATE YOU!"

Aqila stopped mid sprint upon hearing those words. Lev grabbed her wet hair and threw it over her shoulder. Unlike a wet dog in the rain, Lev effortlessly evaporated the baby-blue water with flames bursting out of her pours. Immediately Sartan sent a heavy water splash from the side, but this time Lev evaporated the bubble of deep purple with the raise of one hand. Sartan stumbled backwards bumping into Aqila who stood right behind him.

"Why are you still here?" asked Sartan without looking away from Lev.

Lev attacked just as Aqila answered, and the overwhelming flames drowned out any trace of her voice. A column of fire ripped through the air, and it would have melted right through them had a small wall of purple ice not erected between them in time. The barrier was gone within five seconds, but those five seconds gave Sartan enough time to strike. He thrusted his fist, with stone inside it, right into the flames when they melted through the ice. Aqila watched as his whole body shook and convulsed under the energy that possessed him. The cold air around them vanished right as a column of water vapor devoured Lev's flames adding to its own strength and heat. The vapor was barely visible, but it still shot straight through to Lev.

She recoiled her hand in pain as the steam burned hotter than the flames that Sartan just put out. Without attacking, Lev's eyes widened as she yelled, "YOU PESKY THIEF! NOT EVEN HER STONE WILL NOT SAVE YOU!"

"Run Aqila!" demanded Sartan with waning energy in his voice. "This is my fight! My demise!"

"It is just as equally my fight!" exclaimed Aqila as she disobeyed his demands.

Suddenly, he threw Aqila away, and as she fell on the ground. Aqila rose, turned, and ran to her bike. Once she got on it and started it, she glanced back to see Sartan land a heavy attack on Lev. The force expelling out of Sartan's fist speared through the middle of the fire. The deep cobalt-blue wave sizzled and steamed; most of it turned into vapor before it even hit Lev. Regardless, as Lev fell to the ground Aqila saw an opening to save Sartan and escape. She rode the bike and stopped right next to him.

She then watched him grow violent. Punch after punch sent scolding waves at Lev, and most of the advances landed. A sudden scream came from Sartan's chest as he hastened his assault on Lev. The attacks did no real damage to her, but it slowed her down enough for Aqila and Sartan to live another minute. Sartan's screams quickly deformed into sinister and manic laughter, which was unstable and further deformed into eerie silence. Splashing sounds drowned Aqila's ears as she watched in terror. With each repeated punch, scolding steam shot into their attacker, keeping her on the ground momentarily.

"Don't shoot! He is breaking through the stone! It is the stone that is fighting!" yelled Lev over the chaos. "He is not exactly powerless now but will be once the stone's energy catches up to him!"

Then, more sporadic than an electron, Sartan twisted and turned, attacking Lev with one hand and the goons with another. The vapor strikes from his stone melted right through the faces of the officers. The smell made Aqila verp in her mouth, but she knew they would shoot if Sartan began winning the fight or even escaping. It was either them or her. By the time that last officer lost his life. Sartan had seemingly gathered his emotions...Lev on the other hand had lost hers.

"Worthless!" she exclaimed. The white tattoos that ran up and down her body glowed red with rage, and her pupils, engulfed in flames, focused on Sartan and Aqila. "Just two loose ends to tie up..."

"The moon!" exclaimed Sartan mindlessly as he began to stumble backwards, no longer pinning Lev on the ground with his attacks.

"I fear that I am brighter, PEASANT!" screamed Lev who spontaneously combusted.

Aqila struggled to understand exactly what was happening or why they said that, but she knew that staying there was the worst possible idea she could have. Then without warning, Sartan collapsed on the ground. *No! We have no time for this!* Without thinking, Aqila jumped off the bike to help him up. Sartan smiled as she helped him on to the bike, but not once did he say anything. Their predator did not bother running or attacking; she simply walked towards them with a deep grin burning an unforgettable imprint in Aqila's mind. She attempted to secure him on the bike, but her mouth gaped wide open in response to what his face said. He sat there staring at her with a wide grin and cashed eyes, completely unphased by the dire situation they found themselves in.

"What is wrong with you?" asked Aqila hastily, for she knew Lev was watching them with laughter from behind. When Sartan mumbled to himself while nodding off again she felt heat on her back. Looking over her shoulder Aqila witnessed Lev burning a flame merely ten feet away.

"He is breaking through to the stone!" laughed Lev uncontrollably. Aqila knew that Lev could sense the fear within her, and she also knew that Lev enjoyed every second of watching Aqila's fright trump her logic. "He can no longer protect your over-pedestalized persona!"

Aqila chose not to waste breath replying to Lev's untruthful mockery. Instead, she jumped on to the back of the bike and held Sartan in place. It only took seconds to do this, and it took even less time to hit the gas. As Lev angrily shrank in the side mirror she missed the bike closely with a strand of fire. The dim headlights led her through the bike paths deeper into the forest, hopefully down the same paths her companions took. Lev was completely out of sight now, but she heard a violent scream that could belong to no one else echo through the night. She then heard a deafening explosion far behind her. Flames and smoke rose up into the moon-filled, night sky. *This can only mean one thing...I HAVE TO HURRY!* Swerving through the dark trees she only sped up. That is when she slowed down and stopped to witness it in all of its glory.

Through the thick forest of pine needles behind her stood a column of flames that had magically erected into the sky instantaneously. It was visible from beneath the treeline and brighter than the mid-day sun. The flames curdled and formed into a shape more recognizable by Aqila. Behind them now stood a burning lioness. The animal stretched over the treeline but kept itself way under the clouds. Smoke billowed out of the enigma's fur which mostly blended the creature into the night sky. The gaping mouth dropped orange puddles of flaming liquids out onto the plants below, and there were two red streaks running down the underside of the lioness, each of which glowed maroon and each of which perfectly matched those of the marks on Lev when she crossed their path on the highway out of Dursnia. This instance of Lev was incredibly more terrifying, as it lingered at least half a mile into the sky. Although she did not know where Aqila had driven off to, Lev roared in their general direction, sending a wave of fire scorching through the forest towards them. The gust of hot winds nearly knocked her off the bike when the flames stopped just two tree lengths away from her. Aqila cursed, revved the bike up, and drove down the path as quickly as the bike would allow her. It was not quick enough in the slightest, for in her mirrors she could see the flaming lioness beginning to stand up on all fours. *There is no way she can see me. Is there?* Contemplating such things would only lead to her demise as she was brought back to her reality when the path took a sharp right to miss a creek.

Swerving to miss a thick tree, Aqila nearly threw Sartan off her bike. He had begun slipping off the bike, and since she knew that picking him up off the ground would be a death sentence, she regripped his hands to prevent him from flinging off. Sartan's lifeless body slumped over the front, and Aqila watched the glistening gem slip out of his hand. The neon, blue gemstone shimmered brilliantly beneath the bright chasm of fire behind her that illuminated the sky. The gemstone lingered in the air when the bike dragged her forward into reality, and she knew that it was necessary not to leave it behind as it slipped out of reach onto the quickly receding ground behind her. She brought the vehicle to a stop, glancing back at Lev hoping she was even further away than previously, but upon bringing her attention back to the wheel it was too late. It all happened so fast. The bike hit the dirt, and Aqila rolled into a ditch. Despite the mild pain from the crash, Aqila shoveled her pity aside and rose to her feet.

"The stone has to be here somewhere," murmured Aqila under her breath as she glanced over to Sartan who lay motionless next to the bike. "I did not drive that far…"

She jogged over towards the last place she saw the stone around and hastily scanned the pathway. It was nowhere to be seen in the darkness of the night. The burning flames from Lev's colossal form only added a sense of impending doom rather than assisting with extra light. They served as a constant reminder of what was soon to engulf her if she did not catch up with her allies quickly. There were many grooves and holes in the mud, all of which would be a perfect hiding spot for the gem, none of which were the active hiding spot of the gem.

A strong, heated breeze shook the forest that she stood in, distracting her from the search. Upon glancing towards the night sky, Aqila saw two large helicopters flutter by her. Their spotlights were not searching the forest however. Instead, they were focused on Lev. For some reason Aqila was surprised that the lands of Virgo still had some sort of government presence. *After all it is not everyday an enormous, flaming lioness explodes fire all over your sacred palace. An investigative response is understandably here, and it is understandably welcomed on my part.*

The helicopters flew closer to Lev, but Lev still seemed too fragile to do anything. There was no attack on the helicopters, and there was no fire sent thrashing towards their propellers. Aqila watched in curiosity as Lev's colossal lioness form merely analyzed the threats. She sniffed at the helicopters, glanced all around her, and was sturdily standing on all four legs now. Aqila was stepping backwards away from Lev without looking away when she slipped on a tree branch. She landed flat on her back gasping for breath. Unable to move she choked on her own air while watching Lev from the ground. Lev's head had to be at least two miles off the ground. Then she finally roared a bit more seriously.

The trees shook. The ground rattled. All the sounds of the night went silent after she stopped. An unfortunate helicopter was within her line of fire during the roar, and even though no flames came out of her mouth, the helicopter was sent spiraling down towards its doom. Aqila finally caught enough breath to roll over, and with dirt all over her she spotted something glistening in the ground. She clasped her hands around the gemstone and pulled it out of the crater in the dirt it had dug. It instantly fogged up in her hands, but she wasted no time to be awe-inspired by the transformation. The stone slipped into her pants pocket, and she ran back towards Sartan and the bike. Accidentally jabbing Sartan with the handles on the bike, Aqila tried to be quick, but another deep, reverberating echo haunted her. It sounded as if hundreds of steel miners all struck their pics at once into the hardest of stones.

Looking back she realized that Lev had missed. The second helicopter still fluttered anxiously in the air next to Lev's face. It flew further and further from her, but this time Aqila got to put an image to the sound. Lev jumped forward, catching the helicopter in her jaws. The clamping echo shredded the helicopter, and its operators, into a thousand chunks of flaming shrapnel. As the flakes of the helicopter burned towards the ground Aqila could only see it more effectively as meteors during the late heavy bombardment period raining down from Lev's mouth. *I am next!*

Aqila jumped onto the bike, pulling Sartan up with her. The bike refused to start. Aqila kicked it in the side out of anger, but that seemed not to persuade the bike to start. She stood up and walked the bike forward a few steps. When she tried again the bike revved up. There was no arguing, only muttered swearing as she lifted her feet. The bike followed the dirt path in front of her, and this time Sartan did not nearly fall off at every turn. Aqila had a tighter grip around him, but he still was unresponsive making the sharp turns on the trails much harder to take. He was unresponsive, or so she thought.

Sartan mumbled to himself, "Who can hear me?"

"What?" asked Aqila over the rev of the accelerator. When Sartan kept silent, Aqila asked another question, "Why did you turn on Lev for us? Even after what Ferra--"

"I figured Lev would kill everyone," answered Sartan without letting Aqila finish. Aqila processed the answer briefly before he answered another question...one that she never asked. "Yes, I would've called it speeding up the inevitable though. Rather die now than lat---no I don't want to go deeper!"

"What are you talking about?" asked Aqila who was struggling to hold Sartan on the bike with her, safely drive, and maintain a conversation. "We just have to worry about getting distance from Lev right now. We can worry about deep stuff when we are safer."

Immediately after saying that, Sartan dropped his head forward causing Aqila to lose control of the bike. She gripped the brakes hastily and swerved left to miss a thick trunk. Once stopped, Sartan hung halfway over the front of the bike, and she struggled to fix him back on the seat. He was entirely unconscious now. She sighed heavily before revving forward once more. Her headlights gleamed on the path in front of her, and she followed it religiously, swerving around branches and beside trunks. The dirt moiled under the tires, but Lev did not get any further away. Aqila could see the black eyes of the flaming giant look right back at her in her mirrors. Figuring it was her headlights that Lev was chasing, Aqila knew that with the helicopters gone she would be the next to perish, of course that is if she could catch her. Aqila shifted gears and the trees passing by her sides tripled in quantity. The cold breeze froze her face, but it was much better than a scorching death. The hand that held the throttle down went numb from gripping so tightly and being sliced by the cold. *She is gaining on me...*

There was no time for thinking, per usual. Aqila could hear the echoes of motorcycles revving through a tunnel in the distance. *I hope that is the rest of them.* Once the last echo faded away under her own bike's mechanical sounds, she could hear the train-like roars of the flaming Lev thumping up the space between them. After turning a thick chunk of trees, Aqila could see a far into the distance as she reached an oasis within the forest. The dirty path that she had been traveling on faded into multiple bike trails going towards the side of a mountain. A large plain separated the forest she was in and the mountains in the distance. The mountains dwarfed Lev, and if they dwarfed Lev they might just be her safety net.

The field paths were bumpier than the paths deep within the forest. Tiny rocks and the hard ground threw her off track to the left and the right. She struggled to follow the light tracks left behind by the previous bikes, especially at increasing velocities. Pale light from the moon up above lit up the entire landscape. For a moment Aqila forgot what was happening. She peacefully scraped through the land around ninety miles per hour. The wind had turned her hands into frozen ice chunks, and her face was not much luckier. Mountains in the nearing distance stretched out endlessly both ways. Before she knew it she could see a tunnel meant for travelers in the side of one of the mountains. It was lit up with lights which hung from the ceiling, and somebody stood next to their bike at the entrance.

Suddenly, a bright burst of dark red light lit up the fields. Behind her, Lev had reached the edge of the now blazing forest. On all fours, she pounced forward closing a third of their distance off in one leap. When she landed the whole Earth shook, and flames crept forward towards them. Aqila twisted the throttle as much as it would obey and feared that the bike would break down from over-use before she could make it to the tunnel. *Make it to the tunnel! Make it to the tunnel!* Aqila was closing the gap between her and whoever was standing by their bike at the entrance of the tunnel, but Lev was also closing the gap between her prey.

Lev leapt forward once more, and this time she was more than halfway to the tunnel itself. The impact of her landing on the ground was so strong that Aqila nearly flew off the bike as it wobbled to the left and right uncontrollably. Aqila watched the beast walk after her as if it were no challenge to catch up. The distance between them shrank even as Aqila's speedometer went past the last number. She could now tell that it was Jaako who was waiting for her at the tunnel, but even he had got back on his bike by now. Before she got to the tunnel he began riding off. She was only seconds from the tunnel when a glance into her mirror dropped her heartbeat.

A gaping mouth was wide open lunging forwards. The black teeth dripped with maroon flames that were close enough to make Aqila sweat, and the jaws were wide enough to engulf her whole, along with a few dozen other bikers…simultaneously. She closed her eyes and wished for the best. Deafening flames surrounded her, and she felt a bump in the ground. She opened her eyes to see herself peacefully, but hastily, zooming through the paved tunnel. In her mirror the entrance to the tunnel was completely filled with a black-furred lioness's nose. Within seconds she had caught up to Jaako who was going half her speed.

"Rasw owojo wjofaoi!"

"What!?" screamed back Aqila.

He shook his head and sped up down the tunnel. The tunnel took a sharp curve up ahead, and Aqila glanced back at Lev one more time to see if she had gotten into the tunnel or if she was going around it. To her surprise Lev was still at the entrance. Except now her mouth gaped wide open as if she were waiting for somebody to drive right into it. Aqila briefly watched, and deep within Lev's throat a light shimmered brighter and brighter. Then it dawned on her.

"FASTER!!" she screamed as loudly as she could over the engine of her bike revving up again.

She took the curve when Jaako caught up to her, and he must have heard her screams as he then left her in the dust. The end of the tunnel was in her sights immediately after the curve, but she had Lev's most recent attack fresh in her mind. Her concerns proved to be well warranted as well. In her mirror she could see the curve she just came around quickly receding, but she also witnessed it be consumed by maroon flames. The flames quickly churned over themselves to catch up to Aqila.

Looking back up at the exit, Jaako had just made it out. He instantly slowed down and took a ninety degree right turn straight out of the way of the tunnel. She did not even attempt to recreate such a feat upon reaching the end of the tunnel. The flames had begun nipping her butt, so she knew she would not be able to slow down at all. With no other option that would result in life, Aqila just kept driving straight into the forest upon exiting the tunnel. Luckily for her there was a straight dirt path to follow. Then after a few seconds the path twisted and turned, so when she barely swerved and got out of the line of fire in time without crashing she was ecstatic. She instantly stopped the bike and looked at the flames. Burning endlessly, the beam of fire shot out at least another sixty feet. It stayed burning in the circular form it had chased her in for a good thirty seconds before dwindling down to decently sized fires that had started on their own.

She immediately got back on the bike with Sartan and drove back to the roasted tunnel's exit to find Jaako who, accompanied by everyone else, met her on the now flaming path she had almost lost her life to. The flames lit up the dark night, and a feeling of relief flushed the faces of everyone around her, except Sartan of course. That relief subsided within Aqila, and in its place grew a strong sense of betrayal.

"Why did you all leave me to face Lev alone!?!?" accused Aqila. "I could have died and you all would have been waiting here for Lev???"

"Why did you stay and try to save Sartan?" snapped Ferran. Aqila refused to get off her bike, and instead held Sartan's unconscious body firmly on the steering. "I knew that's what you'd do the second he attacked Lev. It didn't even matter anyways! Look at him!"

"Is he okay?" asked Emilia nervously.

"I don't know!" exclaimed Aqila. "Lev laughed at me and said he is breaking through, but whatever that means is beyond me."

Jaako nodded in understanding while Emilia and Octavia blinked in shared confusion with the rest of the group. Jaako then stated, "I can explain what that means later, but I know Lev won't let a mountain stop her from getting us."

"That is true," replied Caleb, who was getting on a bike with Ferran. Ferran, still on his transport, left his feet on the ground to keep balance as Caleb continued, "If we follow the river South then it will take us to a coastal town. If we make it that far we can ditch the bikes and lose Lev."

"We never lose Lev," stated Aqila as she revved up her bike for another trip. "Where is the river?"

"From what the workers were saying it shouldn't be that much further down the trail," answered Caleb. "We have been going East, so when we hit it go right and follow it down the banks. There is a very slim chance Lev will be able to catch us if we keep putting distance between her. If the river is frozen then we are in even better luck!"

"Are we really that far South?" asked Emilia.

"Of course, we are closer to the Southern Tropic then we are to death," answered Caleb with a laugh. "It looks like this region has barely missed the blizzard whose aftermath we went through on the way here."

"Then what are we waiting on?" asked Ferran.

Everyone looked around at each other with blank stares. The interaction was brief, for when they all heard a lioness's roar echo through the tunnel waiting sounded preposterous. It was a race not to be the last one going down the trail, and Aqila, still buzzing from the adrenaline high, sped right to the front.

Chapter 21
The Angler of Answers
Sartan

Aqila fell to the ground behind him as Sartan focused on Lev once more. Lev was about to attack. The hairs on his skin twitched, and warmth he had never felt before coerced his blood to the very tips of his fingers. Lev's flames scattered around him in what appeared to be a sickly retreat, but instead of doing what flames did best they were chilling compared to the heat of the gemstone tucked tightly within his palm. Unlike the previous two stones, the Cancer Gemstone took over him much faster and much mercilessly. Almost instantly his vision blurred as boiling tears ran down his face uncontrollably and without reason. Not one tear managed to reach his chin as they all evaporated off his face due to the heat he expelled. The cold was unforgiving, but he quickly realized that the heat was equally unforgiving if not more so.

All the excess energy within him had nowhere to go. His tears stopped suddenly, and he started, against his will, spontaneously screaming. "FUCK YOU JILENOS RHARTHKAAA!!!" With the stone still inside his palm he forced more and more boiling water out of it to expel some energy. Lev now laid on the ground from when she was countered by his boiling water. The first strike hit her in the arm, but every attack following it was countered by fire. The flames were nullified by the water, but Sartan was vastly untrained in this art, especially when compared to Lev. Running on anger and adrenaline, Sartan's body disobeyed his mind as it kept Lev on the ground defending herself. Suddenly his off hand began exploding gusts of vapor ten times the temperature of the boiling water that ran down his face into the many guards that surrounded him. Within seconds each one was dead, and his body finally began to obey his mind. He stopped attacking Lev and the guards, of which none remained, and took one step backwards. This was when the moon, which wasn't full just hours ago, flashed in his retinas at full brightness and color. It was so overbearing he lost his balance and couldn't see anything other than the lunar surface.

Sartan exclaimed, "The moon!?"

Immediately afterwards he blinked, and everything went black. He felt his body hit the ground beneath him, but after that he felt nothing. Even all the sound around him went silent.

When he opened his eyes again all he could hear was a calm breeze that flowed peacefully through possibly unobstructed skies. The sound of wind was accompanied with a soft splashing of waves on sand. A seagull chirped in the distance, but when Sartan looked around he only saw objects under the night sky: pines, a bonfire, Aqila, the bike, and of course Lev. It was almost as if his senses had betrayed him. In the midst of his confusion he couldn't resist finding humor in the entire situation. A large smile strapped his face when he realized that Aqila was pulling him on the bike with her. He watched her lips wiggle and her eyes bulge, but he wasn't affected by her visible concern nor did he hear her words of worry. His worry-free smile was the only thing that he could manage to respond with.

Everything began moving ten times faster. The bike went from accelerating violently within a time frame that should have ripped his skin off, and he was suddenly clipping down a trail with thick trees closing in around him. He closed his eyes, fulfilled with life. *If I die right now, then I die right now. Aqila won't crash though. We will be fine.* Then the stone took complete control. His vision was filled with nothing but blue, light blue to be exact. He no longer was on the bike, but now he laid in soft, hot sand. The beach sounds that he was restricted to earlier had only grown stronger. Directly above him he saw three white birds flutter by. In the corner of his eyes he could see the smooth sway of a palm tree's leaves.

Determined to get a feel for his new surroundings, Sartan leaned up to realize that the palm tree that stood a mere five feet away from him, was only another fifteen feet from the waves of the ocean…in every direction. The warm sun melted away every single worry. Strangely enough, a full moon hung low in the sky almost as if it was watching over him despite the sun's extreme presence. It all seemed too good to be true.

His smile faded away as he stood up, and confusion took its place like usual. Sartan looked to the ocean for answers. In every direction it rolled out into the horizon, endlessly kissing the light blue sky that hung over it. He heard a ringing sound come from the air. He couldn't place its location. It could place him though. A large wave crashed on the opposite side of the island which splashed him with warm, foamy water.

A regal, feminine voice called out to him, "Why would you use the stone to fight Lev!? For the first use?! Sartan, I do believe I taught you better!"

On the sand a small crab walked by looking towards the ocean. It must've been washed up from the crashing wave, but when Sartan reached for the crab it began running away. Faster than he had expected it to be, the crab burrowed into the sand before he could catch it. The woman reminded him she was still there, "Sartan, focus. Leave the crabs alone and tell me why you thought it would be a good idea to break through the Cancer Gemstone the same moment you decided to turn against her!"

Sartan toiled the command in his mind, and then it all dawned on him. "Lev is trying to kill me now…and I'm unconscious!"

"My boy, I have tried to protect you the best I can, but as you would expect from someone who is dead, my powers are quite limited. Things work differently in the living world, and my affect on them is minute. It doesn't help that you are unconscious!" exclaimed the woman whose voice drifted casually around him just like the waves. "There is nothing you can do about it now, for you are stuck in my realm for the time being."

"I am finally dead aren't I?" asked Sartan stoically. "I am not going to wake up again are I?"

"Only time will tell. You have to rely on your friend Aqila. Your life…despite my best attempts…has officially fallen into her hands. After everything that has happened to you, that would be the last thing I'd want to hear."

"I trust she will try to save me, but if she can't then I know she tried."

"I don't know. She is driving quite recklessly through a forest as we speak. I suppose we shouldn't waste the time we have together, even if it turns out to be futile in the end. The last time we spoke it was predominantly Stir warning you of Ryby. How did that conversation conclude anyway?"

"Who Ryby? He was mostly angry, but I think he was sad about the rest of the Pisces. He urged me not to become the ruler of the Water Signs like Lev planned for me, but our conversation was quite short and shallow in my opinion. His distrust for Lev was heavy, and his anger towards you was heavier."

"Indeed, I despise my killer as much as he does, but for different reasons."

"Your killer?" asked Sartan even though he had been told two separate stories already.

"I killed Ryby, and Lev killed me. It was all a mess, and we might find time to talk about it later. Before I help you understand anything else I have to ask you a question." Sartan nodded, unsure of whether or not she could see him. Then the woman continued with, "Why did you decide to---"

Everything disappeared as if the plug to a television had just been pulled. Sartan spat dirt out of his mouth, and felt his heart racing. His body was chilled; he laid in a ditch hidden under endless pune needles in every direction. There was blood running down his arm, and he could see Aqila approaching him when everything began fading back to that space black. Within seconds everything disappeared again. It was just black. It was just his thoughts.

Senses returned, and with it came back that cozy island. However, this time he stood shoulder deep into the ocean just off the coast of the palm tree's little island. A familiar feeling returned as he began sweating profusely. His heart rate doubled, and he struggled to breath.

"Relax," whispered the voice in his ear. "I'm here for you."

"What…just…happened?!" asked Sartan.

"Aqila crashed the bike, and you flew off. You are hurt, but you aren't dead…yet."

"That's comforting," laughed Sartan as he started walking through the water back towards the island. "What was your question then?"

"Oh no you don't!" exclaimed the voice as the waves Sartan waded through pulled him out further into the ocean. "You are going to meet me, into the water, Sartan."

"I can't swim or breathe in the water!" exclaimed Sartan as he desperately paddled away from the hungry sea. "Just ask your question and let me go."

The waves grew weaker, but not weak enough for Sartan to get to the shore. "Why did you decide to betray Lev, with the Cancer Gemstone at that, right before she killed your allies? I'm aware that seems rhetorical, but she was the only one who knew how to fix your brainwashing."

"It is complicated," replied Sartan who had yet to give up attempting to make it to the receding island. His feet could barely touch the bottom, and he knew the second he couldn't reach he'd be at the mercy of this woman he didn't know he could trust yet.

"What about your brainwashing? She offered to help fix that, did she not?"

"I don't even think I've been brainwashed. Who can remember every single year of their childhood anyways?"

"Sartan, you can't remember almost fourteen years of your childhood!"

"That doesn't matter. Everyone has told me that Lev is a liar and is evil. Don't you want me to go against Lev anyways? Why are you questioning my decision?"

"Stop! She can hear you!" exclaimed the woman quickly.

"Who can hear me?"

"Nevermind that. Listen, I am questioning you so I can understand you better," replied the woman as she commanded the ocean to pull Sartan beneath the waves. Surprisingly, his breathing continued as normal, and the crystal blue water was clear enough to see through as far as the sun's light would venture down. "I fear there are other reasons for you deciding to betray her. Especially with the circumstances of your attack. Do not get me wrong. I am glad you chose to go against tyranny, but your method raises concern for me. Are you infatuated by the girl?"

Sartan closed his eyes and stopped fighting the water. It pulled him further down where light began to fade, and the heat went with it. He took in a deep breath of water and stated, "I figured Lev would kill everyone."

"They certainly would fail to defeat her. Did you want your friends to die?" exclaimed the woman with worry, shaking her voice as it rippled the water around him.

"Yes, I would've called it speeding up the inevitable though. Rather die now than lat-" The current grabbed him and jerked him deeper into the ever growing black abyss without warning. Sartan opened his eyes to see very thin traces of light reach him at his depth. "No, I don't want to go deeper!"

"How did you plan on escaping if it were just you fighting Lev? If you wanted your friends dead would you not have just let Lev kill them? You all might escape now."

"I didn't plan for us to escape," said Sartan as he floated down aimlessly watching the few strands of light dwindle away to nothing. "I planned for Lev to kill us all."

The woman did not reply. Sartan now was in the deep all by himself. He found it strange that no fish had swam by on his entire descent. Not one single fish had been in the water. Not one single shred of hope floated in his mind. He was okay with this fate. *This is still much better than the other water signs. I could hide here forever. This is still better than the living world.*

"Sartan…" began the woman. "…we need to have a talk."

Sartan didn't reply. He just kept floating down to the bottom of the vast ocean. He lost track of time, but after a while the weight of all the water began pressing down on him quite hard, almost as hard as the woman's foreboding words did.

"You are aware that I am Rakovina, the late Cancer Zodiac, correct?"

"Yes."

"You are aware that you have indeed been brainwashed, correct?"

"I haven't."

"I'm telling you, you have."

"I don't believe you."

"Sartan, you have been brainwashed! I know that because I was the one who did it!"

Sartan struggled to reply as he was too unsure whether to be angry or sad. Eventually he said, "You've been dead my whole life, that's impossible."

"I died shortly after your brainwashing. You were about to turn fourteen. I decided it was for your own safety."

"Why was I singled out? Why would you pick me to be brainwashed if you were the Active Cancer Zodiac? Wouldn't you choose someone a little more 'high profile'?"

"That would only cause problems for the mission you had."

"My mission? So now I'm just a soldier in the Zodiac's sick games, and at fourteen!?"

"It is deeper than that Sartan, and you know it!"

"Then what is it!?"

"I feared you would have been killed if they found you, so I hid the Libra Gemstone on you for protection. Your protection at that, not the protection of the gem. I planned for you to be sent to a small town in the middle of Libra's lands, but somehow you ended up in the capital of the Sagittarius lands before finding your way to Dursnia. By then your memory had gotten back to normal, but you don't remember most of the journey to Kreesburg. I died over a month later, so I wasn't able to track your movement until then."

"Who is 'they'!? Why didn't you send anyone with me that could've helped me on those streets?! To me it sounds like you didn't really plan any of this out!"

"I did send protective measures for you. I had three men who were assigned to watch you closely and make sure that you survived unharmed. However, when you traveled across the ocean two of them were killed on a boat when they defended you from one of Lev's assault teams. The third one lost contact with me not much longer. Nevertheless, I died only weeks after the brainwashing, so overseeing the project was impossible."

"I see," said Sartan as he thought it all over. The ocean was bearing down on him now, and he struggled to breath under its immense weight. "It didn't matter. I still lost the stone...and my life."

"Don't say that Sartan! You aren't dead yet. Aqila is trying very hard to keep you alive. She's lost Lev and is zipping down a frozen river with you right now. She also has the stone, so you have nothing to worry about right now."

Sartan's back softly patted down on the mushy bottom. He stood up on it as an ominous white light appeared from nowhere. Soon, the ocean floor grew as clear as the island above. He could see hundreds of crabs, large and small, scattering around him on the ground. Each one was so determined it crawled over the others not even thinking about how they could crush them, yet not one crab fell victim to the weight of the others. Red crabs, white crabs, strange crabs, aggressive crabs they all hustled around in a hive minded manner. Then a swift current swept Sartan off his feet carrying him a short distance before dropping him off only seconds away.

Perhaps it was a harbinger for the crabs, for every single one of them scattered away from Sartan. Each one crawled and swam off behind him, but as he peered into the waves ahead of him he couldn't spot any impending danger, let alone doom. He swiftly spun around in the water to witness a woman drifting towards him.

All of the crabs held up the sun-tanned woman. Her crystal-clear, blue eyes pacified him while her straight black hair flowed down to her waist. She wore a long black dress that left both of her thick yet toned legs mostly exposed because of the current catching it. The golden symbols etched into the edges of the fabric lined all the way up and down the clothing; the symbol, oddly, was quite provocative: 69. There were no shoes on her feet. No jewelry dangled from her torso or fingers, but a thick golden crown glistened on her head. The fact that she was a few inches taller than Sartan made him wonder if he should be intimidated by her or attracted to her. The full red lips that hid under her soft, small nose cemented Sartan's opinion that she was indeed quite attractive. *This is her realm though. She can turn on me and turn into a blobfish with the snap of a finger. I can't trust her appearance.*

"Didn't expect me to look like this, did you?" laughed the woman through her unwavering grin.

Sartan pretended not to notice her beauty, and kept the frown on his face as stable as concrete. The woman rolled her eyes as he refused to be phased. "None of that means anything to me," stated Sartan in frustration. "I just wanted to remember my childhood! I want to know who my parents were so I can put a face to all my problems! I want my past back!"

The woman sighed as she replied, "Your past won't answer any questions you have…rather raise more you aren't ready for."

"I don't care! I want to know what it was like to live carefree!"

"Constantly living in the good old days won't help! It won't change your present, let alone your future!" boomed the woman. "It will only cloud your vision of the future! Which judging by your recent choices, appears to be very blurry to begin with!"

"I don't care! Will I ever see my parents again!?" demanded Sartan angrily.

"Yes with time!" snapped back the woman just as violently.

"WHY WON'T YOU LET ME DIE!?"

"YOU HAVE A PURPOSE!"

"WHAT IS MY PURPOSE?!"

"I DON'T KNOW!"

"WILL I KILL LEV?!"

"DON'T. KNOW."

"WHO IS MY FATHER?!"

"IT MATTERS NOT!!"

"WILL THE GROUP EVEN ACCEPT ME BACK AFTER I BROUGHT LEV TO THEM?!?"

"I. HONESTLY. DON'T. KNOW."

"WHAT IS HAPPENING!?"

"YOU ARE IN PAIN!"

"WHO IS LEUCEMIE!?"

"LISTEN."

"WHO IS MY MOTHER?!"

"Me."

"THEN YOU CAN'T HELP--" Sartan stopped mid sentence. He glared at Rakovina. Deep into her face. She only looked eight years older than him, but he knew Zodiacs were immortal. Her grin had shrunk into a slight frown as a foggy tear floated off her face. She tried to speak to him, but her words cracked everytime she opened her mouth. Sartan failed to make eye contact and instead looked at her hands, unable to believe it. She waved her hand sending all of the crabs around her scattering away feverishly.

"Sartan…I tried…I really tried to keep you in the palace for as long as I could. Lev, Kozoroh-"

"Stop."

"Ryby, Blizenci, they all signed a treaty."

"Stop!"

"A treaty that stated childbearing was too mortal for the Zodiacs."

"Please…"

"I already had been raising you for years by then…they started forming an alliance together to push their policies upon the other Zodiacs. To the world I killed you, but they knew better. They would search the palace until they found you…they would have killed the heir."

"Rakovina…stop."

"You have to hear this Sartan. Today is the day you learn."

"Why? Why did you have to send me away? You could've run away with me."

"You know better…I had an empire on my shoulders. A world to save. I couldn't hide after watching them kill the other Zodiacs. You were sent into what could be called witness protection, and I…I went hunting for the culprits. As you know…I didn't finish my hunt."

"You did it all for me?"

"Mostly…yes, I knew if I wasn't a threat then you wouldn't be either. I couldn't let them catch you to get what they wanted from me though. You were my weakness. My. One. Weakness."

"Why didn't you hide the Cancer Gemstone on me then?"

"I knew that you'd use the stone that you had. If it was a Water Gemstone then you would break through and surrender your innocent ignorance upon meeting me. I feared you would use the stone more than once though. That third time you used the Libra stone, on that helicopter, I really thought you were going to die. I tried my hardest to keep you alive, although in that circumstance, I believe there was nothing I could do."

"Did I have a nice childhood…did you love me?"

"Absolutely, I sacrificed my life so that you could live on. I sacrifice my life so that the world wouldn't be enslaved by the other Zodiacs. I sacrificed centuries of my work for you. No, I sacrificed an entire empire, and one day I hope you can rule it yourself!"

"Do I have what it takes to rule an entire empire though?"

"Certainly! You have royal blood pulsing through your veins, and if you have the gemstone you will always have access to me."

"Am I going to find this Leucemie character at the Pisces Palace?"

"Sweet Leucemie? No. She volunteered to protect Stir's Palace for me. I am unsure if she is still alive. I gave her powers since she volunteered, but that was years ago. Then again her liege died, so she would have to feast to live. Poor Leucemie…I haven't the time to check on her."

"What do you mean by feasting?"

"Oh…well…it's an empirical term. Vassalization under an Active Zodiac. The rules and agreements. Stuff I'll teach you when you are the emperor."

"The Pisces Palace as well…assuming I don't die soon…where is it?"

"The Pisces Palace is a jewel hidden merely by the difficulty of crossing an Antarctic Ocean. Cross the ocean and reach the Southern Pole of the planet. Once in the Antarctic simply travel West off the coast until you see the unmistakable palace itself. The palace will be inland, but I am sure Ryby will assist you in finding it once you are in his area of influence."

"Really…Ryby will help us?"

"He will help you once he realizes you are attempting to create a new Pisces. Just be cautious of the storm zone. He can guide you through it, but I do believe that he is unable to disable it due to its defensive purposes."

"The what?"

Suddenly, the ocean floor below him gave out, and he started to sink further into the depths. All of the sand exploded into the water disappearing like it was salt in a kettle. The only thing that remained was Rakovina and Sartan. Her eyes glowed white in the water while Sartan's vision quickly began adjusting to the lightless setting. No lighting whatsoever this deep meant he was going blind again.

Sartan nervously asked, "Am I leaving your realm?"

"Unfortunately…" Rakovina stated as her eyes became the only source of light.

"Am I…still alive?"

"Yes, you look like you are sleeping in a bed. They must have made it to the coastal town that boy was talking about. It is the next day, and Aqila is watching over you."

In the distance far behind Rakovina, Sartan saw an angler fish swimming about in a patch of light. The light quickly receded, hiding the creature in the darkness, and in the spot that it swam in now floated a deep red orb. "Where is Lev?" asked Sartan.

"I don't know. Probably sniffing around in the forest for you. If you don't move soon she'll find you for sure, but that still doesn't mean she is the smartest council member in the chamber. When you go back please help your allies. They are in desperate need for structure, leadership, and guidance. Aqila saved your life tonight, and you saved her life. You are considered even in my eyes, so please try not to ruin the alliance you misguided children have built."

"Okay…" said Sartan as he rolled his eyes.

Rakovina grinned and drifted off into the darkness. As the light in her eyes twitched out of existence, her voice echoed around him, "I will be watching you Sartan…I will be here for you…you have so much to fight for, and you don't even realize it yet…" Sartan could still see the symbols on her dress fading into the darkness as he sank further into the depths. The red glow from the angler grew brighter though. Brighter and brighter. It glowed more violently than the sun, and Sartan had a strong gut feeling that when the angler got to him he'd wake up. It zig-zagged around him before stopping. He realized that the glowing ball was actually Mars.

"Why does it look like mars?" asked Sartan to himself.

"Oh my child…" echoed Rakovina from somewhere deep within the waves. "An Aries…is waiting for you…"

"Huh?" mumbled Sartan. He could hear Rakovina laughing to herself, humored by his ignorance. He tried to find her by spinning around in circles, but he quickly gave up and glanced back at the angler. Mars floated peacefully in the waters before going parabolic towards him. It wavered to the left. It wavered to the right. As it drew nearer, and quite quickly, he could see the hungry angler's grin widen. It's mouth gaped open, swallowing him whole. He opened his eyes to find himself in a dark room with Aqila sitting on the bed next to him. She looked worried and was taking his temperature. Sartan instantly spat out the thermometer, rolled to the side of the bed, and threw his hands up to his head which had begun vibrating with pain so erratically the cracked, wooden floorboards below him shook.

Chapter 22
A New Route
Aqila

Aqila allowed a few hours to pass, as requested, before she returned to Sartan, who was now sitting up in the bed. All of the gemstones that they had acquired throughout their journey were on her person, four of which Sartan found by himself. She pulled up an ancient, wooden rocking chair next to the mattress on the floor that Sartan sat on. He was just now looking around the room taking in its pine walls and floors. She peered around the unfamiliar cabin as well. In one corner a row of neglected litter boxes fermented, and in another corner of the room on a wobbling table sat a collection of flickering candles whose wicks kept drowning in wax. Behind her was a doorway with no door rather many strands of beads swaying back and forth in a breeze from the other rooms beyond it. Aqila felt like an itchy-icicle in the room as Sartan was wrapped up in the only blanket. No source of heating existed, and she despised the scent of smoke and cat urine that freely drifted in and out of the bead barrier that the owners called a door.

Sartan broke the silence between them asking, "So…where exactly are we? The coastal town?"

"Yes, we escaped Lev and found this desolate town called Cherkton at the end of a wide river. Everything here is wooden cabins and shops lined up on an unimpressive boardwalk," replied Aqila. She watched Sartan think before continuing with, "This married couple let us stay in their cat shack for a few days, but we all have agreed that it would be a better idea if we left this rat trap sooner. There are not a lot of buildings to hide in or around like the larger cities we have been to."

Sartan grabbed his stomach as it growled before asking, "Where are we going after this?"

"You are obviously hungry. You need to eat before we leave."

"I'll get to it. I'd rather know where we are going from here and why everyone else is missing."

Aqila sighed, "Right now I am not too sure what the plan is. We need to find a mode of transport because all of the bikes we rode on self-destructed thirty minutes after we got here. We also will need to find a Pisces who wants to come with us to recreate Pisces."

"How did you manage to find a Virgo who wanted to go with you?" asked Sartan while standing up from the mattress.

She grabbed his shoulders and pressed him back down to the mattress while saying, "No, sit. You are still too weak to be moving around."

"Aqila I'm fine, but I won't be if we can't manage to figure something out really soon."

"I know. I know," replied Aqila as she sat back down in her chair. "We barely even got Octavia and Emilia to come along with us. Now I have the problem of figuring out how I am going to feed and house all of these people. Not to mention...I think the only reason they have yet to run away is because they are afraid of Lev. Jaako just wants adventure in my opinion, but the girls will leave the second they think they can without getting hurt."

"Why did they agree to come?" asked Sartan as he tossed the blanket off him. He then laughed to himself while he stretched his limbs. "Surely this is better than the life they were living before?"

Aqila grinned briefly before she answered his question, "They were having financial issues in Garigo. Octavia was a cop, and Emilia was a waitress. They were very adamant that they could leave us whenever they wanted, but now Octavia is an inactive Virgo on Lev's to-kill list."

Sartan glared out of the cracked window and asked, "Where is everyone now?"

"Nobody slept well, so as soon as it was light out they all ventured onto the boardwalk. They are probably still on the boardwalk negotiating with merchants for transport and food. The woman who let us all sleep in here last night told us that she was forbidden to give us any food."

"Wasn't allowed to give us any food?" asked Sartan rhetorically. "Why wouldn't she be allowed?"

"I am unsure, but I was too creeped out and too cold to question it." Aqila watched him pat at his sides not once but twice before quickly exclaiming, "Relax, I have them! You dropped them during our escape last night."

"I want them back."

"I will. I will," replied Aqila. "Do you promise not to leave if I give them back?"

"That isn't a promise you can force on me this time. Give them back."

Aqila slowly slid her hand into her pocket and pulled out five different gemstones all of which were so large they failed to fit in her tiny palm. She had to slip the green one back into her pocket and hold the white one in a separate hand to prevent dropping them. Three of them were different shades of blue. She then dropped all of the stones into Sartan's open palm. They all clanked as they landed, but Sartan did not slide them into his pocket immediately as she had expected him to do so. Instead he grabbed the white gemstone with his other hand and separated it from the others.

"I don't want this," said Sartan as he tried to hand it back to her.

"Why not?" asked Aqila while reluctantly grabbing it. "You had it when we first met--"

"Well I don't want it now," he said hastily. The rest of the stones found their way to his pockets, but he insisted that she kept the Libra Gemstone.

"Are you going to stay with us?" she asked. She could feel her stomach tank as he hesitated to reply. "The choice is yours...but we all would really appreciate it if you did. I can talk with Ferra---"

"I will for now. It's obvious you need my help with it all. But I don't believe I will stay here much longer to be completely honest with you."

Aqila nodded. Afterwards she stood up to give him a hug. Of course she felt slightly disappointed when he declined. To distract herself she continued, "We should probably go find everyone else to see if they found any food yet."

Sartan agreed with her, and they both went outside avoiding all of the mangy cats as they passed through the beaded door. Immediately after exiting the front door of the mostly empty cabin, they were confronted with the sea. The only thing between the sea and them was a rocky beach, about thirteen shops in a line parallel to the coast, and a rotting boardwalk that stretched both ways for about a mile. Icy winds ripped through her clothes sending chills up her spine. The air smelled of sea salt, and it left her nostrils more desensitized with every breath of the frozen air she inhaled. A weak sun struggled to shine through the graying clouds, so not one inch of blue lined the sky. Even the few islands of grass separated by burnt dirt appeared ghoulish. Dull pines that lacked large portions of needles lined the world behind the cabins for as far as she could see, and a thick river churned chunks of ice into the sea a short stroll to the right.

"I never thought I'd say it," whispered Sartan slowly. "...but I think I miss the desert."

"I could not agree with you more."

The two of them shivered their way down the boardwalk. She has only had the luxury of wearing fresh clothes once the previous night when Sartan surprised her, but since then her clothes have been ripped from falling off the forest motorbike. The relentless breeze snipped at her legs through the tears in her borrowed gray sweats, and her arms grew mountains of goosebumps beneath a gray hoodie with holes burnt into it. Her mind was consumed with returning to the slightly warmer cabin that the strange couple let them bunk in. Seeing Jaako was like seeing a lighthouse's gleam on a stormy night, but as she approached him she realized that her journey was far from over. Everyone else was nowhere to be found when Sartan and Aqila inquired about Jaako's situation. He did not tell them where everyone else was, as he was distracted by his current focus.

"This drunken fool is trying to charge me a negotiation fee!" exclaimed Jaako loud enough to ruffle the feathers of the man standing on a wooden box. The man swayed back and forth quite uneasily in the strong breeze while danglings two separate keys in Jaako's face.

"Yee should've counted-d your tib-bble!" stuttered the man on the box. "Still want the bo-boat? You can suck om ny nip-nipple! HA!"

"OH WOW!" exclaimed Aqila who looked at the other locals for disgust ridden faces. All of the locals who passed by chose not to hear this man's remarks. *This must be common here...sick!*

"Why are you arguing with him?" asked Sartan.

Jaako whispered, "I want his boat, but I didn't want to steal it in broad daylight."

"Is there even law enforcement here?" asked Sartan.

"I haven't seen any, but everyone seems to treat their boats like children, also he has a strap," replied Jaako. On the side of the man's hip was a holstered six-rounder. If he was sober enough to use it or not was the real question.

"Malex! Get over here an-and make yourself krchuseful!" screamed the man from his wooden crate that shook in the wind more than he did. "Virgil is getting lonely!"

Down the wooden docks worked a woman who immediately ran to the man's side. Aqila instantly noticed her disability. One of the woman's forearms was missing, and a nub meshed together with flesh and skin at her elbow. The woman wore a chipper smile and was nimble on her feet. Aqila questioned her agility, but it appeared she had learned how to live with her disability. She happily stood next to the unhygienic man on the crate like a dog would sit at an owner's request. However, upon arriving next to the man, she was slapped across the face hard enough to be thrown on the mossy planks merely missing the rocks off the side of the boardwalk. Her pale, freckle-ridden face glowed beet red as she attempted to get herself off the ground.

"Good gi-girl!" exclaimed the man who still stood on the box.

Aqila felt her blood begin to boil before she spotted a tear drip off the woman's face. There were many ways to teach this man a lesson, but Aqila could not get her mind past shoving him off the boardwalk into the jagged rocks that laid below. Sartan had already lent a helping hand to the woman despite the man's adamant intentions of harm if Sartan did less than breath on the woman. That was when Aqila simply failed to resist her instincts any longer.

"How dare you tell him not to help her when you are the one who smacked her to the ground!"

The man was too drunk to listen to Aqila's lecturing let alone make a coherent response. He bubbled and gurgled at the wind all the while failing to reply. He took a hefty swig out of a flask wobbled around like an inflatable during a windstorm. The woman had been helped up by Sartan, but she immediately ran to the side of the man.

The stumbling man's fluttering eyes then drifted to Aqila as he exclaimed, "Short thing!"

"It's fine friends, he didn't realize how close I was to him," said the woman instinctively.

"There is no way that wasn't intentional!" announced Jaako, who seemed to be just as concerned as Aqila was. "He smacked you right in the face for seemingly no reason!"

"It is fine I promise!" insisted the woman.

Sartan obliged to the woman's requests by furthering the conversation, "So it seems, we were in the middle of negotiating a boat from the man here. Is there any way we could borrow one of his boats?"

"Not for sale!" bellowed the man as he slipped off the crate into the woman's arm. She barely managed to catch his weight before sitting him down on the crate quickly and shakily. "You sho tur der…roken! K…kiss!"

"Yes!" exclaimed the woman hastily, making sure that his request was fulfilled. She planted a plump kiss on his cheek before sitting him down against the crate.

"Are the boats for sale?" pressed Sartan again, refusing to take anything the man said seriously.

"Master said no…I am deeply sorry," replied the woman. Aqila noticed that the woman had bruises up and down her neck. *I can only imagine what scars lay beneath all of the clothing.* The woman then continued, "Even though we could use the money I am going to have to decline any offers you make. If my master says no then there is no negotiating."

"Master?" asked Jaako. "Are you a slave?"

"I like to think of it as indentured servitude. One day if I am good he will let me go free, but I have been with him for so long that I don't quite know what I'd do without his guidance."

"His guidance looks muddled with inebriation," laughed Sartan loud enough just for Aqila to hear. Aqila agreed without replying. *He is the one that really needs the guidance.*

"Master usually isn't this drunk this early in the morning, but with or without the liquor he knows a lot more about life than I do," answered the woman who must've heard Sartan's remarks.

"How old is he?" asked Jaako. "He doesn't force you to…"

"Master is only twenty years older than I," replied Malex with a great smile. "But I don't condemn him for his sexual desires. After all he was raped in his childhood."

"WHAT DOES THAT MEAN?!?!" exclaimed Aqila. "Just because he was raped means that it is okay for him to do it to you?!"

"Master's intentions are holy. He is still traumatized by his previous relationship, and I could never have been as strong as he was. Now that I am with him he hasn't been happier! As long as I do what he says I am to. If I don't then I am punished physically, but I almost always deserve it."

She stared in disbelief. *There is no way that she would be okay with this. He obviously forces her to do things against her will. I refuse to even consider what she means by punishment.* Aqila took a quick glance at the unconscious man who had begun snoring on the misted planks and came to her conclusion. *He has something she wants, he has absolutely brainwashed her, or she is braindead. One of the three.*

Aqila jumped forward a bit as a hand softly padded itself down on her shoulder. When she spun around ready to neutralize the threat, the women behind her were of friendly faces. Emilia smiled gleefully holding two enormous straw baskets of fish dangling from a pole over both shoulders uneasily. Not far behind was her older sister, Octavia, who was suffering from an obvious sickness. Her unusually pale face accented nightly black circles hanging below her eyes. A torn piece of her uniform stuck out of her nostril and was stained brown from the blood. Most understandably, goosebumps shivered down her unnaturally thick, muscly arms.

"We just spent the rest of our money on that fish, and I can't feel my face in this cold" murmured Octavia as she covered her eyes with her palms.

"That is terrible!" exclaimed the woman. "Your friend looks quite ill. That winter storm really has left it frigid here. The cold never bothers me, but it is a cause for concern when you are dressed the way you are. Follow me. "

Aqila stared in disbelief as her companions followed the disabled woman without any question whatsoever. She picked up the man, startling him from his slump despite her missing forearm and walked them down the planks onto one of the fishing boats, which, after looking at it in more depth, appeared large enough to house thirty people on top of the fish it was built to catch. The boat swayed in the waves, and Aqila began to feel shakier than the boat itself. Perhaps it was the frigid breeze or the waves that sloshed the occasional ice chunk into the side of the vessel, but whatever it was something insisted that the boat was not safe.

The group followed Malex into the boat's interior. To her surprise the inside was much more lavish than she had expected. Paintings lined the walls between the portholes, and fluffy black carpet ran all the way across the floor. At the end of the corridor was a large living room with two cats playing around. All of the clean porcelain that rested on redwood tables was unsafe in these conditions. The cats which more accurately label as large kittens scurried away when they noticed the presence of everyone, and by then Malex had already laid the harmlessly drunk man down on a white-leather couch. Directly opposite the couch was an open space that slowly merged into the bridge of the boat.

"Woah!" exclaimed Jaako. "I don't think I have ever been somewhere this fancy. As a welcomed guest that is. Even the fur coats over there on the…golden racks have leather on them!"

Aqila twisted her head to the line of portholes adjacent to a grand piano. Two racks full of different types of clothing were pressed tightly against the wall of the boat. Big yellow and purple jackets and pants coated with peacock feathers and polar bear fur hung from the golden metal bars, and equally unfashionable silk pajamas choked out the greasy biker jackets for room on the rack. Next to the racks were piles of junk and nic-nacs that spilled over down a second corridor, making it entirely impassable.

"You can wear what you want while you are here," said Malex who was struggling to feed a parrot that Aqila just now noticed was slurring hateful words at her. "Nobody ever wants to buy any of it anyways. It is the least I can do for you my friends."

"How do you manage to afford all of this?" asked Octavia slowly.

"Virgil and I make our income by occasionally selling the many items you see around you, but the real catch of our finances is gathered by fishing. Please, don't be shy. Find something a little warmer to wear within our wide selection."

There was an awkward silence before almost all of them scrambled over each other to get first dibs on the clothes…with the exception of Aqila. Her attention was focused on the itches that came out of nowhere. From her shoulders to her knees, just about every inch of her body pulsed with some sort of itch, not simultaneously but consistently. It was almost as if spiderwebs were thrown over her, and she was struggling to escape the invisible sticky strands that tickled her so lightly. She attempted to relieve herself from the itches without alerting anyone else to the problem, but they all knew. She knew it. *They all know.*

"Where is your bathroom?" asked Aqila as clammy chills bubbled up from her feet.

Malex directed her down the hall, but Aqila insisted that she could find it herself after a brief interaction. Once out of sight, Aqila jogged through the boat entering doors that were obviously not bathrooms. Behind the first door that she opened was a miniature, dreary dungeon with a thin mattress and a few books on a nightstand. Unsure as to whether or not she truly just witnessed Malex's bedroom, Aqila quickly shut the door to move down the hallway. A second door merely five feet further into the ship opened to a kitchen with a man slicing tomatoes faster than a jackhammer could pop cement. Aqila shut the door, but the scent of garlic hit her more heavily than she had expected. Now sprinting, Aqila barged through the next door. A porthole was on the corner of a curved wall, and through it she could see the wind relentlessly slicing through the tarps that lined the boardwalk. Inside the room was a queen sized bed, and on it sat a chippy chihuahua enraged with Aqila's presence. Stuffy furs and drapes hung from the entire bedroom, but Aqila did not have the time to nose around, for the chihuahua snipped at her ankles before she could turn around.

She punted the dog across the room before slamming the door shut. In the heated hallway once more, she felt a warm liquid running down her shaky ankles, blood. Tiny teeth marks glistened red through the tears in her pants. She was only able to take two more steps away from the door before collapsing on the floor. Hot saliva dripped out of her mouth, and the carpet spun around her. She tried to get up off her side, but with how weary she was without sleeping that became an objective which proved futile. Vomit slowly spilled down the side of her face and all over the lavish carpeting.

"Let's get you up," said a young man. Aqila slowly turned in her vomit while still clenching her side. Caleb's steady hand was outstretched waiting for Aqila. A smile sat on his face as he waited for her to get up. Next to him stood Ferran, bruised from Sartan's attacks the previous night, but still kicking nonetheless. She reached out and grabbed Caleb's hand, but to her surprise he did not recoil when he saw the vomit on her hands. He merely wiped it off on his leg as Ferran threw an arm around her for stability.

"Are you okay?" asked Ferran as the three of them made their way back down the hall.

"Stop. I am fine," replied Aqila in a cracked voice.

Caleb walked next to her as he said, "You will be fine. You just have to make it through today."

She was not even looking at him, but she could tell just by the way that he calmly said it, he had a smile on his face. A genuine smile. He knew it. She knew it. They all knew it. There was no way for her to get her hands on anything this far from a city. The three of them knew where they were headed next, and that is what scared her the most. Aqila was bright enough to hide the fear, but she wondered if they were already aware.

"I think our best option would be taking this boat. It is large enough for everyone to fit on, and it will get us across the ocean safely," said Aqila who desperately attempted to sway their attention to the mission.

Ferran was quick to reply, "I agree. The only other plausible option would be to walk the coast South, but that is a terrible idea because if Lev finds us then we would be limited on directions to flee."

"Not only that but we would starve and freeze before Lev ever found us," jumped in Caleb.

"I think you are underestimating Lev. I would be surprised if she fails to find us here by the end of the day. She just popped up at the Virgo Palace out of nowhere. She nearly caught us in Garigo, and we would have been dead had Sartan not stopped her."

"Oh, I did. Not. Know. That. Regardless, are the owners of the boat going to let us ride it to the Pisces Palace? We just saw the rest of you go into this boat, so we followed," asked Ferran as they made it back to the living room.

"Not quite," answered Aqila who just now realized that vomit was dripping off half of her clothes. "The owner of the boats is the blackout drunk on the couch."

Malex was showing Jaako how secure a pocket on his newly acquired black jacket was when she turned to say, "Glad to see that you found your…it appears we have had an accident. No?"

"I did not make it in time," apologized Aqila who just could not bring herself to look Malex in the eyes. "I may need to borrow some clothes after all…"

"Honey, that's perfectly fine!" exclaimed the armless woman. She quickly grabbed two items from the golden clothes rack and brought them over to Aqila. The woman kept a smile on her face as she stopped herself right before handing Aqila some heavy, brown trousers and a camo, hunting coat. "I'll bring these to the restroom for you. Let's clean it up before Virgil sobers up or else I'll be in BIG trouble. Come. Show me where the accident is, and I'll get you everything you need to rinse up."

"While you're doing that Ferran and I will tell everyone else what the plan is," said Caleb as Aqila was leading Malex towards the hallway.

"I don't know Caleb. Jaako and I already thought of a pretty good idea," responded Sartan as Aqila walked further away. "We plan on…"

What plan?! I never made a plan! Ferran and Caleb never made a plan with me! When did Sartan and Jaako have time to make a plan!?! Aqila wondered furiously how they all could be so in-tune with each other about the next step they needed to take…without her guidance at that. Then she wondered if she was just so out of it that she failed to notice what was going on around her.

"Ope, I see it!" exclaimed the woman once the vomit was in sight. "You were so close to the bathroom too. Here let's get you all set up before I take care of the mess. I'm sorry! I meant to say accidenté, it is perfectly fine to not make it in time."

Aqila was too focused on simply watching the walls to even realize that the smile she pretended to show off to Malex faded away. She was brought to the very next door down the hall. Inside it was a luxurious, white tiled floor. A small porthole, that Aqila was way too short to even look out of, sat on the far wall supervising her. It gave a natural white glow to the bathroom, and an unnatural golden glimmer came from a micro-chandelier hanging from the center of the ceiling. A perfect porcelain toilet with golden accents sat next to a walk-in shower that, instead of a faucet, had the water fall directly from the ceiling. A giant oval mirror with wooden frames stared right back at Aqila from the otherside of the room. The sink that stood taller than her sat up on a mahogany base next to a rack. On the rack were ten if not fifteen folded towels that hypnotized Aqila with their luxurious patterns.

"Master let me decorate the bathroom, but I bet you would have guessed that on your own," laughed the woman. "All of the shampoos and soaps you will need are already in the shower, and if you need a scrubber or loofa they are in the cabinets under the sink."

"Thank you," replied Aqila as she stared around at the room waiting for the woman to leave.

"I do ask one thing of you however."

"Of course," said Aqila.

"There is a basket in the corner next to the toilet. It would be greatly appreciated that before you cleanse yourself, you put all of your dirty clothing in it and then put the basket outside of the bathroom so we can wash it all."

The new clothes that Aqila had borrowed were already laid on the sink edge, and although Aqila thought the request to be peculiar, she obliged. Once Malex left the room, Aqila took all of her personal belongings that had made it this far, on the sink: her necklace, Libra's ring that Sartan gave her, and a small wallet with nothing in it but spare change and a photo of her family. She refused to let herself take the photo out of the wallet to reminisce and instead stripped out of her vomit ridden clothes. Quickly and gracefully she slung the basket out of the bathroom before anyone could see her. After grabbing the scrubber from beneath the sink and after turning on the shower she caught herself glancing once more at the small black wallet. She shut the sliding glass door to the shower behind her, and took one step forward.

The steaming water trickled down the glass as her dry hand slowly picked up the wallet. Aqila slid the photo out of the wallet and read the back of it. *The Rih Family, 6749 N.Q. Abdul 33, Fabia 32, Ferran 8, Aqila 6.* Written in blue pen, some of the letters smudged together, but it was all readable from Aqila's eyes. A strong cramp burned in her side as she flipped the photo around. On the front stared back four happy faces. It was funny that Ferran's smile was the only one that showed so many teeth. Looking at a Ferran so much younger was strange to her. It was almost like he had grown into a completely different person. He had. She refused to think any further about who Ferran had become or how he had changed. The scrawny little boy sat on his father's lap next to his chubby sister. *Although I lost most of my child chub or had it develop healthily, I still do not believe that a child that age should...Don't go there Aqila.* She quickly averted her gaze away from her younger self upwards towards her mother.

Her mother wore a happy grin, but it just was not quite happy enough to show teeth. Aqila never knew if her mother was ever truly happy, but from her six year perspective on life that was also never a question back then. She never knew what thoughts were being conceived behind her fair skin or under her creamy blonde hair. All she knew was that her mother was there. Every day she was there. Her father, on the other hand, was not. He was always at work. Politics. It was an overtime job when you made it to Beran's cabinet. She gazed left to see her father staring right back at her with a face that only a daughter could love. *Strange. It has been so long that I struggle to remember what life was like before losing them. I would rather not have had them in the first place sometimes. Is it better to not have at all? Or is it worse to have it but lose it all after getting accustomed to it?* Aqila's cramps had waned enough for her to not notice them at all. With goosebumps all over her body she glimpsed down at her bare feet, one of which had a bit of blood trickling on it from the tiny dog bites she previously endured. It snapped her back to reality. *I am nude in a stranger's bathroom looking at a photo of my family questioning life. Get it together Aqila!*

Aqila placed the photo in her wallet, hopped in the shower, and cleaned herself off. After cleaning herself Aqila stood under the hot water for a good ten minutes. She got out of the shower reluctantly, only after pruning all her skin, and put on the clothes that Malex gave her. Before taking a heavy breath to go back out to the living room, Aqila saw a bird fluttering out of the porthole. Surprised she managed to catch a glimpse of anything at her angle, she watched it fly. It dawned on her that the bird was flying quite quickly actually. It held its wings out in a stretched position for at least six seconds before flapping them again in the wind. She took a step closer to the porthole to get a better view and the whole boat wobbled a little. Her stomach engulfed her heart. *WE ARE MOVING!*

Aqila grabbed the few belongings that remained on the countertop and barged through the bathroom door. Within seconds she was in the bridge confronting whoever had decided to move the boat. On the floor in the corner the woman that had treated them with so much hospitality was wiggling in her restraints away from all the controls of the fishing ship. Her master was nowhere to be found, but the culprits of the act glanced in excitement at Aqila.

"WHAT DID YOU GUYS DO!?!" screamed Aqila when she noticed they had a makeshift gag in Malex's mouth. "WHAT IS GOING ON!!?"

"We found transport!" exclaimed Jaako with a laugh that obviously hid his true feelings.

"Do you even know HOW TO DRIVE A BOAT?! OR WHERE WE ARE GOING?"

Sartan stood up from the center chair while stating, "We are going to the Pisces Palace, and we are getting away from Lev. We have transport, housing and a steady source of food now."

"You can not just steal everything from someone who helped us out so much already!" exclaimed Aqila. She tried to cover herself before somebody pressed a possible contradiction in her statement, "I have stolen things before, yes, but when have I ever stolen somebody's entire home?"

"We aren't taking her home away from her in the slightest," argued Sartan who left the ship unmanned. "We're only moving her home. It is still hers in theory."

"Stop trying to justify yourself!" exclaimed Aqila who still was unable to believe what she was witnessing. "What about the other boat? You just left it at the boardwalk, and now somebody else can easily steal it!"

"Nonsense," interrupted Ferran who was reluctantly siding with Sartan. "We kicked off Malex's master, the weird drunk who beat her."

"YOU THREW HIM OVERBOARD!!!" squealed Aqila as she finally ran forward to the windows. The ship was heading straight into the depths of the deep gray wasteland ahead of her, and no shore could be spotted on either the starboard or port side. "He was too drunk to walk! THERE IS NO WAY HE CAN SWIM TO THE SHORE!!!"

"Aqila! Relax!" demanded Caleb who seemed oddly calm for the circumstances. "We left him on the boardwalk. We would've left Malex too, but she would just go get help. This is the best thing we could've done I assure you Aqila."

"Yeah, we threw the cook overboard not the drunk," stated Jaako which only fueled Aqila's rage.

"ARE YOU SERIOUS!" exclaimed Aqila who now, refusing to glance at their prisoner, turned her attention to the girls. "Octavia, Emilia, what do you think about this!"

Octavia was holding her head in her hand, but despite the black craters beneath her weary eyes she managed to reply, "My headache is too loud to keep track of the crimes your friends committed today. I have no jurisdiction anymore, and I am doomed to die from this damn Virgo shit! After all it was either this or risk fleeing Lev on foot. After seeing what she is capable of first hand coupled with my weakened state…I can only feel safe if a whole sea separated us from her."

Aqila looked to Emilia as a last resort. Emilia stared back with a shaky smile as she nodded in agreement of what Octavia had previously stated. *Okay. We are really doing this then.* Aqila nodded in defeat and prevented herself from questioning them anymore. Instead she played a different game, "I see. What is our plan going to be once we get to the palace?"

Jaako started, "Uhhhhh---"

"That's a problem for when we get to the palace," interrupted Caleb.

"No!" exclaimed Octavia and Sartan in unison.

"I don't know what our plan is going to be, but I promise you that I am not doing that again!" demanded Octavia as she rubbed her forehead.

Everyone glanced at each other in confusion before Caleb asked, "Do what again?"

"I'm not going to be your inactive Pisces or whatever. If this is what it feels like after becoming the inactive Zodiac," answered Octavia briskly.

"Octavia…you won't ever have to become an inactive Zodiac again," said Jaako who was trying not to laugh at her ignorance on the matter. "You can only do that for your sign, but you can still become an Active Virgo if we can find your Gemstone."

"Will that hurt as much as this does?" asked Octavia who pounded her fist on the console three times. "My brain is being blasted nonstop! EVERYWHERE!"

Jaako hesitated, "I don't know the answer to that…"

"Emilia," started Sartan. "Can you take your sister and find her somewhere to rest."

"PLEASE!" exclaimed Octavia. "WITH WATER!"

"Certainly! Come on Octavia. Maybe you just need some rest."

After a brief show of unwarranted unwillingness to move, Octavia followed her sister into the ship. Then Aqila finally thought of something. "Wait, if we do not have anyone to be the inactive Pisces Zodiac…why are we already going to the palace?" Everybody stood speechless. It was almost as if everybody was looking around at each other wondering if they could be eligible. Aqila spoke up and sped the process up, "I know that we will not be able to recreate Pisces yet. Jaako and Octavia can not for obvious reasons. Caleb and Emilia are both air signs, so they would not be eligible. I am an Aries, and Ferran is a Scorpio…Unless Sartan is a Pisces…"

"If I were a Pisces I don't think that Ryby would be this mad at me," said Sartan quickly breaking the suspense for Aqila.

"What the fuck does that mean?!" exclaimed Ferran.

"So that means we have to find someone. We have to go back to the land?" said Caleb unconfidently. "But that is the worst option we have!"

"If we don't have anybody to be the inactive Zodiac we have no point in going to the palace. Not to mention that Lev probably suspects we are headed there to begin with," stated Sartan confidently. "At the very least we would be putting distance between Lev for now, but do we have enough fuel to make it there and back to begin with? We would get stranded at the South Po--"

"Since Lev already knows that we are heading towards the Pisces Palace we should get in and out before she shows up," interrupted Ferran. "I would be angrier if we showed up and Lev was already there waiting for us."

Their conversation was halted when they heard a thud on the ground. Malex had fallen over trying to slug her way towards the living room behind the bridge. She was grunting loudly, but it was her squirming in her constraints that caused even more rugged noise. Something deep inside of Aqila told her to untie the woman, and after Jaako asked if she could be a Pisces Aqila went to ungag her without hesitation.

"Kha! We don't have enough fuel to make it there and back! You all have a death wish! We need to turn back now before my master punishes us all!" exclaimed the woman all within a span of eight seconds. She had stopped squirming, but her frantic frame of mind bled through her words.

"You're lying," stated Sartan with a poker face. "If you ever want to see your master again, tell us the truth. How much fuel do we have left?"

"Do you promise to take me back to him if I tell the truth?" asked Malex hesitantly.

"Why would we want to prevent the healthy relationship the two of you obviously have?" asked Ferran with a grin.

"Do not mess with her Ferran!" exclaimed Aqila. "You guys may have managed to get us moving, but she might be the only one who can get us back to the mainland."

"We have enough fuel to make it there and back three times," answered Malex. "Just don't take me away from my master. You can have the boat, you can have my body, you can even have my life as long as I get to see the master again. As long as he knows that this wasn't my fault."

Aqila and Ferran glanced at each other, sharing thoughts for a brief second. *Is she okay?* Then Ferran threw out a reply to her, "We don't want your life, body, or boat. Well, we need the boat temporarily, but you can have it back when we are done with it. We only need you to navigate it for us."

Malex sniffled, "Okay…"

"So do we have a deal?" asked Ferran as he knelt down next to her.

"Wait!" interrupted Sartan. "Are you a Pisces?"

Malex hesitated before answering nervously, "Maybe…"

Sartan looked around at everyone with both eyebrows raised. It was almost as if he was asking everyone else if they agreed with whatever he was thinking, but it was not that difficult for Aqila to guess the jist of his train of thought. *We need a Pisces to recreate the Pisces Zodiac…we have everything else, the gem, the palace, and a means of transport to it…we just need a Pisces…*

"I think you'd make a great Zodiac," started Sartan when nobody said anything else.

"Sartan, no!" whispered Aqila assertively. "Do NOT do this to her. She has already been through enough. She will be stuck running away from Lev if she does."

This time she wasn't the only one disagreeing with Sartan's decision. Caleb said, "She will have to come with us afterwards which means that we will have to bring her master with us too."

Sartan argued back in a whisper, "Yes, but then we will have an ACTIVE ZODIAC."

"There are other ways…" replied Caleb.

"If we don't do it now then Lev might beat us to the palace making it impossible," added Jaako who actively took Sartan's side in the matter. "Waiting to find the perfect candidate might prove fatal."

"And forcing this candidate would not?" fought back Aqila. "If she resents us because of it then we will be in trouble down the road. She will quickly grow to become more powerful than all of us combined. She will be an Active Zodiac!"

The only one who had yet to speak was Ferran. Aqila looked over at Malex, who had noticed this as well, she was staring straight at Ferran almost begging him to not force her to do whatever dark rituals she certainly must have thought they were talking about. "Guys…in Sartan's defense…"

"Ferran!" exclaimed Aqila instantly.

"No no no, hear me out. In Sartan's defense, I would much rather have Malex be the Active Zodiac if that meant Lev couldn't have one of her pawns be it."

"We have all of the Water Gemstones," admitted Sartan hesitantly. "She physically can't without catching us."

"When did we get those!?!" asked Ferran.

"Long story short. I stole them from Lev."

Ferran took a second to process it, but quickly got his mind back on track. "Okay, well even without the gemstones…if we make Malex the Zodiac then we can use the boats as a base of operations. Steady food, transport, and housing for when we go on to the rest of the Zodiacs. It will be helpful having a way to cross water when we finally end up having to kill the big three," stated Ferran.

"It will be impossible to kill Lev! Let alone Lev, Blizenci, and Kozoroh!" exclaimed Aqila.

"Let's not get ahead of ourselves," said Sartan. "We are at Pisces. We have a Pisces right here with us. Why not give her a promotion?"

"Because that simply is not right!" exclaimed Aqila.

"Then what would be right? Going back to the shore and saying it was all just a misunderstanding?" jabbed back Jaako. "Oh, we accidentally stole your home and your slave…sorry!"

"If we make her the Zodiac then we would be countless steps ahead of where we are right now," argued Ferran. "It is the small progress that matters. Things don't have to be perfect this early in our mission, so why try to find someone perfect?"

"I just think that we are taking a step in the wrong direction," stated Caleb. "But you guys do whatever you think is best for us."

"It's a three versus two vote," whispered Ferran. "We need to make her the Zodiac, Aqila."

Aqila finally agreed, "Fine! But when she resents us all do NOT come running to me for help!"

"I guess we should untie her then. She is going to be with us for the next week or so," said Sartan. "I might know where the palace is too..."

Chapter 23
Tracking the Scent of Fear
Lev

It was the next night. A storm brewed in the sky above Lev, but she was focused on the puny mortal she held up against a wall. He slurred over his own words pretending to be unsure of what had happened the day before. The only thing that she managed to squeeze out of the nuisance was his name, Virgil, and that a group of young adults had stolen everything from him yesterday.

Lev dropped her grip on him, and he flopped onto the deck of a large fishing boat. She held her hand out towards the man, not in attempts to help him up but in attempts to cleanse him. Maroon mist rose out of each of the man's pores as a whooshing sound engulfed them. Then Lev stopped, and the man gasped for air as the red mist dissipated into the salty wind.

"We shall try this again Virgil," commanded Lev with a snap of her fingers.

"Wha-what did you do to me?" asked Virgil shakily as if his whole world was just turned upside down. "I think I'm going to get sick."

Lev, while rolling her eyes, stated, "The alcohol was clouding your memory of the day past, so I removed it from your system. Now you and I are going to get to the bottom of---"

SHHHLSSSSPLAT! A steamy combination of salt and fish scented vapor assaulted Lev's nostrils as the man lost his dinner. He quickly began dry-heaving as all of the liquid inside his stomach had previously been blown off in the harsh February winds after his cleansing. By the time Virgil's body had recovered from the whiplash due to swapping between sobriety levels so quickly, Lev had already lost all of her patience.

"Focus! Who took your boat?"

"It was a group of six or seven," clamored the man uncertainly. "I would've beat them if they didn't get me in my slumber! I was outmanned and outgunned! I could not save myself if my life depended on it, but I feel so violated after losing Malex!"

"Malex? Elaborate."

"She was my slave. I lost my chef too!"

"Oh! What bad news!" taunted Lev as she dabbled in sarcasm. Loud thunder rumbled far off the coast as she continued, "I'm quite positive that you have been suffering deathly since your separation. I would hypothesize that they are hurting even more!"

"Exactly! Even worse, they took my more fancier ship!"

"SILENCE!" boomed Lev as she grabbed the man. She swung him over the edge of the boat's railing with one hand, holding him over the icy water a long drop below. "I care not for what you had and had not! I care even less for what you lost and wish to find! TELL ME who took this from you!"

"Please! No! Wait!"

"This group of six or seven...SPEAK WHILE YOU STILL ALLOW YOU THAT PRIVILEGE!"

"There was a man! He argued with me briefly to buy one of the boats, and then another man arrived with a woman!"

"NAMES!"

"I don't know any of their names!" cried the man. "The woman wore tattered and torn sweatpants and a hoodie with dirt on it, and the man had dirt all over his clothes as if he had fallen in the mud multiple times!"

Lev loosened her grip on the man, and he grabbed her arm immediately to prevent slipping away. She continued, "Was he malnourished?"

"Yes!"

"Tall?"

"Very! The woman was short though!"

"Was there only one woman?"

"No!" exclaimed the man while tears ran down his reddened face. "There were three! One was wearing a police uniform! I don't know anything else! PLEASE!"

"An officer you say?"

"YES! That is all I know I PROMISE!"

"You know how to pilot this vessel, correct?"

"Yes! I can take you anywhere, but almost all of the fuel I had was on the other boat! It was enough to take you anywhere in the world and half way back!"

"How much does this one have?"

"Enough to make it to Railsben," answered the man hastily. "I don't have any capital on me though. It is all on the other boat."

"Unfortunately, I am not familiar with this region."

"It is a coastal city only about six hours away by boat. A large river flows all the way from Celsium straight through Railsben. I'm sure you can find faster transport to wherever you want to go from the capital of the Virgo Empire, right?"

"No. We will go to Railsben to obtain all the fuel we can get our hands on. Then you will take me directly South. We will-"

Virgil interrupted Lev, "There is nothing South of Railsben other than the Southern Ocean. What could you possibly hope to find going South?"

"Your other ship," answered Lev as she swung Virgil back over the railing.

She released her grip on the pitiful peasant, and his body flung itself into the metal wall of the ship. He then crumbled down into a ball on the metal plates that Lev stood on. Virgil hastily crawled towards her, and after flinging his arms around her ankles he, with a whimper in his words, begged, "Impossible! The only thing they would even go South for would be the fishing spots at the Eastern Pisces Islands, but those are further East than they are South! We would never catch them going directly South!"

"They wish not to go to the Eastern Pisces Islands. Neither do I."

Virgil's face flipped from red to paper white, "Where…where are we going then?"

"I never said you were allowed to question me," stated Lev abruptly as she kicked him in the face to free herself of the clingy serf. Rain began assaulting them from far above. It was freezing as it bounced off the metal of the boat. Virgil attempted to scoot away from her, but with one step Lev pinned him by the chest beneath her boot. "As my navigator though…you will need to know at the very least we are headed to the Pisces Mainland."

Virgil squirmed, "What!? The Southern Pole?!"

"Precisely, and so is your other ship."

"Why would they want to g---"

"Start the boat."

Chapter 24
Self-Centered Storm
Ferran

He had been watching the white coast for what felt like hours. Over seven days had passed, and it was the beginning of Ferran's turn to watch for signs of a palace. They had traveled so far South that the sun never fully brightened the sky. They were stuck in a twilight dusk. The sun never fully sank below the horizon, but it also refused to rise high enough to counterfeit daylight for more than six hours. The ship was on autopilot as Malex had set it up upon arriving at the Southern Pole over a day ago. Since then they had been traveling Westward watching the wildlife, ice, and waves to kill the time. Lev hung over his mind like a guilty self-pleasure Ferran knew that they were safe on the seas, however he knew far too well she wouldn't be far behind them.

Ferran was the only one in the bridge, and he didn't mind the solitude. For seven days he had been stuck on a boat with everyone, and they had tried everything to pass the time. All anyone could do was wait. He could only wait: wait to cross the ocean, wait to arrive at the South Pole, wait to find the palace. Even watching the enormous chunks of baby-blue ice drift silently next to the boat had become monotonous. Not one iceberg was the same, but they all were too similar to spot meaningful differences. Cold ice glistened with grayish blue tint under the faint sunlight while mountains of snow piled up on the floating cubes. The boat's systems navigated the icebergs with ease, so Ferran didn't have to do anything but wait for signs of the palace. This took away any sense of risk that might have entertained him. He stared out past the icebergs over the endless wasteland that was the mainland of ice and snow squalls. Drifts flew over the edges of the ice sheets, falling to their icy demises in the waters below. In the distance spikes of ice shot straight up from the ground like leafless trees as far as the eye could see, and they were all covered in the snow that drifted between them.

There had been no change in scenery since Ferran took over the post from Emilia. The sun had risen slightly in the sky, but not enough to halt the Vitamin D deficiency he was developing inside the boat. The bridge wasn't much more comfortable than the outside appeared to be. A few chairs on wheels were scattered around the terminals, one of which Ferran occupied. He leaned back in it resting his feet upon the console. Dull, gray walls absorbed the little light that was being produced by two rectangular, fluorescent lights on the weathered ceiling. The rest of the ship felt like a cluttered five-star hotel, but the bridge almost felt like a prison's server room. Cables buzzed on the walls, and pipes from the boiler steamed as they ran up in the corners of the room across the ceiling. Ferran couldn't complain about his time in the cell-like bridge, as he was alone. Then he heard the wheels of one of the chairs roll back. Ferran quickly assessed the situation to see Sartan sitting down next to him.

"Why are you here?" asked Ferran. "You have to watch the next six hours after me. You'll be exhausted by then. I just started about twenty minutes ago."

"I'll be fine. I've been sleeping and can't fall back asleep," answered Sartan.

"Where is everyone else?"

"They are all asleep or trying to fall asleep. Have you seen anything yet?"

Ferran peered out the window thinking if he should even answer him. After all, the black eye that Sartan had given him at the Virgo Palace hadn't healed completely. Deciding not to be petty he hesitantly answered , "No. Not yet."

Sartan replied, "I see…"

"Yep…"

"How is your eye?"

Instead of complying with Sartan's tyrannical demands, Ferran asked a question of his own, "Did she tell you to do this?"

"Who?" asked Sartan, who obviously knew what Ferran was talking about.

"Aqila!"

"She didn't tell me to talk to you at all if that is what you're getting at."

"That is a lie!" exclaimed Ferran who refused to look at Sartan's filthy face. "That is the whole reason you even helped us in the first place!"

"What are you talking about?" asked Sartan while the boat proceeded around the side of a vast iceberg that floated in front of them. "I helped you in the first place because I knew the injury I caused unintentionally would jeopardize your survival in Dursnia. I felt genuinely guilty."

"Of course," murmured Ferran under his breath.

"Ferran," said Sartan after taking a deep breath. "Why do you distrust me so much?"

"Why do I distrust you?! Why would I trust you!?"

Sartan sighed, "I'm being serious. There has been a problem between us ever since we met."

"Yes, that problem is you."

"How?"

"Maybe because you are a complete stranger that nearly killed Aqila and used that as a way to get into the group," stated Ferran as they rounded the iceberg to see an endless ocean ahead of them.

"I may have injured her, but I made up for it almost immediately. If I never found you then you would probably still be looking for a Tansiq scroll in the Sagittarius lands," argued Sartan.

"Does that mean you deserve my trust?"

"Not at all," answered Sartan in contrast to what Ferran expected. "I wouldn't trust someone for just that, but you trust Jaako, Octavia, and Emilia all more than I. Regardless of everything that I've done for the group so far, I've been a part of your 'mission' longer than any of them, yet you still treat me as a liability rather than an asset to the team."

"Because that is what you are," replied Ferran almost instantaneously. "Everyone else is an inactive Zodiac unlike you."

"Emilia isn't. Jaako wasn't for a brief moment either."

"No, but they knew more about restoring the Zodiacs than you ever will," snapped back Ferran who noticed large seals swimming ahead of the boat. They scuttered and scattered away from the boat as if it were a deadly predator. The seals were faster than the boat, but for some reason they didn't just swim to the left or the right to escape the vessel's path, let alone go under the waves.

Sartan spoke out again, returning Ferran's attention back to the conversation he so desperately wanted to die, "You would be surprised what I have learned about the Zodiacs since then. After all, who knew that the palace was further West than it was East on the South Pole?"

"You claim it is, but it has already been a day without a single sighting of anything!"

"Ferran there has to be something more personal that makes you so distrustful of me. Why else would you despise my presence more than anyone else that is on this boat?"

"Why do you even care? You just want to run away back to living on the streets like a vagabond. A clueless hobo that has to resort to hurting others to survive, is that what you want?" asked Ferran who watched the seals continue their parade away from the boat.

"I don't want to go back to living on the streets. I didn't want to do that to begin with, but life had other plans for me then."

Ferran argued, "How could life have other plans for you? You haven't changed. What are you twenty? I still don't understand why you would care if I despise you or if I distrust you."

"Do you really want to know?" asked Sartan rhetorically. "

"I already know. Aqila would absolutely have her world perfected if you stay with us forever to help revive all the Zodiacs, but you don't want to stay. You just want to watch this mission burn in flames while you wrench my gut by doing…maybe you just want to leech off our success instead. Leave as soon as we start to really struggle as your type always does. No, I bet you just want Aqila," stated Ferran as more seals appeared in front of their vessel.

"You would lose that bet," said Sartan with a tint of annoyance in his voice. "This is personal now. I want to help you and not just so I can get in your sister's pants. The fact that you assume that so frequently really says something about you."

"Oh, I bet it really does. How can I believe you thou-"

"Ferran, if I wanted to do that it would have already happened." Ferran was silent. In an attempt not to give Sartan a black eye he glanced away. While his blood boiled within him he stared out the window watching hundreds of seals scutter in front of the boat. Sartan was waiting for a reply while watching the seals as well. Then he continued slowly, "Let's be honest…the group is dysfunctional. We have just been getting lucky by dodging Lev and going from palace to palace. They need our guidance, but there will never be stability if the two of us despise each other. I know I have made some mistakes as well, and

I'm sure you realize deep within your un-introspective and non-pensive heart that you have too. If we can't solve this then we are doomed to fail. If you can't forgive me then I'm leaving the second we get back to the rest of the world, and I will be taking all of the Water Gemstones with me."

"No!" exclaimed Ferran childishly. He had been listening to everything Sartan said while watching the seals, disagreeing with the words in his mind as they came out of Sartan's mouth. "You can't take all of the Water Gemstones!"

"I acquired them all. If I want to then I will."

Ferran thought about it while more seals appeared. The ice around them had also changed over the course of the conversation. Now it looked melted and refrozen. Chunks in the side of the glacier were missing as if torn from existence or instantaneously evaporated. All of the snow that fiercely drifted in the winds had turned into packed ice thicker than thick, and the sheet of ice that once made up the coast now rose so high that Ferran couldn't even see the ice spikes that once sat on top of it. Every iceberg that floated next to the boat grew taller and sharper, yet each one of them was oddly jagged and remolded by extreme temperatures.

Ferran reluctantly replied, "I agree…our team desperately needs our leadership, and if we are constantly at arms with one another then leadership is simply something that we can't provide." Sartan stared at Ferran as if he were waiting for him to say something else. "What? That's it."

Sartan spat out, "You're so full of shit."

"I'm being serious!" exclaimed Ferran. He choked down the food that threatened to jump out of his stomach. "I want you to stay."

Without speaking, Sartan reached into his pocket and threw a glowing gemstone onto the console directly in front of Ferran. It was large and wet, so wet, in fact, that blue water seemed to ooze out of it all over the console. The baby-blue gem quickly went from a muddled cloud of blue to a gemstone so clear and transparent Ferran could see his reflection in it. Ferran picked it up, and instantly the stone re-muddled itself with a fog that killed its clearness.

"Where are the other two stones?" asked Ferran as he ran his fingers across the trilliant cut stone.

"I lied."

"What do you mean?"

"That is all I managed to steal from Lev."

"You're kidding right?"

"No."

Ferran put the wet stone back on the console. "Oh…"

"What?"

"I was being serious Sartan. I want you to stay and all that."

Sartan stared at him with a blank face, "Okay."

"You aren't getting me to admit anything else, so I don't know what you're waiting for."

"That's fine. As long as you promise to work with me. We need to be able to trust each other with our lives in order to finish this group's mission, and right now I don't even trust you with a steak knife," stated Sartan as he took back the gemstone.

"I don't trust you being in a room with a steak knife."

"The feeling is mutual."

"Good."

"We still need to work together though."

"I don't know...like I said I don't trust you with---"

Sartan interrupted and quite aggressively, "I don't care! If we can't trust each other AT ALL then Lev will easily rip us to shreds!"

"FINE! I will think about it."

"Finally! It wasn't that hard!" exclaimed Sartan with a sigh. "Now that you are actually working with me, you aren't going to say anything about this conversation are you?"

Ferran answered without even thinking, "Not at all. Are you?"

"Never."

Suddenly the boat shifted to the right, nearly hitting an iceberg for seemingly no reason. Waves crashed violently on the sides of the boat as it rocked back and forth. The cries of the seals could be heard through the glass. A singular large fish escaped from the hold of the waters as it caught several seals in its gaping, armored jaws. The fish was larger than five tanks crunched together, and it was faster than all of the seals. It grinded them up by the bunches before another one of its kind appeared from the depths below. This one was a third the size of the boat that Ferran sat not so safely in, and it quickly swam after the seals the smaller one had missed. Ferran and Sartan watched the carnage unfold, and as they proceeded past the killing three more of the behemoths appeared in the icy water.

The spree only lasted a few minutes before almost all of the seals were either consumed, maimed, or scattered across the vast ocean. Just when Ferran thought that the armored, marine life were done hunting they turned their sights toward the ship. By now Malex had appeared on the bridge.

"We need to wake everyone up now!" she exclaimed before disappearing back into the halls of the ship. She continued as she ran off to the bedrooms, "We are all not welcomed here!"

"Surely they won't attack the boat, right?" asked Sartan.

"I think we are about to find out," replied Ferran as they watched the largest fish streamline towards the side of the boat.

The attacker splashed under the water barely missing the vessel, but the current it created was so strong that it forced the boat backwards for a brief second. Anything that wasn't bolted down shook. Then before they could recover from the first attack, a smaller fish slammed giant jaws into the side of the boat. This sent the boat drifting sideways towards the coast. Despite the power from the propellers, the vessel failed to make any progress away from the behemoths as each fish repeatedly slammed into the same side one after another.

"They are trying to sink us!" exclaimed Malex who ran back into the room with everybody else trailing behind her.

Ferran and Sartan watched everyone else rub their eyes multiple times. They all looked out the large windows hoping to see the behemoths, but it wasn't long before they all got a good glimpse. With every few seconds that passed one of the fish nudged the boat closer and closer to the shore, exposing themselves to the bridge's line of sight.

"We just have to make it to the shore before they sink us! Quickly let's get the rafts!" exclaimed Malex in her state of panic.

"I am not putting myself in the water with those things," said Ferran who was trying not to have his stomach drop at the thought of being ripped to shreds. "The smallest one had seven seals in its mouth at once! The raft would make us even easier prey!"

"If we don't do something quickly then they are going to sink us!" exclaimed Jaako with a groggy grumble. "Then we would freeze to death before they even got to us!"

"Or drown," interrupted Aqila.

"Or both!" exclaimed Octavia.

"Maybe they just aren't used to this large of a boat in their territory. They could be curious," stated Caleb calmly. After that Ferran failed to follow the chaotic conversation, for everyone began screaming at once.

"Curious!"

"They work for Lev!"

"No! They're hungry beasts!"

"No, they just want to kill! THEY KILL FOR FUN!" screamed Emilia.

Sartan argued, "If they wanted to eat they would've just chased after the remaining seals!"

Everybody was knocked down to the floor when the largest fish slammed itself into the side of the vessel. This of course, only sent everyone into more panic.

After recovering his legs, Ferran had to scream just to be heard over all of the rambling terrors being hypothesized around him, "YOU GUYS ARE GETTING OUT OF CONTROL!"

Octavia was quick to yell back, "OUT OF CONTROL!? WE ARE ABOUT TO DIE!"

"THINK OF A PLAN SOMEBODY!"

"I JUST WOKE UP AND YOU WANT A PLAN!" screamed back Aqila.

Jaako couldn't help himself. He screamed out, "FUCK!"

"SHIT!"

"WE'RE ALL GOING TO DIE!" exclaimed Emilia.

"I'M SORRY MASTER!"

"I HAVE A PLAN!" screamed Ferran once more as he looked out the window seeing the largest behemoth streaming full throttle towards them.

"WHAT!?" yelled back three voices so quickly Ferran couldn't even tell who they came from.

Ferran briefly glanced out the opposite window seeing chunks of the mainland glacier only a few yards away from the boat. He screamed, "BRACE FOR IMPACT!"

Ferran quickly closed his eyes and fell sideways towards a window. He felt the chair bruise his arm before slamming on a wall, and he heard a multitude of screams as everyone else ragdolled after him. When he opened his eyes after the collision was said and done, water wasn't splashing in on him. His acquaintances were getting up and checking themselves for major harm, and the fish had stopped slamming themselves into the boat. Snow and ice had covered most of the windows, but the one thing that Ferran instantly noticed was that he felt sturdy. Relatively sturdy of course, as the boat was completely on its side, and its failing navigation system confirmed his suspicion. They were no longer in the water.

A heavy humm surrounded them before the ship's console turned off. All of the fluids in the pipes around them stopped pumping by, and even the electrical buzz of equipment had dissipated to nothing. Ferran opened a window that had a hefty inch of snow preventing anything from seeing out. Once opened, Ferran and the others could see all the way to the horizon. In the distant waters the beasts that shipwrecked them splashed around menacingly. By now Malex was already on her knees trying to fix the ship's systems, and the others had begun murmuring fears and potential ideas for salvation. Ferran, however, needed a better view of his surroundings. While everyone was concerned with their fates he crawled out of the window onto the side of the ship. The boat was actually only partially on its side, but regardless, Ferran was forced to crawl upwards to get a view. This was of little challenge.

From the very top of the marooned boat he could see everything. He had climbed far enough from his companions to slip out of earshot, and since the ship wasn't on at all he could hear the Antarctic whisper to him. Soft winds pierced through him silently, and the ship's peak was too far from the water for him to hear the waves. The silence whispered to him, and the energy that flooded into his pours made him question things that he'd never even thought of. There was not a single sound other than his own breath, and because of this his thoughts began to sporadically echo in the void with little context. Ferran gave the thoughts practically no attention whatsoever, but the eerie quietness of the Antarctic forced pointless questions into his skull. *Why?* He turned away from the endless ocean and looked for a way down to the ground. *Why do I?* The boat was marooned on the snow and ice, but a thin path ran from the bow into the depths of the arctic landscape. *Why am I?* Ferran's eyes followed the path. Two giant walls of ice rose up on either side of the trail as it climbed a hill of icy snow. *Why?* At his elevation amongst the top of the boat he could barely see over the peak of the mainland glacier. Far off in the distance glistened a bright silver dome. Even in the twilight it still was blinding, so it was a dead give away for Ferran. *The palace? The palace!*

"The palace!" he screamed as he began making his way back into the ship. "We made it!"

As he crawled back through the window he could hear Jaako asking, "What is he screaming about? He didn't fall did he?"

"We made it!" he exclaimed as his feet touched down on the wall within the bridge.

"What?"

"We made it! We're at the palace!" Ferran exclaimed.

"The palace is in the water Ferran," murmured Aqila solemnly. "We will never make it."

"It's time to give up. I'll never see master again, and we will all die here," whispered Malex, who rested her forehead on the heavy pipe network.

Ferran continued without giving much attention to Malex, "What do you mean the palace is in the water? I just saw it!"

A few heads spun from their depressed positions as Emilia, Jaako, Caleb, and even Aqila all exclaimed in unison, "What!?"

"I could see the palace from the top of the boat!" persisted Ferran. He pointed at the windows that couldn't even be seen through with all the snow on them. "It's over that hill."

"Let's get our supplies!" exclaimed Caleb as he got off his butt.

"What if it isn't?" asked Sartan who was leaning up against the now vertical floor.

"Stop being so pessimistic! The least we can do is check," replied Emilia as she made her way towards the living room.

With the boat being on its side now, all of the things inside of it had fallen to one of the walls. For the next thirty minutes everybody had to crawl down a weak, metal wall to stand on another weak wall and look through piles of clothes, debris, and housewarmers that previously lined the living room. Both of the hallways had become impassable from being out of reach or overflown with clutter, and some of the windows had been broken and filled with snow. The two kittens easily managed to crawl past the blockage, but everyone else was stuck in a small portion of the ship. Eventually, they all found enough layers to wear and found a way to crawl out of the boat into the cold and relentless Antarctic.

Towards the peak of the hill, even Ferran had begun to doubt what he previously saw. They left all their food in the ship, and Ferran didn't quite know how far away the palace actually was. He just knew that it probably was over the hill. *What else would shimmer that brightly under this little sunlight?* The trail, oddly enough, was not made of snow rather thick ice. However, this ice looked as though it did not belong. It was not level in the slightest, almost as if it all had frozen separately, and not only that but it also went straight through the glaciers on either side. Clearly it was not a naturally occuring path. With heavy footprints running all the way back to the boat, Octavia was the first to reach the trail's tall summit.

"Well…" she stated as everyone else heaved after her.

"Is the palace up ahead!?" asked Jaako, unable to hold in his anticipation.

"I guess you could say that," replied Octavia as Ferran caught up with her.

The very tip of the silver palace glowed miles ahead of them. The ice spikes that recently lined the landscape had grown tremendously and violently. Now with a silver tint, they towered stories over Ferran with sharp and jagged icicles coming out at every direction. Below the ice spikes were hundreds if not thousands of craters and divots in the landscape all of which varied violently in size and depth. A thin layer of white snow drifted through the entire landscape all the way to his feet that now stood on perfectly clear ice. Other than the snow that drifted on the top of it, nothing fogged the ice on the way down. He could see clearly directly below, through a baby-blue tint, much further than initially anticipated. Swirls in the ice looked like art, but the frequency and randomness of it all was too vast to be just that. Directly ahead of them, past the endless forest of ice spikes and craters, stood a village of massive igloos and cabins. No lights or smoke came from any of them, but they all had a silver glow that lit up the areas around them. Beside the village sat what seemed to be a runway and hangers. He was too far to tell if the plane was moving, but there was no doubt a plane sitting on the runway. Ferran wondered how all of the citizens who lived here could sustain themselves without heavy imports, but the eeriness of it all triumphed over his mind, forcing him to think again. The landscape was a mirror. To him, it all was unnaturally natural.

"It's all abandoned," stated Sartan after taking in the view. "There is no life ahead of us."

"What makes you think that?" asked Octavia.

"Pisces was slain wasn't he?"

"Yes, Lev killed him," answered Aqila quickly.

Sartan hesitated before continuing, "Not quite."

"What?"

"She was here, but she did not kill Ryby."

"Then who did?" asked Jaako. "Because last time I checked, Lev was the one that killed like everybody."

"Rakovina."

"Who the hell is Rakovina?" laughed Emilia as the group began walking forwards on the slippery ice. "That sounds like a type of candy!"

"Cancer did not kill Ryby!" exclaimed Jaako and Aqila in unison.

"Prove it," argued Sartan.

"Prove she did!" exclaimed Jaako. Sartan didn't say anything. Ferran watched as he opened his mouth but stopped before his first syllable. They took five more steps before Jaako, victoriously said, "You can't!"

"I could, but I won't," said Sartan.

Jaako was quick to respond, "Suit yours-" but he stopped mid sentence. Ferran bumped into Caleb, so he looked up from the ice to see a dog sitting no more than seven feet in front of them. How not one member of his group noticed it approach was beyond Ferran, but there was no question that this creature knew they were coming. In front of everybody, a doberman sat upright on its hind legs. Its ears were vertical and listened to everything, possibly even what they had been saying. The dog's neck was thick and muscly, but the fact that its fur was completely white caught Ferran off guard. The dog was albino, yet its light blue eyes glowed as it waited for their next move. A thick mist began growing behind the dog.

"Sartan…" whispered Aqila loud enough for everyone to hear. "You lied…there is life here."

"Is it friendly?" whispered Caleb.

Ferran took a step towards the dog, but it held its frame without moving an inch in the gust of wind that sliced through Ferran. Snow flew into the dog's face. Ice matted its fur. It obviously had been in the elements for quite a bit of time. Ferran slowly crept closer to it, and the entire time he did the mist in the distance behind the dog churned over itself forming a thick cloud of sleet and snow. They no longer could see the palace from where they stood, but the igloos and cabins were still in sight. Once he got within arm's reach of the dog it stood up on all fours, turned around, and walked towards the igloos and snow storm. Every couple of steps it would throw its head over its shoulder to see if Ferran was following, but after the third time of doing this it stopped and resumed the position that it had previously held.

"Does it want us to follow it?" asked Jaako who was picking his earwax with a finger.

Octavia coughed, "So it appears…"

The group followed the dog, and as one would expect it began leading them around the spikes of ice that were clear enough to see a blue tinted reflection in. The snow squall intensified and slowly wrapped around them as they continued towards the palace, but nothing seemed too abstract, excluding the dog of course. That was until Ferran noticed Aqila. While they were walking between two enormous ice spikes Aqila mumbled to herself before sitting down on the ice. Ferran and Sartan stopped briefly to help her up, and when they got her to her feet they asked why she did that. Her eyes were wide, and her pupils were dilated. She gazed past his face, not answering any of his questions. Ferran's first thought was that she had pushed herself near another overdose, but he also knew that there was physically no way she could've gotten her hands on anything.

"Aqila!" he snapped.

Nothing.

Sartan tried as well, "Aqila! Helloooo!"

Ferran glanced back at the group which was quickly disappearing into the intensifying pop up blizzard. "We can't lose them!" he exclaimed mainly to Sartan as he grabbed Aqila's hand to drag her with him after the rest of their group. However, by the time that they caught up to the group the dog was gone. Octavia and Malex were corralling Jaako, Emilia, and Caleb around a large ice spike. Now Ferran knew that the problem wasn't drug related because the three of them stood mindlessly just like Aqila did.

"What are they doing?" asked Ferran.

Without letting them explain, Sartan also asked, "Where did the dog go?"

"We don't know what's going on with them," answered Octavia with a shiver. "Emilia mumbled something about losing weight before walking straight away from us."

"At the same time Jaako mumbled out of this world philosophical jargon about being a man. Our friend Caleb said something around the same time, but I must admit that these pesky winds and whatever Jaako went on about distracted me," stated Malex who surprisingly wasn't shivering for a woman of her size. "After seeing what they did the dog whined and whimpered before booking it to the next coast. We don't know where he went, but by the speed at which he left it looks like he isn't coming back. I do find it weird that a random dog is just walking around here whimpering and all. Very strange creature he was. Made me feel uncomfortable. Like he was watching me with my panties down. All white too! Not a spec of brown or black, or even gray for that matter! For all we know he could've been a ghost. Or worse! A figment of our im-"

"What happened to Aqila, why does she look like that?" asked Octavia who interrupted Malex.

"We don't know. She whispered something before sitting down, and she has looked lost ever since," answered Ferran. "They all have the same buggy, neverending eyes. Like they all saw a ghost."

"They won't respond to anything I say!" exclaimed Octavia as the winds grew louder. "She's walking away from you!"

Both Ferran and Sartan spun around to see Aqila meandering off into the blizzard. It wasn't hard to catch her, but by the time they turned around the other three had started wandering in their own directions. Ferran let go of Aqila to chase after Caleb while Octavia and Malex chased down Emilia and Jaako, respectively. Once they all corralled their friends back to a singular ice spike visibility had dropped tremendously. Snow piled up on what used to be crystal clean ice, and the winds and howls of snow made it hard to hear what was five feet in front of them, let alone see what was twenty feet in front of them. Luckily, Ferran heard a dog bark directly to his side. It was the doberman again, but now it had a leash in its mouth. He quickly noticed the leash was not normal in the slightest. The small hoop that was used to hold the leash was firmly gripped by the dog's razor sharp teeth. When Ferran reached for it the dog growled and showed off its blood red gums, so he reached for the other end. The other end however, had six hoops which were way too large to be thrown over a dog's neck.

"What is this dog doing!" exclaimed Ferran as he held Caleb by the collar in one hand and one of the hoops in his other.

Malex looked over at him after wrangling in Jaako and said, "It's a leash, silly!"

"No shit!" screamed back Ferran who could barely keep his eyes open in the snow.

"It's a leash for us, not for him!" she laughed back through the howling winds. "Put it on them before they run away again."

"There are only six hoops though!" exclaimed Sartan as he grabbed and put a part of the leash around Aqila's neck.

"We only need four!" shouted Octavia as she followed suit.

"Is this really a good idea to leash them to a random dog?!" yelled Ferran while he stared at the doberman's toothy grin. "Didn't he get us stuck in this mess anyways?"

"The dog seems like it knows how to survive here!" exclaimed Malex as she stepped back from Jaako letting him go now that he was leashed to a dog that they randomly found in the Antarctic. "I'd prefer this over them meandering over the ice in their mindless states just to fall off the glacier and freeze or drown!"

"I should have never shot him!" screamed Octavia from the other side of an ice spike.

"What!?" called back Sartan and Malex in unison.

"The driver of that car! The husband! The father! The son! I didn't mean to kill him! I FOLLOWED PROTOCOL! I DIDN'T KNOW!!!" screamed Octavia at the top of her lungs.

"WHAT!" yelled back Ferran.

"She's getting away!" screamed Malex as Octavia shuffled past Ferran and Sartan. Ferran got distracted by Octavia which resulted in Caleb getting loose. Luckily, Ferran still had one of the leashes in his hands, so Caleb didn't get very far. Ferran, upon grabbing Caleb, instantly threw the leash around his neck after he caught him, and then he glanced over at a fear ridden Malex who had just thrown the leash over her own neck.

"What are you doing?" exclaimed Ferran.

"Making sure that I don't get lost!" she yelled back as Ferran's visibility of her quickly faded under the strengthening snow squall. "I'll wait here if you go catch Octavia for me! I have the last leash in my hand!"

"This is bullshit! Why do I have to go save her from herself?!" Ferran screamed back. The snow had grown so strong that he could only see Caleb's leash line extending into a white void. He knew that the dog and Malex were past Caleb just by pure memory, but there was no way he could remember how to get back if he went after Octavia. "It's too risky!"

The storm began throwing heavy rocks as Sartan slammed into Ferran's side knocking them both on the ground. Since the snow was so dry they still slid out of view of Caleb and the leash, the only thing that kept Ferran tethered to his companions. Sartan quickly helped Ferran to his feet after apologizing for the collision.

"We can find Octavia if we hurry!"

"No! We have to get back to everyone else before we become infected with this mindless syndrome!" exclaimed Ferran as he dusted himself off.

"We already are separated from them!" exclaimed Sartan as he reached out his hand. "We might as well return to them with Octavia. After all it has only been thirty seconds she couldn't have gotten far."

Ferran hesitantly grabbed Sartan's forearm so that they wouldn't get separated in the blizzard before reluctantly agreeing to rescue Octavia from herself. They could hear the dog's barking and decided to go the opposite direction to catch up to octavia. They nearly walked straight into several increasingly sharp ice spikes before walking over bite-sized divots in the ice that refused to stop growing larger as they proceeded on their hunt.

Behind them in the far distance, Malex let out a cry, "Octavia walked in a big circle! It was a fearsome fight, but I managed to catch her on the leash! Hurry back my friends, the wild puppy is walking us away from you!"

Her voice was distorted and echoed by the storm, so it was impossible for them to pinpoint an exact direction that it originated from. Ferran knew that she hadn't moved though. He used this knowledge to turn them directly around since they had only traveled in a mostly straight line so far. He expected the divots of ice and the sharp, jagged ice formations to wane as they made their way back to their group but instead both the divots in the ground and ice spikes grew larger, deeper, sharper, and even wider. When the snow grew so thick that Ferran couldn't even see his own feet through it anymore, they took two more steps before slipping into an extremely deep divot. Ferran opened his eyes after the tumble, and Sartan was nowhere to be seen. Ferran was now on flat land again, and he could hear distorted screams from Malex far away.

"I'M SO STUPID MASTER! I'M SO STUPID! NO, YOU ARE SO STUPID! I JUST WANT US TO WORK! TO BE HAPPY!"

"That's definitely not good!" exclaimed Sartan from Ferran's right.

"Sartan!?"

"Ferran?"

By now Ferran could barely see his hands in front of his face, but Sartan's heavy hand plopped down on his shoulder from behind. "Where are we?" Ferran asked once he spun around.

"I don't know, but I think we lost Malex!"

"We won't last much longer out here!" exclaimed Ferran who had begun shivering.

"Give me your scarf!" demanded Sartan.

"I'm already freezing, no!"

"We have to tie our legs together! If one of us goes mindless then the other won't be able to survive or save us at all if we wander off!"

"I agree, but I don't know if I can survive even by myself in these conditions! What if we both go mindless!?"

"We will deal with that when we get there!" exclaimed Sartan as he finished tying the scarf around their left and right leg, forcing them to be stuck together. He began lifting the leg, sending it forward. "We just have to find the dog!"

As Ferran expected, they only managed to take several steps before the scarfed leg got caught on something and failed them. When they both knelt down to unhook whatever caught the cloth they realized something darker. A finger was stuck in the scarf. The skin, flesh, and blood had all been melted away leaving a pure white skeleton behind. As they surveyed the scene, Ferran noticed a golden crown resting in the snow just above the victim's skull. The crown was cracked, and a giant trilliant slot for a gemstone was missing its stone. The crown had very small sideways 69's running across the base of it that were ironed in, and even smaller cracks of black running upwards throughout the crown. To his right, Sartan unhooked the skeletal finger as he continued gazing at the rest of the carcass. The skeleton had no trace of clothes or shoes other than a few pieces of burnt, black fabric. This was something Ferran found quite strange for being in the South Pole. He reached over and handed Sartan the broken crown that lay next to the skeleton's skull.

Sartan's outburst was childish and distracting, "NO! THIS ISN'T!"

Then Ferran realized what was happening, "STAY WITH ME SARTAN! DON'T GIVE IN!"

"NO! THERE IS NO WAY! I DIDN'T EVEN THINK ABOUT THIS!"

"SARTAN!"

"WHAT WERE THE CHANCES! I DON'T CARE ABOUT THE CHANCES! I WASN'T READY TO SEE THIS! I AM NOT READY TO SEE THIS! YOU TOLD THE TRUTH! I BELIEVE YOU NOW! I BELIEVE YOU! YOU WEREN'T LYING TO ME!"

"SARTAN!!!!" screamed Ferran as he smacked Sartan across the face. "DO NOT! LET THE STORM INTO YOUR MIND!"

Sartan slipped the shattered crown that snapped into two pieces into his heavy coat. Then he stood up, which threw Ferran on his back because of their tied leg. The scarf couldn't handle the stress and ripped enough for Ferran to slide out on his way down. Meanwhile, Sartan repeatedly kept refusing to believe what he was seeing as he backed away from the skeleton.

"Ferran, get up!" Sartan exclaimed as he reached out his hand to Ferran.

"You're still conscious!?" asked Ferran while Sartan helped him up.

Sartan cried out, "I don't even know, but we can't stay here! Anywhere but here!"

"Where do we go! WE ARE LOST JUST LIKE THE SKELETON PROBA-"

Howls from a wolf echoed through the wind. Or were they barks? Howls! Barks! Ferran heard the dog nearby, and with the dog came potential salvation! A strong sense of warmth overcame him, killing his shivers, and Sartan admitted he felt warmer just by hearing the dog as well. They both shuffled against the wind towards the heavenly pup. It wasn't long before they could see leash tracks and paw prints in the snow, but Ferran didn't even care if he found salvation at this point. They knelt down to see the tracks better, and followed them up an extremely steep side of the crater they had fallen into. Immediately upon escaping the divot, the winds pierced through him much stronger and aggressively now that he was in the equally blinding somewhat open terrain. A strong sense of tranquility urged him to stop following the albino doberman's tracks and lay down face first in the snow instead. He fought the urge briefly, but within twelve seconds of thinking the fatal thought his face was buried in the snow. Ferran could hear Sartan hollering for him to get up and tugging on his arms; he kept his face stuffed as deep into the snow as he could until he no longer could breath. Then and only then did he sit up to see nothing but an endless white void in every direction. No Sartan. No dog. No worries. No pain.

The feeling was brief as he soon noticed the dog with its six leashes now empty. He rolled his head back as Sartan threw one of the leashes over his head and another over his own. The painlessness was then filled with self-doubt. Once again Sartan disappeared into the void along with the dog and the leashes. The only thing that remained in his world was a blurry flurry of white chunks flying past a long black leash that extended from his throat into the nothingness. He saw this same image four possibly days, as his body obeyed the dog which tugged him forwards. A much greater force than himself pulled him along past an ocean's worth of snowflakes. He could hear screaming from what he thought to be Sartan but not one word was distinguishable let alone comprehensible. Now his mind raced through self-doubts and hard criticisms of himself.

Why am I so awkward? I don't try to be, but it just happens. Nobody can control how awkward they are, right? See! I'm doing it even now! I don't even know if I can control my awkward level because I'm so awkward. This is terrible. I'm terrible. This is why nobody likes me. Nobody likes me. Who cares though? I am the king of my castle! I care though…and my castle is crumbling. It's all because I can't trust. I can't trust because I can't trust, and that is why we are doomed to fail on our mission. Because I am a fucking failure at connection. We are doomed to fail! Because of ME! It is my fault! It's my fault Sartan got captured! It's my fault that Aqila became a junkie! It's my fault that I haven't even tried to talk to her about it over a week after her overdose! A letter doesn't count. I don't count. Where is the ship? No, It's my fault that we even left the ship! It is all on me! The fact that the ship crashed…ME! The fact that nobody in the group likes each other…ME! The fact that we all died in the South Pole…ME! The fact that we have nowhere to live anymore…ME! The fact that literally all that I own, all that any of us own is on our backs…ME! We are vagabonds now, and it is all my fault! Where do I even begin to fix this?! Who can I ask? Me…I can only trust me. Aqila--no. Caleb? No. Jaako seems unstable and unsturdy, but how the hell is Malex going to be an ACTIVE

PISCES if she is brainwashed by her enslaver?! Sartan fucking hates me, and I would too if I were him! I do! I fucking hate me, and I'm not even him! I'm sorry! I'm sorry! I need to be nicer to myself! I need to be understanding even if every single word that comes out of others' mouths are nothing but complete bullshit! Idiocracy! Prejudices and stereotypes! I'm in hell! This is hell. Let me out. LET ME GO! Just kill me already you fucking dog! I'd rather die than be here! Just like all of my friends would rather die than be in the same room as me for more than two minutes!

Ferran tried to scream, but with each puffed breath no sound escaped him. Suddenly the snow squall lessened, and Ferran could see igloos on either side of him. His vision slowly came back to him where he could now see the dog pulling him and Sartan along. The wind of the storm stopped slicing through his frozen coats, and he could finally hear his footsteps again. The snow then stopped completely. He found himself within the village. Wooden cabins, where the builders got the wood baffled him, and igloos surrounded him so thickly that he struggled to see most of the palace up ahead. The igloos were small and made of ice blocks rather than snow, and the cabins watched him trespass through their lands as the chimneys possibly hadn't puffed out smoke for years. As he traveled between more and more igloos he could see the palace in the distance. It easily towered over him, but it was short compared to the Virgo Palace. Certainly most of the palace stretched beneath the ice…right? When it was only a few hundred yards away it looked much more daunting. The dog pulled the two of them closer to the back side of the palace, and when Ferran noticed that he and Sartan were walking next to the dog now he attempted to talk. Oddly enough, nothing came out still. Sartan noticed the action, but wasn't able to respond as the storm had taken away his speech as well. They weren't able to speak again until the doberman finally stopped inside the palace. They entered through the back into a small room, and to Ferran's surprise he was greeted with warm hugs from all his lost friends. He took his leash off and immediately asked them all one question, "What the hell just happened?!"

"The storm hijacked our minds," answered Malex energetically. "I held out. I really did. It was a raging battle, but she got the better of me!"

"I think you two were the only ones that didn't experience the storm like us," answered Octavia. "The last thing I remember was putting a leash on Emilia. Then everything went white. I got lost in my thoughts, and at some point a leash was thrown around my neck. I took it off about five hours ago in this very room when the storm stopped."

"The storm did not stop five hours ago!" exclaimed Sartan as he pointed to the snow that still fell off his coat.

"Yeah, I couldn't see past my nose but five minutes ago," added Ferran.

"From our window we could see all the way to the big wall of ice at the edge of the glacier's shelf by our boat, but we couldn't see the entire wasteland because of all these darn igloos and abandoned cabins," laughed Emilia.

"We would have gone looking for you, but we were completely locked in here until you guys showed up with the dog," said Aqila.

"You didn't try escaping?" asked Sartan.

"We didn't want to make the dog mad." answered Malex.

Ferran and Aqila shared a questioning glance before Aqila added, "We attempted to…but the dog showed up out of nowhere and started growling at us. I regained consciousness inside this room with everyone else. The dog was nowhere to be seen, but there was a leash on all of us for some reason. Malex and Octavia later explained the leash, but nobody can explain how he got the leash or got us into this tiny cabin. Then when we tried to escape he appeared in front of the window growling. There is only the door that leads outside and the window."

"You let a dog stop you from escaping? A dog that's it?" laughed Ferran.

Octavia quickly replied, "No, we seriously tried to, we weren't even able to break the door or window let alone get to fight the angry dog on the outside that waited for us."

"We were getting kind of nervous being trapped in here for so long though," stated Jaako. "I don't really enjoy being trapped in small rooms without a way out. It's a fire hazard."

"Well we opened the door for you," laughed Sartan.

"Finally!" exclaimed Caleb. "Now we can go to the palace like we had planned."

"What?" asked Ferran and Sartan, almost in sync.

"Go to the palace? The whole reason we came to the South Pole in the first place?" taunted Aqila sarcastically.

"Yeah…we're in it…right now?" replied Ferran with a confused smirk on his face. Everyone piled out of the door to view the outer walls of the vast palace. The walls had spherical shapes all along them that highlighted the melodic mirror-like surface of the palace itself. Not one sharp edge jutted out of the palace's side, and when the frosty wind blew around it a low hum verberated throughout the air. The palace, from a glance, was mostly reflective, showing things from odd angles that were behind or beside the viewer. It would've been easier to map a kaleidoscope than to fully understand the intricate details on the structure.

The dog let the group be aware of its growing impatience with growls and grunts, as it must have been watching them gaze at the palace's architecture. Everyone decided to follow the albino doberman which led them around the crystalline walls. No windows or openings were installed anywhere in sight, but Ferran could only assume that some sort of secret window or door was hiding behind a portion of the mirrors. He was too close to the base to see the peak of the building. Unlike previous palace's this one wasn't shaped in a perfect cube, rather lots of bubbly outreaches of rooms of different sizes and shapes. There was no way an architect of any sort was involved in the construction, unless the architect was a fast growing fungus because that is exactly what the shape of the palace bubbled into as they continued around its many corners.

"Look, an entrance!" exclaimed Emilia as the dog led them through an opening in the center of a bubble shaped wall.

There were no doors, just an opening in the wall, so snow had drifted inside onto the white fluorescent lights that lined the floor. A warm breeze glided by as they strolled deeper down the dimly lit hall. Dark gray walls constructed of marble held firmly, and the featureless ceiling remained constant even after the hall took enough twists and turns to incite nausea. It wasn't long before the dog stopped at a heavy metal door at the very end of the churning hallway. It was the first actual door that Ferran had seen, with the exception of the small room everyone else was in, and still it didn't have a window or even a knob. The door had a silver handle bar and sat heavily on a railway. Caleb used this handle to pull the entire door out of the way to the side.

Once the door had been slid out of the way, snow fluttered through the dark opening onto everybody, and with the snow came a cool breeze strong enough to kill an active volcano. They could hear the echoes of the metal door slamming into the wall bounce around in the black room before shrieking past them. Deep hums came from the open and airy room ahead, but the sound's origin in the room was as easy to locate as it was easy to find a needle in a haystack. When they stepped into the frosty room, Ferran's nose was assaulted with the smell of tea trees and greasy oil. Faint blue lights could be seen glowing far above them, but the lights were so faint and far they shrank in comparison to the little bit of light that the hallway showed into the room. He could feel the wet snowflakes landing on his face as he walked further into the darkness. Suddenly, the dog could be heard barking and growling somewhere deep inside the vast emptiness of the room. It echoed around Ferran twice before, once again, the moaning of the ice ridden wind was the only thing that could be heard in the darkness.

"I don't think this is a good idea guys," whispered Caleb who still stood within the lighting of the hallway they all came from. Ferran could see a black silhouette of somebody standing between him and the hallway, but other than that everyone else had been engulfed by the darkness.

"Where else would we go?" responded Sartan who sounded like he had wandered twenty feet into the room already.

"We just have to find the lights," added Aqila. A moment of brief silence passed before Aqila continued again from the opposite side of the expanse, "Jaako make a fire so we can see!"

"I don't know if I can…"

"Everyone is depending on you Jaako!" hollered Ferran in a somewhat supportive measure.

"That totally doesn't stress me out even more!" exclaimed Jaako. "Why is it so dark here to begin with? Can't we just find the lights?"

"Maybe this palace just doesn't have any lights," said Malex curiously. "Does anyone else smell pancakes and tea trees?"

"Not pancakes," answered Ferran before returning his attention back to Jaako. "Come on Jaako, you can make a small flame just so we can see!"

The wind silently hollered before it was interrupted by a hasty spark of pink light exploding off to Ferran's left. The darkness quickly took over, drowning the flame that Jaako had created almost instantly. Jaako didn't stop though; a pink flame sparked into existence after a couple of tries. It was small and cold, but it provided just about as much light as a lantern would. Everyone quickly gathered around Jaako like moths. Every breath that Ferran took burned his nose more as he could finally begin to see the air escape him in Jaako's light. Then they walked down a path that was lined by two elongated metal bumps on either side of the floor. Every step that they took clomped on the silver-flavored marble flooring between the metal guides, but the pink hue instilled confusion when they reached a wall. The wall was far from plain. It possessed light blue coils that ran about like circuits on a motherboard. There were buttons and levers of so many different sizes the wall began to look like climbing rock. It wasn't long before Ferran spotted a double lever that was larger than any of the rest, but like the rest of the inputs it also had a strange inscription of odd shapes and letters above it.

"I think we found the breakers," whispered Octavia as she reached for the double lever.

"Wait!" exclaimed Emilia. "What if it shocks you?"

Octavia glared at Emilia without saying a word. She then continued and pulled the lever completely down, and as it struck into place a heavy clanking sound echoed around the vast opening. The deep hum that had haunted the room up to this point quickly simmered into a high pitched squeal; quick buzzes of electricity took over and ran throughout the air. Loud clattering and mechanical grinding could be heard coming from above them. Then the very first light flickered on for the fastest second any of them have ever lived through. A floor light that they stood on fought years of decay and darkness before finally prevailing with its fluorescence. The electrical room was as bleak as ever. Gray walls, gray walkway, white lights, and a lot of wires, levers, and buttons surrounded them. The opening to a larger room stood wide and awake, ready to be illuminated, and as Ferran strolled back towards the hallway that they came from, which seemed to be a good hundred feet away, the lights between the hallway and him flickered on.

It started with the floor. A checkered pattern of baby-blue lights turned on exposing just how vast the room truly was. At least five-hundred square feet stood before them. Then the lights in the walls revved up casting a thin glaze of sight around the edges of the room. A frozen tea-tree farm was exposed in one of the corners, and in another corner dozens of empty wooden barrels were frozen together in a visceral heap of disorganization and desperation. The lights stopped climbing up the tall walls. For a moment time stopped, and Ferran wondered if this was all of the lights. Then as he had hoped, the ceiling lights flickered on. Dozens of crystalline chandeliers pulsed with electricity as they lit up the vast throne room they inhabited. Their silver gleams shimmered onto the darkness below them revealing a throne room like no other. Of course an enormous silver throne sat at the very center of the room on an elevated pillar of blue lights and marble slabs. It faced a wide pathway that led to an even larger chamber door that dwarfed the throne itself. The doors were cracked just enough to see through to a crispy silver hallway. Back in the throne room on either side of the actual throne sat several tables with dozens of chairs on each side of them. Some of the tables had elaborate three dimensional models of the palace's architecture like the interactive model he saw Sartan messing with in the Sagittarius Palace, and some of the tables were littered with thousands of papers piled on top of one another. One of the tables that Ferran took particular interest in was one that contained maps of all the other palaces. There were only four Palaces that didn't have a map yet: Capricorn's, Cancer's, Libra's, and Leo's. There was patchwork done for a few of them, but it was nothing like the completed maps of the remaining palaces. Even with the strange and minor inaccuracies that Ferran found in the Sagittarius and Virgo Palaces, such as an entrance through a clay hut and the lack of bonfire grounds, the maps were still strangely precise.

"Hey, come look at this!" exclaimed Aqila who had wandered off to a nearby work table.

Ferran hastily snatched the top three finished palace maps before trotting off to Aqila. Everyone gathered around and looked at the papers on the desk without murmuring one word. Most of the papers were letters between the Zodiacs, Kozoroh, Lev, Blizenci, and Ryby. Some of them were letters from Beek and Vodnar begging Ryby for assistance in a war. A few were from Rakovina and Stir with the words: "We know you are up to something!" underlined in multiple spots. However, the most interesting letter was gripped in Aqila's shaky hands. She quietly read it to herself before handing it over to Ferran. He read the letter to the whole group,

Ryby,

We have grown stronger than any opposition. I am aware that you fear attacks from our only remaining assailant, but with Lev on her way to assist in your operation there is no doubt in my mind that Rakovina will postpone any previously planned assault on your palace, especially now that we are deep into July, Lev's month of benefit. If she is smart, and I know too painfully that she is, Rakovina will not attack us for quite some time. This will give us the necessary leverage to tie up our loose ends and solidify our future. I am lending you Lev for the second half of July. Use her to expand your palace; use her to entrench your rule in the Antarctic. If Stir really did cause that much damage then you will need her help more than I will. Use her to get your domestic issues under control and set up a puppet ruler, for I will require both of you to be away from your empires for quite some time. Blizenci's nation is in shambles; he is struggling with domestic affairs and keeping his subjects passive. His war, regardless of its success, cost too much of his time, resources, and focus. Because of this, he is now behind schedule and requires your assistance. It is a necessity to the project at our given time to make sure that we do not lose our last bit of control over the Air Empires, for if we do then the lands of the Air Zodiacs will quickly slip back into the palms of the peasants. After you finish recovering your lands from Stir's brutal onslaught, take Lev with you to assist

Blizenci in the repair of his empire. You have your orders, and so do your allies. Now don't let Lev's powers, the strongest they will be for a whole year, go to waste down there.

Your New

Liege, Kozoroh

Ferran stood speechless. He gazed around at his companions. A majority of which shared his enthrallment. Even Octavia was wide eyed. Sartan then vigorously searched the table. It was obvious that he didn't find whatever it was that he was looking for, but he did manage to find a letter from Ryby that was never sent. In fact, it very well could've been Ryby's last letter. He read it aloud,

Kozoroh,

Lev has proven to be very effective in rebuilding the damage Stir dealt. So effective in fact, that I do not believe Blizenci will require both of us to assist him in solidifying his rule. We have already completed repairs and have started on improvements. The foreign resources and labor that Lev brought with her was more than enough to fix the palace, and I believe that we should use her strength to terminate our last actual threat, Rakovina. Rakovina is quite literally the only being that can single handedly stop us. Domestic affairs are much simpler to solve than foreign ones, and once she is gone we can announce our plans for Zodiacal representation. There would be no reprimandation for an invasion of her land as she has no allies left that are strong enough to defend her, and with her out of the way we could openly begin phase three. It would save us decades of toying with governments and puppets. I humbly request a reassignment as I believe this task to be overkill and time consuming.

Your Loyal

Vassal, Ryby

"Was that letter ever sent?" asked Caleb immediately.

"I doubt it wholeheartedly," replied Aqila. "When is the date on it?"

"July 23, 6756 N.Q."

"This was definitely not sent then," stated Aqila. "Ryby was killed around that time."

Sartan stuffed the letter into his pocket before looking over some of the others in more detail. As this happened Ferran heard a deep bark echo around him. Everyone's eyes beamed down on the mighty throne, and next to the icy seat stood the albino doberman, attent unwavering. The dog stood motionless, and the chill of the room finally sank in. It had been almost four years since life occupied these halls, since somebody had sat in that throne. Now broken glass let snow flutter in through the ceiling, and even after turning on the electricity, no heat pumped throughout the palace. The palace was cold and dead. The dog must've been aware that they were there to change that.

"WOOOF!"

"He knows, doesn't he?" asked Ferran hesitantly.

Octavia asked, "He knows what?"

Meanwhile Malex responded confidently, "He knows. The dog definitely knows."

She began strolling over towards the dog as she took in the sights of the throne room. Ferran and Sartan followed behind her, and with every step that they trekked towards the throne, the dog's tail whipped back and forth. It swung to the right before swinging back to the left methodically and robotically. The closer they got the faster the oscillations became. By the time Malex had reached the dog he was already on his back ready for a stomach rub. Sharp teeth crept out of a gummy smile as she showered him in affection. The dog flipped and flopped at the feet of the seat, and it didn't notice that Malex had sat down on the throne until Ferran spoke out.

"Are you sure you want to do this Malex?"

"How could I deny this spiritual pup what he wants!" replied Malex as the dog regained its regal and formal stature.

"We have already gone over all of the possible outcomes of this decision multiple times," added Aqila who appeared next to Ferran. "Your life will never be the same after this."

"I..."

Sartan interrupted, "You will have the power to overthrow your master, but you will endure a gruesome transformation first."

"I..."

"This is what we've all been waiting for since our embarkment! Make this moment a fulfilling and memorable one, Malex!" exclaimed Caleb.

"It was more of a hijacking but..."

Ferran could feel the Pisces Gemstone in Sartans hand begin to vibrate. With a quick glance he witnessed its unique bright blue glow seep out of the crevasses in Sartan's fist. He asked, "How do we even do this?"

"I don't know," answered Sartan truthfully. "But from what I understand I just attack her with the Pisces Gemstone, and the stone and the palace will do the rest of the work."

"I don't know if I'm completely ready now that I think about it…" muttered Malex from the throne. "Maybe I could just have a moment to think about it really fast…"

"I see no problem with that," said Aqila as she began walking towards the throne.

The dog immediately began running directly down the path that the throne faced as Ferran pulled Aqila back from the throne. "I don't think giving her any more time to think it over is necessary," he said. He glanced at the dog who ran out two large doors at the end of the walkway before turning back to Aqila, "After all, she agreed to this a while ago."

"I did!" exclaimed Malex who began rubbing her nub with her only hand.

"Wait," began Jaako. "Doesn't it have to be night in order to start the inauguration?"

"I don't know, but I have lost track of what night and day truly mean this far South!" exclaimed Ferran. "Surely it won't matter since it is always night here!"

Malex asked, "Why is everyone screaming? I don't know about this my friends…I must admit it is a lot different when it is actually happening. I don't want to live forever if that means I have to watch my master di-."

Sartan pulled back his fist and exclaimed, "I am sure you'll be powerful enough to save him from death too!"

He then shot his fist forward lunging a baby-blue stream of ice water directly into her chest. Immediately, Malex's head shot backwards into the throne as if she was now possessed by a poltergeist. Her mouth and eyes fumed a bright white gleam straight upwards through the broken window atop the ceiling. The beam quickly expanded exponentially until all that Ferran could see was a blinding white light. In the distance he could hear the dog whine and whimper, but that was quickly muffled by the deafening hum that seeped out from Malex. The sound began to shake the palace itself, and only grew louder as time passed. Now blinded and deafened by the transformation, Ferran threw himself onto the floor knowing that a lethal shockwave was due to ensue. What he thought was a smart move turned out to be a mistake, for when the explosion trucked into him, he rolled all the way into the wall on the far side of the room. He hit his head on the floor multiple times as his body was dragged by the icy water. There was no extreme damage, but the room itself wasn't as lucky.

When the explosion of water finally evaporated away with the blinding light and deafening hum, Ferran was quick to notice that all of the tables, trees, and unbolted structures inside the throne room had been tossed like toy cars into the walls. One table in particular had impaled the wall next to the electrical room, and the group's luck really treated them well as not one of the chandelier crystals had sliced through any of them. Instead, since they were hanging above the blast, they all had been sent flying upwards where they harpooned the bubble shaped ceiling of the throne room. Ferran quickly made his way back to the throne where all of his companions gathered in shock.

Malex's glowing eyes had turned from white to the infamous baby-blue that appeared so frequently around the palace. Unfortunately, the light in her eyes quickly faded away as she slumped over in the seat. Her chest stopped moving with the wind that exited and entered her body, and after a quick check Octavia confirmed that her pulse had dropped low enough to kill a bear in hibernation. Alive but unconscious and probably very weak, Malex survived the transformation. Maybe his sister's incident had distracted him last time, but Ferran had never seen someone grow so weak after becoming an inactive Zodiac.

Caleb asked, "Is she going to die?"

"It looks like she has already started dying," answered Octavia hastily. She was laying Malex down on her back. "I'm going to start compressions!"

"We can NOT have her die!" exclaimed Aqila. "That will put us b--"

"She won't die." echoed a deep, manly voice from across the vast room. Ferran swung his curious head around. At the main entrance to the throne room stood a muscly man in royal robes that Ferran never thought he would see. In one hand he held, by its neck, the entire albino doberman that had assisted Ferran and his crew through the wastes of the merciless winter-wonderland they found themselves in. Its carcass, streaked red, flopped on the cold ground with a wet thud. Then the jewelry-covered emperor continued, "She is weak. She'll be unconscious for days if not weeks, but she won't die. Not from the transformation at least…"

Chapter 25
Airy Entrance, Airy Exit
Sartan

His ginger goatee and short, ginger hair violently contrasted with his pale skin. The royal robes and clothes were glistening gray, gold, and orange above the fluorescent floor lights, and the peculiar gemstone on the man's crown merely confirmed what Sartan already knew. The orange and blue eyes were more than enough for Sartan to sweat a bit; he had seen this man before, less than a month ago. The man took a slight step forwards, and a heated breeze billowed his golden robes around before knocking Octavia right off her feet, quite literally.

From the ground Octavia gasped, "That's Blizenci! Why is Blizenci here?!"

"I would like to ask the same question, but per usual Lev is trailing behind," boomed Blizenci calmly from across the throne room. His voice carried the weight of a man who had lived an eventful and long life, raspy and deep, yet his face told Sartan that he was probably only in his thirties. He took another step, and with it came another gust of heated air. His voice then crackled its way over to their ears, "I apologize. This wasn't very professional of me. My name is Blizenci, and I presume that you are the murderous fugitives that Lev has been hunting for way too long. Am I correct?"

"Murderous fugitives?" asked Aqila.

"That is precisely how she described you, and your friend Sartan didn't object to that description of you. Alas, that was when he was helping Lev chase you, so I am quite sure that the story has changed multiple times since then," replied Blizenci as he took another stride towards them.

"We never killed anybody!" exclaimed Caleb.

Blizenci laughed maniacally, "Of course not! The numerous police officers, inhabitants of Garigo, and workers at the Virgo Palace would like to debate that statement."

"That is different!" exclaimed Jaako. "They were trying to kill us! It was a life or death decision!"

"Yes, the dozens of hospitalized elders that inhabited the nursing home were just mercilessly hunting for your pure souls!" exclaimed Blizenci sarcastically. "How could I forget that you are a hero who is fighting for rightful change! Everything you do is heroic and for a good cause."

"We didn't intend to kill anybody!" exclaimed Caleb.

"How many people have you guys killed?" whispered Emilia nervously.

Blizenci strode closer to the throne as his booming voice cracked, "Intended or not, you've killed countless innocents in a war of aggression and ignorance! What are you even fighting for? To replace the fallen Zodiacs? They are dead for a reason, and the remaining Zodiacs have been hard at work to find a solution that works for everybody. By taking things into your own hands you have only polluted the air and made the truth harder to breathe for everybody."

"Hard at work doing what?" asked Ferran shakily.

"Protective measures that prevent murderous nobodies from infiltrating holy sites such as the palaces. We have created a safer world for our subjects to dwell in, and we are working on expanding the reaches of that world to those who currently don't have any form of Zodiacal representation."

Sartan asked, "What would Ryby think of what you are doing? Or Rakovina?"

"Ryby and Rakovina don't think because they are deceased. If you are going to attempt to look intelligent I'd suggest that you avoid topics that you know nothing about," countered Blizenci who now stood directly in front of them. Octavia had gathered herself, but still hid behind Sartan and the others.

Sartan requested, "Then may I ask you a question?"

"You get one question for the whole group. I have other things to deal with after this."

"Deal!" exclaimed Sartan.

"Wait!" exclaimed Aqila.

Sartan didn't even tilt his head towards Aqila. Instead he went straight into his question, "Rakovina and Ryby can't communicate since they are dead right? Well, why did Ryby demand that I not help Lev? Why did Stir openly show his distrust towards the three living Zodiacs in his cave?"

"You are joking right?" laughed Blizenci. "How would you even be able to communicate with the deceased? You are simply delusional."

"Then how did we find our way to the Pisces Palace?" asked Sartan. "We had no clue where it was, but Rakovina was more than willing to let me in on the secret."

Blizenci's smile slumped into a snarl as he asked, "You used a Tansiq Scroll didn't you?"

"Nope. Ryby was afraid that if I kept helping Lev all of the Pisces would die, but that doesn't make much sense now does it?" taunted Sartan.

"You aren't a Pisces are you?"

"Nope, but for some odd reason Ryby thought that Lev was going to make me the Wagustus of the Water Zodiacs."

Blizenci stared blankly at Sartan before curling his lips. "So you…are telling me…that you might have some knowledge as to what has really happened over the past decade?"

"Precisely."

"You are idiotic," laughed Blizenci uncontrollably. "I was going to kill you regardless, and you used your only question to confirm my suspicions and to confirm something that you already knew! Of all my years I have never seen somebody burn their own brain cells so effectively! What is your trick? Were you born this stupid, or did you just huff glue all through school? I bet you aren't even aware that your life is nearing its end. Do you understand the vastness of death? Eternal. Forever!"

"Master Blizenci," stuttered Octavia as she jumped around Sartan's side. "I'm an officer in Garigo, and my sister and I have been tracking these fugitives since their departure from our illustrious city. We have been waiting for the perfect moment to arrest them, and I believe that right now would be the best time to-"

"Silence traitor," boomed Blizenci as he wiped tears of laughter off his face. "You…" he cracked into broken laughter. "You all will perish. I would let you live a peaceful life in the countryside of my lands, even with all that you know, but with how mentally challenged you are I am sure you would manage to fuck that up too. Your fate has been decided, and your God is here to enforce it."

"Wait, don't kill us!" exclaimed Octavia as she dropped to her knees. "You are literally my hero!"

Heavy winds hastily brewed around Blizenci as he laughed, "Well, then I guess this would be an exciting story. Too bad you won't be alive to hear about it!" He raised both of his arms, and winds ruffled between everybody. Sartan clenched his fist preparing to attack before it was too late.

"WAIT!" screamed a woman from the entrance to the throne room.

"How many of these sleazers are there!?" exclaimed Blizenci as he turned to the voice.

At the doors stood a woman in all black laboratory clothes. Her brown hair was slicked back with gel, and thick glasses rested on her nose. She had two revolvers holstered on her hips, and black latex gloves strapped on her tiny hands. Behind her stood four more similarly clothed individuals. All of which were masked and awaiting her orders. She walked forward without saying anything.

Blizenci exclaimed, "Now who in the hell are you!?"

The woman replied as she spun both of the revolvers into her palms, "The Butcher." She then let off two rounds that sung past Blizenci on both sides. With a quick flick of his wrists a smooth breeze caught the rounds and threw them on the ground. Had Blizenci not stopped the shots Jaako and Aqila would be on the floor gasping for air.

"Excuse me?" asked Blizenci as he gracefully walked towards the threat. "What the hell do you think you are doing?"

"You have your orders and so do I," replied the woman as she raised her left hand straight upwards into the air. All four of the goons behind her whipped out their pistols and aimed them at Blizenci. Four loud pops exploded, but not one of the bullets made it to Blizenci. Sartan wasn't sure which was more impressive: the fact that Blizenci managed to reflect all of the rounds with a burst of wind, or that the woman who claimed she was 'The Butcher' jumped into the air and spun to dodge it.

"Quick, let's get away while he's distracted," whispered Aqila as she motioned for Octavia to pick up Malex's lifeless body.

"Where would we go? The boat is shipwrecked," stated Jaako.

"Ours is, but both Blizenci and this Butcher lady had to have some sort of way to get here," added Caleb who was helping Octavia grab Malex.

"Wait," whispered Sartan as one of The Butcher's guards cried out for help. "Let's try to fight this time. We almost beat Lev, so we can probably beat Blizenci if we all try."

"Absolutely not!" exclaimed Aqila as they made their way to the small hallway.

Three more shots popped off, one of which flew right by Sartan's head, before an entire arm flopped down next to them. Blizenci had already killed two of The Butcher's agents, but The Butcher had managed to land a couple shots off on Blizenci. They didn't affect him hardly at all, but it showed Sartan that it was possible to kill a Zodiac.

"My targets are getting away because of you!" exclaimed The Butcher who vaulted directly over Blizenci. She then shot off three rounds from her revolvers at them.

Blizenci pulled a current of air so strongly that the whole group was knocked off their feet, and the bullets that The Butcher shot at them got caught in the winds and flew straight back towards the woman who fired them. She quickly jumped up, dodging the shots and winds. Two of the bullets sank into Blizenci's stomach. He cried out, "They are not YOUR targets!"

"Yes they are!" she exclaimed before an explosion of heated air sent her flying through the room.

She dropped one of her revolvers, and it slid across the floor next to Sartan. He quickly grabbed it and tossed it to Ferran, as he already had the gemstones he could use to defend himself. On the other side of the room Blizenci finished off the last two guards that The Butcher brought with her. Despite the fact that he could see Octavia and Caleb carry Malex out of the room he still focused on The Butcher. Ferran was able to send one round through Blizenci's side before a click made the revolver useless. Blizenci grabbed at his side while making a hasty and complex hand movement. Suddenly, a burst of air sent the royal flying, gracefully, across the room towards where The Butcher had landed.

"Let's go while they're distracted!" exclaimed Aqila who tugged on Sartan's arm. He glanced back at her unsure of whether or not he should fight or run. In that brief second the fear that dripped off Aqila's face made the decision for him. Sartan then looked back at the fight to see how much time they had before Blizenci would be chasing them again, but instead he got a black boot to the face. The Butcher did a backflip off Sartan's face after Blizenci threw her across the room. She quickly slipped a pocket knife out of her belt and poised it at Sartan's throat, now that he lay dazed and confused on his back.

Luckily, Ferran managed to tackle The Butcher just before she could butcher Sartan. She wrestled with him, and he quickly lost dominance. By the time Sartan regained awareness of his surroundings, she was standing behind Ferran choking him out with her arms. Ferran's face turned purple, and right as Sartan thought he was going to pop like a grape, Jaako lodged the fallen knife just below The Butcher's ribcage, a decision that pierced everybody's eardrums as violently as the blade pierced her skin. She dropped to the floor, but Ferran fell faster. Thinking that was over, Sartan peered around for Blizenci. Blizenci trudged quickly towards away from Jaako, and held his entire arm back as if he were about to punch something right in front of him.

All that Sartan had time to scream was, "Jaako!"

Jaako didn't see Blizenci riling up for an attack. Instead he gripped both of The Butcher's hands in a dance for his life. In one of her hands was the knife that she pulled out from her own side, still dripping with warm blood. They spun around in circles while fighting each other for dominance, and that single fact is what saved Jaako's life. The two of them completed one firm rotation while dodging kicks and headbutts. Both of them were clueless to Blizenci's assault, so when it hit The Butcher in the back she cried out in painful surprise, much more deafening than when the knife was inserted directly into her side. The clothes on her back instantly caught fire, and her grip on Jaako was vaporized. The knife dropped to the floor, and Jaako fell down next to it. However, the heated winds did not stop their barrage of destruction. All of the clothes on The Butcher's back disintegrated under the heat of the winds, and the skin started to drip off her body. Sartan's ears started ringing as all that he could hear was the cries of The Butcher until the winds melted through to her lungs. By then Blizenci had stopped sending the winds into her, but the damage was already done. Her body flopped forwards onto the cold floor that Jaako scurried away from. The back half of her person was melted into a puddled red soup of meat and bone, and that puddled red soup spontaneously combusted into a visceral, steaming heap of barf inducing scents and sights which shook Sartan and his choice not to run away as Aqila suggested.

"I apologize for the unconventional methods of termination, but I grew too annoyed with that one to show her a merciful death," said Blizenci solemnly.

"Why was it so hot? Why did she catch on fire?" cried Jaako who was wiping away sweat and holding his nose while rising to his feet.

"I'm a Summer Zodiac, so my powers are extremely hot."

"Gemini is May. May is spring," coughed Jaako who was still struggling to get the scent of a burning body out of his nose.

"True, but May is one of the closest to the Summer Solstice. You should see what the hotter two Zodiacs are capable of. Anyways, back to business. I will try not to give you the same fate," stated Blizenci while he patted dust off his shoulders.

It wasn't until this moment that Sartan noticed his heartbeat could be felt inside his stomach. The room spun around him from his previous blow, and his ears still rang out from The Butcher's ghastly cries. He gasped for air. His hands were dripping with sweat. The room no longer was frozen in the slightest, and not one snowflake drifted around. Instead the heat that Blizenci created haunted him like the reaper. Steam had started gathering around Sartan's feet, and he watched Blizenci stretch out his arms.

"I'm not dying here!" yelled Emilia as she ran to Blizenci fists drawn. One swift flick of his wrist later and Emilia was on her side by Blizenci's feet. A whoosh of wind left her coughing next to the wall far from everybody.

Blizenci cracked his knuckles and neck. "Okay…now I'm ready."

Unsure how to even start a fight of this scale, Sartan sent a weak strike of icy water towards the Active Gemini Zodiac. The strike was countered almost instantly, and before Sartan could exhale he was spinning around in circles twice each second. He flopped onto the floor. Screams came from his left and right. Sartan slipped another gemstone into his off hand and sent an uncoordinated strike towards the master of air. He missed terribly. Blizenci wasn't even paying attention to him. Regardless, heavy winds still managed to punish him for the mistake. Now Sartan crawled to his feet halfway across the room. Bruises lined his arms and legs from being tossed by the winds. His joints ached. He spun around looking for Blizenci. Pink flames flew past him, and almost immediately an entire table zipped into them. An explosion of splinters and paper accompanied by a scream echoed from somewhere in the room. Sartan then was whooshed across the room again. This time he landed next to Ferran.

Sartan then slipped the last gemstone into his hand as he rose to face Blizenci once more. Blizenci pulled Emilia back into the throne room with a gusty breeze. With a violent stream of water vapor Sartan knocked Blizenci onto his side. As Blizenci fell over a cyclone of wind pulled crystals that previously were part of the chandeliers into the air. They flew around for a few rotations then fell from the sky shattering on impact with the floor. Strike after strike Sartan tried and nearly froze Blizenci with waves of water. An explosion of wind knocked him off his feet again. This time the wind was knocked out of him, and he laid on the ground gasping for breath. A heavy foot pressed down on his chest. Blizenci pressed harder onto his chest to the point Sartan could feel his chest cavity begin to cave inwards on itself. Sartan tried to strike at Blizenci, but he was one instance ahead of him. Sartan's fists were now pinned to the floor under endless winds. Still gasping for air, Sartan watched Blizenci begin blowing air out of his mouth. A current of increasingly hot air slammed Sartan's head back down onto the unforgiving, hard ground. The wind was so strong that Sartan couldn't catch a breath. His heart started skipping beats. The pins on his hands were tighter than handcuffs, and the pressure he felt in his chest was so heavy that his limbs and extremities went numb. The hairs on his face began to smolder in the heat. He heard loud screams and calls, but couldn't comprehend what was being said. Sartan's body was giving out; his peripherals began fading. The last thing that Sartan saw before everything was consumed by darkness was a scarlet-red, jet flame expanding upwards out of Blizenci's chest.

Seconds later the hot winds stopped pressing his face; the weight on his chest was relieved. A strong scent of burning hair and flesh overwhelmed his nostrils, and a strong burning sensation returned to his extremities and limbs. A loud thud rang in his ears, and somebody pulled him up to his feet. Suddenly a high pitched squeal, similar to a propane tank on the edge of explosion, began ringing out. His vision slowly fluttered back as well as the aching in his joints. His bruises burned and screamed out where Aqila gripped his arm tightly. His arms and hands were bloody and itchy, but he managed to maintain a grip on the three gemstones. He glanced around as she led him to the main entrance. Blizenci layed convulsing not too far from the throne, and Jaako helped Ferran limp towards the giant, metal doors.

"Is he dead?" coughed Sartan. A sharp itch verberated throughout his chest after speaking.

"Unlikely," answered Aqila in a crackly, broken voice. "I sent a jet flame from my gemstone through his chest and up into his neck, but he will probably recover in a few minutes."

Next to one of the walls laid the albino Doberman. Its neck was snapped, and a bit of blood trickled out onto the floor. On the other side of the giant doors was a short hallway that led to another set of enormous doors. These doors were still open and let snow from the outside world flutter into the palace. He felt a warm liquid drip off Aqila's face. It was blood, but he was still gasping for air too much to concern her with it. Up ahead of them Emilia stood just outside the palace doors waving for them to hurry up with one hand and holding her shoulder with the other. Dirt and blood was smudged all over her pained face.

"Hurry up!" she exclaimed. "They left a plane!"

Sartan gripped Aqila's arms tighter as she forced him to limp faster towards the door. After they broke through the doors of the palace, Sartan could see Octavia and Caleb standing about one hundred yards away on the nearby runway. Upon seeing them, Caleb ran towards a private jet not too far from one of three hangers. Sartan closed his eyes as Aqila shuffled him in pain across the frozen pavement towards the plane. The wind was a lot stronger than it was earlier, and it was just as hot as the winds that Blizenci created inside the throne room. If he didn't have the weight of Aqila holding him up, he might've been blown away. After walking quite a distance, he opened his eyes back to the world where black clouds were gathering in the far distance. Sartan finally caught his breath when Octavia was helping him up the steps of the airplane. She sat him down in the back seat that overlooked the palace before going back outside to help Jaako and Ferran inside.

"Wheels up!" she screamed seconds before the door clicked shut. "Let's go!"

"Wait," coughed Sartan. "Who's flying us?"

"Caleb and I," answered Octavia without even looking. She kept trudging through the cabin without any regards to her companions.

"We're actually going to die," stated Ferran as he strapped a seatbelt around his body. He refused to glance away from the seat in front of him as he said this.

Sartan saw Malex unconscious and strapped in the seat ahead of him, and Emilia was already strapped in the seat adjacent. He instantly slipped all three of the gemstones into his pockets as he locked himself into his seat next to Aqila.

The plane screeched as it lifted off the icy runway. The wind was even stronger higher up in the air, so the plane rocked back and forth as it rose up around the palace. Sartan, holding a deep cut in his arm, looked out of his window. The third circle around the palace was their last, as a deafening explosion of gales ripped the roof off the throne room. The roof splintered off into thousands of pieces that began rotating around the palace, and an annoying alarm began beeping inside of the plane. It must've been a built in weather warning system as his pilots never turned it off.

"Guys…let's get away from that palace!" exclaimed Jaako who was sitting in the seat ahead of Sartan. "I don't like how that roof is floating around!"

Sartan could see inside of the throne room from the plane, but there was no sign of Blizenci inside the palace. The plane lurched away from the palace hesitantly as air currents tugged it backwards. They managed to escape the quickly forming tornado that was pulling the ice spikes straight out of the ground. Far below right at the edge of the ice spike region slowly passed two figures. Then as they flew over them, two identical fishing boats passed by. One of which they stole from a drunkard.

"We just passed over Lev!" exclaimed Sartan.

"Not a chance!" screamed back Caleb from the cockpit. Immediately after that response a large fire ball exploded merely ten feet away from the plane. Caleb then screamed over the plane's intercom, "Aaand if you look directly below us, you can see that we just passed over Lev!"

Aqila cried out, "And if you look to your right, you can see several tornadoes forming!"

"Oh shit!"

"And if you look to your left, you can see another several tornadoes forming," yelled Jaako.

"We are clear up ahead!" exclaimed Octavia. "The skies start to go back to their melancholic gray not too far past the coast!"

A quickly forming tornado pulled the plane to the right, but if it didn't the fireball that exploded to the left of the plane would've ended the plane. The jet corrected its course dodging both Lev's attacks and the weak tornado that would soon pose a threat to Lev as well. Sartan heard the explosion of another several fireballs outside of the jet, and he saw seven more streaking flames in the tornadoes that had formed far off to the left of the jet. All of the tornadoes slowly churned over each other under the black clouds. Then the skies out of his window went back to the normal, dark-gray skies that had presided since their arrival in the Antarctic. The loud beeping that had started earlier finally turned off.

"Did we make it?" asked Sartan hesitantly.

A few moments of silence ensued before Caleb turned on the plane's intercom and said confidently, "We made it!" Octavia and Caleb screamed in the cockpit in excitement, but everyone in the cabin merely sighed in relief.

"Are you guys not excited we made it!?" called back Octavia.

"A lot of us are in too much severe pain to be excited, Octavia!" snapped back Ferran.

Octavia ran out from the cockpit leaving Caleb piloting the plane all alone, "Right! I'll find the first aid kit! Just hang in here guys!"

Chapter 26
The Final Pisces
Lev

Nine days later under the gray, Antarctic skies, Lev still waited in what remained of the palace. Plane parts and even portions of the ship that she took to get there were scattered around the ranges of ice. Enormous chunks of ice from the igloos had pierced through the walls of the palace, and the cabins that created a village just past the igloos had been thrown to the far reaches of the glacier that everything rested so delicately on. The rescue ship that she had commed for waited off the coast miles from the palace. She could see the dreadnought towering over the glacier even from outside the palace doors. Its cannons alone were larger than the fishing boat she took to get here, and the bridge towered at least fifty feet above the rest of the ship. Such an extravagant vessel could only mean one thing. Lev walked back into the palace and informed Virgil it was time to begin their hike to the shore and that she would leave him here if he wasn't fast enough. But upon walking back outdoors, the very second the snow ridden winds began slicing through Lev's shirt again, she was forced to stand and wait for Virgil. Five men stood in front of them, and the four on the outside were armed with very heavy weaponry, aimed directly at her. The four armed personnel all had masks and cloaks that hid more weapons beneath. In their arms were heavy rail rifles pointed directly at her. The rail rifles were all connected to one another with long and flexible, black cables. One of the guns had a large gemstone glowing inside of the barrel, and she knew just by looking at the black, oval stone, Aquarius's power was being collected.

Their masks made their voices robotic and inhuman. In unison, the four guards stoically demanded, "Kneel."

Lev exclaimed in refusal, "I am not kneeling for your pitiful guards!"

The man in the middle stepped forwards. He didn't have a mask or cloak on, but his voice was still deeper and more precise than his guards, "Lev. Obey their demand."

Lev sighed before dropping to her knees. The snow burned her bare skin, and she refused to look up at the men in front of her in preference to the footprints she left in the snow earlier.

"My liege, I did not think you were going to rescue me personally. Had I known that I---"

"Silence," hissed the man in the middle. Lev still stared down at the snow, so the man took two hefty steps forward. His black boots pressed deeply into the snow just below Lev's head. "You will refer to your liege as master."

"I am NOT going to…" Lev bit her tongue. She stared at the thick, combat boots that sat motionless before her. There was no objection to her statement. Instead, all that she could hear was the crisp winds hollering as they chipped away at the tips of her ears and nose. She knew he was waiting for her to change her mind. "Yes…master."

"Your gaze."

Lev swallowed her pride and tilted her head backwards. She stared directly into the man's cold, brown eyes before continuing, "Master Kozoroh, had I known that you were going to rescue me personally I would never have bothered you. You have very important tasks, and I could have found a way off this glacier if I had no other choice. I could've made a raft and risked crossing the ocean, or I could've commed the Virgo Palace to see if they had any rescue ships."

"You commed for my assistance, immediately. Why didn't Blizenci assist you with escaping this wasteland?"

"He claimed he would, but I didn't want to put all of my faith in him."

"He failed to rescue you?"

"What?" asked Lev in confusion. "He never tried to? He flew back to his lands after a brief conversation with me."

"And he chose not to take you with him?"

"Clearly," answered Lev hastily. She immediately realized her mistake and attempted to resolve it before he noticed. "I apologize, but he flew without a plane. I can't fly across an entire ocean after all, I am not an Air Zodiac like he is."

"Was he in a hurry to leave the Antarctic? Tell me, what would Blizenci be doing here at the South Pole if it was unrelated to the reason you are currently here?"

"I--"

"That merely raises more questions, does it not? Why would you be here either? Especially if you had fugitives who were to be neutralized all the way back in the lands of Virgo."

"You see master, I was--"

"Not to mention my informants across the waters have found some peculiar light patterns coming from this very location. If their calculations are correct, and they always are…then an Active Pisces Zodiac now roams the Earth. I would certainly hope that you had nothing to do with that, as your assignment was to prevent a group of what you called 'young adults' from recreating any type of Zodiacs. Ironically that is the very thing that has transpired."

"But master I can explain!"

"Now. You and I both know that you need the Pisces Gemstone to create an Active Pisces Zodiac, but after Rakovina killed Ryby his Gemstone was kept safely in none other than…your possession. How would you explain this turn of events? Please…my precious Lev. Please explain…"

"I…I groomed Sartan to be the Wagustus of the Water Signs…he then turned on me at the Virgo Palace, stealing all of the Water Gemstones I had."

"Please remind me," said Kozoroh. "How many of the Water Gemstones did you have in your possession again? Two?"

"I had all of them," sniffled Lev, whose head was tilted all the way back in order to look up at Kozoroh. "They have all of the Water Gemstones. They have an Earth Gemstone. They have the Aries Gemstone, and they have the Libra Gemstone."

"So you haven't been precisely truthful with me Lev," said Kozoroh as he grabbed Lev's long and black, braided hair. He pulled her head even further back past the point where joints began popping. "You did take care of these heathens…right?"

"No…" whispered Lev as she closed her eyes. "By the time I got here…they were flying off in the last working plane…"

"I see," stated Kozoroh as he pulled Lev's head to the left and the right, toying with her. "Now where does that put Blizenci in all of this? He was here was he not? All of this destruction couldn't have been a result of those fiends you have been hunting…It was almost as if…dozens of tornadoes ripped through our late friend Ryby's lands…"

"Blizenci…" Lev's voice was shaky and unstable. She was holding back tears of fear. Kozoroh knelt down in front of her and softly grabbed her face by the chin releasing her hair. He tilted her head down to match his brown eyes. He nodded slowly while Lev's words cracked and churned as they got stuck in her throat. "Blizenci…this is all Blizenci's fault!"

"I know…" whispered Kozoroh as he stroked the side of Lev's face. He then stood back up. "You see I find it extremely ironic that Blizenci claimed this was all your fault when I spoke with him. He said that only if Lev was able to communicate better with him. If only you were fighting the fugitives with him at the same time…"

"I didn't even know he would come here!" exclaimed Lev as she stared upwards at her liege. "By the time I arrived he had already been 'defeated' by the fugitives he had no right to hunt. Emphasis on defeated, as he easily could have killed them all. He wanted them to get away! HE WANTED YOU TO THINK THAT THIS WAS ALL MY FAULT! THI---"

"Silence," whispered Kozoroh. "I care not for the 'he said she said'. I care about results. You had an assignment that got off track all the way at the Sagittarius Palace. As far as I am concerned you have failed time after time to kill these ruffians and get back to actual work. Whether or not Blizenci set you up is irrelevant at this point in time. I have already dealt with him and his influence on this little incident we find ourselves recovering from."

"There would not have been an incident if Blizenci never---"

"Blizenci is not your concern. Do you understand?"

Lev bowed her head down and whispered, "Yes."

Kozoroh continued, "You were to kill a few peasants, and now we have three Zodiacs to kill. You failed. Not only that but you have been extremely…disloyal…with your ONLY master, Lev. One could presume that a disestablishment of my power by your hands is in the works. Well, the idea of that action sounds plausible, but commitment in that idea would…nevermind that. Lev, you will obviously not be allowed back into your own lands until given different orders. Your De Jure land that is. Your levies and taxes will be raised along with your feudal requirements."

"Understood master," replied Lev as she tried not to gag the words out.

"I find it pathetic that an ACTIVE Zodiac has failed to terminate a small group of rowdy peasants. Even worse, the ONLY two Active Zodiacs in the world, FAILED to communicate any type of plan to deal with these pesky peasants, and now I have to come all the way across the globe to bail you out of the problem you created all on your own."

"I apologize master, but Blizenci--"

"BLIZENCI IS NOT YOUR PROBLEM AND HAS ALREADY BEEN DEALT WITH!" cracked Kozoroh. "Blizenci underestimated the abilities of these peons just as you have; he paid a similarly hefty price for your overconfidence. I wasn't there when it happened, and my agent that was assisting him, one of the best, obviously did not have the required training for our enemies. One can only assume that he was not taking the threat as seriously as he should've, something I suspect you are guilty of as well. Tell me Lev, from your experiences are your fugitives belligerent and adroit in the art of Zodiacal combat?"

"Negative master. There is only one that could pose a threat, but that is merely because I trained him. I would have no issue--" Lev bit her tongue when she realized that she had made a mistake.

"You TRAINED, one of them?" boomed Kozoroh. "I should have ordered you to terminate Sartan? You groomed one of the targets for a Wagustus position. Never have I witnessed such a disobedient and inflated ego. This entire situation is entirely your fault. How are you expected to run one empire, let alone three, if you can't kill several peasants."

"I understand master."

"No!" exclaimed Kozoroh. "You don't. We need to reiterate the relationship the two of us have here. Your powers may be tied to the sun, but you are far from the center of my solar system. I give you orders. You obey, no questions asked."

"Yes, master."

"You will be punished immediately. Any land outside of your De Jure Leo lands has effectively been revoked permanently. Whether or not I grant it back depends on how efficiently the threat you created has been dealt with," stated Kozoroh in a firm voice as thick veins bulged in his throat. "Not only that but your moves will be monitored by my newly formed group of agents designed to assist and guide you on your tasks."

Lev's lip flared up briefly before she replied, "Of...of course master."

"Surrender any gemstones in your possession."

"Master--"

"IMMEDIATELY."

Lev glared at the guards who held the sparking, rail rifles directly at her. Their coils sparked with electricity which had to be derived from the gemstone, but the weapons didn't flinch an inch within the steady arms of their holders. The weapons couldn't kill her, but she had already learned the hard way once that they possessed the ability to temporarily paralyze even an Active Zodiac such as herself. She bowed her head low as she slipped a gemstone directly into Kozoroh's palm. Her very own Leo Gemstone fell resentfully into Kozoroh's mostly unwrinkled hand.

"You and I both know that your powers will be limited without this, but you will still be able to accomplish the tasks I will assign you without it. I will return the stone when I find you deserve it again. Your actions will ALWAYS have consequences Empress Lev."

"Most certainly master," whispered Lev. Her vision blurred with tears that she so desperately fought to keep from escaping. The severity of her punishment is always subject to change, and she knows that Kozoroh hasn't made his final decision. She also knows that he won't make her punishment less severe if he does decide to amend it.

"And who is this man?" asked Kozoroh unexpectedly.

Lev immediately remembered that she told Virgil to follow her earlier, but he trailed behind, just now exiting the palace. "He is the man that got me across the waters to begin with. His slave escaped with his ship, and now he wants revenge. His slave is the new Pisces--"

"Good. This Pisces we have to kill is untrained and a previous slave," laughed Kozoroh. "Now, kill her master. Terminate him."

"But--"

"Terminate."

"But master, we can use him as bait. We can--"

"Lev," began Kozoroh in a calm tone.

With that she understood. Lev rose to her feet and nodded solemnly. Virgil stared in disbelief as she turned to face him. He began stepping back from her, but it was all in vain. With the clinch of her fist and a flick of her wrist Virgil's stomach slopped out of his body onto the snow. Steam escaped the opening as the flames tore through him. Intestines flopped out of the ever growing hole and hung over his rear. The victim's glossy gaze drifted past Lev as anything louder than a squeak out of his gaping mouth failed to manifest itself. Engulfed in the inferno, he dropped to his knees before collapsing into a visceral heap of flaming chunks of flesh. Lev watched at ease merely feet away while the charring of Virgil's flesh misted the air with a bloody red haze. *If it were up to me I would've kept you around a short bit longer.*

"Now was that so hard?" asked Kozoroh from behind her.

As she turned to face him she replied, "It was done swiftly and with ease."

"Then why were the fugitives not taken care of…swiftly and with ease?" pressed Kozoroh. Lev attempted to reply however as Kozoroh stepped next to Virgil's roasting body he continued, "On to our next bit of business. The palace. Raze it."

"Just the palace?" asked Lev as her heart skipped a beat.

"Everything. Burn it all." demanded Kozoroh while he turned and walked away from Lev. "I will be waiting for you on the ship, and I expect not one brick goes unsoldered."

"Of course master!" exclaimed Lev as she watched Kozoroh leave her next to the smoldering man he forced her to terminate.

"You can take as long as you wish, but we leave at midnight," Kozoroh commanded without looking back.

Lev didn't reply. She watched Kozoroh march to the dreadnought in silence. The wind whispered through the stillness to her, and it snipped at her fingers as it did. Gray skies muddled her vision of the landscapes around her, but she could have been blind and still saw that Kozoroh played her. After everything that she had done for him this is how he is going to treat her. Even after she dealt with so many of the late Zodiacs on his demand, he decides to tighten her feudal obligations! Lev could feel her blood begin to boil as it pumped through her arteries.

She stepped back from the palace to see it in all its greatness. Its bubbly structure towered above her with the faintest of glistens shimmering in the dim light. Pure and clean, crystal extrusions had begun growing out of it, and they already started emitting a nearly invisible, blue glow. The palace was already alive though its heart, weak and defenseless, could have been anywhere in the world by now. Its halls breathed, and its walls slowly pulsed with those taunting blue lucencies. With Kozoroh far out of earshot Lev took one final step back from the palace. She was too late.

"I could've easily prevented this…" mumbled Lev to herself. "I SHOULD HAVE PREVENTED THIS! NO! No…HE IS A FOOL FOR THINKING THIS IS MY FAULT! HIS MIND GAMES WON'T WORK ON ME! I KNOW THIS ISN'T MY FAULT! IF BLIZENCI WASN'T INCOMPETENT---IF HE ACTUALLY USED HIS BRAIN!"

Lev sent a column of flames into the side of the palace, and to her surprise it merely sizzled into the air. "REAAAAAA!!! Why didn't I kill them all IMMEDIATELY!?!?" Fists full of flames frantically flew attacks into the palace without mercy. This time the walls cracked and crumbled. The dim blue glows faded to black within the crystals as they shattered in the extreme conditions.

"I FAILED!!" screamed Lev as the colossal palace entry tumbled to the ground before her. "WHY?! WHY COULD I NOT CATCH EIGHT PEASANTS?!!? HOW COULD I NOT! EEAAAAAAARGH!! NOW I'M BANNED FROM MY OWN DAMN LANDS!? MY COFFERS ARE GOING TO DRY UP PAYING TAXES, AND MY EMPIRE WILL SHRINK TREMENDOUSLY IN MILITARY MIGHT COMPARED TO KOZOROH'S. FUCK!"

Dark red fire burst from her mouth, and she cracked a twirling harpoon of flames through several of the palace walls simultaneously. Bricks of foundation flew past Lev's shoulders, and the snow began melting around her feet. Lev's skin was hot to the touch. Fire trickled out of her palms as the flames in her eyes sizzled with each blink, roasting away her eyebrows. Her gaping mouth was an angry firebox grasping for more fuel to guzzle. At this point she could feel the blood in her veins bubble with energy. Every man-made item on her caught flame and blew away in the wind, but the fire stuck, burning straight off her bare skin. As the dark red fire roasted away on Lev's skin, the palace crumbled one brick at a time.

The palace walls were the first to go. Once engulfed in the conflagration, the ancient walls that Lev had helped repair years ago lasted but moments. Since the town had been ravaged by tornadoes just over a week before, debris was scattered throughout the ice roads, and half of the work was already done for her. The wax was already wicked; she just needed to light the candles. Fire blazed over wooden floorboards and bookshelves that lay abandoned in the streets, and swirling pikes of red smashed through the remaining igloos like a fist through putty. Her screams of absolute salinity wrestled with the roars of the flames that engulfed both her and the town. Even the howling winds failed to do anything other than fuel her ever growing flames. The ice below her cracked and creaked as it grew weak under all of the heat, and an idea crossed Lev's mind upon noticing it.

She sprinted back to the palace now that every single square inch of the town was sweating beneath some form of flame or fire. Lev walked through the flames into the burning behemoth of a structure. By now the walls had crumbled, and all that remained was the heap of debris that still blazed ferociously within the frame of the overall structure. After running through the dark red flames eating at the throne room, Lev glared at the ashen throne that laid on its side far from the pillar of marble it initially rested on, and luckily the palace did not extend downwards beneath the throne room. Because of this the foundation of the throne room had been upturned, and chunks of melting ice and snow kissed the blazing bricks and flames. As the pupils and irises of her eyes were hidden behind raging flames of crispy red that streaked the sides of her neck and body, Lev held out both of her burning hands towards the throne. Two beams of smoldering energy gushed just below the indestructible throne. Thirty seconds passed, and the throne still sat unaffected other than the orange glow it had attained from the heat. The ice and snow below it, however, melted violently. Streams of sweat sizzled on Lev's shoulders as they mixed with the flames engulfing her body, and the throne began slipping below the ground. A pool of water had melted and now completely submerged the throne, violently hissing while doing so. The ice at the bottom of the ever growing pool melted while the water on top bubbled and boiled into the air.

  "This isn't a fun little distraction from my work anymore...you made my name WEAK in the eyes of my liege and the world!" exclaimed Lev whose pours fizzed from excreting sweat directly into her flames. "I'm going to put all of my efforts into finding and killing you, Sartan." She intensified the spirals of fire entering the deep hole. The throne could barely be seen now, for bubbles of the boiling water were thick and plentiful. The steam coming from the boiling water kissed the smoke of the violently burning palace she stood in so intimately that her sight became a thing of the past. Lev stopped when she felt the resistance of the ice snap away under the pressure of her flames. Once she could feel the flames flow freely into the depths of the ice hole she made, a grin snuck across her face. The throne was now on its merry little way to the ocean floor. Not only the ocean floor, but the ocean floor deep beneath the South Pole. "Never," whispered Lev sternly. "NEVER AGAIN, WILL THERE BE... ANOTHER...PISCES!"

Chapter 27
Sartan
No More Running

Outside of the plane window thousands of feet below him Sartan watched green fields of grass creep by. The sun shone brightly into the cabin of the plane, and they have grown accustomed to the smooth flying that the autopilot provided. Unlike the boat that got them to the South Pole, the plane that got them out of it had much less room to wander off in, and this slight inconvenience forced everyone to be dangerously close. Malex, most likely undergoing a dramatic transformation, was still unconscious in her seat. The environment inside the cabin hummed in relief from escaping the tornadic formation back at the palace, from making it across the sea, and most importantly from when Jaako stated that he watched one of the tornadoes rip Lev's boat into a thousand shreds of shrapnel. With Lev stuck at the Pisces Palace, Sartan didn't need to stay with the group anymore. The case was the same for Octavia and Emilia, even Jaako to an extent.

Aqila made this clear when she finally asked, "Lev will surely find her way out of the South Pole, but that may not be for months if not years. I just need to know something…Octavia, what are you going to do when we land?"

Octavia rolled her head towards Aqila and gazed quietly with her glossy, green eyes. "After the past few weeks I am positive there will be no shortage of action…but now that we don't have to worry about Lev…"

"Oh," interrupted Aqila. "I understand."

"Now, I know that you really need a Virgo," continued Octavia whose eyes drifted to her sister. "If what Blizenci claimed you have done is true then you are undoubtedly a terrible group of people who should be tried for your crimes. After surviving attacks from Blizenci himself though, I am sure none of your crimes were premeditated or intentional. DO NOT show me otherwise because I can tell just by the way that Emilia is sadly looking at her feet…she wants to stay with you guys, and quite honestly, I don't know what else we would do."

Instantaneously Jaako screamed out with joy, "YES! I knew it!"

"Calm down," said Ferran as his attention fluttered away from a book he found on the plane. "You seem oddly excited for no reason."

"I am excited too," said Caleb who stood in the cockpit's doorway. "You guys are all family to me. Why would you want to leave after everything we've been through together anyways?"

Ferran was quick to criticize the statement, "Caleb, how can you say that when they've only been with us for a max of a month?"

"I could not agree with you more," said Sartan with a slight smile. "I don't even know any of your full names."

Ferran glared at Sartan before asking him, "So now that Lev isn't an immediate threat are you going to ditch us the second you get your feet on solid ground?" Everyone waited patiently for Sartan's response. Curious eyes snapped back and forth between Sartan's face and Ferran's face while Sartan took a heavy breath. Before a reply flowed out of his mouth Ferran continued, "The only thing that you ever cared about was living a sad lonely life, and if Lev isn't hunting you with every cell in her body you just might be able to get what you want."

Sartan swallowed. Right as Ferran was about to continue he stated, "I have decided…that your mission, this cause that you are fighting for, however irrelevant it seemed at first…is in reality deeply personal to me."

"What the hell does that mean?!" exclaimed Ferran.

"Ferran!" interrupted Aqila, saving Sartan from having to answer that question. "He was captured by Lev, so I am sure that this has become very personal for him!"

"Well how is it personal?" pressed Ferran.

"That does not matter," said Aqila. "He should not have to tell you everything for you to trust him as long as our mission is deeply personal to him!"

"Fine!" exclaimed Ferran hastily. "But does that mean he is staying to help us for good now?"

This time Aqila did not save Sartan from the question. Instead all the eyes in the room slowly landed on Sartan who was waiting for somebody to step in and change the subject. "I…I guess I am…"

"YES!!!" screamed Jaako. "SARTAN!!!"

Ferran stared in disbelief as if a judge had just sentenced him to death, and although they didn't scream in excitement like Jaako, everybody else nodded slowly while smiles crept across their lips. Caleb wrapped his arms around Ferran in an expression of affection. To Sartan's surprise Ferran reluctantly embraced his friend in his arms. Suddenly arms coiled around Sartan's sides, and Aqila threw herself into him. The second Jaako noticed that Emilia was practically tackled.

"Oh, what the hell. Can't have a sandwich without the door hinge!" exclaimed Octavia as she grabbed Emilia and Jaako with one arm. Sartan, while trying not to laugh, attempted to question her strange choice of words, but before he could she slung her other arm around him. Caleb took initiative to force Ferran into the growing group hug. The hug lasted a solid seven seconds before Ferran pushed himself away from everyone, and Sartan immediately jumped out of the moshpit after noticing that. It wasn't until Octavia pulled away when the unnecessary show of care finally died. The only lucky one was Malex because she slept silently in her chair through the entire thing.

"So what is the plan?" asked Sartan to bring logic back into the plane.

"We party!" exclaimed Jaako as he threw his arms up.

"That's a terrible idea," said Ferran.

"Actually I wouldn't object to a bit of controlled stress relief," laughed Octavia.

"I am okay with it, but I would like to view it more as a celebration for our accomplishments," added Sartan.

Aqila slowly stated, "I disagree feeling like it is a bad idea…I do not think that we should-"

"Why not?" asked Sartan as he sat down in one of the chairs, cutting her off mid sentence. "Think about all of the things we have done. Who else can say that they have recreated THREE Zodiacs?! Actually, about a third of us on this plane are Zodiacs now!"

"That scares me," commented Octavia. "If this plane goes down then everything that you guys have worked for is over."

Aqila quickly replied, "Do not say it like that. You helped us too."

Octavia blushed but still continued, "We need to land to ensure we all don't die."

Caleb said, "We will be fine! Octavia knows how to fly a plane or we have a really good autopilot and made it this far, why would it suddenly explode now."

"BEEP. BEEP. BEEP!" laughed Emilia mockingly.

"Oh, I don't know why it could fail…maybe operator error," whispered Ferran slyly with a smirk on his face. Sartan watched everyone who didn't laugh at Emilia's joke either get caught in an existential crisis or begin laughing at Ferran's.

Octavia, however, was quick to respond, "Hey!"

"That reminds me," stated Sartan. "Where are we right now?"

With a shuffle of feet Caleb ran into the cockpit and back out to the cabin. "We are about twenty minutes into Libra lands, but the autopilot is set to take us as far as we can go with the fuel we have."

"And where is that?"

"A metropolis just a few miles into the Taurus Empire," answered Caleb.

"Why so far?"

"I figured we would want to use this opportunity to put as much distance between us and Lev as we could. How would that be done better if we didn't put ourselves practically on the opposite side of the planet?"

"Honesty…" interrupted Aqila. "I do not care where we are going as long as all of us are going there together, and Lev is far away."

For the first time everyone agreed. Unified by a common threat and relieved by common success everyone relaxed in the safety of the jet. Sartan knew that none of this would've been possible without him, and he knew that if just one of these unbearable strangers he had grown to tolerate wasn't there for him at the Pisces Palace his face would be a bubbling slop smeared into a frosty, marble floor thousands of miles away, despite Octavia's brief attempt at selling out to Blizenci. When Caleb taunted the thought of everyone being a family it invigorated him briefly but ultimately reminded him of Rakovina. How much had he forgotten? He refused to let himself slip down that rabbit hole at this moment. They had just stranded Lev and possibly even killed Blizenci. All that had threatened his survival perished, and although he didn't remember everything yet, Sartan knew that the best memories were about to happen. His gaze drifted out of the window. Fluffy, white clouds floated by, and brilliant, blue skies stared right back into his curious, wide eyes. Even the lilac air-machine's losing battle to fight the unbathed, bloody scents that they produced failed to wipe the smile off Sartan. He brushed off his bruises and scrapes as the plane softly flew under the midday sun towards a land that none of them had ever claimed to set foot on. It flew towards a land rich with history and entrenched in tradition. A land full of life. A land full of opportunity.

Author Bio:

An aspiring and somewhat youthful author, X.V.V. has always had excess creativity flowing through them, so with little outlets for said creativity, they finally gripped the pen. Although X.V.V. is just now beginning to dabble in the magic of Fictional Adventures, X.V.V. has been reading this as well as similar genres since early childhood. In their very first project, X.V.V. attempts to explore the more entertaining side of Astrology while still managing to emphasize some inaccuracies of Zodiac based stereotypes and diving deep into themes of emotion, the complications of trust from others' perspectives (rather distrust), and ways of coping with stress or past traumatic experiences. X.V.V. has been working on this large project since August 10, 2020. Without a question, writing a majority of the plot during an uncertain and global pandemic brings changing perspectives and outlooks to the book that are unique to the twenty-twenties. Viewing all of the characters as pieces to a grand chess set, X.V.V. never lets the reader grasp the absolute state of the board, let alone the next four moves of the antagonizing forces.